Robert Louis Stevenson

TALES OF
THE SOUTH SEAS

Island Landfalls
The Ebb-Tide
The Wrecker

Edited and Introduced by
JENNI CALDER

CANONGATE
CLASSICS
72

This edition first published as a Canongate
Classic in 1996 by Canongate Books Ltd
14 High Street, Edinburgh EH1 1TE.

Introduction and Notes © 1987, 1996
Jenni Calder

Island Landfalls first published as a Canongate
Classic in 1987

Professor Barry Menikoff's edition of
The Beach of Falesá is reproduced
by permission of Stanford University Press
and Edinburgh University Press.

The publishers gratefully acknowledge
general subsidy from the Scottish Arts Council
towards the Canongate Classics series
and a specific grant towards the
publication of this title.

Set in 10pt Plantin by Hewer Text Composition
Services, Edinburgh. Printed and bound in
Great Britain by Mackays of Chatham PLC, Chatham, Kent

Canongate Classics
Series Editor: Roderick Watson
Editorial Board: Tom Crawford, J.B. Pick,
Cairns Craig

British Library Cataloguing in Publication Data
A catalogue record is available on request
ISBN 0–86241–643 4

Beset by chronic ill health and in perennial search of sunshine and clean air, Robert Louis Stevenson (1850–94) spent the last seven years of his life travelling in North America and the South Seas. He craved news of his native land, and his advisors in Britain encouraged him to produce more books and stories on Scottish themes. Indeed, Stevenson's most famous later novels, *The Master of Ballantrae* (1888), *Catriona* (1893), and *Weir of Hermiston* (1896), were all produced during the Pacific years, or from what was to become his home when he settled at Vailima on the island of Upolu in Samoa.

Yet Stevenson had become increasingly aware of the white man's failings and the colonial exploitation of the island peoples, and some of his finest writing relates to this issue. At a time when exiled Scots around the world were enjoying the fashion for a more homely 'Kailyard' fiction, Stevenson produced *The Beach at Falesá* and *The Ebb-Tide* in imaginative response to the South Pacific experience. Jenni Calder's selection from Stevenson's creative prose, essays and letters will help to remind readers that he had a penetrating artistic and human interest in cultures far from the shores of Forth and the Weaver's Stone.

Contents

Introduction

It was ill health that drove Robert Louis Stevenson away from Scotland. It was an urge for new and adventurous places and experiences that drew him to the Pacific. In June 1888 he and members of his family sailed out of San Francisco Bay on the schooner yacht *Casco*. For the next six and a half years, until his death on 3 December 1894, Stevenson was never out of Pacific regions.

For the first two of those years he wandered from island to island, on the *Casco*, the *Equator* and the *Janet Nichol*, and spent some time in Australia. It was hopeful voyaging, relished for its own sake, and most of the time with the bonus of good health. Sometimes there were pauses of weeks or months, stays occasioned by personal inclination, or the exigencies of Pacific trade, Pacific weather or Pacific ships. Wherever he was, and for whatever reason, Stevenson was continually alert to sights, sounds and happenings that were new, fresh and vivid. Many of his letters catch the exoticism and excitement of it all.

> This climate; these voyagings; these landfalls at dawn; new islands peaking from the morning bank; new forested harbours; new passing alarms of squalls and surf; new interests of gentle natives, – the whole tale of my life is better to me than any poem.[1]

But Stevenson was not carried away by the romance and adventure of the Pacific, although some of his published work up until that time might have suggested such a response. Another letter, written within days of the one above, suggests his awareness of some of the contradictions and difficulties of the islands.

> The Pacific is a strange place; the 19th century only exists there in spots: all round, it is a no man's land of the ages, a stir-about of epochs and races, barbarisms and civilisations, virtues and crimes.[2]

The Pacific was a challenge because it not only lived up

to his most extravagant ideas of adventure, the ideas that had flowered in *Treasure Island*, but it also presented him with realities that were tantalising and instructive. His understanding of human nature and human history, which is so apparent in *Kidnapped*, in *Strange Case of Dr Jekyll and Mr Hyde*, in stories such as 'Thrawn Janet' and 'The Merry Men', was sharpened and extended.

By the end of 1890 Stevenson, his wife Fanny, and a fluctuating entourage were more or less settled in Vailima, the home he built near Apia on the Samoan island of Upolu. Throughout these years, whether at sea, or encamped in a palm-thatched hut, or living in squalor or in splendour – he sampled both extremes – at Vailima, he was writing. Both the world that he had left and the world in which he was now living were the subject of his pen.

The content of his writing was more diverse and wide-ranging than at any other time of his life. In the early months of his travels he was working on *The Master of Ballantrae*, which he had begun in a sub-arctic winter spent in the Adirondacks in New York State, and finished in a beach house at Waikiki. But although at this distance he could recreate Scotland and Scots, Scottish habits and Scottish speech, the Pacific environment equally commanded his attention. He kept a journal, and when he could he wrote letters. The opportunities to send them were irregular, so there were necessarily long silences. Stories began to suggest themselves, plots and people unfolded from the endless fascination of the Pacific. Yet all the time Scotland was never very far from his mind.

Soon he found himself concerned with much more than simply recording impressions. His interest in the peoples and cultures he encountered became involvement, both personal and, after a while, political. This is reflected in his writing, and worried greatly those at home who would have been happier to see him as a spinner of the picturesque, making delightful capital out of exotic sensations, than as an investigator of colonialism and its impact. But Stevenson could not close his eyes to what he saw going on around him, especially as it provided him with such rich material for continuing an exploration of moral ambiguity that was already a primary current in his work.

He began to write fiction directly inspired by his South Sea experience: *The Wrecker*, in collaboration with his stepson Lloyd Osbourne, *The Ebb-Tide*, begun as *The Pearl Fisher* with Lloyd, set aside and later worked over again by Stevenson alone, the short stories 'The Bottle Imp' and 'The Isle of Voices' aimed at a Polynesian audience, and the masterly novella *The Beach of Falesá*. At the same time his growing understanding of expansionist politics and of the native Polynesians led him to engage with the warring interests of the colonial powers in the Pacific. Inevitably, he wrote about that too.

Stevenson's interest in Samoa and the political situation there had been aroused during a six month stay in Hawaii. There he spent many enjoyable and interesting hours in the company of King Kalakaua, a convivial, extravagant and plausible figure who consumed quantities of champagne and had serious if ambivalent convictions about traditional Polynesian values. Kalakaua had an interest in Samoa, for he felt that a possible solution to colonial squabbling could be that he should take the islands under his wing. At this time Samoa was uneasily supervised by a trio of powers – Germany, Britain and the United States – a situation created by the 1868 Treaty of Berlin, the great nineteenth-century colonial carve-up. Of the three, Germany dominated, both politically and economically, the political influence owing a great deal to Germany's long-established economic presence.

Stevenson was outraged by the political manoeuvrings and manipulations of all three powers, none of which showed much regard for the needs or traditions of the Samoans. His indignation was sharply expressed in a series of letters to *The Times* which rehearsed, with an ironic wit that surely owed something to his Edinburgh legal training, a tale of imperialist treachery and doublethink. Once in Samoa Stevenson openly allied himself with the chief Mataafa, a man for whom he had great personal regard and political respect. Mataafa was the main rival to the German-backed puppet chief Malietoa. The British, while recognizing privately Mataafa's claims, disliked him because he was a Catholic, and were anyway reluctant to disturb a situation that suited them quite well. Stevenson was regarded as an interfering innocent, causing trouble through his naive idealism -- words often used to dismiss the awkwardly honest. The situation erupted into war in July 1883, much of the conflict enacted literally in the Stevensons' back yard. Not content with sending lengthy correspondence to *The Times* Stevenson produced his own account of the situation and the background to the conflict in a book which he called *A Footnote to History*.

We do not usually think of Stevenson as being either a 'straight' historian or a political commentator, but there is clear evidence of his attraction to historical fact. An interest in Scottish history was reflected in more than his fiction and essays: he had applied for the Chair of History and Constitutional Law at Edinburgh University, a post for which he was academically ill-qualified and didn't get. Nevertheless, the intellectual and psychological challenge of Scotland's past always appealed to him, and more significant, perhaps, was his project to write a history of Scotland.

In Samoa Stevenson's involvement in events and his determination to set the record straight was as much the result of his highly developed sense of justice as of the magnetism of historical fact. He was witness to words and actions that were hypocritical, deceitful, and manipulative. He could not stand back from such a state of affairs. He felt a moral obligation to commit to paper – his only effective weapon – his understanding of events. But amongst his friends and associates at home there was alarm. At an early stage in his career Stevenson had been identified as a torch-carrier for a revitalised fiction. In 1878 Leslie Stephen, a highly respected member of the literary establishment, had written to Stevenson saying that he was on the lookout for a new novelist, a Scott or a Dickens or a George Eliot, suggesting that perhaps Stevenson could be the answer. It was an extraordinary profession of faith in a young man who was in the early stages of his literary career, and that aura, the feeling that he was destined for great things, clung to him. From the other side of the world it looked as if Stevenson was spending his time in wild and ill-conceived political adventures with a gang of savages. It did not conform with an image of him as not merely a serious novelist, but as the saviour of English literature at a time when it was judged to be in the doldrums.

What Stevenson realized was that such adventures were not only the stuff of history, they were the stuff of fiction. Although he had gained a reputation as a fine weaver of imaginative tales he was no ivory-tower fabulist. To write he had to live, and for the first time in his life he was well and strong enough to throw himself into the thick of things, whether it was the struggle against the jungle growth on his Vailima land, or riding secretly across the island to consort with the rebels, or tending the wounded in the aftermath of battle, or the emotional conflicts that were a part of daily life amongst the Vailima extended family.

Stevenson's refusal to withdraw was partly the result of his unending enthusiasm for life, partly of moral conviction. Both these aspects of his mind and personality are evident in his writing. They were if anything heightened by his South Seas experience, and certainly reflected in the material brought together in this volume. In it we can see three levels of response, in the letters, in the extracts from his book *In the South Seas*, and in the fiction. In the letters, with which the selection begins, there is all the lively immediacy of instant communication. From them we get a vivid picture of the activities that filled his days, the demanding physical work, the even more intense demands of writing, and the serendipity for which he had a particular talent. These were years in which, in some respects, Stevenson tasted a freedom from conventional restrictions which previously had been overshadowed by parental and social authority. One of those parents, his mother, had travelled with him and was as aware as anyone of the lack of restraint. 'It is a strange, irresponsible, half-savage life,' she wrote, '& I sometimes wonder if we shall ever be able to return to civilised habits again.'[3]

The absence of civilisation suited Stevenson wonderfully.

He would have loved this description, written after his death, and would have recognised himself immediately.

> . . . I met a little group of three European strangers –
> two men and a woman. The latter wore a print gown,
> large gold crescent earrings, a Gilbert-Island hat of
> plaited straw, encircled by a wreath of small shells, a
> scarlet silk scarf round her neck, and a brilliant plaid
> shawl across her shoulders; her bare feet were encased
> in white canvas shoes, and across her back was slung
> a guitar. . . . The younger of her two companions was
> dressed in a striped pyjama suit – the undress costume
> of most European traders in these seas – a slouch hat
> of native make, dark blue sun-spectacles, and over
> his shoulders a banjo. The other man was dressed
> in a shabby suit of white flannels that had seen many
> better days, a white drill yachting cap with a prominent
> peak, a cigarette in his mouth, a photographic camera
> in his hand. Both the men were bare-footed. They
> had, evidently, just landed from the little schooner
> now lying placidly at anchor, and my first thought
> was that, probably, they were wandering players en
> route to New Zealand, compelled by their poverty to
> take the cheap conveyance of a trading vessel.[4]

They were not, of course, wandering players, but Stevenson, his wife, and Lloyd Osbourne. This was written by W.E. Clarke, missionary on Upolu, subsequently a respected friend of Stevenson who had no great sympathy for the missionary breed on the whole, and mentioned in one of the letters included here.

It was in many ways a delightful existence, but Stevenson had to work, especially once the bills for Vailima started coming in. There was a large and proliferating household to maintain, which was not only a financial burden but often an emotional and psychological one too. There were extreme pressures and profound anxieties, money problems, illness and unhappiness amongst the members of the household, worries over work in hand that foundered. Indeed, all of this almost certainly contributed to his death, brought by a sudden brain haemorrhage. These pressures hardly surface in his letters, for he did not like to dwell on his difficulties and was concerned that the folk at home should not worry.

Nor do we detect them in his more literary writing during this period.

In the South Seas represents another level of response to the Pacific, considered, ordered, and crafted. If the writing here is without the spontaneity of the letters, it still has sparkle and humour, and Stevenson's avid interest in all he encountered is apparent. The scenery was intoxicating; the expanses of ocean, the islands taking shape as they approached, the mountains, streams and forests, the stretches of sand and shore – all these he found irresistible. The people were equally a temptation. He became absorbed by island customs and behaviour, by beliefs and folklore, and comparisons with Scotland came readily. It wasn't just homesickness that kept Scotland in the forefront of his mind throughout his time in the Pacific, but the chords that were struck by anything from a mountainside to a myth. Sometimes it was the very unlikeliness of similarity that made the discovery such a delight. Most striking of all is Stevenson's sense of a common humanity. He recognized that the fears and vulnerabilities of the South Sea islanders were little different from those of men and women everywhere.

From time to time the modern reader may be brought up sharply by words or phrases that suggest a colonialist condescension. Stevenson, for example, refers to the adult Samoan workers on his Vailima land as 'boys'. 'Nigger' appears to describe blacks of African origin. And the paternalism of some of his attitudes at times reads uncomfortably. But it would be ungenerous and misleading to be overcritical. This was the language of the times, and he was in fact far ahead of his time in his respect for the islanders and his interest in them as individuals with a culture of their own. There is no doubt that he enjoyed being gaffer at Vailima, but he shared in their work and although he was of course in a position of power (even if he didn't have the political influence he would have liked) he was very aware that he was also in a position of responsibility. He was disgusted by white exploitation of the islanders, angry at the way many missionaries totally disregarded Samoan traditions, and saddened at the erosion of human spirit, in victims and perpetrators alike, that followed from the diminishment of a people.

Always uncompromisingly himself Stevenson was at the same time genuinely internationalist and sought out common ground with whomever he encountered. During an enforced stay at Tautira on Tahiti while the *Casco*'s masts were being repaired, he established a flourishing relationship with the local chieftain, Ori a Ori. They feasted each other, and swapped songs and stories. When on Christmas Day 1888 the *Casco* pointed north for Hawaii the handsome Ori and another local dignitary, the aristocratic Princess Moë, wept; Louis and Fanny Stevenson wept also. They left behind them not only good friends, but a wonderful source of story and fable.

This and other meetings inspired the stories 'The Bottle Imp' and 'The Isle of Voices'. Stevenson readily adapted to the resonance and cadences of myth, for legendary tales had suffused his own upbringing. If he had absorbed such sources into his Scottish fiction, he was equally primed to make something of the Polynesian story-telling to which he was now exposed. Thus 'The Bottle Imp' is an ancient tale with a contemporary feel, and it provides an interesting glimpse of some of the incidentals of the Polynesian encounter with whites. The scene and the viewpoint are Polynesian, and the white presence is not conspicuous. If readers are inclined to question the success of Stevenson's attempt at getting under the skin of his Polynesian characters, it is worth noting that the fable itself has an impulsion that overrides this. 'The Isle of Voices' has a more specifically Polynesian reference, and Stevenson's grasp on the tale is less confident. But there is an ambience, a personalised environment, that still remains powerful.

Stevenson was acutely aware of the kinship between traditional story-telling in the Pacific and in Scotland. He continually drew parallels between Scottish and Polynesian customs, traditions and tribes. He recognized that this was a useful way of gaining the confidence of the islanders from whom he sought acceptance. As an amateur anthropologist he was unusual for that time, since he looked at alien cultures as much in terms of their similarities with his own as of their differences. At the same time he seems to have shared the belief held by even the most enlightened investigators that tribal societies represented a primitive

stage in human evolution which would inevitably give
way to 'civilisation'. What was less usual was his regret
at the loss this would entail, and his indignation at
what he described as '. . . the unjust (yet I can see
the inevitable) extinction of Polynesian Islanders by our
shabby civilisation'.

There is no doubt that his sensitivity towards this loss
was a direct result of his engagement with his own cultural
origins. There was mutual nourishment. As his writing
responded to the challenge of the Pacific he was also
probing and examining the Scottish past and the Scottish
character. The traditions of Border reiving and rivalry
which play so important a part in *Weir of Hermiston*,
his last substantial piece of fiction, have their parallels
in Pacific life. The authoritarian attitudes of the novel's
Lord Braxfield towards human frailty were not dissimilar
to those of the imperialist powers towards the native
populations. The harsh landscapes and harsher actions
of Scotland might have seemed very different from the
sun-dazzled, easy-going South Seas, yet the roots of human
behaviour were sustained by the same kind of needs and
feelings.

In the South Seas is not a continuous record of Stevenson's
travels. It is a series of worked up, almost self-contained
pieces. His letters, some of them written over several
days, convey a sense of day-to-day living, of a con-
tinuum, a pattern of progress and setbacks, of events
not just following upon each other but entangled with
each other. Life is tidier in the book version of these
events. Hindsight and the literary imagination lend shape
and meaning. I am not suggesting that reality is being
tampered with, but literary skills are at work and an
inevitable process of selection and reordering is going
on. Stevenson was a conscious and deliberate crafts-
man, and this process was part of his commitment,
of his sense of responsibility as a writer. The directness of his style can be pleasantly informal, yet at the
same time there is a literary, almost an ornate quality. Stevenson combines close observation, an awareness of language as well as of sensation, sympathetic
humour, and a strong feeling for the potential absurdity
that lies in the clash of mutual ignorance. Here is an

example, taken from 'The Maroon', one of the pieces
included here.

> It chanced one day that I was ashore in the cove
> with Mrs Stevenson and the ship's cook. Except for
> the *Casco* lying outside, and a crane or two, and the
> ever-busy wind and sea, the face of the world was
> of a prehistoric emptiness; life appeared to stand
> stockstill, and the sense of isolation was profound
> and refreshing. On a sudden, the tradewind, coming
> in a gust over the isthmus, struck and scattered the
> fans of the palms above the den; and, behold! in two
> of the tops there sat a native, motionless as an idol and
> watching us, you would have said, without a wink.
> The next moment the tree closed, and the glimpse
> was gone. This discovery of human presences latent
> overhead in a place where we had supposed ourselves
> alone, the immobility of our tree-top spies, and the
> thought that perhaps at all hours we were similarly
> supervised, struck us with a chill. Talk languished on
> the beach. As for the cook (whose conscience was not
> clear), he never afterwards set foot on shore, and twice,
> when the *Casco* appeared to be driving on the rocks,
> it was amusing to observe that man's alacrity; death,
> he was persuaded, awaiting him upon the beach. It
> was more than a year later, in the Gilberts, that the
> explanation dawned upon myself. The natives were
> drawing palm-tree wine, a thing forbidden by law;
> and when the wind thus suddenly revealed them,
> they were doubtless more troubled than ourselves.

Here is an incident contained in a paragraph. Hindsight
rounds the story off. The visual context, the island
ambience, the culture clash are all there. And so is the
author, taking a step back, looking at himself and his
companions. The writer of first person documentary has
to be observer, participant and artist. Stevenson highlights
these roles by adopting a tone of mild irony, which also
softens the nuts and bolts of his style, and maintains the
distance between observer and actor. Twentieth-century
writers would probably feel it was not so important to be
scrupulous about distinguishing these roles, yet Stevenson's
control of tone gives a true modernity to his prose.

It is now around one hundred years since Stevenson was in the Pacific. From this distance we can see that he was engaged in one of the most important arenas of nineteenth-century history, both geographically and psychologically. We are now aware of the long-term effects of imperialism and are living with their consequences. What Stevenson witnessed, and what he recorded with considerable acuity, was colonialism in action in the Pacific one hundred years after the voyages of Captain Cook in the 1770s and 80s, a convenient date for locating the origins of imperialism in that part of the world.

Literary convention associates one great novelist in particular with the exploration and exposure of the tensions and conflicts inherent not just in the confrontation between imperialist powers and native populations, but in the sensations of the representatives of imperialism. This writer is Joseph Conrad, and his *Heart of Darkness* has become an emblem of the rotten core of exploitation. But a parallel and a companion to Conrad's great novella can be found in the earlier and equally impressive story by Stevenson, *The Beach of Falesá*.

Stevenson saw the Pacific as a huge melting-pot, or perhaps 'stew' is a more appropriate word, remembering that he wrote about the islands as 'a stir-about of epochs and races, barbarisms and civilisations, virtues and crimes'. He did not mean that these attributes belonged to one race or another. What his fiction tells us is that this 'stir-about' was a melange of peoples, none of which had any special claim to virtue or criminality. His particular interest, as it was Conrad's later, was in the moral and psychological effects of an environment of exoticism and exploitation on people with differing backgrounds and assumptions.

All Stevenson's fiction reveals a pre-eminent concern with the moral dimensions of man – of man in particular, rather than woman. Before coming to the Pacific he had examined moral ambivalence in the context mainly of Scotland's past, although his most famous venture into this territory, *Strange Case of Dr Jekyll and Mr Hyde*, was ostensibly set in London. Scottish history offered event after event, situation after situation, which seemed to demonstrate and confirm what Stevenson saw as fundamental divisions within humankind, between emotional life and

the instinct for survival – sometimes an instinct for evil –
and the need for controlled social relations. Towards the
end of his life he wrote to his cousin Bob, who had been
a close companion of his experimental youth, 'The prim
obliterated polite face of life, and the broad, bawdy, and
orgiastic – or maenadic – foundation, form a spectacle to
which no habit reconciles me.'[6] He did not have to search
far in Scotland's past to find extremes of feeling and belief,
extremes that led to violence of action and language.

In spite of *Jekyll and Hyde*, where in fact the extremes of
behaviour are not entirely convincing, Stevenson has not
had the reputation of a writer engaged with violence. Yet
we need look no further than *Treasure Island* or *Kidnapped*
to find naked conflict starkly expressed. The adventure story
genre of course accommodates violence quite comfortably.
In *The Master of Ballantrae* it is rather more sinister. But
physical violence is only one aspect of confrontation. In
the unfinished *Weir of Hermiston* there is an attempt to
illuminate the whole spectrum of division and extremity
through one powerfully knotted plot. The bold language of
the elder Kirstie warning the hero Archie about the dangers
of his relationship with a young and vulnerable girl catches
the essence of at least part of Stevenson's concern. Kirstie's
words echo those of Stevenson's to Bob.

> Man, do ye no' comprehend that it's God's wull
> we should be blendit and glamoured, and have nae
> command over our ain members at a time like that?
> My bairn . . . think o' the puir lass! have pity upon
> her, Erchie! and O, be wise for twa! Think o' the risk
> she rins! I have seen ye, and what's to prevent ithers?
> I saw ye once in the Hags, in my ain howf, and I
> was wae to see ye there – in pairt for the omen, for I
> think there's a weird on the place – and in pairt for
> puir nakit envy and bitterness o' hairt. It's strange ye
> should forgather there tae! God, but yon puir, thrawn,
> auld Covenanter's seen a heap o' human natur since
> he lookit his last on the musket-barrels, if he never
> saw nane afore . . .

Even without specific knowledge of the references here, to
the Covenanting conflicts and martyrdoms for example,
the vibrance of Kirstie's language alerts us to many of

the aspects of human feelings and behaviour that were a preoccupation during Stevenson's years at Vailima. On the one hand there was human nature, willed by God, as the Calvinists believed, to lead to sin unless kept in check. On the other hand were the rules and rigid structures imposed to keep humanity under control, but which themselves were dangerous in their capacity to distort.

Weir of Hermiston is set in eighteenth-century Scotland. Stevenson was living in late nineteenth-century Samoa. The wayward Archie is fenced in with social, moral and judicial rules. What was the situation in the Pacific? There was certainly plenty of opportunity to witness human nature in the raw. Traditional tribal life was breaking down. It had once been firmly stratified and organised, contrary to how it seemed to white incomers who were only too ready to exploit economic innocence and an apparently easy-going sexuality. There was a system of morality that was as strong, however different, as anything devised in the Christian world. To the whites, tribal life looked like moral anarchy while they themselves were a long way from the accustomed boundaries of behaviour – indeed that was part of the place's attraction. The result was a breeding ground of moral ambivalence which fascinated Stevenson.

The novelist could no longer write about human nature in terms of a contest between Dr Jekyll and Mr Hyde, or a balance between prim, whiggish, sensible David Balfour and flamboyant, self-conceited, courageous Alan Breck. The edges of moral responsibility and the margins of moral judgment were too blurred. All around him were people whose customary moral and social structures were destroyed or left behind. This is the territory he explores in the novel *The Ebb-Tide* (1893) where he looks at the varieties of disintegration exhibited in three individuals who find themselves 'on the beach' in Tahiti, a form of destitution that was common in the islands. One of *The Ebb-Tide*'s characters shows himself to be totally evil. Another is desperately weak and when a figure of authority appears, he submits thankfully to that dubious power. The third, the central character, struggles to maintain his self-respect by seeking resources within himself.

The Beach of Falesá is equally a moral tale. Wiltshire, the hero, is a small-time trader. By the end of the nineteenth century the focus of white trading in the Pacific was copra, dried coconut meat valuable for its oil. Coconuts were plentiful, native labour to collect them not difficult to harness. Stevenson himself had taken a close look at the copra trade as the *Equator* had made her way from island to island. 'The mystery of the copra trade tormented me,' he wrote in 'Around Our House' (*In the South Seas*), 'as I sat and watched the profits drip on the stair and sands.' Traders like Wiltshire, established on island stations, had come to expect an easy time. They offered cheap trade goods in exchange for the copra the islanders brought in, cheated the islanders whenever they could – everyone, it seemed, cheerfully watered the copra to bump up the weight, hence the dripping profits – and assumed there would be no lack of bodily comforts. Women were available, liquor was cheap, and sunshine inexhaustible.

Stevenson's Wiltshire is no different from any other trader, and in many respects this is still true at the end of the story. He does not change, and his identity as hero does not blot out his shortcomings. He retains the prejudices and limitations with which he started out. We are in no doubt that he is in the business of exploitation, and although there is a certain charm in his frankness the reader quickly recognises him as an ordinary and unremarkable sort of man. The tone and rhythm of his thought and speech tell us this. But they also tell us that, plain man though he is, he is not unresponsive to his surroundings. He appreciates the setting moon, the scent of the mountains, the prospect of fresh experience.

Stevenson's portrayal through the first person of a character who gives away more about himself than he states is a fine achievement. As the oblique unfolding of personality is continued, deeper levels of moral ambivalence are revealed. Wiltshire has no scruples about cheating the natives, yet he is troubled, not so much by exploitation itself as by the hypocrisy that surrounds it. His feelings about the marriage to Uma, the island girl who is acquired for him, demonstrate this. He does not object to being provided with a woman. That he sees as an unexceptionable part of the life of the white man in the islands. But he is unhappy about the phony marriage, although he rationalises and in the course of rationalizing unwraps a whole nexus of ambivalence and double standards. 'A man might easily feel cheap for less,' is his comment on the worthless marriage certificate. 'But it was the practice in these parts, and (as I told myself) not the least the fault of us White Men but of the missionaries. If they had let the natives be, I had never needed this deception, but taken all the wives I wished, and left them when I pleased, with a clear conscience.'

By any standards Wiltshire's morality is dubious. He is ready to exploit the islanders both economically and sexually. When Uma first appears he and his supposed ally Case size her up like a marketable object, an impression confirmed by Case's 'That's pretty' – not 'she's pretty'. The image modulates from object to animal to child. Wiltshire describes her as having 'a sly, strange, blindish look between a cat's and a baby's' and then, 'she looked up at men quick and timid like a child dodging a blow'. It is only later and, significantly, away from Case, that he sees her differently. 'She showed the best bearing for a bride conceivable, serious and still; and I thought shame to stand up with her in that mean house and before that grinning negro' (the latter not an islander but an associate of the degenerate Randall). Wiltshire has not only become aware of Uma as an individual; that awareness has implications for his sense of himself.

The two strands of the story are closely interwoven, with Uma providing the binding force. One strand follows Wiltshire's discovery of his love and respect for Uma, and his wish to do the decent thing by her. The other is the story of how he destroys Case, more out of self-preservation than a sense of public duty. He has considerable courage, but he does not see himself as champion of the native.

The story that Wiltshire tells proceeds like the peeling of an onion. With each episode, in themselves inexplicable and incomplete, he reveals more of himself and adds to his own understanding. He makes it quite clear that he acts throughout largely through self-interest, although concern for another, Uma, has translated self-interest onto a more heroic level. Yet he emerges as a decent and relatively honourable man, if not honest with the islanders at least honest with himself, and not attempting to disguise his prejudices.

The most striking feature of *The Beach of Falesá*, and

the feature that disturbed some contemporary readers, is its frankness. Its frankness about sex distressed its first editor. Readers one hundred years later probably feel that the story's frankness about exploitation and deceit is more significant. In many ways it is more direct than anything Conrad was to write later, and this is largely because Stevenson's vehicle is a man of limited understanding and imagination. He is not preoccupied with his own soul or a struggle to come to terms with guilt or collusion. Wiltshire has no problems of that kind. He adjusts cheerfully. When his modest ambition of returning to England and running a pub fades, because of his commitment to his family, he accepts it. He lives comfortably with his own prejudices, assuming, probably rightly, that they are the norm. All this is clear in the final paragraph. But much more than that is clear. Stevenson, through his inadvertent hero, precisely exposes an ambivalence that is at the heart of imperialism.

> My public house? Not a bit of it, nor ever likely; I'm stuck here, I fancy: I don't like to leave the kids, you see; and there's no use talking – they're better here than what they would be in a white man's country. Though Ben took the eldest up to Auckland, where he's been schooled with the best. But what bothers me is the girls. They're only half castes of course; I know that as well as you do, and there's nobody thinks less of half castes than I do; but they're mine, and about all I've got; I can't reconcile my mind to their taking up with kanakas, and I'd like to know where I'm to find them whites?

Falesá was a kind of breakthrough for Stevenson. Most of his fiction had drawn back from the problems of the contemporary world by placing character and action in the past. But we know Stevenson was keen to take on the confusions and contradictions of late Victorian life. In Scotland all kinds of inhibitions stood in the way of his tackling these in fiction, not the least of which was the unacceptability of being honest about sex. In the South Seas these inhibitions dwindled. At the same time, the circumstances and environment heightened just those ambiguities and contradictions that so fascinated him.

In a letter to Colvin he claimed that *Falesá* was the first ever realistic story to be set in the South Seas.

> Everybody else who has tried, that I have seen, got carried away by the romance, and ended in a kind of sugar candy sham epic, and the whole effect was lost – there was no etching, no human grin, consequently no conviction. Now I have got the smell and the look of the thing a good deal. You will know more about the South Seas after you have read my little tale than if you had read a library.

Stevenson had begun both *The Wrecker* (1892) and *The Ebb-Tide* (serialised in 1893 but not published in book form until shortly before his death) before tackling *The Beach of Falesá*. *The Wrecker* was conceived as an adventure story, a 'police' tale, but nevertheless it, too, captures something of the flavour of moral and physical disintegration which features with particular power and subtlety in *The Ebb-Tide*. *The Wrecker* can be read as a kind of introduction to the latter novel, as it tells us a great deal about white activity in the Pacific islands. It is a story of the making and breaking of fortunes and reputations, of duplicity and desperation, of weakness and fear. Although slow to get started, once the action reaches San Francisco, which Stevenson describes as the city which 'keeps the doors of the Pacific, and is the port of entry to another world and an earlier epoch in man's history', it moves into a higher gear. Through his hero, Loudon Dodd, Stevenson catches the tenor of his own excitement when he himself was in San Francisco longing to voyage westward.

Although *The Wrecker* was jointly written with Lloyd Osbourne, it draws directly on Stevenson's own experience, his Edinburgh background and his spells in Paris as well as America's Pacific coast and the islands. There are echoes of circumstances and phrases that appear in *In the South Seas* and the letters. The book was conceived on *The Equator* and writing began when Stevenson and his family were in the Gilbert Islands. The vigour and immediacy of the chapters that describe the voyages and crews of the *Norah Creina*, the *Flying Scud* and the *Currency Lass* are striking. The picture of San Francisco as the centre of a web of wheeling and dealing around the multiplicitous possibilities of the Pacific is also vivid. The view is very much from the ocean's eastern rim and provides a different perspective from Stevenson's other island writing.

The two main characters, Loudon Dodd and his friend and partner Jim Pinkerton (the Scottish flavour of both names is probably significant), exist in a kind of social and moral limbo, which again helps to prepare the way for *The Ebb-Tide*. They are both on the make. They are both ready to shut their eyes to irregularity and fraud. Yet they are both likeable, especially Pinkerton with his eager and almost innocent belief in each new enterprise. Dodd's cool self-interest is unsettled as he gradually unravels the mystery of the *Flying Scud*, the wreck he and Pinkerton purchase as a speculative venture, but the moral ambivalence of the story is not fully explored. The strength of the book lies in its detailing of the Pacific ambience and the people who were part of the exploitative world of ships and trade and speculation.

It is *The Ebb-Tide* which picks up and pursues some of the implications of both Wiltshire's story and the tale of the *Flying Scud*, and examines the theme of moral degeneration in uncompromising detail. If *Falesá* is a distillation of all that Stevenson experienced in the Pacific, *The Ebb-Tide* is a challenging exploration of moral and cultural assumptions about race and colonial intrusion.

It centres on four characters, all men: the novel is womanless – it is not sexual morality that is at issue here, although one of the characters agonises over his failure as husband and father. Like the characters in *Jekyll and Hyde* (and most of those in *The Wrecker*, although Pinkerton's marriage is part of his salvation) these men are adrift from family and community. Stevenson himself described them in a letter to Henry James as 'a troop of swine' and worried about the grimness of the story, but in fact it is the different ways in which four individuals react to their particular circumstances that provide the novel's crucial and provocative tension. Each is off-course in his own way. The three men 'on the beach' in Tahiti at the beginning of the story are desperately looking for any chance of pulling themselves out of a destitution that is the more intense because they are white. They consider themselves superior, yet in reality are more helpless than the native islanders. Huish is a Cockney, cunning and totally unprincipled. Davis is an American sea captain who lost his ship through drunken inadequacy. Herrick is an educated Englishman with pretensions to respectability. In the early scenes of the book Stevenson skilfully reveals the different threads of weakness, self-deception and self-interest in the three men, against a background of social and cultural fragmentation. The environment is all-important, for they are not only without money, possessions and prospects in a place where white men expect to succeed; they are deprived of all the props and supports on which men and women in a conventionally structured society depend.

To draw the most out of a clash of character and cultures, Stevenson employs a technique he had used successfully before. He confines his characters first on a schooner, which they take over with bogus credentials when smallpox kills the captain and the mate, then on an island. The schooner provides an opportunity for crime, in which all three men collude, but their own little world also begins to fragment as anger and guilt come to the surface. When they come upon an uncharted island presided over by Attwater, they are ripe to succumb to his gentlemanly certainties. But the island is not the tropical paradise that it might seem, and there is almost no escape.

The psychological and symbolic resonances of the story are extensive. Three men who are outcasts from the conventional, western, 'civilised' world, first seek restitution through crime, then find the possibility of refuge on an idyllic island under the control of an upper-class, Cambridge-educated dictator. In fact, Stevenson is describing environments which are built on exploitation and composed of layer upon layer of illusion and deceit. Assumed names and assumed histories (an integral part of *The Wrecker*, where some characters have several identities), the schooner's cargo of champagne which proves to be water, the imposed regime of white superiority founded on violence and trickery, and – perhaps most striking of all – the island itself, which features on no chart and rises mysteriously out of the sea, 'the undiscovered, the scarce-believed in', all challenge the reader's preconceptions. Herrick, the most sympathetic of the characters and most subject to conscience, gazes at the island as the schooner approaches.

> The isle was like the rim of a great vessel sunken
> in the waters; it was like the embankment of an
> annular railway grown upon with wood: so slender
> it seemed amidst the outrageous breakers, so frail
> and pretty, he would scarce have wondered to see it
> sink and disappear without a sound, and the waves
> close smoothly over its descent.

The fragile beauty has a sinister quality which grows
stronger as Herrick encounters Attwater and explores
the island. Attwater has built his pearl-fishing kingdom
on savage exploitation of the islanders, but he offers all
the certainties and comforts of control. The responses of
Herrick, Davis and Huish to what they find, and the physical
and psychological struggles involved, bring the story to its
conclusion.

The climate, the ocean, the seductive environment of
the tropical island, all play their part in this parable of
moral breakdown. The examination of four men removed
from accustomed codes and constraints and ignorant of
social and cultural mores of the people they exploit is
inseparable from the environment. There is no 'sugar
candy' here, or at least only in the sense that candy can
be corrupting. Of the four characters, Attwater is wholly
corrupted by power though his sophisticated veneer is
flawless. Huish, who in spite of a kind of impudent
courage is evil ('the devil . . . looked out of his face'),
is shot by Attwater. Davis, the weakest of the four,
becomes Attwater's puppet: absolute power requires pup-
pets. Only Herrick, perhaps, escapes, and he is deeply
compromised.

The Ebb-Tide continues Stevenson's fascinated exploration of humanity's tenuous hold on right and wrong, which
had begun in his earliest work. He began to write in the
context of mid-Victorian Scotland, where moral absolutes
were fiercely delineated. *The Ebb-Tide*, his last complete
novel and undoubtedly one of his best, is informed by the
other side of the Victorian coin, the imperialist intrusions
on which Britain's and Scotland's nineteenth-century success depended. It delivers a message about ambivalence,
reminding us that the codes on which we depend are

flawed, while sailing on a chartless ocean is dangerous. He had long since questioned the Calvinist determinism of his upbringing. *The Ebb-Tide* shows him probing aspects and implications of human behaviour which were normally disguised. Like *The Beach of Falesá*, it is a remarkably radical book and strikingly modern in tone. In his short life Stevenson travelled a long way, both in miles and in understanding of the human predicament.

This collection of Stevenson's South Sea writings enables the reader to trace part of this journey and to see some of the ways in which the writer about Scotland's contentious past became also an investigator of Britain's imperialist present. It shows Stevenson in all his moods, boyishly enthusiastic, keenly appreciative of the absurd, nostalgic, uncertain, deeply serious – all the qualities that have attracted readers to Stevenson for more than a hundred years.

Jenni Calder

NOTES TO INTRODUCTION

1. Letter to James Payne, *The Letters of Robert Louis Stevenson*, ed. Sidney Colvin (London 1911), vol. iii, p.131.

2. Letter to Sidney Colvin, *ibid.*, p.134.

3. Margaret Stevenson, *From Saranac to the Marquesas and Beyond* (London 1903), p.63.

4. W.E. Clarke, *Reminiscences of Robert Louis Stevenson*, n.d., no page numbers.

5. In Arthur Johnstone, *Recollections of Robert Louis Stevenson in the Pacific* (London 1905), p.103.

6. Letter to R.A.M. Stevenson, *Letters*, vol. iv, p.303.

7. Robert Louis Stevenson, *Weir of Hermiston*, Skerryvore Edition (London 1925), p.129.

8. Letter to Sidney Colvin, *Letters*, vol. iii, p.292.

ISLAND LANDFALLS:
Reflections from the South Seas
by Robert Louis Stevenson

selected and introduced by
JENNI CALDER

Letters

Throughout his life Stevenson was a prolific letter writer. While in the South Seas he wrote to many of his friends in England and Scotland, most regularly to Sidney Colvin, who acted as his literary agent in London. From the following letters, written between the ages of thirty-nine and forty-one, we get a flavour of Stevenson's experiences and responses in the Pacific which has a spontaneous liveliness often muted in his more polished work. His delight in fresh encounters and his boyish enthusiasm are expressed in the letters without inhibition. But an attentiveness to detail and nuance is also apparent, and a disarming directness. When he wrote for publication, there were times that Stevenson felt he had to curb his frankness and subdue his criticism. This was less likely to be true of his letters.

The text of the letters in this selection is taken from the Swanston edition of Stevenson's work, 1925, which includes some letters not published in earlier editions.

Yacht 'Casco', at sea, near the Paumotus
7 A.M., *September 6th, 1888, with a dreadful pen.*

My Dear Charles, – Last night as I lay under my blanket in the cockpit, courting sleep, I had a comic seizure. There was nothing visible but the southern stars, and the steersman there out by the binnacle lamp; we were all looking forward to a most deplorable landfall on the morrow, praying God we should fetch a tuft of palms which are to indicate the Dangerous Archipelago; the night was as warm as milk, and all of a sudden I had a vision of – Drummond Street. It came on me like a flash of lightning: I simply returned thither, and into the past. And when I remember all I hoped and feared as I pickled about Rutherford's[2] in the rain and the east wind; how I feared I should make a mere shipwreck, and yet timidly hoped not; how I feared I should never have a friend, far less a wife, and yet passionately hoped I might; how I hoped (if I did not take to drink) I should possibly write one little book, etc. etc. And then now – what a change! I feel somehow as if I should like the incident set upon a brass plate at the corner of that dreary thoroughfare for all students to read, poor devils, when their hearts are down. And I felt I must write one word to you. Excuse me if I write little: when I am at sea, it gives me a headache; when I am in port, I have my diary crying 'Give, give.' I shall have a fine book of travels, I feel sure; and will tell you more of the South Seas after very few months than any other writer has done – except Herman Melville[3] perhaps, who is a howling cheese. Good luck to you, God bless you. – Your affectionate friend,   R.L.S.

1. Baxter was an old friend and fellow-student of Stevenson's. An Edinburgh lawyer, he handled Stevenson's financial affairs while he was abroad.

2. A public house in Drummond Street, a stone's throw from Edinburgh University's Old College, and still standing.

3. Stevenson had read Melville's *Typee* (1846), a record of a four month stay in the Marquesas, with great enthusiasm.

TO THOMAS ARCHER[1]

Tautira, Island of Tahiti [November 1888].

Dear Tomarcher, – This is a pretty state of things! seven o'clock and no word of breakfast! And I was awake a good deal last night, for it was full moon, and they had made a great fire of cocoa-nut husks down by the sea, and as we have no blinds or shutters, this kept my room very bright. And then the rats had a wedding or a school-feast under my bed. And then I woke early, and I have nothing to read except Virgil's *Æneid*, which is not good fun on an empty stomach, and a Latin dictionary, which is good for naught, and by some humorous accident, your dear papa's article on Skerryvore. And I read the whole of that, and very impudent it is, but you must not tell your dear papa I said so, or it might come to a battle in which you might lose either a dear papa or a valued correspondent, or both, which would be prodigal. And still no breakfast; so I said 'Let's write to Tomarcher.'

This is a much better place for children than any I have hitherto seen in these seas. The girls (and sometimes the boys) play a very elaborate kind of hopscotch. The boys play horses exactly as we do in Europe; and have very good fun on stilts, trying to knock each other down, in which they do not often succeed. The children of all ages go to church and are allowed to do what they please, running about the aisles, rolling balls, stealing mama's bonnet and publicly sitting on it, and at last going to sleep in the middle of the floor. I forgot to say that the whips to play horses, and the balls to roll about the church – at least I never saw them used elsewhere – grow ready made on trees; which is rough on toy-shops. The whips are so good that I wanted to play horses myself; but no such luck! my hair is grey, and I am a great big, ugly man. The balls are rather hard, but very light and quite round. When you grow up and become offensively rich, you can charter a ship in the port of London, and have it come back to you entirely loaded with these balls; when you could satisfy your mind as to

1. 'Tomarcher' was the son of writer, critic and translator William Archer, who had visited Stevenson in his Bournemouth house, called Skerryvore after the famous Stevenson lighthouse in the Hebrides.

3

their character, and give them away when done with to your uncles and aunts. But what I really wanted to tell you was this: besides the tree-top toys (Hush-a-by, toy-shop, on the tree-top!), I have seen some real *made* toys, the first hitherto observed in the South Seas.

This was how. You are to imagine a four-wheeled gig; one horse; in the front seat two Tahiti natives, in their Sunday clothes, blue coat, white shirt, kilt (a little longer than the Scotch) of a blue stuff with big white or yellow flowers, legs and feet bare; in the back seat me and my wife, who is a friend of yours; under our feet, plenty of lunch and things: among us a great deal of fun in broken Tahitian, one of the natives, the sub-chief of the village, being a great ally of mine. Indeed we have exchanged names; so that he is now Rui, the nearest they can come to Louis, for they have no *l* and no *s* in their language. Rui is six feet three in his stockings, and a magnificent man. We all have straw hats, for the sun is strong. We drive between the sea, which makes a great noise, and the mountains; the road is cut through a forest mostly of fruit trees, the very creepers, which take the place of our ivy, heavy with a great and delicious fruit, bigger than your head and far nicer, called Barbedine. Presently we came to a house in a pretty garden, quite by itself, very nicely kept, the doors and windows open, no one about, and no noise but that of the sea. It looked like a house in a fairy-tale, and just beyond we must ford a river, and there we saw the inhabitants. Just in the mouth of the river, where it met the sea waves, they were ducking and bathing and screaming together like a covey of birds: seven or eight little naked brown boys and girls as happy as the day was long; and on the banks of the stream beside them, real toys – toy ships, full rigged, and with their sails set, though they were lying in the dust on their beam ends. And then I knew for sure they were all children in a fairy-story, living alone together in that lonely house with the only toys in all the island; and that I had myself driven, in my four-wheeled gig, into a corner of the fairy-story, and the question was, should I get out again? But it was all right; I guess only one of the wheels of the gig had got into the fairy-story; and the next jolt the whole thing vanished, and we drove on in our sea-side forest as before, and I have the honour to be Tomarcher's valued correspondent, TERIITERA, which he was previously known as

ROBERT LOUIS STEVENSON

TO R.A.M. STEVENSON[1]

Honolulu, Hawaiian Islands, February 1889.

My Dear Rob, – My extremely foolhardy venture is practically over. How foolhardy it was I don't think I realised. We had a very small schooner, and, like most yachts, over-rigged and over-sparred, and like many American yachts on a very dangerous sail plan. The waters we sailed in are, of course, entirely unlighted, and very badly charted; in the Dangerous Archipelago, through which we were fools enough to go, we were perfectly in ignorance of where we were for a whole night and half the next day, and this in the midst of invisible islands and rapid and variable currents; and we were lucky when we found our whereabouts at last. We have twice had all we wanted in the way of squalls: once, as I came on deck, I found the green sea over the cockpit coamings and running down the companion like a brook to meet me; at that same moment the foresail sheet jammed and the captain had no knife; this was the only occasion on the cruise that ever I set a hand to a rope, but I worked like a Trojan, judging the possibility of haemorrhage better than the certainty of drowning. Another time I saw a rather singular thing: our whole ship's company as pale as paper from the the captain to the cook; we had a black squall astern on the port side and a white squall ahead to starboard; the complication passed off innocuous, the black squall only fetching us with its tail, and the white one slewing off somewhere else. Twice we were a long while (days) in the close vicinity of hurricane weather, but again luck prevailed, and we saw none of it. These are dangers incident to these seas and small craft. What was an amazement, and at the same time a powerful stroke of luck, both our masts were rotten, and we found it out – I was going to say in time, but it was stranger and

1. Bob Stevenson was Stevenson's cousin, son of Alan Stevenson, the designer of the Skerryvore lighthouse. Three years older than Stevenson, he was a favourite playmate in childhood and a valued friend as a young man.

luckier than that. The head of the main-mast hung over so that hands were afraid to go to the helm; and less than three weeks before – I am not sure it was more than a fortnight – we had been nearly twelve hours beating off the lee shore of Eimeo (or Moorea, next island to Tahiti) in half a gale of wind with a violent head sea: she would neither tack nor wear once, and had to be boxed off with the mainsail – you can imagine what an ungodly show of kites we carried – and yet the mast stood. The very day after that, in the southern bight of Tahiti, we had a near squeak, the wind suddenly coming calm; the reefs were close in with, my eye! what a surf! The pilot thought we were gone, and the captain had a boat cleared, when a lucky squall came to our rescue. My wife, hearing the order given about the boats, remarked to my mother, 'Isn't that nice? We shall soon be ashore!' Thus does the female mind unconsciously skirt along the verge of eternity. Our voyage up here was most disastrous – calms, squalls, head sea, waterspouts of rain, hurricane weather all about, and we in the midst of the hurricane season, when even the hopeful builder and owner of the yacht had pronounced these seas unfit for her. We ran out of food, and were quite given up for lost in Honolulu: people had ceased to speak to Belle[2] about the *Casco*, as a deadly subject.

But the perils of the deep were part of the programme; and though I am very glad to be done with them for a while and comfortably ashore, where a squall does not matter a snuff to any one, I feel pretty sure I shall want to get to sea again ere long. The dreadful risk I took was financial, and double-headed. First, I had to sink a lot of money in the cruise, and if I didn't get health, how was I to get it back? I have got health to a wonderful extent; and as I have the most interesting matter for my book, bar accidents, I ought to get all I have laid out and a profit. But, second (what I own I never considered till too late), there was the danger of collisions, of damages and heavy repairs, of disablement, towing, and salvage; indeed, the cruise might have turned round and cost me double. Nor will this danger be quite over till I hear the yacht is in San Francisco; for though I

2. Mrs. Isobel Strong, daughter of Stevenson's wife
   Fanny Osbourne. Belle was living in Honolulu
   with her artist husband Joe Strong.

have shaken the dust of her deck from my feet, I fear (as a point of law) she is still mine till she gets there.

From my point of view, up to now the cruise has been a wonderful success. I never knew the world was so amusing. On the last voyage we had grown so used to sea-life that no one wearied, though it lasted a full month, except Fanny, who is always ill. All the time our visits to the islands have been more like dreams than realities: the people, the life, the beachcombers, the old stories and songs I have picked up, so interesting; the climate, the scenery, and (in some places) the women, so beautiful. The women are handsomest in Tahiti, the men in the Marquesas; both as fine types as can be imagined. Lloyd reminds me, I have not told you one characteristic incident of the cruise from a semi-naval point of view. One night we were going ashore in Anaho Bay;[3] the most awful noise on deck; the breakers distinctly audible in the cabin; and there I had to sit below, entertaining in my best style a negroid native chieftain, much the worse for rum! You can imagine the evening's pleasure.

This naval report on cruising in the South Seas would be incomplete without one other trait. On our voyage up here I came one day into the dining-room, the hatch in the floor was open, the ship's boy was below with a baler, and two of the hands were carrying buckets as for a fire; this meant that the pumps had ceased working.

One stirring day was that in which we sighted Hawaii. It blew fair, but very strong; we carried jib, foresail, and mainsail, all single-reefed, and she carried her lee rail under water and flew. The swell, the heaviest I have ever been out in – I tried in vain to estimate the height, *at least* fifteen feet – came tearing after us about a point and a half off the wind. We had the best hand – old Louis – at the wheel; and really, he did nobly, and had noble luck, for it never caught us once. At times it seemed we must have it; Louis would look over his shoulder with the queerest look and dive down his neck into his shoulders; and then it missed us somehow, and only sprays came over our quarter, turning the little outside lane of deck into a mill race as deep as to the cockpit coamings. I never remember anything more delightful and exciting. Pretty soon after we were lying absolutely becalmed under

3. The Stevenson party had spent some time at
Anaho Bay in the Gilbert Islands.

the lee of Hawaii, of which we had been warned; and
the captain never confessed he had done it on purpose,
but when accused, he smiled. Really, I suppose he did
quite right, for we stood committed to a dangerous race,
and to bring her to the wind would have been rather a
heart-sickening manoeuvre.

                                                    R.L.S.

TO MISS ADELAIDE BOODLE[1]
                            Honolulu, April 6th, 1889.

My Dear Miss Boodle, – Nobody writes a letter better
than my Gamekeeper: so gay, so pleasant, so engagingly
particular, answering (by some delicate instinct) all the
questions she suggests. It is a shame you should get such
a poor return as I can make, from a mind essentially and
originally incapable of the art epistolary. I would let the
paper-cutter take my place; but I am sorry to say the
little wooden seaman did after the manner of seamen,
and deserted in the Societies.[2] The place he seems to have
stayed at – seems, for his absence was not observed till we
were near the Equator – was Tautira,[3] and, I assure you, he
displayed good taste, Tautira being as 'nigh hand heaven'
as a paper-cutter or anybody has a right to expect.

I think all our friends will be very angry with us, and I
give the grounds of their probable displeasure bluntly – we
are not coming home for another year. My mother[4] returns
next month. Fanny, Lloyd, and I push on again among
the islands on a trading schooner, the *Equator* – first for
the Gilbert group, which we shall have an opportunity to
explore thoroughly; then, if occasion serve, to the Marshalls
and Carolines; and if occasion (or money) fail, to Samoa,

1. A neighbour in Bournemouth who became very
    friendly with both Fanny and Louis Stevenson.
    Stevenson nicknamed her 'the Gamekeeper'.

2. The Society Islands, of which Tahiti is the largest.

3. On the opposite side of Tahiti from Papeete,
    the island's main town and capital of French
    Polynesia. The Stevensons had spent a very happy
    time there.

4. Stevenson's mother, Margaret Isabella Balfour
    Stevenson, recently widowed, accompanied him
    for the first part of the South Seas trip.

and back to Tahiti. I own we are deserters, but we have excuses. You cannot conceive how these climates agree with the wretched house-plant of Skerryvore: he wonders to find himself sea-bathing, and cutting about the world loose, like a grown-up person. They agree with Fanny too, who does not suffer from her rheumatism, and with Lloyd also. And the interest of the islands is endless; and the sea, though I own it is a fearsome place, is very delightful. We had applied for places in the American missionary ship, the *Morning Star*, but this trading schooner is a far preferable idea, giving us more time and a thousandfold more liberty; so we determined to cut off the missionaries with a shilling.

The Sandwich Islands[5] do not interest us very much; we live here, oppressed with civilisation, and look for good things in the future. But it would surprise you if you came out tonight from Honolulu (all shining with electric lights, and all in a bustle from the arrival of the mail, which is to carry you these lines) and crossed the long wooden causeway along the beach, and came out on the road through Kapiolani park, and seeing a gate in the palings, with a tub of gold-fish by the wayside, entered casually in. The buildings stand in three groups by the edge of the beach, where an angry little spitfire sea continually spirts and thrashes with impotent irascibility, the big seas breaking further out upon the reef. The first is a small house, with a very large summer parlour, or *lanai*, as they call it here, roofed, but practically open. There you will find the lamps burning and the family sitting about the table, dinner just done: my mother, my wife, Lloyd, Belle, my wife's daughter, Austin her child, and tonight (by way of rarity) a guest. All about the walls our South Sea curiosities, war clubs, idols, pearl shells, stone axes, etc.; and the walls are only a small part of a lanai, the rest being glazed or latticed windows, or mere open space.

You will see there no sign of the Squire, however; and being a person of a humane disposition, you will only glance in over the balcony railing at the merry-makers in the summer parlour, and proceed further afield after the Exile. You look round, there is beautiful green turf, many

5. Hawaiian Islands.

trees of an outlandish sort that drop thorns – look out if
your feet are bare; but I beg your pardon, you have not
been long enough in the South Seas – and many oleanders
in full flower. The next group of buildings is ramshackle,
and quite dark; you make out a coach-house door, and
look in – only some cocoanuts; you try round to the left
and come to the sea front, where Venus and the moon are
making luminous tracks on the water, and a great swell rolls
and shines on the outer reef; and here is another door – all
these places open from the outside – and you go in, and find
photography, tubs of water, negatives steeping, a tap, and a
chair and an inkbottle, where my wife is supposed to write;
round a little further, a third door, entering which you find
a picture upon the easel and a table sticky with paints; a
fourth door admits you to a sort of court, where there is a
hen sitting – I believe on a fallacious egg. No sign of the
Squire in all this. But right opposite the studio door you
have observed a third little house, from whose open door
lamplight streams and makes hay of the strong moonlight
shadows. You had supposed it made no part of the grounds,
for a fence runs round it lined with oleander; but as the
Squire is nowhere else, is it not just possible he may be
here? It is a grim little wooden shanty; cobwebs bedeck
it; friendly mice inhabit its recesses; the mailed cockroach
walks upon the wall; so also, I regret to say, the scorpion.
Herein are two pallet beds, two mosquito curtains, strung
to the pitch-boards of the roof, two tables laden with books
and manuscripts, three chairs, and, in one of the beds, the
Squire busy writing to yourself, as it chances, and just at
this moment somewhat bitten by mosquitoes. He has just
set fire to the insect powder, and will be all right in no
time; but just now he contemplates large white blisters,
and would like to scratch them, but knows better. The
house is not bare; it has been inhabited by Kanakas,[6] and
– you know what children are! – the bare wood walls are
pasted over with pages from the *Graphic, Harper's Weekly*,
etc. The floor is matted, and I am bound to say the matting
is filthy. There are two windows and two doors, one of
which is condemned; on the panels of that last a sheet of

6. In the Hawaiian language Kanaka is the word for
   man, but was widely used to refer to all native
   Pacific islanders.

paper is pinned up, and covered with writing. I cull a few plums: –

A duck-hammock for each person.
A patent organ like the commandant's at Taiohae.[7]
Cheap and bad cigars for presents.
Revolvers.
Permanganate of potass.
Liniment for the head and sulphur.
Fine tooth-comb.

What do you think this is? Simply life in the South Seas foreshortened. These are a few of our desiderata for the next trip, which we jot down as they occur.

There, I have really done my best and tried to send you something like a letter – one letter in return for all your dozens. Pray remember us all to yourself, Mrs Boodle, and the rest of your house. I do hope your mother will be better when this comes. I shall write and give you a new address when I have made up my mind as to the most probable, and I do beg you will continue to write from time to time and give us airs from home. Tomorrow – think of it – I must be off by a quarter to eight to drive in to the palace and breakfast with his Hawaiian Majesty at 8.30: I shall be dead indeed. Please give my news to Scott, I trust he is better; give him my warm regards. To you we all send all kinds of things, and I am the absentee Squire,

ROBERT LOUIS STEVENSON

---

7. A village in the Marquesas Islands.

TO SIDNEY COLVIN

Honolulu, June 1889

My Dear Colvin, – I am just home after twelve days journey to Molokai,[1] seven of them at the leper settlement, where I can only say that the sight of so much courage, cheerfulness, and devotion strung me too high to mind the infinite pity and horror of the sights. I used to ride over from Kalawao to Kalaupapa (about three miles across the promontory, the cliff-wall, ivied with forest and yet inaccessible from steepness, on my left), go to the Sisters' home, which is a miracle of neatness, play a game of croquet with seven leper girls (90° in the shade), get a little old-maid meal served me by the Sisters, and ride home again, tired enough, but not too tired. The girls have all dolls, and loved dressing them. You who know so many ladies delicately clad, and they who know so many dressmakers, please make it known it would be an acceptable gift to send scraps for doll dressmaking to the Reverend Sister Maryanne, Bishop Home, Kalaupapa, Molokai, Hawaiian Islands.

I have seen sights that cannot be told, and heard stories that cannot be repeated: yet I never admired my poor race so much, nor (strange as it may seem) loved life more than in the settlement. A horror of moral beauty broods over the place: that's like bad Victor Hugo,[2] but it is the only way I can express the sense that lived with me all these days. And this even though it was in great part Catholic, and my sympathies flew never with so much difficulty as towards Catholic virtues. The passbook kept with heaven stirs me to anger and laughter. One of the sisters calls the place 'the ticket office to heaven'. Well, what is the odds? They do their darg, and do it with kindness and efficiency incredible; and we must take folk's virtues as we find them, and love the better part. Of old Damien,[3] whose weaknesses and worse perhaps I heard fully, I think only the more. It was a European

1. One of the Hawaiian Islands, on which there was a leper colony. Stevenson made a point of visiting Molokai during his stay in Honolulu.

2. Stevenson came to admire the French novelist, though with certain reservations.

3. Father Damien was the Belgian priest who

peasant: dirty, bigoted, untruthful, unwise, tricky, but superb with generosity, residual candour and fundamental good-humour: convince him he had done wrong (it might take hours of insult) and he would undo what he had done and like his corrector better. A man, with all the grime and paltriness of mankind, but a saint and hero all the more for that. The place as regards scenery is grand, gloomy, and bleak. Mighty mountain walls descending sheer along the whole face of the island into the sea unusually deep; the front of the mountain ivied and furred with clinging forest, one viridescent cliff: about half-way from east to west, the low, bare, stony promontory edged in between the cliff and the ocean; the two little towns (Kalawao and Kalaupapa) seated on either side of it, as bare almost as bathing machines upon a beach; and the population – gorgons and chimaeras dire. All this tear of the nerves I bore admirably; and the day after I got away, rode twenty miles along the opposite coast and up into the mountains: they call it twenty, I am doubtful of the figures: I should guess it nearer twelve; but let me take credit for what residents allege; and I was riding again the day after, so I need say no more about health. Honolulu does not agree with me at all: I am always out of sorts there, with slight headache, blood to the head, etc. I had a good deal of work to do and did it with miserable difficulty; and yet all the time I have been gaining strength, as you see, which is highly encouraging. By the time I am done with this cruise I shall have the material for a very singular book of travels: names of strange stories and characters, cannibals, pirates, ancient legends, old Polynesian poetry, – never was so generous a farrago. I am going down now to get the story of a shipwrecked family, who were fifteen months on an island with a murderer: there is a specimen. The Pacific is a strange place; the nineteenth century only exists there in spots: all round, it is a no man's land of

presided over the leper colony. Although he never
met Damien, who died before Stevenson's visit
to Molokai, he admired him greatly. Damien
was considered a reprobate by many. Stevenson
defended him against what he considered
sanctimonious Protestant attack in 'An Open
Letter to the Rev. Dr Hyde of Honolulu' (1890).

the ages, a stir-about of epochs and races, barbarisms and civilisations, virtues and crimes.

It is good of you to let me stay longer, but if I had known how ill you were, I should be now on my way home. I had chartered my schooner and made all arrangements before (at last) we got definite news. I feel highly guilty; I should be back to insult and worry you a little. Our address till further notice is to be c/o R. Towns and Co., Sydney. That is final: I only got the arrangement made yesterday; but you may now publish it abroad. – Yours ever,

R.L.S.

TO SIDNEY COLVIN
Schooner 'Equator,' Apaiang Lagoon
22nd August, 1889.

My Dear Colvin, – The missionary ship is outside the reef trying (vainly) to get in; so I may have a chance to get a line off. I am glad to say I shall be home by June next for the summer, or we shall know the reason why. For God's sake be well and jolly for the meeting. I shall be, I believe, a different character from what you have seen this long while. This cruise is up to now a huge success, being interesting, pleasant, and profitable. The beachcomber is perhaps the most interesting character here; the natives are very different, on the whole, from Polynesians: they are moral, stand-offish (for good reasons), and protected by a dark tongue. It is delightful to meet the few Hawaiians (mostly missionaries) that are dotted about, with their Italian *brio* and their ready friendliness. The whites are a strange lot, many of them good, kind, pleasant fellows; others quite the lowest I have ever seen even in the slums of cities. I wish I had time to narrate to you the doings and character of three white murderers (more or less proven) I have met. One, the only undoubted assassin of the lot, quite gained my affection in his big home out of a wreck, with his New Hebrides wife in her savage turban of hair and yet a perfect lady, and his three adorable little girls in Rob Roy Macgregor dresses, dancing to the hand organ, performing circus on the floor with startling effects of nudity, and curling up together on a mat to sleep, three sizes, three attitudes, three Rob Roy dresses, and six little clenched fists: the murderer meanwhile brooding and gloating over his chicks, till your whole heart went out to him; and yet his crime on the face of it was dark: disembowelling, in his own house, an old man of seventy, and him drunk.

It is lunch-time, I see, and I must close up with my warmest love to you. I wish you were here to sit upon me when required. Ah! if you were but a good sailor! I will never leave the sea, I think; it is only here that a Briton lives: my poor grandfather, it is from him I inherit the taste, I fancy, and he was round many islands in his day: but I, please God, shall beat him at that before the recall is sounded. Would you be surprised to learn that I contemplate becoming a shipowner? I do, but it is a secret. Life is far better fun than people dream who fall asleep among the chimney stacks and telegraph wires.

Love to Henry James and others near. – Ever yours, my dear fellow

ROBERT LOUIS STEVENSON.

TO SIDNEY COLVIN
Equator Town,[1] *Apemama, October* 1889.

No *Morning Star* came, however; and so now I try to send this to you by the schooner *J. L. Tiernan.* We have been about a month ashore, camping out in a kind of town the king set up for us: on the idea that I was really a 'big chief' in England. He dines with us sometimes, and sends up a cook for a share of our meals when he does not come himself. This sounds like high living! alas, undeceive yourself. Salt junk is the mainstay; a low island, except for cocoanuts, is just the same as a ship at sea: brackish water, no supplies, and very little shelter. The king is a great character – a thorough tyrant, very much of a gentleman, a poet, a musician, a historian, or perhaps rather more a genealogist – it is strange to see him lying in his house among a lot of wives (nominal wives) writing the History of Apemama in an account-book; his description of one of his own songs, which he sang to me himself, as 'about sweethearts, and trees, and the sea – and no true, all-the-same lie', seems

1. At Apemama in the Gilberts King Tembinoka constructed a compound of huts for the Stevenson party's stay. It was known as 'Equator Town', after the schooner *Equator* in which they were voyaging.

about as compendious a definition of lyric poetry as a man could ask. Tembinoka is here the great attraction: all the rest is heat and tedium and villainous dazzle, and yet more villainous mosquitoes. We are like to be here, however, many a long week before we get away, and then whither? A strange trade this voyaging: so vague, so bound-down, so helpless. Fanny has been planting some vegetables, and we have actually onions and radishes coming up: ah, onion-despiser, were you but awhile in a low island, how your heart would leap at sight of a coster's barrow! I think I could shed tears over a dish of turnips. No doubt we shall all be glad to say farewell to low islands – I had near said for ever. They are very tame; and I begin to read up the directory, and pine for an island with a profile, a running brook, or were it only a well among the rocks. The thought of a mango came to me early this morning and set my greed on edge; but you do not know what a mango is, so—

I have been thinking a great deal of you and the Monument[2] of late, and even tried to get my thought into a poem, hitherto without success. God knows how you are: I begin to weary dreadfully to see you – well, in nine months, I hope; but that seems a long time. I wonder what has befallen me too, that flimsy part of me that lives (or dwindles) in the public mind; and what has befallen *The Master*,[3] and what kind of a Box[4] the Merry Box has been found. It is odd to know nothing of all this. We had an old woman to do devil-work for you about a month ago, in a Chinaman's house on Apaiang[5] (August 23rd or 24th). You should have seen the crone with a noble masculine face, like that of an old crone [*sic*], a body like a man's (naked all but the feathery female girdle), knotting cocoanut leaves and muttering spells: Fanny and I, and the good captain of the *Equator*, and the Chinaman and his native wife and

2. Stevenson referred thus to the British Museum, where Colvin was Curator of Prints.
3. *The Master of Ballantrae*, recently published.
4. *The Wrong Box*, written in collaboration with Lloyd Osbourne before leaving the United States for the Pacific, and recently published.
5. One of the Gilbert Islands.

sister-in-law, all squatting on the floor about the sibyl; and a crowd of dark faces watching from behind her shoulder (she sat right in the doorway) and tittering aloud with strange, appalled, embarrassed laughter at each fresh adjuration. She informed us you were in England, not travelling and now no longer sick; she promised us a fair wind the next day, and we had it, so I cherish the hope she was as right about Sidney Colvin. The shipownering has rather petered out since I last wrote, and a good many other plans besides.

Health? Fanny very so-so; I pretty right upon the whole, and getting through plenty work: I know not quite how, but it seems to me not bad and in places funny.

South Sea Yarns:[6]

1. *The Wrecker*		R.L.S.
2. *The Pearl Fisher* }	*by*	*and*
3. *The Beachcombers.*		LLOYD O.

The Pearl Fisher, part done, lies in Sydney. It is *The Wrecker* we are now engaged upon: strange ways of life, I think, they set forth: things that I can scarce touch upon, or even not at all, in my travel book; and the yarns are good, I do believe. *The Pearl Fisher* is for the *New York Ledger:* the yarn is a kind of Monte Cristo one. *The Wrecker* is the least good as a story, I think; but the characters seem to me good. *The Beachcombers* is more sentimental. These three scarce touch the outskirts of the life we have been viewing; a hot-bed of strange characters and incidents: Lord, how different from Europe or the Pallid States! Farewell. Heaven knows when this will get to you. I burn to be in Sydney and have news.

R.L.S.

TO SIDNEY COLVIN

In the Mountain, Apia, Samoa
Monday, November 2, 1890.

My Dear Colvin, – This is a hard and interesting and

6. *The Wrecker* (1892) had been begun, in collaboration with Lloyd Osbourne, a few months earlier. *The Pearl Fisher* was begun by Lloyd Osbourne in Honolulu the previous spring. The final version was written by Stevenson and published as *The Ebb Tide* (1893). *The Beachcombers* was never written.

beautiful life that we lead now. Our place is in a deep cleft of Vaea Mountain, some six hundred feet above the sea, embowered in a forest, which is our strangling enemy, and which we combat with axes and dollars. I went crazy over outdoor work, and had at last to confine myself to the house, or literature must have gone by the board. *Nothing* is so interesting as weeding, clearing, and pathmaking; the over-sight of labourers becomes a disease; it is quite an effort not to drop into the farmer; and it does make you feel so well. To come down covered with mud and drenched with sweat and rain after some hours in the bush, change, rub down, and take a chair in the verandah, is to taste a quiet conscience. And the strange thing that I mark is this: if I go out and make sixpence, bossing my labourers and plying the cutlass or the spade, idiot conscience applauds me: if I sit in the house and make twenty pounds, idiot conscience wails over my neglect and the day wasted. For near a fortnight I did not go beyond the verandah; then I found my rush of work run out, and went down for the night to Apia; put in Sunday afternoon with our consul, 'a nice young man', dined with my friend H. J. Moors[1] in the evening, went to church – no less – at the white and half-white church – I had never been before, and was much interested; the woman I sat next *looked* a full-blood native, and it was in the prettiest and readiest English that she sang the hymns; back to Moors', where we yarned of the islands, being both wide wanderers, till bedtime; bed, sleep, breakfast, horse saddled; round to the mission, to get Mr Clarke[2] to be my interpreter; over with him to the King's whom I have not called on since my return; received by that mild old gentleman; have some interesting talk with him about Samoan superstitions and my land –

1. Henry Moors was a trader in Apia who acted as agent for the building of Vailima. He was a close associate of Stevenson and wrote about their relationship in *With Stevenson in Samoa* (1910).

2. W.E. Clarke was from the London Missionary Society and a man for whom Stevenson, often critical of missionaries, had considerable regard. See the passage quoted in the Introduction.

the scene of a great battle in his (Malietoa Laupepa's[3]) youth – the place where we have cleared the platform of his fort – the gully of the stream full of dead bodies – the fight rolled off up Vaea mountain-side; back with Clarke to the mission; had a bit of lunch and consulted over a queer point of missionary policy just arisen, about our new Town Hall and the balls there – too long to go into, but a quaint example of the intricate questions which spring up daily in the missionary path.

Then off up the hill; Jack very fresh, the sun (close on noon) staring hot, the breeze strong and pleasant; the ineffable green country all around – gorgeous little birds (I think they are humming-birds, but they say not) skirmishing in the wayside flowers. About a quarter way up I met a native coming down with the trunk of a cocoa palm across his shoulder; his brown breast glistening with sweat and oil: 'Talofa' – 'Talofa, alii – You see that white man? He speak for you.' 'White man he gone up here?' – 'Ioe' (Yes) – 'Tofa, alii' – 'Tofa, soifua!' I put Jack up the steep path, till he is all as white as a shaving stick – Brown's euxesis, wish I had some – past Tanugamanomo, a bush village – see into the houses as I pass – they are open sheds scattered on a green – see the brown folk sitting there, suckling kids, sleeping on their stiff wooden pillows – then on through the wood-path – and here I find the mysterious white man (poor devil!) with his twenty years' certificate of good behaviour as a book-keeper, frozen out by the strikes in the colonies, come up here on a chance, no work to be found, big hotel bill, no ship to leave in – come up to beg twenty dollars because he heard I was a Scotchman, offering to leave his portmanteau in pledge. Settle this, and on again; and here my house comes in view, and a war whoop fetches my wife and Henry (or Simelé), our Samoan boy, on the front balcony; and I am home again, and only sorry that I shall have to go down again to Apia this day week. I could, I would, dwell here unmoved, but there are things to be attended to.

Tuesday, 3rd. – I begin to see the whole scheme of letter-writing; you sit down every day and pour out an equable stream of twaddle.

3. The puppet king of Samoa, supported by the Germans.

This morning all my fears were fled, and all the trouble had fallen to the lot of Peni himself, who deserved it; my field was full of weeders and I am again able to justify the ways of God. All morning I worked at *The South Seas*, and finished the chapter I had stuck upon on Saturday. Fanny, awfully hove-to with rheumatics and injuries received upon the field of sport and glory, chasing pigs, was unable to go up and down stairs, so she sat upon the back verandah, and my work was chequered by her cries. 'Paul, you take a spade to do that – dig a hole first. If you do that, you'll cut your foot off! Here, you boy, what you do there? You no get work? You go find Simelé; he give you work. Peni, you tell this boy he go find Simelé: suppose Simelé no give him work, you tell him go 'way. I no want him here. That boy no good.' – *Peni* (from the distance in reassuring tones), 'All right, sir!' – *Fanny* (after a long pause), 'Peni, you tell that boy go find Simelé! I no want him stand here all day. He no do nothing.' – Luncheon, beef, soda-scones, fried bananas, pine-apple in claret, coffee. Try to write a poem; no go. Play the flageolet. Then sneakingly off to farmering and pioneering. Four gangs at work on our place; a lively scene; axes crashing and smoke blowing; all the knives are out. But I rob the garden party of one without a stock, and you should see my hand – cut to ribbons. Now I want to do my path up the Vaituliga single-handed, and I want it to burst on the public complete. Hence, with devilish ingenuity, I begin it at different places; so that if you stumble on one section, you may not even then suspect the fullness of my labours. Accordingly I started in a new place, below the wire, and hoping to work up to it. It was perhaps lucky I had so bad a cutlass, and my smarting hand bade me stay before I had got up to the wire, but just in season, so that I was only the better of my activity, not dead beat as yesterday.

A strange business it was, and infinitely solitary; away above, the sun was in the high tree-tops; the lianas noosed and sought to hang me; the saplings struggled, and came up with that sob of death that one gets to know so well; great, soft, sappy trees fell at a lick of the cutlass, little tough switches laughed at and dared my best endeavour. Soon, toiling down in that pit of verdure, I heard blows on the far side, and then laughter. I confess a chill settled on my heart. Being so dead alone, in a place where by rights none should be beyond me, I was aware, upon interrogation, if those blows had drawn nearer, I should (of course quite unaffectedly) have executed a strategic movement to the rear; and only the other day I was lamenting my insensibility to superstition! Am I beginning to be sucked in? Shall I become a midnight twitterer like my neighbours? At times I thought the blows were echoes; at times I thought the laughter was from birds. For our birds are strangely human in their calls. Vaea Mountain about sundown sometimes rings with shrill cries, like the hails of merry, scattered children. As a matter of fact, I believe stealthy woodcutters from Tanugamanono were above me in the wood and answerable for the blows; as for the laughter, a woman and two children asked Fanny's leave to go up shrimp-fishing in the burn; beyond doubt, it was these I heard. Just at the right time I returned; to wash down, change, and begin this snatch of letter before dinner was ready, and to finish it afterwards . . .

Dinner: stewed beef and potatoes, baked bananas, new loaf-bread hot from the oven, pine-apple in claret. These are great days: we have been low in the past; but now we are as belly-gods, enjoying all things.

Vailima, Apia,[2] Samoa, December 29th, 1890

My Dear Henry James, – It is terrible how little everybody writes, and how much of that little disappears in the capacious maw of the Post Office. Many letters, both from and to me, I now know to have been lost in transit: my eye is on the Sydney Post Office, a large ungainly structure with a tower, as being not a hundred miles from the scene of disappearance; but then I have no proof. The *Tragic Muse* you announced to me as coming; I had already ordered it from a Sydney bookseller: about two months ago he advised me that his copy was in the post; and I am still tragically museless.

News, news, news. What do we know of yours? What do you care for ours? We are in the midst of the rainy season, and dwell among alarms of hurricanes, in a very unsafe little two-storied wooden box 650 feet above and about three miles from the sea-beach. Behind us, till the other slope of the island, desert forest, peaks, and loud torrents; in front green slopes to the sea, some fifty miles of which we dominate. We see the ships as they go out and in to the dangerous roadstead of Apia; and if they lie far out, we can even see their topmasts while they are at anchor. Of sounds of men, beyond those of our own labourers, there reach us, at very long intervals, salutes from the warships in harbour, the bell of the cathedral church, and the low of the conch-shell calling the labour boys on the German plantations. Yesterday, which was Sunday – the *quantième* is most likely erroneous; you can now correct it – we had a visitor – Baker of Tonga. Heard you ever of him? He is a great man here: he is accused of theft, rape, judicial murder, private poisoning, abortion, misappropriation of public moneys – oddly enough, not forgery, nor arson: you would be amused if you knew how thick the accusations fly in this South Sea world. I make no doubt my own character is something illustrious; or if not yet, there is a good time coming.

1. The novelist and critic Henry James was a close friend of Stevenson, and had visited him often in Bournemouth. *The Tragic Muse* (1889) was his most recent novel.

2. The main town on the island of Upolu, and Samoa's capital.

But all our resources have not of late been Pacific. We have had enlightened society: La Farge[3] the painter, and your friend Henry Adams:[4] a great privilege – would it might endure. I would go oftener to see them, but the place is awkward to reach on horseback. I had to swim my horse the last time I went to dinner; and as I have not yet returned the clothes I had to borrow, I dare not return in the same plight; it seems inevitable – as soon as the wash comes in, I plump straight into the American consul's shirt or trousers! They, I believe, would come oftener to see me but for the horrid doubt that weights upon our commissariat department; we have *often* almost nothing to eat; a guest would simply break the bank; my wife and I have dined on one avocado pear; I have several times dined on hard bread and onions. What would you do with a guest at such narrow seasons? – eat him? or serve up a labour boy fricaseed?

Work? work is now arrested, but I have written, I should think, about thirty chapters of the South Sea book; they will all want rehandling, I dare say. Gracious, what a strain is a long book! The time it took me to design this volume, before I could dream of putting pen to paper, was excessive; and then think of writing a book of travels on the spot, when I am continually extending my information, revising my opinions, and seeing the most finely finished portions of my work come part by part in pieces. Very soon I shall have no opinions left. And without an opinion, how to string artistically vast accumulations of fact? Darwin[5] said no one could observe without a theory; I suppose he was right; 'tis a fine point of metaphysic; but I will take my

3. John La Farge was an American artist, and friend of another American artist Will Low, a companion of Stevenson in France in the 1870s.

4. American historian and friend of Henry James. He and La Farge were rather appalled at the Stevenson household. Adams described Stevenson as 'a bundle of sticks in a bag, with dirty striped pyjamas' and Fanny Stevenson as 'an Apache squaw'.

5. Stevenson was intrigued by the theories of Charles Darwin, whose *Origin of Species* was published in 1859.

oath, no man can write without one – at least the way he would like to, and my theories melt, melt, melt, and as they melt the thaw-waters wash down my writing and leave unideal tracts – wastes instead of cultivated farms.

Kipling[6] is by far the most promising young man who has appeared since – ahem – I appeared. He amazes me by his precocity and various endowment. But he alarms me by his copiousness and haste. He should shield his fire with both hands 'and draw up all his strength and sweetness in one ball'. ('Draw all his strength and all His sweetness up into one ball'? I cannot remember Marvell's[7] words.) So the critics have been saying to me; but I was never capable of – and surely never guilty of – such a debauch of production. At this rate his works will soon fill the habitable globe; and surely he was armed for better conflicts than these succinct sketches and flying leaves of verse? I look on, I admire, I rejoice for myself; but in a kind of ambition we all have for our tongue and literature I am wounded. If I had this man's fertility and courage, it seems to me I could heave a pyramid.

Well, we begin to be the old fogies now; and it was high time *something* rose to take our places. Certainly Kipling has the gifts; the fairy godmothers were all tipsy at his christening: what will he do with them?

I am going to manage to send a long letter every month to Colvin, which, I dare say, if it is ever of the least interest, he will let you see. My wife is now better, and I hope will be reasonably right. We are a very crazy couple to lead so rough a life, but we manage excellently: she is handy and inventive, and I have one quality, I don't grumble. The nearest I came was the other day: when I had finished dinner, I thought awhile, then had my horse saddled, rode down to Apia, and dined again – I must say with unblunted appetite; that is my best excuse. Goodbye, my dear James; find an hour to write to us, and register your letter. – Yours affectionately,

R.L.S.

6. Rudyard Kipling's first stories were being
   published in the 1880s.

7. Stevenson is quoting, slightly inaccurately, from
   the seventeenth-century poet Andrew Marvell's
   poem 'To His Coy Mistress'. The lines should
   read 'Let us roll all our strength and all/Our
   Sweetness up into one ball.'

TO SIDNEY COLVIN

Tuesday, Dec., 1891.

Sir, – I have the honour to report further explorations of the river Vaea, with accompanying sketch plan. The party under my command consisted of one horse, and was extremely insubordinate and mutinous, owing to not being used to go into the bush, and being half-broken anyway – and that the wrong half. The route indicated for my party was up to the bed of the so-called river Vaea, which I accordingly followed to a distance of perhaps two or three furlongs eastward from the house of Vailima, where the stream being quite dry, the bush thick, and the ground very difficult, I decided to leave the main body of the force under my command tied to a tree, and push on myself with the point of the advance guard, consisting of one man. The valley had become very narrow and airless; foliage close shut above; dry bed of the stream much excavated, so that I passed under fallen trees without stooping. Suddenly it turned sharp to the north, at right angles to its former direction; I heard living water, and came in view of a tall face of rock and the stream spraying down it; it might have been climbed, but it would have been dangerous, and I had to make my way up the steep earth banks, where there is nowhere any footing for man, only for trees, which made the rounds of my ladder. I was near the top of this climb, which was very hot and steep, and the pulses were buzzing all over my body, when I made sure there was one external sound in my ears, and paused to listen. No mistake; a sound of a mill-wheel thundering, I thought, close by yet below me, a huge mill-wheel, yet not going steadily, but with a *schottisch*[1] movement, and at each fresh impetus shaking the mountain. There, where I was, I just put down the sound of the mystery of the bush; where no sound now surprises me – and any sound alarms; I only thought it would give Jack a fine fright, down where he stood tied to a tree by himself, and he was badly enough scared when I left him. The good folks at home identified it; it was a sharp earthquake.

1. An energetic dance, similar to a polka.

At the top of the climb I made my way again to the watercourse; it is here running steady and pretty full; strange these intermittencies – and just a little below the main stream is quite dry, and all the original brook has gone down some lava gallery of the mountain – and just a little further below, it begins picking up from the left hand in little boggy tributaries, and in the inside of a hundred yards has grown a brook again. The general course of the brook was, I guess, s.e.; the valley still very deep and whelmed in wood. It seemed a swindle to have made so sheer a climb and still find yourself at the bottom of a well. But gradually the thing seemed to shallow, the trees to seem poorer and smaller; I could see more and more of the silver sprinkles of sky among the foliage instead of the sombre piling up of tree behind tree. And here I had two scares – first, away up on my right hand I heard a bull low; I think it was a bull from the quality of the low, which was singularly songful and beautiful; the bulls belong to me, but how did I know that the bull was aware of that? and my advance guard not being at all properly armed, we advanced with great precaution until I was satisfied that I was passing eastward of the enemy. It was during this period that a pool of the river suddenly boiled up in my face in a little fountain. It was in a very dreary, marshy part among dilapidated trees that you see through holes in the trunks of; and if any kind of beast or elf or devil had come out of that sudden silver ebullition I declare I do not think I should have been surprised. It was perhaps a thing as curious – a fish, with which these head waters of the stream are alive. They are some of them as long as my finger, should be easily caught in these shallows, and some day I'll have a dish of them.

Very soon after I came to where the stream collects in another banana swamp, with the bananas bearing well. Beyond, the course is again quite dry; it mounts with a sharp turn a very steep face of the mountain, and then stops abruptly at the lip of the plateau, I suppose the top of Vaea mountain: plainly no more springs here – there was no smallest furrow of a watercourse beyond – and my task might be said to be accomplished. But such is the animated spirit in the service that the whole advance guard expressed a sentiment of disappointment that an exploration, so far successfully conducted, should come to stop in the most promising view of fresh successes. And though unprovided either with compass or cutlass, it was determined to push some way along the plateau, marking our direction by the laborious process of bending down, sitting upon, and thus breaking the wild cocoanut trees. This was the less regretted by all from a delightful discovery made of a huge banyan tree growing here in the bush, with flying-buttressed flying buttresses, and huge arcs of trunk hanging high overhead and trailing down new complications of root. I climbed some way up what seemed the original beginning; it was easier to climb than a ship's rigging, even rattled; everywhere there was a foot-hold and hand-hold. It was judged wise to return and rally the main body, who had now been left alone for perhaps forty minutes in the bush.

The return was effected in good order, but unhappily I only arrived (like so many other explorers) to find my main body or rear-guard in a condition of mutiny; the work, it is to be supposed, of terror. It is right I should tell you the Vaea has a bad name, an *aitu fatine* – female devil of the woods – succubus – haunting it, and doubtless Jack had heard of her; perhaps, during my absence, saw her; lucky Jack! Anyway, he was neither to hold nor to bind, and finally, after nearly smashing me by accident, and from mere scare and insubordination several times, deliberately set in to kill me; but poor Jack! the tree he selected for that purpose was a banana! I jumped off and gave him the heavy end of my whip over the buttocks! Then I took and talked in his ear in various voices; you should have heard my alto – it was a dreadful, devilish note – I *knew* Jack *knew* it was an *aitu*. Then I mounted him again, and he carried me fairly steadily. He'll learn yet. He has to learn to trust absolutely to his rider; till he does, the risk is always great in thick bush, where a fellow must try different passages, and put back and forward and pick his way by hair's-breadths.

The expedition returned to Vailima in time to receive the visit of the R.C. Bishop. He is a superior man, much above the average of priests.

Thursday. – Yesterday the same expedition set forth to the southward by what is known as Carruthers' Road. At a fallen tree which completely blocks the way, the main body was as before left behind, and the advance guard of one now proceeded with the exploration. At the great tree known as *Mepi Tree*, after Maben the surveyor, the expedition struck forty yards due west till it struck the top of a steep bank which it descended. The whole bottom of the ravine is filled with sharp lava blocks quite unrolled and very difficult and dangerous to walk among; no water in the course, scarce any sign of water. And yet surely water must have made this bold cutting in the plateau. And if so, why is the lava sharp? My science gave out; but I could not but think it ominous and volcanic. The course of the stream was tortuous, but with a resultant direction a little by west of north; the sides a whole way exceeding steep the expedition buried under fathoms of foliage. Presently water appeared in the bottom, a good quantity; perhaps thirty or forty cubic feet, with pools and waterfalls. A tree that stands all along the banks here must be very fond of water; its roots lie close-packed down the stream, like hanks of guts, so as to make often a corrugated walk, each root ending in a blunt tuft of filaments, plainly to drink water. Twice there came in small tributaries from the left or western side – the whole plateau having a smartish inclination to the east; one of the tributaries is a handsome little web of silver hanging in the forest. Twice I was startled by birds; one that barked like a dog; another that whistled loud ploughman's signals, so that I vow I was thrilled, and thought I had fallen among runaway blacks, and regretted my cutlass which I had lost and left behind while taking bearings. A good many fishes in the brook, and many cray-fish; one of the last with a queer glow-worm head. Like all our brooks, the water is pure as air, and runs over red stones like rubies. The foliage along the banks very thick and high, the place close, the walking exceedingly laborious. By the time the expedition reached the fork, it was felt exceedingly questionable whether the *morale* of the force were sufficiently good to undertake more extended operations. A halt was called, the men refreshed with water and a bath, and it was decided at a drumhead council of war to continue the descent of the Embassy Water straight for Vailima, whither the expedition returned, in rather poor condition, and wet to the waist, about 4 P.M.

Thus in two days the two main watercourses of this country have been pretty thoroughly explored, and I conceive my instructions fully carried out. The main body of the second expedition was brought back by another officer despatched for that purpose from Vailima. Casualties: one horse wounded; one man bruised; no deaths – as yet, but the bruised man feels today as if his case was mighty serious.

In the South Seas

The following excerpts are from the book *In the South Seas* which Stevenson based on the journals he kept during his voyaging on the *Casco* and the *Equator*, and while visiting the Marquesas, the Paumotus (or Dangerous Archipelago, now Tuamotu) and the Gilbert Islands (now Kiribati). The Marquesas and Tuamotu are part of Polynesia, a collection of widely scattered volcanic islands and coral atolls. Culturally and historically the Polynesian islands have much in common, but, as Stevenson recorded, there are many differences in detail of character, belief and lifestyle. Kiribati belongs to the Micronesian group, although just next door, Tuvali (the old Ellice Islands) is in Polynesia.

The *Casco's* first landfall was at Nukahiva in the Marquesas on 28 July 1888, where the Americans had established a whaling station early in the century. It was whaling that first drew Americans and Europeans in significant numbers to the Pacific. From the Marquesas the *Casco* sailed westward through the Dangerous Archipelago, an experience that proved as alarming as the name suggests, to Fakarava atoll, the administrative centre of this group of islands. In early October they carried on to Tahiti, where repairs to the *Casco* kept them until December. They left on Christmas Day 1888 to sail north, for Honolulu.

The Stevensons were six months in Hawaii where, amongst other activities including socializing with King Kalakaua, Stevenson finished *The Master of Ballantrae*, and revised *The Wrong Box*. In June 1889 they left on a trading schooner, the *Equator*, which took them to Butaritari and Apemama in the Gilbert Islands. The following pieces describe aspects of Stevenson's experience in the Marquesas, at Fakarava, and in the Gilberts.

from The Marquesas

MAKING FRIENDS

The impediment of tongues was one that I particularly over-estimated. The languages of Polynesia are easy to smatter, though hard to speak with elegance. And they are extremely similar, so that a person who has a tincture of one or two may risk, not without hope, an attempt upon the others.

And again, not only is Polynesian easy to smatter, but interpreters abound. Missionaries, traders, and broken white folk living on the bounty of the natives, are to be found in almost every isle and hamlet; and even where these are unserviceable, the natives themselves have often scraped up a little English, and in the French zone (though far less commonly) a little French-English, or an efficient pidgin, what is called to the westward 'Beach-la-Mar', comes easy to the Polynesian; it is now taught, besides, in the schools of Hawaii; and from the multiplicity of British ships, and the nearness of the States on the one hand and the colonies on the other, it may be called, and will almost certainly become, the tongue of the Pacific. I will instance a few examples. I met in Majuro a Marshall Island boy who spoke excellent English; this he had learned in the German firm in Jaluit,[1] yet did not speak one word of German. I heard from a gendarme who had taught school in Rapa-iti[2] that while the children had the utmost difficulty or reluctance to learn French, they picked up English on the wayside, and as if by accident. On one of the most out-of-the-way atolls in the Carolines, my friend Mr Benjamin Hird was amazed to find the lads playing cricket on the beach and

1. Majuro, Jaluit. Both in the Marshall Islands, Micronesia.
2. A small volcanic island 300 miles southeast of the Tubai Islands.

32

talking English; and it was in English that the crew of the
Janet Nicoll,[1] a set of black boys from different Melanesian
islands, communicated with other natives throughout the
cruise, transmitted orders, and sometimes jested together
on the fore-hatch. But what struck me perhaps most of
all was a word I heard on the verandah of the Tribunal at
Noumea.[2] A case had just been heard – a trial for infanticide
against an ape-like native woman; and the audience were
smoking cigarettes as they awaited the verdict. An anxious,
amiable French lady, not far from tears, was eager for
acquittal, and declared she would engage the prisoner
to be her children's nurse. The bystanders exclaimed at
the proposal; the woman was a savage, said they, and
spoke no language. '*Mais, vous savez,*' objected the fair
sentimentalist; '*ils apprennent si vite l'anglais!*'

But to be able to speak to people is not all. And in the
first stage of my relations with natives I was helped by
two things. To begin with, I was the showman of the
Casco. She, her fine lines, tall spars, and snowy decks,
the crimson fittings of the saloon, and the white, the gilt,
and the repeating mirrors of the tiny cabin, brought us a
hundred visitors. The men fathomed out her dimensions
with their arms, as their fathers fathomed out the ships of
Cook;[3] the women declared the cabins more lovely than
a church; bouncing Junos were never weary of sitting
in the chairs and contemplating in the glass their own
bland images; and I have seen one lady strip up her
dress, and, with cries of wonder and delight, rub herself
bare-breeched upon the velvet cushions. Biscuit, jam, and
syrup was the entertainment; and, as in European parlours,
the photograph album went the round. This sober gallery,
their everyday costumes and physiognomies, had become
transformed, in three weeks' sailing, into things wonderful

1. *SS Janet Nicholl*, the trading steamer in which the
   Stevensons left Sydney and visited the Gilberts,
   the Marshalls and New Caledonia. The spelling
   '*Nicholl*' is incorrect.

2. Capital of New Caledonia, part of the Melanesian
   group, in the West Pacific.

3. Captain James Cook, who made three expeditions
   to the Pacific in the 1770s and initiated British
   involvement in that part of the world.

and rich and foreign; alien faces, barbaric dresses, they
were now beheld and fingered, in the swerving cabin,
with innocent excitement and surprise. Her Majesty was
often recognised, and I have seen French subjects kiss her
photograph; Captain Speedy – in an Abyssinian war-dress,
supposed to be the uniform of the British army – met with
much acceptance; and the effigies of Mr Andrew Lang[6]
were admired in the Marquesas. There is the place for
him to go when he shall be weary of Middlesex and
Homer.

It was perhaps yet more important that I had enjoyed
in my youth some knowledge of our Scots folk of the
Highlands and the Islands. Not much beyond a century
has passed since these were in the same convulsive and
transitionary state as the Marquesans of today. In both
cases an alien authority enforced, the clans disarmed,
the chiefs deposed, new customs introduced, and chiefly
that fashion of regarding money as the means and object
of existence. The commercial age, in each, succeeding
at a bound to an age of war abroad and patriarchal
communism at home. In one the cherished practice of
tattooing, in the other a cherished costume, proscribed.
In each a main luxury cut off: beef, driven under cloud of
night from Lowland pastures, denied to the meat-loving
Highlander; long-pig, pirated from the next village, to the
man-eating Kanaka. The grumbling, the secret ferment,
the fears and resentments, the alarms and sudden councils
of Marquesan chiefs, reminded me continually of the
days of Lovat and Struan. Hospitality, tact, natural fine
manners, and a touchy punctilio, are common to both
races: common to both tongues the trick of dropping
medial consonants. Here is a table of two widespread
Polynesian words: –

	House.	Love.*
Tahitian	FARE	AROHA
New Zealand	WHARE	

6. Scottish historian, poet and folklorist, and friend
   of Stevenson.

* Where that word is used as a salutation I give that
   form. [R.L.S.]

Samoan	FALE	TALOFA
Manihiki	FALE	ALOHA
Hawaiian	HALE	ALOHA
Marquesan	HA'E	KAOHA

The elision of medial consonants, so marked in these Marquesan instances, is no less common both in Gaelic and the Lowland Scots. Stranger still, that prevalent Polynesian sound, the so-called catch, written with an apostrophe, and often or always the gravestone of a perished consonant, is to be heard in Scotland to this day. When a Scot pronounces water, better, or bottle – *wa'er, be'er*, or *bo'le* – the sound is precisely that of the catch; and I think we may go beyond, and say, that if such a population could be isolated, and this mispronunciation should become the rule, it might prove the first stage of transition from *t* to *k*, which is the disease of Polynesian languages. The tendency of the Marquesans, however, is to urge against consonants, or at least on the very common letter *l*, a war of mere extermination. A hiatus is agreeable to any Polynesian ear; the ear even of the stranger soon grows used to these barbaric voids; but only in the Marquesan will you find such names as *Haaii* and *Paaaeua*, when each individual vowel must be separately uttered.

These points of similarity between a South Sea people and some of my own folk at home ran much in my head in the islands; and not only inclined me to view my fresh acquaintances with favour, but continually modified my judgment. A polite Englishman comes today to the Marquesans and is amazed to find the men tattooed; polite Italians came not long ago to England and found our fathers stained with woad; and when I paid the return visit as a little boy, I was highly diverted with the backwardness of Italy: so insecure, so much a matter of the day and hour, is the pre-eminence of race. It was so that I hit upon a means of communication which I recommend to travellers. When I desired any detail of savage custom, or of superstitious belief, I cast back in the story of my fathers, and fished for what I wanted with some trait of equal barbarism: Michael Scott,[1] Lord Derwentwater's head, the second-sight, the Water Kelpie, – each of these I have found to be a killing bait; the black bull's head of Stirling procured me the legend of *Rahero*;[2] and what I knew of the Cluny Macphersons, or of the Appin Stewarts, enabled me to learn, and helped me to understand, about the *Tevas*[3] of Tahiti. The native was no longer ashamed, his sense of kinship grew warmer, and his lips were opened. It is this sense of kinship that the traveller must rouse and share; or he had better content himself with travels from the blue bed to the brown. And the presence of one Cockney titterer will cause a whole party to walk in clouds of darkness.

The hamlet of Anaho stands on a margin of flat land between the west of the beach and the spring of the impending mountains. A grove of palms, perpetually ruffling its green fans, carpets it (as for a triumph) with fallen branches, and shades it like an arbour. A road runs from end to end of the covert among beds of flowers, the milliner's shop of the community; and here and there, in the grateful twilight, in an air filled with a diversity of scents, and still within hearing of the surf upon the reef, the native houses stand in scattered neighbourhood. The same word, as we have seen, represents in many tongues of Polynesia, with scarce a shade of difference, the abode of man. But although the word be the same, the structure itself continually varies; and the Marquesan, among the most backward and barbarous of islanders, is yet the most commodiously lodged. The grass huts of Hawaii, the birdcage houses of Tahiti, or the open shed, with the crazy Venetian blinds, of the polite Samoan – none of these can be compared with the Marquesan *paepae-hae*, or dwelling platform. The paepae is an oblong terrace built without cement of black volcanic stone, from twenty to

1. Michael Scott etc. These all feature in Scottish legend. Stevenson was fascinated by the common cultural ground he discovered.

2. 'The Song of Rahero', a narrative poem in ballad form which Stevenson based on a story heard from Princess Moë at Tautira.

3. A Tahitian tribal name, which Stevenson compares with warlike figures and clans in Scottish history.

fifty feet in length, raised from four to eight feet from the earth, and accessible by a broad stair. Along the back of this, and coming to about half its width, runs the open front of the house, like a covered gallery: the interior sometimes neat and almost elegant in its bareness, the sleeping space divided off by an endlong coaming, some bright raiment perhaps hanging from a nail, and a lamp and one of White's sewing-machines the only marks of civilisation. On the outside, at one end of the terrace, burns the cooking-fire under a shed; at the other there is perhaps a pen for pigs; the remainder is the evening lounge and *al fresco* banquet-hall of the inhabitants. To some houses water is brought down the mountain in bamboo pipes, perforated for the sake of sweetness. With the Highland comparison in my mind, I was struck to remember the sluttish mounds of turf and stone in which I have sat and been entertained in the Hebrides and the North Islands. Two things, I suppose, explain the contrast. In Scotland wood is rare, and with materials so rude as turf and stone the very hope of neatness is excluded. And in Scotland it is cold. Shelter and a hearth are needs so pressing that a man looks not beyond; he is out all day after a bare bellyful, and at night when he saith, 'Aha, it is warm!' he has not appetite for more. Or if for something else, then something higher; a fine school of poetry and song arose in these rough shelters, and an air like '*Lochaber no more*' is an evidence of refinement more convincing, as well as more imperishable, than a palace.

To one such dwelling platform a considerable troop of relatives and dependants resort. In the hour of the dusk, when the fire blazes, and the scent of cooked breadfruit fills the air, and perhaps the lamp glints already between the pillars of the house, you shall behold them silently assemble to this meal, men, women, and children; and the dogs and pigs frisk together up the terrace stairway, switching rival tails. The strangers from the ship were soon equally welcome: welcome to dip their fingers in the wooden dish, to drink cocoa-nuts, to share the circulating pipe, and to hear and hold high debate about the misdeeds of the French, the Panama Canal, or the geographical position of San Francisco and New Yo'ko. In a Highland hamlet,

quite out of reach of any tourist, I have met the same plain
and dignified hospitality.

I have mentioned two facts – the distasteful behaviour
of our earliest visitors, and the case of the lady who
rubbed herself upon the cushions – which would give
a very false opinion of Marquesan manners. The great
majority of Polynesians are excellently mannered; but the
Marquesan stands apart, annoying and attractive, wild,
shy, and refined. If you make him a present he affects to
forget it, and it must be offered him again at his going: a
pretty formality I have found nowhere else. A hint will get
rid of any one or any number; they are so fiercely proud
and modest; while many of the more lovable but blunter
islanders crowd upon a stranger, and can be no more driven
off than flies. A slight or an insult the Marquesan seems
never to forget. I was one day talking by the wayside with
my friend Hoka, when I perceived his eyes suddenly to flash
and his stature to swell. A white horseman was coming down
the mountain, and as he passed, and while he paused to
exchange salutations with myself, Hoka was still staring
and ruffling like a gamecock. It was a Corsican who had
years before called him *cochon sauvage – coçon chauvage*, as
Hoka mispronounced it. With people so nice and so touchy,
it was scarce to be supposed that our company of greenhorns
should not blunder into offences. Hoka, on one of his visits,
fell suddenly in a brooding silence, and presently after left
the ship with cold formality. When he took me back into
favour, he adroitly and pointedly explained the nature of
my offence: I had asked him to sell cocoa-nuts; and in
Hoka's view articles of food were things that a gentleman
should give, not sell; or at least that he should not sell to
any friend. On another occasion I gave my boat's crew a
luncheon of chocolate and biscuits. I had sinned, I could
never learn how, against some point of observance; and
though I was drily thanked, my offerings were left upon
the beach. But our worst mistake was a slight we put on
Toma, Hoka's adoptive father, and in his own eyes the
rightful chief of Anaho. In the first place, we did not call
upon him, as perhaps we should, in his fine new European
house, the only one in the hamlet. In the second, when we
came ashore upon a visit to his rival, Taipi-kikino, it was
Toma whom we saw standing at the head of the beach,

a magnificent figure of a man, magnificently tattooed, and it was of Toma that we asked our question: 'Where is the chief?' 'What chief?' cried Toma, and turned his back on the blasphemers. Nor did he forgive us. Hoka came and went with us daily; but, alone I believe of all the countryside, neither Toma nor his wife set foot on board the *Casco*. The temptation resisted it is hard for a European to compute. The flying city of Laputa[1] moored for a fortnight in St James's Park affords but a pale figure of the *Casco* anchored before Anaho; for the Londoner has still his change of pleasures, but the Marquesan passes to his grave through an unbroken uniformity of days.

On the afternoon before it was intended we should sail, a valedictory party came on board: nine of our particular friends equipped with gifts and dressed as for a festival. Hoka, the chief dancer and singer, the greatest dandy of Anaho, and one of the handsomest young fellows in the world – sullen, showy, dramatic, light as a feather and strong as an ox – it would have been hard, on that occasion, to recognise, as he sat there stooped and silent, his face heavy and grey. It was strange to see the lad so much affected; stranger still to recognise in his last gift one of the curios we had refused on the first day, and to know our friend, so gaily dressed, so plainly moved at our departure, for one of the half-naked crew that had besieged and insulted us on our arrival: strangest of all, perhaps, to find, in that carved handle of a fan, the last of those curiosities of the first day which had now all been given to us by their possessors – their chief merchandise, for which they had sought to ransom us as long as we were strangers, which they pressed on us for nothing as soon as we were friends. The last visit was not long protracted. One after another they shook hands and got down into their canoe; when Hoka turned his back immediately upon the ship, so that we saw his face no more. Taipi, on the other hand, remained standing and facing us with gracious valedictory gestures; and when Captain Otis dipped the ensign, the whole party saluted with their hats. This was the farewell; the episode of our visit to Anaho was held concluded; and though the *Casco* remained nearly forty

1. The flying island in the third part of Swift's
   Gulliver's Travels (1726).

hours at her moorings, not one returned on board, and I am inclined to think they avoided appearing on the beach. This reserve and dignity is the finest trait of the Marquesan.

from The Marquesas

THE MAROON

Of the beauties of Anaho books might be written. I remember waking about three, to find the air temperate and scented. The long swell brimmed into the bay, and seemed to fill it full and then subside. Gently, deeply, and silently the *Casco* rolled; only at times a block piped like a bird. Oceanward, the heaven was bright with stars and the sea with their reflections. If I looked to that side, I might have sung with the Hawaiian poet:

> *Ua maomao ka lani, ua kahaea luna,*
> *Ua pipi ka maka o ka hoku.*
> (The heavens were fair, they stretched above,
> Many were the eyes of the stars.)

And then I turned shoreward, and high squalls were overhead; the mountains loomed up black; and I could have fancied I had slipped ten thousand miles away and was anchored in a Highland loch; that when the day came, it would show pine, and heather, and green fern, and roofs of turf sending up the smoke of peats; and the alien speech that should next greet my ears must be Gaelic, not Kanaka.

And day, when it came, brought other sights and thoughts. I have watched the morning break in many quarters of the world; it has been certainly one of the chief joys of my existence, and the dawn that I saw with most emotion shone upon the bay of Anaho. The mountains abruptly overhang the port with every variety of surface and of inclination, lawn, and cliff, and forest. Not one of these but wore its proper tint of saffron, of sulphur, of the clove, and of the rose. The lustre was like that of satin; on the lighter hues there seemed to float an efflorescence; a solemn bloom appeared on the more dark. The light itself was the ordinary light of morning, colourless and clean; and on this ground of jewels, pencilled out the least detail of drawing.

41

Meanwhile, around the hamlet, under the palms, where the blue shadow lingered, the red coals of cocoa husk and the light trails of smoke betrayed the awakening business of the day; along the beach men and women, lads and lasses, were returning from the bath in bright raiment, red and blue and green, such as we delighted to see in the coloured pictures of our childhood; and presently the sun had cleared the eastern hill, and the glow of the day was over all.

The glow continued and increased, the business, from the main part, ceased before it had begun. Twice in the day there was a certain stir of shepherding along the seaward hills. At times a canoe went out to fish. At times a woman or two languidly filled a basket in the cotton patch. At times a pipe would sound out of the shadow of a house, ringing the changes on its three notes, with an effect like *Que le jour me dure* repeated endlessly. Or at times, across a corner of the bay, two natives might communicate in the Marquesan manner with conventional whistlings. All else was sleep and silence. The surf broke and shone around the shores; a species of black crane fished in the broken water; the black pigs were continually galloping by on some affair; but the people might never have awaked, or they might all be dead.

My favourite haunt was opposite the hamlet, where there was a landing in a cove under a lianaed cliff. The beach was lined with palms and a tree called the purao, something between the fig and mulberry in growth, and bearing a flower like a great yellow poppy with a maroon heart. In places rocks encroached upon the sand; the beach would be all submerged; and the surf would bubble warmly as high as to my knees, and play with cocoa-nut husks as our more homely ocean plays with wreck and wrack and bottles. As the reflux drew down, marvels of colour and design streamed between my feet; which I would grasp at, miss, or seize: now to find them what they promised, shells to grace a cabinet or be set in gold upon a lady's finger; now to catch only *maya* of coloured sand, pounded fragments and pebbles, that, as soon as they were dry, became as dull and homely as the flints upon a garden path. I have toiled at this childish pleasure for hours in the strong sun, conscious of my incurable ignorance; but too keenly pleased to be ashamed. Meanwhile, the blackbird (or his tropical understudy) would be fluting in the thickets overhead.

A little further, in the turn of the bay, a streamlet trickled in the bottom of a den, thence spilling down a stair of rock into the sea. The draught of air drew down under the foliage in the very bottom of the den, which was a perfect arbour for coolness. In front it stood open on the blue bay and the *Casco* lying there under her awning and her cheerful colours. Overhead was a thatch of puraos, and over these again palms brandished their bright fans, as I have seen a conjurer make himself a halo out of naked swords. For in this spot, over a neck of low land at the foot of the mountains, the trade-wind streams into Anaho Bay in a flood of almost constant volume and velocity, and of a heavenly coolness.

It chanced one day that I was ashore in the cove with Mr Stevenson and the ship's cook. Except for the *Casco* lying outside, and a crane or two, and the ever-busy wind and sea, the face of the world was of a prehistoric emptiness; life appeared to stand stockstill, and the sense of isolation was profound and refreshing. On a sudden, the trade-wind, coming in a gust over the isthmus, struck and scattered the fans of the palms above the den; and behold! in two of the tops there sat a native, motionless as an idol and watching us, you would have said, without a wink. The next moment the tree closed, and the glimpse was gone. This discovery of human presences latent overhead in a place where we had supposed ourselves alone, the immobility of our tree-top spies, and the thought that perhaps at all hours we were similarly supervised, struck us with a chill. Talk languished on the beach. As for the cook (whose conscience was not clear), he never afterwards set foot on shore, and twice, when the *Casco* appeared to be driving on the rocks, it was amusing to observe that man's alacrity; death, he was persuaded, awaiting him upon the beach. It was more than a year later, in the Gilberts, that the explanation dawned upon myself. The natives were drawing palm-tree wine, a thing forbidden by law; and when the wind thus suddenly revealed them, they were doubtless more troubled than ourselves.

At the top of the den there dwelt an old, melancholy, grizzled man of the name of Tari (Charlie) Coffin. He was

a native of Oahu, in the Sandwich Islands; and had gone to
sea in his youth in the American whalers; a circumstance to
which he owned his name, his English, his down-east twang,
and the misfortune of his innocent life. For one captain,
sailing out of New Bedford,[1] carried him to Nuka-hiva and
marooned him there among the cannibals. The motive for
this act was inconceivably small; poor Tari's wages, which
were thus economised, would scarce have shook the credit
of the New Bedford owners. And the act itself was simply
murder. Tari's life must have hung in the beginning by a
hair. In the grief and terror of that time, it is not unlikely
he went mad, an infirmity to which he was still liable; or
perhaps a child may have taken a fancy to him and ordained
him to be spared. He escaped at least alive, married in the
island, and when I knew him was a widower with a married
son and a granddaughter. But the thought of Oahu haunted
him; its praise was for ever on his lips; he beheld it, looking
back, as a place of ceaseless feasting, song, and dance; and in
his dreams I daresay he revisits it with joy. I wonder what he
would think if he could be carried there indeed, and see the
modern town of Honolulu brisk with traffic, and the palace
with its guards, and the great hotel, and Mr Berger's band
with their uniforms and outlandish instruments; or what
he would think to see the brown faces grown so few and
the white so many; and his father's land sold for planting
sugar, and his father's house quite perished, or perhaps the
last of them struck leprous and immured between the surf
and the cliffs on Molokai. So simply, even in South Sea
Islands, and so sadly, the changes come.

Tari was poor, and poorly lodged. His house was a
wooden frame, run up by Europeans; it was indeed
his official residence, for Tari was the shepherd of the
promontory sheep. I can give a perfect inventory of its
contents: three kegs, a tin biscuit-box, an iron saucepan,
several cocoa-shell cups, a lantern, and three bottles,
probably containing oil; while the clothes of the family
and a few mats were thrown across the open rafters. Upon
my first meeting with this exile he had conceived for me
one of the baseless island friendships, had given me nuts to
drink, and carried me up the den 'to see my house' – the only

1. Massachusetts whaling port.

entertainment that he had to offer. He liked the 'Amelican', he said, and the 'Inglishman', but the 'Flessman' was his abhorrence; and he was careful to explain that if he had thought us 'Fless', we should have had none of his nuts, and never a sight of his house. His distaste for the French I can partly understand, but not at all his toleration of the Anglo-Saxon. The next day he brought me a pig, and some days later one of our party going ashore found him in act to bring a second. We were still strange to the islands; we were pained by the poor man's generosity, which he could ill afford; and, by a natural enough but quite unpardonable blunder, we refused the pig. Had Tari been a Marquesan we should have seen him no more; being what he was, the most mild, long-suffering, melancholy man, he took a revenge a hundred times more painful. Scarce had the canoe with the nine villagers put off from their farewell before the *Casco* was boarded from the other side. It was Tari; coming thus late because he had no canoe of his own, and had found it hard to borrow one; coming thus solitary (as indeed we always saw him), because he was a stranger in the land, and the dreariest of company. The rest of my family basely fled from the encounter. I must receive our injured friend alone; and the interview must have lasted hard upon an hour, for he was loath to tear himself away. 'You go' way. I see you no more – no, sir!' he lamented; and then looking about him with rueful admiration. 'This goodee ship – no, sir! – goodee ship!' he would exclaim: the 'no, sir' thrown out sharply through the nose upon a rising inflection, an echo from New Bedford and the fallacious whaler. From these expressions of grief and praise he would return continually to the case of the rejected pig. 'I like give plesent all 'e same you,' he complained: 'only got pig: you no take him!' He was a poor man; he had no choice of gifts; he had only a pig, he repeated; and I had refused it. I have rarely been more wretched than to see him sitting there, so old, so grey, so poor, so hardly fortuned, of so rueful a countenance, and to appreciate, with growing keenness, the affront which I had so innocently dealt him; but it was one of those cases in which speech is vain.

Tari's son was smiling and inert; his daughter-in-law, a girl of sixteen, pretty, gentle, and grave, more intelligent than most Anaho women, and with a fair share of French; his grandchild, a mite of a creature at the breast. I went up the den one day when Tari was from home, and found the son making a cotton sack, and madame suckling mademoiselle. When I had sat down with them on the floor, the girl began to question me about England; which I tried to describe, piling the pan and the cocoa shells one upon another to represent the houses, and explaining, as best I was able, and by word and gesture, the over-population, the hunger and the perpetual toil. '*Pas de cocotiers? pas de popoi?*' she asked. I told her it was too cold, and went through an elaborate performance, shutting out draughts, and crouching over an imaginary fire, to make sure she understood. But she understood right well; remarked it must be bad for the health, and sat a while gravely reflecting on that picture of unwanted sorrows. I am sure it roused her pity, for it struck in her another thought always uppermost in the Marquesan bosom; and she began with a smiling sadness, and looking on me out of melancholy eyes, to lament the decease of her own people. '*Ici pas de Kanaques*,' said she; and taking me baby from her breast, she held it out to me with both her hands. '*Tenez* – a little baby like this; then dead. All the Kanaques die. Then no more.' The smile, and this instancing by the girl-mother of her own tiny flesh and blood, affected me strangely; they spoke of so tranquil a despair. Meanwhile the husband smilingly made his sack; and the unconscious babe struggled to reach a pot of raspberry jam, friendship's offering, which I had just brought up the den; and in a perspective of centuries I saw their case as ours, death coming in like a tide, and the day already numbered when there should be no more Beretani, and no more of any race whatever, and (what oddly touched me) no more literary works and no more readers.

from The Marquesas

DEPOPULATION

Over the whole extent of the South Seas, from one tropic to
another, we find traces of a bygone state of over-population,
when the resources of even a tropical soil were taxed, and
even the improvident Polynesian trembled for the future.
We may accept some of the ideas of Mr Darwin's theory of
coral islands, and suppose a rise of the sea, or the subsidence
of some former continental area, to have driven into the
tops of the mountains multitudes of refugees. Or we may
suppose, more soberly, a people of sea-rovers, emigrants
from a crowded country, to strike upon and settle island
after island, and as time went on to multiply exceedingly
in their new seats. In either case the end must be the same;
soon or late it must grow apparent that the crew are too
numerous, and the famine is at hand. The Polynesians met
this emergent danger with various expedients of activity
and prevention. A way was found to preserve breadfruit
by packing it in artificial pits; pits forty feet in depth and
of proportionate bore are still to be seen, I am told, in the
Marquesas; and yet even these were insufficient for the
teeming people, and the annals of the past are gloomy
with famine and cannibalism. Among the Hawaiians – a
hardier people, in a more exacting climate – agriculture
was carried far; the land was irrigated with canals; and the
fishponds of Molokai prove the number and diligence of
the old inhabitants. Meanwhile, over all the island world,
abortion and infanticide prevailed. On coral atolls, where
the danger was most plainly obvious, these were enforced
by law and sanctioned by punishment. On Vaitupu, in the
Ellices, only two children were allowed to a couple; on
Nukufetau,[1] but one. On the latter the punishment was

1. An atoll in the Ellice Islands, Southwest Pacific.

47

by fine; and it is related that the fine was sometimes paid, and the child spared.

This is characteristic. For no people in the world are so fond or so long-suffering with children – children make the mirth and the adornment of their homes, serving them for playthings and for picture-galleries. 'Happy is the man that has his quiver full of them.' The stray bastard is contended for by rival families; and the natural and the adopted children play and grow up together undistinguished. The spoiling, and I may almost say the deification, of the child, is nowhere carried so far as in the eastern islands; and furthest, according to my opportunities of observation, in the Paumotu group, the so-called Low or Dangerous Archipelago. I have seen a Paumotuan native turn from me with embarrassment and disaffection because I suggested that a brat would be the better for beating. It is a daily matter in some eastern islands to see a child strike or even stone its mother, and the mother, so far from punishing, scarce ventures to resist. In some, when his child was born, a chief was superseded and resigned his name; as though, like a drone, he had then fulfilled the occasion of his being. And in some the lightest words of children had the weight of oracles. Only the other day, in the Marquesas, if a child conceived a distaste to any stranger, I am assured the stranger would be slain. And I shall have to tell in another place an instance of the opposite: how a child in Manihiki[1] having taken a fancy to myself, her adoptive parents at once accepted the situation and loaded me with gifts.

With such sentiments the necessity for child-destruction would not fail to clash, and I believe we find the trace of divided feeling in the Tahitian brotherhood of Oro. At a certain date a new god was added to the Society-Island Olympus, or an old one refurbished and made popular. Oro was his name, and he may be compared with the Bacchus of the ancients. His zealots sailed from bay to bay, and from island to island; they were everywhere received with feasting; wore fine clothes; sang, danced, acted; gave exhibitions of dexterity and strength; and were the artists, the acrobats, the bards, and the harlots of the group. Their life was public and epicurean; their

---

1. Polynesian island in the central South Pacific.

initiation a mystery; and the highest in the land aspired to join the brotherhood. If a couple stood next in line to a high-chieftaincy, they were suffered, on grounds of policy, to spare one child; all other children, who had a father or a mother in the company of Oro, stood condemned from the moment of conception. A freemasonry, an agnostic sect, a company of artists, its members all under oath to spread unchastity, and all forbidden to leave offspring – I do not know how it may appear to others, but to me the design seems obvious. Famine menacing the islands, and the needful remedy repulsive, it was recommended to the native mind by these trappings of mystery, pleasure, and parade. This is the more probable, and the secret, serious purpose of the institution appears the more plainly, if it be true, that after a certain period of life, the obligation of the votary was changed; at first, bound to be profligate: afterwards, expected to be chaste.

Here, then, we have one side of the case. Man-eating among kindly men, child-murder among child-lovers, industry in a race the most idle, invention in a race the least progressive, this grim, pagan salvation-army of the brotherhood of Oro, the report of early voyagers, the wide-spread vestiges of former habitation, and the universal tradition of the islands, all point to the same fact of former crowding and alarm. And today we are face to face with the reverse. Today in the Marquesas, in the Eight Islands of Hawaii, in Mangareva,[1] in Easter Island,[2] we find the same race perishing like flies. Why this change? Or, grant that the coming of the whites, the change of habits, and the introduction of new maladies and vices, fully explain the depopulation, why is that depopulation not universal? The population of Tahiti, after a period of alarming decrease, has again become stationary. I hear of a similar result among some Maori tribes; in many of the Paumotus a slight increase is to be observed; and the Samoans are today as healthy and at least as fruitful as before the change. Grant that the Tahitians, the Maoris, and the Paumotuans have become inured to the new conditions;

1. Principal island of the Gambiers, French Polynesia.
2. Polynesian volcanic island now belonging to Chile.

and what are we to make of the Samoans, who have never suffered?

Those who are acquainted only with a single group are apt to be ready with solutions. Thus I have heard the mortality of the Maoris attributed to their change of residence – from fortified hill-tops to the low, marshy vicinity of their plantations. How plausible! And yet the Marquesans are dying out in the same houses where their fathers multiplied. Or take opium. The Marquesas and Hawaii are the two groups the most infected with this vice; the population of the one is the most civilised, that of the other by far the most barbarous, of Polynesians; and they are two of those that perish the most rapidly. Here is a strong case against opium. But let us take unchastity, and we shall find the Marquesas and Hawaii figuring again upon another count. Thus, Samoans are the most chaste of Polynesians, and they are to this day entirely fertile; Marquesans are the most debauched: we have seen how they are perishing; Hawaiians are notoriously lax, and they begin to be dotted among deserts. So here is a case stronger still against unchastity; and here also we have a correction to apply. Whatever the virtues of the Tahitian, neither friend nor enemy dares call him chaste; and yet he seems to have outlived the time of danger. One last example: syphilis has been plausibly credited with much of the sterility. But the Samoans are, by all accounts, as fruitful as at first; by some accounts more so; and it is not seriously to be argued that the Samoans have escaped syphilis.

These examples show how dangerous it is to reason from any particular cause, or even from many in a single group. I have in my eye an able and amiable pamphlet by the Rev. S.E. Bishop:[1] 'Why are the Hawaiians Dying Out?' Any one interested in the subject ought to read this tract, which contains real information; and yet Mr Bishop's views would have been changed by an acquaintance with other groups. Samoa is, for the moment, the main and the most instructive exception to the rule. The people are the most chaste and one of the most temperate of island peoples. They have never been tried and depressed with any grave pestilence. Their clothing has scarce been tampered with;

1. Sereno Bishop, Hawaiian-born American missionary.

at the simple and becoming tabard of the girls, Tartuffe,[1] in many another island, would have cried out; for the cool, healthy, and modest lava-lava or kilt, Tartuffe has managed in many another island to substitute stifling and inconvenient trousers. Lastly, and perhaps chiefly, so far from their amusements having been curtailed, I think they have been, upon the whole, extended. The Polynesian falls easily into despondency: bereavement, disappointment, the fear of novel visitations, the decay or proscription of ancient pleasures, easily incline him to be sad; and sadness detaches him from life. The melancholy of the Hawaiian and the emptiness of his new life are striking; and the remark is yet more apposite to the Marquesas. In Samoa, on the other hand, perpetual song and dance, perpetual games, journeys, and pleasures, make an animated and a smiling picture of the island life. And the Samoans are today the gayest and the best entertained inhabitants of our planet. The importance of this can scarcely be exaggerated. In a climate and upon a soil where a livelihood can be had for the stooping, entertainment is a prime necessity. It is otherwise with us, where life presents us with a daily problem, and there is a serious interest, and some of the heat of conflict, in the mere continuing to be. So, in certain atolls, where there is no great gaiety, but man must bestir himself with some vigour for his daily bread, public health and the population are maintained; but in the lotos islands, with the decay of pleasures, life itself decays. It is from this point of view that we may instance, among other causes of depression, the decay of war. We have been so long used in Europe to that dreary business of war on the great scale, trailing epidemics and leaving pestilential corpses in its train, that we have almost forgotten its original, the most healthful, if not the most humane, of all field sports – hedge-warfare. From this, as well as from the rest of his amusements and interests, the islander, upon a hundred islands, has been recently cut off. And to this, as well as to so many others, the Samoan still makes good a special title.

Upon the whole, the problem seems to me to stand thus: – Where there have been fewest changes, important and unimportant, salutary or hurtful, there the race

  1. Character in Molière's play of the same name, a religious hypocrite.

survives. Where there have been most, important and unimportant, salutary or hurtful, there it perishes. Each change, however small, augments the sum of new conditions to which the race has to become inured. There may seem, *a priori*, no comparison between the change from 'sour toddy' to bad gin, and that from the island kilt to a pair of European trousers. Yet I am far from persuaded that the one is any more hurtful than the other; and the unaccustomed race will sometimes die of pin-pricks. We are here face to face with one of the difficulties of the missionary. In Polynesian islands he easily obtains pre-eminent authority; the king becomes his *mairedupalais*; he can proscribe, he can command; and the temptation is ever towards too much. Thus (by all accounts) the Catholics in Mangareva, and thus (to my own knowledge) the Protestants in Hawaii, have rendered life in a more or less degree unliveable to their converts. And the mild, uncomplaining creatures (like children in a prison) yawn and await death. It is easy to blame the missionary. But it is his business to make changes. It is surely his business, for example, to prevent war; and yet I have instanced war itself as one of the elements of health. On the other hand, it were, perhaps, easy for the missionary to proceed more gently, and to regard every change as an affair of weight. I take the average missionary; I am sure I do him no more than justice when I suppose that he would hesitate to bombard a village, even in order to convert an archipelago. Experience begins to show us (at least in Polynesian islands) that change of habit is bloodier than a bombardment.

There is one point, ere I have done, where I may go to meet criticism. I have said nothing of faulty hygiene, bathing during fevers, mistaken treatment of children, native doctoring, or abortion – all causes frequently adduced. And I have said nothing of them because they are conditions common to both epochs, and even more efficient in the past than in the present. Was it not the same with unchastity, it may be asked? Was not the Polynesian always unchaste? Doubtless he was so always: doubtless he is more so since the coming of his remarkably chaste visitors from Europe. Take the Hawaiian account of Cook: I have no doubt it is entirely fair. Take Krusenstern's[1] candid, almost innocent, description of a Russian man-of-war at the Marquesas; consider the disgraceful history of missions in Hawaii itself, where (in the war of lust) the American missionaries were once shelled by an English adventurer, and once raided and mishandled by the crew of an American warship; add the practice of whaling fleets to call at the Marquesas, and carry off a complement of women for the cruise; consider, besides, how the whites were at first regarded in the light of demigods, as appears plainly in the reception of Cook upon Hawaii; and again, in the story of the discovery of Tutuila, when the really decent women of Samoa prostituted themselves in public to the French; and bear in mind how it was the custom of the adventurers, and we may almost say the business of the missionaries, to deride and infract even the most salutary tapus. Here we see every engine of dissolution directed at once against a virtue never and nowhere very strong or popular; and the result, even in the most degraded islands, has been further degradation. Mr Lawes, the missionary of Savage Island, told me the standard of female chastity had declined there since the coming of the whites. In heathen time, if a girl gave birth to a bastard, her father or brother would dash the infant down the cliffs; and today the scandal would be small. Or take the Marquesas. Stanislao Moanatini told me that in his own recollection the young were strictly guarded; they were not suffered so much as to look upon one another in the street, but passed (so my informant put it) like dogs; and the odher day the whole school-children of Nuka-hiva and Ua-pu escaped in a body to the woods, and lived there for a fortnight in promiscuous liberty. Readers of travels may perhaps exclaim at my authority, and declare themselves better informed. I should prefer the statement of an intelligent native like Stanislao (even if it stood alone, which it is far from doing) to the report of the most honest traveller. A ship of war comes to a haven, anchors, lands a party, receives and returns a visit, and the captain writes a chapter on the manners of the island. It is not considered

1. Adam Ivan Krusenstern, a Russian explorer, navigator and hydrographer of the late eighteenth and early nineteenth centuries. He was the first Russian to circumnavigate the world.

what class is mostly seen. Yet we should not be pleased if a Lascar foremast hand were to judge England by the ladies who parade Ratcliffe Highway, and the gentlemen who share with them their hire. Stanislao's opinion of a decay of virtue even in these unvirtuous islands has been supported to me by others; his very example, the progress of dissolution amongst the young, is adduced by Mr Bishop in Hawaii. And so far as Marquesans are concerned, we might have hazarded a guess of some decline in manners. I do not think that any race could ever have prospered or multiplied with such as now obtain; I am sure they would have been never at the pains to count paternal kinship. It is not possible to give details; suffice it that their manners appear to be imitated from the dreams of ignorant and vicious children, and their debauches persevered in until energy, reason, and almost life itself are in abeyance.

from The Marquesas

THE STORY OF A PLANTATION

Taahauku, on the south-westerly coast of the island of Hiva-oa – Tahuku, say the slovenly whites – may be called the port of Atuona. It is a narrow and small anchorage, set between low cliffy points, and opening above upon a woody valley: a little French fort, now disused and deserted, overhangs the valley and the inlet. Atuona itself, at the head of the next bay, is framed in a theatre of mountains, which dominate the more immediate settling of Taahauku and give the salient character of the scene. They are reckoned at no higher than four thousand feet; but Tahiti with eight thousand, and Hawaii with fifteen, can offer no such picture of abrupt, melancholy alps. In the morning, when the sun falls directly on their front, they stand like a vast wall: green to the summit, if by any chance the summit should be clear – watercourses here and there delineated on their face, as narrow as cracks. Towards afternoon, the light falls more obliquely, and the sculpture of the range comes in relief, huge gorges sinking into shadow, huge, tortuous buttresses standing edged with sun. At all hours of the day they strike the eye with some new beauty, and the mind with the same menacing gloom.

The mountains, dividing and deflecting the endless airy deluge of the Trade, are doubtless answerable for the climate. A strong draught of wind blew day and night over the anchorage. Day and night the same fantastic and attenuated clouds fled across the heavens, the same dusky cap of rain and vapour fell and rose on the mountain. The landbreezes came very strong and chill, and the sea, like the air, was in perpetual bustle. The swell crowded into the narrow anchorage like sheep into a fold; broke all along both sides, high on the one, low on the other; kept a certain blowhole sounding and smoking like a cannon; and spent itself at last upon the beach.

On the side away from Atuona, the sheltering promontory was a nursery of coco-trees. Some were mere infants, none had attained to any size, none had yet begun to shoot skyward with that whip-like shaft of the mature palm. In the young trees the colour alters with the age and growth. Now all is of a grass-like hue, infinitely dainty; next the rib grows golden, the fronds remaining green as ferns; and then, as the trunk continues to mount and to assume its final hue of grey, the fans put on manlier and more decided depths of verdure, stand out dark upon the distance, glisten against the sun, and flash like silver fountains in the assault of the wind. In this young wood of Taahauku, all these hues and combinations were exampled and repeated by the score. The trees grew pleasantly spaced upon a hilly sward, here and there interspersed with a rack for drying copra, or a tumbledown hut for storing it. Every here and there the stroller had a glimpse of the *Casco* tossing in the narrow anchorage below; and beyond he had ever before him the dark amphitheatre of the Atuona mountains and the cliffy bluff that closes it to seaward. The trade-wind moving in the fans made a ceaseless noise of summer rain; and from time to time, with the sound of a sudden and distant drum-beat, the surf would burst in a sea cave.

At the upper end of the inlet, its low, cliffy lining sinks, at both sides, into a beach. A copra warehouse stands in the shadow of the shoreside trees, flitted about for ever by a clan of dwarfish swallows; and a line of rails on a high wooden staging bends back into the mouth of the valley. Walking on this, the new-landed traveller becomes aware of a broad fresh-water lagoon (one arm of which he crosses), and beyond, of a grove of noble palms, sheltering the house of the trader, Mr Keane. Overhead, the cocos join in a continuous and lofty roof; blackbirds are heard lustily singing; the island cock springs his jubilant rattle and airs his golden plumage; cow-bells sound far and near in the grove; and when you sit in the broad verandah, lulled by this symphony, you may say to yourself, if you are able: 'Better fifty years of Europe . . .' Farther on, the floor of the valley is flat and green, and dotted here and there with stripling coco palms. Through the midst, with many changes of music,

the river trots and brawls; and along its course, where we
should look for willows, puraos grow in clusters, and make
shadowy pools after an angler's heart. A vale more rich and
peaceful, sweeter air, a sweeter voice of rural sounds, I have
found nowhere. One circumstance alone might strike the
experienced: here is a convenient beach, deep soil, good
water, and yet nowhere any paepaes, nowhere any trace of
island inhabitation.

It is but a few years since this valley was a place choked
with jungle, the debatable land and battle-ground of cannibals. Two clans laid claim to it – neither could substantiate
the claim, and the roads lay desert, or were only visited by
men in arms. It is for this very reason that it wears now
so smiling an appearance: cleared, planted, built upon,
supplied with railways, boat-houses, and bath-houses. For,
being no man's land, it was the more readily ceded to a
stranger. The stranger was Captain John Hart: Ima Hati,
'Broken-arm', the natives call him, because when he first
visited the islands his arm was in a sling. Captain Hart,
a man of English birth but an American subject, had
conceived the idea of cotton culture in the Marquesas
during the American War, and was at first rewarded with
success. His plantation at Anaho was highly productive;
island cotton fetched a high price, and the natives used
to debate which was the stronger power, Ima Hati or the
French: deciding in favour of the captain, because, though
the French had the most ships, he had the more money.

He marked Taahauku for a suitable site, acquired it,
and offered the superintendence to Mr Robert Stewart,
a Fifeshire man, already some time in the islands, who
had just been ruined by a war on Tauata. Mr Stewart
was somewhat averse to the adventure, having some
acquaintance with Atuona and its notorious chieftain,
Moipu. He had once landed there, he told me, about dusk,
and found the remains of a man and woman partly eaten.
On his starting and sickening at the sight, one of Moipu's
young men picked up a human foot, and provocatively
staring at the stranger, grinned and nibbled at the heel.
None need be surprised if Mr Stewart fled incontinently
to the bush, lay there all night in a great horror of mind,
and got off to sea again by daylight on the morrow. 'It was
always a bad place, Atuona', commented Mr Stewart, in his

homely Fifeshire voice. In spite of this dire introduction, he accepted the captain's offer, was landed at Taahauku with three Chinamen, and proceeded to clear the jungle.

War was pursued at that time, almost without interval, between the men of Atuona and the men of Haamau; and one day, from the opposite sides of the valley, battle – or I should rather say the noise of battle – raged all the afternoon: the shots and insults of the opposing clans passing from hill to hill over the heads of Mr Stewart and his Chinamen. There was no genuine fighting; it was like a bicker of schoolboys, only some fool had given the children guns. One man died of his exertions in running, the only casualty. With night the shots and insults ceased; the men of Haamau withdrew; and victory, on some occult principle, was scored to Moipu. Perhaps, in consequence, there came a day when Moipu made a feast, and a party from Haamau came under safe-conduct to eat of it. These passed early by Taahauku, and some of Moipu's young men were there to be a guard of honour. They were not long gone before there came down from Haamau, a man, his wife, and a girl of twelve, their daughter, bringing fungus. Several Atuona lads were hanging round the store; but the day being one of truce none apprehended danger. The fungus was weighed and paid for; the man of Haamau proposed he should have his axe ground in the bargain; and Mr Stewart demurring at the trouble, some of the Atuona lads offered to grind it for him, and set it on the wheel. While the axe was grinding, a friendly native whispered Mr Stewart to have a care of himself, for there was trouble in hand; and, all at once, the man of Haamau was seized, and his head and arm stricken from his body, the head at one sweep of his own newly sharpened axe. In the first alert, the girl escaped among the cotton; and Mr Stewart, having thrust the wife into the house and locked her in from the outside, supposed the affair was over. But the business had not passed without noise, and it reached the ears of an older girl who had loitered by the way, and who now came hastily down the valley, crying as she came for her father. Her, too, they seized and beheaded; I know not what they had done with the axe, it was a blunt knife that served their butcherly turn upon the girl; and the blood spurted in fountains and painted them from head to foot. Thus horrible from crime, the party returned to Atuona, carrying the heads to Moipu. It may be fancied how the feast broke up; but it is notable that the guests were honourably suffered to retire. These passed back through Taahauku in extreme disorder; a little after the valley began to be overrun with shouting and triumphing braves; and a letter of warning coming at the same time to Mr Stewart, he and his Chinamen took refuge with the Protestant missionary in Atuona. That night the store was gutted, and the bodies cast in a pit and covered with leaves. Three days later the schooner had come in; and things appearing quieter, Mr Stewart and the captain landed in Taahauku to compute the damage and to view the grave, which was already indicated by the stench. While they were so employed, a party of Moipu's young men, decked with red flannel to indicate martial sentiments, came over the hills from Atuona, dug up the bodies, washed them in the river, and carried them away on sticks. That night the feast began.

Those who knew Mr Stewart before this experience declare the man to be quite altered. He stuck, however, to his post; and somewhat later, when the plantation was already well established, and gave employment to sixty Chinamen and seventy natives, he found himself once more in dangerous times. The men of Haamau, it was reported, had sworn to plunder and erase the settlement; letters came continually from the Hawaiian missionary, who acted as intelligence department; and for six weeks Mr Stewart and three other whites slept in the cotton-house at night in a rampart of bales, and (what was their best defence) ostentatiously practised rifle-shooting by day upon the beach. Natives were often there to watch them; the practice was excellent; and the assault was never delivered – if it ever was intended, which I doubt, for the natives are more famous for false rumours than for deeds of energy. I was told the late French war was a case in point; the tribes on the beach accusing those in the mountains of designs which they had never the hardihood to entertain. And the same testimony to their backwardness in open battle reached me from all sides. Captain Hart once landed after an engagement in a certain bay; one man had his hand hurt, an old woman and two children had been slain; and the captain improved the occasion by poulticing the hand, and

taunting both sides upon so wretched an affair. It is true
these wars were often merely formal – comparable with
duels to the first blood. Captain Hart visited a bay where
such a war was being carried on between two brothers, one
of whom had been thought wanting in civility to the guests
of the other. About one-half of the population served day
about upon alternate sides, so as to be well with each
when the inevitable peace should follow. The forts of
the belligerents were over against each other, and close
by. Pigs were cooking. Well-oiled braves, with well-oiled
muskets, strutted on the paepae or sat down to feast. No
business, however needful, could be done, and all thoughts
were supposed to be centred in this mockery of war. A few
days later, by a regrettable accident, a man was killed; it
was felt at once the thing had gone too far, and the quarrel
was instantly patched up. But the more serious wars were
prosecuted in a similar spirit; a gift of pigs and a feast made
their inevitable end; the killing of a single man was a great
victory, and the murder of defenceless solitaries counted a
heroic deed.

The foot of the cliffs, about all these islands, is the place
of fishing. Between Taahauku and Atuona we saw men, but
chiefly women, some nearly naked, some in thin white or
crimson dresses, perched in little surf-beat promontories –
the brown precipice overhanging them, and the convolvulus
overhanging that, as if to cut them off the more completely
from assistance. There they would angle much of the
morning; and as fast as they caught any fish, eat them,
raw and living, where they stood. It was such helpless ones
that the warriors from the opposite island of Tauata slew,
and carried home and ate, and were thereupon accounted
mighty men of valour. Of one such exploit I can give the
account of an eye-witness. 'Portuguese Joe', Mr Keane's
cook, was once pulling an oar in an Atuona boat, when
they spied a stranger in a canoe with some fish and a piece
of tapu. The Atuona men cried upon him to draw near and
have a smoke. He complied, because, I suppose, he had no
choice; but he knew, poor devil, what he was coming to,
and (as Joe said) 'he didn't seem to care about the smoke'.
A few questions followed, as to where he came from, and
what was his business. These he must needs answer, as he
must needs draw at the unwelcome pipe, his heart the while

drying in his bosom. And then, of a sudden, a big fellow in Joe's boat leaned over, plucked the stranger from his canoe, struck him with a knife in the neck – inward and downward, as Joe showed in pantomine more expressive than his words – and held him under water, like a fowl, until his struggles ceased. Whereupon the long-pig was hauled on board, the boat's head turned about for Atuona, and these Marquesan braves pulled home rejoicing. Moipu was on the beach and rejoiced with them on their arrival. Poor Joe toiled at his oar that day with a white face, yet he had no fear for himself. 'They were very good to me – gave me plenty grub: never wished to eat white man,' said he.

If the most horrible experience was Mr Stewart's, it was Captain Hart himself who ran the nearest danger. He had bought a piece of land from Timau, chief of a neighbouring bay, and put some Chinese there to work. Visiting the station with one of the Godeffroys,[1] he found his Chinamen trooping to the beach in terror; Timau had driven them out, seized their effects, and was in war attire with his young men. A boat was despatched to Taahauku for reinforcement; as they awaited her return, they could see, from the deck of the schooner, Timau and his young men dancing the war-dance on a hill-top till past twelve at night; and so soon as the boat came (bringing three gendarmes, armed with chasse-pots, two white men from Taahauku station, and some native warriors) the party set out to seize the chief before he should awake. Day was not come, and it was a very bright moonlight morning, when they reached the hill-top where (in a house of palm-leaves) Timau was sleeping off his debauch. The assailants were fully exposed, the interior of the hut quite dark; the position far from sound. The gendarmes knelt with their pieces ready, and Captain Hart advanced alone. As he drew near the door he heard the snap of a gun cocking from within, and in sheer self-defence – there being no other escape – sprang into the house and grappled Timau. 'Timau, come with me!' he cried. But Timau – a great fellow, his eyes blood-red with the abuse of kava, six foot three in stature – cast him on one side; and the captain, instantly expecting to be either shot or brained,

1. The German firm J.C. Godeffroy and Son led the exploitation of copra in the Pacific.

discharged his pistol in the dark. When they carried Timau
out at the door into the moonlight, he was already dead,
and, upon his unlooked-for termination of their sally, the
whites appeared to have lost all conduct, and retreated to
the boats, fired upon by the natives as they went. Captain
Hart, who almost rivals Bishop Dordillon in popularity,
shared with him the policy of extreme indulgence to the
natives, regarding them as children, making light of their
defects, and constantly in favour of mild measures. The
death of Timau has thus somewhat weighed upon his
mind; the more so, as the chieftain's musket was found
in the house unloaded. To a less delicate conscience the
matter will seem light. If a drunken savage elects to cock a
fire-arm, a gentleman advancing towards him in the open
cannot wait to make sure if it be charged.

I have touched on the captain's popularity. It is one of
the things that most strikes a stranger in the Marquesas. He
comes instantly on two names, both new to him, both locally
famous, both mentioned by all with affection and respect –
the bishop's and the captain's. It gave me a strong desire to
meet with the survivor, which was subsequently gratified –
to the enrichment of these pages. Long after that again, in
the Place Dolorous – Molokai – I came once more on the
traces of that affectionate popularity. There was a blind
white leper there, an old sailor – 'an old tough' he called
himself – who had long sailed among the eastern islands.
Him I used to visit, and, being fresh from the scenes of
his activity, gave him the news. This (in the true island
style) was largely a chronicle of wrecks; and it chanced
I mentioned the case of one not very successful captain,
and how he had lost a vessel for Mr Hart; thereupon the
blind leper broke forth in lamentation. 'Did he lose a ship
of John Hart's?' he cried; 'poor John Hart! Well, I'm sorry
it was Hart's,' with needless force of epithet, which I neglect
to reproduce.

Perhaps, if Captain Hart's affairs had continued to
prosper, his popularity might have been different. Success
wins glory, but it kills affection, which misfortune fosters.
And the misfortune which overtook the captain's enterprise
was truly singular. He was at the top of his career. Ile Masse
belonged to him, given by the French as an indemnity
for the robberies at Taahauku. But the Ile Masse was

only suitable for cattle; and his two chief stations were Anaho, in Nukahiva, facing the north-east, and Taahauku in Hiva-oa, some hundred miles to the southward, and facing the south-west. Both these were on the same day swept by a tidal wave, which was not felt in any other bay or island of the group. The south coast of Hiva-oa was bestrewn with building timber and camphor-wood chests, containing goods; which, on the promise of a reasonable salvage, the natives very honestly brought back, the chests apparently not opened, and some of the wood after it had been built into their houses. But the recovery of such jetsam could not affect the result. It was impossible the captain should withstand this partiality of fortune; and with his fall the prosperity of the Marquesas ended. Anaho is truly extinct, Taahauku but a shadow of itself; nor has any new plantation arisen in their stead.

from The Paumotus

A HOUSE TO LET IN A LOW ISLAND

Never populus, it was yet by a chapter of accidents that I found the island[1] so deserted that no sound of human life diversified the hours; that we walked in that trim public garden of a town, among closed houses, without even a lodging-bill in a window to prove some tenancy in the back quarters; and, when we visited the Government bungalow, that Mr Donat, acting Vice-President, greeted us alone, and entertained us with cocoa-nut punches in the Sessions Hall and seat of judgment of that widespread archipelago, our glasses standing arrayed with summonses and census returns. The unpopularity of a late Vice-President had begun the movement of exodus, his native employés resigning court appointments and retiring each to his own cocoa-patch in the remoter districts of the isle. Upon the back of that, the Governor in Papeete[2] issued a decree: All land in the Paumotus must be defined and registered by a certain date. Now, the folk of the archipelago are half nomadic; a man can scarce be said to belong to a particular atoll; he belongs to several, perhaps, holds a stake and counts cousinship in half a score; and the inhabitants of Rotoava in particular, man, woman, and child, and from the gendarme to the Mormon prophet and the schoolmaster, owned – I was going to say land – owned at least coral blocks and growing coco-palms in some adjacent isle. Thither – from the gendarme to the babe in arms, the pastor followed by his flock, the schoolmaster carrying along with him his scholars, and the scholars with their books and slates – they had taken ship some two days previous to our arrival,

1. Stevenson had arrived at the port of Rotoava on Fakarava atoll in the Paumotus group.
2. Main town of Tahiti and capital of French Polynesia.

and were all now engaged disputing boundaries. Fancy overhears the shrillness of their disputation mingle with the surf and scatter sea-fowl. It was admirable to observe the completeness of their flight, like that of hibernating birds; nothing left but empty houses, like old nests to be reoccupied in spring; and even the harmless necessary dominie borne with them in their transmigration. Fifty odd set out, and only seven, I was informed, remained. But when I made a feast on board the *Casco*, more than seven, and nearer seven times seven, appeared to be my guests. Whence they appeared, how they were summoned, whither they vanished when the feast was eaten, I have no guess. In view of Low Island tales, and that awful frequentation which makes men avoid the seaward beaches of an atoll, some two score of those that ate with us may have returned, for the occasion, from the kingdom of the dead.

It was this solitude that put it in our minds to hire a house, and become, for the time being, in-dwellers of the isle – a practice I have ever since, when it was possible, adhered to. Mr Donat placed us, with that intent, under the convoy of one Taniera Mahinui, who combined the incongruous characters of catechist and convict. The reader may smile, but I affirm he was well qualified for either part. For that of convict, first of all, by a good substantial felony, such as in all lands casts the perpetrator in chains and dungeons. Taniera was a man of birth – the chief a while ago, as he loved to tell, of a district in Anaa of 800 souls. In an evil hour it occurred to the authorities in Papeete to charge the chiefs with the collection of the taxes. It is a question if much were collected; it is certain that nothing was handed on; and Taniera, who had distinguished himself by a visit to Papeete and some high living in restaurants, was chosen for the scapegoat. The reader must understand that not Taniera but the authorities in Papeete were first in fault. The charge imposed was disproportioned. I have not yet heard of any Polynesian capable of such a burden; honest and upright Hawaiians – one in particular, who was admired even by the whites as an inflexible magistrate – have stumbled in the narrow path of the trustee. And Taniera, when the pinch came, scorned to denounce accomplices; others had shared the spoil, he bore the penalty alone. He was condemned in five years. The period, when I had the pleasure of his friendship, was not yet expired; he still drew prison rations, the sole and not unwelcome reminder of his chains, and, I believe, looked forward to the date of his enfranchisement with mere alarm. For he had no sense of shame in the position; complained of nothing but the defective table of his place of exile; regretted nothing but the fowls and eggs and fish of his own more favoured island. And as for his parishioners, they did not think one hair the less of him. A schoolboy, mulcted in ten thousand lines of Greek and dwelling sequestered in the dormitories, enjoys unabated consideration from his fellows. So with Taniera: a marked man, not a dishonoured; having fallen under the lash of the unthinkable gods; a Job, perhaps, or say a Taniera in the den of lions. Songs are likely made and sung about this saintly Robin Hood. On the other hand, he was even highly qualified for his office in the Church; being by nature a grave, considerate, and kindly man; his face rugged and serious, his smile bright; the master of several trades, a builder both of boats and houses; endowed with a fine pulpit voice; endowed besides with such a gift of eloquence that at the grave of the late chief of Fakarava he set all the assistants weeping. I never met a man of a mind more ecclesiastical; he loved to dispute and to uniform himself of doctrine and the history of sects; and when I showed him the cuts in a volume of Chambers's *Encyclopaedia* – except for the one of an ape – reserved his whole enthusiasm for cardinals' hats, censers, candlesticks, and cathedrals. Methought when he looked upon the cardinal's hat a voice said low in his ear: 'Your foot is on the ladder.'

Under the guidance of Taniera we were soon installed in what I believe to have been the best-appointed private house in Fakarava. It stood just beyond the church in an oblong patch of cultivation. More than three hundred sacks of soil were imported from Tahiti for the Residency garden; and this must shortly be renewed, for the earth blows away, sinks in crevices of the coral, and is sought for at last in vain. I know not how much earth had gone to the garden of my villa; some at least, for an alley of prosperous bananas ran to the gate, and over the rest of the enclosure, which was covered with the usual clinker-like fragments of smashed coral, not only coco-palms and mikis but also fig-trees flourished, all of a delicious greenness. Of course there was no blade of grass. In front a picket fence divided us from the white road, the palm-fringed margin of the lagoon, and the lagoon itself, reflecting clouds by day and stars by night. At the back, a bulwark of uncemented coral enclosed us from the narrow belt of bush and the nigh ocean beach where the seas thundered, the roar and wash of them still humming in the chambers of the house.

This itself was of one story, verandahed front and back. It contained three rooms, three sewing-machines, three sea-chests, chairs, tables, a pair of beds, a cradle, a double-barrelled gun, a pair of enlarged coloured photographs, a pair of coloured prints after Wilkie and Mulready,[1] and a French lithograph with the legend: '*Le brigade du Général Lepasset brûlant son drapeau devant Metz.*' Under the stilts of the house a stove was rusting, till we drew it forth and put it in commission. Not far off was the burrow in the coral whence we supplied ourselves with brackish water. There was live stock, besides, on the estate – cocks and hens and a brace of ill-regulated cats, whom Taniera came every morning with the sun to feed on grated cocoa-nut. His voice was our regular réveillé, ringing pleasantly about the garden: 'Pooty – pooty – poo – poo – poo!'

Far as we were from the public offices, the nearness of the chapel made our situation what is called eligible in advertisements, and gave us a side look on some native life. Every morning, as soon as he had fed the fowls, Taniera set the bell agoing in the small belfry; and the faithful, who were not very numerous, gathered to prayers. I was once present: it was the Lord's day, and seven females and eight males composed the congregation. A woman played precentor starting with a longish note; the catechist joined in upon the second bar; and then the faithful in a body. Some had printed hymn-books which they followed; some of the rest filled up with 'eh – eh – eh', the Paumotuan tol-de-rol. After the hymn, we had an antiphonal prayer or two; and then Taniera rose from the front bench, where he had been sitting in his catechist's robes, passed within the altar-rails, opened his Tahitian Bible, and began to preach from notes. I understood one word – the name of

1. Sir David Wilkie, historical and genre painter, 1785–1841. William Mulready, genre painter in the Wilkie style, 1786–1863.

God; but the preacher managed his voice with taste, used rare and expressive gestures, and made a strong impression of sincerity. The plain service, the vernacular Bible, the hymn-tunes mostly on an English pattern – 'God save the Queen', I was informed, a special favourite – all, save some paper flowers upon the altar, seemed not merely but austerely Protestant. It is thus the Catholics have met their low island proselytes half-way.

Taniera had the keys of our house; it was with him I made my bargain, if that could be called a bargain in which all was remitted to my generosity; it was he who fed the cats and poultry, he who came to call and pick a meal with us like an acknowledged friend; and we long fondly supposed he was our landlord. This belief was not to bear the test of experience; and, as my chapter has to relate, no certainty succeeded it.

We passed some days of airless quiet and great heat; shell-gatherers were warned from the ocean beach, where sunstroke waited them from ten till four; the highest palm hung motionless, there was no voice audible but that of the sea on the far side. At last, about four of a certain afternoon, long cats-paws flawed the face of the lagoon; and presently in the tree-tops there awoke the grateful bustle of the trades, and all the houses and alleys of the island were fanned out. To more than one enchanted ship, that had lain long becalmed in view of the green shore, the wind brought deliverance; and by daylight on the morrow a schooner and two cutters lay moored in the port of Rotoava. Nor only in the outer sea, but in the lagoon itself, a certain traffic woke with the reviving breeze; and among the rest one François, a half-blood, set sail with the first light in his own half-decked cutter. He had held before a court appointment; being, I believe, the Residency sweeper-out. Trouble arising with the unpopular Vice-Resident, he had thrown his honours down, and fled to the far parts of the atoll to plant cabbages – or at least coco-palms. Thence he was now driven by such need as even a Cincinnatus[1]

---

1. Lucius Octavius Cincinnatus, 5th century B.C.
   Roman senator who put devotion to the republic
   before personal fame and power. Appointed
   Dictator in a crisis, he resigned and returned to
   his farm when the danger was past.

must acknowledge, and fared for the capital city, the seat of his late functions, to exchange half a ton of copra for necessary flour. And here, for a while, the story leaves to tell of his voyaging.

It must tell, instead, of our house, where, toward seven at night, the catechist came suddenly in with his pleased air of being welcome; armed besides with a considerable bunch of keys. These he proceeded to try on the sea-chests, drawing each in turn from its place against the wall. Heads of strangers appeared in the doorway and volunteered suggestions. All in vain. Either they were the wrong keys or the wrong boxes, or the wrong man was trying them. For a little Taniera fumed and fretted; then had recourse to the more summary method of the hatchet; one of the chests was broken open, and an armful of clothing, male and female, baled out and handed to the strangers on the verandah.

These were François, his wife, and their child. About eight A.M., in the midst of the lagoon, their cutter had capsized in jibbing. They got her righted, and though she was still full of water put the child on board. The mainsail had been carried away, but the jib still drew her sluggishly along, and François and the woman swam astern and worked the rudder with their hands. The cold was cruel; the fatigue, as time went on, became excessive; and in that preserve of sharks, fear haunted them. Again and again, François, the half-breed, would have desisted and gone down; but the woman, whole blood of an amphibious race, still supported him with cheerful words. I am reminded of a woman of Hawaii who swam with her husband, I dare not say how many miles, in a high sea, and came ashore at last with his dead body in her arms. It was about five in the evening, after nine hours' swimming, that François and his wife reached land at Rotoava. The gallant fight was won, and instantly the more childish side of native character appears. They had supped, and told and retold their story, dripping as they came; the flesh of the woman, Mrs Stevenson helped to shift, was cold as stone; and François, having changed to a dry cotton shirt and trousers, passed the remainder of the evening on my floor and between open doorways, in a thorough draught. Yet François, the son of a French father, speaks excellent French himself and seems intelligent.

It was our first idea that the catechist, true to his evangelical vocation, was clothing the naked from his superfluity. Then it came out that François was but dealing with his own. The clothes were his, so was the chest, so was the house. François was in fact the landlord. Yet you observe he had hung back on the verandah while Taniera tried his 'prentice hand upon the locks; and even now, when his true character appeared, the only use he made of the estate was to leave the clothes of his family drying on the fence. Taniera was still the friend of the house, still fed the poultry, still came about us on his daily visits, François, during the remainder of his stay, holding bashfully aloof. And there was stranger matter. Since François had lost the whole load of his cutter, the half ton of copra, an axe, bowls, knives, and clothes – since he had in a manner to begin the world again, and his necessary flour was not yet bought or paid for – I proposed to advance him what he needed on the rent. To my enduring amazement he refused, and the reason he gave – if that can be called a reason which but darkens counsel – was that Taniera was his friend. His friend, you observe; not his creditor. I inquired into that, and was assured that Taniera, an exile in a strange isle, might possibly be in debt himself, but certainly was no man's creditor.

Very early one morning we were awakened by a bustling presence in the yard, and found our camp had been surprised by a tall, lean, old native lady, dressed in what were obviously widow's weeds. You could see at a glance she was a notable woman, a housewife, sternly practicable, alive with energy, and with fine possibilities of temper. Indeed there was nothing native about her but the skin; and the type abounds, and is everywhere respected, nearer home. It did us good to see her scour the grounds, examining the plants and chickens; watering, feeding, trimming them; taking angry, purpose-like possession. When she neared the house our sympathy abated; when she came to the broken chest I wished I were elsewhere. We had scarce a word in common; but her whole lean body spoke for her with indignant eloquence. 'My chest!' it cried, with a stress on the possessive. 'My chest – broken open! This is a fine state of things!' I hastened to lay the blame where it belonged – on François and his wife – and found I had made things worse instead of better. She repeated the names at first with incredulity, then with despair. A while she seemed stunned, next fell to disembowelling the box, piling the goods on the floor, and visibly computing the extent of François's ravages; and presently after she was observed in high speech with Taniera, who seemed to hang an ear like one reproved.

Here, then, by all known marks, should be my land-lady at last; here was every character of the proprietor fully developed. Should I not approach her on the still depending question of my rent? I carried the point to an adviser. 'Nonsense!' he cried. 'That's the old woman, the mother. It doesn't belong to her. I believe that's the man the house belongs to,' and he pointed to one of the coloured photographs on the wall. On this I gave up all desire of understanding; and when the time came for me to leave, in the judgment-hall of the archipelago, and with the awful countenance of the acting Governor, I duly paid my rent to Taniera. He was satisfied, and so was I. But what had he to do with it? Mr Donat, acting magistrate and a man of kindred blood, could throw no light upon the mystery; a plain private person, with a taste for letters, cannot be expected to do more.

from The Gilberts

At Honolulu we had said farewell to the *Casco* and to
Captain Otis, and our next adventure was made in
changed conditions. Passage was taken for myself, my
wife, Mr Osbourne, and my China boy, Ah Fu, on a
pigmy trading schooner, the *Equator*, Captain Dennis Reid;
and on a certain bright June day in 1889, adorned in the
Hawaiian fashion with the garlands of departure, we drew
out of port and bore with a fair wind for Micronesia.

The whole extent of the South Seas is desert of ships;
more especially that part where we were now to sail.
No post runs in these islands; communication is by
accident; where you may have designed to go is one
thing, where you shall be able to arrive is another. It
was my hope, for instance, to have reached the Carolines,
and returned to the light of day by way of Manila and
the China ports; and it was in Samoa that we were
destined to re-appear and be once more refreshed with
the sight of mountains. Since the sunset faded from the
peaks of Oahu six months had intervened, and we had
seen no spot of earth so high as an ordinary cottage.
Our path had been still on the flat sea, our dwellings
upon erected coral, our diet from the pickle-tub or out
of tins; I had learned to welcome shark's flesh for a
variety; and a mountain, an onion, an Irish potato or
a beef-steak, had been long lost to sense and dear to
aspiration.

The two chief places of our stay, Butaritari and Apemama,
lie near the line; the latter within thirty miles. Both enjoy
a superb ocean climate, days of blinding sun and bracing
winds, nights of a heavenly brightness. Both are somewhat
wider than Fakarava, measuring perhaps (at the widest) a
quarter of a mile from beach to beach. In both, a course

kind of *taro*[1] thrives; its culture is a chief business of the natives, and the consequent mounds and ditches make miniature scenery and amuse the eye. In all else they show the customary features of an atoll: the low horizon, the expanse of the lagoon, the sedge-like rim of palm-tops, the sameness and smallness of the land, the hugely superior size and interest of sea and sky. Life on such islands is in many points like life on shipboard. The atoll, like the ship, is soon taken for granted; and the islanders, like the ship's crew, become soon the centre of attention. The isles are populous, independent, seats of kinglets, recently civilised, little visited. In the last decade many changes have crept in; women no longer go unclothed till marriage; the widow no longer sleeps at night and goes abroad by day with the skull of her dead husband; and, fire-arms being introduced, the spear and the sharktooth sword are sold for curiosities. Ten years ago all these things and practices were to be seen in use; yet ten years more, and the old society will have entirely vanished. We came in a happy moment to see its institutions still erect and (in Apemama) scarce decayed.

Populous and independent – warrens of men, ruled over with some rustic pomp – such was the first and still the recurring impression of these tiny lands. As we stood across the lagoon for the town of Butaritari, a stretch of the low shore was seen to be crowded with the brown roofs of houses; those of the palace and king's summer parlour (which are of corrugated iron) glittered near one end conspicuously bright; the royal colours flew hard by on a tall flagstaff; in front, on an artificial islet, the gaol played the part of a martello. Even upon this first and distant view, the place had scarce the air of what it truly was, a village; rather of that which it was also, a petty metropolis, a city rustic and yet royal.

The lagoon is shoal. The tide being out, we waded for some quarter of a mile in tepid shallows, and stepped ashore at last into a flagrant stagnancy of sun and heat. The lee side of a line island after noon is indeed a breathless place; on the ocean beach the trade will be still blowing, boisterous and cool; out in the lagoon it will be blowing also, speeding the canoes; but the screen of bush completely intercepts

1. A food plant with starchy roots and succulent leaves.

it from the shore, and sleep and silence and companies of mosquitoes brood upon the towns.

We may thus be said to have taken Butaritari by surprise. A few inhabitants were still abroad in the north end, at which we landed. As we advanced, we were soon done with encounter, and seemed to explore a city of the dead. Only, between the posts of open houses, we could see the townsfolk stretched in the siesta, sometimes a family together veiled in a mosquito net, sometimes a single sleeper on a platform like a corpse on a bier.

The houses were of all dimensions, from those of toys to those of churches. Some might hold a battalion, some were so minute they could scarce receive a pair of lovers; only in the playroom, when the toys are mingled, do we meet such incongruities of scale. Many were open sheds; some took the form of roofed stages; others were walled and the walls pierced with little windows. A few were perched on piles in the lagoon; the rest stood at random on a green, through which the roadway made a ribbon of sand, or along the embankments of a sheet of water like a shallow dock. One and all were the creatures of a single tree; palm-tree wood and palm-tree leaf their materials; no nail had been driven, no hammer sounded, in their building, and they were held together by lashings of palm-tree sinnet.

In the midst of the thoroughfare, the church stands like an island, a lofty and dim house with rows of windows; a rich tracery of framing sustains the roof; and through the door at either end the street shows in a vista. The proportions of the place, in such surroundings, and built of such materials, appeared august; and we threaded the nave with a sentiment befitting visitors in a cathedral. Benches run along either side. In the midst, on a crazy dais, two chairs stand ready for the king and queen when they shall choose to worship; over their heads a hoop, apparently from a hogshead, depends by a strip of red cotton; and the hoop (which hangs askew) is dressed with streamers of the same material, red and white.

This was our first advertisement of the royal dignity, and presently we stood before its seat and centre. The palace is built of imported wood upon a European plan; the roof of corrugated iron, the yard enclosed with walls, the gate surmounted by a sort of lychhouse. It cannot be called spacious; a labourer in the States is sometimes more commodiously lodged; but when we had the chance to see it within, we found it was enriched (beyond all island expectation) with coloured advertisements and cuts from illustrated papers. Even before the gate some of the treasures of the crown stand public: a bell of good magnitude, two pieces of cannon, and a single shell. The bell cannot be rung nor the guns fired; they are curiosities, proofs of wealth, a part of the parade of the royalty, and stand to be admired like statues in a square. A straight gut of water like a canal runs almost to the palace door; the containing quay-walls excellently built of coral; over against the mouth, by what seems an effect of landscape art, the martello-like islet of the gaol breaks the lagoon. Vassal chiefs with tribute, neighbour monarchs come a-roving, might here sail in, view with surprise these extensive public works, and be awed by these mouths of silent cannon. It was impossible to see the place and not to fancy it designed for pageantry. But the elaborate theatre then stood empty; the royal house deserted, its doors and windows gaping; the whole quarter of the town immersed in silence. On the opposite bank of the canal, on a roofed stage, an ancient gentleman slept publicly, sole visible inhabitant; and beyond on the lagoon a canoe spread a striped lateen, the sole thing moving.

The canal is formed on the south by a pier or causeway with a parapet. As the far end the parapet stops, and the quay expands into an oblong peninsula in the lagoon, the breathing-place and summer parlour of the king. The midst is occupied by an open house or permanent marquee – called here a maniapa, or, as the word is now pronounced, a maniap' – at the lowest estimation forty feet by sixty. The iron roof, lofty but exceedingly low-browed, so that a woman must stoop to enter, is supported externally on pillars of coral, within by a frame of wood. The floor is of broken coral, divided in aisles by the uprights of the frame; the house far enough from shore to catch the breeze, which enters freely and disperses the mosquitoes; and under the low eaves the sun is seen to glitter and the waves to dance on the lagoon.

It was now some while since we had met any but slumberers; and when we had wandered down the pier and stumbled at last into this bright shed, we were surprised to find it occupied by a society of a wakeful people, some twenty souls in all, the court and guardsmen of Butaritari. The court ladies were busy making mats; the guardsmen yawned and sprawled. Half a dozen rifles lay on a rock and a cutlass was leaned against a pillar: the armoury of these drowsy musketeers. At the far end, a little closed house of wood displayed some tinsel curtains, and proved, upon examination, to be a privy of the European model. In front of this, upon some mats, lolled Tebureimoa, the king[1]; behind him, on the panels of the house, two crossed rifles represented fasces. He wore pyjamas which sorrowfully misbecame his bulk; his nose was hooked and cruel, his body overcome with sodden corpulence, his eye timorous and dull; he seemed at once oppressed with drowsiness and held awake by apprehension: a pepper rajah muddled with opium, and listening for the march of a Dutch army, looks perhaps not otherwise. We were to grow better acquainted, and first and last I had the same impression; he seemed always drowsy, yet always to hearken and start; and, whether from remorse or fear, there is no doubt he seeks a refuge in the abuse of drugs.

The rajah displayed no sign of interest in our coming. But the queen, who sat beside him in a purple sacque, was more accessible; and there was present an interpreter so willing that his volubility became at last the cause of our departure. He had greeted us upon our entrance: – 'That is the honourable King, and I am his interpreter,' he had said, with more stateliness than truth. For he held no appointment in the court, seemed extremely ill-acquainted with the island language, and was present, like ourselves, upon a visit of civility. Mr Williams was his name: an American darkey, runaway ship's cook, and bar-keeper at *The Land we Live in* tavern, Butaritari. I never knew a man who had more words in his command or less truth

1. Tebureimoa, Nantemat' by name and a carpenter to trade was the last of four brothers who had been kings of Butaritari before him. He earned the nick-name 'Mr Corpse' because of his bloody service as hatchetman to his oldest brother, the tyrant Nakaeia. He proved to be a weak and guilt-ridden figure when finally installed as king in his own right.

to communicate; neither the gloom of the monarch, nor my own efforts to be distant, could in the least abash him; and when the scene closed, the darkey was left talking.

The town still slumbered, or had but just begun to turn and stretch itself; it was still plunged in heat and silence. So much the more vivid was the impression that we carried away of the house upon the islet, the Micronesian Saul wakeful amid his guards, and his unmelodious David, Mr Williams, chattering through the drowsy hours.

from The Gilberts

AROUND OUR HOUSE

When we left the palace we were still but seafarers ashore; and within the hour we had installed our goods in one of the six foreign houses of Butaritari, namely, that usually occupied by Maka, the Hawaiian missionary. Two San Francisco firms are here established, Messrs Crawford and Messrs Wightman Brothers; the first hard by the palace of the mid town, the second at the north entry; each with a store and bar-room. Our house was in the Wightman compound, betwixt the store and bar, within a fenced enclosure. Across the road a few native houses nestled in the margin of the bush, and the green wall of palms rose solid, shutting out the breeze. A little sandy cove of the lagoon ran in behind, sheltered by a verandah pier, the labour of queens' hands. Here, when the tide was high, sailed boats lay to be loaded; when the tide was low, the boats took ground some half a mile away, and an endless series of natives descended the pier stair, tailed across the sand in strings and clusters, waded to the waist with the bags of copra, and loitered backward to renew their charge. The mystery of the copra trade tormented me, as I sat and watched the profits drip on the stair and the sands.[1]

In front, from shortly after four in the morning until nine at night, the folk of the town streamed by us intermittently along the road: families going up the island to make copra on their lands; women bound for the bush to gather flowers against the evening toilet; and, twice a day, the

1. Copra is dried coconut kernel from which coconut-oil could be extracted for use in food fats, soap, detergents and candles. Sold by weight, it is heavier when moist.

toddy-cutters,[1] each with his knife and shell. In the first grey of the morning, and again late in the afternoon, these would straggle past about their tree-top business, strike off here and there into the bush, and vanish from the face of earth. At about the same hour, if the tide be low in the lagoon, you are likely to be bound yourself across the island for a bath, and may enter close at their heels alleys of the palm wood. Right in front, although the sun is not yet risen, the east is already lighted with preparatory fires, and the huge accumulations of the trade-wind cloud glow with and heliograph the coming day. The breeze is in your face; overhead in the tops of the palms, its playthings, it maintains a lively bustle; look where you will, above or below, there is no human presence, only the earth and shaken forest. And right overhead the song of an invisible singer breaks from the thick leaves; from farther on a second tree-top answers; and beyond again, in the bosom of the woods, a still more distant minstrel perches and sways and sings. So, all round the isle, the toddy-cutters sit on high, and are rocked by the trade, and have a view far to seaward, where they keep watch for sails, and like huge birds utter their songs in the morning. They sing with a certain lustiness and Bacchic glee; the volume of sound and the articulate melody fall unexpected from the tree-top, whence we anticipate the chattering of fowls. And yet in a sense these songs also are but chatter; the words are ancient, obsolete, and sacred; few comprehend them, perhaps no one perfectly; but it was understood the cutters 'prayed to have good toddy, and sang of their old wars'. The prayer is at least answered; and when the foaming shell is brought to your door, you have a beverage well 'worthy of a grace'. All forenoon you may return and taste; it only sparkles, and sharpens, and grows to be a new drink, not less delicious; but with the progress of the day the fermentation quickens and grows acid; in twelve hours it will be yeast for bread, in two days more a devilish intoxicant, the counsellor of crime.

The men are of a marked Arabian cast of features, often bearded and moustached, often gaily dressed, some with bracelets and anklets, all stalking hidalgo-like, and accepting salutations with a haughty lip. The hair (with

1. A toddy-palm is a coconut or other palm, the juice of which can be fermented to make toddy.

the dandies of either sex) is worn turban-wise in a frizzled bush; and like the daggers of the Japanese, a pointed stick (used for a comb) is thrust gallantly among the curls. The women from this bush of hair look forth enticingly: the race cannot be compared with the Tahitian for female beauty; I doubt even if the average be high; but some of the prettiest girls, and one of the handsomest women I ever saw, were Gilbertines. Butaritari, being the commercial centre of the group, is Europeanised; the coloured sacque or the white shift are common wear, the latter for the evening; the trade hat, loaded with flowers, fruit, and ribbons, is unfortunately not unknown; and the characteristic female dress of the Gilberts no longer universal. The *ridi* is its name: a cutty petticoat or fringe of the smoked fibre of cocoa-nut leaf, not unlike tarry string; the lower edge not reaching the mid-thigh, the upper adjusted so low upon the haunches that it seems to cling by accident. A sneeze, you think, and the lady must surely be left destitute. 'The perilous, hairbreadth ridi' was our word for it; and in the conflict that rages over women's dress it has the misfortune to please neither side, the prudish condemning it as insufficient, the more frivolous finding it unlovely in itself. Yet if a pretty Gilbertine would look her best, that must be her costume. In that, and naked otherwise, she moves with an incomparable liberty and grace and life, that marks the poetry of Micronesia. Bundle her in a gown, the charm is fled, and she wriggles like an Englishwoman.

Towards dusk the passers-by became more gorgeous. The men broke out in all the colours of the rainbow – or at least of the trade-room, – and both men and women began to be adorned and scented with new flowers. A small white blossom is the favourite, sometimes sown singly in a woman's hair like little stars, now composed in a thick wreath. With the night, the crowd sometimes thickened in the road, and the padding and brushing of bare feet became continuous; the promenades mostly grave, the silence only interrupted by some giggling and scampering of girls; even the children quiet. At nine, bed-time struck on a bell from the cathedral, and the life of the town ceased. At four the next morning the signal is repeated in the darkness, and the innocent prisoners set free; but for seven hours all must lie – I was about to say within doors, of a place where doors, and even walls, are an exception – housed, at least, under their airy roofs and clustered in the tents of the mosquito-nets. Suppose a necessary errand to occur, suppose it imperative to send abroad, the messenger must then go openly, advertising himself to the police with a huge brand of cocoa-nut, which flares from house to house like a moving bonfire. Only the police themselves go darkling, and grope in the night of misdemeanants. I used to hate their treacherous presence; their captain in particular, a crafty old man in white, lurked nightly about my premises till I could have found it in my heart to beat him. But the rogue was privileged.

Not one of the eleven resident traders came to town, no captain cast anchor in the lagoon, but we saw him ere the hour was out. This was owing to our position between the store and the bar – the *Sans Souci*, as the last was called. Mr Rick was not only Messrs Wightman's manager, but consular agent for the States; Mrs Rick was the only white woman on the island, and one of the only two in the archipelago; their house besides, with its cool verandahs, its bookshelves, its comfortable furniture, could not be rivalled nearer than Jaluit or Honolulu. Every one called in consequence, save such as might be prosecuting a South Sea quarrel, hingeing on the price of copra and the odd cent, or perhaps a difference about poultry. Even these, if they did not appear upon the north, would be presently visible to the southward, the *Sans Souci* drawing them as with cords. In an island with a total population of twelve white persons, one of the two drinking-shops might seem superfluous; but every bullet has its billet, and the double accommodation of Butaritari is found in practice highly convenient by the captains and crews of ships: *The Land we Live in* being tacitly resigned to the forecastle, the *Sans Souci* tacitly reserved for the afterguard. So aristocratic were my habits, so commanding was my fear of Mr Williams, that I have never visited the first; but in the other, which was the club or rather the casino of the island, I regularly passed my evenings. It was small, but neatly fitted, and at night (when the lamp was lit) sparkled with glass and glowed with coloured pictures like a theatre at Christmas. The pictures were advertisements, the glass coarse enough, the carpentry amateur; but the effect, in that incongruous isle, was of unbridled luxury and inestimable expense. Here songs were sung, tales told, tricks performed, games played. The Ricks, ourselves, Norwegian Tom the bar-keeper, a captain or two from the ships, and perhaps three or four traders come down the island in their boats or by the road on foot, made up the usual company. The traders, all bred to the sea, take a humorous pride in their new business; 'South Sea Merchants' is the title they prefer. 'We are all sailors here' – 'Merchants, if you please' – '*South Sea* Merchants' – was a piece of conversation endlessly repeated, that never seemed to lose in savour. We found them at all times simple, genial, gay, gallant, and obliging; and, across some interval of time, recall with pleasure the traders of Butaritari. There was one black sheep indeed. I tell of him here where he lived, against my rule; for in this case I have no measure to preserve, and the man is typical of a class of ruffians that once disgraced the whole field of the South Seas, and still linger in the rarely visited isles of Micronesia. He had the name on the beach of 'a perfect gentleman when sober', but I never saw him otherwise than drunk. The few shocking and savage traits of the Micronesian he has singled out with the skill of a collector, and planted in the soil of his original baseness. He has been accused and acquitted of a treacherous murder; and has since boastfully owned it, which inclines me to suppose him innocent. His daughter is defaced by his erroneous cruelty, for it was his wife he had intended to disfigure, and, in the darkness of the night and the frenzy of cocoa-brandy, fastened on the wrong victim. The wife has since fled and harbours in the bush with natives; and the husband still demands from deaf ears her forcible restoration. The best of his business is to make natives drink, and then advance the money for the fine upon a lucrative mortgage. 'Respect for whites' is the man's word: 'What is the matter with this island is the want of respect for whites.' On his way to Butaritari, while I was there, he spied his wife in the bush with certain natives and made a dash to capture her; whereupon one of her companions drew a knife, and the husband retreated: 'Do you call that proper respect for whites?' he cried. At an early stage of the acquaintance we proved our respect for his kind of white by forbidding him our enclosure under pain of death. Thenceforth he lingered often in the neighbourhood with I knew not what sense of envy or design of mischief; his white, handsome face (which I beheld with loathing) looked in upon us at all hours across the fence; and once, from a safe distance, he avenged himself by shouting a recondite island insult, to us quite inoffensive, on his English lips incredibly incongruous.

Our enclosure, round which this composite of degradations wandered, was of some extent. In one corner was a trellis with a long table of rough boards. Here the Fourth of July feast had been held not long before with memorable consequences, yet to be set forth; here we took our meals; here entertained to a dinner the king and notables of Makin. In the midst was the house, with a verandah front and back, and three rooms within. In the verandah we slung our man-of-war hammocks, worked there by day, and slept at night. Within were beds, chairs, a round table, a fine hanging lamp, and portraits of the royal family of Hawaii. Queen Victoria proves nothing; Kalakaua[1] and Mrs Bishop[2] are diagnostic; and the truth is we were the stealthy tenants of the parsonage. On the day of our arrival Maka was away; faithless trustees unlocked his doors; and the dear rigorous man, the sworn foe of liquor and tobacco, returned to find his verandah littered with cigarettes and his parlour horrible with bottles. He made but one condition—on the round table, which he used in the celebration of the sacraments, he begged us to refrain from setting liquor; in all else he bowed to the accomplished fact, refused rent, retired across the way into a native house, and, plying in his boat, beat the remotest quarters of the isle for provender. He found us pigs – I could not fancy where – no other pigs were visible; he brought us fowls and taro; when we gave our feast to the monarch and gentry, it was he who supplied the wherewithal, he who

1. King of Hawaii, whom Stevenson got to know well during the six month stay at Waikiki.
2. Probably a reference to Bernice Pauaohi Bishop, after whom Honolulu's Bishop Museum was founded in 1889, the year Stevenson was in Hawaii. She was the wife of missionary Charles Reed Bishop and a member of the Hawaiian royal family.

superintended the cooking, he who asked grace at table, and when the king's health was proposed, he also started the cheering with an English hip-hip-hip. There was never a more fortunate conception; the heart of the fatted king exulted in his bosom at the sound.

Take him for all in all, I have never known a more engaging creature than this parson of Butaritari: his mirth, his kindness, his noble, friendly feelings, brimmed from the man in speech and gesture. He loved to exaggerate, to act and overact the momentary part, to exercise his lungs and muscles, and to speak and laugh with his whole body. He had the morning cheerfulness of birds and healthy children; and his humour was infectious. We were next neighbours and met daily, yet our salutations lasted minutes at a stretch – shaking hands, slapping shoulders, capering like a pair of Merry-Andrews, laughing to split our sides upon some pleasantry that would scarce raise a titter in an infant-school. It might be five in the morning, the toddy-cutters just gone by, the road empty, the shade of the island lying far on the lagoon: and the ebullition cheered me for the day.

Yet I always suspected Maka of a secret melancholy; these jubilant extremes could scarce be constantly maintained. He was besides long, and lean, and lined, and corded, and a trifle grizzled; and his Sabbath countenance was even saturnine. On that day we made a procession to the church, or (as I must always call it) the cathedral; Maka (a blot on the hot landscape) in tall hat, black frockcoat, black trousers; under his arm the hymn-book and the Bible; in his face, a reverent gravity: – beside him Mary his wife, a quiet, wise, and handsome elderly lady, seriously attired: – myself following with singular and moving thoughts. Long before, to the sound of bells and streams and birds, through a green Lothian glen, I had accompanied Sunday by Sunday a minister in whose house I lodged; and the likeness, and the difference, and the series of years and deaths, profoundly touched me. In the great, dusky, palm-tree cathedral the congregation rarely numbered thirty: the men on one side, the women on the other, myself posted (for a privilege) amongst the women, and the small missionary contingent gathered close around the platform, we were lost in that round vault. The lessons were read antiphonally, the flock was catechised, a blind youth repeated weekly a long string of psalms, hymns were sung – I never heard worse singing, – and the sermon followed. To say I understood nothing were untrue; there were points that I learned to expect with certainty; the name of Honolulu, that of Kalakaua, the word Cap'n-man-o'-wa', the word ship, and a description of a storm at sea, infallibly occurred; and I was not seldom rewarded with the name of my own Sovereign in the bargain. The rest was but sound to the ears, silence for the mind; a plain expanse of tedium, rendered unbearable by heat, a hard chair, and the sight through the wide doors of the more happy heathen on the green. Sleep breathed on my joints and eyelids, sleep hummed in my ears; it reigned in the dim cathedral. The congregation stirred and stretched; they moaned, they groaned aloud; they yawned upon a singing note, as you may sometimes hear a dog when he has reached the tragic bitterest of boredom. In vain the preacher thumped the table; in vain he singled and addressed by name particular hearers. I was myself perhaps a more effective excitant; and at least to one old gentleman the spectacle of my successful struggles against sleep – and I hope they were successful – cheered the flight of time. He, when he was not catching flies or playing tricks upon his neighbours, gloated with a fixed, truculent eye upon the stages of my agony; and once, when the service was drawing towards a close, he winked at me across the church.

I write of the service with a smile; yet I was always there – always with respect for Maka, always with admiration for his deep seriousness, his burning energy, the fire of his roused eye, the sincere and various accents of his voice. To see him weekly flogging a dead horse and blowing a cold fire was a lesson in fortitude and constancy. It may be a question whether if the mission were fully supported, and he was set free from business avocations, more might not result; I think otherwise myself; I think not neglect but rigour had reduced his flock, that which has once provoked a revolution, and which today, in a man so lively and engaging, amazes the beholder. No song, no dance, no tobacco, no liquor, no alleviative of life – only toil and church-going; so says a voice from his face; and the face is the face of the Polynesian Esau, but the voice is the voice of a Jacob from a different world.

And a Polynesian at the best makes a singular missionary in the Gilberts, coming from a country recklessly unchaste to one conspicuously strict; from a race hag-ridden with bogies to one comparatively bold against the terrors of the dark. The thought was stamped one morning in my mind, when I chanced to be abroad by moonlight, and saw all the town lightless, but the lamp faithfully burning by the missionary's bed. It requires no law, no fire, and no scouting police, to withhold Maka and his countrymen from wandering in the night unlighted.

from The Gilberts

A TALE OF A TAPU[1]

On the morrow of our arrival (Sunday, 14th July 1889) our photographers were early stirring. Once more we traversed a silent town; many were yet abed and asleep; some sat drowsily in their open houses; there was no sound of intercourse or business. In that hour before the shadows, the quarter of the palace and canal seemed like a landing-place in the *Arabian Nights* or from the classic poets; here were the fit destination of some 'faery frigot', here some adventurous prince might step ashore among new characters and incidents; and the island prison, where it floated on the luminous face of the lagoon, might have passed for the repository of the Grail. In such a scene, and at such an hour, the impression received was not so much of foreign travel – rather of past ages; it seemed not so much degrees of latitude that we had crossed, as centuries of time that we had re-ascended; leaving, by the same steps, home and today. A few children followed us, mostly nude, all silent; in the clear, weedy waters of the canal some silent damsels waded, baring their brown thighs; and to one of the maniap's before the palace gate we were attracted by a low but stirring hum of speech.

The oval shed was full of men sitting cross-legged. The king was there in striped pyjamas, his rear protected by four guards with Winchesters, his air and bearing marked by unwonted spirit and decision; tumblers and black bottles went the round; and the talk, throughout loud, was general and animated. I was inclined at first to view this scene with suspicion. But the hour appeared unsuitable for a carouse; drink was besides forbidden equally by the law of the land and the canons of the church; and while I was yet hesitating,

1. A taboo, a proscription.

the king's rigorous attitude disposed of my last doubt. We had come, thinking to photograph him surrounded by his guards, and at the first word of the design his piety revolted. We were reminded of the day – the Sabbath, in which thou shalt take no photographs – and returned with a flea in our ear, bearing the rejected camera.

At church, a little later, I was struck to find the throne unoccupied. So nice a Sabbatarian might have found the means to be present; perhaps my doubts revived; and before I got home they were transformed to certainties. Tom, the bar-keeper of the *Sans Souci*, was in conversation with two emissaries from the court. The 'keen', they said, wanted 'din', failing which 'perandi'.* No din, was Tom's reply, and no perandi; but 'pira' if they pleased. It seems they had no use for beer, and departed sorrowing.

'Why, what is the meaning of all this?' I asked. 'Is the island on the spree?'

Such was the fact. On the 4th of July a feast had been made, and the king, at the suggestion of the whites, had raised the tapu against liquor. There is a proverb about horses; it scarce applies to the superior animal, of whom it may be rather said, that any one can start him drinking, not any twenty can prevail on him to stop. The tapu, raised ten days before, was not yet re-imposed; for ten days the town had been passing the bottle or lying (as we had seen it the afternoon before) in hoggish sleep; and the king, moved by the Old Men and his own appetites, continued to maintain the liberty, to squander his savings on liquor, and to join in and lead the debauch. The whites were the authors of this crisis; it was upon their own proposal that the freedom had been granted at the first; and for a while, in the interests of trade, they were doubtless pleased it should continue. That pleasure had now sometime ceased; the bout had been prolonged (it was conceded) unduly; and it now began to be a question how it might conclude. Hence Tom's refusal. Yet that refusal was avowedly only for the moment, and it was avowedly unavailing; the king's foragers, denied by Tom at the *Sans Souci*, would be supplied at *The Land we Live in* by the gobbling Mr Williams.

The degree of the peril was not easy to measure at

* Gin and brandy. [R.L.S.]

the time, and I am inclined to think now it was easy to exaggerate. Yet the conduct of drunkards even at home is always matter for anxiety; and at home our populations are not armed from the highest to the lowest with revolvers and repeating rifles, neither do we go on a debauch by the whole townful – and I might rather say, by the whole polity – king, magistrates, police, and army joining in one common scene of drunkenness. It must be thought besides that we were here in barbarous islands, rarely visited, lately and partly civilised. First and last, a really considerable number of whites have perished in the Gilberts, chiefly through their own misconduct; and the natives have displayed in at least one instance a disposition to conceal an accident under a butchery, and leave nothing but dumb bones. This last was the chief consideration against a sudden closing of the bars; the bar-keepers stood in the immediate breach and dealt direct with madmen; too surly a refusal might at any moment precipitate a blow, and the blow might prove the signal for a massacre.

Monday, 15th – At the same hour we returned to the same maniap'. Kümmel (of all drinks) was served in tumblers; in the midst sat the crown prince, a fatted youth, surrounded by fresh bottles and busily plying the corkscrew; and king, chief, and commons showed the loose mouth, the uncertain joints, and the blurred and animated eye of the early drinker. It was plain we were impatiently expected; the king retired with alacrity to dress, the guards were despatched after their uniforms; and we were left to await the issue of these preparations with a shedful of tipsy natives. The orgie had proceeded further than on Sunday. The day promised to be of great heat; it was already sultry, the courtiers were already fuddled; and still the kümmel continued to go round, and the crown prince to play butler. Flemish freedom followed upon Flemish excess; and a funny dog, a handsome fellow, gaily dressed, and with a full turban of frizzed hair, delighted the company with a humorous courtship of a lady in a manner not to be described. It was our diversion, in this time of waiting, to observe the gathering of the guards. They have European arms, European uniforms, and (to their sorrow) European shoes. We saw one warrior (like Mars) in the article of being armed; two men and a stalwart woman were scarce strong enough to boot him; and after a single appearance on parade the army is crippled for a week.

At last, the gates under the king's house opened; the army issued, one behind another, with guns and epaulettes; the colours stooped under the gateway; majesty followed in his uniform bedizened with gold lace; majesty's wife came next in a hat and feathers, and an ample trained silk gown; the royal imps succeeded; there stood the pageantry of Makin marshalled on its chosen theatre. Dickens might have told how serious they were; how tipsy; how the king melted and streamed under his cocked hat; how he took station by the larger of his two cannons – austere, majestic, but not truly vertical; how the troops huddled, and were straightened out, and clubbed again; how they and their firelocks raked at various inclinations like the masts of ships; and how an amateur photographer reviewed, arrayed, and adjusted them, to see his dispositions change before he reached the camera.

The business was funny to see; I do not know that it is graceful to laugh at; and our report of these transactions was received on our return with the shaking of grave heads.

The day had begun ill; eleven hours divided us from sunset; and at any moment, on the most trifling chance, the trouble might begin. The Wightman compound was in a military sense untenable, commanded on three sides by houses and thick bush; the town was computed to contain over a thousand stand of excellent new arms; and retreat to ships, in the case of an alert, was a recourse not to be thought of. Our talk that morning must have closely reproduced the talk in English garrisons before the Sepoy mutiny;[1] the sturdy doubt that any mischief was in prospect, the sure belief that (should any come) there was nothing left but to go down fighting, the half amused, half anxious attitude of mind in which we were awaiting fresh developments.

The kümmel soon ran out; we were scarce returned before the king had followed us in quest of more. Mr Corpse was now divested of his more awful attitude, the lawless bulk of him again encased in striped pyjamas; a guardsman brought up the rear with his rifle at the trail; and his majesty was

1. The Indian Mutiny of 1857, in which many of the Sepoy troops of the East India Company's Bengal army mutinied.

further accompanied by a Rarotongan[1] whalerman and
the playful courtier with the turban of frizzed hair. There
was never a more lively deputation. The whalerman was
gapingly, tearfully tipsy; the courtier walked on air; the king
himself was even sportive. Seated in a chair in the Ricks'
sitting-room, he bore the brunt of our prayers and menaces
unmoved. He was even rated, plied with historic instances,
threatened with the men-of-war, ordered to restore the tapu
on the spot – and nothing in the least affected him. It should
be done tomorrow, he said; today it was beyond his power,
today he durst not. 'Is that royal?' cried indignant Mr Rick.
No, it was not royal; had the king been of a royal character
we should ourselves have held a different language; and
royal or not, he had the best of the dispute. The terms
indeed were hardly equal; for the king was the only man
who could restore the tapu, but the Ricks were not the only
people who sold drink. He had but to hold his ground on
the first question, and they were sure to weaken on the
second. A little struggle they still made for the fashion's
sake; and then one exceedingly tipsy deputation departed,
greatly rejoicing, a case of brandy wheeling beside them in
a barrow. The Rarotongan (whom I had never seen before)
wrung me by the hand like a man bound on a far voyage.
'My dear frien'!' he cried, 'good-bye, my dear frien'!' –
tears of kümmel standing in his eyes; the king lurched as he
went, the courtier ambled – a strange party of intoxicated
children to be intrusted with that barrowful of madness.

You could never say the town was quiet; all morning
there was a ferment in the air, an aimless movement and
congregation of natives in the street. But it was not before
half-past one that a sudden hubbub of voices called us from
the house, to find the whole white colony already gathered
on the spot as by concerted signal. The *Sans Souci* was
overrun with rabble, the stair and verandah thronged.
From all these throats an inarticulate babbling cry went
up incessantly; it sounded like the bleating of young lambs,
but angrier. In the road his royal highness (whom I had seen
so lately in the part of butler) stood crying upon Tom; on
the top step, tossed in the hurly-burly, Tom was shouting
to the prince. Yet a while the pack swayed about the bar,

1. Rarotonga, the largest of the Cook Islands, a
scattered Polynesian group in the Central Pacific.

vociferous. Then came a brutal impulse; the mob reeled, and returned and was rejected; the stair showed a stream of heads; and there shot into view, through the disbanding ranks, three men violently dragging in their midst a fourth. By his hair and his hands, his head forced as low as his knees, his face concealed, he was wrenched from the verandah and whisked along the road into the village, howling as he disappeared. Had his face been raised, we should have seen it bloodied, and the blood was not his own. The courtier with the turban of frizzed hair had paid the costs of this disturbance with the lower part of one ear.

So the brawl passed with no other casualty than might seem comic to the inhumane. Yet we looked round on serious faces and – a fact that spoke volumes – Tom was putting up the shutters on the bar. Custom might go elsewhither, Mr Williams might profit as he pleased, but Tom had had enough of bar-keeping for that day. Indeed the event had hung on a hair. A man had sought to draw a revolver – on what quarrel I could never learn, and perhaps he himself could not have told; one shot, when the room was so crowded, could scarce have failed to take effect; where many were armed and all tipsy, it could scarce have failed to draw others; and the woman who spied the weapon and the man who seized it may very well have saved the white community.

The mob insensibly melted from the scene; and for the rest of the day our neighbourhood was left in peace and a good deal in solitude. But the tranquility was only local; *din* and *perandi* still flowed in other quarters; and we had one more sight of Gilbert Island violence. In the church, where we had wandered photographing, we were startled by a sudden piercing outcry. The scene, looking forth from the doors of that great hall of shadow, was unforgettable. The palms, the quaint and scattered houses, the flag of the island streaming from its tall staff, glowed with intolerable sunshine. In the midst two women rolled fighting on the grass. The combatants were the more easy to be distinguished, because the one was stripped to the *ridi* and the other wore a holoku[1] (sacque) of some lively

1. A dress rather like a nightgown introduced after
   European contact in an effort to make Polynesian
   women cover themselves modestly.

colour. The first was uppermost, her teeth locked in her adversary's face, shaking her like a dog; the other impotently fought and scratched. So for a moment we saw them wallow and grapple there like vermin; then the mob closed and shut them in.

It was a serious question that night if we should sleep ashore. But we were travellers, folk that had come far in quest of the adventurous; on the first sign of an adventure it would have been a singular inconsistency to have withdrawn; and we sent on board instead for our revolvers. Mindful of Taahauku, Mr Rick, Mr Osbourne, and Mrs Stevenson held an assault of arms on the public highway, and fired at bottles to the admiration of the natives. Captain Reid of the *Equator* stayed on shore with us to be at hand in case of trouble, and we retired to bed at the accustomed hour, agreeably excited by the day's events. The night was exquisite, the silence enchanting; yet as I lay in my hammock looking on the strong moonshine and the quiescent palms, one ugly picture haunted me of the two women, the naked and the clad, locked in that hostile embrace. The harm done was probably not much, yet I could have looked on death and massacre with less revolt. The return to these primeval weapons, the vision of man's beastliness, of his ferality, shocked in me a deeper sense than that with which we count the cost of battles. There are elements in our state and history which it is a pleasure to forget, which it is perhaps the better wisdom not to dwell on. Crime, pestilence, and death are in the day's work; the imagination readily accepts them. It instinctively rejects, on the contrary, whatever shall call up the image of our race upon its lowest terms, as the partner of beasts, beastly itself, dwelling pell-mell and hugger-mugger, hairy man with hairy woman, in the caves of old. And yet to be just to barbarous islanders we must not forget the slums and dens of our cities: I must not forget that I have passed dinnerward through Soho, and seen that which cured me of my dinner.

A TALE OF A TAPU. PART TWO

Tuesday, July 16.—It rained in the night, sudden and loud, in Gilbert Island fashion. Before the day, the crowing of a cock aroused me and I wandered in the compound and along the street. The squall was blown by, the moon shone with incomparable lustre, the air lay dead as in a room, and yet all the isle sounded as under a strong shower, the eaves thickly pattering, the lofty palms dripping at larger intervals and with a louder note. In this bold nocturnal light the interior of the houses lay inscrutable, one lump of blackness, save when the moon glinted under the roof, and made a belt of silver, and drew the slanting shadows of the pillars on the floor. Nowhere in all the town was any lamp or ember; not a creature stirred; I thought I was alone to be awake; but the police were faithful to their duty; secretly vigilant, keeping account of time; and a little later, the watchman struck slowly and repeatedly on the cathedral bell; four o'clock, the warning signal. It seemed strange that, in a town resigned to drunkenness and tumult, curfew and réveillé should still be sounded and still obeyed.

The day came, and brought little change. The place still lay silent; the people slept, the town slept. Even the few who were awake, mostly women and children, held their peace and kept within under the strong shadow of the thatch, where you must stop and peer to see them. Through the deserted streets, and past the sleeping houses, a deputation took its way at an early hour to the palace; the king was suddenly awakened, and must listen (probably with a headache) to unpalatable truths. Mrs Rick, being a sufficient mistress of that difficult tongue, was spokeswoman; she explained to the sick monarch that I was an intimate personal friend of Queen Victoria's; that immediately on my return I should make her a report upon Butaritari; and that if my house should have been again invaded by natives, a man-of-war would be despatched to make reprisals. It was scarce the fact – rather a just and necessary parable of the fact, corrected for latitude; and it certainly told upon the king. He was much affected; he had conceived the notion (he said) that I was a man of some importance, but not dreamed it was as bad as this; and the missionary house was tapu'd under a fine of fifty dollars.

So much was announced on the return of the deputation; not any more; and I gathered subsequently that much more had passed. The protection gained was welcome. It had been the most annoying and not the least alarming feature of the day before, that our house was periodically filled with tipsy natives, twenty or thirty at a time, begging drink, fingering our goods, hard to be dislodged, awkward to quarrel with. Queen Victoria's friend (who was soon promoted to be her son) was free from these intrusions. Not only my house, but my neighbourhood as well, was left in peace; even on our walks abroad we were guarded and prepared for; and, like great persons visiting a hospital, saw only the fair side. For the matter of a week we were thus suffered to go out and in and live in a fool's paradise, supposing the king to have kept his word, the tapu to be revived and the island once more sober.

Tuesday, July 23.—We dined under a bare trellis erected for the Fourth of July; and here we used to linger by lamplight over coffee and tobacco. In that climate evening approaches without sensible chill; the wind dies out before sunset; heaven glows a while and fades, and darkens into the blueness of the tropical night; swiftly and insensibly the shadows thicken, the stars multiply their number; you look around you and the day is gone. It was then that we would see our Chinaman draw near across the compound in a lurching sphere of light, divided by his shadows; and with the coming of the lamp the night closed about the table. The faces of the company, the spars of the trellis, stood out suddenly bright on a ground of blue and silver, faintly designed with palm-tops and the peaked roofs of houses. Here and there the gloss upon a leaf, or the fracture of a stone, returned an isolated sparkle. All else had vanished. We hung there, illuminated like a galaxy of stars *in vacuo*; we sat, manifest and blind, amid the general ambush of the darkness; and the islanders, passing with light footfalls and low voices in the sand of the road, lingered to observe us, unseen.

On Tuesday the dusk had fallen, the lamp had just been brought, when a missile struck the table with a rattling smack and rebounded past my ear. Three inches to one side and this page had never been written; for the thing travelled like a cannon ball. It was supposed at the time to be a nut, though even at the time I thought it seemed a small one and fell strangely.

Wednesday, July 24. – The dusk had fallen once more, and the lamp been just brought out, when the same business was repeated. And again the missile whistled past my ear.

One nut I had been willing to accept; a second, I rejected utterly. A cocoa-nut does not come slinging along on a windless evening, making an angle of about fifteen degrees with the horizon; cocoa-nuts do not fall on successive nights at the same hour and spot; in both cases, besides, a specific moment seemed to have been chosen, that when the lamp was just carried out, a specific person threatened, and that the head of the family. I may have been right or wrong, but I believed I was the mark of some intimidation; believed the missile was a stone, aimed not to hit, but to frighten.

No idea makes a man more angry. I ran into the road, where the natives were as usual promenading in the dark; Maka joined me with a lantern; and I ran from one to another, glared in quite innocent faces, put useless questions, and proffered idle threats. Thence I carried my wrath (which was worthy the son of any queen in history) to the Ricks. They heard me with depression, assured me this trick of throwing a stone into a family dinner was not new; that it meant mischief, and was of a piece with the alarming disposition of the natives. And then the truth, so long concealed from us, came out. The king had broken his promise, he had defied the deputation; the tapu was still dormant, *The Land we Live in* still selling drink, and that quarter of the town disturbed and menaced by perpetual broils. But there was worse ahead: a feast was now preparing for the birthday of the little princess; and the tributary chiefs of Kuma and Little Makin were expected daily. Strong in a following of numerous and somewhat savage clansmen, each of these was believed, like a Douglas of old, to be of doubtful loyalty. Kuma (a little pot-bellied fellow) never visited the place, never entered the town, but sat on the beach on a mat, his gun across his knees, parading his mistrust and scorn; Karaiti of Makin, although he was more bold, was not supposed to be more friendly; and not only were these vassals jealous of the throne, but the followers on either side shared in the animosity. Brawls had already taken place; blows had passed which might at any moment be repaid in blood. Some of the strangers were already here and already drinking; if the debauch continued after the bulk of them had come, a collision, perhaps a revolution, was to be expected.

The sale of drink is in this group a measure of the jealousy of traders; one begins, the others are constrained to follow; and to him who has the most gin, and sells it the most recklessly, the lion's share of copra is assured. It is felt by all to be an extreme expedient, neither safe, decent, nor dignified. A trader on Tarawa,[1] heated by an eager rivalry, brought many cases of gin. He told me he sat afterwards day and night in his house till it was finished, not daring to arrest the sale, not venturing to go forth, the bush all round him filled with howling drunkards. At night, above all, when he was afraid to sleep, and heard shots and voices about him in the darkness, his remorse was black.

'My God!' he reflected, 'if I was to lose my life on such a wretched business!' Often and often, in the story of the Gilberts, this scene has been repeated; and the remorseful trader sat beside his lamp, longing for the day, listening with agony for the sound of murder, registering resolutions for the future. For the business is easy to begin, but hazardous to stop. The natives are in their way a just and law-abiding people, mindful of their debts, docile to the voice of their own institutions; when the tapu is re-enforced they will cease drinking; but the white who seeks to antedate the movement by refusing liquor does so at his peril.

Hence, in some degree, the anxiety and helplessness of Mr Rick. He and Tom, alarmed by the rabblement of the *Sans Souci*, had stopped the sale; they had done so without danger, because *The Land we Live in* still continued selling; it was claimed, besides, that they had been the first to begin. What step could be taken? Could Mr Rick visit Mr Muller (with whom he was not on terms) and address him thus: 'I was getting ahead of you, now you are getting ahead of me, and I ask you to forgo your profits. I got my place closed in safety, thanks to your continuing; but now I think you have continued long enough. I begin to be alarmed; and because I am afraid I ask you to confront a certain danger'? It was not to be thought of. Something else had to be found; and there was one person at one end of the town who was at least not interested in copra. There was little else to be said in favour of myself as an ambassador. I had arrived in the Wightman schooner, I was living in the Wightman compound, I was the daily associate of the

1. Tarawa. Also known as the Knox Islands, part of the Gilbert group.

Wightman coterie. It was egregious enough that I should now intrude unasked in the private affairs of Crawford's agent, and press upon him the sacrifice of his interests and the venture of his life. But bad as I might be, there was none better; since the affair of the stone I was, besides, sharp-set to be doing, the idea of a delicate interview attracted me, and I thought it policy to show myself abroad.

The night was very dark. There was service in the church, and the building glimmered through all its crevices like a dim Kirk Allowa'.[1] I saw few other lights, but was indistinctly aware of many people stirring in the darkness, and a hum and splutter of low talk that sounded stealthy. I believe (in the old phrase) my beard was sometimes on my shoulder as I went. Muller's was but partly lighted, and quite silent, and the gate was fastened. I could by no means manage to undo the latch. No wonder, since I found it afterwards to be four or five feet long – a fortification in itself. As I still fumbled, a dog came on the inside and snuffed suspiciously at my hands, so that I was reduced to calling 'House ahoy!' Mr Muller came down and put his chin across the paling in the dark. 'Who is that?' said he, like one who has no mind to welcome strangers.

'My name is Stevenson,' said I.

'O, Mr Stevens! I didn't know you. Come inside.'

We stepped into the dark store, when I leaned upon the counter and against the wall. All the light came from the sleeping-room, where I saw his family being put to bed; it struck full in my face, but Mr Muller stood in shadow. No doubt he expected what was coming, and sought the advantage of position; but for a man who wished to persuade and had nothing to conceal, mine was the preferable.

'Look here,' I began, 'I hear you are selling to the natives.'

'Others have done that before me,' he returned pointedly.

'No doubt,' said I, 'and I have nothing to do with the past, but the future. I want you to promise you will handle these spirits carefully.'

1. Alloway in Ayrshire is the birthplace of Robert Burns. In Burns's famous poem 'Tam o'Shanter' Tam encounters 'warlocks and witches' in Alloway kirkyard during a drunken ride home.

'Now what is your motive in this?' he asked, and then, with a sneer, 'Are you afraid of your life?'

'That is nothing to the purpose,' I replied. 'I know, and you know, these spirits ought not to be used at all.'

'Tom and Mr Rick have sold them before.'

'I have nothing to do with Tom and Mr Rick. All I know is I have heard them both refuse.'

'No, I suppose you have nothing to do with them. Then you are just afraid of your life.'

'Come now,' I cried, being perhaps a little stung, 'you know in your heart I am asking a reasonable thing. I don't ask you to lose your profit – though I would prefer to see no spirits brought here, as you would—'

'I don't say I wouldn't. I didn't begin this,' he interjected.

'No, I don't suppose you did,' said I. 'And I don't ask you to lose; I ask you to give me your word, man to man, that you will make no native drunk.'

Up to now Mr Muller had maintained an attitude very trying to my temper; but he had maintained it with difficulty, his sentiment being all upon my side; and here he changed ground for the worse. 'It isn't me that sells,' said he.

'No, it's that nigger,' I agreed. 'But he's yours to buy and sell; you have your hand on the nape of his neck; and I ask you – I have my wife here – to use the authority you have.'

He hastily returned to his old ward. 'I don't deny I could if I wanted,' said he. 'But there's no danger, the natives are all quiet. You're just afraid of your life.'

I do not like to be called a coward, even by implication; and here I lost my temper and propounded an untimely ultimatum. 'You had better put it plain,' I cried. 'Do you mean to refuse me what I ask?'

'I don't want either to refuse it or grant it,' he replied.

'You'll find you have to do the one thing or the other, and right now!' I cried, and then, striking into a happier vein, 'Come,' said I, 'you're a better sort than that. I see what's wrong with you – you think I came from the opposite camp. I see the sort of man you are, and you know that what I ask is right.'

Again he changed ground. 'If the natives get any drink, it isn't safe to stop them,' he objected.

'I'll be answerable for the bar,' I said. 'We are three men and four revolvers; we'll come at a word, and hold the place against the village.'

'You don't know what you're talking about; it's too dangerous!' he cried.

'Look here,' said I, 'I don't mind much about losing that life you talk so much of; but I mean to lose it the way I want to, and that is, putting a stop to all this beastliness.'

He talked a while about his duty to the firm; I minded not at all, I was secure of victory. He was but waiting to capitulate, and looked about for any potent to relieve the strain. In the gush of light from the bedroom door I spied a cigar-holder on the desk. 'That is well coloured,' said I.

'Will you take a cigar?' said he.

I took it and held it up unlighted. 'Now,' said I, 'you promise me.'

'I promise you you won't have any trouble from natives that have drunk at my place,' he replied.

'That is all I ask,' said I, and showed it was not by immediately offering to try his stock.

So far as it was anyway critical our interview here ended. Mr Muller had thenceforth ceased to regard me as an emissary from his rivals, dropped his defensive attitude, and spoke as he believed. I could make out that he would already, had he dared, have stopped the sale himself. Not quite daring, it may be imagined how he resented the idea of interference from those who had (by his own statement) first led him on, then deserted him in the breach, and now (sitting themselves in safety) egged him on to a new peril, which was all gain to them, all loss to him. I asked him what he thought of the danger from the feast.

'I think worse of it than any of you,' he answered. 'They were shooting around here last night, and I heard the balls too. I said to myself, "That's bad." What gets me is why you should be making this row up at your end. I should be the first to go.'

It was a thoughtless wonder. The consolation of being second is not great; the fact, not the order of going – there was our concern.

Scott talks moderately of looking forward to a time of

fighting 'with a feeling that resembled pleasure'. The resemblance seems rather an identity. In modern life, contact is ended; man grows impatient of endless manoeuvres; and to approach the fact, to find ourselves where we can push our advantage home, and stand a fair risk, and see at last what we are made of, stirs the blood. It was so at least with all my family, who bubbled with delight at the approach of trouble; and we sat deep into the night like a pack of schoolboys, preparing the revolvers and arranging plans against the morrow. It promised certainly to be a busy and eventful day. The Old Men were to be summoned to confront me on the question of the tapu; Muller might call us at any moment to garrison his bar; and suppose Muller to fail, we decided in a family council to take that matter into our own hands, *The Land we Live in* at the pistol's mouth, and with the polysyllabic Williams, dance to a new tune. As I recall our humour, I think it would have gone hard with the mulatto.

Wednesday, July 24. – It was as well, and yet it was disappointing that these thunder-clouds rolled off in silence. Whether the Old Men recoiled from an interview with Queen Victoria's son, whether Muller had secretly intervened, or whether the step flowed naturally from the fears of the king and the nearness of the feast, the tapu was early that morning re-enforced; not a day too soon, from the manner the boats began to arrive thickly, and the town was filled with the big rowdy vassals of Karaiti.

The effect lingered for some time on the minds of the traders; it was with the approval of all present that I helped to draw up a petition to the United States, praying for a law against the liquor trade in the Gilberts; and it was at this request that I added, under my own name, a brief testimony of what had passed; – useless pains; since the whole reposes, probably unread and possibly unopened, in a pigeon-hole at Washington.

Sunday, July 28. – This day we had the afterpiece of the debauch. The king and queen, in European clothes, and followed by armed guards, attended church for the first time, and sat perched aloft in a precarious dignity under the barrel-hoops. Before sermon his majesty clambered from the dais, stood lopsidedly upon the gravel floor, and in a few words abjured drinking. The queen followed suit with a yet briefer allocution. All the men in church were next addressed in turn; each held up his right hand, and the affair was over – throne and church were reconciled.

from The Gilberts

HUSBAND AND WIFE

The trader accustomed to the manners of Eastern Polynesia
has a lesson to learn among the Gilberts. The *ridi* is but a
spare attire; as late as thirty years back the women went
naked until marriage; within ten years the custom lingered;
and these facts, above all when heard in description, conveyed a very false idea of the manners of the group. A very
intelligent missionary described it (in its former state) as a
'Paradise of naked women' for the resident whites. It was
at least a platonic Paradise, where Lothario ventured at his
peril. Since 1860, fourteen whites have perished on a single
island, all for the same cause, all found where they had no
business, and speared by some indignant father of a family;
the figure was given me by one of their contemporaries
who had been more prudent and survived. The strange
persistence of these fourteen martyrs might seem to point to
monomania or a series of romantic passions; gin is the more
likely key. The poor buzzards sat alone in their houses by an
open case; they drank; their brain was fired; they stumbled
towards the nearest houses on chance; and the dart went
through their liver. In place of a Paradise the trader found
an archipelago of fierce husbands and of virtuous women.
'Of course if you wish to make love to them, it's the same
as anywhere else,' observed a trader innocently; but he and
his companions rarely so choose.

The trader must be credited with a virtue; he often
makes a kind and loyal husband. Some of the worst
beachcombers in the Pacific, some of the last of the
old school, have fallen in my path, and some of them
were admirable to their native wives, and one made a
despairing widower. The position of a trader's wife in
the Gilberts is, besides, unusually enviable. She shares the
immunities of her husband. Curfew in Butaritari sounds

for her in vain. Long after the bell is rung and the great
island ladies are confined for the night to their own roof,
this chartered libertine may scamper and giggle through
the deserted streets or go down to bathe in the dark. The
resources of the store are at her hand; she goes arrayed
like a queen, and feasts delicately every day upon tinned
meats. And she who was perhaps of no regard or station
among natives sits with captains, and is entertained on
board of schooners. Five of these privileged dames were
some time our neighbours. Four were handsome skittish
lasses, gamesome like children, and like children liable to
fits of pouting. They wore dresses by day, but there was a
tendency after dark to strip these lendings and to career and
squall about the compound in the aboriginal *ridi*. Games
of cards were continually played, with shells for counters;
their course was much marred by cheating; and the end of
a round (above all if a man was of the party) resolved itself
into a scrimmage for the counters. The fifth was a matron. It
was a picture to see her sail to church on a Sunday, a parasol
in hand, a nursemaid following, and the baby buried in
a trade hat and armed with a patent feeding-bottle. The
service was enlivened by her continual supervision and
correction of the maid. It was impossible not to fancy the
baby was a doll, and the church some European playroom.
All these women were legitimately married. It is true that
the certificate of one, when she proudly showed it, proved
to run thus, that she was 'married for one night', and her
gracious partner was at liberty to 'send her to hell' the next
morning; but she was none the wiser or the worse for the
dastardly trick. Another, I heard, was married on a work of
mine in a pirated edition; it answered the purpose as well as
a Hall Bible. Notwithstanding all these allurements of social
distinction, rare food and raiment, a comparative vacation
from toil, and legitimate marriage contracted on a pirated
edition, the trader must sometimes seek long before he
can be mated. While I was in the group one had been
eight months on the quest, and he was still a bachelor.

Within strictly native society the old laws and practices were harsh, but not without a certain stamp of
high-mindedness. Stealthy adultery was punished with
death; open elopement was properly considered virtue
in comparison, and compounded for a fine in land. The

male adulterer alone seems to have been punished. It is correct manners for a jealous man to hang himself; a jealous woman had a different remedy – she bites her rival. Ten or twenty years ago it was a capital offence to raise a woman's *ridi*; to this day it is still punished with a heavy fine; and the garment itself is still symbolically sacred. Suppose a piece of land to be disputed in Butaritari, the claimant who shall first hang a *ridi* on the tapu-post has gained his cause, since no one can remove or touch it but himself.

The *ridi* was the badge not of the woman but the wife, the mark not of her sex but of her station. It was the collar on the slave's neck, the brand on merchandise. The adulterous woman seems to have been spared; were the husband offended, it would be a poor consolation to send his draught cattle to the shambles. Karaiti, to this day, calls his eight wives 'his horses', some trader having explained to him the employment of these animals on farms; and Nanteitei hired out his wives to do mason-work. Husbands, at least when of high rank, had the power of life and death; even whites seem to have possessed it; and their wives, when they had trangressed beyond forgiveness, made haste to pronounce the formula of deprecation – *I Kana Kim*. This form of words had so much virtue that a condemned criminal, repeating it on a particular day to the king who had condemned him, must be instantly released. It is an offer of abasement, and, strangely enough, the reverse – the imitation – is a common vulgar insult in Great Britain to this day. I give a scene between a trader and his Gilbert Island wife, as it was told me by the husband, now one of the oldest residents, but then a freshman in the group.

'Go and light a fire,' said the trader, 'and when I have brought this oil I will cook some fish.'

The woman grunted at him, island fashion.

'I am not a pig that you should grunt at me,' said he.

'I know you are not a pig,' said the woman, 'neither am I your slave.'

'To be sure you are not my slave, and if you do not care to stop with me, you had better go home to your people,' said he. 'But in the meantime go and light the fire; and when I have brought this oil I will cook some fish.'

She went as if to obey; and presently when the trader

looked she had built a fire so big that the cook-house was catching in flames.

'*I Kana Kim!*' she cried, as she saw him coming; but he recked not, and hit her with a cooking-pot. The leg pierced her skull, blood spouted, it was thought she was a dead woman, and the natives surrounded the house in a menacing expectation. Another white was present, a man of older experience. 'You will have us both killed if you go on like this,' he cried. 'She had said *I Kana Kim!*' If she had not said *I Kana Kim* he might have struck her with a caldron. It was not the blow that made the crime, but the disregard of an accepted formula.

Polygamy, the particular sacredness of wives, their semi-servile state, their seclusion in kings' harems, even their privilege of biting, all would seem to indicate a Mohammedan society and the opinion of the soullessness of woman. And not so in the least. It is a mere appearance. After you have studied these extremes in one house, you may go to the next and find all reversed, the woman the mistress, the man only the first of her thralls. The authority is not with the husband as such, nor the wife as such. It resides in the chief or the chief-woman; in him or her who had inherited the lands of the clan, and stands to the clansman in the place of parent, exacting their service, answerable for their fines. There is but the one source of power and the one ground of dignity – rank. The king married a chief-woman; she became his menial, and must work with her hands on Messrs Wightman's pier. The king divorced her; she regained at once her former state and power. She married the Hawaiian sailor, and behold the man is her flunkey and can be shown the door at pleasure. Nay, and such low-born lords are even corrected physically, and, like grown but dutiful children, must endure the discipline.

We were intimate in one such household, that of Nei Takauti and Nan Tok'; I put the lady first of necessity. During one week of fool's paradise, Mrs Stevenson had gone alone to the sea-side of the island after shells. I am very sure the proceeding was unsafe; and she soon perceived a man and woman watching her. Do what she would, her guardians held her steadily in view; and when the afternoon began to fall, and they thought she had stayed long enough, took her in charge, and by signs and broken

English ordered her home. On the way the lady drew from her earring-hole a clay-pipe, the husband lighted it, and it was handed to my unfortunate wife, who knew not how to refuse the incommodious favour; and when they were all come to our house, the pair sat down beside her on the floor, and improved the occasion with prayer. From that day they were our family friends; bringing thrice a day the beautiful island garlands of white flowers, visiting us any evening, and frequently carrying us down to their own maniap' in return, the woman leading Mrs Stevenson by the hand like one child with another.

Nan Tok', the husband, was young, extremely hand-some, of the most approved good humour, and suffering in his precarious station from suppressed high spirits. Nei Takauti, the wife, was getting old; her grown son by a former marriage had just hanged himself before his mother's eyes in despair at a well-merited rebuke. Perhaps she had never been beautiful, but her face was full of character, her eye of sombre fire. She was a high chief-woman, but by a strange exception for a person of her rank, was small, spare, and sinewy, with lean small hands and corded neck. Her full dress of an evening was invariably a white chemise – and for adornment, green leaves (or sometimes white blossoms) stuck in her hair and thrust through her huge earring-holes. The husband on the contrary changed to view like a kaleidoscope. Whatever pretty thing my wife might have given to Nei Takauti – a string of beads, a ribbon, a piece of bright fabric – appeared the next evening on the person of Nan Tok'. It was plain he was a clothes-horse; that he wore livery; that, in a word, he was his wife's wife. They reversed the parts indeed, down to the least particular; it was the husband who showed himself the ministering angel in the hour of pain, while the wife displayed the apathy and heartlessness of the proverbial man.

When Nei Takauti had a headache Nan Tok' was full of attention and concern. When the husband had a cold and a racking toothache the wife heeded not, except to jeer. It is always the woman's part to fill and light the pipe; Nei Takauti handed hers in silence to the wedded page; but she carried it herself, as though the page were not entirely trusted. Thus she kept the money, but it was he who ran the errands, anxiously sedulous. A cloud on her

face dimmed instantly his beaming looks; on an early visit
to their maniap' my wife saw he had cause to be wary. Nan
Tok' had a friend with him, a giddy young thing, of his own
age and sex; and they had worked themselves into that stage
of jocularity when consequences are too often disregarded.
Nei Takauti mentioned her own name. Instantly Nan Tok'
held up two fingers, his friend did likewise, both in an
ecstasy of slyness. It was plain the lady had two names;
and from the nature of their merriment, and the wrath that
gathered on her brow, there must be something ticklish in
the second. The husband pronounced it; a well-directed
cocoa-nut from the hand of his wife caught him on the
side of the head, and the voices and the mirth of these
indiscreet young gentlemen ceased for the day.

The people of Eastern Polynesia are never at a loss; their
etiquette is absolute and plenary; in every circumstance it
tells them what to do and how to do it. The Gilbertines
are seemingly more free, and pay for their freedom (like
ourselves) in frequent perplexity. This was often the case
with the topsy-turvy couple. We had once supplied them
during a visit with a pipe and tobacco; and when they had
smoked and were about to leave; they found themselves
confronted with a problem; should they take or leave what
remained of the tobacco. The piece of plug was taken up,
it was laid down again, it was handed back and forth, and
argued over, till the wife began to look haggard and the
husband elderly. They ended by taking it, and I wager
were not yet clear of the compound before they were sure
they had decided wrong. Another time they had been given
each a liberal cup of coffee, and Nan Tok' with difficulty
and disaffection made an end of his. Nei Takauti had taken
some, she had no mind for more, plainly conceived it would
be a breach of manners to set down the cup unfinished,
and ordered her wedded retainer to dispose of what was
left. 'I have swallowed all I can, I cannot swallow more,
it is a physical impossibility,' he seemed to say; and his
stern officer reiterated her commands with secret imperative
signals. Luckless dog! but in mere humanity we came to the
rescue and removed the cup.

I cannot but smile over this funny household; yet I
remember the good souls with affection and respect.
Their attention to ourselves was surprising. The garlands

are much esteemed, the blossoms must be sought far and wide; and though they had many retainers to call to their aid, we often saw themselves passing afield after the blossoms, and the wife engaged with her own hands in putting them together. It was no want of heart, only that disregard so incident to husbands, that made Nei Takauti despise the sufferings of Nan Tok'. When my wife was unwell she proved a diligent and kindly nurse; and the pair, to the extreme embarrassment of the sufferer, became fixtures in the sick-room. This rugged, capable, imperious old dame, with the wild eyes, had deep and tender qualities: her pride in her young husband it seemed that she dissembled, fearing possibly to spoil him; and when she spoke of her dead son there came something tragic in her face. But I seemed to trace in the Gilbertines a virility of sense and sentiment which distinguishes them (like their harsh and uncouth language) from their brother islanders in the east.

Fiction

Throughout his time in the Pacific Stevenson was writing fiction, both short stories and full-length novels. Of the three shorter pieces included here, 'The Bottle Imp' was probably written first, during Stevenson's first stay in Samoa in December 1889 and January 1890. It was published in instalments in the New York *Herald* in February 1891, and in *Black and White* (London) in March and April. 'The Isle of Voices' was written in the autumn of 1892 and published in the *National Observer* in February 1893. *The Beach of Falesá* was begun in November 1890, but most of it was written during the following September. It was serialised in the *Illustrated London News* in July and August 1892, but Stevenson was put under pressure to make a number of alterations. The editor felt changes were needed to render the story more palatable to his readers. Stevenson was extremely unhappy about this, and referred to the published version as 'slashed and gaping ruins'.[1]

Thanks to the researches of Professor Barry Menikoff, the full extent of the changes forced on the manuscript are now known, and reproduced here is Stevenson's original text. All three stories appeared in *Island Night's Entertainments* (1893) although Stevenson would have preferred to keep the two stories 'The Bottle Imp' and 'The Isle of Voices', written for a Polynesian audience, separate from *The Beach of Falesá*. I have brought them together here as they are equally the products of Stevenson's sympathetic interest in the South Seas.

The two full-length novels show different approaches to

1. Letter to J.M. Barrie, *The Letters of Robert Louis Stevenson*, ed. Bradford A. Booth and Ernest Mehew, vol. VII, p.413.

Stevenson's Pacific experiences. *The Wrecker*, a collaboration between Lloyd Osbourne and Stevenson, was begun in the summer of 1889 and finished nearly two years later. It, too, was serialised, in *Scribner's Magazine* from August 1891 to the following July, before being published in volume form in 1892. It was Lloyd Osbourne who started on *The Ebb-Tide*, while the Stevenson party was staying in Honolulu in 1889. Later work on the novel was by Stevenson alone, who completed it in 1893. Although it is now recognised as being almost entirely the work of Stevenson, it was first published under both names. After serialisation in the magazine *To-day*, from November 1893 to February 1894, and in *McClure's Magazine* (USA) from February to July 1896 the book was published in the United States in July of that year and in Britain in September.

Apart from *The Beach of Falesá*, the text of the stories and novels is taken from the Edinburgh Edition, the collected edition of Stevenson's work in preparation at the time of his death.

THE BOTTLE IMP

There was a man of the Island of Hawaii, whom I shall call Keawe; for the truth is, he still lives, and his name must be kept secret; but the place of his birth was not far from Honaunau, where the bones of Keawe the Great lie hidden in a cave. This man was poor, brave, and active; he could read and write like a schoolmaster; he was a first-rate mariner besides, sailed for some time in the island steamers, and steered a whaleboat on the Hamakua coast. At length it came in Keawe's mind to have a sight of the great world and foreign cities, and he shipped on a vessel bound to San Francisco.

This is a fine town, with a fine harbour, and rich people uncountable; and, in particular, there is one hill which is covered with palaces. Upon this hill Keawe was one day taking a walk with his pocket full of money, viewing the great houses upon either hand with pleasure. 'What fine houses these are!' he was thinking, 'and how happy must those people be who dwell in them, and take no care for the morrow!' The thought was in his mind when he came abreast of a house that was smaller than some others, but all finished and beautified like a toy; the steps of that house shone like silver, and the borders of the garden bloomed

NOTE: Any student of that very unliterary product, the English drama of the early part of the century, will here recognise the name and the root idea of a piece once rendered popular by the redoubtable O. Smith. The root idea is there, and identical, and yet I hope I have made it a new thing. And the fact that the tale has been designed and written for a Polynesian audience may lend it some extraneous interest nearer home.   R.L.S.

like garlands, and the windows were bright like diamonds; and Keawe stopped and wondered at the excellence of all he saw. So stopping, he was aware of a man that looked forth upon him through a window so clear that Keawe could see him as you see a fish in a pool upon the reef. The man was elderly, with a bald head and a black beard; and his face was heavy with sorrow, and he bitterly sighed. And the truth of it is, that as Keawe looked in upon the man, and the man looked out upon Keawe, each envied the other.

All of a sudden the man smiled and nodded, and beckoned Keawe to enter, and met him at the door of the house.

'This is a fine house of mine,' said the man, and bitterly sighed. 'Would you not care to view the chambers?'

So he led Keawe all over it, from the cellar to the roof, and there was nothing there that was not perfect of its kind, and Keawe was astonished.

'Truly,' said Keawe, 'this is a beautiful house; if I lived in the like of it I should be laughing all day long. How comes it, then, that you should be sighing?'

'There is no reason,' said the man, 'why you should not have a house in all points similar to this, and finer, if you wish. You have some money, I suppose?'

'I have fifty dollars,' said Keawe; 'but a house like this will cost more than fifty dollars.'

The man made a computation. 'I am sorry you have no more,' said he, 'for it may raise you trouble in the future; but it shall be yours at fifty dollars.'

'The house?' asked Keawe.

'No, not the house,' replied the man; 'but the bottle. For I must tell you, although I appear to you so rich and fortunate, all my fortune, and this house itself and its garden, came out of a bottle not much bigger than a pint. This is it.'

And he opened a lockfast place, and took out a round-bellied bottle with a long neck; the glass of it was white like milk, with changing rainbow colours in the grain. Within-sides something obscurely moved, like a shadow and a fire.

'This is the bottle,' said the man; and, when Keawe laughed, 'You do not believe me?' he added. 'Try, then, for yourself. See if you can break it.'

So Keawe took the bottle up and dashed it on the floor till he was weary; but it jumped on the floor like a child's ball, and was not injured.

'This is a strange thing,' said Keawe. 'For by the touch of it, as well as by the look, the bottle should be of glass.'

'Of glass it is,' replied the man, sighing more heavily than ever; 'but the glass of it was tempered in the flames of hell. An imp lives in it, and that is the shadow we behold there moving; or so I suppose. If any man buy this bottle the imp is at his command; all that he desires – love, fame, money, houses like this house, ay, or a city like this city – all are his at the word uttered. Napoleon had this bottle, and by it he grew to be the king of the world; but he sold it at last, and fell. Captain Cook had this bottle, and by it he found his way to so many islands; but he, too, sold it, and was slain upon Hawaii. For, once it is sold, the power goes and the protection; and unless a man remain content with what he has, ill will befall him.'

'And yet you talk of selling it yourself?' Keawe said.

'I have all I wish, and I am growing elderly,' replied the man. 'There is one thing the imp cannot do – he cannot prolong life; and, it would not be fair to conceal from you, there is a drawback to the bottle; for if a man die before he sells it, he must burn in hell for ever.'

'To be sure, that is a drawback and no mistake,' cried Keawe. 'I would not meddle with the thing. I can do without a house, thank God; but there is one thing I could not be doing with one particle, and that is to be damned.'

'Dear me, you must not run away with things,' returned the man. 'All you have to do is to use the power of the imp in moderation, and then sell it to someone else, as I do to you, and finish your life in comfort.'

'Well, I observe two things,' said Keawe. 'All the time you keep sighing like a maid in love, that is one; and, for the other, you sell this bottle very cheap.'

'I have told you already why I sigh,' said the man. 'It is because I fear my health is breaking up; and, as you said yourself, to die and go to the devil is a pity for any one. As for why I sell so cheap, I must explain to you there is a peculiarity about the bottle. Long ago, when the devil brought it first upon earth, it was extremely expensive, and was sold first of all to Prester John[1] for many millions of dollars; but it cannot be sold at all, unless sold at a loss. If you sell it for as much as you paid for it, back it comes to you again like a homing pigeon. It follows that the price has kept falling in these centuries, and the bottle is now remarkably cheap. I bought it myself from one of my great neighbours on this hill, and the price I paid was only ninety dollars. I could sell it for as high as eighty-nine dollars and ninety-nine cents, but not a penny dearer, or back the thing must come to me. Now, about this there are two bothers. First, when you offer a bottle so singular for eighty odd dollars, people do not suppose you to be jesting. And second – but there is no hurry about that – and I need not go into it. Only remember it must be coined money that you sell it for.'

'How am I to know that this is all true?' asked Keawe.

'Some of it you can try at once,' replied the man. 'Give me your fifty dollars, take the bottle, and wish your fifty dollars back into your pocket. If that does not happen, I pledge you my honour I will cry off the bargain and restore your money.'

'You are not deceiving me?' said Keawe.

The man bound himself with a great oath.

'Well, I will risk that much,' said Keawe, 'for that can do no harm.' And he paid over his money to the man, and the man handed him the bottle.

'Imp of the bottle,' said Keawe, 'I want my fifty dollars back.' And sure enough he had scarce said the word before his pocket was as heavy as ever.

'To be sure this is a wonderful bottle,' said Keawe.

'And now good-morning to you, my fine fellow, and the devil go with you for me!' said the man.

'Hold on,' said Keawe, 'I don't want any more of this fun. Here, take your bottle back.'

'You have bought it for less than I paid for it,' replied the man, rubbing his hands. 'It is yours now; and, for my

---

1. Legendary Christian ruler in the East. The legend had its origins in the eleventh and twelfth centuries. Later, Prester John was associated with Ethiopia.

part, I am only concerned to see the back of you.' And with that he rang for his Chinese servant, and had Keawe shown out of the house.

Now, when Keawe was in the street, with the bottle under his arm, he began to think. 'If all is true about this bottle, I may have made a losing bargain,' thinks he. 'But perhaps the man was only fooling me.' The first thing he did was to count his money; the sum was exact – forty-nine dollars American money, and one Chili piece. 'That looks like the truth,' said Keawe. 'Now I will try another part.'

The streets in that part of the city were as clean as a ship's decks, and though it was noon, there were no passengers. Keawe set the bottle in the gutter and walked away. Twice he looked back, and there was the milky round-bellied bottle where he left it. A third time he looked back, and turned a corner; but he had scarce done so, when something knocked upon his elbow, and behold! it was the long neck sticking up; and as for the round belly, it was jammed into the pocket of his pilotcoat.

'And that looks like the truth', said Keawe.

The next thing he did was to buy a corkscrew in a shop, and go apart into a secret place in the fields. And there he tried to draw the cork, but as often as he put the screw in, out it came again, and the cork as whole as ever.

'This is some new sort of cork,' said Keawe, and all at once he began to shake and sweat, for he was afraid of that bottle.

On his way back to the port-side he saw a shop where a man sold shells and clubs from the wild islands, old heathen deities, old coined money, pictures from China and Japan, and all manner of things that sailors bring in their sea-chests. And here he had an idea. So he went in and offered the bottle for a hundred dollars. The man of the shop laughed at him at the first, and offered him five; but, indeed, it was a curious bottle – such glass was never blown in any human glassworks, so prettily the colours shone under the milky white, and so strangely the shadow hovered in the midst; so, after he had disputed a while after the manner of his kind, the shopman gave Keawe sixty silver dollars for the thing, and set it on a shelf in the midst of his window.

'Now,' said Keawe, 'I have sold that for sixty which I

bought for fifty – or, to say truth, a little less, because one of my dollars was from Chili. Now I shall know the truth upon another point.'

So he went back on board his ship, and, when he opened his chest, there was the bottle, and had come more quickly than himself. Now Keawe had a mate on board whose name was Lopaka.

'What ails you?' said Lopaka, 'that you stare in your chest?'

They were alone in the ship's forecastle, and Keawe bound him to secrecy, and told all.

'This is a very strange affair,' said Lopaka; 'and I fear you will be in trouble about this bottle. But there is one point very clear – that you are sure of the trouble, and you had better have the profit in the bargain. Make up your mind what you want with it; give the order, and if it is done as you desire, I will buy the bottle myself; for I have an idea of my own to get a schooner, and go trading through the islands.'

'That is not my idea,' said Keawe; 'but to have a beautiful house and garden on the Kona Coast, where I was born, the sun shining in at the door, flowers in the garden, glass in the windows, pictures on the walls, and toys and fine carpets on the tables, for all the world like the house I was in this day – only a story higher, and with balconies all about like the King's palace; and to live there without care and make merry with my friends and relatives.'

'Well,' said Lopaka, 'let us carry it back with us to Hawaii; and if all comes true, as you suppose, I will buy the bottle, as I said, and ask a schooner.'

Upon that they were agreed, and it was not long before the ship returned to Honolulu, carrying Keawe and Lopaka, and the bottle. They were scarce come ashore when they met a friend upon the beach, who began at once to condole with Keawe.

'I do not know what I am to be condoled about,' said Keawe.

'Is it possible you have not heard,' said the friend, 'your uncle – that good old man – is dead, and your cousin – that beautiful boy – was drowned at sea?'

Keawe was filled with sorrow, and, beginning to weep and to lament, he forgot about the bottle. But Lopaka was thinking to himself, and presently, when Keawe's grief was a little abated, 'I have been thinking,' said Lopaka. 'Had not your uncle lands in Hawaii, in the district of Kaü?'

'No,' said Keawe, 'not in Kaü; they are on the mountain side – a little way south of Hookena.'

'These lands will now be yours?' asked Lopaka.

'And so they will,' says Keawe, and began again to lament for his relatives.

'No,' said Lopaka, 'do not lament at present. I have a thought in my mind. How if this should be the doing of the bottle? For here is the place ready for your house.'

'If this be so,' cried Keawe, 'it is a very ill way to serve me by killing my relatives. But it may be indeed; for it was in just such a station that I saw the house with my mind's eye.'

'The house, however, is not yet built,' said Lopaka.

'No, nor like to be!' said Keawe; 'for though my uncle has some coffee and ava[1] and bananas, it will not be more than will keep me in comfort; and the rest of that land is the black lava.'

'Let us go to the lawyer,' said Lopaka; 'I have still this idea in my mind.'

Now, when they came to the lawyer's, it appeared Keawe's uncle had grown monstrous rich in the last days, and there was a fund of money.

'And here is the money for the house!' cried Lopaka.

'If you are thinking of a new house,' said the lawyer, 'here is the card of a new architect, of whom they tell me great things.'

'Better and better!' cried Lopaka. 'Here is all made plain for us. Let us continue to obey orders.'

So they went to the architect, and he had drawings of houses on his table.

'You want something out of the way,' said the architect. 'How do you like this?' and he handed a drawing to Keawe.

Now, when Keawe set eyes on the drawing, he cried out aloud, for it was the picture of his thought exactly drawn.

---

1. The palm-lily tree, which yields an intoxicating liquor.

'I am in for this house,' thought he. 'Little as I like the way it comes to me, I am in for it now, and I may as well take the good along with the evil.'

So he told the architect all that he wished, and how he would have that house furnished, and about the pictures on the wall and the knickknacks on the tables; and he asked the man plainly for how much he would undertake the whole affair.

The architect put many questions, and took his pen and made a computation; and when he had done he named the very sum that Keawe had inherited.

Lopaka and Keawe looked at one another and nodded.

'It is quite clear,' thought Keawe, 'that I am to have this house, whether or no. It comes from the devil, and I fear I will get little good by that; and of one thing I am sure, I will make no more wishes as long as I have this bottle. But with the house I am saddled, and I may as well take the good along with the evil.'

So he made his terms with the architect, and they signed a paper; and Keawe and Lopaka took ship again and sailed to Australia; for it was concluded between them they should not interfere at all, but leave the architect and the bottle imp to build and adorn that house at their own pleasure.

The voyage was a good voyage, only all the time Keawe was holding in his breath, for he had sworn he would utter no more wishes, and take no more favours from the devil. The time was up when they got back. The architect told them that the house was ready, and Keawe and Lopaka took a passage in the *Hall*, and went down Kona way to view the house, and see if all had been done fitly according to the thought that was in Keawe's mind.

Now, the house stood on the mountain side, visible to ships. Above, the forest ran up into the clouds of rain; below, the black lava fell in cliffs, where the kings of old lay buried. A garden bloomed about that house with every hue of flowers; and there was an orchard of papaia on the one hand and an orchard of bread-fruit on the other, and right in front, toward the sea, a ship's mast had been rigged up and bore a flag. As for the house, it was three stories high, with great chambers and broad balconies on each. The windows were of glass, so excellent that it was as clear as water and as bright as day. All manner of furniture adorned the chambers. Pictures hung upon the wall in golden frames: pictures of ships, and men fighting, and of the most beautiful women, and of singular places; nowhere in the world are there pictures of so bright a colour as those Keawe found hanging in his house. As for the knickknacks, they were extraordinary fine; chiming clocks and musical boxes filled with pictures, weapons of price from all quarters of the world, and the most elegant puzzles to entertain the leisure of a solitary man. And as no one would care to live in such chambers, only walk through and view them, the balconies were made so broad that a whole town might have lived upon them in delight; and Keawe knew not which to prefer, whether the back porch, where you got the land-breeze, and looked upon the orchards and the flowers, or the front balcony, where you could drink the wind of the sea, and look down the steep wall of the mountain and see the *Hall* going by once a week or so between Hookena and the hills of Pele, or the schooners plying up the coast for wood and ava and bananas.

When they had viewed all, Keawe and Lopaka sat on the porch.

'Well,' asked Lopaka, 'is it all as you designed?'

'Words cannot utter it,' said Keawe. 'It is better than I dreamed, and I am sick with satisfaction.'

'There is but one thing to consider,' said Lopaka; 'all this may be quite natural, and the bottle imp have nothing whatever to say to it. If I were to buy the bottle, and got no schooner after all, I should have put my hand in the fire for nothing. I gave you my word, I know; but yet I think you would not grudge me one more proof.'

'I have sworn I would take no more favours,' said Keawe. 'I have gone already deep enough.'

'This is no favour I am thinking of,' replied Lopaka. 'It is only to see the imp himself. There is nothing to be gained by that, and so nothing to be ashamed of; and yet, if I once saw him, I should be sure of the whole matter. So indulge me so far, and let me see the imp; and, after that, here is the money in my hand, and I will buy it.'

'There is only one thing I am afraid of,' said Keawe. 'The imp may be very ugly to view: and if you once set eyes upon him you might be very undesirous of the bottle.'

'I am a man of my word,' said Lopaka. 'And here is the money betwixt us.'

'Very well,' replied Keawe. 'I have a curiosity myself. – So, come, let us have one look at you, Mr. Imp.'

Now as soon as that was said the imp looked out of the bottle, and in again, swift as a lizard; and there sat Keawe and Lopaka turned to stone. The night had quite come, before either found a thought to say or voice to say it with; and then Lopaka pushed the money over and took the bottle.

'I am a man of my word,' said he, 'and had need to be so, or I would not touch this bottle with my foot. Well, I shall get my schooner, and a dollar or two for my pocket; and then I will be rid of this devil as fast as I can. For to tell you the plain truth, the look of him has cast me down.'

'Lopaka,' said Keawe, 'do not you think any worse of me than you can help; I know it is night, and the roads bad, and the pass by the tombs an ill place to go by so late, but I declare since I have seen that little face, I cannot eat or sleep or pray till it is gone from me. I will give you a lantern, and a basket to put the bottle in, and any picture or fine thing in all my house that takes your fancy; – and be gone at once, and go sleep at Hookena with Nahinu.'

'Keawe,' said Lopaka, 'many a man would take this ill; above all, when I am doing you a turn so friendly as to keep my word and buy the bottle; and for that matter, the night, and the dark, and the way by the tombs, must be all tenfold more dangerous to a man with such a sin upon his conscience, and such a bottle under his arm. But for my part, I am so extremely terrified myself, I have not the heart to blame you. Here I go then; and I pray God you may be happy in your house, and I fortunate with my schooner, and both get to heaven in the end in spite of the devil and his bottle.'

So Lopaka went down the mountain; and Keawe stood in his front balcony, and listened to the clink of the horse's shoes, and watched the lantern go shining down the path, and along the cliff of caves where the old dead are buried; and all the time he trembled and clasped his hands, and prayed for his friend, and gave glory to God that he himself was escaped out of that trouble.

But the next day came very brightly, and that new house of

his was so delightful to behold that he forgot his terrors. One day followed another, and Keawe dwelt there in perpetual joy. He had his place on the back porch; it was there he ate and lived, and read the stories in the Honolulu newspapers; but when any one came by they would go in and view the chambers and the pictures. And the fame of the house went far and wide; it was called *Ka-Hale Nui* – the Great House – in all Kona; and sometimes the Bright House, for Keawe kept a Chinaman, who was all day dusting and furbishing; and the glass and the gilt, and the fine stuffs, and the pictures, shone as bright as the morning. As for Keawe himself, he could not walk in the chambers without singing, his heart was so enlarged; and when ships sailed by upon the sea, he would fly his colours on the mast.

So time went by, until one day Keawe went upon a visit as far as Kailua to certain of his friends. There he was well feasted; and left as soon as he could the next morning, and rode hard, for he was impatient to behold his beautiful house; and, besides, the night then coming on was the night in which the dead of old days go abroad in the sides of Kona; and having already meddled with the devil, he was the more chary of meeting with the dead. A little beyond Honaunau, looking far ahead, he was aware of a woman bathing in the edge of the sea; and she seemed a well-grown girl, but he thought no more of it. Then he saw her white shift flutter as she put it on, and then her red holoku; and by the time he came abreast of her she was done with her toilet, and had come up from the sea, and stood by the track side in her red holoku, and she was all freshened with the bath, and her eyes shone and were kind. Now Keawe no sooner beheld her than he drew rein.

'I thought I knew every one in this country,' said he. 'How comes it that I do not know you?'

'I am Kokua, daughter of Kiano,' said the girl, 'and I have just returned from Oahu. Who are you?'

'I will tell you who I am in a little,' said Keawe, dismounting from his horse, 'but not now. For I have a thought in my mind, and if you knew who I was, you might have heard of me, and would not give me a true answer. But tell me, first of all, one thing: Are you married?'

At this Kokua laughed out aloud. 'It is you who ask questions,' she said. 'Are you married yourself?'

'Indeed, Kokau, I am not,' replied Keawe, 'and never thought to be until this hour. But here is the plain truth. I have met you here at the roadside, and I saw your eyes, which are like the stars, and my heart went to you as swift as a bird. And so now, if you want none of me, say so, and I will go on to my own place; but if you think me no worse than any other young man, say so, too, and I will turn aside to your father's for the night, and tomorrow I will talk with the good man.'

Kokua said never a word, but she looked at the sea and laughed.

'Kokua,' said Keawe, 'if you say nothing, I will take that for the good answer; so let us be stepping to your father's door.'

She went ahead of him, still without speech; only sometimes she glanced back and glanced away again, and she kept the strings of her hat in her mouth.

Now, when they had come to the door, Kiano came out on his verandah, and cried out and welcomed Keawe by name. At that the girl looked over, for the fame of the great house had come to her ears; and, to be sure, it was a great temptation. All that evening they were very merry together; and the girl was as bold as brass under the eyes of her parents, and made a mock of Keawe, for she had a quick wit. The next day he had a word with Kiano, and found the girl alone.

'Kokua', said he, 'you made a mock of me all the evening; and it is still time to bid me go. I would not tell you who I was, because I have so fine a house, and I feared you would think too much of that house, and too little of the man that loves you. Now you know all, and if you wish to have seen the last of me, say so at once.'

'No,' said Kokua; but this time she did not laugh, nor did Keawe ask for more.

This was the wooing of Keawe; things had gone quickly; but so an arrow goes, and the ball of a rifle swifter still, and yet both may strike the target. Things had gone fast, but they had gone far also, and the thought of Keawe rang in the maiden's head; she heard his voice in the breach of the surf upon the lava, and for this young man that she had seen but twice she would have left father and mother in her native islands. As for Keawe himself, his horse flew up the path of the mountain under the cliff of tombs, and the sound of the hoofs, and the sound of Keawe singing to himself for pleasure, echoed in the caverns of the dead. He came to the Bright House, and still he was singing. He sat and ate in the broad balcony, and the Chinaman wondered at his master, to hear how he sang between the mouthfuls. The sun went down into the sea, and the night came; and Keawe walked the balconies by lamplight, high on the mountains, and the voice of his singing startled men on ships.

'Here am I now upon my high place,' he said to himself. 'Life may be no better; this is the mountain top; and all shelves about me toward the worse. For the first time I will light up the chambers, and bathe in my fine bath with the hot water and the cold, and sleep alone in the bed of my bridal chamber.'

So the Chinaman had word, and he must rise from sleep and light the furnaces; and as he wrought below, beside the boilers, he heard his master singing and rejoicing above him in the lighted chambers. When the water began to be hot the Chinaman cried to his master; and Keawe went into the bathroom; and the Chinaman heard him sing as he filled the marble basin; and heard him sing, and the singing broken, as he undressed; until of a sudden the song ceased. The Chinaman listened, and listened; he called up the house to Keawe to ask if all were well, and Keawe answered him 'Yes', and bade him go to bed; but there was no more singing in the Bright House; and all night long the Chinaman heard his master's feet go round and round the balconies without repose.

Now the truth of it was this; as Keawe undressed for his bath, he spied upon his flesh a patch like a patch of lichen on a rock, and it was then that he stopped singing. For he knew the likeness of that patch, and knew that he was fallen in the Chinese Evil.*

Now, it is a sad thing for any man to fall into this sickness. And it would be a sad thing for any one to leave a house so beautiful and so commodious, and depart from all his friends to the north coast of Molokai between the mighty

* Leprosy [R.L.S.]

cliff and the sea-breakers. But what was that to the case of the man Keawe, he who had met his love but yesterday, and won her but that morning, and now saw all his hopes break, in a moment, like a piece of glass?

A while he sat upon the edge of the bath; then sprang, with a cry, and ran outside; and to and fro, to and fro, along the balcony, like one despairing.

'Very willingly could I leave Hawaii, the home of my fathers,' Keawe was thinking. 'Very lightly could I leave my house, the high-placed, the many-windowed, here upon the mountains. Very bravely could I go to Molokai, to Kalaupapa by the cliffs, to live with the smitten and to sleep there, far from my fathers. But what wrong have I done, what sin lies upon my soul, that I should have encountered Kokua coming cool from the seawater in the evening? Kokua, the soul-ensnarer! Kokua, the light of my life! Her may I never wed, her may I look upon no longer, her may I no more handle with my loving hand; and it is for this, it is for you, O Kokua! that I pour my lamentations!'

Now you are to observe what sort of man Keawe was, for he might have dwelt there in the Bright House for years, and no one been the wiser of his sickness; but he reckoned nothing of that, if he must lose Kokua. And again, he might have wed Kokua even as he was; and so many would have done, because they have the souls of pigs; but Keawe loved the maid manfully, and he would do her no hurt and bring her in no danger.

A little beyond the midst of the night, there came in his mind the recollection of the bottle. He went round to the back porch, and called to memory the day when the devil had looked forth; and at the thought ice ran in his veins.

'A dreadful thing is the bottle,' thought Keawe, 'and dreadful is the imp, and it is a dreadful thing to risk the flames of hell. But what other hope have I to cure my sickness or to wed Kokua? What!' he thought, 'would I beard the devil once, only to get me a house, and not face him again to win Kokua?'

Thereupon he called to mind it was the next day the *Hall* went by on her return to Honolulu. 'There must I go first,' he thought, 'and see Lopaka. For the best hope that I have now is to find that same bottle I was so pleased to be rid of.'

Never a wink could he sleep; the food stuck in his throat; but he sent a letter to Kiano, and, about the time when the steamer would be coming, rode down beside the cliff of the tombs. It rained; his horse went heavily; he looked up at the black mouths of the caves, and he envied the dead that slept there and were done with trouble; and called to mind how he had galloped by the day before, and was astonished. So he came down to Hookena, and there was all the country gathered for the steamer as usual. In the shed before the store they sat and jested and passed the news; but there was no matter of speech in Keawe's bosom, and he sat in their midst and looked without on the rain falling on the houses, and the surf beating among the rocks, and the sighs arose in his throat.

'Keawe of the Bright House is out of spirits,' said one to another. Indeed, and so he was, and little wonder.

Then the *Hall* came, and the whaleboat carried him on board. The after-part of the ship was full of Haoles,* who had been to visit the volcano, as their custom is; and the midst was crowded with Kanakas, and the forepart with wild bulls from Hilo and horses from Kaü; but Keawe sat apart from all in his sorrow, and watched for the house of Kiano. There it sat, low upon the shore in the black rocks, and shaded by the cocoa palms, and there by the door was a red holoku, no greater than a fly, and going to and from with a fly's busyness. 'Ah, queen of my heart,' he cried, 'I'll venture my dear soul to win you!'

Soon after, darkness fell, and the cabins were lit up, and the Haoles sat and played at the cards and drank whisky as their custom is; but Keawe walked the deck all night; and all the next day, as they steamed under the lee of Maui or of Molokai, he was still pacing to and fro like a wild animal in a menagerie.

Towards evening they passed Diamond Head, and came to the pier of Honolulu. Keawe stepped out among the crowd and began to ask for Lopaka. It seemed he had become the owner of a schooner – none better in the islands

* Whites [R.L.S.]

– and was gone upon an adventure as far as Pola-Pola or Kahiki; so there was no help to be looked for from Lopaka. Keawe called to mind a friend of his, a lawyer in the town (I must not tell his name), and inquired of him. They said he was grown suddenly rich, and had a fine new house upon Waikiki shore; and this put a thought in Keawe's head, and he called a hack and drove to the lawyer's house.

The house was all brand new, and the trees in the garden no greater than walking-sticks, and the lawyer, when he came, had the air of a man well pleased.

'What can I do to serve you?' said the lawyer.

'You are a friend of Lopaka's,' replied Keawe, 'and Lopaka purchased from me a certain piece of goods that I thought you might enable me to trace.'

The lawyer's face became very dark. 'I do not profess to misunderstand you, Mr Keawe,' said he, 'though this is an ugly business to be stirring in. You may be sure I know nothing, but yet I have a guess, and if you would apply in a certain quarter I think you might have news.'

And he named the name of a man, which, again, I had better not repeat. So it was for days, and Keawe went from one to another, finding everywhere new clothes and carriages, and fine new houses, and men everywhere in great contentment, although, to be sure, when he hinted at his business their faces would cloud over.

'No doubt I am upon the track,' thought Keawe. 'These new clothes and carriages are all the gifts of the little imp, and these glad faces are the faces of men who have taken their profit and got rid of the accursed thing in safety. When I see pale cheeks and hear sighing, I shall know I am near the bottle.'

So it befell at last that he was recommended to a Haole in Beritania Street. When he came to the door, about the hour of the evening meal, there were the usual marks of the new house, and the young garden, and the electric light shining in the windows; but when the owner came, a shock of hope and fear ran through Keawe; for here was a young man, white as a corpse, and black about the eyes, the hair shedding from his head, and such a look in his countenance as a man may have when he is waiting for the gallows.

'Here it is, to be sure,' thought Keawe, and so with this

man he noways veiled his errand. 'I am come to buy the bottle,' said he.

At the word the young Haole of Beritania Street reeled against the wall.

'The bottle!' he gasped. 'To buy the bottle!' Then he seemed to choke, and seizing Keawe by the arm carried him into a room and poured out wine in two glasses.

'Here is my respects,' said Keawe, who had been much about with Haoles in his time. 'Yes,' he added, 'I am come to buy the bottle. What is the price by now?'

At that word the young man let his glass slip through his fingers, and looked upon Keawe like a ghost.

'The price,' says he; 'the price! You do not know the price?'

'It is for that I am asking you,' returned Keawe. 'But why are you so much concerned? Is there anything wrong about the price?'

'It has dropped a great deal in value since your time, Mr Keawe,' said the young man, stammering.

'Well, well, I shall have the less to pay for it,' says Keawe. 'How much did it cost you?'

The young man was as white as a sheet. 'Two cents,' said he.

'What!' cried Keawe, 'two cents? Why, then, you can only sell it for one. And he who buys it——' The words died upon Keawe's tongue; he who bought it could never sell it again, the bottle and the bottle imp must abide with him until he died, and when he died must carry him to the red end of hell.

The young man of Beritania Street fell upon his knees. 'For God's sake, buy it!' he cried. 'You can have all my fortune in the bargain. I was mad when I bought it at that price. I had embezzled money at my store; I was lost else; I must have gone to jail.'

'Poor creature,' said Keawe, 'you would risk your soul upon so desperate an adventure, and to avoid the proper punishment of your own disgrace; and you think I could hesitate with love in front of me. Give me the bottle, and the change, which I make sure you have all ready. Here is a five-cent piece.'

It was as Keawe supposed; the young man had the change ready in a drawer; the bottle changed hands, and Keawe's fingers were no sooner clasped upon the stalk than he had breathed his wish to be a clean man. And, sure enough, when he got home to his room, and stripped himself before a glass, his flesh was whole like an infant's. And here was the strange thing: he had no sooner seen this miracle than his mind changed within him, and he cared naught for the Chinese Evil, and little enough for Kokua; and had but the one thought, that here he was bound to the bottle imp for time and for eternity, and had no better hope but to be a cinder for ever in the flames of hell. Away ahead of him he saw them blaze with his mind's eye, and his soul shrank, and darkness fell upon the light.

When Keawe came to himself a little, he was aware it was the night when the band played at the hotel. Thither he went, because he feared to be alone; and there, among happy faces, walked to and fro, and heard the tunes go up and down, and saw Berger beat the measure, and all the while he heard the flames crackle, and saw the red fire burning in the bottomless pit. Of a sudden the band played *Hiki-ao-ao*; that was a song that he had sung with Kokua, and at the strain courage returned to him.

'It is done now,' he thought, 'and once more let me take the good along with the evil.'

So it befell that he returned to Hawaii by the first steamer, and as soon as it could be managed he was wedded to Kokua, and carried her up the mountain side to the Bright House.

Now it was with these two, that when they were together, Keawe's heart was stilled; but so soon as he was alone he fell into a brooding horror, and heard the flames crackle, and saw the red fire burn in the bottomless pit. The girl, indeed, had come to him wholly; her heart leapt in her side at the sight of him, her hand clung to his; and she was so fashioned from the hair upon her head to the nails upon her toes that none could see her without joy. She was pleasant in her nature. She had the good word always. Full of song she was, and went to and fro in the Bright House, the brightest thing in its three stories, carolling like the birds. And Keawe beheld and heard her with delight, and then must shrink upon the side, and weep and groan to think upon the price that he had paid for her; and then he must dry his eyes, and wash his face, and go and sit with her on the broad balconies, joining in her songs, with a sick spirit, answering her smiles.

There came a day when her feet began to be heavy and her songs more rare; and now it was not Keawe only that would weep apart, but each would sunder from the other and sit in opposite balconies with the whole width of the Bright House betwixt. Keawe was so sunk in his despair he scarce observed the change, and was only glad he had more hours to sit alone and brood upon his destiny, and was not so frequently condemned to pull a smiling face on a sick heart. But one day, coming softly through the house, he heard the sound of a child sobbing, and there was Kokua rolling her face upon the balcony floor, and weeping like the lost.

'You do well to weep in this house, Kokua,' he said. 'And yet I would give the head off my body that you (at least) might have been happy.'

'Happy!' she cried. 'Keawe, when you lived alone in your Bright House you were the word of the island for a happy man; laughter and song were in your mouth, and your face was as bright as the sunrise. Then you wedded poor Kokua; and the good God knows what is amiss in her – but from that day you have not smiled. O!' she cried, 'what ails me? I thought I was pretty, and I knew I loved him. What ails me that I throw this cloud upon my husband?'

'Poor Kokua,' said Keawe. He sat down by her side, and sought to take her hand; but that she plucked away. 'Poor Kokua!' he said again. 'My poor child – my pretty. And I had thought all this while to spare you! Well, you shall know all. Then, at least, you will pity poor Keawe; then you will understand how much he loved you in the past – that he dared hell for your possession – and how much he loves you still (the poor condemned one), that he can yet call up a smile when he beholds you.'

With that he told her all, even from the beginning.

'You have done this for me?' she cried. 'Ah, well, then what do I care!' – and she clasped and wept upon him.

'Ah, child!' said Keawe, 'and yet, when I consider of the fire of hell, I care a good deal!'

'Never tell me,' said she; 'no man can be lost because he loved Kokua, and no other fault. I tell you, Keawe, I shall save you with these hands, or perish in your company.

What! you loved me, and gave your soul, and you think I will not die to save you in return?'

'Ah, my dear! you might die a hundred times, and what difference would that make?' he cried, 'except to leave me lonely till the time comes of my damnation?'

'You know nothing,' said she. 'I was educated in a school in Honolulu; I am no common girl. And I tell you, I shall save my lover. What is this you say about a cent? But all the world is not American. In England they have a piece they call a farthing, which is about half a cent. Ah! sorrow!' she cried, 'that makes it scarcely better, or the buyer must be lost, and we shall find none so brave as my Keawe! But then, there is France: they have a small coin there which they call a centime, and these go five to the cent, or thereabout. We could not do better. Come, Keawe, let us go to the French islands; let us go to Tahiti as fast as ships can bear us. There we have four centimes, three centimes, two centimes, one centime; four possible sales to come and go on; and two of us to push the bargain. Come, my Keawe! kiss me, and banish care. Kokua will defend you.'

'Gift of God!' he cried. 'I cannot think that God will punish me for desiring aught so good! Be it as you will, then; take me where you please: I put my life and my salvation in your hands.'

Early the next day Kokua was about her preparations. She took Keawe's chest that he went with sailoring; and first she put the bottle in a corner; and then packed it with the richest of their clothes and the bravest of the knickknacks in the house. 'For,' said she, 'we must seem to be rich folks, or who will believe in the bottle?' All the time of her preparation she was as gay as a bird; only when she looked upon Keawe the tears would spring in her eye, and she must run and kiss him. As for Keawe, a weight was off his soul; now that he had his secret shared, and some hope in front of him, he seemed like a new man, his feet went lightly on the earth, and his breath was good to him again. Yet was terror still at his elbow; and ever and again, as the wind blows out a taper, hope died in him, and he saw the flames toss and the red fire burn in hell.

It was given out in the country they were gone pleasuring to the States, which was thought a strange thing, and yet not so strange as the truth, if any could have guessed it.

So they went to Honolulu in the *Hall*, and thence in the *Umatilla* to San Francisco with a crowd of Haoles, and at San Francisco took their passage by the mail brigantine, the *Tropic Bird*, for Papeete, the chief place of the French in the south islands. Thither they came, after a pleasant voyage, on a fair day of the Trade Wind, and saw the reef with the surf breaking, and Motuiti with its palms, and the schooner riding within-side, and the white houses of the town low down along the shore among green trees, and overhead the mountains and the clouds of Tahiti, the wise island.

It was judged the most wise to hire a house, which they did accordingly, opposite the British Consul's, to make a great parade of money, and themselves conspicuous with carriages and horses. This it was easy to do, so long as they had the bottle in their possession; for Kokua was more bold than Keawe, and, whenever she had a mind, called on the imp for twenty or a hundred dollars. At this rate they soon grew to be remarked in the town; and the strangers from Hawaii, their riding and their driving, the fine holokus and the rich lace of Kokua, became the matter of much talk.

They got on well after the first with the Tahitian language, which is indeed like to the Hawaiian, with a change of certain letters; and as soon as they had any freedom of speech, began to push the bottle. You are to consider it was not an easy subject to introduce; it was not easy to persuade people you were in earnest, when you offered to sell them for four centimes the spring of health and riches inexhaustible. It was necessary besides to explain the dangers of the bottle; and either people disbelieved the whole thing and laughed, or they thought the more of the darker part, became overcast with gravity, and drew away from Keawe and Kokua, as from persons who had dealings with the devil. So far from gaining ground, these two began to find they were avoided in the town; the children ran away from them screaming, a thing intolerable to Kokua; Catholics crossed themselves as they went by; and all persons began with one accord to disengage themselves from their advances.

Depression fell upon their spirits. They would sit at night in their new house, after a day's weariness, and not exchange one word, or the silence would be broken by Kokua bursting suddenly into sobs. Sometimes they would pray together;

sometimes they would have the bottle out upon the floor, and sit all evening watching how the shadow hovered in the midst. At such times they would be afraid to go to rest. It was long ere slumber came to them, and, if either dozed off, it would be to wake and find the other silently weeping in the dark, or, perhaps, to wake alone, the other having fled from the house and the neighbourhood of that bottle, and to pace under the bananas in the little garden, or to wander on the beach by moonlight.

One night it was so when Kokua awoke. Keawe was gone. She felt in the bed, and his place was cold. Then fear fell upon her, and she sat up in bed. A little moonshine filtered through the shutters. The room was bright, and she could spy the bottle on the floor. Outside it blew high, the great trees of the avenue cried aloud, and the fallen leaves rattled in the verandah. In the midst of this Kokua, was aware of another sound; whether of a beast or of a man she could scarce tell, but it was as sad as death, and cut her to the soul. Softly she arose, set the door ajar, and looked forth into the moonlit yard. There, under the bananas, lay Keawe, his mouth in the dust, and as he lay he moaned.

It was Kokua'a first thought to run forward and console him; her second potently withheld her. Keawe had borne himself before his wife like a brave man; it became her little in the hour of weakness to intrude upon his shame. With the thought she drew back into the house.

'Heaven!' she thought, 'how careless have I been – how weak! It is he, not I, that stands in this eternal peril; it was he, not I, that took the curse upon his soul. It is for my sake, and for the love of a creature of so little worth and such poor help, that he now beholds so close to him the flames of hell – ay, and smells the smoke of it, lying without there in the wind and moonlight. Am I so dull of spirit that never till now I have surmised my duty, or have I seen it before and turned aside? But now, at least, I take up my soul in both the hands of my affection; now I say farewell to the white steps of heaven and the waiting faces of my friends. A love for a love, and let mine be equalled with Keawe's! A soul for a soul, and be it mine to perish!'

She was a deft woman with her hands, and was soon apparelled. She took in her hands the change – the precious centimes they kept ever at their side; for this coin is little used, and they had made provision at a Government office. When she was forth in the avenue clouds came on the wind, and the moon was blackened. The town slept, and she knew not whither to turn till she heard one coughing in the shadow of the trees.

'Old man,' said Kokua, 'what do you here abroad in the cold night?'

The old man could scarce express himself for coughing, but she made out that he was old and poor, and a stranger in the island.

'Will you do me a service?' said Kokua. 'As one stranger to another, and as an old man to a young woman, will you help a daughter of Hawaii?'

'Ah,' said the old man. 'So you are the witch from the Eight Islands, and even my old soul you seek to entangle. But I have heard of you, and defy your wickedness.'

'Sit down here,' said Kokua, 'and let me tell you a tale.' And she told him the story of Keawe from the beginning to the end.

'And now,' said she, 'I am his wife, whom he bought with his soul's welfare. And what should I do? If I went to him myself and offered to buy it, he would refuse. But if you go, he will sell it eagerly; I will await you here; you will buy it for four centimes, and I will buy it again for three. And the Lord strengthen a poor girl!'

'If you meant falsely,' said the old man, 'I think God would strike you dead.'

'He would!' cried Kokua. 'Be sure he would. I could not be so treacherous – God would not suffer it.'

'Give me the four centimes and await me here,' said the old man.

Now, when Kokua stood alone in the street, her spirit died. The wind roared in the trees, and it seemed to her the rushing of flames of hell; the shadows tossed in the light of the street lamp, and they seemed to her the snatching hands of evil ones. If she had had the strength, she must have run away, and if she had had the breath she must have screamed aloud; but in truth she could do neither, and stood and trembled in the avenue, like an affrighted child.

Then she saw the old man returning, and he had the bottle in his hand.

'I have done your bidding,' said he. 'I left your husband

weeping like a child; tonight he will sleep easy.' And he held the bottle forth.

'Before you give it me,' Kokua panted, 'take the good with the evil – ask to be delivered from your cough.'

'I am an old man,' replied the other, 'and too near the gate of the grave to take a favour from the devil. – But what is this? Why do you not take the bottle? Do you hesitate?'

'Not hesitate!' cried Kokua. 'I am only weak. Give me a moment. It is my hand resists, my flesh shrinks back from the accursed thing. One moment only!'

The old man looked upon Kokua kindly. 'Poor child!' said he, 'you fear; your soul misgives you. Well, let me keep it. I am old, and can never more be happy in this world, and as for the next—'

'Give it me!' gasped Kokua. 'There is your money. Do you think I am so base as that? Give me the bottle.'

'God bless you, child,' said the old man.

Kokua concealed the bottle under her holoku, said farewell to the old man, and walked off along the avenue, she cared not whither. For all roads were now the same to her, and led equally to hell. Sometimes she walked, and sometimes ran; sometimes she screamed out loud in the night, and sometimes lay by the wayside in the dust and wept. All that she had heard of hell came back to her; she saw the flames blaze, and she smelt the smoke, and her flesh withered on the coals.

Near day she came to her mind again, and returned to the house. It was even as the old man said – Keawe slumbered like a child. Kokua stood and gazed upon his face.

'Now, my husband,' said she, 'it is your turn to sleep. When you wake it will be your turn to sing and laugh. But for poor Kokua, alas! that meant no evil – for poor Kokua, no more sleep, no more singing, no more delight, whether in earth or heaven.'

With that she lay down in the bed by his side, and her misery was so extreme that she fell in a deep slumber instantly.

Late in the morning her husband woke her and gave her the good news. It seemed he was silly with delight, for he paid no heed to her distress, ill though she dissembled it. The words stuck in her mouth, it mattered not; Keawe did the speaking. She ate not a bite, but who was to observe it? for Keawe cleared the dish. Kokua saw and heard him, like some strange thing in a dream; there were times when she forgot or doubted, and put her hands to her brow; to know herself doomed and hear her husband babble seemed so monstrous.

All the while Keawe was eating and talking, and planning the time of their return, and thanking her for saving him, and fondling her, and calling her the true helper after all. He laughed at the old man that was fool enough to buy that bottle.

'A worthy old man he seemed,' Keawe said. 'But no one can judge by appearances. For why did the old reprobate require the bottle?'

'My husband,' said Kokua humbly, 'his purpose may have been good.'

Keawe laughed like an angry man.

'Fiddle-de-dee!' cried Keawe. 'An old rogue, I tell you, and an old ass to boot. For the bottle was hard enough to sell at four centimes; and at three it will be quite impossible. The margin is not broad enough, the thing begins to smell of scorching – brrr!' said he, and shuddered. 'It is true I bought it myself at a cent, when I knew not there were smaller coins. I was a fool for my pains; there will never be found another: and whoever has that bottle now will carry it to the pit.'

'O my husband!' cried Kokua. 'Is it not a terrible thing to save oneself by the eternal ruin of another? It seems to me I could not laugh. I would be humbled. I would be filled with melancholy. I would pray for the poor holder.'

Then Keawe, because he felt the truth of what she said, grew the more angry. 'Heighty-teighty!' cried he. 'You may be filled with melancholy if you please. It is not the mind of a good wife. If you thought at all of me you would sit shamed.'

Thereupon he went out, and Kokua was alone.

What chance had she to sell that bottle at two centimes? None, she perceived. And if she had any, here was her husband hurrying her away to a country where there was nothing lower than a cent. And here – on the morrow of her sacrifice – was her husband leaving her and blaming her.

She would not even try to profit by what time she had,

but sat in the house, and now had the bottle out and viewed it with unutterable fear, and now, with loathing, hid it out of sight.

By and by Keawe came back, and would have her take a drive.

'My husband, I am ill,' she said. 'I am out of heart. Excuse me, I can take no pleasure.'

Then was Keawe more wroth than ever. With her, because he thought she was brooding over the case of the old man; and with himself, because he thought she was right, and was ashamed to be so happy.

'This is your truth,' cried he, 'and this your affection! Your husband is just saved from eternal ruin, which he encountered for the love of you – and you can take no pleasure! Kokua, you have a disloyal heart.'

He went forth again furious, and wandered in the town all day. He met friends, and drank with them; they hired a carriage and drove into the country, and there drank again. All the time Keawe was ill at ease, because he was taking this pastime while his wife was sad, and because he knew in his heart that she was more right than he; and the knowledge made him drink the deeper.

Now there was an old brutal Haole drinking with him, one that had been a boatswain of a whaler, a runaway, a digger in gold mines, a convict in prisons. He had a low mind and a foul mouth; he loved to drink and to see others drunken; and he pressed the glass upon Keawe. Soon there was no more money in the company.

'Here, you!' says the boatswain, 'you are rich, you have been always saying. You have a bottle or some foolishness.'

'Yes,' says Keawe, 'I am rich; I will go back and get some money from my wife, who keeps it.'

'That's a bad idea, mate,' said the boatswain. 'Never you trust a petticoat with dollars. They're all false as water; you keep an eye on her.'

Now this word stuck in Keawe's mind; for he was muddled with what he had been drinking.

'I should not wonder but she was false, indeed,' thought he. 'Why else should she be so cast down at my release? But I will show her I am not the man to be fooled. I will catch her in the act.'

Accordingly, when they were back in town, Keawe bade the boatswain wait for him at the corner, by the old calaboose, and went forward up the avenue alone to the door of his house. The night had come again; there was a light within, but never a sound; and Keawe crept about the corner, opened the back-door softly, and looked in.

There was Kokua on the floor, the lamp at her side; before her was a milk-white bottle, with a round belly and a long neck; and as she viewed it, Kokua wrung her hands.

A long time Keawe stood and looked in the doorway. At first he was struck stupid; and then fear fell upon him that the bargain had been made amiss, and the bottle had come back to him as it came at San Francisco; and at that his knees were loosened, and the fumes of the wine departed from his head like mists off a river in the morning. And then he had another thought; and it was a strange one, that made his cheeks to burn.

'I must make sure of this,' thought he.

So he closed the door, and went softly round the corner again, and then came noisily in, as though he were but now returned. And, lo! by the time he opened the front door no bottle was to be seen; and Kokua sat in a chair and started up like one awakened out of sleep.

'I have been drinking all day and making merry,' said Keawe. 'I have been with good companions, and now I only come back for money, and return to drink and carouse with them again.'

Both his face and voice were as stern as judgment, but Kokua was too troubled to observe.

'You do well to use your own, my husband,' said she, and her words trembled.

'O, I do well in all things,' said Keawe, and he went straight to the chest and took out money. But he looked besides in the corner where they kept the bottle, and there was no bottle there.

At that the chest heaved upon the floor like a sea-billow, and the house span about him like a wreath of smoke, for he saw he was lost now, and there was no escape. 'It is what I feared,' he thought. 'It is she who has bought it.'

And then he came to himself a little and rose up; but the sweat streamed on his face as thick as the rain and as cold as the well-water.

'Kokua,' said he, 'I said to you today what ill became me. Now I return to carouse with my jolly companions,' and at that he laughed a little quietly. 'I will take more pleasure in the cup if you forgive me.'

She clasped his knees in a moment; she kissed his knees with flowing tears.

'O,' she cried, 'I asked but a kind word!'

'Let us never one think hardly of the other,' said Keawe, and was gone out of the house.

Now, the money that Keawe had taken was only some of that store of centime pieces they had laid in at their arrival. It was very sure he had no mind to be drinking. His wife had given her soul for him, now he must give his for hers; no other thought was in the world with him.

At the corner, by the old calaboose, there was the boatswain waiting.

'My wife has the bottle,' said Keawe, 'and, unless you help me to recover it, there can be no more money and no more liquor tonight.'

'You do not mean to say you are serious about that bottle?' cried the boatswain.

'There is the lamp,' said Keawe. 'Do I look as if I was jesting?'

'That is so,' said the boatswain. 'You look as serious as a ghost.'

'Well, then,' said Keawe, 'here are two centimes; you must go to my wife in the house, and offer her these for the bottle, which (if I am not much mistaken) she will give you instantly. Bring it to me here, and I will buy it back from you for one; for that is the law with this bottle, that it still must be sold for a less sum. But whatever you do, never breathe a word to her that you come from me.'

'Mate, I wonder are you making a fool of me?' asked the boatswain.

'It will do you no harm if I am,' returned Keawe.

'That is so, mate,' said the boatswain.

'And if you doubt me,' added Keawe, 'you can try. As soon as you are clear of the house, wish to have your pocket full of money, or a bottle of the best rum, or what you please, and you will see the virtue of the thing.'

'Very well, Kanaka,' says the boatswain. 'I will try; but if you are having your fun out of me, I will take my fun out of you with a belaying-pin.'

So the whaler-man went off up the avenue; and Keawe stood and waited. It was near the same spot where Kokua had waited the night before; but Keawe was more resolved, and never faltered in his purpose; only his soul was bitter with despair.

It seemed a long time he had to wait before he heard a voice singing in the darkness of the avenue. He knew the voice to be the boatswain's; but it was strange how drunken it appeared upon a sudden.

Next, the man himself came stumbling into the light of the lamp. He had the devil's bottle buttoned in his coat; another bottle was in his hand; and even as he came in view he raised it to his mouth and drank.

'You have it,' said Keawe. 'I see that.'

'Hands off!' cried the boatswain, jumping back. 'Take a step near me and I'll smash your mouth. You thought you could make a cat's-paw of me, did you?

'What do you mean?' cried Keawe.

'Mean?' cried the boatswain, 'This is a pretty good bottle, this is; that's what I mean. How I got it for two centimes I can't make out; but I'm sure you shan't have it for one.'

'You mean you won't sell it?' gasped Keawe.

'No, *sir*!' cried the boatswain. 'But I'll give you a drink of the rum, if you like.'

'I tell you,' said Keawe, 'the man who has that bottle goes to hell.'

'I reckon I'm going anyway,' returned the sailor; 'and this bottle's the best thing to go with I've struck yet. No, sir!' he cried again, 'this is my bottle now, and you can go and fish for another.'

'Can this be true?' Keawe cried. 'For your own sake, I beseech you, sell it me!'

'I don't value any of your talk,' replied the boatswain. 'You thought I was a flat; now you see I'm not; and there's an end. If you won't have a swallow of the rum I'll have one myself. Here's your health, and good-night to you!'

So off he went down the avenue towards town, and there goes the bottle out of the story.

But Keawe ran to Kokua light as the wind; and great was their joy that night; and great, since then, has been the peace of all their days in the Bright House.

Keola was married with Lehua, daughter of Kalamake,
the wise man of Molokai, and he kept his dwelling with
the father of his wife. There was no man more cunning
than that prophet; he read the stars, he could divine by
the bodies of the dead, and by the means of evil creatures:
he could go alone into the highest parts of the mountain,
into the region of the hobgoblins, and there he would lay
snares to entrap the spirits of ancient.

For this reason no man was more consulted in all the
Kingdom of Hawaii. Prudent people bought, and sold,
and married, and laid out their lives by his counsels; and
the King had him twice to Kona to seek the treasures of
Kamehameha.[1] Neither was any man more feared: of his
enemies, some had dwindled in sickness by the virtue of
his incantations, and some had been spirited away, the life
and the clay both, so that folk looked in vain for so much
as a bone of their bodies. It was rumoured that he had
the art or the gift of the old heroes. Men had seen him at
night upon the mountains, stepping from one cliff to the
next; they had seen him walking in the high forest, and his
head and shoulders were above the trees.

This Kalamake was a strange man to see. He was come of
the best blood in Molokai and Maui, of a pure descent; and
yet he was more white to look upon than any foreigner: his
hair the colour of dry grass, and his eyes red and very blind,
so that 'Blind as Kalamake, that can see across tomorrow'
was a byword in the islands.

Of all these doings of his father-in-law, Keola knew a

1. Dynastic name of the late eighteenth- and
   nineteenth-century kings of Hawaii. Kamehameha
   I united the Hawaiian Islands.

143

little by the common repute, a little more he suspected, and the rest he ignored. But there was one thing troubled him. Kalamake was a man that spared for nothing, whether to eat or to drink or to wear; and for all he paid in bright new dollars. 'Bright as Kalamake's dollars' was another saying in the Eight Isles. Yet he neither sold, nor planted, nor took hire – only now and then for his sorceries – and there was no source conceivable for so much silver coin.

It chanced one day Keola's wife was gone upon a visit to Kaunakakai, on the lee side of the island, and the men were forth at the sea-fishing. But Keola was an idle dog, and he lay in the verandah and watched the surf beat on the shore and the birds fly about the cliff. It was a chief thought with him always – the thought of the bright dollars. When he lay down to bed he would be wondering why they were so many, and when he woke at morn he would be wondering why they were all new; and the thing was never absent from his mind. But this day of all days he made sure in his heart of some discovery. For it seems he had observed the place where Kalamake kept his treasure, which was a lockfast desk against the parlour wall, under the print of Kamehameha the Fifth, and a photograph of Queen Victoria with her crown; and it seems again that, no later than the night before, he found occasion to look in, and behold! the bag lay there empty. And this was the day of the steamer; he could see her smoke off Kalaupapa; and she must soon arrive with a month's goods, tinned salmon and gin, and all manner of rare luxuries for Kalamake.

'Now if he can pay for his goods today,' Keola thought, 'I shall know for certain that the man is a warlock, and the dollars come out of the Devil's pocket.'

While he was thinking, there was his father-in-law behind him, looking vexed.

'Is that the steamer?' he asked.

'Yes,' said Keola. 'She has but to call at Pelekunu, and then she will be here.'

'There is no help for it then,' returned Kalamake, 'and I must take you in my confidence, Keola, for the lack of any one better. Come here within the house.'

So they stepped together into the parlour, which was a very fine room, papered and hung with prints, and furnished with a rocking-chair, and a table and a sofa in the European style. There was a shelf of books besides, and a family Bible in the midst of the table, and the lockfast writing-desk against the wall; so that any one could see it was the house of a man of substance.

Kalamake made Keola close the shutters of the windows, while he himself locked all the doors and set open the lid of the desk. From this he brought forth a pair of necklaces hung with charms and shells, a bundle of dried herbs, and the dried leaves of trees, and a green branch of palm.

'What I am about,' said he, 'is a thing beyond wonder. The men of old were wise; they wrought marvels, and this among the rest; but that was at night, in the dark, under the fit stars and in the desert. The same will I do here in my own house and under the plain eye of day.'

So saying, he put the Bible under the cushion of the sofa so that it was all covered, brought out from the same place a mat of a wonderfully fine texture, and heaped the herbs and leaves on sand in a tin pan. And then he and Keola put on the necklaces and took their stand upon the opposite corners of the mat.

'The time comes,' said the warlock; 'be not afraid.'

With that he set flame to the herbs, and began to mutter and wave the branch of palm. At first the light was dim because of the closed shutters; but the herbs caught strongly afire, and the flames beat upon Keola, and the room glowed with the burning: and next the smoke rose and made his head swim and his eyes darken, and the sound of Kalamake muttering ran in his ears. And suddenly, to the mat on which they were standing came a snatch or twitch, that seemed to be more swift than lightning. In the same wink the room was gone and the house, the breath all beaten from Keola's body. Volumes of light rolled upon his eyes and head, and he found himself transported to a beach of the sea, under a strong sun, with a great surf roaring: he and the warlock standing there on the same mat, speechless, gasping and grasping at one another, and passing their hands before their eyes.

'What was this?' cried Keola, who came to himself the first, because he was the younger. 'The pang of it was like death.'

'It matters not,' panted Kalamake. 'It is now done.'

'And in the name of God where are we?' cried Keola.

'That is not the question,' replied the sorcerer. 'Being here, we have matter in our hands, and that we must attend to. Go, while I recover my breath, into the borders of the wood, and bring me the leaves of such and such a herb, and such and such a tree, which you will find to grow there plentifully – three handfuls of each. And be speedy. We must be home again before the steamer comes; it would seem strange if we had disappeared.' And he sat on the sand and panted.

Keola went up the beach, which was of shining sand and coral, strewn with singular shells; and he thought in his heart –

'How do I not know this beach? I will come here again and gather shells.'

In front of him was a line of palms against the sky; not like the palms of the Eight Islands, but tall and fresh and beautiful, and hanging out withered fans like gold among the green, and he thought in his heart –

'It is strange I should not have found this grove. I will come here again, when it is warm, to sleep.' And he thought, 'How warm it has grown suddenly!' For it was winter in Hawaii, and the day had been chill. And he thought also, 'Where are the grey mountains? And where is the high cliff with the hanging forest and the wheeling birds?' And the more he considered, the less he might conceive in what quarter of the islands he was fallen.

In the border of the grove, where it met the beach, the herb was growing, but the tree farther back. Now, as Keola went toward the tree, he was aware of a young woman who had nothing on her body, but a belt of leaves.

'Well!' thought Keola, 'they are not very particular about their dress in this part of the country.' And he paused, supposing she would observe him and escape; and, seeing that she still looked before her, stood and hummed aloud. Up she leaped at the sound. Her face was ashen; she looked this way and that, and her mouth gaped with the terror of her soul. But it was a strange thing that her eyes did not rest upon Keola.

'Good-day,' said he. 'You need not be so frightened; I will not eat you.' And he had scarce opened his mouth before the young woman fled into the bush.

'These are strange manners,' thought Keola. And, not thinking what he did, ran after her.

As she ran, the girl kept crying in some speech that was not practised in Hawaii, yet some of the words were the same, and he knew she kept calling and warning others. And presently he saw more people running – men, women and children, one with another, all running and crying like people at a fire. And with that he began to grow afraid himself, and returned to Kalamake, bringing the leaves. Him he told what he had seen.

'You must pay no heed,' said Kalamake. 'All this is like a dream and shadows. All will disappear and be forgotten.'

'It seemed none saw me,' said Keola.

'And none did,' replied the sorcerer. 'We walk here in the broad sun invisible by reason of these charms. Yet they hear us; and therefore it is well to speak softly, as I do.'

With that he made a circle round the mat with stones, and in the midst he set the leaves.

'It will be your part,' said he, 'to keep the leaves alight, and feed the fire slowly. While they blaze (which is but for a little moment) I must do my errand; and before the ashes blacken, the same power that brought us carries us away. Be ready now with the match; and do you call me in good time, lest the flames burn out and I be left.'

As soon as the leaves caught, the sorcerer leaped like a deer out of the circle, and began to race along the beach like a hound that has been bathing. As he ran he kept stooping to snatch shells; and it seemed to Keola that they glittered as he took them. The leaves blazed with a clear flame that consumed them swiftly; and presently Keola had but a handful left, and the sorcerer was far off, running and stopping.

'Back!' cried Keola. 'Back! The leaves are near done.'

At that Kalamake turned, and if he had run before, now he flew. But fast as he ran, the leaves burned faster. The flame was ready to expire when, with a great leap, he bounded on the mat. The wind of his leaping blew it out; and with that the beach was gone, and the sun and the sea, and they stood once more in the dimness of the shuttered parlour, and were once more shaken and blinded; and on the mat betwixt them lay a pile of shining dollars. Keola ran to the shutters; and there was the steamer tossing in the swell close in.

The same night Kalamake took his son-in-law apart, and gave him five dollars in his hand.

'Keola,' said he, 'if you are a wise man (which I am doubtful of) you will think you slept this afternoon on the verandah, and dreamed as you were sleeping. I am a man of few words, and I have for my helpers people of short memories.'

Never a word more said Kalamake, nor referred again to that affair. But it ran all the while in Keola's head – if he were lazy before he would now do nothing.

'Why should I work,' thought he, 'when I have a father-in-law who makes dollars of sea-shells?'

Presently his share was spent. He spent it all upon fine clothes. And then he was sorry:

'For,' thought he, 'I had done better to have bought a concertina, with which I might have entertained myself all day long.' And then he began to grow vexed with Kalamake.

'This man has the soul of a dog,' thought he. 'He can gather dollars when he pleases on the beach, and he leaves me to pine for a concertina! Let him beware: I am no child, I am as cunning as he, and hold his secret.' With that he spoke to his wife Lehua, and complained of her father's manners.

'I would let my father be,' said Lehua. 'He is a dangerous man to cross.'

'I care that for him!' cried Keola; and snapped his fingers. 'I have him by the nose. I can make him do what I please.' And he told Lehua the story.

But she shook her head.

'You may do what you like,' said she; 'but as sure as you thwart my father, you will be no more heard of. Think of this person, and that person; think of Hua, who was a noble of the House of Representatives, and went to Honolulu every year; and not a bone or a hair of him was found. Remember Kamau, and how he wasted to a thread, so that his wife lifted him with one hand. Keola, you are a baby in my father's hands; he will take you with his thumb and finger and eat you like a shrimp.'

Now Keola was truly afraid of Kalamake, but he was vain too; and these words of his wife incensed him.

'Very well,' said he, 'if that is what you think of me, I will show how much you are deceived.' And he went straight to where his father-in-law was sitting in the parlour.

'Kalamake,' said he, 'I want a concertina.'

'Do you indeed?' said Kalamake.

'Yes,' said he, 'and I may as well tell you plainly, I mean to have it. A man who picks up dollars on the beach can certainly afford a concertina.'

'I had no idea you had so much spirit,' replied the sorcerer. 'I thought you were a timid, useless lad, and I cannot describe how much pleased I am to find I was mistaken. Now I begin to think I may have found an assistant and successor in my difficult business. A concertina? You shall have the best in Honolulu. And tonight, as soon as it is dark, you and I will go and find the money.'

'Shall we return to the beach?' asked Keola.

'No, no!' replied Kalamake; 'you must begin to learn more of my secrets. Last time I taught you to pick shells; this time I shall teach you to catch fish. Are you strong enough to launch Pili's boat?'

'I think I am,' returned Keola. 'But why should we not take your own, which is afloat already?'

'I have a reason which you will understand thoroughly before tomorrow,' said Kalamake. 'Pili's boat is the better suited for my purpose. So, if you please, let us meet there as soon as it is dark; and in the meanwhile let us keep our own counsel, for there is no cause to let the family into our business.'

Honey is not more sweet than was the voice of Kalamake, and Keola could scarce contain his satisfaction.

'I might have had my concertina weeks ago,' thought he, 'and there is nothing needed in this world but a little courage.'

Presently after he spied Lehua weeping, and was half in a mind to tell her all was well.

'But no,' thinks he; 'I shall wait till I can show her the concertina; we shall see what the chit will do then. Perhaps she will understand in the future that her husband is a man of some intelligence.'

As soon as it was dark father and son-in-law launched Pili's boat and set the sail. There was a great sea, and it blew strong from the leeward; but the boat was swift and light and dry, and skimmed the waves. The wizard had a lantern, which he lit and held with his finger through the ring; and the two sat in the stern and smoked cigars, of which Kalamake had always a provision, and spoke like friends of magic and the great sums of money which they could make by its exercise, and what they should buy first, and what second; and Kalamake talked like a father.

Presently he looked all about, and above him at the stars, and back at the island, which was already three parts sunk under the sea, and he seemed to consider ripely his position.

'Look!' says he, 'there is Molokai already behind us, and Maui like a cloud; and by the bearing of these three stars I know I am come where I desire. This part of the sea is called the Sea of the Dead. It is in this place extraordinarily deep, and the floor is all covered with the bones of men, and in the holes of this part gods and goblins keep their habitation. The flow of the sea is to the north, stronger than a shark can swim, and any man who shall here be thrown out of a ship it bears away like a wild horse into the uttermost ocean. Presently he is spent and goes down, and his bones are scattered with the rest, and the gods devour his spirit.'

Fear came on Keola at the words, and he looked, and by the light of the stars and the lantern the warlock seemed to change.

'What ails you?' cried Keola, quick and sharp.

'It is not I who am ailing,' said the wizard; 'but there is one here very sick.'

With that he changed his grasp upon the lantern, and, behold! as he drew his finger from the ring, the finger stuck and the ring was burst, and his hand was grown to be of the bigness of three.

At that sight Keola screamed and covered his face.

But Kalamake held up the lantern. 'Look rather at my face!' said he – and his head was huge as a barrel; and still he grew and grew as a cloud grows on a mountain, and Keola sat before him screaming, and the boat raced on the great seas.

'And now,' said the wizard, 'what do you think about that concertina? and are you sure you would not rather have a flute? No?' says he; 'that is well, for I do not like my family to be changeable of purpose. But I begin to think I had better get out of this paltry boat, for my bulk swells to a very unusual degree, and if we are not the more careful, she will presently be swamped.'

With that he threw his legs over the side. Even as he did so, the greatness of the man grew thirty-fold and forty-fold as swift as sight or thinking, so that he stood in the deep seas to the armpits, and his head and shoulders rose like a high isle, and the swell beat and burst upon his bosom, as it beats and breaks against a cliff. The boat ran still to the north, but he reached out his hand, and took the gunwhale by the finger and thumb, and broke the side like a biscuit, and Keola was spilled into the sea. And the pieces of the boat the sorcerer crushed into the hollow of his hand and flung miles away into the night.

'Excuse me taking the lantern,' said he; 'for I have a long wade before me, and the land is far, and the bottom of the sea uneven, and I feel the bones under my toes.'

And he turned and went off walking with great strides; and as often as Keola sank in the trough he could see him no longer; but as often as he was heaved upon the crest, there he was striding and dwindling, and he held the lamp high over his head, and the waves broke white about him as he went.

Since first the islands were fished out of the sea there was never a man so terrified as this Keola. He swam indeed, but he swam as puppies swim when they are cast in to drown, and knew not wherefore. He could but think of the hugeness of the swelling of the warlock, of that face which was great as a mountain, of those shoulders that were broad as an isle, and of the seas that beat on them in vain. He thought, too, of the concertina, and shame took hold upon him; and of the dead men's bones, and fear shook him.

Of a sudden he was aware of something dark against the stars that tossed, and a light below, and a brightness of the cloven sea; and he heard speech of men. He cried out aloud and a voice answered; and in a twinkling the bows of a ship hung above him on a wave like a thing balanced, and swooped down. He caught with his two hands in the chains of her, and the next moment was buried in the rushing seas, and the next hauled on board by seamen.

They gave him gin and biscuit and dry clothes, and asked him how he came where they found him, and whether the light which they had seen was the lighthouse Lae o Ka Laau. But Keola knew white men are like children and only believe their own stories; so about himself he told them what he pleased, and as for the light (which was Kalamake's lantern) he vowed he had seen none.

This ship was a schooner bound for Honolulu, and then to trade in the low islands; and by a very good chance for Keola she had lost a man off the bowsprit in a squall. It was no use talking. Keola durst not stay in the Eight Islands. Word goes so quickly, and all men are so fond to talk and carry news, that if he hid in the north end of Kauai or in the south end of Kaü, the wizard would have wind of it before a month, and he must perish. So he did what seemed the most prudent, and shipped sailor in the place of the man who had been drowned.

In some ways the ship was a good place. The food was extraordinarily rich and plenty, with biscuits and salt beef every day, and pea-soup and puddings made of flour and suet twice a week, so that Keola grew fat. The captain also was a good man, and the crew no worse than other whites. The trouble was the mate, who was the most difficult man to please Keola had ever met with, and beat and cursed him daily, both for what he did and what he did not. The blows that he dealt were very sore, for he was strong; and the words he used were very unpalatable, for Keola was come of a good family and accustomed to respect. And what was the worst of all, whenever Keola found a chance to sleep, there was the mate awake and stirring him up with a rope's end. Keola saw it would never do; and he made up his mind to run away.

They were about a month out from Honolulu when they made the land. It was a fine starry night, the sea was smooth as well as the sky fair; it blew a steady trade; and there was the island on their weather bow, a ribbon of palm-trees lying flat along the sea. The captain and the mate looked at it with the night-glass, and named the name of it, and talked of it, beside the wheel where Keola was steering. It seemed it was an isle where no traders came. By the captain's way, it was an isle besides where no man dwelt; but the mate thought otherwise.

'I don't give a cent for the directory,' said he. 'I've been past here one night in the schooner *Eugenie*; it was just such a night as this; they were fishing with torches, and the beach was thick with lights like a town.'

'Well, well,' says the captain, 'it's steep-to, that's the great point; and there ain't any outlying dangers by the chart, so we'll just hug the lee side of it. – Keep her romping full, don't I tell you!' he cried to Keola, who was listening so hard that he forgot to steer.

And the mate cursed him, and swore that Kanaka was for no use in the world, and if he got started after him with a belaying-pin, it would be a cold day for Keola.

And so the captain and mate lay down on the house together, and Keola was left to himself.

'This island will do very well for me,' he thought; 'if no traders deal there, the mate will never come. And as for Kalamake, it is not possible he can ever get as far as this.'

With that he kept edging the schooner nearer in. He had to do this quietly, for it was the trouble with these white men, and above all with the mate, that you could never be sure of them; they would all be sleeping sound, or else pretending, and if a sail shook they would jump to their feet and fall on you with a rope's end. So Keola edged her up little by little, and kept all drawing. And presently the land was close on board, and the sound of the sea on the sides of it grew loud.

With that the mate sat up suddenly upon the house.

'What are you doing?' he roars. 'You'll have the ship ashore!'

And he made one bound for Keola, and Keola made another clean over the rail and plump into the starry sea. When he came up again, the schooner had payed off on her true course, and the mate stood by the wheel himself, and Keola heard him cursing. The sea was smooth under the lee of the island; it was warm besides, and Keola had his sailor's knife, so he had no fear of sharks. A little way before him the trees stopped; there was a break in the line of the land like the mouth of a harbour; and the tide, which was then flowing, took him up and carried him through. One minute he was without, and the next within; had floated there in a wide shallow water, bright with ten thousand stars, and all about him was the ring of the land, with its string of palm-trees. And he was amazed, because this was a kind of island he had never heard of.

The time of Keola in that place was in two periods – the period when he was alone, and the period when he was there with the tribe. At first he sought everywhere and found no man; only some houses standing in a hamlet, and the marks of fires. But the ashes of the fires were cold and the rains had washed them away; and the winds had blown, and some of the huts were overthrown. It was here he took his dwelling; and he made a fire drill, and a shell hook, and fished and cooked his fish, and climbed after green cocoa-nuts, the juice of which he drank, for in all the isle there was no water. The days were long to him, and the nights terrifying. He made a lamp of cocoa-shell, and drew the oil of the ripe nuts, and made a wick of fibre; and when evening came he closed up his hut, and lit his lamp, and lay and trembled till morning. Many a time he thought in his heart he would have been better in the bottom of the sea, his bones rolling there with the others.

All this while he kept by the inside of the island, for the huts were on the shore of the lagoon, and it was there the palms grew best, and the lagoon itself abounded with good fish. And to the outer side he went once only, and he looked but the once at the beach of the ocean, and came away shaking. For the look of it, with its bright sand, and strewn shells, and strong sun and surf, went sore against his inclination.

'It cannot be,' he thought, 'and yet it is very like. And how do I know? These white men, although they pretend to know where they are sailing, must take their chance like other people. So that after all we may have sailed in a circle, and I may be quite near to Molokai, and this may be the very beach where my father-in-law gathers his dollars.'

So after that he was prudent, and kept to the land side.

It was perhaps a month later, when the people of the place arrived – the fill of six great boats. They were a fine race of men, and spoke a tongue that sounded different from the tongue of Hawaii, but so many of the words were the same that it was not difficult to understand. The men besides were very courteous, and the women very towardly; and they made Keola welcome, and built him a house, and gave him a wife; and, what surprised him the most, he was never sent to work with the young men.

And now Keola had three periods. First he had a period of being very sad, and then he had a period when he was pretty merry. Last of all came the third, when he was the most terrified man in the four oceans.

The cause of the first period was the girl he had to wife. He was in doubt about the island, and he might have been in doubt about the speech, of which he had heard so little when he came there with the wizard on the mat. But about his wife there was no mistake conceivable, for she was the same girl that ran from him crying in the wood. So he had sailed all this way, and might as well have stayed in Molokai; and had left home and wife and all his friends for no other cause but to escape his enemy, and the place he had come to was that wizard's hunting-ground, and the shore where he walked invisible. It was at this period when he kept the most close to the lagoon side, and, as far as he dared, abode in the cover of his hut.

The cause of the second period was talk he heard from his wife and the chief islanders. Keola himself said little. He was never so sure of his new friends, for he judged they were too civil to be wholesome, and since he had grown better acquainted with his father-in-law the man had grown more cautious. So he told them nothing of himself, but only his name and descent, and that he came from the Eight Islands, and what fine islands they were; and about the king's palace in Honolulu, and how he was a chief friend of the king and the missionaries. But he put many questions and learned much. The island where he was was called the Isle of Voices; it belonged to the tribe, but they made their home upon another, three hours' sail to the southward. There they lived and had their permanent houses, and it was a rich island, where were eggs and chickens and pigs, and ships came trading with rum and tobacco. It was there the schooner had gone after Keola deserted; there, too, the mate had died, like the fool of a white man as he was. It seems, when the ship came, it was the beginning of the sickly season in that isle; when the fish of the lagoon are poisonous, and all who eat of them swell up and die. The mate was told of it; he saw the boats preparing, because in that season the people leave that island and sail to the Isle of Voices; but he was a fool of a white man, who would believe no stories but his own, and he caught one of these fish, cooked it and ate it, and swelled up and died, which was good news to Keola. As for the Isle of Voices, it lay solitary the most part of the year; only now and then a boat's crew came for copra, and in the bad season, when the fish at the main isle were poisonous, the tribe dwelt there in a body. It had its name from a marvel, for it seemed the seaside of it was all beset with invisible devils; day and night you heard them talking one with another in strange tongues; day and night little fires blazed up and were extinguished on the beach; and what was the cause of these doings no man might conceive. Keola asked them if it were the same in their island where they stayed, and they told him no, not there; nor yet in any other of some hundred isles that lay all about them in that sea; but it was a thing peculiar to the Isle of Voices. They told him also that these fires and voices were ever on the seaside and in the seaward fringes of the wood, and a man might dwell by the lagoon two thousand years (if he could live so long) and never be any way troubled; and even on the seaside the devils did no harm if let alone. Only once a chief had cast a spear at one of the voices, and the same night he fell out of a cocoa-nut palm and was killed.

Keola thought a good bit with himself. He saw he would be all right when the tribe returned to the main island, and right enough where he was, if he kept by the lagoon, yet he had a mind to make things righter if he could. So he told the high chief he had once been in an isle that was pestered the same way, and the folk had found a means to cure that trouble.

'There was a tree growing in the bush there,' says he, 'and it seems these devils came to get the leaves of it. So the people of the isle cut down the tree wherever it was found, and the devils came no more.'

They asked what kind of tree this was, and he showed them the tree of which Kalamake burned the leaves. They found it hard to believe, yet the idea tickled them. Night after night the old men debated it in their councils, but the high chief (though he was a brave man) was afraid of the matter, and reminded them daily of the chief who cast a spear against the voices and was killed, and the thought of that brought all to a stand again.

Though he could not yet bring about the destruction of the trees, Keola was well enough pleased, and began to look about him and take pleasure in his days; and, among other things, he was the kinder to his wife, so that the girl began to love him greatly. One day he came to the hut, and she lay on the ground lamenting.

'Why,' said Keola, 'what is wrong with you now?'

She declared it was nothing.

The same night she woke him. The lamp burned very low, but he saw by her face she was in sorrow.

'Keola', she said, 'put your ear to my mouth that I may whisper, for no one must hear us. Two days before the boats begin to be got ready, go you to the seaside of the isle and lie in a thicket. We shall choose that place beforehand, you and I; and hide food; and every night I shall come near by there singing. So when a night comes and you do not hear me, you shall know we are clean gone out of the island, and you may come forth again in safety.

The soul of Keola died within him.

'What is this?' he cried, 'I cannot live among devils. I will not be left behind upon this isle. I am dying to leave it.'

'You will never leave it alive, my poor Keola,' said the girl; 'for to tell you the truth, my people are eaters of men; but this they keep secret. And the reason they will kill you before we leave is because in our island ships come, and Donat-Kimaran comes and talks for the French, and there is a white trader there in a house with a verandah, and a catechist. O, that is a fine place indeed! The trader has barrels filled with flour; and a French warship once came in the lagoon and gave everybody wine and biscuit. Ah, my poor Keola, I wish I could take you there, for great is my love to you, and it is the finest place in the seas except Papeete.'

So now Keola was the most terrified man in the four oceans. He had heard tell of eaters of men in the south islands, and the thing had always been a fear to him; and here it was knocking at his door. He had heard besides, by travellers, of their practices, and how when they are in a mind to eat a man they cherish and fondle him like a mother with a favourite baby. And he saw this must be his own case; and that was why he had been housed, and fed, and wived, and liberated from all work; and why the old men and the chiefs discoursed with him like a person of weight. So he lay on his bed and railed upon his destiny; and the flesh curdled on his bones.

The next day the people of the tribe were very civil, as their way was. They were elegant speakers, and they made beautiful poetry, and jested at meals, so that a missionary must have died laughing. It was little enough Keola cared for their fine ways; all he saw was the white teeth shining in their mouths, and his gorge rose at the sight; and when they were done eating, he went and lay in the bush like a dead man.

The next day it was the same, and then his wife followed him.

'Keola,' she said, 'if you do not eat, I tell you plainly you will be killed and cooked tomorrow. Some of the old chiefs are murmuring already. They think you are fallen sick and must lose flesh.'

With that Keola got to his feet, and anger burned in him.

'It is little I care one way or the other,' said he. 'I am between the devil and the deep sea. Since die I must, let me die the quickest way; and since I must be eaten at the best of it, let me rather be eaten by hobgoblins than by men. Farewell,' said he, and he left her standing, and walked to the seaside of the island.

It was all bare in the strong sun; there was no sign of man, only the beach was trodden, and all about him as he went the voices talked and whispered, and the little fires sprang up and burned down. All tongues of the earth were spoken there; the French, the Dutch, the Russian, the Tamil, the Chinese. Whatever land knew sorcery, there were some of its people whispering in Keola's ear. That beach was thick as a cried fair, yet no man seen; and as he walked he saw the shells vanish before him, and no man to pick them up. I think the devil would have been afraid to be alone in such a company: but Keola was past fear and courted death. When the fires sprang up, he charged for them like a bull. Bodiless voices called to and fro; unseen hands poured sand upon the flames; and they were gone from the beach before he reached them.

'It is plain Kalamake is not here,' he thought, 'or I must have been killed long since.'

With that he sat him down in the margin of the wood, for he was tired, and put his chin upon his hands. The business before his eyes continued: the beach babbled with voices, and the fires sprang up and sank, and the shells vanished and were renewed again even while he looked.

'It was a by-day when I was here before,' he thought, 'for it was nothing to this.'

And his head was dizzy with the thought of these millions and millions of dollars, and all these hundreds and hundreds of persons culling them upon the beach and flying in the air higher and swifter than eagles.

'And to think how they have fooled me with their talk of mints,' says he, 'and that money was made there, when it is clear that all the new coin in all the world is gathered on these sands! But I will know better the next time!' said he.

And at last, he knew not very well how or when, sleep fell on Keola, and he forgot the island and all his sorrows.

Early the next day, before the sun was yet up, a bustle woke him. He awoke in fear, for he though the tribe had caught him napping; but it was no such matter. Only, on the beach in front of him, the bodiless voices called and shouted one upon another, and it seemed they all passed and swept beside him up the coast of the island.

'What is afoot now?' thinks Keola. And it was plain to him it was something beyond ordinary, for the fires were not lighted nor the shells taken, but the bodiless voices kept posting up the beach, and hailing and dying away; and others following, and by the sound of them these wizards should be angry.

'It is not me they are angry at,' thought Keola, 'for they pass me close.'

As when hounds go by, or horses in a race, or city folk coursing to a fire, and all men join and follow after, so it was now with Keola; and he knew not what he did, nor why he did it, but there, lo and behold! he was running with the voices.

So he turned one point of the island, and this brought him in view of a second; and there he remembered the wizard trees to have been growing by the score together in a wood. From this point there went up a hubbub of men

crying not to be described; and by the sound of them, those
that he ran with shaped their course of the same quarter.
A little nearer, and there began to mingle with the outcry
the crash of many axes. And at this a thought came at last
into his mind that the high chief had consented; that the
men of the tribe had set-to cutting down these trees; that
word had gone about the isle from sorcerer to sorcerer, and
these were all now assembling to defend their trees. Desire
of strange things swept him on. He posted with the voices,
crossed the beach, and came into the borders of the wood,
and stood astonished. One tree had fallen, others were part
hewed away. There was the tribe clustered. They were back
to back, and bodies lay, and blood flowed among their feet.
The hue of fear was on all their faces: their voices went up
to heaven shrill as a weasel's cry.

Have you seen a child when he is all alone and has a
wooden sword, and fights, leaping and hewing with the
empty air? Even so the man-eaters huddled back to back,
and heaved up their axes, and laid on, and screamed as
they laid on, and behold! no man to contend with them!
only here and there Keola saw an axe swinging over against
them without hands; and time and again a man of the tribe
would fall before it, clove in twain or burst asunder, and
his soul sped howling.

For a while Keola looked upon this prodigy like one that
dreams, and then fear took him by the midst as sharp as
death, that he should behold such doings. Even in that
same flash the high chief of the clan espied him standing,
and pointed and called out his name. Thereat the whole
tribe saw him also, and their eyes flashed, and their teeth
clashed.

'I am too long here,' thought Keola, and ran further out of the wood and down the beach, not caring
whither.

'Keola!' said a voice close by upon empty sand.

'Lehua! is that you?' he cried, and gasped, and looked
in vain for her; but by the eyesight he was stark alone.

'I saw you pass before,' the voice answered; 'but you
would not hear me. – Quick! get the leaves and herbs, and
let us free.'

'You are there with the mat?' he asked.

'Here, at your side,' said she. And he felt her arms about

him. – Quick! the leaves and the herbs, before my father can get back!'

So Keola ran for his life, and fetched the wizard fuel: and Lehua guided him back, and set his feet upon the mat, and made the fire. All the time of its burning the sound of battle towered out of the wood; the wizards and the man-eaters hard at fight; the wizards, the viewless ones, roaring out aloud like bulls upon a mountain, and the men of the tribe replying shrill and savage out of the terror of their souls. And all the time of the burning, Keola stood there and listened, and shook, and watched how the unseen hands of Lehua poured the leaves. She poured them fast, and the flame burned high, and scorched Keola's hands; and she speeded and blew the burning with her breath. The last leaf was eaten, the flame fell, and the shock followed, and there were Keola and Lehua in the room at home.

Now, when Keola could see his wife at last he was mighty pleased, and he was mighty pleased to be home again in Molokai and sit down beside a bowl of poi[1] – for they make no poi on board ships, and there was none in the Isle of Voices – and he was out of the body with pleasure to be clean escaped out of the hands of the eaters of men. But there was another matter not so clear, and Lehua and Keola talked of it all night and were troubled. There was Kalamake left upon the isle. If, by the blessing of God, he could but stick there, all were well; but should he escape and return to Molokai, it would be an ill day for his daughter and her husband. They spoke of his gift of swelling, and whether he could wade that distance in the seas. But Keola knew by this time where that island was – and that is to say, in the Low or Dangerous Archipelago. So they fetched the atlas and looked upon the distance in the map, and by what they could make of it, it seemed a far way for an old gentleman to walk. Still, it would not do to make too sure of a warlock like Kalamake, and they determined at last to take counsel of a white missionary.

So the first one that came by, Keola told him everything. And the missionary was very sharp on him for taking the second wife in the low island; but for all

---

1. A fermented porridge made from the ground-up roots of the taro plant.

the rest, he vowed he could make neither head nor
tail of it.

'However,' says he, 'if you think this money of your
father's ill gotten, my advice to you would be, give some
of it to the lepers and some to the missionary fund. And
as for this extraordinary rigmarole, you cannot do better
than keep it to yourselves.'

But he warned the police at Honolulu that, by all he
could make out, Kalamake and Keola had been coining
false money, and it would not be amiss to watch them.

Keola and Lehua took his advice, and gave many dollars
to the lepers and the fund. And no doubt the advice must
have been good, for from that day to this Kalamake has
never more been heard of. But whether he was slain in the
battle by the trees, or whether he is still kicking his heels
upon the Isle of Voices, who shall say?

The Beach of Falesá

ONE. A SOUTH SEA BRIDAL

I saw that island first when it was neither night nor morning. The moon was to the west, setting but still broad and bright. To the east, and right amidships of the dawn, which was all pink, the daystar sparkled like a diamond. The land breeze blew in our faces and smelt strong of wild lime and vanilla: other things besides, but these were the most plain; and the chill of it set me sneezing. I should say I had been for years on a low island near the line, living for the most part solitary among natives. Here was a fresh experience; even the tongue would be quite strange to me; and the look of these woods and mountains, and the rare smell of them, renewed my blood.

The captain blew out the binnacle lamp.

'There,' said he, 'there goes a bit of smoke, Mr Wiltshire, behind the break of the reef. That's Falesá[1] where your station is, the last village to the east; nobody lives to windward, I don't know why. Take my glass, and you can make the houses out.'

I took the glass; and the shores leaped nearer, and I saw the tangle of woods and the breach of the surf, and the brown roofs and the black insides of houses peeped among the trees.

'Do you catch a bit of white there to the east'ard?' the captain continued. 'That's your house. Coral built, stands high, verandah you could walk on three abreast: best station in the South Pacific. When old Adams saw it, he took and shook me by the hand. – "I've dropped into a soft thing here," says he. – "So you have," says I, "and time too!"

1. A fictional place. The word means 'sacred house'.
   Stevenson knew the meaning of the word, and
   presumably chose it deliberately.

Poor Johnny! I never saw him again but the once, and
then he had changed his tune – couldn't get on with the
natives, or the whites, or something; and the next time we
came round, there he was dead and buried. I took and put
up a bit of a stick to him: "John Adams, *obit* eighteen and
sixty eight. Go thou and do likewise." I missed that man;
I never could see much harm in Johnny.'

'What did he die of?' I inquired.

'Some kind of a sickness,' says the captain. 'It appears it
took him sudden. Seems he got up in the night, and filled
up on Pain-Killer and Kennedy's Discovery: no go – he was
booked beyond Kennedy. Then he had tried to open a case
of gin; no go again – not strong enough. Then he must have
turned to and run out on the verandah, and capsized over
the rail. When they found him the next day, he was clean
crazy – carried on all the time about somebody watering
his copra. Poor John!'

'Was it thought to be the island?' I asked.

'Well, it was thought to be the island, or the trouble, or
something,' he replied. 'I never could hear but what it was
a healthy place. Our last man, Vigours, never turned a hair.
He left because of the beach; said he was afraid of Black
Jack and Case and Whistling Jimmie, who was still alive
at the time but got drowned soon afterward when drunk.
As for old Captain Randall, he's been here any time since
eighteen forty, forty five. I never could see much harm in
Billy, nor much change. Seems as if he might live to be
old Kafoozleum. No, I guess it's healthy.'

'There's a boat coming now,' said I. 'She's right in the
pass; looks to be a sixteen foot whale; two white men in
the stern sheets.'

'That's the boat that drowned Whistling Jimmie!' cried
the captain. 'Let's see the glass. Yes: that's Case, sure
enough, and the darkie. They've got a gallows bad
reputation, but you know what a place the beach is for
talking. My belief, that Whistling Jimmie was the worst
of the trouble; and he's gone to glory, you see. What'll
you bet they ain't after gin? Lay you five to two they take
six cases.'

When these two traders came aboard I was pleased with
the looks of them at once, or rather, with the looks of both,
and the speech of one. I was sick for white neighbours after

my four years at the line, which I always counted years
of prison; getting tabooed, and going down to the Speak
House to see and get it taken off; buying gin, and going
on a break, and then repenting; sitting in my house at
night with the lamp for company; or walking on the beach
and wondering what kind of a fool to call myself for being
where I was. There were no other whites upon my island;
and when I sailed to the next, rough customers made the
most of the society. Now to see these two when they came
aboard, was a pleasure. One was a negro to be sure; but
they were both rigged out smart in striped pyjamas and
straw hats, and Case would have passed muster in a city.
He was yellow and smallish; had a hawk's nose to his face,
pale eyes, and his beard trimmed with scissors. No man
knew his country, beyond he was of English speech; and
it was clear he came of a good family and was splendidly
educated. He was accomplished too; played the accordion
first rate; and give him a piece of string or a cork or a
pack of cards, and he could show you tricks equal to
any professional. He could speak when he chose fit for
a drawing room; and when he chose he could blaspheme
worse than a Yankee boatswain and talk smut to sicken a
kanaka. The way he thought would pay best at the moment,
that was Case's way; and it always seemed to come natural
and like as if he was born to it. He had the courage of a
lion and the cunning of a rat; and if he's not in Hell today,
there's no such place. I know but one good point to the
man; that he was fond of his wife and kind to her. She
was a Sāmoa woman, and dyed her hair red, Sāmoa style;
and when he came to die (as I have to tell of) they found
one strange thing, that he had made a will like a christian
and the widow got the lot. All his, they said, and all Black
Jack's, and the most of Billy Randall's in the bargain; for
it was Case that kept the books. So she went off home in
the schooner *Manu'a*, and does the lady to this day in her
own place.

But of all this, on that first morning, I knew no more
than a fly. Case used me like a gentleman and like a friend,
made me welcome to Falesá, and put his services at my
disposal, which was the more helpful from my ignorance
of the native. All the early part of the day, we sat drinking
better acquaintance in the cabin, and I never heard a man

talk more to the point. There was no smarter trader, and none dodgier, in the islands. I remember one bit of advice he gave that morning, and one yarn he told. The bit of advice was this. 'Whenever you get hold of any money,' says he – 'any christian money, I mean – the first thing to do is to fire it up to Sydney to the bank. It's only a temptation to a copra merchant; some day, he'll be in a row with the other traders, and he'll get his shirt out and buy copra with it. And the name of the man that buys copra with gold is Damfool,' says he. That was the advice; and this was the yarn, which might have opened my eyes to the danger of that man for a neighbour, if I had been anyway suspicious. It seems Case was trading somewhere in the Ellices. There was a man Miller a Dutchman there, who had a strong hold with the natives and handled the bulk of what there was. Well one fine day a schooner got wrecked in the lagoon, and Miller bought her (the way these things are usually managed) for an old song, which was the ruin of him. For having a lot of trade on hand that had cost him practically nothing, what does he do but begin cutting rates? Case went round to the other traders. 'Wants to lower prices?' says Case. 'All right, then. He has five times the turn-over of any of us; if buying at a loss is the game, he stands to lose five times more. Let's give him the bed rock; let's bilge the——!' And so they did, and five months after, Miller had to sell out his boat and station, and begin again somewhere in the Carolines.

All this talk suited me, and my new companion suited me, and I thought Falesá seemed to be the right kind of a place; and the more I drank, the lighter my heart. Our last trader had fled the place at half an hour's notice, taking a chance passage in a labour ship from up west; the captain, when he came, had found the station closed, the keys left with the native pastor, and a letter from the runaway confessing he was fairly frightened of his life. Since then the firm had not been represented and of course there was no cargo; the wind besides was fair, the captain hoped he could make his next island by dawn, with a good tide; and the business of landing my trade was gone about lively. There was no call for me to fool with it, Case said; nobody would touch my things, everyone was honest in Falesá, only about chickens or an odd knife or an odd stick of tobacco; and the best I could do was to sit quiet till the vessel left, then come straight to his house, see old Captain Randall, the father of the Beach, take pot luck, and go home to sleep when it got dark. So it was high noon, and the schooner was under way, before I set my foot on shore at Falesá.

I had a glass or two on board, I was just off a long cruise and the ground heaved under me like a ship's deck. The world was like all new painted; my foot went along to music; Falesá might have been Fiddler's Green, if there is such a place, and more's the pity if there isn't! It was good to foot the grass, to look aloft at the green mountains, to see the men with their green wreaths and the women in their bright dresses, red and blue. On we went, in the strong sun and the cool shadow, liking both; and all the children in the town came trotting after with their shaven heads and their brown bodies, and raising a thin kind of a cheer in our wake, like crowing poultry.

'By the by,' says Case, 'we must get you a wife.'

'That's so,' said I, 'I had forgotten.'

There was a crowd of girls about us, and I pulled myself up and looked among them like a Bashaw. They were all dressed out for the sake of the ship being in; and the women of Falesá are a handsome lot to see. If they have a fault, they are a trifle broad in the beam; and I was just thinking so when Case touched me.

'That's pretty,' says he.

I saw one coming on the other side alone. She had been fishing; all she wore was a chemise, and it was wetted through, and a cutty sark at that. She was young and very slender for an island maid, with a long face, a high forehead, and a sly, strange, blindish look between a cat's and a baby's.

'Who's she?' said I. 'She'll do.'

'That's Uma,' said Case, and he called her up and spoke to her in the native. I didn't know what he said; but when he was in the midst, she looked up at me quick and timid like a child dodging a blow; then down again; and presently smiled. She had a wide mouth, the lips and the chin cut like any statue's; and the smile came out for a moment and was gone. There she stood with her head bent and heard Case to an end; spoke back in the pretty Polynesian voice, looking him full in the face; heard him again in answer; and then with an obeisance started off. I had just a share of the bow, but never another shot of her eye; and there was no more word of smiling.

'I guess it's all right,' said Case. 'I guess you can have her. I'll make it square with the old lady. You can have your pick of the lot for a plug of tobacco,' he added, sneering.

I suppose it was the smile stuck in my memory, for I spoke back sharp. 'She doesn't look that sort,' I cried.

'I don't know that she is,' said Case. 'I believe she's as right as the mail. Keeps to herself, don't go round with the gang, and that. O, no, don't you misunderstand me – Uma's on the square.' He spoke eager I thought, and that surprised and pleased me. 'Indeed,' he went on, 'I shouldn't make so sure of getting her, only she cottoned to the cut of your jib. All you have to do is to keep dark and let me work the mother my own way; and I'll bring the girl round to the captain's for the marriage.'

I didn't care for the word marriage, and I said so.

'O, there's nothing to hurt in the marriage,' says he. 'Black Jack's the chaplain.'

By this time we had come in view of the house of these three white men; for a negro is counted a white man – and so is a Chinese! a strange idea, but common in the islands. It was a board house with a strip of ricketty verandah. The store was to the front, with a counter, scales and the poorest possible display of trades: a case or two of tinned meats; a barrel of hard bread; a few bolts of cotton stuff, not to be compared with mine; the only thing well represented being the contraband – fire arms and liquor. 'If these are my only rivals,' thinks I, 'I should do well in Falesá.' Indeed there was only the one way they could touch me, and that was with the guns and drink.

In the back room was old Captain Randall, squatting on the floor native fashion, fat and pale, naked to the waist, gray as a badger and his eyes set with drink. His body was covered with gray hair and crawled over by flies; one was in the corner of his eye – he never heeded; and the mosquitoes hummed about the man like bees. Any clean-minded man would have had the creature out at once and buried him; and to see him, and think he was seventy, and remember he had once commanded a ship, and come ashore in his smart togs, and talked big in bars and consulates, and sat in club verandahs, turned me sick and sober.

He tried to get up when I came in, but that was hopeless, so he reached me a hand instead and stumbled out some salutation.

'Papa's pretty full this morning,' observed Case. 'We've had an epidemic here; and Captain Randall takes gin for a prophylactic – don't you, papa?'

'Never took such thing my life!' cried the captain, indignantly. 'Take gin for my health's sake, Mr Wha's-ever-your-name. 'S a preacaution'ry measure.'

'That's all right, papa,' said Case. 'But you'll have to brace up. There's going to be a marriage, Mr Wiltshire here is going to get spliced.'

The old man asked to whom.

'To Uma,' said Case.

'Uma?' cried the captain. 'Wha's he want Uma for? 'S he come here for his health, anyway? Wha' 'n hell's he want Uma for?'

'Dry up papa,' said Case. 'Tain't you that's to marry her. I guess you're not her godfather and godmother, I guess Mr Wiltshire's going to please himself.'

With that he made an excuse to me that he must move about the marriage, and left me alone with the poor wretch that was his partner and (to speak truth) his gull. Trade and station belonged both to Randall; Case and the negro were parasites; they crawled and fed upon him like the flies, he none the wiser. Indeed I have no harm to say of Billy Randall, beyond the fact that my gorge rose at him, and the time I now passed in his company was like a nightmare.

The room was stifling hot and full of flies; for the house was dirty and low and small, and stood in a bad place, behind the village, in the borders of the bush, and sheltered from the trade. The three men's beds were on the floor, and a litter of pans and dishes. There was no standing furniture, Randall, when he was violent, tearing it to laths. There I sat, and had a meal which was served us by Case's wife; and there I was entertained all day by that remains of man, his tongue stumbling among low old jokes and long old stories, and his own wheezy laughter always ready, so that he had no sense of depression. He was nipping gin all the while; sometimes he fell asleep and awoke again whimpering and shivering, and every now and again he would ask me why in Hell I wanted to marry Uma. 'My friend,' I was telling myself all day, 'you must not be an old gentleman like this.'

It might be four in the afternoon perhaps, when the backdoor was thrust slowly open, and a strange old native woman crawled into the house almost on her belly. She was swathed in black stuff to her heels; her hair was gray in swatches; her face was tattooed, which was not the practise in that island; her eyes big and bright and crazy. These she fixed upon me with a wrapt expression that I saw to be part acting; she said no plain word, but smacked and mumbled with her lips, and hummed aloud, like a child over its Christmas pudding. She came straight across the house heading for me, and as soon as she was alongside, caught up my hand and purred and crooned over it like a great cat. From this she slipped into a kind of song.

'Who in the devil's this?' cried I, for the thing startled me.

'It's Faavao,' says Randall, and I saw he had hitched along the floor into the farthest corner.

'You ain't afraid of her?' I cried.

'Me 'fraid!' cried the captain. 'My dear friend, I defy her! I don't let her put her foot in here. Only I suppose 's diff'ent today for the marriage. 'S Uma's mother.'

'Well, suppose it is, what's she carrying on about?' I asked, more irritated, perhaps more frightened than I cared to show; and the captain told me she was making up a quantity of poetry in my praise because I was to marry Uma. 'All right, old lady,' says I, with rather a failure of a laugh. 'Anything to oblige. But when you're done with my hand, you might let me know.'

She did as though she understood; the song rose into a cry and stopped; the woman crouched out of the house the same way that she came in, and must have plunged straight into the bush, for when I followed her to the door she had already vanished.

'These are rum manners,' said I.

''S a rum crowd,' said the captain, and to my surprise he made the sign of the cross on his bare bosom.

'Hillo!' says I, 'are you a papist?'

He repudiated the idea with contempt. 'Hard-shell Baptis',' said he. 'But, my dear friend, the papists got some good ideas too; and tha' 's one of 'em. You take my advice, and whenever you come across Uma or Faavao or Vigours or any of that crowd, you take a leaf out o' the priests, and do what I do: savvy?' says he, repeated the sign, and winked his dim eye at me. 'No, *sir*!' he broke out again, 'no papists here!' and for a long time entertained me with his religious opinions.

I must have been taken with Uma from the first, or I should certainly have fled from that house and got into the clean air, and the clean sea or some convenient river. Though it's true I was committed to Case; and besides I could never have held my head up in that island, if I had run from a girl upon my wedding night.

The sun was down, the sky all on fire and the lamp had been sometime lighted, when Case came back with Uma and the negro. She was dressed and scented; her kilt was of fine tapa,[1] looking richer in the folds than any silk; and behind which was of the colour of dark honey, she wore bare only for some half a dozen necklaces of seeds and flowers; and behind her ears and in her hair, she had the scarlet flowers of the hybiscus. She showed the best bearing for a bride conceivable, serious and still; and I thought shame to stand up with her in that mean house and before that grinning negro. I thought shame I say; for the mountebank was dressed with a big paper collar, the book he made believe to read from was an odd volume of a novel, and the words of his service not fit to be set down. My conscience smote me when we joined hands; and when she got her certificate, I was tempted to throw up in bargain and confess. Here is the document: it was Case that wrote it, signatures and all, in a leaf out of the ledger.

This is to certify that *Uma* daughter of *Faavao* of Falesá island of——, is illegally married to *Mr John Wiltshire* for one night, and Mr John Wiltshire is at liberty to send her to hell next morning.

John Blackamoor
Chaplain to the Hulks

Extracted from the register
by William T. Randall
Master Mariner.

1. Bark cloth, a material made in many parts of the Pacific.

That was a nice paper to put in a girl's hand and see her hide away like gold. A man might easily feel cheap for less. But it was the practise in these parts, and (as I told myself) not the least the fault of us White Men but of the missionaries. If they had let the natives be, I had never needed this deception, but taken all the wives I wished, and left them when I pleased, with a clear conscience.

The more ashamed I was, the more hurry I was in to be gone; and our desires thus jumping together, I made the less remark of a change in the traders. Case had been all eagerness to keep me; now, as though he had attained a purpose, he seemed all eagerness to have me go. Uma, he said, could show me to my house, and the three bade us farewell indoors.

The night was nearly come; the village smelt of trees, and flowers and the sea, and breadfruit cooking; there came a fine roll of sea from the reef, and from a distance, among the woods and houses, many pretty sounds of men and children. It did me good to breathe free air; it did me good to be done with the captain and see, instead, the creature at my side. I felt for all the world as though she were some girl at home in the old country, and forgetting myself for a minute, took her hand to walk with. Her fingers nestled into mine; I heard her breathe deep and quick; and all at once she caught my hand to her face and pressed it there. 'You good!' she cried, and ran ahead of me, and stopped and looked back and smiled, and ran ahead of me again; thus guiding me through the edge of the bush and by a quiet way to my own house.

The truth is Case had done the courting for me in style; told her I was mad to have her and cared nothing for the consequence; and the poor soul, knowing that which I was still ignorant of, believed it every word, and had her head nigh turned with vanity and gratitude. Now of all this I had no guess; I was one of those most opposed to any nonsense about native women, having seen so many whites eaten up by their wives' relatives and made fools of in the bargain; and I told myself I must make a stand at once and bring her to her bearings. But she looked so quaint and pretty as she ran away and then awaited me, and the thing was done so like a child or a kind of dog, that the best I could do was just to follow her whenever she went on, to listen for the fall of her bare feet, and to watch in the dusk for the shining of her body. And there was another thought came in my head. She played kitten with me now when we were alone; but in the house she had carried it the way a countess might, so proud and humble. And what with her dress – for all there was so little of it, and that native enough – what with her fine tapa and fine scents, and her red flowers and seeds that were quite as bright as jewels, only larger – it came over me she was a kind of a countess really, dressed to hear great singers at a concert, and no even mate for a poor trader like myself.

She was the first in the house; and while I was still without, I saw a match flash and the lamplight kindle in the windows. The station was a wonderful fine place, coral built, with quite a wide verandah, and the main room high and wide. My chest and cases had been piled in, and made rather of a mess; and there, in the thick of the confusion, stood Uma by the table, awaiting me. Her shadow went all the way up behind her into the hollow of the iron roof; she stood against it bright, the lamplight shining on her skin. I stopped in the door, and she looked at me, not speaking, with eyes that were eager and yet daunted. Then she touched herself on the bosom. 'Me – your wifie,' she said. It had never taken me like that before; but the want of her took and shook all through me, like the wind in the luff of a sail.

I could not speak, if I had wanted; and if I could, I would not. I was ashamed to be so much moved about a native, ashamed of the marriage too, and the certificate she had treasured in her kilt; and I turned aside and made believe to rummage among my cases. The first thing I lighted on was a case of gin, the only one that I had brought; and partly for the girl's sake, and partly for the horror of the recollection of old Randall, took a sudden resolve. I prized the lid off; one by one, I drew the bottles with a pocket corkscrew, and sent Uma out to pour the stuff from the verandah.

She came back after the last, and looked at me puzzled like.

'Why you do that?' she asked.

'No good,' said I, for I was now a little better master of my tongue. 'Man he drink, he no good.'

She agreed with this but kept considering. 'Why you

bring him?' she asked presently. 'Suppose you no want drink, you no bring him, I think.'

'That's all right,' said I. 'One time I want drink too much; now no want. You see I no savvy I get one little wifie. Suppose I drink gin, my little wifie he 'fraid.'

To speak to her kindly was about more than I was fit for; I had made my vow I would never let on to weakness with a native; and I had nothing for it but to stop.

She stood looking gravely down at me where I sat by the open case. 'I think you good man,' she said. And suddenly she had fallen before me on the floor. 'I belong you all-e-same pig!' she cried.

TWO. THE BAN

I came on the verandah just before the sun rose on the morrow. My house was the last on the east; there was a cape of woods and cliffs behind that hid the sunrise. To the west, a swift cold river ran down, and beyond was the green of the village, dotted with cocoapalms and breadfruits and houses. The shutters were some of them down and some open; I saw the mosquito bars still stretched, with shadows of people new wakened sitting up inside; and all over the green others were stalking silent, wrapped in their many-coloured sleeping clothes like Bedouins in bible pictures. It was mortal still and solemn and chilly; and the light of the dawn on the lagoon was like the shining of a fire.

But the thing that troubled me was nearer hand. Some dozen young men and children made a piece of a half circle, flanking my house; the river divided them, some were on the near side, some on the far, and one on a boulder in the midst; and they all sat silent, wrapped in their sheets, and stared at me and my house as straight as pointer dogs. I thought it strange as I went out. When I had bathed and come back again, and found them all there, and two or three more along with them, I thought it stranger still. What could they see to gaze at in my house? I wondered, and went in.

But the thought of these starers stuck in my mind, and presently I came out again. The sun was now up, but it was still behind the cape of woods: say quarter of an hour had come and gone. The crowd was greatly increased, the far bank of the river was lined for quite a way; perhaps thirty grown folk, and of children twice as many, some standing, some squatted on the ground, and all staring at my house. I have seen a house in a South Sea village

175

thus surrounded, but then a trader was thrashing his wife inside, and she singing out. Here was nothing: the stove was alight, the smoke going up in a Christian manner; all was shipshape and Bristol fashion. To be sure, there was a stranger come; but they had a chance to see that stranger yesterday and took it quiet enough. What ailed them now? I leaned my arms on the rail and stared back. Devil a wink they had in them. Now and then I could see the children chatter, but they spoke so low not even the hum of their speaking came my length. The rest were like graven images; they stared at me, dumb and sorrowful, with their bright eyes; and it came upon me things would look not much different, if I were on the platform of the gallows, and these good folk had come to see me hanged.

I felt I was getting daunted, and began to be afraid I looked it, which would never do. Up I stood, made believe to stretch myself, came down the verandah stair, and strolled towards the river. There went a short buzz from one to the other, like what you hear in theatres when the curtain goes up; and some of the nearest gave back the matter of a pace. I saw a girl lay one hand on a young man and make a gesture upward with the other; at the same time she said something in the native with a gasping voice. Three little boys sat beside my path, where I must pass within three feet of them. Wrapped in their sheets, with their shaved heads and bits of topknots, and queer faces, they looked like figures on a chimney piece. Awhile they sat their ground, solemn as judges; I came up hand over fist, doing my five knots, like a man that meant business; and I thought I saw a sort of a wink and gulp in the three faces. The one jumped up (he was the farthest off) and ran for his mammy. The other two, trying to follow suit, got foul, came to ground together bawling, wriggled right out of their sheets – and in a moment there were all three of them, two mother naked, scampering for their lives and singing out like pigs. The natives, who would never let a joke slip even at a burial, laughed and let up, as short as a dog's bark.

They say it scares a man to be alone. No such thing. What scares him in the dark or the high bush, is that he can't make sure, and there might be an army at his elbow. What scares him worst is to be right in the midst of a crowd, and have no guess of what they're driving at. When that laugh stopped, I stopped too. The boys had not yet made their offing, they were still on the full stretch going the one way, when I had already gone about ship and was sheering off the other. Like a fool I had come out, doing my five knots, like a fool I went back again. It must have been the funniest thing to see, and what knocked me silly, this time no one laughed; only one old woman gave a kind of pious moan, the way you have heard dissenters in their chapels at the sermon.

'I never saw such damfool kanakas as your people here,' I said once to Uma, glancing out of the window at the starers.

'Savvy nothing,' says Uma, with a kind of a disgusted air that she was good at.

And that was all the talk we had upon the matter, for I was put out, and Uma took the thing so much as a matter of course, that I was fairly ashamed.

All day, off and on, now fewer and now more, the fools sat about the west end of my house and across the river, waiting for the show, whatever that was – fire to come down from heaven, I suppose, and consume me bones and baggage. But by evening, like real islanders, they had wearied of the business; and got away and had a dance instead in the big house of the village, where I heard them singing and clapping hands till maybe ten at night; and the next day, it seemed they had forgotten I existed. If fire had come down from heaven or the earth opened and swallowed me, there would have been nobody to see the sport or take the lesson, or whatever you like to call it. But I was to find they hadn't forgot either, and kept an eye lifting for phenomena over my way.

I was hard at it both these days getting my trade in order, and taking stock of what Vigours had left. This was a job that made me pretty sick, and kept me from thinking on much else. Ben had taken stock the trip before, I knew I could trust Ben; but it was plain somebody had been making free in the meantime. I found I was out by what might easy cover six months salary and profit; and I could have kicked myself all round the village to have been such a blamed ass, sitting boozing with that Case, instead of attending to my own affairs and taking stock.

However, there's no use crying over spilt milk. It was done now and couldn't be undone. All I could do was to get what was left of it, and my new stuff (my own choice) in order, to go round and get after the rats and cockroaches, and to fix up that store regular Sydney style. A fine show I made of it; and the third morning, when I had lit my pipe and stood in the doorway and looked in – and turned and looked far up the mountain, and saw the cocoanuts waving, and saw the island dandies, and reckoned up the yards of print they wanted for their kilts and dresses – I felt as if I was in the right place to make a fortune, and go home again, and start a public house. There was I sitting in that verandah, in as handsome a piece of scenery as you could find, a splendid sun, and a fine, fresh healthy trade that stirred up a man's blood like seabathing; and the whole thing was clean gone from me, and I was dreaming England, which is after all a nasty, cold, muddy hole, with not enough light to see to read by – and dreaming the looks of my public, by a kant of a broad highroad like an avenue and with the sign on a green tree.

So much for the morning, but the day passed and the devil any one looked near me, and from all I knew of natives in other islands, I thought this strange. People laughed a little at our firm, and their fine stations, and at this station of Falesá in particular: all the copra in the district wouldn't pay for it (I had heard them say) in fifty years; which I supposed was an exaggeration. But when the day went and no business came at all, I began to get down-hearted, and about three in the afternoon, I went out for a stroll to cheer me up. On the green I saw a white man coming with a cassock on, by which and by the face of him, I knew he was a priest. He was a good natured old soul to look at, gone a little grizzled, and so dirty you could have written with him on a piece of paper.

'Good day, sir,' says I.

He answered me eagerly in native.

'Don't you speak any English?' said I.

'Franch,' says he.

'Well,' said I, 'I'm sorry, but I can't do anything there.'

He tried me awhile in the French, and then again in native, which he seemed to think was the best chance.

I made out he was after more than passing the time of day with me, but had something to communicate, and I listened the harder. I heard the names of Adams and Case and of Randall – Randall the oftenest; and the word 'poison' or something like it; and a native word that he said very often. I went home repeating it to myself.

'What does *fussy-ocky* mean?' I asked of Uma, for that was as near as I could come to it.

'Make dead,' said she.

'The devil does it!' says I. 'Did ever you hear that Case had poisoned Johnny Adams?'

'Every man he savvy that,' says Uma, scornful like. 'Give him white sand – bad sand. He got the bottle still. Suppose he give you gin, you no take him.'

Now I had heard much the same sort of story in other islands, and the same white powder always to the front, which made me think the less of it. For all that I went over to Randall's place, to see what I could pick up, and found Case on the door step cleaning a gun.

'Good shooting here?' says I.

'A one,' says he. 'The bush is full of all kinds of birds. I wish copra was as plenty,' says he, I thought slyly, 'but there don't seem anything doing.'

I could see Black Jack in the store serving a customer.

'That looks like business, though,' said I.

'That's the first sale we've made in three weeks,' said he.

'You don't tell me?' says I. 'Three weeks? Well, well.'

'If you don't believe me,' he cries, a little hot, 'you can go and look at the copra house. It's half empty to this blessed hour.'

'I shouldn't be much the better for that, you see,' says I. 'For all I can tell, it might have been whole empty yesterday.'

'That's so,' says he, with a bit of a laugh.

'By the by,' I said, 'what sort of a party is that priest? Seems rather a friendly sort.'

At this Case laughed right out loud. 'Ah,' says he, 'I see what ails you now! Galuchet's been at you.' *Father Galoshes* was the name he went by mostly, but Case always gave it the French quirk, which was another reason we had for thinking him above the common.

'Yes, I have seen him,' says I. 'I made out he didn't think much of you or Captain Randall.'

'That he don't!' says Case. 'It was the trouble about poor Adams. The last day, when he lay dying, there was young Buncombe round. Ever met Buncombe?'

I told him no.

'He's a cure, is Buncombe!' laughs Case. 'Well, Buncombe took it in his head that as there was no other clergyman about, bar kanaka pastors, we ought to call in Father Galuchet, and have the old man administered and take the sacrament. It was all the same to me, you may suppose; but I said I thought Adams was the fellow to consult. He was jawing away about watered copra and a sight of foolery. "Look here," I said. "You're pretty sick. Would you like to see Galoshes?" He sat right up on his elbow. "Get the priest," says he, "get the priest, don't let me die here like a dog." He spoke kind of fierce and eager, but sensible enough; there was nothing to say against that; so we went and asked Galuchet if he would come. You bet he would! He jumped in his dirty linen at the thought of it. But we had reckoned without Papa. He's a hard-shell Baptist, is Papa; no papists need apply; and he took and locked the door. Buncombe told him he was bigoted, and I thought he would have had a fit. "Bigoted!" he says. "Me bigoted? Have I lived to hear it from a jackanapes like you?" And he made for Buncombe, and I had to hold them apart — and there was Adams in the middle, gone luny again and carrying on about copra like a born fool. It was good as the play, and I was about knocked out of time with laughing, when all of a sudden Adams sat up, clapped his hands to his chest, and went into the horrors.[1] He died hard, did John Adams,' says Case with a kind of a sudden sternness.

'And what became of the priest?' I asked.

'The priest?' says Case. 'O, he was hammering on the door outside, and crying on the natives to come and beat it in, and singing out it was a soul he wished to save, and that. He was in a hell of a taking was the priest. But what

1. Delirium tremens. It is tempting to think that when in *Heart of Darkness* Conrad invokes 'the horror' it might be an echo of Stevenson.

would you have? Johnny had slipped his cable; no more
Johnny in the market! and the administration racket clean
played out. Next thing, word came to Randall the priest
was praying upon Johnny's grave. Papa was pretty full,
and got a club, and lit out straight for the place; and
there was Galoshes on his knees, and a lot of natives
looking on. You wouldn't think papa cared that much
about anything, unless it was liquor; but he and the priest
stuck to it two hours, slanging each other in native; and
every time Galoshes tried to kneel down, papa went for
him with the club. There never were such larks in Falesá.
The end of it was that Captain Randall knocked over with
some kind of a fit or stroke, and the priest got in his goods
after all. But he was the angriest priest you ever heard of;
and complained to the chiefs about the outrage, as he called
it. That was no account, for our chiefs are protestant here;
and anyway he had been making trouble about the drum
for morning school, and they were glad to give him a
wipe. Now he swears old Randall gave Adams poison or
something, and when the two meet they grin at each other
like baboons.'

He told this story as natural as could be, and like a man
that enjoyed the fun; though now I come to think of it
after so long, it seems rather a sickening yarn. However
Case never set up to be soft, only to be square and hearty
and a man all round; and to tell the truth, he puzzled me
entirely.

I went home, and asked Uma if she were a *Popey*, which
I had made out to be the native word for catholics.

'*E le ai*!' says she – she always used the native when she
meant 'no' more than usually strong, and indeed there's
more of it. 'No good, popey,' she added.

Then I asked her about Adams and the priest, and she
told me much the same yarn in her own way. So that I
was left not much farther on; but inclined upon the whole,
to think the bottom of the matter was the row about the
sacrament, and the poisoning only talk.

The next day was a Sunday, when there was no business
to be looked for. Uma asked me in the morning if I was
going to 'pray'; I told her she bet not; and she stopped
home herself with no more words. I thought this seemed
unlike a native, and a native woman, and a woman that

had new clothes to show off; however, it suited me to the ground and I made the less of it. The queer thing was that I came next door to going to church after all, a thing I'm little likely to forget. I had turned out for a stroll, and heard the hymn tune up. You know how it is; if you hear folk singing, it seems to draw you; and pretty soon I found myself alongside the church. It was a little long low place, coral built, rounded off at both ends like a whale boat, a big native roof on the top of it, windows without sashes and doorways without doors. I stuck my head into one of the windows, and the sight was so new to me – for things went quite different in the islands I was acquainted with – that I stayed and looked on. The congregation sat on the floor on mats, the women on one side, the men on the other; all rigged out to kill, the women with dresses and trade hats, the men in white jackets and shirts. The hymn was over; the pastor, a big, buck kanaka, was in the pulpit preaching for his life; and by the way he wagged his hand, and worked his voice, and made his points, and seemed to argue with the folk, I made out he was a gun at the business. Well, he looked up suddenly and caught my eye; and I give you my word he staggered in the pulpit. His eyes bulged out of his head, his hand rose and pointed at me like as if against his will, and the sermon stopped right there.

It isn't a fine thing to say for yourself, but I ran away; and if the same kind of a shock was given me, I should run away again tomorrow. To see that palavering kanaka struck all of a heap at the mere sight of me, gave me a feeling as if the bottom had dropped out of the world. I went right home, and stayed there, and said nothing. You might think I would tell Uma, but that was against my system. You might have thought I would have gone over and consulted Case; but the truth was I was ashamed to speak of such a thing, I thought everyone would blurt out laughing in my face. So I held my tongue, and thought all the more, and the more I thought, the less I liked the business.

By Monday night, I got it clearly in my head I must be tabooed. A new store to stand open two days in a village, and not a man or woman come to see the trade, was past believing.

'Uma,' said I, 'I think I'm tabooed.'

'I think so,' said she.

I thought awhile whether I should ask her more, but it's a bad idea to set natives up with any notion of consulting them, so I went to Case. It was dark, and he was sitting alone, as he did mostly, smoking on the stairs.

'Case,' said I, 'here's a queer thing. I'm tabooed.'

'O, fudge!' says he. 'Tain't the practise in these islands.'

'That may be, or it mayn't,' said I. 'It's the practise where I was before; you can bet I know what it's like; and I tell it you for a fact: I'm tabooed.'

'Well,' said he; 'it ain't possible. However I'll tell you what I'll do; just to put your mind at rest, I'll go round and find out for sure. Just you waltz in and talk to papa.'

'Thank you,' I said, 'I'd rather stay right out here on the verandah: your house is so close.'

'I'll call papa out here, then,' says he.

'My dear fellow,' I says, 'I wish you wouldn't. The fact is I don't take to Mr. Randall.'

Case laughed, took a lantern from the store, and set out into the village. He was gone perhaps quarter of an hour, and he looked mighty serious when he came back.

'Well,' said he, clapping down the lantern on the verandah steps, 'I would never have believed it. I don't know where the impudence of these kanakas 'll go next, they seem to have lost all idea of respect for whites. What we want is a man of war: a German, if we could – they know how to manage kanakas.'

'I *am* tabooed then?' I cried.

'Something of the sort,' said he. 'It's the worst thing of the kind I've heard yet. But I'll stand by you, Wiltshire, man to man. You come round here tomorrow about nine and we'll have it out with the chiefs. They're afraid of me; or they used to be, but their heads are so big now I don't know what to think. Understand me, Wiltshire, I don't count this your quarrel,' he went on with a great deal of resolution; 'I count it all of our quarrel, I count it the White Man's Quarrel, and I'll stand to it through thick and thin, and there's my hand on it.'

'Have you found out what's the reason?' I asked.

'Not yet,' said Case. 'But we'll fix them down tomorrow.'

Altogether I was pretty well pleased with his attitude,

and almost more the next day when we met to go before the chiefs, to see him so stern and resolved. The chiefs awaited us in one of their big oval houses, which was marked out to us from a long way off by the crowd about the eaves, a hundred strong if there was one, men, women and children. Many of the men were on their way to work and wore green wreaths; and it put me in thoughts of the first of May at home. This crowd opened and buzzed about the pair of us as we went in, with a sudden angry animation. Five chiefs were there, four mighty stately men, the fifth old and puckered. They sat on mats in their white kilts and jackets; they had fans in their hands like fine ladies; and two of the younger ones wore catholic medals, which gave me matter of reflection. Our place was set and the mats laid for us over against these grandees on the near side of the house; the midst was empty; the crowd, close at our backs, murmured and craned and jostled to look on, and the shadows of them tossed in front of us on the clean pebbles of the floor. I was just a hair put out by the excitement of the commons, but the quiet, civil appearance of the chiefs reassured me: all the more when their spokesman began and made a long speech in a low tone of voice, sometimes waving his hand toward Case, sometimes toward me, and sometimes knocking with his knuckles on the mat. One thing was clear: there was no sign of anger in the chiefs.

'What's he been saying?' I asked, when he had done.

'O, just that they're glad to see you, and they understand by me you wish to make some kind of a complaint, and you're to fire away, and they'll do the square thing.'

'It took a precious long time to say that,' said I.

'O, the rest was sawder and *bonjour* and that,' says Case – 'you know what kanakas are!'

'Well, they don't get much *bonjour* out of me,' said I. 'You tell who I am. I'm a white man, and a British Subject, and no end of a big chief at home; and I've come here to do them good and bring them civilisation; and no sooner have I got my trade sorted out, than they go and taboo me and no one dare come near my place! Tell them I don't mean to fly in the face of anything legal; and if what they want's a present, I'll do what's fair. I don't blame any man looking out for himself, tell them, for that's human nature;

but if they think they're going to come any of their native ideas over me, they'll find then selves mistaken. And tell them plain, that I demand the reason of this treatment as a White Man and a British Subject.'

That was my speech. I know how to deal with kanakas; give them plain sense and fair dealing, and I'll do them that much justice, they knuckle under every time. They haven't any real government or any real law, that's what you've got to knock into their heads; and even if they had, it would be a good joke if it was to apply to a white man. It would be a strange thing if we came all this way and couldn't do what we pleased. The mere idea has always put my monkey up, and I rapped my speech out pretty big. Then Case translated it, or made believe to, rather; and the first chief replied, and then a second and a third, all in the same style, easy and genteel but solemn underneath. Once a question was put to Case, and he answered it, and all hands (both chiefs and commons) laughed out loud and looked at me. Last of all, the puckered old fellow and the big young chief that spoke first, started in to put Case through a kind of catechism. Sometimes I made out that Case was trying to fence, and they stuck to him like hounds, and the sweat ran down his face, which was no very pleasant sight to me; and at some of his answers, the crowd moaned and murmured, which was a worse hearing. It's a cruel shame I knew no native; for (as I now believe) they were asking Case about my marriage, and he must have had a tough job of it to clear his feet. But leave Case alone: he had the brains to run a parliament.

'Well, is that all?' I asked, when a pause came.

'Come along,' says he, mopping his face. 'I'll tell you outside.'

'Do you mean they won't take the taboo off?' I cried.

'It's something queer,' said he. 'I'll tell you outside. Better come away.'

'I won't take it at their hands,' cried I. 'I ain't that kind of a man. You don't find me turn my back on a parcel of kanakas.'

'You'd better,' said Case.

He looked at me with a signal in his eye; and the five chiefs looked at me civilly enough but kind of pointed; and the people looked at me and craned and jostled. I remembered the folks that watched my house, and how the pastor had jumped in his pulpit at the bare sight of me; and the whole business seemed so out of the way that I rose and followed Case. The crowd opened again to let us through, but wider than before, the children on the skirts running and singing out; and as we two white men walked away, they all stood and watched us.

'And now,' said I, 'what is all this about?'

'The truth is I can't rightly make it out myself. They have a down on you,' says Case.

'Taboo a man because they have a down on him!' I cried. 'I never heard the like.'

'It's worse than that, you see,' said Case. 'You ain't tabooed, I told you that couldn't be. The people won't go near you, Wiltshire; and there's where it is.'

'They won't go near me? What do you mean by that? Why won't they go near me?' I cried.

Case hesitated. 'Seems they're frightened,' says he, in a low voice.

I stopped dead short. 'Frightened?' I repeated. 'Are you gone crazy, Case? What are they frightened of?'

'I wish I could make out,' Case answered, shaking his head. 'Appears like one of their tomfool superstitions. That's what I don't cotton to,' he said; 'it's like the business about Vigours.'

'I'd like to know what you mean by that, and I'll trouble you to tell me,' says I.

'Well, you know, Vigours lit out and left all standing,' said he. 'It was some superstition business – I never got the hang of it – but it began to look bad before the end.'

'I've heard a different story about that,' said I, 'and I had better tell you so. I heard he ran away because of you.'

'O, well, I suppose he was ashamed to tell the truth,' says Case, 'I guess he thought it silly. And it's a fact that I packed him off. "What would you do, old man?" says he—"Get," says I, "and not think twice about it." I was the gladdest kind of man to see him clear away. It ain't my notion to turn back on a mate when he's in a tight place; but there was that much trouble in the village that I couldn't see where it might likely end. I was a fool to be so much about with Vigours. They cast it up to me today; didn't you hear Maea – that's the young chief, the big one

John Menzies
Glasgow Airport
VAT Reg. No. 270 3484 66
Registered Office:
John Menzies (UK) Ltd.
8/11 St. John's Lane, London

01.10.96 TALES OF   5.99

                    TOTAL   5.99
Cash Payment   10.00

                    CHANGE   4.01

Thankyou for shopping at
John Menzies

17/10/96 18:42 Tn:027763 Op:0384 1610/01

– ripping out about "Vika"? That was him they were after; they don't seem to forget it, somehow.'

'This is all very well,' said I, 'but it don't tell me what's wrong; it don't tell me what they're afraid of – what their idea is.'

'Well, I wish I knew,' said Case. 'I can't say fairer than that.'

'You might have asked, I think,' says I.

'And so I did,' says he; 'but you must have seen for yourself, unless you're blind, that the asking got the other way. I'll go far as I dare for another white man; but when I find I'm in the scrape myself, I think first of my own bacon. The loss of me is I'm too good natured. And I'll take the freedom of telling you, you show a queer kind of gratitude to a man who's got into all this mess along of your affairs.'

'There's a thing I'm thinking of,' said I. 'You were a fool to be so much about with Vigours. One comfort, you haven't been much about with me. I notice you've never been inside my house. Own up, now: you had word of this before?'

'It's a fact I haven't been,' said he. 'It was an oversight and I'm sorry for it, Wiltshire. But about coming now, I'll be quite plain.'

'You mean you won't?' I asked.

'Awfully sorry, old man, but that's the size of it,' says Case.

'In short, you're afraid?' says I.

'In short, I'm afraid,' says he.

'And I'm still to be tabooed for nothing?' I asked.

'I tell you you're not tabooed,' said he. 'The kanakas won't go near you, that's all. And who's to make 'em? We traders have a lot of gall, I must say; we make these poor kanakas take back their laws, and take up their taboos, and that, whenever it happens to suit us. But you don't mean to say you expect a law obliging people to deal in your store whether they want to or not? You don't mean to tell me you've got the gall for that! And if you had, it would be a queer thing to propose to me. I would just like to point out to you, Wiltshire, that I'm a trader myself.'

'I don't think I would talk of gall if I was you,' said I. 'Here's about what it comes to, as well as I can make out.

None of the people are to trade with me, as they're all to trade with you. You're to have the copra, and I'm to go to the devil and shake myself. And I don't know any native, and you're the only man here worth mention that speaks English, and you have the gall to up and hint to me my life's in danger, and all you've got to tell me is, you don't know why?'

'Well, it is all I have to tell you,' said he. 'I don't know, I wish I did.'

'And so you turn your back and leave me to myself: is that the position?' says I.

'If you like to put it nasty,' says he. 'I don't put it so. I say merely I'm going to keep clear of you, or if I don't I'll get in danger for myself.'

'Well,' said I, 'you're a nice kind of a white man!'

'O, I understand you're riled,' said he. 'I would be myself. I can make excuses.'

'All right,' I said, 'go and make excuses somewhere else. Here's my way, there's yours.'

With that we parted, and I went straight home, in a holy temper, and found Uma trying on a lot of trade goods like a baby.

'Here,' I said, 'you quit that foolery. Here's a pretty mess to have made – as if I wasn't bothered enough anyway! And I thought I told you to get dinner?'

And then I believe I gave her a bit of the rough side of my tongue, as she deserved. She stood up at once, like a sentry to his officer; for I must say she was always well brought up and had a great respect for whites.

'And now,' says I, 'you belong round here, you're bound to understand this. What am I tabooed for anyway? or if I ain't tabooed, what makes the folks afraid of me?'

She stood and looked at me with eyes like saucers.

'You no savvy?' she gasps at last.

'No,' said I. 'How would you expect me to? We don't have any such craziness where I come from.'

'Ese no tell you?' she asked again.

(*Ese* was the name the natives had for Case; it may mean foreign, or extraordinary; or it might mean a mummy apple; but most like it was only his own name misheard and put in the kanaka spelling.)

'Not much!' said I.

'Damn Ese,' she cried.

You might think it was funny to hear this kanaka girl come out with a big swear. No such thing. There was no swearing in her; no, nor anger; she was beyond anger, and meant the word simple and serious. She stood there straight as she said it; I cannot justly say that ever I saw a woman look like that before or after, and it struck me mum. Then she made a kind of an obeisance, but it was the proudest kind, and threw her hands out open.

'I 'shamed,' she said. 'I think you savvy. Ese he tell me you savvy, he tell me you no mind – tell me you love me too much. Taboo belong me,' she said, touching herself on the bosom, as she had done upon our wedding night. 'Now I go 'way, taboo he go 'way too. Then you get too much copra. You like more better, I think. Tofá, alii,' says she in the native – 'Farewell, chief!'

'Hold on,' I cried. 'Don't be in such a blamed hurry.'

She looked at me sidelong with a smile. 'You see, you get copra,' says she, the same as you might offer candies to a child.

'Uma,' said I, 'hear reason. I didn't know, and that's a fact; and Case seems to have played it pretty mean upon the pair of us. But I do know now, and I don't mind: I love you too much. You no go 'way, you no leave me, I too much sorry.'

'You no love me!' she cried, 'you talk me bad words!' And she threw herself in a corner on the floor, and began to cry.

Well, I'm no scholar, but I wasn't born yesterday, and I thought the worst of that trouble was over. However, there she lay – her back turned, her face to the wall – and shook with sobbing like a little child, so that her feet jumped with it. It's strange how it hits a man when he's in love; for there's no use mincing things; kanaka and all, I was in love with her, or just as good. I tried to take her hand, but she would none of that. 'Uma,' I said, 'there's no sense in carrying on like this. I want you stop here, I want my little wifie, I tell you true.'

'No tell me true!' she sobbed.

'All right,' says I, 'I'll wait till you're through with this.' And I sat right down beside her on the floor, and set to smoothe her hair with my hand. At first she wriggled away when I touched her; then she seemed to notice me no more; then her sobs grew gradually less and presently stopped; and the next thing I knew, she raised her face to mine.

'You tell me true? You like me stop?' she asked.

'Uma,' I said, 'I would rather have you than all the copra in the South Seas,' which was a very big expression, and the strangest thing was that I meant it.

She threw her arms about me, sprang close up, and pressed her face to mine in the island way of kissing, so that I was all wetted with her tears and my heart went out to her wholly. I never had anything so near me as this little brown bit of a girl. Many things went together and all helped to turn my head. She was pretty enough to eat; it seemed she was my only friend in that queer place; I was ashamed that I had spoken rough to her; and she was a woman, and my wife, and a kind of a baby besides that I was sorry for; and the salt of her tears was in my mouth. And I forgot Case and the natives; and I forgot that I knew nothing of the story, or only remembered it to banish the remembrance; and I forgot that I was to get no copra and so could make no livelihood; and I forgot my employers, and the strange kind of service I was doing them, when I preferred my fancy to their business; and I forgot even that Uma was no true wife of mine, but just a maid beguiled, and that in a pretty shabby style. But that is to look too far on. I will come to that part of it next.

It was late before we thought of getting dinner. The stove was out, and gone stone-cold; but we fired up after awhile, and cooked each a dish, helping and hindering each other, and making a play of it like children. I was so greedy of her nearness that I sat down to dinner with my lass upon my knee, made sure of her with one hand, and ate with the other. Ay, and more than that. She was the worst cook I suppose God made; the things she set her hand to, it would have sickened an entire horse to eat of; yet I made my meal that day on Uma's cookery, and can never call to mind to have been better pleased.

I didn't pretend to myself, and I didn't pretend to her. I saw I was clean gone; and if she was to make a fool of me, she must. And I suppose it was this that set her talking, for now she made sure that we were friends. A lot she told me, sitting in my lap and eating my dish, as I ate hers, from foolery: a lot about herself and her mother and Case, all which would be very tedious and fill sheets if I set it down in Beach de Mar, but which I must give a hint of in plain English – and one thing about myself, which had a very big effect on my concerns, as you are soon to hear.

It seems she was born in one of the Line islands; had been only two or three years in these parts, where she had come with a white man who was married to her mother and then died; and only the one year in Falesá. Before that, they had been a good deal on the move, trekking about after the white man, who was one of these rolling stones that keep going round after a soft job. They talk about looking for gold at the end of the rainbow; but if a man wants an employment that'll last him till he dies, let him start out on the soft-job hunt. There's meat and drink in it too, and beer and skittles; for you never hear of them starving and rarely see them sober; and as for steady sport, cockfighting isn't in the same county with it. Anyway, this beachcomber carried the woman and her daughter all over the shop, but mostly to out of the way islands, where there were no police and he thought perhaps the soft-job hung out. I've my own view of this old party; but I was just as glad he had kept Uma clear of Apia and Papeete and these flash towns. At last he struck Fale-alii on this island, got some trade the Lord knows how! muddled it all away in the usual style, and died worth next to nothing, bar a bit of land at Falesá that he had got for a bad debt, which was what put it in the minds of the mother and daughter to come there and live. It seems Case encouraged them all he could, and helped to get their house built. He was very kind those days, and gave Uma trade, and there is no doubt he had his eye on her from the beginning. However, they had scarce settled, when up turned a young man, a native, and wanted to marry her. He was a small chief, and had some fine mats and old songs in his family, and was 'very pretty', Uma said; and altogether it was an extraordinary match for a penniless girl and an out-islander.

At the first word of this, I got downright sick with jealousy.

'And you mean to say you would have married him!' I cried.

'*Ioe*,' says she. 'I like too much!'

'Well!' I said. 'And suppose I had come round after?'

'I like you more better now,' said she. 'But suppose I marry Ioane, I one good wife. I no common kanaka: good girl!' says she.

Well, I had to be pleased with that; but I promise you I didn't care about the business one little bit, and liked the end of that yarn better than the beginning. For it seems this proposal of marriage was the start of all the trouble. It seems, before that, Uma and her mother had been looked down upon of course for kinless folk and out-islanders, but nothing to hurt; and even when Ioane came forward there was less trouble at first than might have been looked for. And then all of a sudden, about six months before my coming, Ioane backed out and left that part of the island, and from that day to this, Uma and her mother had found themselves alone. None called at their house, none spoke to them on the roads. If they went to church, the other women drew their mats away and left them in a clear space by themselves. It was a regular excommunication, like what you read of in the middle ages; and the cause or sense of it beyond guessing. It was some *tala pepelo*, Uma said, some lie, some calumny; and all she knew of it was that the girls who had been jealous of her luck with Ioane used to twit her with his desertion, and cry out, when they met her alone in the woods, that she would never be married. 'They tell me no man he marry me. He too much 'fraid,' she said.

The only soul that came about them after this desertion was Master Case; even he was chary of showing himself, and turned up mostly by night; and pretty soon he began to table his cards and make up to Uma. I was still sore about Ioane, and when Case turned up in the same line of business, I cut up downright rough.

'Well,' I said sneering, 'and I suppose you thought Case "very pretty" and "liked too much".'

'Now you talk silly,' said she. 'White man he come here, I marry him all-e-same kanaka; very well then, he marry me all-e-same white woman. Suppose he no marry, he go 'way, woman he stop. All-e-same thief; empty hand, Tonga-heart – no can love! Now you come marry me; you big heart – you no 'shamed island girl. That thing I love you for too much. I proud.'

I don't know that ever I felt sicker all the days of my

life. I laid down my fork and I put away 'the island girl';
I didn't seem somehow to have any use for either; and I
went and walked up and down in the house, and Uma
followed me with her eyes, for she was troubled, and
small wonder! But troubled was no word for it with me;
I so wanted, and so feared, to make a clean breast of the
sweep that I had been.

And just then there came a sound of singing out of the
sea; it sprang up suddenly clear and near, as the boat turned
the headland; and Uma, running to the window, cried out
it was 'Misi' come upon his rounds.

I thought it was a strange thing I should be glad to have
a missionary; but if it was strange, it was still true.

'Uma,' said I, 'you stop here in this room, and don't
budge a foot out of it till I come back.'

THREE. THE MISSIONARY

As I came out on the verandah, the mission boat was shooting for the mouth of the river. She was a long whale boat painted white; a bit of an awning astern; a native pastor crouched on the wedge of the poop, steering; some four and twenty paddles flashing and dipping, true to the boat-song; and the missionary under the awning, in his white clothes, reading in a book, and set him up! It was pretty to see and hear; there's no smarter sight in the islands than a missionary boat with a good crew and a good pipe to them; and I considered it for half a minute with a bit of envy perhaps, and then strolled towards the river.

From the opposite side there was another man aiming for the same place, but he ran and got there first. It was Case; doubtless his idea was to keep me apart from the missionary who might serve me as interpreter; but my mind was upon other things, I was thinking how he had jockeyed us about the marriage, and tried his hand on Uma before; and at the sight of him, rage flew in my nostrils.

'Get out of that, you low, swindling thief!' I cried.

'What's that you say?' says he.

I gave him the word again, and rammed it down with a good oath. 'And if ever I catch you within six fathoms of my house,' I cried, 'I'll clap a bullet in your measly carcase.'

'You must do as you like about your house,' said he, 'where I told you I have no thought of going. But this is a public place.'

'It's a place where I have private business,' said I. 'I have no idea of a hound like you eavesdropping, and I give you notice to clear out.'

'I don't take it though,' says Case.

'I'll show you, then,' said I.

'We'll have to see about that,' said he.

He was quick with his hands, but he had neither the height nor the weight, being a flimsy creature alongside a man like me; and besides I was blazing to that height of wrath that I could have bit into a chisel. I gave him first the one and then the other, so that I could hear his head rattle and crack, and he went down straight.

'Have you had enough?' cries I. But he only looked up white and blank, and the blood spread upon his face like wine upon a napkin. 'Have you had enough?' I cried again. 'Speak up, and don't lie malingering there, or I'll take my feet to you!'

He sat up at that, and held his head – by the look of him you could see it was spinning – and the blood poured on his pyjamas.

'I've had enough for this time,' says he, and he got up staggering and went off by the way that he had come.

The boat was close in; I saw the missionary had laid his book to one side, and I smiled to myself. 'He'll know I'm a man, anyway,' thinks I.

This was the first time, in all my years in the Pacific, I had ever exchanged two words with any missionary; let alone asked one for a favour. I didn't like the lot, no trader does; they look down upon us and make no concealment; and besides they're partly kanakaised, and suck up with natives instead of with other white men like themselves. I had on a rig of clean, striped pyjamas, for of course I had dressed decent to go before the chiefs; but when I saw the missionary step out of his boat in the regular uniform, while duck clothes, pith helmet, white shirt and tie, and yellow boots to his feet, I could have bunged stones at him. As he came nearer, queering me pretty curious (because of the fight I suppose) I saw he looked mortal sick, for the truth was he had a fever on and had just had a chill in the boat.

'Mr Tarleton, I believe?' says I, for I had got his name.

'And you, I suppose, are the new trader?' says he.

'I want to tell you first that I don't hold with missions,' I went on, 'and that I think you and the likes of you do a sight of harm, filling up the natives with old wives' tales and bumptiousness.'

'You are perfectly entitled to your opinions,' says he, looking a bit ugly, 'but I have no call to hear them.'

'It so happens that you've got to hear them,' I said. 'I'm no missionary nor missionary lover; I'm no kanaka nor favourer of kanakas: I'm just a trader, I'm just a common, low, god-damned white man and British subject, the sort you would like to wipe your boots on. I hope that's plain.'

'Yes, my man,' said he. 'It's more plain than creditable. When you are sober, you'll be sorry for this.'

He tried to pass on, but I stopped him with my hand. The kanakas were beginning to growl; guess they didn't like my tone, for I spoke to that man as free as I would to you.

'Now you can't say I've deceived you,' said I, 'and I can go on. I want a service, I want two services in fact; and if you care to give me them, I'll perhaps take more stock in what you call your christianity.'

He was silent for a moment. Then he smiled. 'You are rather a strange sort of man,' says he.

'I'm the sort of a man God made me,' says I. 'I don't set up to be a gentleman,' I said.

'I am not quite so sure,' said he. 'And what can I do for you, Mr——?'

'Wiltshire,' I says, 'though I'm mostly called Welsher; but Wiltshire is the way it's spelt, if the people on the beach could only get their tongues about it. And what do I want? Well, I'll tell you the first thing. I'm what you call a sinner – what I call a sweep – and I want you to help me make it up to a person I've deceived.'

He turned and spoke to his crew in the native. 'And now I am at your service,' said he, 'but only for the time my crew are dining. I must be much farther down the coast before night. I was delayed at Papa-mālūlū till this morning, and I have an engagement in Fale-alii tomorrow night.'

I led the way to my house in silence and rather pleased with myself for the way I had managed the talk, for I like a man to keep his self-respect.

'I was sorry to see you fighting,' says he.

'O, that's part of a yarn I want to tell you,' I said. 'That's service number two. After you've heard it, you'll let me know whether you're sorry or not.'

We walked right in through the store, and I was surprised

to find Uma had cleared away the dinner things. This was so unlike her ways, that I saw she had done it out of gratitude, and liked her the better. She and Mr Tarleton called each other by name, and he was very civil to her seemingly. But I thought little of that; they can always find civility for a kanaka; it's us white men they lord it over. Besides I didn't want much Tarleton just then: I was going to do my pitch.

'Uma,' said I, 'give us your marriage certificate.' She looked put out. 'Come,' said I. 'You can trust me. Hand it up.'

She had it about her person as usual; I believe she thought it was a pass to heaven, and if she died without having it handy she would go to hell. I couldn't see where she put it the first time, I couldn't see now where she took it from; it seemed to jump in her hand like that Blavatsky[1] business in the papers. But it's the same way with all island women, and I guess they're taught it when young.

'Now,' said I, with the certificate in my hand, 'I was married to this girl by Black Jack the negro. The certificate was wrote by Case, and it's a dandy piece of literature, I promise you. Since then I've found that there's a kind of cry in the place against this wife of mine, and so long as I keep her, I cannot trade. Now what would any man do in my place, if he was a man?' I said. 'The first thing he would do is this, I guess.' And I took and tore up the certificate and bunged the pieces on the floor.

'*Aué!*' cried Uma, and began to clap her hands, but I caught one of them in mine.

'And the second thing that he would do,' said I, 'if he was what I would call a man, and you would call a man, Mr Tarleton, is to bring the girl right before you or any other missionary, and to up and say: "I was wrong married to this wife of mine, but I think a heap of her, and now I want to be married to her right." Fire away, Mr Tarleton. And I guess you'd better do it in native, it'll please the old lady,' I said, giving her the proper name of a man's wife upon the spot.

So we had in two of the crew to witness, and were spliced

---

1. Madame Blavatsky, the spiritualist, who was active
   at the time Stevenson was writing.

in our own house; and the parson prayed a good bit, I must say, but not so long as some, and shook hands with the pair of us.

'Mr Wiltshire,' he says, when he had made out the lines and packed off the witnesses, 'I have to thank you for a very lively pleasure. I have rarely performed the marriage ceremony with more grateful emotions.'

That was what you would call talking. He was going on besides with more of it, and I was ready for as much taffy as he had in stock, for I felt good. But Uma had been taken up with something half through the marriage, and cut straight in.

'How your hand he get hurt?' she asked.

'You ask Case's head, old lady,' says I.

She jumped with joy, and sang out.

'You haven't made much of a christian of this one,' says I to Mr Tarleton.

'We didn't think her one of our worst,' says he, 'when she was at Fale-alii; and if Uma bears malice, I shall be tempted to fancy she has good cause.'

'Well, there we are at service number two,' said I. 'I want to tell you our yarn, and see if you can let a little daylight in.'

'Is it long?' he asked.

'Yes,' I said, 'it's a goodish bit of a yarn.'

'Well, I'll give you all the time I can spare,' says he, looking at his watch. 'But I must tell you fairly I haven't eaten since five this morning; and unless you can let me have something, I am not likely to eat again before seven or eight tonight.'

'By God, we'll give you dinner!' I cried.

I was a little caught up at my swearing, just when all was going straight; and so was the missionary I suppose, but he made believe to look out of the window and thanked us.

So we ran him up a bit of a meal. I was bound to let the old lady have a hand in it, to show off; so I deputised her to brew the tea. I don't think I ever met such tea as she turned out. But that was not the worst, for she got round with the salt-box, which she considered an extra European touch, and turned my stew into sea water. Altogether, Mr Tarleton had a devil of a dinner of it; but he had plenty entertainment by the way, for all the while that we were cooking, and afterwards when he was making believe to eat, I kept posting him up on Master Case and the beach of Falesá, and he putting questions that showed he was following close.

'Well,' said he at last, 'I am afraid you have a dangerous enemy. This man Case is very clever and seems really wicked. I must tell you I have had my eye on him for nearly a year, and have rather had the worst of our encounters. About the time when the last representative of your firm ran so suddenly away, I had a letter from Namu, the native pastor, begging me to come to Falesá at my earliest convenience, as his flock were all "adopting catholic practices." I had great confidence in Namu; I fear it only shows how easily we are deceived. No one could hear him preach and not be persuaded he was a man of extraordinary parts. All our islanders easily acquire a kind of eloquence, and can roll out and illustrate with a great deal of vigour and fancy secondhand sermons; but Namu's sermons are his own, and I cannot deny that I have found them means of grace. Moreover he has a keen curiosity in secular things, does not fear work, is clever at carpentering, and has made himself so much respected among the neighbouring pastors that we call him, in a jest which is half serious, the Bishop of the East. In short I was proud of the man; all the more puzzled by his letter; and took occasion to come this way. The morning before my arrival, Vigours had been set on board the *Lion*, and Namu was perfectly at ease, apparently ashamed of his letter, and quite unwilling to explain it. This of course I could not allow; and he ended by confessing that he had been much concerned to find his people using the sign of the cross, but since he had learned the explanation his mind was satisfied. For Vigours had the Evil Eye, a common thing in a country of Europe called Italy, where men were often struck dead by that kind of devil; and it appeared the sign of the cross was a charm against its power.

'"And I explain it, Misi," said Namu in this way. "The country in Europe is a Popey country, and the devil of the Evil Eye may be a catholic devil, or at least used to catholic ways. So then I reasoned thus; if this sign of the cross were used in a Popey manner, it would be sinful; but when it is used only to protect men from a devil, which is a thing harmless in itself, the sign too must be harmless. For the sign is neither good nor bad, even as a bottle is neither good nor bad. But if the bottle be full of gin, the gin is bad; and if the sign be made in idolatry, so is the idolatry bad." And very like a native pastor, he had a text apposite about the casting out of devils.

"'And who has been telling you about the Evil Eye?' I asked.

'He admitted it was Case. Now I am afraid you will think me very narrow, Mr Wiltshire, but I must tell you I was displeased, and cannot think a trader at all a good man to advise or have an influence upon my pastors. And besides there had been some flying talk in the country of old Adams and his being poisoned, to which I had paid no great heed; but it came back to me at the moment.

"'And is this Case a man of sanctified life?" I asked.

'He admitted he was not; for though he did not drink, he was profligate with women and had no religion.

"'Then," said I, "I think the less you have to do with him the better."

'But it is not easy to have the last word with a man like Namu; he was ready in a moment with an illustration. "Misi," said he, "you have told me there were wise men, not pastors, not even holy, who knew many things useful to be taught, about trees for instance, and beasts, and to print books, and about the stones that are burned to make knives of. Such men teach you in your college, and you learn from them, but take care not to learn to be unholy. Misi, Case is my college."

'I knew not what to say. Mr Vigours had evidently been driven out of Falesá by the machinations of Case and with something not very unlike the collusion of my pastor. I called to mind it was Namu who had reassured me about Adams and traced the rumour to the ill will of the priest. And I saw I must inform myself more thoroughly from an impartial source. There is an old rascal of a chief here, Faiaso, whom I daresay you saw today at the council; he has been all his life turbulent and sly, a great fomenter of rebellions, and a thorn in the side of the mission and the island. For all that he is very shrewd, and except in politics or about his own misdemeanours, a teller of the truth. I went to his house, told him what I had heard, and besought him to be frank. I do not think I had ever a more painful interview. Perhaps you will understand me, Mr Wiltshire, if I tell you that I am perfectly serious in these old wives' tales with which you reproached me, and as anxious to do well for these islands as you can be to please and to protect your pretty wife. And you are to remember that I thought Namu a paragon, and was proud of the man as one of the first ripe fruits of the mission. And now I was informed that he had fallen in a sort of dependence upon Case. The beginning of it was not corrupt; it began doubtless in fear and respect produced by trickery and pretence; but I was shocked to find that another element had been lately added, that Namu helped himself in the store, and was believed to be deep in Case's debt. Whatever the trader said, that Namu believed with trembling. He was not alone in this; many in the village lived in similar subjection; but Namu's case was the most influential, it was through Namu Case had wrought most evil; and with a certain following among the chiefs, and the pastor in his pocket, the man was as good as master of the village. You know something of Vigours and Adams; but perhaps you have never heard of old Underhill, Adams' predecessor. He was a quiet, mild old fellow, I remember, and we were told he had died suddenly: white men die very suddenly in Falesá. The truth, as I now heard it, made my blood run cold. It seems he was struck with a general palsy, all of him dead but one eye, which he continually winked. Word was started that the helpless old man was now a devil; and this vile fellow Case worked upon the natives' fears, which he professed to share, and pretended he durst not go into the house alone. At last a grave was dug, and the living body buried at the far end of the village. Namu, my pastor, whom I had helped to educate, offered up prayer at the hateful scene.

'I felt myself in a very difficult position. Perhaps too it was my duty to have denounced Namu and had him deposed; perhaps I think so now; but at the time, it seemed less clear. He had a great influence, it might prove greater than mine. The natives are prone to superstition; perhaps by stirring them up, I might but ingrain and spread these dangerous fancies. And Namu besides, apart from this novel and accursed influence, was a good pastor, an able man

and spiritually minded. Where should I look for a better?
how was I to find as good? At that moment with Namu's
failure fresh in my view, the work of my life appeared a
mockery; hope was dead in me; I would rather repair such
tools as I had, than go abroad in quest of others that must
certainly prove worse; and a scandal is, at the best, a thing
to be avoided when humanly possible. Right or wrong
then, I determined on a quiet course. All that night I
denounced and reasoned with the erring pastor; twitted
him with his ignorance and want of faith; twitted him
with his wretched attitude, making clean the outside of the
cup and platter, callously helping at a murder, childishly
flying in excitement about a few childish, unnecessary
and inconvenient gestures; and long before day, I had
him on his knees and bathed in tears of what seemed a
genuine repentance. On Sunday I took the pulpit in the
morning and preached from First Kings, nineteenth, on
the fire, the earthquake and the voice: distinguishing the
true spiritual power, and referring with such plainness as I
dared to recent events in Falesá. The effect produced was
great; and it was much increased, when Namu rose in his
turn, and confessed that he had been wanting in faith and
conduct, and was convinced of sin. So far, then all was
well; but there was one unfortunate circumstance. It was
nearing the time of our 'May' in the island, when the native
contributions to the mission are received; it fell in my duty to
make a notification on the subject; and this gave my enemy
his chance, by which he was not slow to profit.

'News of the whole proceedings must have been carried
to Case as soon as church was over; and the same afternoon
he made an occasion to meet me in the midst of the village.
He came up with so much intentness and animosity that I
felt it would be damaging to avoid him.

'"So," he says in native, "here is the holy man. He has
been preaching against me, but that was not in his heart.
He has been preaching the love of God, but that was not in
his heart – it was between his teeth. Will you know what was
in his heart?" cried he. "I will show it you." And making a
snatch at my head, he made believe to pluck out a dollar,
and held it in the air.

'There went that rumour through the crowd with which
Polynesians receive a prodigy. As for myself, I stood

amazed. The thing was a common conjuring trick, which I have seen performed at home a score of times; but how was I to convince the villagers of that? I wished I had learned legerdemain instead of Hebrew, that I might have paid the fellow out with his own coin. But there I was, I could not stand there silent, and the best that I could find to say was weak.

'"I will trouble you not to lay hands on me again," said I.

'"I have no such thought," said he, "nor will I deprive you of your dollar. Here it is," he said, and flung it at my feet. I am told it lay where it fell three days.'

'I must say it was well played,' said I.

'O, he is clever,' said Mr Tarleton, 'and you can now see for yourself how dangerous. He was a party to the horrid death of the paralytic; he is accused of poisoning Adams; he drove Vigours out of the place by lies that might have led to murder; and there is no question but he has now made up his mind to rid himself of you. How he means to try, we have no guess; only be sure it's something new. There is no end to his readiness and invention.'

'He gives himself a sight of trouble,' says I. 'And after all, what for?'

'Why, how many tons of copra may they make in this district?' asked the missionary.

'I daresay as much as sixty tons,' says I.

'And what is the profit to the local trader?' he asked.

'You may call it three pounds,' said I.

'Then you can reckon for yourself how much he does it for,' said Mr Tarleton. 'But the more important thing is to defeat him. It is clear he spread some report against Uma, in order to isolate and have his wicked will of her; failing of that, and seeing a new rival come upon the scene, he used her in a different way. Now the first point to find out is about Namu. Uma, when people began to leave you and your mother alone, what did Namu do?'

'Stop away all-e-same,' says Uma.

'I fear the dog has returned to his vomit,' said Mr Tarleton. 'And now what am I to do for you? I will speak to Namu, I will warn him he is observed; it will be strange if he allow anything to go on amiss, when he is put upon his guard. At the same time, this precaution may fail, and then you must turn elsewhere. You have two people at hand to whom you might apply. There is first of all the priest, who might protect you by the catholic interest; they are a wretchedly small body, but they count two chiefs. And then there is old Faiaso. Ah, if it had been some years ago, you would have needed no one else; but his influence is much reduced, it has gone into Maea's hands, and Maea, I fear, is one of Case's jackalls. In fine, if the worst comes to the worst, you must send up or come yourself to Fale-alii, and though I am not due at this end of the island for a month, I will see what can be done.'

So Mr Tarleton said farewell; and half an hour later, the crew were singing and the paddles flashing in the missionary boat.

FOUR. DEVIL-WORK

Near a month went by without much doing. The same night of our marriage, Galoshes called round, made himself mighty civil, and got into a habit of dropping in about dark and smoking his pipe with the family. He could talk to Uma of course, and started to teach me native and French at the same time. He was a kind old buffer, though the dirtiest you would wish to see, and he muddled me up with foreign languages worse than the tower of Babel.

That was one employment we had, and it made me feel less lonesome; but there was no profit in the thing; for though the priest came and sat and yarned, none of his folks could be enticed into my store; and if it hadn't been for the other occupation I struck out, there wouldn't have been a pound of copra in the house. This was the idea: Fa'avao (Uma's mother) had a score of bearing trees. Of course, we could get no labour, being all as good as tabooed. And the two women and I turned to make copra with our own hands. It was copra to make your mouth water, when it was done – I never understood how much the natives cheated me till I had made that four hundred pounds of my own hand – and it weighed so light, I felt inclined to take and water it myself.

When we were at the job, a good many kanakas used to put in the best of the day looking on, and once that nigger turned up. He stood back with the natives, and laughed, and did the big don and the funny dog, till I began to get riled.

'Here, you, nigger!' says I.

'I don't address myself to you, sah,' says the nigger. 'Only speak to gen'le'um.'

'I know,' says I, 'but it happens I was addressing myself to you, Mr Black Jack. And all I want to know is just this: did you see Case's figurehead about a week ago?'

'No, sah,' says he.

'That's all right, then,' says I; 'for I'll show you the own brother to it, only black, in the inside of about two minutes.'

And I began to walk towards him, quite slow and my hands down; only there was trouble in my eye, if anybody took the pains to look.

'You're a low, obstropulous fellow, sah,' says he.

'You bet!' says I.

By that time he thought I was about as near as was convenient, and lit out so it would have done your heart good to see him travel. And that was all I saw of that precious gang, until what I am about to tell you.

It was one of my chief employments these days to go pot-hunting in the woods, which I found (as Case had told me) very rich in game. I have spoken of the cape, which shut up the village and my station from the east. A path went about the end of it, and led into the next bay. A strong wind blew here daily, and as the line of the barrier reef stopped at the end of the cape, a heavy surf ran on the shores of the bay. A little cliffy hill cut the valley in two parts, and stood close on the beach; and at high water the sea broke right on the face of it, so that all passage was stopped. Woody mountains hemmed the place all round; the barrier to the east was particularly steep and leafy; the lower parts of it, along the sea, falling in sheer black cliffs streaked with cinnabar; the upper part lumpy with the tops of the great trees. Some of the trees as black as your shoes. Many birds hovered round the bay, some of them snow white; and the flying-fox (or vampire) flew there in broad daylight, gnashing its teeth.

For a long while I came as far as this shooting and went no farther. There was no sign of any path beyond; and the cocoapalms in the front of the foot of the valley were the last this way. For the whole 'eye' of the island, as natives call the windward end, lay desert. From Falesá round about to Papa-mālūlū, there was neither house, nor man, nor planted fruit tree; and the reef being mostly absent and the shores bluff, the sea beat direct among crags, and there was scarce a landing place.

I should tell you that after I began to go in the woods, although no one offered to come near my store, I found people willing enough to pass the time of day with me where nobody could see them. And as I had begun to pick up native, and most of them had a word or two of English, I began to hold little odds and ends of conversation, not to much purpose, to be sure, but they took off the worst of the feeling. For it's a miserable thing to be made a leper of.

It chanced one day, towards the end of the month, that I was sitting in this bay in the edge of the bush, looking east, with a kanaka. I had given him a fill of tobacco, and we were making out to talk as best we could; indeed he had more English than most.

I asked him if there was no road going eastward.

'One time one road,' said he. 'Now he dead.'

'Nobody he go there?' I asked.

'No good,' said he. 'Too much devil he stop there.'

'Oho!' says I, 'got-um plenty devil, that bush?'

'Man devil, woman devil: too much devil,' said my friend. 'Stop there all-e-time. Man he go there, no come back.'

I thought, if this fellow was so well posted on devils and spoke of them so free, which is not common, I had better fish for a little information about myself and Uma.

'You think me one devil?' I asked again.

'No think devil,' said he soothingly. 'Think all-e-same fool.'

'Uma, she devil?' I asked again.

'No, no: no devil; devil stop bush,' said the young man.

I was looking in front of me across the bay, and I saw the hanging front of the woods pushed suddenly open, and Case with a gun in his hand step forth into the sunshine on the black beach. He was got up in light pyjamas, near white, his gun sparkled, he looked mighty conspicuous; and the land crabs scuttled from all round him to their holes.

'Hullo, my friend,' says I, 'you no talk all-e-same true. Ese he go, he come back.'

'Ese no all-e-same. Ese *Tiapolo*,' says my friend; and with a good bye, slunk off among the trees.

I watched Case all round the beach, where the tide was low; and let him pass me on the homeward way to Falesá. He was in deep thought; and the birds seemed to know it, trotting quite near him on the sand and wheeling and calling in his ears. Where he passed nearest me, I could see by the working of his lips that he was talking in to himself, and what pleased me mightily, he had still my trademark on his brow. I tell you the plain truth, I had a mind to give him a gunfull in his ugly mug, but I thought better of it.

All this time, and all the time I was following home, I kept repeating that native word, which I remembered by 'Polly, put the kettle on and make us all some tea': tea-a-pollo.

'Uma,' says I, when I got back, 'what does Tiapolo mean?'

'Devil,' says she.

'I thought *aitu* was the word for that?' I said.

'*Aitu* 'nother kind of devil,' said she; 'stop bush, eat kanaka. Tiapolo big-chief devil, stop home; all-e-same Christian devil.'

'Well then,' said I. 'I'm no further forward. How can Case be Tiapolo?'

'No all-e-same,' said she. 'Ese belong Tiapolo; Tiapolo too much like; Ese all-e-same his son. Suppose Ese he wish something, Tiapolo he make him.'

'That's mighty convenient for Ese,' says I. 'And what kind of things does he make for him?'

Well, out came a rigmarole of all sorts of stories, many of which (like the blue dollar he took from Mr Tarleton's head) were plain enough to me, but others I could make nothing of; and the thing that most surprised the kanakas was what surprised me least; namely, that he could go in the desert among all the *aitus*. Some of the boldest, however, had accompanied him, and had heard him speak with the dead and give them orders, and safe in his protection, had returned unscathed. Some said he had a church there where he worshipped Tiapolo, and Tiapolo appeared to him; others swore there was no sorcery at all, that he performed his miracles by the power of prayer, and the church was no church but a prison in which he had confined a dangerous *aitu*. Namu had been in the bush with him once, and returned glorifying God for these wonders. Altogether I began to have a glimmer of the man's position, and the means by which he had acquired it, and though I saw he was a tough nut to crack, I was noways cast down.

'Very well,' said I, 'I'll have a look at Master Case's place of worship myself, and we'll see about the glorifying.'

At this time Uma fell in a terrible taking; if I went in the high brush, I should never return; none could go there but by the protection of Tiapolo.

'I'll chance it on God's,' said I. 'I'm a good sort of a fellow, Uma, as fellows go; and I guess God'll con me through.'

She was silent for awhile. 'I think,' said she, mighty solemn; and then presently: 'Victoreea he big chief?'

'You bet,' said I.

'He like you too much?' she asked again.

I told her with a grin I believed the old lady was rather partial to me.

'All right,' said she. 'Victoreea he big chief, like you too much; no can help you here in Falesá; no can do, too far off. Maea he small chief; stop here; suppose he like you, make you all right. All-e-same God and Tiapolo. God he big chief, got too much work. Tiapolo he small chief, he like too much make-see, work very hard.'

'I'll have to hand you over to Mr Tarleton,' said I. 'Your theology's out of its bearings, Uma.'

However we stuck at this business all the evening, and with the stories she told me of the desert and its dangers, she came near frightening herself into a fit. I don't remember half a quarter of them of course, for I paid little heed; but two come back to me kind of clear.

About six miles up the coast there is a sheltered cove, they call *Fanga-anaana*, 'the haven full of caves'. I've seen it from the sea myself, as near as I could get my boys to venture in, and it's a little strip of yellow sand. Black cliffs overhang it full of the black mouths of caves, great trees overhang the cliffs and dangle down lianas, and in one place, about the middle, a big brook pours over in a cascade. Well, there was a boat going by here with six young men of Falesá, 'all very pretty,' Uma said, which was the loss of them. It blew strong, there was a heavy head sea; and by the time they opened Fanga-anaana, and saw the white cascade and the shady beach, they were all tired and thirsty, and their water had run out. One proposed to land and get a drink; and being reckless fellows, they were all of the same mind except the youngest. Lotu was his name; he was a very good young gentleman and very wise; and he held out they were crazy, telling them the place was given over to spirits and devils and the dead, and there were no living folk nearer than six miles the one way and maybe twelve the other. But they laughed at his words; and being five to one, pulled in, beached the boat, and landed. It was a wonderful pleasant place, Lotu said, and the water excellent. They walked round the beach, but could see nowhere any way to mount the cliffs, which made them easier in their mind; and at last they sat down to make a meal on the food they had brought with them. They were scarce set, when there came out of the mouth of one of the black caves six of the most beautiful ladies ever seen; they had flowers in their hair, and the most beautiful breasts, and necklaces of scarlet seeds; and began to jest with these young gentlemen, and the young gentlemen to jest back with them, all but Lotu. As for Lotu, he saw there could be no living women in such a place, and ran, and flung himself in the bottom of the boat, and covered his face, and prayed. All the time the business lasted, Lotu made one clean break of prayer; and that was all he knew of it, until his friends came back, and made him sit up, and they put to sea again out of the bay, which was now quite desert, and no word of the six ladies. But what frightened Lotu worst, not one of the five remembered anything of what had passed, but they were all like drunken men, and sang and laughed in the boat, and skylarked. The wind freshened and came squally, the sea rose extraordinary high; it was such weather as any man in the islands would have turned back to and fled home to Falesá; but these five were like crazy folk, and cracked on all sail, and drove their boat into the seas. Lotu went to the bailing; none of the others thought to help him, but sang and skylarked and carried on, and spoke singular things beyond a man's comprehension, and laughed out loud when they said them. So the rest of that day, Lotu bailed for his life in the bottom of the boat, and was all drenched with sweat and cold sea water; and none heeded him. Against all expectation, they came safe in a dreadful tempest to Papa-mālūlū, where the palms were singing out and the cocoanuts flying like cannon balls about the village green; and the same night the five young gentlemen sickened and spoke never a reasonable word until they died.

'And do you mean to tell me you can swallow a yarn like that?' I asked.

She told me the thing was well known, and with handsome young men alone, it was even common. But this was the only case where five had been slain the same day and in a company by the love of the women devils; and it had made a great stir in the island; and she would be crazy if she doubted.

'Well anyway,' says I, 'you needn't be frightened about me. I've got no use for the women devils; you're all the women I want, and all the devil too, old lady.'

To that she answered there were other sorts, and she had seen one with her own eyes. She had gone one day alone to the next bay, and perhaps got too near the margin of the bad place. The boughs of the high bush overshadowed her from the kant of the hill; but she herself was outside in a flat place, very stony and growing full of young mummy-apples, four and five feet high. It was a dark day in the rainy season; and now there came squalls that tore off the leaves and sent them flying, and now it was all still as in a house. It was in one of these still times, that a whole gang of birds and flying-foxes came pegging out of the bush like creatures frightened. Presently after she heard a rustle nearer hand, and saw coming out of the margin of the trees among the mummy-apples, the appearance of a lean, gray, old boar. It seemed to think as it came, like a person, and all of a sudden, as she looked at it coming, she was aware it was no boar but a thing that was a man with a man's thoughts. At that she ran, and the pig after her, and as the pig ran it hollered aloud, so that the place rang with it.

'I wish I had been there with my gun,' said I. 'I guess the pig would have hollered so as to surprise himself.'

But she told me a gun was of no use with the like of these, which were the spirits of the dead.

Well, this kind of talk put in the evening, which was the best of it; but of course it didn't change my notion; and the next day, with my gun and a good knife, I set off upon a voyage of discovery. I made as near as I could for the place where I had seen Case come out; for if it was true he had some kind of establishment in the bush, I reckoned I should find a path. The beginning of the desert was marked off by a wall – to call it so, for it was more of a long mound of stones;

they say it reached right across the island, but how they know it is another question, for I doubt if anyone has made the journey in a hundred years; the natives sticking chiefly to the sea and their little colonies along the coast, and that part being mortal high and steep and full of cliffs. Up to the west side of the wall, the ground has been cleared, and there are cocoapalms, and mummy-apples, and guavas, and lots of sensitive.[1] Just across, the bush begins outright; high bush at that: trees going up like the masts of ships, and ropes of liana hanging down like a ship's rigging, and nasty orchids growing in the forks like funguses. The ground, where there was no underwood, looked to be a heap of boulders. I saw many green pigeons which I might have shot, only I was there with a different idea; a number of butterflies flopped up and down along the ground like dead leaves; sometimes I would hear a bird calling, sometimes the wind overhead, and always the sea along the coast.

But the queerness of the place, it's more difficult to tell of; unless to one who has been alone in the high bush himself. The brightest kind of a day, it is always dim down there. A man can see to the end of nothing; whichever way he looks, the wood shuts up, one bough folding with another, like the fingers of your hand; and whenever he listens, he hears always something new – men talking, children laughing, the strokes of an axe a far way ahead of him, and sometimes a sort of quick, stealthy scurry near at hand that makes him jump and look to his weapons. It's all very well for him to tell himself that he's alone, bar trees and birds; he can't make out to believe it: whichever way he turns, the whole place seems to be alive and looking on. Don't think it was Uma's yarns that put me out; I don't value native talk a fourpenny piece: it's a thing that's natural in the bush, and that's the end of it.

As I got near the top of the hill, for the ground of the wood goes up in this place steep as a ladder, the wind began to sound straight on, and the leaves to toss and switch open and let in the sun. This suited me better; it

1. Sensitive plant. Stevenson had a close acquaintance with sensitive plant as it grew profusely at Vailima and was very hard to eradicate.

was the same noise all the time and nothing to startle. Well, I had got to a place where there was an underwood of what they call wild cocoanut – mighty pretty with its scarlet fruits – when there came a sound of singing in the wind that I thought I had never heard the like of. It was all very fine to tell myself it was the branches; I knew better. It was all very fine to tell myself it was a bird; I knew never a bird that sang like that. It rose, and swelled, and died away, and swelled again; and now I thought it was like some one weeping, only prettier; and now I thought it was like harps; and there was one thing I made sure of, it was a sight too sweet to be wholesome in a place like that. You may laugh if you like; but I declare I called to mind the six young ladies that came, with their scarlet necklaces, out of the cave at Fanga-anaana, and wondered if they sang like that. We laugh at the natives and their superstitions; but see how many traders take them up, splendidly educated white men, that have been bookkeepers (some of them) and clerks in the old country! It's my belief a superstition grows up in a place like the different kinds of weeds; and as I stood there, and listened to that wailing, I twittered in my shoes.

You may call me a coward to be frightened; I thought myself brave enough to go on ahead. But I went mighty carefully, with my gun cocked, spying all about me like a hunter, fully expecting to see a handsome young woman sitting somewhere in the bush, and fully determined (if I did) to try her with a charge of duckshot. And sure enough I had not gone far, when I met with a queer thing. The wind came on the top of the wood in a strong puff, the leaves in front of me burst open, and I saw for a second something hanging in a tree. It was gone in a wink, the puff blowing by and the leaves closing. I tell you the truth; I had made up my mind to see an *aitu*; and if the thing had looked like a pig or a woman, it wouldn't have given me the same turn. The trouble was that it seemed kind of square; and the idea of a square thing that was alive and sang, knocked me sick and silly. I must have stood quite a while; and I made pretty certain it was right out of the same tree that the singing came. Then I began to come to myself a bit.

'Well,' says I, 'if this is really so, if this is a place where there are square things that sing, I'm gone up anyway. Let's have my fun for my money.'

But I thought I might as well take the off-chance of a prayer being any good; so I plumped on my knees and prayed out loud; and all the time I was praying, the strange sounds came out of the tree, and went up and down, and changed, for all the world like music; only you could see it wasn't human – there was nothing there that you could whistle.

As soon as I had made an end in proper style, I laid down my gun, stuck my knife between my teeth, walked right up to that tree, and began to climb. I tell you my heart was like ice. But presently, as I went up, I caught another glimpse of the thing, and that relieved me, for I thought it seemed woundy like a box; and when I had got right up to it, I near fell out of the tree with laughter. A box it was, sure enough, and a candle box at that, with the brand upon the side of it; and it had banjo strings stretched so as to sound when the wind blew. I believe they call the thing a Tyrolean harp, whatever that may mean.

'Well, Mr Case,' said I, 'you've frightened me once. But I defy you to frighten me again,' I says, and slipped down the tree, and set out again to find my enemy's head office, which I guessed would not be far away.

The undergrowth was thick in this part. I couldn't see before my nose, and must burst my way through by main force and ply the knife as I went, slicing the cords of the lianas and slashing down whole trees at a blow. I call them trees for the bigness, but in truth they were just big weeds and sappy to cut through like a carrot. From all this crowd and kind of vegetation, I was just thinking to myself the place might have once been cleared, when I came on my nose over a pile of stones, and saw in a moment it was some kind of a work of man. The Lord knows when it was made or when deserted; for this part of the island has lain undisturbed since long before the whites came. A few steps beyond, I hit into a path I had been always looking for. It was narrow but well beaten, and I saw that Case had plenty of disciples. It seems indeed it was a piece of fashionable boldness to venture up here with the trader; and a young man scarce reckoned himself grown, till he had got his breech tattooed for one thing, and seen Case's devils for another. This is mighty like kanakas; but if you look at it another way, it's mighty like white folks too.

A bit along the path, I was brought to a clean stand and had to rub my eyes. There was a wall in front of me, the path passing it by a gap; it was tumble down and plainly very old, but built of big stones very well laid; and there is no native alive today upon that island that could dream of such a piece of building. Along all the top of it was a line of queer figures, idols, or scare-crows, or what not. They had carved and painted faces, ugly to view their eyes and teeth were of shell; their hair and their bright clothes blew in the wind, and some of them worked with the tugging. There are islands up west, where they make these kinds of figures till today; but if ever they were made in this island, the practise and the very recollection of it are now long forgotten. And the singular thing was that all these bogies were as fresh as toys out of a shop.

Then it came in my mind what Case had let out to me the first day, that he was a good forger of island curiosities: a thing by which so many traders turn an honest penny. And with that I saw the whole business, and how this display served the man a double purpose: first of all to season his curiosities, and then to frighten those that came to visit him.

But I should tell you (what made the thing more curious) that all the time the Tyrolean harps were harping round me in the trees, and even while I looked a green and yellow bird (that I suppose was building) began to tear the hair off the head of one of the figures.

A little farther on, I found the last curiosity of the museum. The first I saw of it was a longish mound of earth with a twist to it. Digging off the earth with my hands, I found underneath tarpaulin stretched on boards, so that this was plainly the roof of a cellar. It stood right on the top of the hill, and the entrance was on the far side, between two rocks, like the entrance to a cave. I went in as far as the bend, and looking round the corner, saw a shining face. It was big and ugly like a pantomime mask, and the brightness of it waxed and dwindled, and at times it smoked.

'Oho,' says I, 'luminous paint!'

And I must say I rather admired the man's ingenuity.

With a box of tools and a few mighty simple contrivances, he had made out to have a devil of a temple. Any poor kanaka brought up here in the dark, with the harps whining all round him, and shown that smoking face in the bottom of a hole, would make no kind of doubt but he had seen and heard enough devils for a lifetime. It's easy to find out what kanakas think. Just go back to yourself anyway round from ten to fifteen years old, and there's an average kanaka. There are some pious, just as there are pious boys; and the most of them, like the boys again, are middling honest and yet think it rather larks to steal, and are easy scared and rather like to be so. I remembered a boy I was at school with at home, who played the Case business. He didn't know anything, that boy; he couldn't do anything; he had no luminous paint and no Tyrolean harps; he just boldly said he was a sorcerer, and frightened us out of our boots, and we loved it. And then it came in my mind how the master had once flogged that boy, and the surprise we were all in to see the sorcerer catch it and bum like anybody else. Thinks I to myself: 'I must find some way of fixing it so for Master Case.' And the next moment I had my idea.

I went back by the path which, when once you had found it, was quite plain and easy walking; and when I stepped out on the black sands, who should I see but Master Case himself?' I cocked my gun and held it handy; and we marched up and passed without a word, each keeping the tail of his eye on the other; and no sooner had we passed, than we each wheeled round like fellows drilling and stood face to face. We had each taken the same notion in his head, you see, that the other fellow might give him the load of a gun in the stern.

'You've shot nothing,' says Case.

'I'm not on the shoot today,' says I.

'Well, the devil go with you for me,' says he.

'The same to you,' says I.

But we stuck just the way we were; no fear of either of us moving.

Case laughed. 'We can't stop here all day, though,' said he.

'Don't let me detain you,' says I.

He laughed again. 'Look here, Wiltshire, do you think me a fool?' he asked.

'More of a knave if you want to know,' says I.

'Well, do you think it would better me to shoot you here on this open beach?' said he, 'because I don't. Folks come fishing every day. There may be a score of them up the valley now, making copra; there may be half a dozen on the hill behind you after pigeons; they might be watching us this minute, and I shouldn't wonder. I give you my word I don't want to shoot you. Why should I? You don't hinder me any; you haven't got one pound of copra but what you made with your own hands like a negro slave. You're vegetating, that's what I call it; and I don't care where you vegetate, nor yet how long. Give me your word you don't mean to shoot me, and I'll give you a lead and walk away.'

'Well,' said I, 'you're frank and pleasant, ain't you? and I'll be the same. I don't mean to shoot you today. Why should I? This business is beginning; it ain't done yet, Mr Case. I've given you one turn already, I can see the marks of my knuckles on your head to this blooming hour; and I've more cooking for you. I'm not a paralee like Underhill; my name ain't Adams and it ain't Vigours; and I mean to show you that you've met your match.'

'This is a silly way to talk,' said he. 'This is not the talk to make me move on with.'

'All right,' said I. 'Stay where you are. I ain't in any hurry, and you know it. I can put in the day on this beach, and never mind. I ain't got any copra to bother with. I ain't got any luminous paint to see to.'

I was sorry I said that last, but it whipped out before I knew. I could see it took the wind out of his sails, and he stood and stared at me with his brow drawn up. Then I suppose he made up his mind he must get to the bottom of this.

'I take you at your word,' says he, and turned his back, and walked right into the devil's bush.

I let him go of course, for I had passed my word. But I watched him as long as he was in sight, and after he was gone, lit out for cover as lively as you would want to see, and went the rest of the way home under the bush. For I didn't trust him sixpenceworth. One thing I saw: I had been ass enough to give him warning; and that which I meant to do, I must do at once.

You would think I had had about enough excitement for one morning; but there was another turn waiting me. As soon as I got far enough round the cape to see my house, I made out there were strangers there; a little farther, and no doubt about it, there were a couple of armed sentries squatting at my door. I could only suppose the trouble about Uma must have come to a head, and the station been seized. For aught I could think Uma was taken up already, and these armed men were waiting to do the like by me.

However, as I came nearer, which I did at top speed, I saw there was a third native sitting on the verandah like a guest, and Uma was talking with him like a hostess. Nearer still I made out it was the big young chief Maea, and that he was smiling away and smoking; and what was he smoking? – none of your European cigarettes fit for a cat; not even the genuine, big, knock-me-down native article, that a fellow can really put in the time with, if his pipe is broke; but a cigar, and one of my Mexicans at that, that I could swear to. At sight of this, my heart started beating; and I took a wild hope in my head that the trouble was over, and Maea had come round.

Uma pointed me out to him, as I came up, and he met me at the head of my own stairs like a thorough gentleman.

'Vilivili,' said he, which was the best they could make of my name, 'I pleased.'

There is no doubt when an island chief wants to be civil he can do it. I saw the way things were from the word go. There was no call for Uma to say to me: 'He no 'fraid Ese now; come bring copra.' I tell you I shook hands with that kanaka like as if he was the best white man in Europe.

The fact was Case and he had got after the same girl, or Maea suspected it and concluded to make hay of the trader on the chance. He had dressed himself up, got a couple of retainers cleaned and armed to kind of make the thing more public, and just waiting till Case was clear of the village, came round to put the whole of his business my way. He was rich as well as powerful, I suppose that man was worth fifty thousand nuts per annum. I gave him the price of the beach and a quarter cent better, and as for credit, I would have advanced him the inside of the store and the fittings besides, I was so pleased to see him.

I must say he bought like a gentleman: rice and tins and biscuit enough for a week's feast, and stuffs by the bolt. He was agreeable besides; he had plenty fun to him; and we cracked jests together, mostly through Uma for interpreter, because he had mighty little English, and my native was still off colour. One thing I made out: he could never really have thought much harm of Uma; he could never have been really frightened, and must just have made believe from dodginess and because he thought Case had a strong pull in the village and could help him on.

This set me thinking that both he and I were in a tightish place. What he had done was to fly in the face of the whole village, and the thing might cost him his authority. More than that, after my talk with Case on the beach, I thought it might very well cost me my life. Case had as good as said he would pot me if ever I got copra; he would come home to find the best business in the village had changed hands, and the best thing I thought I could do was to get in first with the potting.

'See here, Uma,' says I, 'tell him I'm sorry I made him wait, but I was looking for Case's Tiapolo store in the bush.'

'He want savvy if you no 'fraid?' translated Uma.

I laughed out. 'Not much!' says I. 'Tell him the place is a blooming toyshop! Tell him in England we give these things to the kids to play with.'

'He want savvy if you hear devil sing?' she asked next.

'Look here,' I said, 'I can't do it now because I've got no banjo strings in stock; but the next time the ship comes round, I'll have one of these same contraptions right here in my verandah, and he can see for himself how much devil there is to it. Tell him, as soon as I can get the strings, I'll make one for his picaninnies. The name of the concern is a Tyrolean harp; and you can tell him the name means in English, that nobody but damfools give a cent for it.'

This time he was so pleased he had to try his English again. 'You talk true?' says he.

'Rather!' said I. 'Talk all-e-same bible. Bring out a bible here, Uma, if you've got such a thing, and I'll kiss it. Or I'll tell you what's better still,' says I, taking a header. 'Ask him if he's afraid to go up there himself by day.'

It appeared he wasn't; he could venture as far as that by day in company.

'That's the ticket, then!' said I. 'Tell him the man's a fraud and the place foolishness, and if he'll go up there tomorrow, he'll see all that's left of it. But tell him this, Uma, and mind he understands it; if he gets talking, it's bound to come to Case and I'm a dead man. I'm playing his game, tell him, and if he says one word, my blood will be at his door and be the damnation of him here and after.'

She told him, and he shook hands with me up to the hilts, and says he: 'No talk. Go up tomollow. You my friend?'

'No, sir!' says I. 'No such foolishness. I've come here to trade, tell him, and not to make friends. But as to Case, I'll send that man to glory.'

So off Maea went, pretty well pleased, as I could see.

FIVE. NIGHT IN THE BUSH

Well, I was committed now; Tiapolo had to be smashed up before next day; and my hands were pretty full, not only with preparations, but with argument. My house was like a mechanics' debating society; Uma was so made up that I shouldn't go into the bush by night, or that if I did I was never to come back again. You know her style of arguing, you've had a specimen about Queen Victoria and the devil; and I leave you to fancy if I was tired of it before dark.

At last, I had a good idea; what was the use of casting my pearls before her? I thought: some of her own chopped hay would be likelier to do the business.

'I'll tell you what, then,' said I. 'You fish out your bible, and I'll take that up along with me. That'll make me right.'

She swore a bible was no use.

'That's just your blamed kanaka ignorance,' said I. 'Bring the bible out.'

She brought it, and I turned to the title page where I thought there would likely be some English, and so there was. 'There!' said I. 'Look at that! *"London: printed for the British and Foreign Bible Society, Blackfriars"*'; and the date, which I can't read, owing to its being in these X's. There's no devil in hell can look near the Bible Society, Blackfriars. Why, you silly!' I said, 'how do you suppose we get along with our own *aitus* at home? All Bible Society!'

'I think you no got any,' said she. 'White man he tell me you no got.'

'Sounds likely, don't it?' I asked. 'Why would these islands all be chock full of them, and none in Europe?'

'Well, you no got breadfruit,' said she.

I could have tore my hair. 'Now, look here, old lady,' said I, 'you dry up, for I'm tired of you. I'll take the bible, which'll put me as straight as the mail; and that's the last word I've got to say.'

The night fell extraordinary dark, clouds coming up with sundown and overspreading all; not a star showed; there was only an end of a moon, and that not due before the small hours. Round the village, what with the lights and the fires in the open houses and the torches of many fishers moving on the reef, it kept as gay as an illumination; but the sea and the mountains and woods were all clean gone. I suppose it might be eight o'clock when I took the road, loaden like a donkey. First there was that bible, a book as big as your head, which I had let myself in for by my own tomfoolery. Then there was my gun and knife and lantern and patent matches, all necessary. And then there was the real plant of the affair in hand, a mortal weight of gunpowder, a pair of dynamite fishing-bombs, and two or three pieces of slow match that I had hauled out of the tin cases and spliced together the best way I could; for the match was only trade stuff, and a man would be crazy that trusted it. Altogether, you see, I had the materials of a pretty good blow up. Expense was nothing to me; I wanted that thing done right.

As long as I was in the open, and had the lamp in my house to steer by, I did well. But when I got to the path, it fell so dark I could make no headway, walking into trees and swearing there, like a man looking for the matches in his bedroom. I knew it was risky to light up; for my lantern would be visible all the way to the point of the cape; and as no one went there after dark, it would be talked about and come to Case's ears. But what was I to do? I had either to give the business over and lose caste with Maea, or light up, take my chance, and get through the thing the smartest I was able.

As long as I was on the path, I walked hard; but when I came to the black beach, I had to run. For the tide was now nearly flowed; and to get through with my powder dry between the surf and the steep hill, took all the quickness I possessed. As it was even, the wash caught me to the knees and I came near falling on a stone. All this time, the hurry I was in, and the free air and the smell of the sea, kept my spirits lively; but when I was once in the bush and began to climb the path, I took it easier. The

fearsomeness of the wood had been a good bit rubbed off
for me by Master Case's banjo strings and graven images;
yet I thought it was a dreary walk, and guessed, when the
disciples went up there, they must be badly scared. The
light of the lantern, striking among all these trunks, and
forked branches, and twisted rope's-ends of lianas, made
the whole place, or all that you could see it, a kind of a
puzzle of turning shadows. They came to meet you, solid
and quick like giants, and then span off and vanished; they
hove up over your head like clubs, and flew away into the
night like birds. The floor of the bush glimmered with dead
wood, the way the matchbox used to shine after you had
struck a lucifer. Big cold drops fell on me from the branches
overhead like sweat. There was no wind to mention, only a
little icy breath of a land breeze that stirred nothing; and
the harps were silent.

The first landfall I made was when I got through the
bush of wild cocoanuts, and came in view of the bogies on
the wall. Mighty queer they looked by the shining of the
lantern, with ther painted faces, and shell eyes, and their
clothes and their hair hanging. One after another I pulled
them all up and piled them in a bundle on the cellar roof,
so as they might go to glory with the rest. Then I chose a
place behind one of the big stones at the entrance, buried
my powder and the two shells, and arranged my match
along the passage. And then I had a look at the smoking
head, just for good-bye. It was doing fine.

'Cheer up,' says I. 'You're booked.'

It was my first idea to light up and be getting homeward;
for the darkness, and the glimmer of the dead wood, and the
shadows of the lantern made me lonely. But I knew where
one of the harps hung; it seemed a pity it shouldn't go with
the rest; and at the same time I couldn't help letting on to
myself that I was mortal tired of my employment and would
like best to be at home and have the door shut. I stepped out
of the cellar, and argued it fore and back. There was a sound
of the sea far down below me on the coast; nearer hand, not
a leaf stirred; I might have been the only living creature this
side Cape Horn. Well, as I stood there thinking, it seemed
the bush woke and became full of little noises. Little noises
they were, and nothing to hurt – a bit of a crackle, a bit of
a brush – but the breath jumped right out of me and my

throat went as dry as a biscuit. It wasn't Case I was afraid of, which would have been common sense; I never thought of Case; what took me, as sharp as the cholic, was the old wives' tales, the devil-women and the man-pigs. It was the toss of a penny whether I should run; but I got a purchase on myself, and stepped out, and held up the lantern (like a fool) and looked all round.

In the direction of the village and the path, there was nothing to be seen; but when I turned inland, it's a wonder to me I didn't drop. There – coming right up out of the desert and the bad bush – there, sure enough, was a devil-woman, just the way I had figured she would look. I saw the light shine on her bare arms and her bright eyes. And there went out of me a yell so big that I thought it was my death.

'Ah! No sing out!' says the devil-woman, in a kind of a high whisper. 'Why you talk big voice? Put out light! Ese he come.'

'My God Almighty, Uma, is that you?' says I.

'*Ioe*,' says she. 'I come quick. Ese here soon.'

'You come alone?' I asked. 'You no 'fraid?'

'Ah, too much 'fraid!' she whispered, clutching me. 'I think die.'

'Well,' says I, with a kind of a weak grin. 'I'm not the one to laugh at you, Mrs Wiltshire, for I'm about the worst scared man in the South Pacific myself.'

She told me in two words what brought her. I was scarce gone, it seems, when Faavao came in; and the old woman had met Black Jack running as hard as he was fit from our house to Case's. Uma neither spoke nor stopped, but lit right out to come and warn me. She was so close at my heels that the lantern was her guide across the beach, and afterwards, by the glimmer of it in the trees, she got her line up hill. It was only when I had got to the top or was in the cellar, that she wandered – Lord knows where! – and lost a sight of precious time, afraid to call out lest Case was at the heels of her, and falling in the bush so that she was all knocked and bruised. That must have been when she got too far to the southward, and how she came to take me in the flank at last, and frighten me beyond what I've got the words to tell of.

Well, anything was better than a devil-woman; but I thought her yarn serious enough. Black Jack had no call to be about my house, unless he was set there to watch; and it looked to me as if my tomfool word about the paint and perhaps some chatter of Maea's had got us all in a clove hitch. One thing was clear: Uma and I were here for the night; we daren't try to go home before day, and even then it would be safer to strike round up the mountain and come in by the back of the village, or we might walk into an ambuscade. It was plain too that the mine should be sprung immediately, or Case might be in time to stop it.

I marched into the tunnel, Uma keeping tight hold of me, opened my lantern and lit the match. The first length of it burned like a spill of paper; and I stood stupid, watching it burn, and thinking we were going aloft with Tiapolo, which was none of my views. The second took to a better rate, though faster than I cared about; and at that I got my wits again, hauled Uma clear of the passage, blew out and dropped the lantern; and the pair of us groped our way into the bush until I thought it might be safe, and lay down together by a tree.

'Old lady,' I said, 'I won't forget this night. You're a trump, and that's what's wrong with you.'

She humped herself close up to me. She had run out the way she was with nothing on but her kilt; and she was all wet with the dews and the sea on the black beach, and shook straight on with cold and the terror of the dark and the devils.

'Too much 'fraid,' was all she said.

The far side of Case's hill goes down near as steep as a precipice into the next valley. We were on the very edge of it, and I could see the dead wood shine and hear the sea sound far below. I didn't care about the position, which left me no retreat, but I was afraid to change. Then I saw I had made a worse mistake about the lantern, which I should have left lighted, so that I could have had a crack at Case when he stepped into the shine of it. And even if I hadn't the wit to do that, it seemed a senseless thing to leave the good lantern to blow up with the graven images; the thing belonged to me, after all, and was worth money, and might come in handy. If I could have trusted the match, I might have run in still and rescued it. But who was going to trust the match? You know what trade is; the stuff was good enough for kanakas to go fishing with, where they've got to look lively anyway, and the most they risk is only to have their hand blown off; but for any one that wanted to fool around a blow-up like mine, that match was rubbish.

Altogether, the best I could do was to lie still, see my shot gun handy, and wait for the explosion. But it was a solemn kind of a business; the blackness of the night was like solid; the only thing you could see was the nasty, bogy glimmer of the dead wood, and that showed you nothing but itself; and as for sounds, I stretched my ears till I thought I could have heard the match burn in the tunnel, and that bush was as silent as a coffin. Now and then there was a bit of a crack, but whether it was near or far, whether it was Case stubbing his toes within a few yards of me or a tree breaking miles away, I knew no more than the babe unborn.

And then all of a sudden Vesuvius went off. It was a long time coming; but when it came (though I say it that shouldn't) no man could ask to see a better. At first it was just a son of a gun of a row, and a spout of fire, and the wood lighted up so that you could see to read. And then the trouble began. Uma and I were half buried under a waggonful of earth, and glad it was no worse; for one of the rocks at the entrance of the tunnel was fired clean into the air, fell within a couple of fathom of where we lay, and bounded over the edge of the hill, and went pounding down into the next valley. I saw I had rather under-calculated our distance, or overdone the dynamite and powder, which you please.

And presently I saw I had made another slip. The noise of the thing began to die off, shaking the island; the dazzle was over; and yet the night didn't come back the way that I expected. For the whole wood was scattered with red coals and brands from the explosion; they were all round me on the flat, some had fallen below in the valley, and some stuck and flared in the treetops. I had no fear of fire, for these forests are too wet to kindle. But the trouble was that the place was all lit up, not very bright but good enough to get a shot by; and the way the coals were scattered, it was just as likely Case might have the advantage of myself. I looked all round for his white face, you may be sure; but there was not a sign of him. As for Uma, the life seemed to have been knocked right out of her by the bang and blaze of it.

There was one bad point in my game. One of the blessed graven images had come down all afire, hair and clothes and body, not four yards away from me. I cast a mighty noticing glance all round; there was still no Case; and I made up my mind I must get rid of that burning stick before he came, or I should be shot there like a dog.

It was my first idea to have crawled; and then I thought speed was the main thing, and stood half up to make a rush. The same moment, from somewhere between me and the sea, there came a flash and a report, and a rifle bullet screeched in my ear. I swung straight round, and up with my gun. But the brute had a Winchester; and before I could as much as see him, his second shot knocked me over like a ninepin. I seemed to fly in the air, then came down by the run and lay half a minute silly; and then I found my hands empty and my gun had flown over my head as I fell. It makes a man mighty wide awake to be in the kind of box that I was in. I scarce knew where I was hurt, or whether I was hurt or not, but turned right over on my face to crawl after my weapon. Unless you have tried to get about with a smashed leg, you don't know what pain is, and I let a howl out like a bullock's.

This was the unluckiest noise that I ever made in my life. Up to then, Uma had stuck to her tree like a sensible woman, knowing she would be only in the way. But as soon as she heard me sing out, she ran forward – the Winchester cracked again – and down she went.

I had sat up, leg and all, to stop her; but when I saw her tumble, I clapped down again where I was, lay still, and felt the handle of my knife. I had been scurried and put out before. No more of that for me; he had knocked over my girl, I had got to fix him for it; and I lay there and gritted my teeth, and footed up the chances. My leg was broke, my gun was gone, Case had still ten shots in his Winchester, it looked a kind of hopeless business. But I never despaired nor thought upon despairing: that man had got to go.

For a goodish bit, not one of us let on. Then I heard Case begin to move nearer in the bush, but mighty careful. The image had burned out; there were only a few coals left here and there; and the wood was main dark, but had a kind of a low glow in it like a fire on its last legs. It was by this that I made out Case's head looking at me over a big tuft of ferns; and at the same time the brute saw me and shouldered his Winchester. I lay quite still and as good as looked into the barrel; it was my last chance; but I thought my heart would have come right out of its bearings. Then he fired. Lucky for me it was no shot gun, for the bullet struck within an inch of me and knocked the dirt in my eyes.

Just you try and see if you can lie quiet, and let a man take a sitting shot at you, and miss you by a hair! But I did, and lucky too. Awhile Case stood with the Winchester at the port-arms; then he gave a little laugh to himself, and stepped round the ferns.

'Laugh!' thought I. 'If you had the wit of a louse, you would be praying!'

I was all as taut as a ship's hauser or the spring of a watch; and as soon as he came within reach of me, I had him by the ankle, plucked the feet right from under him, laid him out, and was upon the top of him, broken leg and all, before he breathed. His Winchester had gone the same road as my shot gun; it was nothing to me; I defied him now. I'm a pretty strong man anyway, but I never knew what strength was till I got hold of Case. He was knocked out of time by the rattle he came down with, and threw up his hands together, more like a frightened woman, so that I caught both of them with my left. This wakened him up, and he fixed his teeth in my forearm like a weasel. Much I cared! My leg gave me all the pain I had any use for; and I drew my knife, and got it in the place.

'Now,' said I, 'I've got you; and you're gone up, and a good job too. Do you feel the point of that? That's for Underhill. And there's for Adams. And now here's for Uma, and that's going to knock your blooming soul right out of you.'

With that, I gave him the cold steel for all I was worth. His body kicked under me like a spring sofa; he gave a dreadful kind of a long moan, and lay still.

'I wonder if you're dead. I hope so,' I thought, for my head was swimming. But I wasn't going to take chances; I had his own example too close before me for that; and I tried to draw the knife out to give it him again. The blood came over my hands, I remember, hot as tea; and with that

I fainted clean away and fell with my head on the man's mouth.

When I came to myself, it was pitch dark; the cinders had burned out, there was nothing to be seen but the shine of the dead wood; and I couldn't remember where I was, nor why I was in such pain, nor what I was all wetted with. Then it came back; and the first thing I attended to was to give him the knife again a half a dozen times up to the handle. I believe he was dead already; but it did him no harm and did me good.

'I bet you're dead now,' I said, and then I called to Uma.

Nothing answered; and I made a move to go and grope for her, fouled my broken leg, and fainted again.

When I came to myself the second time, the clouds had all cleared away except a few that sailed there, white as cotton. The moon was up, a tropic moon. The moon at home turns a wood black; but even this old but-end of a one showed up that forest as green as by day. The night birds – or rather they're a kind of early morning bird – sang out with their long, falling notes like nightingales. And I could see the dead man that I was still half resting on, looking right up into the sky with his open eyes, no paler than when he was alive; and a little way off, Uma tumbled on her side. I got over to her the best way I was able; and when I got there, she was broad awake and crying and sobbing to herself with no more noise than an insect. It appears she was afraid to cry out loud, because of the *aitus*. Altogether she was not much hurt, but scared beyond belief; she had come to her senses a long while ago, cried out to me, heard nothing in reply, made out we were both dead, and had lain there ever since, afraid to budge a finger. The ball had ploughed up her shoulder; and she had lost a main quantity of blood; but I soon had that tied up the way it ought to be with the tail of my shirt and a scarf I had on, got her head on my sound knee and my back against a trunk, and settled down to wait for morning. Uma was for neither use nor ornament; and could only clutch hold of me, and shake, and cry; I don't suppose there was ever anybody worse scared, and to do her justice, she had had a lively night of it. As for me, I was in a good bit of pain and fever, but not so bad when I sat still; and every time I looked over to Case, I could have sung and whistled. Talk about meat and drink! to see that man lying there dead as a herring filled me full.

The night birds stopped after a while; and then the light began to change, the east came orange, the whole wood began to whirr with singing like a musical box, and there was the broad day.

I didn't expect Maea for a long while yet; and indeed I thought there was an off chance he might go back on the whole idea and not come at all. I was the better pleased when, about an hour after daylight, I heard sticks smashing and a lot of kanakas laughing and singing out to keep their courage up. Uma sat up quite brisk at the first word of it; and presently we saw a party come stringing out of the path, Maea in front and behind him a white man in a pith helmet. It was Mr Tarleton who had turned up late last night in Falesá, having left his boat and walked the last stage with a lantern.

They buried Case upon the field of glory, right in the hole where he had kept the smoking head. I waited till the thing was done; and Mr Tarleton prayed, which I thought tomfoolery, but I'm bound to say he gave a pretty sick view of the dear departed's prospects, and seemed to have his own ideas of hell. I had it out with him afterwards, told him he had scamped his duty, and what he had ought to have done was to up like a man and tell the kanakas plainly Case was damned, and a good riddance; but I never could get him to see it my way. Then they made me a litter of poles and carried me down to the station. Mr Tarleton set my leg, and made a regular missionary splice of it, so that I limp to this day. That done, he took down my evidence, and Uma's and Maea's, wrote it all out fair, and had us sign it; and then he got the chiefs and marched over to Papa Randall's to seize Case's papers.

All they found was a bit of a diary, kept for a good many years, and all about the price of copra and chickens being stolen and that; and the books of the business, and the will I told you of in the beginning, by both of which the whole thing (stock lock and barrel) appeared to belong to the Sāmoa woman. It was I that bought her out, at a mighty reasonable figure, for she was in a hurry to get home. As for Randall and the black, they had to tramp;

got into some kind of a station on the Papa-mālūlū side; did very bad business, for the truth is neither of the pair was fit for it; and lived mostly on fish, which was the means of Randall's death. It seems there was a nice shoal in one day, and papa went after them with dynamite; either the match burned too fast or papa was full, or both, but the shell went off (in the usual way) before he threw it; and where was papa's hand? Well, there's nothing to hurt in that; the islands up north are all full of one-handed men, like the parties in the Arabian Nights; but either Randall was too old, or he drank too much, and the short and the long of it was that he died. Pretty soon after, the nigger was turned out of the islands for stealing from white men, and went off to the west, where he found men of his own colour, in case he liked that, and the men of his own colour took and ate him at some kind of a corroborree and I'm sure I hope he was to their fancy!

So there was I left alone in my glory at Falesá; and when the schooner came round I filled her up and gave her a deck cargo half as high as the house. I must say Mr Tarleton did the right thing by us; but he took a meanish kind of a revenge.

'Now, Mr Wiltshire,' said he, 'I've put you all square with everybody here. It wasn't difficult to do, Case being gone; but I have done it, and given my pledge besides that you will deal fairly with the natives. I must ask you to keep my word.'

Well, so I did. I used to be bothered about my balances, but I reasoned it out this way. We all have queerish balances, and the natives all know it and water their copra in a proportion; so that it's fair all round. But the truth is, it did use to bother me; and though I did well in Falesá, I was half-glad when the firm moved me on to another station, where I was under no kind of pledge, and could look my balances in the face.

As for the old lady, you know her as well as I do. She's only the one fault; if you don't keep your eye lifting, she would give away the roof off the station. Well, it seems it's natural in kanaka. She's turned a powerful big woman now, and could throw a London bobby over her shoulder. But that's natural in kanakas too; and there's no manner of doubt that she's an A one wife.

Mr Tarleton's gone home, his trick being over; he was the best missionary I ever struck, and now it seems he's parsonizing down Somerset ways. Well, that's best for him; he'll have no kanakas there to get luny over.

My public house? Not a bit of it, nor ever likely; I'm stuck here, I fancy; I don't like to leave the kids, you see; and there's no use talking – they're better here than what they would be in a white man's country. Though Ben took the eldest up to Auckland, where he's being schooled with the best. But what bothers me is the girls. They're only half castes of course; I know that as well as you do, and there's nobody thinks less of half castes than I do; but they're mine, and about all I've got; I can't reconcile my mind to their taking up with kanakas, and I'd like to know where I'm to find them whites?

THE EBB-TIDE
A TRIO AND QUARTETTE

by Robert Louis Stevenson
in collaboration with
Lloyd Osbourne

'There is a tide in the affairs of men'

Contents

NOTE

On the pronunciation of a name very
frequently repeated on these pages, the
reader may take for a guide:
'It was the schooner *Farallone*.'

R.L.S.
L.O.

Stevenson and I little knew, when we began our collaboration, that we were afterwards to raise such a hornets' nest about our ears. The critics resented such an unequal partnership, and made it impossible for us to continue it. It may be that they were right; they wanted Stevenson's best, and felt pretty sure they would not get it in our collaboration. But when they ascribed all the good in our three books to Stevenson and all the bad to me, they went a little beyond the mark. It is a pleasure to me to recall that the early part of both *The Wrecker* and *The Ebb-Tide* was almost entirely my own; so also were the storm scenes of the *Norah Creina*; so also the fight on the *Flying Scud*; so also the inception of Huish's scheme, the revelation of it to his companions, his landing on the atoll with the bottle of vitriol in his breast. On the other hand, the Paris portion of *The Wrecker* was all Stevenson's, as well as the concluding chapters of both the South Sea books.

It is not possible to disentangle anything else that was wholly mine or his – the blending was too complete, our method of work too criss-crossed and intimate. For instance, we would begin by outlining the story in a general way; this done, we marshalled it into chapters, with a few explanatory words to each; then it was time for me to write the first draft of Chapter 1. This I would read to him, and if it were satisfactory it was laid to one side; but if it were not, I would rewrite it, embodying his criticisms. Each chapter in turn was fully discussed in advance before I put pen to paper; and in this way, though the actual first draft was in my own hand, the form of the story continually took shape under Stevenson's eyes. When my first draft of the entire book was finished he would rewrite it again from cover to cover.

I can remember nothing more delightful than the days

3

we thus passed together. If our three books are in no wise great, they preserve, it seems to me, something of the zest and exhilaration that went into their making – the good humour, the eagerness.

We were both under the glamour of the Islands – and that life, so strange, so picturesque, so animated, took us both by storm. Kings and beachcombers, pearl-fishers and princesses, traders, slavers, and schooner-captains, castaways, and runaways – what a world it was! And all this in a fairyland of palms, and glassy bays, and little lost settlements nestling at the foot of forest and mountain, with kings to make brotherhood with us, and a dubious white man or two, in earrings and pyjamas, no less insistent to extend to us the courtesies of the "beach."

It was amid such people, and amid such scenes, that *The Ebb-Tide* and *The Wrecker* were written.

PART I
THE TRIO

ONE

Night on the Beach

Throughout the island world of the Pacific, scattered men of many European races and from almost every grade of society carry activity and disseminate disease. Some prosper, some vegetate. Some have mounted the steps of thrones and owned islands and navies. Others again must marry for a livelihood; a strapping, merry, chocolate-coloured dame supports them in sheer idleness; and, dressed like natives, but still retaining some foreign element of gait or attitude, still perhaps with some relic (such as a single eye-glass) of the officer and gentleman, they sprawl in palm-leaf verandahs and entertain an island audience with memoirs of the music-hall. And there are still others, less pliable, less capable, less fortunate, perhaps less base, who continue, even in these isles of plenty, to lack bread.

At the far end of the town of Papeete, three such men were seated on the beach under a *purao* tree.

It was late. Long ago the band had broken up and marched musically home, a motley troop of men and women, merchant clerks and navy officers, dancing in its wake, arms about waist and crowned with garlands. Long ago darkness and silence had gone from house to house about the tiny pagan city. Only the street lamps shone on, making a glow-worm halo in the umbrageous alleys or drawing a tremulous image on the waters of the port. A sound of snoring ran among the piles of lumber by the Government pier. It was wafted ashore from the graceful clipper-bottomed schooners, where they lay moored close in like dinghies, and their crews were stretched upon the deck under the open sky or huddled in a rude tent amidst the disorder of merchandise.

But the men under the *purao* had no thought of sleep. The same temperature in England would have passed without remark in summer; but it was bitter cold for the South

7

Seas. Inanimate nature knew it, and the bottle of cocoanut oil stood frozen in every bird-cage house about the island; and the men knew it, and shivered. They wore flimsy cotton clothes, the same they had sweated in by day and run the gauntlet of the tropic showers; and to complete their evil case, they had no breakfast to mention, less dinner, and no supper at all.

In the telling South Sea phrase, these three men were *on the beach*. Common calamity had brought them acquainted, as the three most miserable English-speaking creatures in Tahiti; and beyond their misery, they knew next to nothing of each other, not even their true names. For each had made a long apprenticeship in going downward; and each, at some stage of the descent, had been shamed into the adoption of an *alias*. And yet not one of them had figured in a court of justice; two were men of kindly virtues; and one, as he sat and shivered under the *purao*, had a tattered Virgil in his pocket.

Certainly, if money could have been raised upon the book, Robert Herrick would long ago have sacrificed that last possession; but the demand for literature, which is so marked a feature in some parts of the South Seas, extends not so far as the dead tongues; and the Virgil, which he could not exchange against a meal, had often consoled him in his hunger. He would study it, as he lay with tightened belt on the floor of the old calaboose, seeking favourite passages and finding new ones only less beautiful because they lacked the consecration of remembrance. Or he would pause on random country walks; sit on the path side, gazing over the sea on the mountains of Eimeo; and dip into the *Aeneid*, seeking *sortes*. And if the oracle (as is the way of oracles) replied with no very certain nor encouraging voice, visions of England at least would throng upon the exile's memory: the busy schoolroom, the green playing-fields, holidays at home, and the perennial roar of London, and the fireside, and the white head of his father. For it is the destiny of those grave, restrained and classic writers, with whom we make enforced and often painful acquaintanceship at school, to pass into the blood and become native in the memory; so that a phrase of Virgil speaks not so much of Mantua or Augustus, but English places and the student's own irrevocable youth.

Robert Herrick was the son of an intelligent, active, and ambitious man, small partner in a considerable London house. Hopes were conceived of the boy; he was sent to a good school, gained there an Oxford scholarship, and proceeded in course to the Western University. With all his talent and taste (and he had much of both) Robert was deficient in consistency and intellectual manhood, wandered in bypaths of study, worked at music or at metaphysics when he should have been at Greek, and took at last a paltry degree. Almost at the same time, the London house was disastrously wound up; Mr Herrick must begin the world again as a clerk in a strange office, and Robert relinquish his ambitions and accept with gratitude a career that he detested and despised. He had no head for figures, no interest in affairs, detested the constraint of hours, and despised the aims and the success of merchants. To grow rich was none of his ambitions; rather to do well. A worse or a more bold young man would have refused the destiny; perhaps tried his future with his pen; perhaps enlisted. Robert, more prudent, possibly more timid, consented to embrace that way of life in which he could most readily assist his family. But he did so with a mind divided; fled the neighbourhood of former comrades; and chose, out of several positions placed at his disposal, a clerkship in New York.

His career thenceforth was one of unbroken shame. He did not drink, he was exactly honest, he was never rude to his employers, yet was everywhere discharged. Bringing no interest to his duties, he brought no attention; his day was a tissue of things neglected and things done amiss; and from place to place and from town to town, he carried the character of one thoroughly incompetent. No man can bear the word applied to him without some flush of colour, as indeed there is none other that so emphatically slams in a man's face the door of self-respect. And to Herrick, who was conscious of talents and acquirements, who looked down upon those humble duties in which he was found wanting, the pain was the more exquisite. Early in his fall, he had ceased to be able to make remittances; shortly after, having nothing but failure to communicate, he ceased writing home; and about a year before this tale begins, turned suddenly upon the streets of San Francisco by a

vulgar and infuriated German Jew, he had broken the last
bonds of self-respect, and upon a sudden impulse, changed
his name and invested his last dollar in a passage on the
mail brigantine, the *City of Papeete*. With what expectation
he had trimmed his flight for the South Seas, Herrick
perhaps scarcely knew. Doubtless there were fortunes to
be made in pearl and copra; doubtless others not more
gifted than himself had climbed in the island world to be
queen's consorts and king's ministers. But if Herrick had
gone there with any manful purpose, he would have kept
his father's name; the *alias* betrayed his moral bankruptcy;
he had struck his flag; he entertained no hope to reinstate
himself or help his straitened family; and he came to the
islands (where he knew the climate to be soft, bread cheap,
and manners easy) a skulker from life's battle and his own
immediate duty. Failure, he had said, was his portion; let
it be a pleasant failure.

It is fortunately not enough to say 'I will be base.'
Herrick continued in the islands his career of failure; but
in the new scene and under the new name, he suffered
no less sharply than before. A place was got, it was lost
in the old style; from the long-suffering of the keepers of
restaurants he fell to more open charity upon the wayside;
as time went on, good nature became weary, and after a
repulse or two, Herrick became shy. There were women
enough who would have supported a far worse and a far
uglier man; Herrick never met or never knew them: or
if he did both, some manlier feeling would revolt, and
he preferred starvation. Drenched with rains, broiling by
day, shivering by night, a disused and ruinous prison for
a bedroom, his diet begged or pilfered out of rubbish
heaps, his associates two creatures equally outcast with
himself, he had drained for months the cup of penitence.
He had known what it was to be resigned, what it was to
break forth in a childish fury of rebellion against fate, and
what it was to sink into the coma of despair. The time
had changed him. He told himself no longer tales of an
easy and perhaps agreeable declension; he read his nature
otherwise; he had proved himself incapable of rising, and
he now learned by experience that he could not stoop to
fall. Something that was scarcely pride or strength, that was
perhaps only refinement, withheld him from capitulation;

but he looked on upon his own misfortune with a growing
rage, and sometimes wondered at his patience.

It was now the fourth month completed, and still there
was no change or sign of change. The moon, racing through
a world of flying clouds of every size and shape and density,
some black as ink stains, some delicate as lawn, threw the
marvel of her Southern brightness over the same lovely
and detested scene: the island mountains crowned with
the perennial island cloud, the embowered city studded
with rare lamps, the masts in the harbour, the smooth
mirror of the lagoon, and the mole of the barrier reef
on which the breakers whitened. The moon shone too,
with bull's-eye sweeps, on his companions; on the stalwart
frame of the American who called himself Brown, and was
known to be a master mariner in some disgrace; and on
the dwarfish person, the pale eyes and toothless smile of a
vulgar and bad-hearted cockney clerk. Here was society for
Robert Herrick! The Yankee skipper was a man at least: he
had sterling qualities of tenderness and resolution; he was
one whose hand you could take without a blush. But there
was no redeeming grace about the other, who called himself
sometimes Hay and sometimes Tomkins, and laughed at
the discrepancy; who had been employed in every store in
Papeete, for the creature was able in his way; who had been
discharged from each in turn, for he was wholly vile; who
had alienated all his old employers so that they passed him
in the street as if he were a dog, and all his old comrades
so that they shunned him as they would a creditor.

Not long before, a ship from Peru had brought an
influenza, and it now raged in the island, and particularly
in Papeete. From all round the *purao* arose and fell a dismal
sound of men coughing, and strangling as they coughed.
The sick natives, with the islander's impatience of a touch
of fever, had crawled from their houses to be cool and,
squatting on the shore or on the beached canoes, painfully
expected the new day. Even as the crowing of cocks goes
about the country in the night from farm to farm, accesses
of coughing arose, and spread, and died in the distance,
and sprang up again. Each miserable shiverer caught the
suggestion from his neighbour, was torn for some minutes
by that cruel ecstasy, and left spent and without voice or
courage when it passed. If a man had pity to spend, Papeete

beach, in that cold night and in that infected season, was a place to spend it on. And of all the sufferers, perhaps the least deserving, but surely the most pitiable, was the London clerk. He was used to another life, to houses, beds, nursing, and the dainties of the sickroom; he lay there now, in the cold open, exposed to the gusting of the wind, and with an empty belly. He was besides infirm; the disease shook him to the vitals; and his companions watched his endurance with surprise. A profound commiseration filled them, and contended with and conquered their abhorrence. The disgust attendant on so ugly a sickness magnified this dislike; at the same time, and with more than compensating strength, shame for a sentiment so inhuman bound them the more straitly to his service; and even the evil they knew of him swelled their solicitude, for the thought of death is always the least supportable when it draws near to the merely sensual and selfish. Sometimes they held him up; sometimes, with mistaken helpfulness, they beat him between the shoulders; and when the poor wretch lay back ghastly and spent after a paroxysm of coughing, they would sometimes peer into his face, doubtfully exploring it for any mark of life. There is no one but has some virtue: that of the clerk was courage; and he would make haste to reassure them in a pleasantry not always decent.

'I'm all right, pals,' he gasped once: 'this is the thing to strengthen the muscles of the larynx.'

'Well, you take the cake!' cried the captain.

'O, I'm good plucked enough,' pursued the sufferer with a broken utterance. 'But it do seem bloomin' hard to me, that I should be the only party down with this form of vice, and the only one to do the funny business. I think one of you other parties might wake up. Tell a fellow something.'

'The trouble is we've nothing to tell, my son,' returned the captain.

'I'll tell you, if you like, what I was thinking,' said Herrick.

'Tell us anything,' said the clerk, 'I only want to be reminded that I ain't dead.'

Herrick took up his parable, lying on his face and speaking slowly and scarce above his breath, not like a man who has anything to say, but like one talking against time.

'Well, I was thinking this,' he began: 'I was thinking I

lay on Papeete beach one night – all moon and squalls and
fellows coughing – and I was cold and hungry, and down
in the mouth, and was about ninety years of age, and had
spent two hundred and twenty of them on Papeete beach.
And I was thinking I wished I had a ring to rub, or had
a fairy godmother, or could raise Beelzebub. And I was
trying to remember how you did it. I knew you made a
ring of skulls, for I had seen that in the *Freischütz*: and that
you took off your coat and turned up your sleeves, for I had
seen Formes do that when he was playing Kaspar, and you
could see (by the way he went about it) it was a business he
had studied; and that you ought to have something to kick
up a smoke and a bad smell, I dare say a cigar might do, and
that you ought to say the Lord's Prayer backwards. Well, I
wondered if I could do that; it seemed rather a feat, you
see. And then I wondered if I would say it forward, and I
thought I did. Well, no sooner had I got to *world without
end,* than I saw a man in a *pariu,* and with a mat under his
arm, come along the beach from the town. He was rather a
hard-favoured old party, and he limped and crippled, and
all the time he kept coughing. At first I didn't cotton to
his looks, I thought, and then I got sorry for the old soul
because he coughed so hard. I remembered that we had
some of that cough mixture the American consul gave the
captain for Hay. It never did Hay a ha'porth of service, but
I thought it might do the old gentleman's business for him,
and stood up. "*Yorana!*" says I. "*Yorana!*" says he. "Look
here," I said, "I've got some first-rate stuff in a bottle; it'll
fix your cough, savvy? *Harry my*[1] and I'll measure you a
tablespoonful in the palm of my hand, for all our plate
is at the bankers.' So I thought the old party came up,
and the nearer he came, the less I took to him. But I had
passed my word, you see.'

'Wot is this bloomin' drivel?' interrupted the clerk. 'It's
like the rot there is in tracts.'

'It's a story; I used to tell them to the kids at home,'
said Herrick. 'If it bores you, I'll drop it.'

'O, cut along!' returned the sick man, irritably. 'It's
better than nothing.'

---

1. Come here.

'Well,' continued Herrick, 'I had no sooner given him the cough mixture than he seemed to straighten up and change, and I saw he wasn't a Tahitian after all, but some kind of Arab, and had a long beard on his chin. "One good turn deserves another," says he. "I am a magician out of the *Arabian Nights*, and this mat that I have under my arm is the original carpet of Mohammed Ben Somebody-or-other. Say the word, and you can have a cruise upon the carpet." "You don't mean to say this is the Travelling Carpet?" I cried. "You bet I do," said he. "You've been to America since last I read the *Arabian Nights*," said I, a little suspicious. "I should think so," said he. "Been everywhere. A man with a carpet like this isn't going to moulder in a semi-detached villa." Well, that struck me as reasonable. "All right," I said; "and do you mean to tell me I can get on that carpet and go straight to London, England?" I said, "London, England," captain, because he seemed to have been so long in your part of the world. "In the crack of a whip," said he. I figured up the time. What is the difference between Papeete and London, captain?'

'Taking Greenwich and Point Venus, nine hours, odd minutes and seconds,' replied the mariner.

'Well, that's about what I made it,' resumed Herrick, 'about nine hours. Calling this three in the morning, I made out I would drop into London about noon; and the idea tickled me immensely. "There's only one bother," I said, "I haven't a copper cent. It would be a pity to go to London and not buy the morning *Standard*." "O!" said he, "you don't realise the conveniences of this carpet. You see this pocket? you've only got to stick your hand in, and you pull it out filled with sovereigns.""

'Double-eagles, wasn't it?' inquired the captain.

'That was what it was!' cried Herrick. 'I thought they seemed unusually big, and I remember now I had to go to the money-changers at Charing Cross and get English silver.'

'O, you went there?' said the clerk. 'Wot did you do? Bet you had a B. and S.!'

'Well, you see, it was just as the old boy said – like the cut of a whip,' said Herrick. 'The one minute I was here on the beach at three in the morning, the next I was in front of the Golden Cross at midday. At first I was dazzled, and covered my eyes, and there didn't seem the smallest change;

the roar of the Strand and the roar of the reef were like the same: hark to it now, and you can hear the cabs and buses rolling and the streets resound! And then at last I could look about, and there was the old place, and no mistake! With the statues in the square, and St Martin's-in-the-Fields, and the bobbies, and the sparrows, and the hacks; and I can't tell you what I felt like. I felt like crying, I believe, or dancing, or jumping clean over the Nelson Column. I was like a fellow caught up out of Hell and flung down into the dandiest part of Heaven. Then I spotted for a hansom with a spanking horse. "A shilling for yourself, if you're there in twenty minutes!" said I to the jarvey. He went a good pace, though of course it was a trifle to the carpet; and in nineteen minutes and a half I was at the door.'

'What door?' asked the captain.

'Oh, a house I know of,' returned Herrick.

'But it was a public-house!' cried the clerk – only these were not his words. 'And w'y didn't you take the carpet there instead of trundling in a growler?'

'I didn't want to startle a quiet street,' said the narrator. 'Bad form. And besides, it was a hansom.'

'Well, and what did you do next?' inquired the captain.

'Oh, I went in,' said Herrick.

'The old folks?' asked the captain.

'That's about it,' said the other, chewing a grass.

'Well, I think you are about the poorest 'and at a yarn!' cried the clerk. 'Crikey, it's like *Ministering Children*! I can tell you there would be more beer and skittles about my little jaunt. I would go and have a B. and S. for luck. Then I would get a big ulster with astrakhan fur, and take my cane and do the la-de-la down Piccadilly. Then I would go to a slap-up restaurant, and have green peas, and a bottle of fizz, and a chump chop – Oh! and I forgot, I'd 'ave some devilled whitebait first – and green gooseberry tart, and 'ot coffee, and some of that form of vice in big bottles with a seal – Benedictine – that's the bloomin' nyme! Then I'd drop into a theatre, and pal on with some chappies, and do the dancing rooms and bars, and that, and wouldn't go 'ome till morning, till daylight doth appear. And the next day I'd have water-cresses, 'am, muffin, and fresh butter; wouldn't I just, O my!'

The clerk was interrupted by a fresh attack of coughing.

'Well, now, I'll tell you what I would do,' said the captain:
'I would have none of your fancy rigs with the man driving
from the mizzen cross-trees, but a plain fore-and-aft hack
cab of the highest registered tonnage. First of all, I would
bring up at the market and get a turkey and a sucking-pig.
Then I'd go to a wine merchant's and get a dozen of
champagne, and a dozen of some sweet wine, rich and
sticky and strong, something in the port or madeira line,
the best in the store. Then I'd bear up for a toy-store, and
lay out twenty dollars in assorted toys for the piccaninnies;
and then to a confectioner's and take in cakes and pies and
fancy bread, and that stuff with the plums in it; and then
to a news-agency and buy all the papers, all the picture
ones for the kids, and all the story papers for the old girl
about the Earl discovering himself to Anna-Mariar and the
escape of the Lady Maude from the private madhouse; and
then I'd tell the fellow to drive home.'

'There ought to be some syrup for the kids,' suggested
Herrick; 'they like syrup.'

'Yes, syrup for the kids, red syrup at that!' said the
captain. 'And those things they pull at, and go pop, and
have measly poetry inside. And then I tell you we'd have
a thanksgiving day and Christmas tree combined. Great
Scott, but I would like to see the kids! I guess they would
light right out of the house, when they saw daddy driving
up. My little Adar— '

The captain stopped sharply.

'Well, keep it up!' said the clerk.

'The damned thing is, I don't know if they ain't starving!'
cried the captain.

'They can't be worse off than we are, and that's one
comfort,' returned the clerk. 'I defy the devil to make me
worse off.'

It seemed as if the devil heard him. The light of the moon
had been some time cut off and they had talked in darkness.
Now there was heard a roar, which drew impetuously
nearer; the face of the lagoon was seen to whiten; and
before they had staggered to their feet, a squall burst in rain
upon the outcasts. The rage and volume of that avalanche
one must have lived in the tropics to conceive; a man panted
in its assault, as he might pant under a shower-bath; and the
world seemed whelmed in night and water.

They fled, groping for their usual shelter – it might be almost called their home – in the old calaboose; came drenched into its empty chambers; and lay down, three sops of humanity on the cold coral floors, and presently, when the squall was overpast, the others could hear in the darkness the chattering of the clerk's teeth.

'I say, you fellows,' he wailed, 'for God's sake, lie up and try to warm me. I'm blymed if I don't think I'll die else!'

So the three crept together into one wet mass, and lay until day came, shivering and dozing off, and continually re-awakened to wretchedness by the coughing of the clerk.

TWO

Morning on the Beach – The Three Letters

The clouds were all fled, the beauty of the tropic day was spread upon Papeete; and the wall of breaking seas upon the reef, and the palms upon the islet, already trembled in the heat. A French man-of-war was going out, homeward bound; she lay in the middle distance of the port, an ant heap for activity. In the night a schooner had come in, and now lay far out, hard by the passage; and the yellow flag, the emblem of pestilence, flew on her. From up the coast, a long procession of canoes headed round the point and towards the market, bright as a scarf with the many-coloured clothing of the natives and the piles of fruit. But not even the beauty and the welcome warmth of the morning, not even these naval movements, so interesting to sailors and to idlers, could engage the attention of the outcasts. They were still cold at heart, their mouths sour from the want of sleep, their steps rambling from the lack of food; and they strung like lame geese along the beach in a disheartened silence. It was towards the town they moved; towards the town whence smoke arose, where happier folk were breakfasting; and as they went, their hungry eyes were upon all sides, but they were only scouting for a meal.

A small and dingy schooner lay snug against the quay, with which it was connected by a plank. On the forward deck, under a spot of awning, five Kanakas who made up the crew, were squatted round a basin of fried feis,[1] and drinking coffee from tin mugs.

'Eight bells: knock off for breakfast!' cried the captain with a miserable heartiness. 'Never tried this craft before; positively my first appearance; guess I'll draw a bumper house.'

---

1. *Fei* is the hill banana.

He came close up to where the plank rested on the grassy quay; turned his back upon the schooner, and began to whistle that lively air, 'The Irish Washerwoman.' It caught the ears of the Kanaka seamen like a preconcerted signal; with one accord they looked up from their meal and crowded to the ship's side, fei in hand and munching as they looked. Even as a poor brown Pyrenean bear dances in the streets of English towns under his master's baton; even so, but with how much more of spirit and precision, the captain footed it in time to his own whistling, and his long morning shadow capered beyond him on the grass. The Kanakas smiled on the performance; Herrick looked on heavy-eyed, hunger for the moment conquering all sense of shame; and a little farther off, but still hard by, the clerk was torn by the seven devils of the influenza.

The captain stopped suddenly, appeared to perceive his audience for the first time, and represented the part of a man surprised in his private hour of pleasure.

'Hello!' said he.

The Kanakas clapped hands and called upon him to go on.

'No, *sir!*' said the captain. 'No eat, no dance. Savvy?'

'Poor old man!' returned one of the crew. 'Him no eat?'

'Lord, no!' said the captain. 'Like-um too much eat. No got.'

'All right. Me got,' said the sailor; 'you tome here. Plenty toffee, plenty fei. Nutha man him tome too.'

'I guess we'll drop right in,' observed the captain; and he and his companions hastened up the plank. They were welcomed on board with the shaking of hands; place was made for them about the basin; a sticky demijohn of molasses was added to the feast in honour of company, and an accordion brought from the forecastle and significantly laid by the performer's side.

'*Ariana*,'[1] said he lightly, touching the instrument as he spoke; and he fell to on a long savoury fei, made an end of it, raised his mug of coffee, and nodded across at the spokesman of the crew. 'Here's your health,

1. By-and-bye.

old man; you're a credit to the South Pacific,' said
he.

With the unsightly greed of hounds they glutted themselves with the hot food and coffee; and even the clerk
revived and the colour deepened in his eyes. The kettle
was drained, the basin cleaned; their entertainers, who
had waited on their wants throughout with the pleased
hospitality of Polynesians, made haste to bring forward a
dessert of island tobacco and rolls of pandanus leaf to serve
as paper; and presently all sat about the dishes puffing like
Indian Sachems.

'When a man 'as breakfast every day, he don't know
what it is,' observed the clerk.

'The next point is dinner,' said Herrick; and then with
a passionate utterance: 'I wish to God I was a Kanaka!'

'There's one thing sure,' said the captain. 'I'm about
desperate, I'd rather hang than rot here much longer.'
And with the word he took the accordion and struck up.
'Home, sweet home.'

'O, drop that!' cried Herrick, 'I can't stand that.'

'No more can I,' said the captain. 'I've got to play
something though: got to pay the shot, my son.' And he
struck up 'John Brown's Body' in a fine sweet baritone:
'Dandy Jim of Carolina,' came next; 'Rorin the Bold,'
'Swing low, Sweet Chariot,' and 'The Beautiful Land'
followed. The captain was paying his shot with usury, as he
had done many a time before; many a meal had he bought
with the same currency from the melodious-minded natives,
always, as now, to their delight.

He was in the middle of 'Fifteen Dollars in the Inside
Pocket,' singing with dogged energy, for the task went
sore against the grain, when a sensation was suddenly to
be observed among the crew.

'*Tapena Tom harry my*,'[1] said the spokesman, pointing.

And the three beachcombers, following his indication,
saw the figure of a man in pyjama trousers and a white
jumper approaching briskly from the town.

'That's Tapena Tom, is it?' said the captain, pausing in
his music. 'I don't seem to place the brute.'

---

1. 'Captain Tom is coming.'

'We'd better cut,' said the clerk. ''E's no good.'

'Well,' said the musician deliberately, 'one can't most generally always tell. I'll try it on, I guess. Music has charms to soothe the savage Tapena, boys. We might strike it rich; it might amount to iced punch in the cabin.'

'Hiced punch? O my!' said the clerk. 'Give him something 'ot, captain. "Way down the Swannee River"; try that.'

'No, *sir*! Looks Scotch,' said the captain; and he struck, for his life, into 'Auld Lang Syne.'

Captain Tom continued to approach with the same business-like alacrity; no change was to be perceived in his bearded face as he came swinging up the plank: he did not even turn his eyes on the performer.

> 'We twa hae paidled in the burn
> Frae morning tide till dine,'

went the song.

Captain Tom had a parcel under his arm, which he laid on the house roof, and then turning suddenly to the strangers: 'Here, you!' he bellowed, 'be off out of that!'

The clerk and Herrick stood not on the order of their going, but fled incontinently by the plank. The performer, on the other hand, flung down the instrument and rose to his full height slowly.

'What's that you say?' he said. 'I've half a mind to give you a lesson in civility.'

'You set up any more of your gab to me,' returned the Scotsman, 'and I'll show ye the wrong side of a jyle. I've heard tell of the three of ye. Ye're not long for here, I can tell ye that. The Government has their eyes upon ye. They make short work of damned beachcombers, I'll say that for the French.'

'You wait till I catch you off your ship!' cried the captain: and then, turning to the crew, 'Good-bye, you fellows!' he said. 'You're gentlemen, anyway! The worst nigger among you would look better upon a quarter-deck than that filthy Scotchman.'

Captain Tom scorned to reply; he watched with a hard smile the departure of his guests; and as soon as the last foot was off the plank; turned to the hands to work cargo.

The beachcombers beat their inglorious retreat along the shore; Herrick first, his face dark with blood, his knees trembling under him with the hysteria of rage. Presently, under the same *purao* where they had shivered the night before, he cast himself down, and groaned aloud, and ground his face into the sand.

'Don't speak to me, don't speak to me. I can't stand it,' broke from him.

The other two stood over him perplexed.

'Wot can't he stand now?' said the clerk. "Asn't he 'ad a meal? *I'm* lickin' my lips.'

Herrick reared up his wild eyes and burning face. 'I can't beg!' he screamed, and again threw himself prone.

'This thing's got to come to an end,' said the captain with an intake of the breath.

'Looks like signs of an end, don't it?' sneered the clerk.

'He's not so far from it, and don't you deceive yourself,' replied the captain. 'Well,' he added in a livelier voice, 'you fellows hang on here, and I'll go and interview my representative.'

Whereupon he turned on his heel, and set off at a swinging sailor's walk towards Papeete.

It was some half hour later when he returned. The clerk was dozing with his back against the tree: Herrick still lay where he had flung himself; nothing showed whether he slept or waked.

'See, boys!' cried the captain, with that artificial heartiness of his which was at times so painful, 'here's a new idea.' And he produced note paper, stamped envelopes, and pencils, three of each. 'We can all write home by the mail brigantine; the consul says I can come over to his place and ink up the addresses.'

'Well, that's a start, too,' said the clerk. 'I never thought of that.'

'It was that yarning last night about going home that put me up to it,' said the captain.

'Well, 'and over,' said the clerk. 'I'll 'ave a shy,' and he retired a little distance to the shade of a canoe.

The others remained under the *purao*. Now they would write a word or two, now scribble it out; now they would sit biting at the pencil end and staring seaward; now their eyes would rest on the clerk, where he sat propped on the canoe, leering and coughing, his pencil racing glibly on the paper.

'I can't do it,' said Herrick suddenly. 'I haven't got the heart.'

'See here,' said the captain, speaking with unwonted gravity; 'it may be hard to write, and to write lies at that; and God knows it is; but it's the square thing. It don't cost anything to say you're well and happy, and sorry you can't make a remittance this mail; and if you don't, I'll tell you what I think it is – I think it's about the high-water mark of being a brute beast.'

'It's easy to talk,' said Herrick. 'You don't seem to have written much yourself, I notice.'

'What do you bring in me for?' broke from the captain. His voice was indeed scarce raised above a whisper, but emotion clanged in it. 'What do you know about me? If you had commanded the finest barque that ever sailed from Portland; if you had been drunk in your berth when she struck the breakers in Fourteen Island Group, and hadn't had the wit to stay there and drown, but came on deck, and given drunken orders, and lost six lives – I could understand your talking then! There,' he said more quietly, 'that's my yarn, and now you know it. It's a pretty one for the father of a family. Five men and a woman murdered. Yes, there was a woman on board, and hadn't no business to be either. Guess I sent her to Hell, if there is such a place. I never dared go home again; and the wife and the little ones went to England to her father's place. I don't know what's come to them,' he added, with a bitter shrug.

'Thank you, captain,' said Herrick. 'I never liked you better.'

They shook hands, short and hard, with eyes averted, tenderness swelling in their bosoms.

'Now, boys! to work again at lying!' said the captain.

'I'll give my father up,' returned Herrick with a writhen smile. 'I'll try my sweetheart instead for a change of evils.'

And here is what he wrote:

'Emma, I have scratched out the beginning to my father, for I think I can write more easily to you. This is my last farewell to all, the last you will ever hear or see of an unworthy friend and son. I have failed in life; I am quite broken down and disgraced. I pass under a false name; you will have to tell my father that with all your kindness. It is my own fault.

I know, had I chosen, that I might have done well; and yet I swear to you I tried to choose. I could not bear that you should think I did not try. For I loved you all; you must never doubt me in that, you least of all. I have always unceasingly loved, but what was my love worth? and what was I worth? I had not the manhood of a common clerk, I could not work to earn you; I have lost you now, and for your sake I could be glad of it. When you first came to my father's house – do you remember those days? I want you to – you saw the best of me then, all that was good in me. Do you remember the day I took your hand and would not let it go – and the day on Battersea Bridge, when we were looking at a barge, and I began to tell you one of my silly stories, and broke off to say I loved you? That was the beginning, and now here is the end. When you have read this letter, you will go round and kiss them all good-bye, my father and mother, and the children, one by one, and poor uncle; and tell them all to forget me, and forget me yourself. Turn the key in the door; let no thought of me return; be done with the poor ghost that pretended he was a man and stole your love. Scorn of myself grinds in me as I write. I should tell you I am well and happy, and want for nothing. I do not exactly make money, or I should send a remittance; but I am well cared for, have friends, live in a beautiful place and climate, such as we have dreamed of together, and no pity need be wasted on me. In such places, you understand, it is easy to live, and live well, but often hard to make sixpence in money. Explain this to my father, he will understand. I have no more to say; only linger, going out, like an unwilling guest. God in heaven bless you. Think of me to the last, here, on a bright beach, the sky and sea immoderately blue, and the great breakers roaring outside on a barrier reef, where a little isle sits green with palms. I am well and strong. It is a more pleasant way to die than if you were crowding about me on a sick-bed. And yet I am dying. This is my last kiss. Forgive, forget the unworthy.'

So far he had written, his paper was all filled, when there returned a memory of evenings at the piano, and that song, the masterpiece of love, in which so many have found the expression of their dearest thoughts. '*Einst, O wunder!*' he added. More was not required; he knew that in his love's heart the context would spring up, escorted with fair images and harmony; of how all through life her name should tremble in his ears, her name be everywhere repeated in the sounds of nature; and when death came, and he lay dissolved, her memory lingered and thrilled among his elements.

> 'Once, O wonder! once from the ashes of my heart
> Arose a blossom— '

Herrick and the captain finished their letters about the same time; each was breathing deep, and their eyes met and were averted as they closed the envelopes.

'Sorry I write so big,' said the captain gruffly. 'Came all of a rush, when it did come.'

'Same here,' said Herrick. 'I could have done with a ream when I got started; but it's long enough for all the good I had to say.'

They were still at the addresses when the clerk strolled up, smirking and twirling his envelope, like a man well pleased. He looked over Herrick's shoulder.

'Hullo,' he said, 'you ain't writing 'ome.'

'I am, though,' said Herrick; 'she lives with my father. Oh, I see what you mean,' he added. 'My real name is Herrick. No more Hay' – they had both used the same *alias* – 'no more Hay than yours, I dare say.'

'Clean bowled in the middle stump!' laughed the clerk. 'My name's 'Uish if you want to know. Everybody has a false nyme in the Pacific. Lay you five to three the captain 'as.'

'So I have too,' replied the captain; 'and I've never told my own since the day I tore the title page out of my Bowditch and flung the damned thing into the sea. But I'll tell it to you, boys. John Davis is my name. I'm Davis of the *Sea Ranger*.'

'Dooce you are!' said Hush. 'And what was she? a pirate or a slyver?'

'She was the fastest barque out of Portland, Maine,' replied the captain; 'and for the way I lost her, I might as well have bored a hole in her side with an auger.'

'Oh, you lost her, did you?' said the clerk. ''Ope she was insured?'

No answer being returned to this sally, Huish, still

brimming over with vanity and conversation, struck into another subject.

'I've a good mind to read you my letter,' said he. 'I've a good fist with a pen when I choose, and this is a prime lark. She was a barmaid I ran across in Northampton; she was a spanking fine piece, no end of style; and we cottoned at first sight like parties in the play. I suppose I spent the chynge of a fiver on that girl. Well, I 'appened to remember her nyme, so I wrote to her, and told her 'ow I had got rich, and married a queen in the Hislands, and lived in a blooming palace. Such a sight of crammers! I must read you one bit about my opening the nigger parliament in a cocked 'at. It's really prime.'

The captain jumped to his feet. 'That's what you did with the paper that I went and begged for you?' he roared.

It was perhaps lucky for Huish – it was surely in the end unfortunate for all – that he was seized just then by one of his prostrating accesses of cough; his comrades would have else deserted him, so bitter was their resentment. When the fit had passed, the clerk reached out his hand, picked up the letter, which had fallen to the earth, and tore it into fragments, stamp and all.

'Does that satisfy you?' he asked sullenly.

'We'll say no more about it,' replied Davis.

THREE

The Old Calaboose – Destiny at the Door

The old calaboose, in which the waifs had so long harboured, is a low, rectangular enclosure of building at the
corner of a shady western avenue and a little townward of
the British consulate. Within was a grassy court, littered
with wreckage and the traces of vagrant occupation. Six or
seven cells opened from the court: the doors, that had once
been locked on mutinous whalermen, rotting before them
in the grass. No mark remained of their old destination,
except the rusty bars upon the windows.

The floor of one of the cells had been a little cleared; a
bucket (the last remaining piece of furniture of the three
caitiffs) stood full of water by the door, a half cocoanut shell
beside it for a drinking cup; and on some ragged ends of mat
Huish sprawled asleep, his mouth open, his face deathly.
The glow of the tropic afternoon, the green of sunbright
foliage, stared into that shady place through door and
window; and Herrick, pacing to and fro on the coral floor,
sometimes paused and laved his face and neck with tepid
water from the bucket. His long arrears of suffering, the
night's vigil, the insults of the morning, and the harrowing
business of the letter, had strung him to that point when
pain is almost pleasure, time shrinks to a mere point, and
death and life appear indifferent. To and fro he paced like
a caged brute; his mind whirling through the universe of
thought and memory; his eyes, as he went, skimming the
legends on the wall. The crumbling whitewash was all full
of them: Tahitian names, and French, and English, and
rude sketches of ships under sail and men at fisticuffs.

It came to him of a sudden that he too must leave upon
these walls the memorial of his passage. He paused before
a clean space, took the pencil out, and pondered. Vanity,
so hard to dislodge, awoke in him. We call it vanity at
least; perhaps unjustly. Rather it was the bare sense of his

27

existence prompted him; the sense of his life, the one thing wonderful, to which he scarce clung with a finger. From his jarred nerves there came a strong sentiment of coming change; whether good or ill he could not say: change, he knew no more – change, with inscrutable veiled face, approaching noiseless. With the feeling, came the vision of a concert room, the rich hues of instruments, the silent audience, and the loud voice of the symphony. 'Destiny knocking at the door,' he thought; drew a stave on the plaster, and wrote in the famous phrase from the Fifth Symphony. 'So,' thought he, 'they will know that I loved music and had classical tastes. They? He, I suppose: the unknown, kindred spirit that shall come some day and read my *memor querela*. Ha, he shall have Latin too!' And he added: *terque quaterque beati Queis ante ora patrum.*

He turned again to his uneasy pacing, but now with an irrational and supporting sense of duty done. He had dug his grave that morning; now he had carved his epitaph; the folds of the toga were composed, why should he delay the insignificant trifle that remained to do? He paused and looked long in the face of the sleeping Huish, drinking disenchantment and distaste of life. He nauseated himself with that vile countenance. Could the thing continue? What bound him now? Had he no rights? – only the obligation to go on, without discharge or furlough, bearing the unbearable? *Ich trage unerträgliches*, the quotation rose in his mind; he repeated the whole piece, one of the most perfect of the most perfect of poets; and a phrase struck him like a blow: *Du, stolzes Herz, du hast es ja gewollt*. Where was the pride of his heart? And he raged against himself, as a man bites on a sore tooth, in a heady sensuality of scorn. 'I have no pride, I have no heart, no manhood,' he thought, 'or why should I prolong a life more shameful than the gallows? Or why should I have fallen to it? No pride, no capacity, no force. Not even a bandit! and to be starving here with worse than banditti – with this trivial hell-hound!' His rage against his comrade rose and flooded him, and he shook a trembling fist at the sleeper.

A swift step was audible. The captain appeared upon the threshold of the cell, panting and flushed, and with a foolish face of happiness. In his arms he carried a loaf of bread and bottles of beer; the pockets of his coat were bulging with cigars. He rolled his treasures on the floor, grasped Herrick by both hands, and crowed with laughter.

'Broach the beer!' he shouted. 'Broach the beer, and glory hallelujah!'

'Beer?' repeated Huish, struggling to his feet.

'Beer it is!' cried Davis. 'Beer and plenty of it. Any number of persons can use it (like Lyon's tooth-tablet) with perfect propriety and neatness. Who's to officiate?'

'Leave me alone for that,' said the clerk. He knocked the necks off with a lump of coral, and each drank in succession from the shell.

'Have a weed,' said Davis. 'It's all in the bill.'

'What is up?' asked Herrick.

The captain fell suddenly grave. 'I'm coming to that,' said he. 'I want to speak with Herrick here. You, Hay – or Huish, or whatever your name is – you take a weed and the other bottle, and go and see how the wind is down by the *purao*. I'll call you when you're wanted!'

'Hay? Secrets? That ain't the ticket,' said Huish.

'Look here, my son,' said the captain, 'this is business, and don't you make any mistake about it. If you're going to make trouble, you can have it your own way and stop right here. Only get the thing right: if Herrick and I go, we take the beer. Savvy?'

'Oh, I don't want to shove my oar in,' returned Huish. 'I'll cut right enough. Give me the swipes. You can jaw till you're blue in the face for what I care. I don't think it's the friendly touch: that's all.' And he shambled grumbling out of the cell into the staring sun.

The captain watched him clear of the courtyard; then turned to Herrick.

'What is it?' asked Herrick thickly.

'I'll tell you,' said Davis. 'I want to consult you. It's a chance we've got. What's that?' he cried, pointing to the music on the wall.

'What?' said the other. 'Oh, that! It's music; it's a phrase of Beethoven's I was writing up. It means Destiny knocking at the door.'

'Does it?' said the captain, rather low; and he went near and studied the inscription; 'and this French?' he asked, pointing to the Latin.

'O, it just means I should have been luckier if I had

died at home,' returned Herrick impatiently. 'What is this business?'

'Destiny knocking at the door,' repeated the captain; and then, looking over his shoulder. 'Well, Mr Herrick, that's about what it comes to,' he added.

'What do you mean? Explain yourself,' said Herrick.

But the captain was again staring at the music. 'About how long ago since you wrote up this truck?' he asked.

'What does it matter?' exclaimed Herrick. 'I dare say half an hour.'

'My God, it's strange!' cried Davis. 'There's some men would call that accidental: not me. That— ' and he drew his thick finger under the music – 'that's what I call Providence.'

'You said we had a chance,' said Herrick.

'Yes, *sir*!' said the captain, wheeling suddenly face to face with his companion. 'I did so. If you're the man I take you for, we have a chance.'

'I don't know what you take me for,' was the reply. 'You can scarce take me too low.'

'Shake hands, Mr Herrick,' said the captain. 'I know you. You're a gentleman and a man of spirit. I didn't want to speak before that bummer there; you'll see why. But to you I'll rip it right out. I got a ship.'

'A ship?' cried Herrick. 'What ship?'

'That schooner we saw this morning off the passage.'

'The schooner with the hospital flag?'

'That's the hooker,' said Davis. 'She's the *Farallone*, hundred and sixty tons register, out of 'Frisco for Sydney, in California champagne. Captain, mate, and one hand all died of the smallpox, same as they had round in the Paumotus, I guess. Captain and mate were the only white men; all the hands Kanakas; seems a queer kind of outfit from a Christian port. Three of them left and a cook; didn't know where they were; I can't think where they were either, if you come to that; Wiseman must have been on the booze, I guess, to sail the course he did. However, there *he* was, dead; and here are the Kanakas as good as lost. They bummed around at sea like the babes in the wood; and tumbled end-on upon Tahiti. The consul here took charge. He offered the berth to Williams; Williams had never had the smallpox and backed down. That was when I came

in for the letter paper; I thought there was something up
when the consul asked me to look in again; but I never let
on to you fellows, so's you'd not be disappointed. Consul
tried M'Neil; scared of smallpox. He tried Capirati, that
Corsican and Leblue, or whatever his name is, wouldn't
lay a hand on it; all too fond of their sweet lives. Last of all,
when there wasn't nobody else left to offer it to, he offers it to
me. "Brown, will you ship captain and take her to Sydney?"
says he. "Let me choose my own mate and another white
hand," says I, "for I don't hold with this Kanaka crew
racket; give us all two months' advance to get our clothes
and instruments out of pawn, and I'll take stock tonight, fill
up stores, and get to sea tomorrow before dark!" That's what
I said. "That's good enough," says the consul, "and you can
count yourself damned lucky, Brown," says he. And he said
it pretty meaningful-appearing, too. However, that's all one
now. I'll ship Huish before the mast – of course I'll let him
berth aft – and I'll ship you mate at seventy-five dollars and
two months' advance.'

'Me mate? Why, I'm a landsman!' cried Herrick.

'Guess you've got to learn,' said the captain. 'You don't
fancy I'm going to skip and leave you rotting on the beach
perhaps? I'm not that sort, old man. And you're handy
anyway; I've been shipmates with worse.'

'God knows I can't refuse,' said Herrick. 'God knows I
thank you from my heart.'

'That's all right,' said the captain. 'But it ain't all.' He
turned aside to light a cigar.

'What else is there?' asked the other, with a pang of
undefinable alarm.

'I'm coming to that,' said Davis, and then paused a little.
'See here,' he began, holding out his cigar between his finger
and thumb, 'suppose you figure up what this'll amount to.
You don't catch on? Well, we get two months' advance;
we can't get away from Papeete – our creditors wouldn't
let us go – for less; it'll take us along about two months to
get to Sydney; and when we get there, I just want to put
it to you squarely: What the better are we?'

'We're off the beach at least,' said Herrick.

'I guess there's a beach at Sydney,' returned the captain;
'and I'll tell you one thing, Mr Herrick – I don't mean to
try. No, *sir*! Sydney will never see me.'

'Speak out plain,' said Herrick.

'Plain Dutch,' replied the captain. 'I'm going to own that schooner. It's nothing new; it's done every year in the Pacific. Stephens stole a schooner the other day, didn't he? Hayes and Pease stole vessels all the time. And it's the making of the crowd of us. See here – you think of that cargo. Champagne! why, it's like as if it was put up on purpose. In Peru we'll sell that liquor off at the pier-head, and the schooner after it, if we can find a fool to buy her; and then light out for the mines. If you'll back me up, I stake my life I carry it through.'

'Captain,' said Herrick, with a quailing voice, 'don't do it!'

'I'm desperate,' returned Davis. 'I've got a chance; I may never get another. Herrick, say the word; back me up; I think we've starved together long enough for that.'

'I can't do it. I'm sorry. I can't do it. I've not fallen as low as that,' said Herrick, deadly pale.

'What did you say this morning?' said Davis. 'That you couldn't beg? It's the one thing or the other, my son.'

'Ah, but this is the jail!' cried Herrick. 'Don't tempt me. It's the jail.'

'Did you hear what the skipper said on board that schooner?' pursued the captain. 'Well, I tell you he talked straight. The French have let us alone for a long time; it can't last longer; they've got their eye on us; and as sure as you live, in three weeks you'll be in jail whatever you do. I read it in the consul's face.'

'You forget, captain,' said the young man. 'There is another way. I can die; and to say truth, I think I should have died three years ago.'

The captain folded his arms and looked the other in the face. 'Yes,' said he, 'yes, you can cut your throat; that's a frozen fact; much good may it do you! And where do I come in?'

The light of a strange excitement came in Herrick's face. 'Both of us,' said he, 'both of us together. It's not possible you can enjoy this business. Come,' and he reached out a timid hand, 'a few strokes in the lagoon – and rest!'

'I tell you, Herrick, I'm 'most tempted to answer you the way the man does in the Bible, and say, "*Get thee behind me, Satan!*"' said the captain. 'What! you think I would go

drown myself, and I got children starving? Enjoy it? No, by
God, I do not enjoy it! but it's the row I've got to hoe, and
I'll hoe it till I drop right here. I have three of them, you
see, two boys and the one girl, Adar. The trouble is that
you are not a parent yourself. I tell you, Herrick, I love
you,' the man broke out; 'I didn't take to you at first, you
were so anglified and tony, but I love you now; it's a man
that loves you stands here and wrestles with you. I can't go
to sea with the bummer alone; it's not possible. Go drown
yourself, and there goes my last chance – the last chance of
a poor miserable beast, earning a crust to feed his family.
I can't do nothing but sail ships, and I've no papers. And
here I get a chance, and you go back on me! Ah, you've
no family, and that's where the trouble is!'

'I have indeed,' said Herrick.

'Yes, I know,' said the captain, 'you think so. But no
man's got a family till he's got children. It's only the kids
count. There's something about the little shavers . . . I can't
talk of them. And if you thought a cent about this father
that I hear you talk of, or that sweetheart you were writing
to this morning, you would feel like me. You would say,
What matters laws, and God, and that? My folks are hard
up, I belong to them, I'll get them bread, or, by God! I'll get
them wealth, if I have to burn down London for it. That's
what you would say. And I'll tell you more: your heart is
saying so this living minute. I can see it in your face. You're
thinking, Here's poor friendship for the man I've starved
along of, and as for the girl that I set up to be in love with,
here's a mighty limp kind of a love that won't carry me as
far as 'most any man would go for a demijohn of whisky.
There's not much *ro*mance to that love, anyway; it's not
the kind they carry on about in songbooks. But what's the
good of my carrying on talking, when it's all in your inside
as plain as print? I put the question to you once for all. Are
you going to desert me in my hour of need? – you know if
I've deserted you – or will you give me your hand, and try
a fresh deal, and go home (as like as not) a millionaire? Say
no, and God pity me! Say yes, and I'll make the little ones
pray for you every night on their bended knees. "God bless
Mr Herrick!" that's what they'll say, one after the other,
the old girl sitting there holding stakes at the foot of the
bed, and the damned little innocents . . .' He broke off.

'I don't often rip out about the kids,' he said; 'but when I do, there's something fetches loose.'

'Captain,' said Herrick faintly, 'is there nothing else?'

'I'll prophesy if you like,' said the captain with renewed vigour. 'Refuse this, because you think yourself too honest, and before a month's out you'll be jailed for a sneak-thief. I give you the word fair. I can see it, Herrick, if you can't; you're breaking down. Don't think, if you refuse this chance, that you'll go on doing the evangelical; you're about through with your stock; and before you know where you are, you'll be right out on the other side. No, it's either this for you; or else it's Caledonia. I bet you never were there, and saw those white, shaved men, in their dust clothes and straw hats, prowling around in gangs in the lamplight at Noumea; they look like wolves, and they look like preachers, and they look like the sick; Huish is a daisy to the best of them. Well, there's your company. They're waiting for you, Herrick, and you got to go; and that's a prophecy.'

And as the man stood and shook through his great stature, he seemed indeed like one in whom the spirit of divination worked and might utter oracles. Herrick looked at him, and looked away; it seemed not decent to spy upon such agitation; and the young man's courage sank.

'You talk of going home,' he objected. 'We could never do that.'

'*We* could,' said the other. 'Captain Brown couldn't, nor Mr Hay, that shipped mate with him couldn't. But what's that to do with Captain Davis or Mr Herrick, you galoot?'

'But Hayes had these wild islands where he used to call,' came the next fainter objection.

'We have the wild islands of Peru,' retorted Davis. 'They were wild enough for Stephens, no longer agone than just last year. I guess they'll be wild enough for us.'

'And the crew?'

'All Kanakas. Come, I see you're right, old man. I see you'll stand by.' And the captain once more offered his hand.

'Have it your own way then,' said Herrick. 'I'll do it: a strange thing for my father's son. But I'll do it. I'll stand by you, man, for good or evil.'

'God bless you!' cried the captain, and stood silent. 'Herrick,' he added with a smile, 'I believe I'd have died in my tracks, if you'd said, No!'

And Herrick, looking at the man, half believed so also.

'And now we'll go break it to the bummer,' said Davis.

'I wonder how he'll take it,' said Herrick.

'Him? Jump at it!' was the reply.

FOUR

The Yellow Flag

The schooner *Farallone* lay well out in the jaws of the pass, where the terrified pilot had made haste to bring her to her moorings and escape. Seen from the beach through the thin line of shipping, two objects stood conspicuous to seaward: the little isle, on the one hand, with its palms and the guns and batteries raised forty years before in defence of Queen Pomare's capital; the outcast *Farallone*, upon the other, banished to the threshold of the port, rolling there to her scuppers, and flaunting the plague-flag as she rolled. A few sea birds screamed and cried about the ship; and within easy range, a man-of-war guard boat hung off and on and glittered with the weapons of marines. The exuberant daylight and the blinding heaven of the tropics picked out and framed the pictures.

A neat boat, manned by natives in uniform, and steered by the doctor of the port, put from shore towards three of the afternoon, and pulled smartly for the schooner. The fore-sheets were heaped with sacks of flour, onions, and potatoes, perched among which was Huish dressed as a foremast hand; a heap of chests and cases impeded the action of the oarsmen; and in the stern, by the left hand of the doctor, sat Herrick, dressed in a fresh rig of slops, his brown beard trimmed to a point, a pile of paper novels on his lap, and nursing the while between his feet a chronometer, for which they had exchanged that of the *Farallone*, long since run down and the rate lost.

They passed the guard boat, exchanging hails with the boatswain's mate in charge, and drew near at last to the forbidden ship. Not a cat stirred, there was no speech of man; and the sea being exceeding high outside, and the reef close to where the schooner lay, the clamour of the surf hung round her like the sound of battle.

'*Ohé la goëlette!*' sang out the doctor, with his best voice.

Instantly, from the house where they had been stowing away stores, first Davis, and then the ragamuffin, swarthy crew made their appearance.

'Hullo, Hay, that you?' said the captain, leaning on the rail. 'Tell the old man to lay her alongside, as if she was eggs. There's a hell of a run of sea here, and his boat's brittle.'

The movement of the schooner was at that time more than usually violent. Now she heaved her side as high as a deep sea steamer's, and showed the flashing of her copper; now she swung swiftly toward the boat until her scuppers gurgled.

'I hope you have sea legs,' observed the doctor. 'You will require them.'

Indeed, to board the *Farallone*, in that exposed position where she lay, was an affair of some dexterity. The less precious goods were hoisted roughly in; the chronometer, after repeated failures, was passed gently and successfully from hand to hand; and there remained only the more difficult business of embarking Huish. Even that piece of dead weight (shipped A.B. at eighteen dollars, and described by the captain to the consul as an invaluable man) was at last hauled on board without mishap; and the doctor, with civil salutations, took his leave.

The three co-adventurers looked at each other, and Davis heaved a breath of relief.

'Now let's get this chronometer fixed,' said he, and led the way into the house. It was a fairly spacious place; two state-rooms and a good-sized pantry opened from the main cabin; the bulkheads were painted white, the floor laid with waxcloth. No litter, no sign of life remained; for the effects of the dead men had been disinfected and conveyed on shore. Only on the table, in a saucer, some sulphur burned, and the fumes set them coughing as they entered. The captain peered into the starboard stateroom, where the bed-clothes still lay tumbled in the bunk, the blanket flung back as they had flung it back from the disfigured corpse before its burial.

'Now, I told these niggers to tumble that truck overboard,' grumbled Davis. 'Guess they were afraid to lay hands on it. Well, they've hosed the place out; that's as much as can be expected, I suppose. Huish, lay on to these blankets.'

'See you blooming well far enough first,' said Huish, drawing back.

'What's that?' snapped the captain. 'I'll tell you, my young friend, I think you make a mistake. I'm captain here.'

'Fat lot I care,' returned the clerk.

'That so?' said Davis. 'Then you'll berth forward with the niggers! Walk right out of this cabin.'

'Oh, I dessay!' said Huish. 'See any green in my eye? A lark's a lark.'

'Well, now, I'll explain this business, and you'll see (once for all) just precisely how much lark there is to it,' said Davis. 'I'm captain, and I'm going to be it. One thing of three. First, you take my orders here as cabin steward, in which case you mess with us. Or second, you refuse, and I pack you forward – and you get as quick as the word's said. Or, third and last, I'll signal that man-of-war and send you ashore under arrest for mutiny.'

'And, of course, I wouldn't blow the gaff? O no!' replied the jeering Huish.

'And who's to believe you, my son?' inquired the captain. 'No, *sir*! There ain't no lark about my captainising. Enough said. Up with these blankets.'

Huish was no fool, he knew when he was beaten; and he was no coward either, for he stepped to the bunk, took the infected bed-clothes fairly in his arms, and carried them out of the house without a check or tremor.

'I was waiting for the chance,' said Davis to Herrick. 'I needn't do the same with you, because you understand it for yourself.'

'Are you going to berth here?' asked Herrick, following the captain into the stateroom, where he began to adjust the chronometer in its place at the bed-head.

'Not much!' replied he. 'I guess I'll berth on deck. I don't know as I'm afraid, but I've no immediate use for confluent smallpox.'

'I don't know that I'm afraid either,' said Herrick. 'But the thought of these two men sticks in my throat; that captain and mate dying here, one opposite to the other. It's grim. I wonder what they said last?'

'Wiseman and Wishart?' said the captain. 'Probably mighty small potatoes. That's a thing a fellow figures out for himself one way, and the real business goes quite another. Perhaps Wiseman said, "Here old man, fetch up the gin, I'm feeling powerful rocky." And perhaps Wishart said, "Oh, hell!"'

'Well, that's grim enough,' said Herrick.

'And so it is,' said Davis. 'There; there's that chronometer fixed. And now it's about time to up anchor and clear out.'

He lit a cigar and stepped on deck.

'Here, you! What's *your* name?' he cried to one of the hands, a lean-flanked, clean-built fellow from some far western island, and of a darkness almost approaching to the African.

'Sally Day,' replied the man.

'Devil it is,' said the captain. 'Didn't know we had ladies on board. Well, Sally, oblige me by hauling down that rag there. I'll do the same for you another time.' He watched the yellow bunting as it was eased past the cross-trees and handed down on deck. 'You'll float no more on this ship,' he observed. 'Muster the people aft, Mr Hay,' he added, speaking unnecessarily loud, 'I've a word to say to them.'

It was with a singular sensation that Herrick prepared for the first time to address a crew. He thanked his stars indeed, that they were natives. But even natives, he reflected, might be critics too quick for such a novice as himself; they might perceive some lapse from that precise and cut-and-dry English which prevails on board a ship; it was even possible they understood no other; and he racked his brain, and overhauled his reminiscences of sea romance for some appropriate words.

'Here, men! tumble aft!' he said. 'Lively now! All hands aft!'

They crowded in the alleyway like sheep.

'Here they are, sir,' said Herrick.

For some time the captain continued to face the stern; then turned with ferocious suddenness on the crew, and seemed to enjoy their shrinking.

'Now,' he said, twisting his cigar in his mouth and toying with the spokes of the wheel, 'I'm Captain Brown. I command this ship. This is Mr Hay, first officer. The other white man is cabin steward, but he'll stand watch and do his trick. My orders shall be obeyed smartly. You savvy,

"*smartly*"? There shall be no growling about the kaikai,
which will be above allowance. You'll put a handle to the
mate's name, and tack on "sir" to every order.I give you.
If you're smart and quick, I'll make this ship comfortable
for all hands.' He took the cigar out of his mouth. 'If you're
not,' he added, in a roaring voice, 'I'll make it a floating
hell. Now, Mr Hay, we'll pick watches, if you please.'

'All right,' said Herrick.

'You will please use "sir" when you address me, Mr Hay,'
said the captain. 'I'll take the lady. Step to starboard,
Sally.' And then he whispered in Herrick's ear: 'take the
old man.'

'I'll take you, there,' said Herrick.

'What's your name?' said the captain. 'What's that you
say? Oh, that's no English; I'll have none of your highway
gibberish on my ship. We'll call you old Uncle Ned, because
you've got no wool on the top of your head, just the place
where the wool ought to grow. Step to port, Uncle. Don't
you hear Mr Hay has picked you? Then I'll take the white
man. White Man, step to starboard. Now which of you two
is the cook? You? Then Mr Hay takes your friend in the
blue dungaree. Step to port, Dungaree. There, we know
who we all are: Dungaree, Uncle Ned, Sally Day, White
Man, and Cook. All F.F.V.'s I guess. And now, Mr Hay,
we'll up anchor, if you please.'

'For Heaven's sake, tell me some of the words,' whispered
Herrick.

An hour later, the *Farallone* was under all plain sail, the
rudder hard a-port, and the cheerfully clanking windlass
had brought the anchor home.

'All clear, sir,' cried Herrick from the bow.

The captain met her with the wheel, as she bounded like
a stag from her repose, trembling and bending to the puffs.
The guard boat gave a parting hail, the wake whitened and
ran out; the *Farallone* was under weigh.

Her berth had been close to the pass. Even as she forged
ahead Davis slewed her for the channel between the pier
ends of the reef, the breakers sounding and whitening to
either hand. Straight through the narrow band of blue,
she shot to seaward: and the captain's heart exulted as
he felt her tremble underfoot, and (looking back over
the taffrail) beheld the roofs of Papeete changing position

on the shore and the island mountains rearing higher in the wake.

But they were not yet done with the shore and the horror of the yellow flag. About midway of the pass, there was a cry and a scurry, a man was seen to leap upon the rail, and, throwing his arms over his head, to stoop and plunge into the sea.

'Steady as she goes,' the captain cried, relinquishing the wheel to Huish.

The next moment he was forward in the midst of the Kanakas, belaying pin in hand.

'Anybody else for shore?' he cried, and the savage trumpeting of his voice, no less than the ready weapon in his hand, struck fear in all. Stupidly they stared after their escaped companion, whose black head was visible upon the water, steering for the land. And the schooner meanwhile slipt like a racer through the pass, and met the long sea of the open ocean with a souse of spray.

'Fool that I was, not to have a pistol ready!' exclaimed Davis. 'Well, we go to sea short-handed, we can't help that. You have a lame watch of it, Mr Hay.'

'I don't see how we are to get along,' said Herrick.

'Got to,' said the captain. 'No more Tahiti for me.'

Both turned instinctively and looked astern. The fair island was unfolding mountain top on mountain top; Eimeo, on the port board, lifted her splintered pinnacles; and still the schooner raced to the open sea.

'Think!' cried the captain with a gesture, 'yesterday morning I danced for my breakfast like a poodle dog.'

FIVE

The Cargo of Champagne

The ship's head was laid to clear Eimeo to the north, and the captain sat down in the cabin, with a chart, a ruler, and an epitome.

'East a half no'the,' said he, raising his face from his labours. 'Mr Hay, you'll have to watch your dead reckoning; I want every yard she makes on every hair's-breadth of a course. I'm going to knock a hole right straight through the Paumotus, and that's always a near touch. Now, if this South East Trade ever blew out of the S.E., which it don't, we might hope to lie within half a point of our course. Say we lie within a point of it. That'll just about weather Fakarava. Yes, sir, that's what we've got to do, if we tack for it. Brings us through this slush of little islands in the cleanest place: see?' And he showed where his ruler intersected the wide-lying labyrinth of the Dangerous Archipelago. 'I wish it was night, and I could put her about right now; we're losing time and easting. Well, we'll do our best. And if we don't fetch Peru, we'll bring up to Ecuador. All one, I guess. Depreciated dollars down, and no questions asked. A remarkable fine institution, the South American don.'

Tahiti was already some way astern, the Diadem rising from among broken mountains – Eimeo was already close aboard, and stood black and strange against the golden splendour of the west – when the captain took his departure from the two islands, and the patent log was set.

Some twenty minutes later, Sally Day, who was continually leaving the wheel to peer in at the cabin clock, announced in a shrill cry 'Fo'bell,' and the cook was to be seen carrying the soup into the cabin.

'I guess I'll sit down and have a pick with you,' said Davis to Herrick. 'By the time I've done, it'll be dark, and we'll clap the hooker on the wind for South America.'

In the cabin at one corner of the table, immediately below

the lamp, and on the lee side of a bottle of champagne, sat Huish.

'What's this? Where did that come from?' asked the captain.

'It's fizz, and it came from the after-'old, if you want to know,' said Huish, and drained his mug.

'This'll never do,' exclaimed Davis, the merchant seaman's horror of breaking into cargo showing incongruously forth on board that stolen ship. 'There was never any good came of games like that.'

'You byby!' said Huish. 'A fellow would think (to 'ear him) we were on the square! And look 'ere, you've put this job up 'ansomely for me, 'aven't you? I'm to go on deck and steer while you two sit and guzzle, and I'm to go by nickname, and got to call you "sir" and "mister." Well, you look here, my bloke: I'll have fizz *ad lib.*, or it won't wash. I tell you that. And you know mighty well, you ain't got any man-of-war to signal now.'

Davis was staggered. 'I'd give fifty dollars this had never happened,' he said weakly.

'Well, it '*as* 'appened, you see,' returned Huish. 'Try some; it's devilish good.'

The Rubicon was crossed without another struggle. The captain filled a mug and drank.

'I wish it was beer,' he said with a sigh. 'But there's no denying it's the genuine stuff and cheap at the money. Now, Huish, you clear out and take your wheel.'

The little wretch had gained a point, and he was gay. 'Ay, ay, sir,' said he, and left the others to their meal.

'Pea soup!' exclaimed the captain. 'Blamed if I thought I should taste pea soup again!'

Herrick sat inert and silent. It was impossible after these months of hopeless want to smell the rough, high-spiced sea victuals without lust, and his mouth watered with desire of the champagne. It was no less impossible to have assisted at the scene between Huish and the captain, and not to perceive, with sudden bluntness, the gulf where he had fallen. He was a thief among thieves. He said it to himself. He could not touch the soup. If he had moved at all, it must have been to leave the table, throw himself overboard, and drown – an honest man.

'Here,' said the captain, 'you look sick, old man; have
a drop of this.'

The champagne creamed and bubbled in the mug; its
bright colour, its lively effervescence, seized his eye. 'It is
too late to hesitate,' he thought; his hand took the mug
instinctively; he drank, with unquenchable pleasure and
desire of more; drained the vessel dry, and set it down
with sparkling eyes.

'There is something in life after all!' he cried. 'I had forgot
what it was like. Yes, even this is worth while. Wine, food,
dry clothes – why, they're worth dying, worth hanging, for!
Captain, tell me one thing: why aren't all the poor folk
foot-pads?'

'Give it up,' said the captain.

'They must be damned good,' cried Herrick. 'There's
something here beyond me. Think of that calaboose!
Suppose we were sent suddenly back.' He shuddered as
though stung by a convulsion, and buried his face in his
clutching hands.

'Here, what's wrong with you?' cried the captain. There
was no reply; only Herrick's shoulders heaved, so that the
table was shaken. 'Take some more of this. Here, drink
this. I order you to. Don't start crying when you're out of
the wood.'

'I'm not crying,' said Herrick, raising his face and showing
his dry eyes. 'It's worse than crying. It's the horror of that
grave that we've escaped from.'

'Come now, you tackle your soup; that'll fix you,' said
Davis kindly. 'I told you you were all broken up. You
couldn't have stood out another week.'

'That's the dreadful part of it!' cried Herrick. 'Another
week and I'd have murdered someone for a dollar! God!
and I know that? And I'm still living? It's some beastly
dream.'

'Quietly, quietly! Quietly does it, my son. Take your pea
soup. Food, that's what you want,' said Davis.

The soup strengthened and quieted Herrick's nerves;
another glass of wine, and a piece of pickled pork and
fried banana completed what the soup began; and he was
able once more to look the captain in the face.

'I didn't know I was so much run down,' he said.

'Well,' said Davis, 'you were as steady as a rock all

day: now you've had a little lunch, you'll be as steady as a rock again.'

'Yes,' was the reply, 'I'm steady enough now, but I'm a queer kind of a first officer.'

'Shucks!' cried the captain. 'You've only got to mind the ship's course, and keep your slate to half a point. A babby could do that, let alone a college graduate like you. There ain't nothing *to* sailoring, when you come to look it in the face. And now we'll go and put her about. Bring the slate; we'll have to start our dead reckoning right away.'

The distance run since the departure was read off the log by the binnacle light and entered on the slate.

'Ready about,' said the captain. 'Give me the wheel, White Man, and you stand by the mainsheet. Boom tackle, Mr Hay, please, and then you can jump forward and attend head sails.'

'Ay, ay, sir,' responded Herrick.

'All clear forward?' asked Davis.

'All clear, sir.'

'Hard a-lee!' cried the captain. 'Haul in your slack as she comes,' he called to Huish. 'Haul in your slack, put your back into it; keep your feet out of the coils.' A sudden blow sent Huish flat along the deck, and the captain was in his place. 'Pick yourself up and keep the wheel hard over!' he roared. 'You wooden fool, you wanted to get killed, I guess. Draw the jib,' he cried a moment later; and then to Huish, 'Give me the wheel again, and see if you can coil that sheet.'

But Huish stood and looked at Davis with an evil countenance. 'Do you know you struck me?' said he.

'Do you know I saved your life?' returned the other, not deigning to look at him, his eyes travelling instead between the compass and the sails. 'Where would you have been, if that boom had swung out and you bundled in the clack? No, *sir*, we'll have no more of you at the mainsheet. Seaport towns are full of mainsheet-men; they hop upon one leg, my son, what's left of them, and the rest are dead. (Set your boom tackle, Mr Hay.) Struck you, did I? Lucky for you I did.'

'Well,' said Huish slowly, 'I daresay there may be somethink in that. 'Ope there is.' He turned his back elaborately on the captain, and entered the house, where the speedy explosion of a champagne cork showed he was attending to his comfort.

Herrick came aft to the captain. 'How is she doing now?' he asked.

'East and by no'the a half no'the,' said Davis. 'It's about as good as I expected.'

'What'll the hands think of it?' said Herrick.

'Oh, they don't think. They ain't paid to,' says the captain.

'There was something wrong, was there not? between you and— ' Herrick paused.

'That's a nasty little beast, that's a biter,' replied the captain, shaking his head. 'But so long as you and me hang in, it don't matter.'

Herrick lay down in the weather alleyway; the night was cloudless, the movement of the ship cradled him, he was oppressed besides by the first generous meal after so long a time of famine; and he was recalled from deep sleep by the voice of Davis singing out: 'Eight bells!'

He rose stupidly, and staggered aft, where the captain gave him the wheel.

'By the wind,' said the captain. 'It comes a little puffy; when you get a heavy puff, steal all you can to windward, but keep her a good full.'

He stepped towards the house, paused and hailed the forecastle.

'Got such a thing as a concertina forward?' said he. 'Bully for you, Uncle Ned. Fetch it aft, will you?'

The schooner steered very easy; and Herrick, watching the moon-whitened sails, was overpowered by drowsiness. A sharp report from the cabin startled him; a third bottle had been opened; and Herrick remembered the *Sea Ranger* and Fourteen Island Group. Presently the notes of the accordion sounded, and then the captain's voice:

> 'O honey, with our pockets full of money,
> We will trip, trip, trip, we will trip it on the quay,
> And I will dance with Kate, and Tom will dance
>   with Sall,
> When we're all back from South Amerikee.'

So it went to its quaint air; and the watch below lingered and listened by the forward door, and Uncle Ned was to be seen in the moonlight nodding time; and Herrick smiled at the wheel, his anxieties a while forgotten. Song followed song; another cork exploded; there were voices raised, as though the pair in the cabin were in disagreement; and presently it seemed the breach was healed; for it was now the voice of Huish that struck up, to the captain's accompaniment—

> 'Up in a balloon, boys,
>   Up in a balloon,
> All among the little stars
>   And round about the moon.'

A wave of nausea overcame Herrick at the wheel. He wondered why the air, the words (which were yet written with a certain knack), and the voice and accent of the singer, should all jar his spirit like a file on a man's teeth. He sickened at the thought of his two comrades drinking away their reason upon stolen wine, quarrelling and hiccupping and waking up, while the doors of the prison yawned for them in the near future. 'Shall I have sold my honour for nothing?' he thought; and a heat of rage and resolution glowed in his bosom – rage against his comrades – resolution to carry through this business if it might be carried; pluck profit out of shame, since the shame at least was now inevitable; and come home, home from South America – how did the song go? – 'with his pockets full of money':

> 'O honey, with our pockets full of money,
> We will trip, trip, trip, we will trip it on the quay:'

so the words ran in his head; and the honey took on visible form, the quay rose before him and he knew it for the lamplit Embankment, and he saw the lights of Battersea bridge bestride the sullen river. All through the remainder of his trick, he stood entranced, reviewing the past. He had been always true to his love, but not always sedulous to recall her. In the growing calamity of his life, she had swum more distant, like the moon in mist. The letter of farewell, the dishonourable hope that had surprised and corrupted him in his distress, the changed scene, the sea, the night and the music – all stirred him to the roots of manhood. 'I *will* win her,' he thought, and ground his teeth. 'Fair or foul, what matters if I win her?'

'Fo' bell, matey. I think um fo' bell' – he was suddenly recalled by these words in the voice of Uncle Ned.

'Look in at the clock, Uncle,' said he. He would not look himself, from horror of the tipplers.

'Him past, matey,' repeated the Hawaiian.

'So much the better for you, Uncle,' he replied; and he gave up the wheel, repeating the directions as he had received them.

He took two steps forward and remembered his dead reckoning. 'How has she been heading?' he thought; and he flushed from head to foot. He had not observed or had forgotten; here was the old incompetence; the slate must be filled up by guess. 'Never again!' he vowed to himself in silent fury, 'never again. It shall be no fault of mine if this miscarry.' And for the remainder of his watch, he stood close by Uncle Ned, and read the face of the compass as perhaps he had never read a letter from his sweetheart.

All the time, and spurring him to the more attention, song, loud talk, fleering laughter and the occasional popping of a cork, reached his ears from the interior of the house; and when the port watch was relieved at midnight, Huish and the captain appeared upon the quarter-deck with flushed faces and uneven steps, the former laden with bottles, the latter with two tin mugs. Herrick silently passed them by. They hailed him in thick voices, he made no answer, they cursed him for a churl, he paid no heed although his belly quivered with disgust and rage. He closed-to the door of the house behind him, and cast himself on a locker in the cabin – not to sleep he thought – rather to think and to despair. Yet he had scarce turned twice on his uneasy bed, before a drunken voice hailed him in the ear, and he must go on deck again to stand the morning watch.

The first evening set the model for those that were to follow. Two cases of champagne scarce lasted the four-and-twenty hours, and almost the whole was drunk by Huish and the captain. Huish seemed to thrive on the excess; he was never sober, yet never wholly tipsy; the food and the sea air had soon healed him of his disease, and he began to lay on flesh. But with Davis things went worse. In the drooping, unbuttoned figure that sprawled all day upon the lockers, tippling and reading novels; in the fool who made of the evening watch a public carouse on the quarter-deck, it would have been hard to recognise the vigorous seaman of Papeete roads. He kept himself reasonably well in hand till he had taken the sun and yawned and blotted through his calculations; but from the moment he rolled up the chart, his hours were passed in slavish self-indulgence or in hoggish slumber. Every other branch of his duty was neglected, except maintaining a stern discipline about the dinner table. Again and again Herrick would hear the cook called aft, and see him running with fresh tins, or carrying away again a meal that had been totally condemned. And the more the captain became sunk in drunkenness, the more delicate his palate showed itself. Once, in the forenoon, he had a bo'sun's chair rigged over the rail, stripped to his trousers, and went overboard with a pot of paint. 'I don't like the way this schooner's painted,' said he, 'and I've taken a down upon her name.' But he tired of it in half an hour, and the schooner went on her way with an incongruous patch of colour on the stern, and the word *Farallone* part obliterated and part looking through. He refused to stand either the middle or the morning watch. It was fine-weather sailing, he said; and asked, with a laugh, 'Who ever heard of the old man standing watch himself?' To the dead reckoning which Herrick still tried to keep, he would pay not the least attention nor afford the least assistance.

'What do we want of dead reckoning?' he asked. 'We get the sun all right, don't we?'

'We mayn't get it always though,' objected Herrick. 'And you told me yourself you weren't sure of the chronometer.'

'Oh, there ain't no flies in the chronometer!' cried Davis.

'Oblige me so far, captain,' said Herrick stiffly. 'I am anxious to keep this reckoning, which is a part of my duty; I do not know what to allow for current, nor how to allow for it. I am too inexperienced; and I beg of you to help me.'

'Never discourage zealous officer,' said the captain, unrolling the chart again, for Herrick had taken him over his day's work and while he was still partly sober. 'Here it is: look for yourself; anything from west to west no'the-west, and anyways from five to twenty-five miles.

That's what the A'm'ralty chart says; I guess you don't expect to get on ahead of your own Britishers?'

'I am trying to do my duty, Captain Brown,' said Herrick, with a dark flush, 'and I have the honour to inform you that I don't enjoy being trifled with.'

'What in thunder do you want?' roared Davis. 'Go and look at the blamed wake. If you're trying to do your duty, why don't you go and do it? I guess it's no business of mine to go and stick my head over the ship's rump? I guess it's yours. And I'll tell you what it is, my fine fellow, I'll trouble you not to come the dude over me. You're insolent, that's what's wrong with you. Don't you crowd me, Mr Herrick, Esquire.'

Herrick tore up his papers, threw them on the floor, and left the cabin.

'He's turned a bloomin' swot, ain't he?' sneered Huish.

'He thinks himself too good for his company, that's what ails Herrick, Esquire,' raged the captain. 'He thinks I don't understand when he comes the heavy swell. Won't sit down with us, won't he? won't say a civil word? I'll serve the son of a gun as he deserves. By God, Huish, I'll show him whether he's too good for John Davis!'

'Easy with the names, cap',' said Huish, who was always the more sober. 'Easy over the stones, my boy!'

'All right, I will. You're a good sort, Huish. I didn't take to you at first, but I guess you're right enough. Let's open another bottle,' said the captain; and that day, perhaps because he was excited by the quarrel, he drank more recklessly, and by four o'clock was stretched insensible upon the locker.

Herrick and Huish supped alone, one after the other, opposite his flushed and snorting body. And if the sight killed Herrick's hunger, the isolation weighed so heavily on the clerk's spirit, that he was scarce risen from table ere he was currying favour with his former comrade.

Herrick was at the wheel when he approached, and Huish leaned confidentially across the binnacle.

'I say, old chappie,' he said, 'you and me don't seem to be such pals somehow.'

Herrick gave her a spoke or two in silence; his eye, as it skirted from the needle to the luff of the foresail, passed the man by without speculation. But Huish was really dull, a

thing he could support with difficulty, having no resources
of his own. The idea of a private talk with Herrick, at this
stage of their relations, held out particular inducements
to a person of his character. Drink besides, as it renders
some men hyper-sensitive, made Huish callous. And it
would almost have required a blow to make him quit his
purpose.

'Pretty business, ain't it?' he continued; 'Dyvis on the
lush? Must say I thought you gave it 'im AI today. He
didn't like it a bit; took on hawful after you were gone.—
"'Ere," says I, "'old on, easy on the lush," I says. "'Errick
was right, and you know it. Give 'im a chanst," I says.—
"'Uish," sezee, "don't you gimme no more of your jaw,
or I'll knock your bloomin' eyes out." Well, wot can I do,
'Errick? But I tell you, I don't 'arf like it. It looks to me
like the *Sea Rynger* over again.'

Still Herrick was silent.

'Do you 'ear me speak?' asked Huish sharply. 'You're
pleasant, ain't you?'

'Stand away from that binnacle,' said Herrick.

The clerk looked at him, long and straight and black;
his figure seemed to writhe like that of a snake about to
strike; then he turned on his heel, went back to the cabin
and opened a bottle of champagne. When eight bells were
cried, he slept on the floor beside the captain on the locker;
and of the whole starboard watch, only Sally Day appeared
upon the summons. The mate proposed to stand the watch
with him, and let Uncle Ned lie down; it would make
twelve hours on deck, and probably sixteen, but in this
fair-weather sailing, he might safely sleep between his
tricks of wheel, leaving orders to be called on any sign
of squalls. So far he could trust the men, between whom
and himself a close relation had sprung up. With Uncle
Ned he held long nocturnal conversations, and the old
man told him his simple and hard story of exile, suffering,
and injustice among cruel whites. The cook, when he found
Herrick messed alone, produced for him unexpected and
sometimes unpalatable dainties, of which he forced himself
to eat. And one day, when he was forward, he was surprised
to feel a caressing hand run down his shoulder, and to hear
the voice of Sally Day crooning in his ear: 'You gootch man!'
He turned, and, choking down a sob, shook hands with the

negrito. They were kindly, cheery, childish souls. Upon the
Sunday each brought forth his separate Bible – for they were
all men of alien speech even to each other, and Sally Day
communicated with his mates in English only, each read or
made believe to read his chapter, Uncle Ned with spectacles
on his nose; and they would all join together in the singing of
missionary hymns. It was thus a cutting reproof to compare
the islanders and the whites aboard the *Farallone*. Shame
ran in Herrick's blood to remember what employment he
was on, and to see these poor souls – and even Sally Day,
the child of cannibals, in all likelihood a cannibal himself
– so faithful to what they knew of good. The fact that he
was held in grateful favour by these innocents served like
blinders to his conscience, and there were times when he
was inclined, with Sally Day, to call himself a good man. But
the height of his favour was only now to appear. With one
voice, the crew protested; ere Herrick knew what they were
doing, the cook was aroused and came a willing volunteer;
all hands clustered about their mate with expostulations
and caresses; and he was bidden to lie down and take his
customary rest without alarm.

'He tell you tlue,' said Uncle Ned. 'You sleep. Evely man
hae he do all light. Evely man he like you too much.'

Herrick struggled, and gave way; choked upon some
trivial words of gratitude; and walked to the side of the
house, against which he leaned, struggling with emotion.

Uncle Ned presently followed him and begged him to
lie down.

'It's no use, Uncle Ned,' he replied. 'I couldn't sleep.
I'm knocked over with all your goodness.'

'Ah, no call me Uncle Ned no mo'!' cried the old man.
'No my name! My name Taveeta, all-e-same Taveeta King
of Islael. Wat for he call that Hawaii? I think no savvy
nothing – all-e-same Wise-a-mana.'

It was the first time the name of the late captain had
been mentioned, and Herrick grasped the occasion. The
reader shall be spared Uncle Ned's unwieldy dialect, and
learn in less embarrassing English, the sum of what he now
communicated. The ship had scarce cleared the Golden
Gates before the captain and mate had entered on a
career of drunkenness, which was scarcely interrupted
by their malady and only closed by death. For days and

weeks they had encountered neither land nor ship; and seeing themselves lost on the huge deep with their insane conductors, the natives had drunk deep of terror.

At length they made a low island, and went in; and Wiseman and Wishart landed in the boat.

There was a great village, a very fine village, and plenty Kanakas in that place; but all mighty serious; and from every here and there in the back parts of the settlement, Taveeta heard the sounds of island lamentation. 'I no savvy *talk* that island,' said he. 'I savvy hear um *cly*. I think, Hum! too many people die here!' But upon Wiseman and Wishart the significance of that barbaric keening was lost. Full of bread and drink, they rollicked along unconcerned, embraced the girls who had scarce energy to repel them, took up and joined (with drunken voices) in the death wail, and at last (on what they took to be an invitation) entered under the roof of a house in which was a considerable concourse of people sitting silent. They stooped below the eaves, flushed and laughing; within a minute they came forth again with changed faces and silent tongues; and as the press severed to make way for them, Taveeta was able to perceive, in the deep shadow of the house, the sick man raising from his mat a head already defeatured by disease. The two tragic triflers fled without hesitation for their boat, screaming on Taveeta to make haste; they came aboard with all speed of oars, raised anchor and crowded sail upon the ship with blows and curses, and were at sea again – and again drunk – before sunset. A week after, and the last of the two had been committed to the deep. Herrick asked Taveeta where that island was, and he replied that, by what he gathered of folks' talk as they went up together from the beach, he supposed it must be one of the Paumotus. This was in itself probable enough, for the Dangerous Archipelago had been swept that year from east to west by devastating smallpox; but Herrick thought it a strange course to lie from Sydney. Then he remembered the drink.

'Were they not surprised when they made the island?' he asked.

'Wise-a-mana he say "dam! what this?"' was the reply.

'O, that's it then,' said Herrick. 'I don't believe they knew where they were.'

'I think so too,' said Uncle Ned. 'I think no savvy. This

one mo' betta,' he added, pointing to the house where the drunken captain slumbered: 'Take-a-sun all-e-time.'

The implied last touch completed Herrick's picture of the life and death of his two predecessors; of their prolonged, sordid, sodden sensuality as they sailed, they knew not whither, on their last cruise. He held but a twinkling and unsure belief in any future state; the thought of one of punishment he derided; yet for him (as for all) there dwelt a horror about the end of the brutish man. Sickness fell upon him at the image thus called up; and when he compared it with the scene in which himself was acting, and considered the doom that seemed to brood upon the schooner, a horror that was almost superstitious fell upon him. And yet the strange thing was, he did not falter. He who had proved his incapacity in so many fields, being now falsely placed amid duties which he did not understand, without help, and it might be said without countenance, had hitherto surpassed expectation; and even the shameful misconduct and shocking disclosures of that night seemed but to nerve and strengthen him. He had sold his honour; he vowed it should not be in vain; 'it shall be no fault of mine if this miscarry,' he repeated. And in his heart he wondered at himself. Living rage no doubt supported him; no doubt also, the sense of the last cast, of the ships burned, of all doors closed but one, which is so strong a tonic to the merely weak, and so deadly a depressant to the merely cowardly.

For some time the voyage went otherwise well. They weathered Fakarava with one board; and the wind holding well to the southward and blowing fresh, they passed between Ranaka and Ratiu, and ran some days north-east by east-half-east under the lee of Takume and Honden, neither of which they made. In about 14° South and between 134° and 135° West, it fell a dead calm with rather a heavy sea. The captain refused to take in sail, the helm was lashed, no watch was set, and the *Farallone* rolled and banged for three days, according to observation, in almost the same place. The fourth morning, a little before day, a breeze sprang up and rapidly freshened. The captain had drunk hard the night before; he was far from sober when he was roused; and when he came on deck for the first time at half-past eight, it was plain he had already drunk deep again at breakfast. Herrick avoided his eye; and resigned the deck with indignation to a man more than half-seas over.

By the loud commands of the captain and the singing out of fellows at the ropes, he could judge from the house that sail was being crowded on the ship; relinquished his half-eaten breakfast; and came on deck again, to find the main and the jib topsails set, and both watches and the cook turned out to hand the staysail. The *Farallone* lay already far over; the sky was obscured with misty scud; and from the windward an ominous squall came flying up, broadening and blackening as it rose.

Fear thrilled in Herrick's vitals. He saw death hard by; and if not death, sure ruin. For if the *Farallone* lived through the coming squall, she must surely be dismasted. With that their enterprise was at an end, and they themselves bound prisoners to the very evidence of their crime. The greatness of the peril and his own alarm sufficed to silence him. Pride, wrath, and shame raged without issue in his mind; and he shut his teeth and folded his arms close.

The captain sat in the boat to windward, bellowing orders and insults, his eyes glazed, his face deeply congested; a bottle set between his knees, a glass in his hand half empty. His back was to the squall, and he was at first intent upon the setting of the sail. When that was done, and the great trapezium of canvas had begun to draw and to trail the lee-rail of the *Farallone* level with the foam, he laughed out an empty laugh, drained his glass, sprawled back among the lumber in the boat, and fetched out a crumpled novel.

Herrick watched him, and his indignation glowed red hot. He glanced to windward where the squall already whitened the near sea and heralded its coming with a singular and dismal sound. He glanced at the steersman, and saw him clinging to the spokes with a face of a sickly blue. He saw the crew were running to their stations without orders. And it seemed as if something broke in his brain; and the passion of anger, so long restrained, so long eaten in secret, burst suddenly loose and shook him like a sail. He stepped across to the captain and smote his hand heavily on the drunkard's shoulder.

'You brute,' he said, in a voice that tottered, 'look behind you!'

'Wha's that?' cried Davis, bounding in the boat and upsetting the champagne.

'You lost the *Sea Ranger* because you were a drunken sot,' said Herrick. 'Now you're going to lose the *Farallone*. You're going to drown here the same way as you drowned others, and be damned. And your daughter shall walk the streets, and your sons be thieves like their father.'

For the moment, the words struck the captain white and foolish. 'My God!' he cried, looking at Herrick as upon a ghost; 'my God, Herrick!'

'Look behind you, then!' reiterated the assailant.

The wretched man, already partly sobered, did as he was told, and in the same breath of time leaped to his feet. 'Down staysail!' he trumpeted. The hands were thrilling for the order, and the great sail came with a run, and fell half overboard among the racing foam. 'Jib topsail-halyards! Let the stays'l be,' he said again.

But before it was well uttered, the squall shouted aloud and fell, in a solid mass of wind and rain commingled, on the *Farallone*; and she stooped under the blow, and lay like a thing dead. From the mind of Herrick reason fled; he clung in the weather rigging, exulting; he was done with life, and he gloried in the release; he gloried in the wild noises of the wind and the choking onslaught of the rain; he gloried to die so, and now, amid this coil of the elements. And meanwhile, in the waist up to his knees in water – so low the schooner lay – the captain was hacking at the foresheet with a pocket knife. It was a question of seconds, for the *Farallone* drank deep of the encroaching seas. But the hand of the captain had the advance; the foresail boom tore apart the last strands of the sheet and crashed to leeward; the *Farallone* leaped up into the wind and righted; and the peak and throat halyards, which had long been let go, began to run at the same instant.

For some ten minutes more she careered under the impulse of the squall; but the captain was now master of himself and of his ship, and all danger at an end. And then, sudden as a trick change upon the stage, the squall blew by, the wind dropped into light airs, the sun beamed forth again upon the tattered schooner; and the captain, having secured the foresail boom and set a couple of hands to the pump, walked aft, sober, a little pale, and with the sodden end of a cigar still stuck between his teeth even as the squall had found it. Herrick followed him; he could scarce recall the violence of his late emotions, but he felt there was a scene to go through, and he was anxious and even eager to go through with it.

The captain, turning at the house end, met him face to face, and averted his eyes. 'We've lost the two tops'ls and the stays'l,' he gabbled. 'Good business, we didn't lose any sticks. I guess you think we're all the better without the kites.'

'That's not what I'm thinking,' said Herrick, in a voice strangely quiet, that yet echoed confusion in the captain's mind.

'I know that,' he cried, holding up his hand. 'I know what you're thinking. No use to say it now. I'm sober.'

'I have to say it, though,' returned Herrick.

'Hold on, Herrick; you've said enough,' said Davis. 'You've said what I would take from no man breathing but yourself; only I know it's true.'

'I have to tell you, Captain Brown,' pursued Herrick, 'that I resign my position as mate. You can put me in irons or shoot me, as you please; I will make no resistance – only, I decline in any way to help or to obey you; and I suggest you should put Mr Huish in my place. He will make a worthy first officer to your captain, sir.' He smiled, bowed, and turned to walk forward.

'Where are you going, Herrick?' cried the captain, detaining him by the shoulder.

'To berth forward with the men, sir,' replied Herrick, with the same hateful smile. 'I've been long enough aft here with you – gentlemen.'

'You're wrong there,' said Davis. 'Don't you be too quick with me; there ain't nothing wrong but the drink – it's the old story, man! Let me get sober once, and then you'll see,' he pleaded.

'Excuse me, I desire to see no more of you,' said Herrick.

The captain groaned aloud. 'You know what you said about my children?' he broke out.

'By rote. In case you wish me to say it you again?' asked Herrick.

'Don't!' cried the captain, clapping his hands to his ears.

'Don't make me kill a man I care for! Herrick, if you see me put a glass to my lips again till we're ashore, I give you leave to put a bullet through me; I beg you to do it! You're the only man aboard whose carcase is worth losing; do you think I don't know that? do you think I ever went back on you? I always knew you were in the right of it – drunk or sober, I knew that. What do you want? – an oath? Man, you're clever enough to see that this is sure-enough earnest.'

'Do you mean there shall be no more drinking?' asked Herrick, 'neither by you nor Huish? that you won't go on stealing my profits and drinking my champagne that I gave my honour for? and that you'll attend to your duties, and stand watch and watch, and bear your proper share of the ship's work, instead of leaving it all on the shoulders of a landsman, and making yourself the butt and scoff of native seamen? Is that what you mean? If it is, be so good as to say it categorically.'

'You put these things in a way hard for a gentleman to swallow,' said the captain. 'You wouldn't have me say I was ashamed of myself? Trust me this once; I'll do the square thing, and there's my hand on it.'

'Well, I'll try it once,' said Herrick. 'Fail me again . . .'

'No more now!' interrupted Davis. 'No more, old man! Enough said. You've a riling tongue when your back's up, Herrick. Just be glad we're friends again, the same as what I am; and go tender on the raws; I'll see as you don't repent it. We've been mighty near death this day – don't say whose fault it was! – pretty near hell, too, I guess. We're in a mighty bad line of life, us two, and ought to go easy with each other.'

He was maundering; yet it seemed as if he were maundering with some design, beating about the bush of some communication that he feared to make, or perhaps only talking against time in terror of what Herrick might say next. But Herrick had now spat his venom; his was a kindly nature, and, content with his triumph, he had now begun to pity. With a few soothing words, he sought to conclude the interview, and proposed that they should change their clothes.

'Not right yet,' said Davis. 'There's another thing I want to tell you first. You know what you said about my children? I want to tell you why it hit me so hard;

I kind of think you'll feel bad about it too. It's about my little Adar. You hadn't ought to have quite said that – but of course I know you didn't know. She – she's dead, you see.'

'Why, Davis!' cried Herrick. 'You've told me a dozen times she was alive! Clear your head, man! This must be the drink.'

'No, *sir*,' said Davis. 'She's dead. Died of a bowel complaint. That was when I was away in the brig *Oregon*. She lies in Portland, Maine. "Adar, only daughter of Captain John Davis and Mariar his wife, aged five." I had a doll for her on board. I never took the paper off'n that doll, Herrick; it went down the way it was with the *Sea Ranger*, that day I was damned.'

The Captain's eyes were fixed on the horizon, he talked with an extraordinary softness but a complete composure; and Herrick looked upon him with something that was almost terror.

'Don't think I'm crazy neither,' resumed Davis. 'I've all the cold sense that I know what to do with. But I guess a man that's unhappy's like a child; and this is a kind of a child's game of mine. I never could act up to the plain-cut truth, you see; so I pretend. And I warn you square; as soon as we're through with this talk, I'll start in again with the pretending. Only, you see, she can't walk no streets,' added the captain, 'couldn't even make out to live and get that doll!'

Herrick laid a tremulous hand upon the captain's shoulder.

'Don't do that!' cried Davis, recoiling from the touch. 'Can't you see I'm all broken up the way it is? Come along, then; come along, old man; you can put your trust in me right through; come along and get dry clothes.'

They entered the cabin, and there was Huish on his knees prising open a case of champagne.

'Vast, there!' cried the captain. 'No more of that. No more drinking on this ship.'

'Turned teetotal, 'ave you?' inquired Huish. 'I'm agreeable. About time, eh? Bloomin' nearly lost another ship, I fancy.' He took out a bottle and began calmly to burst the wire with the spike of a corkscrew.

'Do you hear me speak?' cried Davis.

'I suppose I do. You speak loud enough,' said Huish. 'The trouble is that I don't care.'

Herrick plucked the captain's sleeve. 'Let him free now,' he said. 'We've had all we want this morning.'

'Let him have it then,' said the captain. 'It's his last.'

By this time the wire was open, the string was cut, the head of gilded paper was torn away; and Huish waited, mug in hand, expecting the usual explosion. It did not follow. He eased the cork with his thumb; still there was no result. At last he took the screw and drew it. It came out very easy and with scarce a sound.

'Illo!' said Huish. ''Ere's a bad bottle.'

He poured some of the wine into the mug; it was colourless and still. He smelt and tasted it.

'W'y, wot's this?' he said. 'It's water!'

If the voice of trumpets had suddenly sounded about the ship in the midst of the sea, the three men in the house could scarcely have been more stunned than by this incident. The mug passed round; each sipped, each smelt of it; each stared at the bottle in its glory of gold paper as Crusoe may have stared at the footprint; and their minds were swift to fix upon a common apprehension. The difference between a bottle of champagne and a bottle of water is not great; between a shipload of one or the other lay the whole scale from riches to ruin.

A second bottle was broached. There were two cases standing ready in a stateroom; these two were brought out, broken open, and tested. Still with the same result: the contents were still colourless and tasteless, and dead as the rain in a beached fishing-boat.

'Crikey!' said Huish.

'Here, let's sample the hold!' said the captain, mopping his brow with a back-handed sweep; and the three stalked out of the house, grim and heavy-footed.

All hands were turned out; two Kanakas were sent below, another stationed at a purchase; and Davis, axe in hand, took his place beside the coamings.

'Are you going to let the men know?' whispered Herrick.

'Damn the men!' said Davis. 'It's beyond that. We've got to know ourselves.'

Three cases were sent on deck and sampled in turn;

from each bottle, as the captain smashed it with the axe, the champagne ran bubbling and creaming.

'Go deeper, can't you?' cried Davis to the Kanakas in the hold.

The command gave the signal for a disastrous change. Case after case came up, bottle after bottle was burst and bled mere water. Deeper yet, and they came upon a layer where there was scarcely so much as the intention to deceive; where the cases were no longer branded, the bottles no longer wired or papered, where the fraud was manifest and stared them in the face.

'Here's about enough of this foolery!' said Davis. 'Stow back the cases in the hold, Uncle, and get the broken crockery overboard. Come with me,' he added to his co-adventurers, and led the way back into the cabin.

SIX

The Partners

Each took a side of the fixed table; it was the first time they had sat down at it together; but now all sense of incongruity, all memory of differences, was quite swept away by the presence of the common ruin.

'Gentlemen,' said the captain, after a pause, and with very much the air of a chairman opening a board-meeting, 'we're sold.'

Huish broke out in laughter. 'Well, if this ain't the 'ighest old rig!' he cried. 'And Dyvis, 'ere, who thought he had got up so bloomin' early in the mornin'! We've stolen a cargo of spring water! Oh, my crikey!' and he squirmed with mirth.

The captain managed to screw out a phantom smile.

'Here's Old Man Destiny again,' said he to Herrick, 'but this time I guess he's kicked the door right in.'

Herrick only shook his head.

'O Lord, it's rich!' laughed Huish. 'It would really be a scrumptious lark if it 'ad 'appened to somebody else! And wot are we to do next? Oh, my eye! with this bloomin' schooner, too?'

'That's the trouble,' said Davis. 'There's only one thing certain: it's no use carting this old glass and ballast to Peru. No, *sir*, we're in a hole.'

'O my, and the merchant!' cried Huish; 'the man that made this shipment! He'll get the news by the mail brigantine; and he'll think of course we're making straight for Sydney.'

'Yes, he'll be a sick merchant,' said the captain. 'One thing: this explains the Kanaka crew. If you're going to lose a ship, I would ask no better myself than a Kanaka crew. But there's one thing it don't explain; it don't explain why she came down Tahiti ways.'

'W'y, to lose her, you byby!' said Huish.

'A lot you know,' said the captain. 'Nobody wants to lose a schooner; they want to lose her *on her course*, you skeericks! You seem to think underwriters haven't got enough sense to come in out of the rain.'

'Well,' said Herrick, 'I can tell you (I am afraid) why she came so far to the eastward. I had it of Uncle Ned. It seems these two unhappy devils, Wiseman and Wishart, were drunk on the champagne from the beginning – and died drunk at the end.'

The captain looked on the table.

'They lay in their two bunks, or sat here in this damned house,' he pursued, with rising agitation, 'filling their skins with the accursed stuff, till sickness took them. As they sickened and the fever rose, they drank the more. They lay here howling and groaning, drunk and dying, all in one. They didn't know where they were, they didn't care. They didn't even take the sun, it seems.'

'Not take the sun?' cried the captain, looking up. 'Sacred Billy! what a crowd!'

'Well, it don't matter to Joe!' said Huish. 'Wot are Wiseman and the t'other buffer to us?'

'A good deal, too,' says the captain. 'We're their heirs, I guess.'

'It is a great inheritance,' said Herrick.

'Well, I don't know about that,' returned Davis. 'Appears to me as if it might be worse. 'Tain't worth what the cargo would have been of course, at least not money down. But I'll tell you what it appears to figure up to. Appears to me as if it amounted to about the bottom dollar of the man in 'Frisco.'

''Old on,' said Huish. 'Give a fellow time; 'ow's this, umpire?'

'Well, my sons,' pursued the captain, who seemed to have recovered his assurance, 'Wiseman and Wishart were to be paid for casting away this old schooner and its cargo. We're going to cast away the schooner right enough; and I'll make it my private business to see that we get paid. What were W. and W. to get? That's more'n I can tell. But W. and W. went into this business themselves, they were on the crook. Now *we're* on the square, *we* only stumbled into it; and that merchant has just got to squeal, and I'm the man to see that he squeals good.

No, *sir*! there's some stuffing to this *Farallone* racket after all.'

'Go it, cap!' cried Huish. 'Yoicks! Forrard! 'Old 'ard! There's your style for the money! Blow me if I don't prefer this to the hother.'

'I do not understand,' said Herrick. 'I have to ask you to excuse me; I do not understand.'

'Well now, see here, Herrick,' said Davis, 'I'm going to have a word with you anyway upon a different matter, and it's good that Huish should hear it too. We're done with this boozing business, and we ask your pardon for it right here and now. We have to thank you for all you did for us while we were making hogs of ourselves; you'll find me turn-to all right in future; and as for the wine, which I grant we stole from you, I'll take stock and see you paid for it. That's good enough, I believe. But what I want to point out to you is this. The old game was a risky game. The new game's as safe as running a Vienna Bakery. We just put this *Farallone* before the wind, and run till we're well to looard of our port of departure and reasonably well up with some other place, where they have an American Consul. Down goes the *Farallone*, and good-bye to her! A day or so in the boat; the consul packs us home, at Uncle Sam's expense, to 'Frisco; and if that merchant don't put the dollars down, you come to me!'

'But I thought,' began Herrick; and then broke out; 'oh, let's get on to Peru!'

'Well, if you're going to Peru for your health, I won't say no!' replied the captain. 'But for what other blame' shadow of a reason you should want to go there, gets me clear. We don't want to go there with this cargo; I don't know as old bottles is a lively article anywheres; leastways, I'll go my bottom cent, it ain't Peru. It was always a doubt if we could sell the schooner; I never rightly hoped to, and now I'm sure she ain't worth a hill of beans; what's wrong with her, I don't know; I only know it's something, or she wouldn't be here with this truck in her inside. Then again, if we lose her, and land in Peru, where are we? We can't declare the loss, or how did we get to Peru? In that case the merchant can't touch the insurance; most likely he'll go bust; and don't you think you see the three of us on the beach of Callao?'

'There's no extradition there,' said Herrick.

'Well, my son, and we want to be extraded,' said the captain. 'What's our point? We want to have a consul extrade us as far as San Francisco and that merchant's office door. My idea is that Samoa would be found an eligible business centre. It's dead before the wind; the States have a consul there, and 'Frisco steamers call, so's we could skip right back and interview the merchant.'

'Samoa?' said Herrick. 'It will take us for ever to get there.'

'Oh, with a fair wind!' said the captain.

'No trouble about the log, eh?' asked Huish.

'No, *sir*,' said Davis. '*Light airs and baffling winds. Squalls and calms. D. R.: five miles. No obs. Pumps attended.* And fill in the barometer and thermometer off of last year's trip.' 'Never saw such a voyage,' says you to the consul. 'Thought I was going to run short . . .' He stopped in mid career. ''Say,' he began again, and once more stopped. 'Beg your pardon, Herrick,' he added with undisguised humility, 'but did you keep the run of the stores?'

'Had I been told to do so, it should have been done, as the rest was done, to the best of my little ability,' said Herrick. 'As it was, the cook helped himself to what he pleased.'

Davis looked at the table.

'I drew it rather fine, you see,' he said at last. 'The great thing was to clear right out of Papeete before the consul could think better of it. Tell you what: I guess I'll take stock.'

And he rose from table and disappeared with a lamp in the lazarette.

''Ere's another screw loose,' observed Huish.

'My man,' said Herrick, with a sudden gleam of animosity, 'it is still your watch on deck, and surely your wheel also?'

'You come the 'eavy swell, don't you, ducky?' said Huish. 'Stand away from that binnacle. Surely your w'eel, my man. Yah.'

He lit a cigar ostentatiously, and strolled into the waist with his hands in his pockets.

In a surprisingly short time, the captain reappeared; he did not look at Herrick, but called Huish back and sat down.

'Well,' he began, 'I've taken stock – roughly.' He paused
as if for somebody to help him out; and none doing so,
both gazing on him instead with manifest anxiety, he yet
more heavily resumed. 'Well, it won't fight. We can't do
it; that's the bed rock. I'm as sorry as what you can be,
and sorrier. We can't look near Samoa. I don't know as
we could get to Peru.'

'Wot-ju mean?' asked Huish brutally.

'I can't 'most tell myself,' replied the captain. 'I drew it
fine; I said I did; but what's been going on here gets me!
Appears as if the devil had been around. That cook must
be the holiest kind of fraud. Only twelve days, too! Seems
like craziness. I'll own up square to one thing: I seem to
have figured too fine upon the flour. But the rest – my
land! I'll never understand it! There's been more waste on
this twopenny ship than what there is to an Atlantic Liner.'
He stole a glance at his companions; nothing good was to
be gleaned from their dark faces; and he had recourse to
rage. 'You wait till I interview that cook!' he roared and
smote the table with his fist. 'I'll interview the son of a
gun so's he's never been spoken to before. I'll put a bead
upon the— '

'You will not lay a finger on the man,' said Herrick.
'The fault is yours and you know it. If you turn a savage
loose in your store-room, you know what to expect. I will
not allow the man to be molested.'

It is hard to say how Davis might have taken this defiance;
but he was diverted to a fresh assailant.

'Well!' drawled Huish, 'you're a plummy captain, ain't
you? You're a blooming captain! Don't you set up any of
your chat to me, John Dyvis: I know you now, you ain't
any more use than a bloomin' dawl! Oh, you "don't know",
don't you? Oh, it "gets you", do it? Oh, I dessay! W'y, we
en't you 'owling for fresh tins every blessed day? 'Ow often
'ave I 'eard you send the 'ole bloomin' dinner off and tell
the man to chuck it in the swill tub? And breakfast? Oh,
my crikey! breakfast for ten, and you 'ollerin' for more! And
now you "can't 'most tell"! Blow me, if it ain't enough to
make a man write an insultin' letter to Gawd! You dror it
mild, John Dyvis; don't 'andle me; I'm dyngerous.'

Davis sat like one bemused; it might even have been
doubted if he heard, but the voice of the clerk rang about

the cabin like that of a cormorant among the ledges of the cliff.

'That will do, Huish,' said Herrick.

'Oh, so you tyke his part, do you? you stuck-up sneerin' snob! Tyke it then. Come on, the pair of you. But as for John Dyvis, let him look out! He struck me the first night aboard, and I never took a blow yet but wot I gave as good. Let him knuckle down on his marrow bones and beg my pardon. That's my last word.'

'I stand by the Captain,' said Herrick. 'That makes us two to one, both good men; and the crew will all follow me. I hope I shall die very soon; but I have not the least objection to killing you before I go. I should prefer it so; I should do it with no more remorse than winking. Take care – take care, you little cad!'

The animosity with which these words were uttered was so marked in itself, and so remarkable in the man who uttered them that Huish stared, and even the humiliated Davis reared up his head and gazed at his defender. As for Herrick, the successive agitations and disappointments of the day had left him wholly reckless; he was conscious of a pleasant glow, an agreeable excitement; his head seemed empty, his eyeballs burned as he turned them, his throat was dry as a biscuit; the least dangerous man by nature, except in so far as the weak are always dangerous, at that moment he was ready to slay or to be slain with equal unconcern.

Here at least was the gage thrown down, and battle offered; he who should speak next would bring the matter to an issue there and then; all knew it to be so and hung back; and for many seconds by the cabin clock, the trio sat motionless and silent.

Then came an interruption, welcome as the flowers in May.

'Land ho!' sang out a voice on deck. 'Land a weatha bow!'

'Land!' cried Davis, springing to his feet. 'What's this? There ain't no land here.'

And as men may run from the chamber of a murdered corpse, the three ran forth out of the house and left their quarrel behind them, undecided.

The sky shaded down at the sea level to the white of

opals; the sea itself, insolently, inkily blue, drew all about
them the uncompromising wheel of the horizon. Search it
as they pleased, not even the practised eye of Captain Davis
could descry the smallest interruption. A few filmy clouds
were slowly melting overhead; and about the schooner, as
around the only point of interest, a tropic bird, white as a
snowflake, hung, and circled, and displayed, as it turned,
the long vermilion feather of its tail. Save the sea and the
heaven, that was all.

'Who sang out land?' asked Davis. 'If there's any boy
playing funny dog with me, I'll teach him skylarking!'

But Uncle Ned contentedly pointed to a part of the
horizon, where a greenish, filmy iridescence could be
discerned floating like smoke on the pale heavens.

Davis applied his glass to it, and then looked at
the Kanaka. 'Call that land?' said he. 'Well, it's more
than I do.'

'One time long ago,' said Uncle Ned, 'I see Anaa
all-e-same that, four five hours befo' we come up. Capena
he say sun go down, sun go up again; he say lagoon
all-e-same milla.'

'All-e-same *what*?' asked Davis.

'Milla, sah,' said Uncle Ned.

'Oh, ah! mirror,' said Davis. 'I see; reflection from the
lagoon. Well, you know, it is just possible, though it's
strange I never heard of it. Here, let's look at the chart.'

They went back to the cabin, and found the position of
the schooner well to windward of the archipelago in the
midst of a white field of paper.

'There! you see for yourselves,' said Davis.

'And yet I don't know,' said Herrick, 'I somehow think
there's something in it. I'll tell you one thing too, captain;
that's all right about the reflection; I heard it in Papeete.'

'Fetch up that Findlay, then!' said Davis. 'I'll try
it all ways. An island wouldn't come amiss, the way
we're fixed.'

The bulky volume was handed up to him, broken-backed
as is the way with Findlay; and he turned to the place and
began to run over the text, muttering to himself and turning
over the pages with a wetted finger.

'Hullo!' he exclaimed. 'How's this?' And he read aloud.
'*New Island*. According to M. Delille this island, which

from private interests would remain unknown, lies, it is said, in lat. 12° 49′ 10″ S. long. 133° 6′ W. In addition to the position above given Commander Matthews, H.M.S. *Scorpion*, states that an island exists in lat. 12° 0′ S. long. 133° 16′ W. This must be the same, if such an island exists, which is very doubtful, and totally disbelieved in by South Sea traders.'

'Golly!' said Huish.

'It's rather in the conditional mood,' said Herrick.

'It's anything you please,' cried Davis, 'only there it is! That's our place, and don't you make any mistake.'

'"Which from private interests would remain unknown,"' read Herrick, over his shoulder. 'What may that mean?'

'It should mean pearls,' said Davis. 'A pearling island the government don't know about? That sounds like real estate. Or suppose it don't mean anything. Suppose it's just an island; I guess we could fill up with fish, and cocoanuts, and native stuff, and carry out the Samoa scheme hand over fist. How long did he say it was before they raised Anaa? Five hours, I think?'

'Four or five,' said Herrick.

Davis stepped to the door. 'What breeze had you that time you made Anaa, Uncle Ned?' said he.

'Six or seven knots,' was the reply.

'Thirty or thirty-five miles,' said Davis. 'High time we were shortening sail, then. If it is an island, we don't want to be butting our head against it in the dark; and if it isn't an island, we can get through it just as well by daylight. Ready about!' he roared.

And the schooner's head was laid for that elusive glimmer in the sky, which began already to pale in lustre and diminish in size, as the stain of breath vanishes from a window pane. At the same time she was reefed close down.

PART II
THE QUARTETTE

SEVEN

The Pearl-Fisher

About four in the morning, as the captain and Herrick sat together on the rail, there arose from the midst of the night in front of them the voice of breakers. Each sprang to his feet and stared and listened. The sound was continuous, like the passing of a train; no rise or fall could be distinguished; minute by minute the ocean heaved with an equal potency against the invisible isle; and as time passed, and Herrick waited in vain for any vicissitude in the volume of that roaring, a sense of the eternal weighed upon his mind. To the expert eye the isle itself was to be inferred from a certain string of blots along the starry heaven. And the schooner was laid to and anxiously observed till daylight.

There was little or no morning bank. A brightening came in the east; then a wash of some ineffable, faint, nameless hue between crimson and silver; and then coals of fire. These glimmered a while on the sea line, and seemed to brighten and darken and spread out, and still the night and the stars reigned undisturbed; it was as though a spark should catch and glow and creep along the foot of some heavy and almost incombustible wall-hanging, and the room itself be scarce menaced. Yet a little after, and the whole east glowed with gold and scarlet, and the hollow of heaven was filled with the daylight.

The isle – the undiscovered, the scarce believed-in – now lay before them and close aboard; and Herrick thought that never in his dreams had he beheld anything more strange and delicate. The beach was excellently white, the continuous barrier of trees inimitably green; the land perhaps ten feet high, the trees thirty more. Every here and there, as the schooner coasted northward, the wood was intermitted; and he could see clear over the inconsiderable strip of land (as a man looks over a wall) to the lagoon within – and clear over that again to where the far side of the atoll prolonged its pencilling of trees against the morning sky. He tortured himself to find analogies. The isle was like the rim of a great vessel sunken in the waters; it was like the embankment of an annular railway grown upon with wood: so slender it seemed amidst the outrageous breakers, so frail and pretty, he would scarce have wondered to see it sink and disappear without a sound, and the waves close smoothly over its descent.

Meanwhile the captain was in the forecross-trees, glass in hand, his eyes in every quarter, spying for an entrance, spying for signs of tenancy. But the isle continued to unfold itself in joints, and to run out in indeterminate capes, and still there was neither house nor man, nor the smoke of fire. Here a multitude of sea-birds soared and twinkled, and fished in the blue waters; and there, and for miles together, the fringe of cocoa-palm and pandanus extended desolate, and made desirable green bowers for nobody to visit, and the silence of death was only broken by the throbbing of the sea.

The airs were very light, their speed was small; the heat intense. The decks were scorching underfoot, the sun flamed overhead, brazen, out of a brazen sky; the pitch bubbled in the seams, and the brains in the brain-pan. And all the while the excitement of the three adventurers glowed about their bones like a fever. They whispered, and nodded, and pointed, and put mouth to ear, with a singular instinct of secrecy, approaching that island underhand like eavesdroppers and thieves; and even Davis from the cross-trees gave his orders mostly by gestures. The hands shared in this mute strain, like dogs, without comprehending it; and through the roar of so many miles of breakers, it was a silent ship that approached an empty island.

At last they drew near to the break in that interminable gangway. A spur of coral sand stood forth on the one hand; on the other a high and thick tuft of trees cut off the view; between was the mouth of the huge laver. Twice a day the ocean crowded in that narrow entrance and was heaped between these frail walls; twice a day, with the return of the ebb, the mighty surplusage of water must struggle to escape. The hour in which the *Farallone* came there was the hour of flood. The sea turned (as with the instinct of the homing pigeon) for the vast receptacle, swept eddying through the gates, was transmuted, as it did so, into a wonder of watery and silken hues, and brimmed into the inland sea beyond. The schooner looked up close-hauled, and was caught and carried away by the influx like a toy. She skimmed; she flew; a momentary shadow touched her decks from the shore-side trees; the bottom of the channel showed up for a moment and was in a moment gone; the next, she floated on the bosom of the lagoon, and below, in the transparent chamber of waters, a myriad of many-coloured fishes were sporting, a myriad pale flowers of coral diversified the floor.

Herrick stood transported. In the gratified lust of his eye, he forgot the past and the present; forgot that he was menaced by a prison on the one hand and starvation on the other; forgot that he was come to that island, desperately foraging, clutching at expedients. A drove of fishes, painted like the rainbow and billed like parrots, hovered up in the shadow of the schooner, and passed clear of it, and glinted in the submarine sun. They were beautiful, like birds, and their silent passage impressed him like a strain of song.

Meanwhile, to the eye of Davis in the cross-trees, the lagoon continued to expand its empty waters, and the long succession of the shore-side trees to be paid out like fishing line off a reel. And still there was no mark of habitation. The schooner, immediately on entering, had been kept away to the nor'ard where the water seemed to be the most deep; and she was now skimming past the tall grove of trees, which stood on that side of the channel and denied further view. Of the whole of the low shores of the island, only this bight remained to be revealed. And suddenly the curtain was raised; they began to open out a haven, snugly elbowed there, and beheld, with an astonishment beyond words, the roofs of men.

The appearance, thus 'instantaneously disclosed' to those on the deck of the *Farallone*, was not that of a city, rather of a substantial country farm with its attendant hamlet: a long line of sheds and store-houses; apart, upon the one side, a deep-verandah'ed dwelling-house; on the other, perhaps a dozen native huts; a building with a belfry and some rude offer at architectural features that might be thought to mark it out for a chapel; on the beach in front some heavy boats drawn up, and a pile of timber running forth into the burning shallows of the lagoon. From a flagstaff at the pierhead, the red ensign of England was displayed. Behind, about, and over, the same tall grove of palms, which had masked the settlement in the beginning, prolonged its roof of tumultuous green fans, and turned and ruffled overhead, and sang its silver song all day in the wind. The place had the indescribable but unmistakable appearance of being in commission; yet there breathed from it a sense of desertion that was almost poignant, no human figure was to be observed going to and fro about the houses, and there was no sound of human industry or enjoyment. Only, on the top of the beach and hard by the flagstaff, a woman of exorbitant stature and as white as snow was to be seen beckoning with uplifted arm. The second glance identified her as a piece of naval sculpture, the figure-head of a ship that had long hovered and plunged into so many running billows, and was now brought ashore to be the ensign and presiding genius of that empty town.

The *Farallone* made a soldier's breeze of it; the wind, besides, was stronger inside than without under the lee of the land; and the stolen schooner opened out successive objects with the swiftness of a panorama, so that the adventurers stood speechless. The flag spoke for itself; it was no frayed and weathered trophy that had beaten itself to pieces on the post, flying over desolation; and to make assurance stronger, there was to be descried in the deep shade of the verandah, a glitter of crystal and the fluttering of white napery. If the figure-head at the pier end, with its perpetual gesture and its leprous whiteness, reigned alone in that hamlet as it seemed to do, it would not have reigned long. Men's hands had been busy, men's feet stirring there, within the circuit of the clock. The *Farallones* were sure of it; their eyes dug in the deep shadow of the palms for some one hiding; if intensity of looking might have prevailed, they would have pierced the walls of houses; and there came to them, in these pregnant seconds, a sense of being watched and played with, and of a blow impending, that was hardly bearable.

The extreme point of palms they had just passed enclosed a creek, which was thus hidden up to the last moment from the eyes of those on board; and from this, a boat put suddenly and briskly out, and a voice hailed.

'Schooner ahoy!' it cried. 'Stand in for the pier! In two cables' lengths you'll have twenty fathoms water and good holding ground.'

The boat was manned with a couple of brown oarsmen in scanty kilts of blue. The speaker, who was steering, wore white clothes, the full dress of the tropics; a wide hat shaded his face; but it could be seen that he was of stalwart size, and his voice sounded like a gentleman's. So much could be made out. It was plain, besides, that the *Farallone* had been descried some time before at sea, and the inhabitants were prepared for its reception.

Mechanically the orders were obeyed, and the ship berthed; and the three adventurers gathered aft beside the house and waited, with galloping pulses and a perfect vacancy of mind, the coming of the stranger who might mean so much to them. They had no plan, no story prepared; there was no time to make one; they were caught red-handed and must stand their chance. Yet this anxiety was chequered with hope. The island being undeclared, it was not possible the man could hold any office or be in a position to demand their papers. And beyond that, if there was any truth in Findlay, as it now seemed there should be, he was the representative of the 'private reasons,' he must see their coming with a profound disappointment; and perhaps (hope whispered) he would be willing and able to purchase their silence.

The boat was by that time forging alongside, and they were able at last to see what manner of man they had to do with. He was a huge fellow, six feet four in height, and of a build proportionately strong, but his sinews seemed to be dissolved in a listlessness that was more than languor. It was only the eye that corrected this impression; an eye of an unusual mingled brilliancy and softness, sombre as coal and with lights that outshone the topaz; an eye of unimpaired health and virility; an eye that bid you beware of the man's devastating anger. A complexion, naturally dark, had been tanned in the island to a hue hardly distinguishable from that of a Tahitian; only his manners and movements, and the living force that dwelt in him, like fire in flint, betrayed the European. He was dressed in white drill, exquisitely made; his scarf and tie were of tender-coloured silks; on the thwart beside him there leaned a Winchester rifle.

'Is the doctor on board?' he cried as he came up. 'Dr Symonds, I mean? You never heard of him? Nor yet of the *Trinity Hall*? Ah!'

He did not look surprised, seemed rather to affect it in politeness; but his eye rested on each of the three white men in succession with a sudden weight of curiosity that was almost savage. 'Ah, *then*!' said he, 'there is some small mistake, no doubt, and I must ask you to what I am indebted for this pleasure?'

He was by this time on the deck, but he had the art to be quite unapproachable; the friendliest vulgarian, three parts drunk, would have known better than take liberties; and not one of the adventurers so much as offered to shake hands.

'Well,' said Davis, 'I suppose you may call it an accident. We had heard of your island, and read that thing in the Directory about the *private reasons*, you see; so when we saw the lagoon reflected in the sky, we put her head for it at once, and so here we are.'

''Ope we don't intrude!' said Huish.

The stranger looked at Huish with an air of faint surprise, and looked pointedly away again. It was hard to be more offensive in dumb show.

'It may suit me, your coming here,' he said. 'My own schooner is overdue, and I may put something in your way in the meantime. Are you open to a charter?'

'Well, I guess so,' said Davis; 'it depends.'

'My name is Attwater,' continued the stranger. 'You, I presume, are the captain?'

'Yes, sir. I am the captain of this ship: Captain Brown,' was the reply.

'Well, see 'ere!' said Huish, 'better begin fair! 'E's skipper on deck right enough, but not below. Below, we're all equal, all got a lay in the adventure; when it comes to business, I'm as good as 'e; and what I say is, let's go into the 'ouse and have a lush, and talk it over among pals. We've some prime fizz,' he said, and winked.

The presence of the gentleman lighted up like a candle the vulgarity of the clerk; and Herrick instinctively, as one shields himself from pain, made haste to interrupt.

'My name is Hay,' said he, 'since introductions are going. We shall be very glad if you will step inside.'

Attwater leaned to him swiftly. 'University man?' said he.

'Yes, Merton,' said Herrick, and the next moment blushed scarlet at his indiscretion.

'I am of the other lot,' said Attwater: 'Trinity Hall, Cambridge. I called my schooner after the old shop. Well! this is a queer place and company for us to meet in, Mr Hay,' he pursued, with easy incivility to the others. 'But do you bear out . . . I beg this gentleman's pardon, I really did not catch his name.'

'My name is 'Uish, sir,' returned the clerk, and blushed in turn.

'Ah!' said Attwater. And then turning again to Herrick, 'Do you bear out Mr Whish's description of your vintage? or was it only the unaffected poetry of his own nature bubbling up?'

Herrick was embarrassed; the silken brutality of their visitor made him blush; that he should be accepted as an equal, and the others thus pointedly ignored, pleased him in spite of himself, and then ran through his veins in a recoil of anger.

'I don't know,' he said. 'It's only California; it's good enough, I believe.'

Attwater seemed to make up his mind. 'Well then, I'll tell you what: you three gentlemen come ashore this evening and bring a basket of wine with you; I'll try and find the food,' he said. 'And by the by, here is a question I should have asked you when I come on board: have you had smallpox?'

'Personally, no,' said Herrick. 'But the schooner had it.'

'Deaths?' from Attwater.

'Two,' said Herrick.

'Well, it is a dreadful sickness,' said Attwater.

''Ad you any deaths?' asked Huish, ''ere on the island?'

'Twenty-nine,' said Attwater. 'Twenty-nine deaths and thirty-one cases, out of thirty-three souls upon the island. – That's a strange way to calculate, Mr Hay, is it not? Souls! I never say it but it startles me.'

'Oh, so that's why everything's deserted?' said Huish.

'That is why, Mr Whish,' said Attwater; 'that is why the house is empty and the graveyard full.'

'Twenty-nine out of thirty-three!' exclaimed Herrick, 'Why, when it came to burying – or did you bother burying?'

'Scarcely,' said Attwater; 'or there was one day at least when we gave up. There were five of the dead that morning, and thirteen of the dying, and no one able to go about except the sexton and myself. We held a council of war, took the . . . empty bottles . . . into the lagoon, and . . . buried them.' He looked over his shoulder, back at the bright water. 'Well, so you'll come to dinner, then? Shall we say half-past six. *So* good of you!'

His voice, in uttering these conventional phrases, fell at once into the false measure of society; and Herrick unconsciously followed the example.

'I am sure we shall be very glad,' he said. 'At half-past six? Thank you so very much.'

'"For my voice has been turned to the note of the gun
That startles the deep when the combat's begun,"'

quoted Attwater, with a smile, which instantly gave way to an air of funereal solemnity. 'I shall particularly expect Mr Whish,' he continued. 'Mr Whish, I trust you understand the invitation?'

'I believe you, my boy!' replied the genial Huish.

'That is right then; and quite understood, is it not?' said Attwater. 'Mr Whish and Captain Brown at six-thirty without fault – and you, Hay, at four sharp.'

And he called his boat.

During all this talk, a load of thought or anxiety had weighed upon the captain. There was no part for which nature had so liberally endowed him as that of the genial ship captain. But today he was silent and abstracted. Those who knew him could see that he hearkened close to every syllable, and seemed to ponder and try it in balances. It would have been hard to say what look there was, cold, attentive, and sinister, as of a man maturing plans, which still brooded over the unconscious guest; it was here, it was there, it was nowhere; it was now so little that Herrick chid himself for an idle fancy; and anon it was so gross and palpable that you could say every hair on the man's head talked mischief.

He woke up now, as with a start. 'You were talking of a charter,' said he.

'Was I?' said Attwater. 'Well, let's talk of it no more at present.'

'Your own schooner is overdue, I understand?' continued the captain.

'You understand perfectly, Captain Brown,' said Attwater; 'thirty-three days overdue at noon today.'

'She comes and goes, eh? plies between here and . . .?' hinted the captain.

'Exactly; every four months; three trips in the year,' said Attwater.

'You go in her, ever?' asked Davis.

'No, one stops here,' said Attwater, 'one has plenty to attend to.'

'Stop here, do you?' cried Davis. 'Say, how long?'

'How long, O Lord,' said Attwater with perfect, stern gravity. 'But it does not seem so,' he added, with a smile.

'No, I dare say not,' said Davis. 'No, I suppose not. Not with all your gods about you, and in as snug a berth as this. For it is a pretty snug berth,' said he, with a sweeping look.

'The spot, as you are good enough to indicate, is not entirely intolerable,' was the reply.

'Shell, I suppose?' said Davis.

'Yes, there was shell,' said Attwater.

'This is a considerable big beast of a lagoon, sir,' said the captain. 'Was there a – was the fishing – would you call the fishing anyways *good*?'

'I don't know that I would call it anyways anything,' said Attwater, 'if you put it to me direct.'

'There were pearls too?' said Davis.

'Pearls, too,' said Attwater.

'Well, I give out!' laughed Davis, and his laughter rang cracked like a false piece. 'If you're not going to tell, you're not going to tell, and there's an end to it.'

'There can be no reason why I should affect the least degree of secrecy about my island,' returned Attwater; 'that came wholly to an end with your arrival; and I am sure, at any rate, that gentlemen like you and Mr Whish, I should have always been charmed to make perfectly at home. The point on which we are now differing – if you can call it a difference – is one of times and seasons. I have some information which you think I might impart, and I think

not. Well, we'll see tonight! By-by, Whish!' He stepped
into his boat and shoved off. 'All understood, then?' said
he. 'The captain and Mr Whish at six-thirty, and you, Hay,
at four precise. You understand that, Hay? Mind, I take no
denial. If you're not there by the time named, there will be
no banquet; no song, no supper, Mr Whish!'

White birds whisked in the air above, a shoal of
parti-coloured fishes in the scarce denser medium below;
between, like Mahomet's coffin, the boat drew away briskly
on the surface, and its shadow followed it over the glittering
floor of the lagoon. Attwater looked steadily back over his
shoulders as he sat; he did not once remove his eyes from
the *Farallone* and the group on her quarter-deck beside the
house, till his boat ground upon the pier. Thence, with an
agile pace, he hurried ashore, and they saw his white clothes
shining in the chequered dusk of the grove until the house
received him.

The captain, with a gesture and a speaking countenance,
called the adventurers into the cabin.

'Well,' he said to Herrick, when they were seated,
'there's one good job at least. He's taken to you in
earnest.'

'Why should that be a good job?' said Herrick.

'Oh, you'll see how it pans out presently,' returned Davis.
'You go ashore and stand in with him, that's all! You'll get
lots of pointers; you can find out what he has, and what the
charter is, and who's the fourth man – for there's four of
them, and we're only three.'

'And suppose I do, what next?' cried Herrick. 'Answer
me that!'

'So I will, Robert Herrick,' said the captain. 'But first,
let's see all clear. I guess you know,' he said with an
imperious solemnity, 'I guess you know the bottom is
out of this *Farallone* speculation? I guess you know it's
right out? and if this old island hadn't been turned up
right when it did, I guess you know where you and I and
Huish would have been?'

'Yes, I know that,' said Herrick. 'No matter who's to
blame, I know it. And what next?'

'No matter who's to blame, you know it, right enough,'
said the captain, 'and I'm obliged to you for the reminder.
Now here's this Attwater: what do you think of him?'

'I do not know,' said Herrick. 'I am attracted and repelled. He was insufferably rude to you.'

'And you, Huish?' said the captain.

Huish sat cleaning a favourite briar root; he scarce looked up from that engrossing task. 'Don't ast me what I think of him!' he said. 'There's a day comin', I pray Gawd, when I can tell it him myself.'

'Huish means the same as what I do,' said Davis. 'When that man came stepping around, and saying "Look here, I'm Attwater" – and you knew it was so, by God! – I sized him right straight up. Here's the real article, I said, and I don't like it; here's the real, first-rate, copper-bottomed aristocrat. '*Aw! don't know ye, do I? God damn ye, did God make ye?*' No, that couldn't be nothing but genuine; a man got to be born to that, and notice! smart as champagne and hard as nails; no kind of a fool; no, *sir*! not a pound of him! Well, what's he here upon this beastly island for? I said. *He's* not here collecting eggs. He's a palace at home, and powdered flunkies; and if he don't stay there, you bet he knows the reason why! Follow?'

'O yes, I 'ear you,' said Huish.

'He's been doing good business here, then,' continued the captain. 'For ten years, he's been doing a great business. It's pearl and shell, of course; there couldn't be nothing else in such a place, and no doubt the shell goes off regularly by this *Trinity Hall*, and the money for it straight into the bank, so that's no use to us. But what else is there? Is there nothing else he would be likely to keep here? Is there nothing else he would be bound to keep here? Yes, sir; the pearls! First, because they're too valuable to trust out of his hands. Second, because pearls want a lot of handling and matching; and the man who sells his pearls as they come in, one here, one there, instead of hanging back and holding up – well, that man's a fool, and it's not Attwater.'

'Likely,' said Huish, 'that's w'at it is; not proved, but likely.'

'It's proved,' said Davis bluntly.

'Suppose it was?' said Herrick. 'Suppose that was all so, and he had these pearls – a ten years' collection of them? – Suppose he had? There's my question.'

The captain drummed with his thick hands on the board in front of him; he looked steadily in Herrick's face, and

Herrick as steadily looked upon the table and the pattering fingers; there was a gentle oscillation of the anchored ship, and a big patch of sunlight travelled to and fro between the one and the other.

'Hear me!' Herrick burst out suddenly.

'No, you better hear me first,' said Davis. 'Hear me and understand me. *We've* got no use for that fellow, whatever you may have. He's your kind, he's not ours; he's took to you, and he's wiped his boots on me and Huish. Save him if you can!'

'Save him?' repeated Herrick.

'Save him, if you're able!' reiterated Davis, with a blow of his clenched fist. 'Go ashore, and talk him smooth; and if you get him and his pearls aboard, I'll spare him. If you don't, there's going to be a funeral. Is that so, Huish? does that suit you?'

'I ain't a forgiving man,' said Huish, 'but I'm not the sort to spoil business neither. Bring the bloke on board and bring his pearls along with him, and you can have it your own way; maroon him where you like – I'm agreeable.'

'Well, and if I can't?' cried Herrick, while the sweat streamed upon his face. 'You talk to me as if I was God Almighty, to do this and that! But if I can't?'

'My son,' said the captain, 'you better do your level best, or you'll see sights!'

'O yes,' said Huish. 'O crikey, yes!' He looked across at Herrick with a toothless smile that was shocking in its savagery; and his ear caught apparently by the trivial expression he had used, broke into a piece of the chorus of a comic song which he must have heard twenty years before in London: meaningless gibberish that, in that hour and place, seemed hateful as a blasphemy: 'Hikey, pikey, crikey, fikey, chillingawallaba dory.'

The captain suffered him to finish; his face was unchanged.

'The way things are, there's many a man that wouldn't let you go ashore,' he resumed. 'But I'm not that kind. I know you'd never go back on me, Herrick! Or if you choose to – go, and do it, and be damned!' he cried, and rose abruptly from the table.

He walked out of the house; and as he reached the door, turned and called Huish, suddenly and violently, like the barking of a dog. Huish followed, and Herrick remained alone in the cabin.

'Now, see here!' whispered Davis. 'I know that man. If you open your mouth to him again, you'll ruin all.'

EIGHT

Better Acquaintance

The boat was gone again, and already half-way to the *Farallone*, before Herrick turned and went unwillingly up the pier. From the crown of the beach, the figure-head confronted him with what seemed irony, her helmeted head tossed back, her formidable arm apparently hurling something, whether shell or missile, in the direction of the anchored schooner. She seemed a defiant deity from the island, coming forth to its threshold with a rush as of one about to fly, and perpetuated in that dashing attitude. Herrick looked up at her, where she towered above him head and shoulders, with singular feelings of curiosity and romance, and suffered his mind to travel to and fro in her life-history. So long she had been the blind conductress of a ship among the waves; so long she had stood here idle in the violent sun, that yet did not avail to blister her; and was even this the end of so many adventures? he wondered, or was more behind? And he could have found in his heart to regret that she was not a goddess, nor yet he a pagan, that he might have bowed down before her in that hour of difficulty.

When he now went forward, it was cool with the shadow of many well-grown palms; draughts of the dying breeze swung them together overhead; and on all sides, with a swiftness beyond dragon-flies or swallows, the spots of sunshine flitted, and hovered, and returned. Underfoot, the sand was fairly solid and quite level, and Herrick's steps fell there noiseless as in new-fallen snow. It bore the marks of having been once weeded like a garden alley at home; but the pestilence had done its work, and the weeds were returning. The buildings of the settlement showed here and there through the stems of the colonnade, fresh painted, trim and dandy, and all silent as the grave. Only, here and there in the crypt, there was a rustle and scurry and some crowing of poultry; and from behind the house with the verandahs, he saw smoke arise and heard the crackling of a fire.

The stone houses were nearest him upon his right. The first was locked; in the second, he could dimly perceive, through a window, a certain accumulation of pearl-shell piled in the far end; the third, which stood gaping open on the afternoon, seized on the mind of Herrick with its multiplicity and disorder of romantic things. Therein were cables, windlasses and blocks of every size and capacity; cabin windows and ladders; rusty tanks, a companion hutch; a binnacle with its brass mountings and its compass idly pointing, in the confusion and dusk of that shed, to a forgotten pole; ropes, anchors, harpoons, a blubber dipper of copper, green with years, a steering wheel, a tool chest with the vessel's name upon the top, the *Asia*: a whole curiosity-shop of sea curios, gross and solid, heavy to lift, ill to break, bound with brass and shod with iron. Two wrecks at the least must have contributed to this random heap of lumber; and as Herrick looked upon it, it seemed to him as if the two ships' companies were there on guard, and he heard the tread of feet and whisperings, and saw with the tail of his eye the commonplace ghosts of sailor men.

This was not merely the work of an aroused imagination, but had something sensible to go upon; sounds of a stealthy approach were no doubt audible; and while he still stood staring at the lumber, the voice of his host sounded suddenly, and with even more than the customary softness of enunciation, from behind.

'Junk,' it said, 'only old junk! And does Mr Hay find a parable?'

'I find at least a strong impression,' replied Herrick, turning quickly, lest he might be able to catch, on the face of the speaker, some commentary on the words.

Attwater stood in the doorway, which he almost wholly filled; his hands stretched above his head and grasping the architrave. He smiled when their eyes met, but the expression was inscrutable.

'Yes, a powerful impression. You are like me; nothing so affecting as ships!' said he. 'The ruins of an empire would leave me frigid, when a bit of an old rail that an old shellback leaned on in the middle watch, would bring me up all standing. But come, let's see some more of the island. It's all sand and coral and palm trees; but there's a kind of a quaintness in the place.'

'I find it heavenly,' said Herrick, breathing deep, with head bared in the shadow.

'Ah, that's because you're new from sea,' said Attwater. 'I dare say, too, you can appreciate what one calls it. It's a lovely name. It has a flavour, it has a colour, it has a ring and fall to it; it's like its author – it's half Christian! Remember your first view of the island, and how it's only woods and water; and suppose you had asked somebody for the name, and he had answered – *nemorosa Zacynthos*!'

'*Jam medio apparet fluctu!*' exclaimed Herrick. 'Ye gods, yes, how good!'

'If it gets upon the chart, the skippers will make nice work of it,' said Attwater. 'But here, come and see the diving-shed.'

He opened a door, and Herrick saw a large display of apparatus neatly ordered: pumps and pipes, and the leaded boots, and the huge snouted helmets shining in rows along the wall; ten complete outfits.

'The whole eastern half of my lagoon is shallow, you must understand,' said Attwater; 'so we were able to get in the dress to great advantage. It paid beyond belief, and was a queer sight when they were at it, and these marine monsters' – tapping the nearest of the helmets – 'kept appearing and reappearing in the midst of the lagoon. Fond of parables?' he asked abruptly.

'O yes!' said Herrick.

'Well, I saw these machines come up dripping and go down again, and come up dripping and go down again, and all the while the fellow inside as dry as toast!' said Attwater; 'and I thought we all wanted a dress to go down into the world in, and come up scatheless. What do you think the name was?' he inquired.

'Self-conceit,' said Herrick.

'Ah, but I mean seriously!' said Attwater.

'Call it self-respect, then!' corrected Herrick, with a laugh.

'And why not Grace? Why not God's Grace, Hay?' asked Attwater. 'Why not the grace of your Maker and Redeemer, He who died for you, He who upholds you, He whom you daily crucify afresh? There is nothing here,' – striking on his bosom – 'nothing there' – smiting the wall – 'and nothing there' – stamping – 'nothing but God's Grace! We walk upon it, we breathe it; we live and die by it; it makes the nails and axles of the universe; and a puppy in pyjamas prefers self-conceit!' The huge dark man stood over against Herrick by the line of the divers' helmets, and seemed to swell and glow; and the next moment the life had gone from him. 'I beg your pardon,' said he; 'I see you don't believe in God?'

'Not in your sense, I am afraid,' said Herrick.

'I never argue with young atheists or habitual drunkards,' said Attwater flippantly. 'Let us go across the island to the outer beach.'

It was but a little way, the greatest width of that island scarce exceeding a furlong, and they walked gently. Herrick was like one in a dream. He had come there with a mind divided; come prepared to study that ambiguous and sneering mask, drag out the essential man from underneath, and act accordingly; decision being till then postponed. Iron cruelty, an iron insensibility to the suffering of others, the uncompromising pursuit of his own interests, cold culture, manners without humanity; these he had looked for, these he still thought he saw. But to find the whole machine thus glow with the reverberation of religious zeal, surprised him beyond words; and he laboured in vain, as he walked, to piece together into any kind of whole his odds and ends of knowledge – to adjust again into any kind of focus with itself, his picture of the man beside him.

'What brought you here to the South Seas?' he asked presently.

'Many things,' said Attwater. 'Youth, curiosity, romance, the love of the sea, and (it will surprise you to hear) an interest in missions. That has a good deal declined, which will surprise you less. They go the wrong way to work; they are too parsonish, too much of the old wife, and even the old apple wife. *Clothes, clothes,* are their idea; but clothes are not Christianity, any more than they are the sun in heaven, or could take the place of it! They think a parsonage with roses, and church bells, and nice old women bobbing in the lanes, are part and parcel of religion. But religion is a savage thing, like the universe it illuminates; savage, cold, and bare, but infinitely strong.'

'And you found this island by an accident?' said Herrick.

'As you did!' said Attwater. 'And since then I have had a business, and a colony, and a mission of my own. I was a man of the world before I was a Christian; I'm a man of the world still, and I made my mission pay. No good ever came of coddling. A man has to stand up in God's sight and work up to his weight avoirdupois; then I'll talk to him, but not before. I gave these beggars what they wanted: a judge in Israel, the bearer of the sword and scourge; I was making a new people here; and behold, the angel of the Lord smote them and they were not!'

With the very uttering of the words, which were accompanied by a gesture, they came forth out of the porch of the palm wood by the margin of the sea and full in front of the sun which was near setting. Before them the surf broke slowly. All around, with an air of imperfect wooden things inspired with wicked activity, the crabs trundled and scuttled into holes. On the right, whither Attwater pointed and abruptly turned, was the cemetery of the island, a field of broken stones from the bigness of a child's hand to that of his head, diversified by many mounds of the same material, and walled by a rude rectangular enclosure. Nothing grew there but a shrub or two with some white flowers; nothing but the number of the mounds, and their disquieting shape, indicated the presence of the dead.

'The rude forefathers of the hamlet sleep!'

quoted Attwater as he entered by the open gateway into that unholy close. 'Coral to coral, pebbles to pebbles,' he said, 'this has been the main scene of my activity in the South Pacific. Some were good, and some bad, and the majority (of course and always) null. Here was a fellow, now, that used to frisk like a dog; if you had called him he came like an arrow from a bow; if you had not, and he came unbidden, you should have seen the deprecating eye and the little intricate dancing step. Well, his trouble is over now, he has lain down with kings and councillors; the rest of his acts, are they not written in the book of the chronicles? That fellow was from Penrhyn; like all the Penrhyn islanders he was ill to manage; heady, jealous, violent: the man with the nose! He lies here quiet enough. And so they all lie.

"And darkness was the burier of the dead!"'

He stood, in the strong glow of the sunset, with bowed head; his voice sounded now sweet and now bitter with the varying sense.

'You loved these people?' cried Herrick, strangely touched.

'I?' said Attwater. 'Dear no! Don't think me a philanthropist. I dislike men, and hate women. If I like the islands at all, it is because you see them here plucked of their lendings, their dead birds and cocked hats, their petticoats and coloured hose. Here was one I liked though,' and he set his foot upon a mound. 'He was a fine savage fellow; he had a dark soul; yes, I liked this one. I am fanciful,' he added, looking hard at Herrick, 'and I take fads. I like you.'

Herrick turned swiftly and looked far away to where the clouds were beginning to troop together and amass themselves round the obsequies of day. 'No one can like me,' he said.

'You are wrong there,' said the other, 'as a man usually is about himself. You are attractive, very attractive.'

'It is not me,' said Herrick; 'no one can like me. If you knew how I despised myself – and why!' His voice rang out in the quiet graveyard.

'I knew that you despised yourself,' said Attwater. 'I saw the blood come into your face today when you remembered Oxford. And I could have blushed for you myself, to see a man, a gentleman, with these two vulgar wolves.'

Herrick faced him with a thrill. 'Wolves?' he repeated.

'I said wolves and vulgar wolves,' said Attwater. 'Do you know that today, when I came on board, I trembled?'

'You concealed it well,' stammered Herrick.

'A habit of mine,' said Attwater. 'But I was afraid, for all that: I was afraid of the two wolves.' He raised his hand slowly. 'And now, Hay, you poor lost puppy, what do you do with the two wolves?'

'What do I do? I don't do anything,' said Herrick. 'There is nothing wrong; all is above board; Captain Brown is a good soul; he is a . . . he is . . .' The phantom voice of

Davis called in his ear: 'There's going to be a funeral' and the sweat burst forth and streamed on his brow. 'He is a family man,' he resumed again, swallowing; 'he has children at home – and a wife.'

'And a very nice man?' said Attwater. 'And so is Mr Whish, no doubt?'

'I won't go so far as that,' said Herrick. 'I do not like Huish. And yet . . . he has his merits too.'

'And, in short, take them for all in all, as good a ship's company as one would ask?' said Attwater.

'O yes,' said Herrick, 'quite.'

'So then we approach the other point of why you despise yourself?' said Attwater.

'Do we not all despise ourselves?' cried Herrick. 'Do not you?'

'Oh, I say I do. But do I?' said Attwater. 'One thing I know at least: I never gave a cry like yours. Hay! it came from a bad conscience! Ah, man, that poor diving dress of self-conceit is sadly tattered! Today, now, while the sun sets, and here in this burying place of brown innocents, fall on your knees and cast your sins and sorrows on the Redeemer. Hay— '

'Not Hay!' interrupted the other, strangling. 'Don't call me that! I mean . . . For God's sake, can't you see I'm on the rack?'

'I see it, I know it, I put and keep you there, my fingers are on the screws!' said Attwater. 'Please God, I will bring a penitent this night before His throne. Come, come to the mercy-seat! He waits to be gracious, man – waits to be gracious!'

He spread out his arms like a crucifix, his face shone with the brightness of a seraph's; in his voice, as it rose to the last word, the tears seemed ready.

Herrick made a vigorous call upon himself. 'Attwater,' he said, 'you push me beyond bearing. What am I to do? I do not believe. It is living truth to you; to me, upon my conscience, only folk-lore. I do not believe there is any form of words under heaven by which I can lift the burthen from my shoulders. I must stagger on to the end with the pack of my responsibility; I cannot shift it; do you suppose I would not, if I thought I could? I cannot – cannot – cannot – and let that suffice.'

The rapture was all gone from Attwater's countenance; the dark apostle had disappeared; and in his place there stood an easy, sneering gentleman, who took off his hat and bowed. It was pertly done, and the blood burned in Herrick's face.

'What do you mean by that?' he cried.

'Well, shall we go back to the house?' said Attwater. 'Our guests will soon be due.'

Herrick stood his ground a moment with clenched fists and teeth; and as he so stood, the fact of his errand there slowly swung clear in front of him, like the moon out of clouds. He had come to lure that man on board; he was failing, even if it could be said that he had tried; he was sure to fail now, and knew it, and knew it was better so. And what was to be next?

With a groan he turned to follow his host, who was standing with polite smile, and instantly and somewhat obsequiously led the way in the now darkened colonnade of palms. There they went in silence, the earth gave up richly of her perfume, the air tasted warm and aromatic in the nostrils; and from a great way forward in the wood, the brightness of lights and fire marked out the house of Attwater.

Herrick meanwhile resolved and resisted an immense temptation to go up, to touch him on the arm and breathe a word in his ear: 'Beware, they are going to murder you.' There would be one life saved; but what of the two others? The three lives went up and down before him like buckets in a well, or like the scales of balances. It had come to a choice, and one that must be speedy. For certain invaluable minutes, the wheels of life ran before him, and he could still divert them with a touch to the one side or the other, still choose who was to live and who was to die. He considered the men. Attwater intrigued, puzzled, dazzled, enchanted and revolted him; alive, he seemed but a doubtful good; and the thought of him lying dead was so unwelcome that it pursued him, like a vision, with every circumstance of colour and sound. Incessantly, he had before him the image of that great mass of man stricken down in varying attitudes and with varying wounds; fallen prone, fallen supine, fallen on his side; or clinging to a doorpost with the changing face and the relaxing fingers of the death-agony. He heard the click of the trigger, the thud of the ball, the cry of the victim; he saw the blood flow. And this building up of circumstance was like a consecration of the man, till he seemed to walk in sacrificial fillets. Next he considered Davis, with his thick-fingered, coarse-grained, oat-bread commonness of nature, his indomitable valour and mirth in the old days of their starvation, the endearing blend of his faults and virtues, the sudden shining forth of a tenderness that lay too deep for tears; his children, Adar and her bowel complaint, and Adar's doll. No, death could not be suffered to approach that head even in fancy; with a general heat and a bracing of his muscles, it was borne in on Herrick that Adar's father would find in him a son to the death. And even Huish showed a little in that sacredness; by the tacit adoption of daily life they were become brothers; there was an implied bond of loyalty in their cohabitation of the ship and their passed miseries, to which Herrick must be a little true or wholly dishonoured. Horror of sudden death for horror of sudden death, there was here no hesitation possible: it must be Attwater. And no sooner was the thought formed (which was a sentence) than his whole mind of man ran in a panic to the other side: and when he looked within himself, he was aware only of turbulence and inarticulate outcry.

In all this there was no thought of Robert Herrick. He had complied with the ebb-tide in man's affairs, and the tide had carried him away; he heard already the roaring of the maelstrom that must hurry him under. And in his bedevilled and dishonoured soul there was no thought of self.

For how long he walked silent by his companion Herrick had no guess. The clouds rolled suddenly away; the orgasm was over; he found himself placid with the placidity of despair; there returned to him the power of commonplace speech; and he heard with surprise his own voice say: 'What a lovely evening!'

'Is it not?' said Attwater. 'Yes, the evenings here would be very pleasant if one had anything to do. By day, of course, one can shoot.'

'You shoot?' asked Herrick.

'Yes, I am what you would call a fine shot,' said Attwater. 'It is faith; I believe my balls will go true; if I were to miss once, it would spoil me for nine months.'

'You never miss, then?' said Herrick.

'Not unless I mean to,' said Attwater. 'But to miss nicely is the art. There was an old king one knew in the western islands, who used to empty a Winchester all round a man, and stir his hair or nick a rag out of his clothes with every ball except the last; and that went plump between the eyes. It was pretty practice.'

'You could do that?' asked Herrick, with a sudden chill.

'Oh, I can do anything,' returned the other. 'You do not understand: what must be, must.'

They were now come near to the back part of the house. One of the men was engaged about the cooking fire, which burned with the clear, fierce, essential radiance of cocoanut shells. A fragrance of strange meats was in the air. All round in the verandahs lamps were lighted, so that the place shone abroad in the dusk of the trees with many complicated patterns of shadow.

'Come and wash your hands,' said Attwater, and led the way into a clean, matted room with a cot bed, a safe, a shelf or two of books in a glazed case, and an iron washing-stand. Presently he cried in the native, and there appeared for a moment in the doorway a plump and pretty young woman with a clean towel.

'Hullo!' cried Herrick, who now saw for the first time the fourth survivor of the pestilence, and was startled by the recollection of the captain's orders.

'Yes,' said Attwater, 'the whole colony lives about the house, what's left of it. We are all afraid of devils, if you please! and Taniera and she sleep in the front parlour, and the other boy on the verandah.'

'She is pretty,' said Herrick.

'Too pretty,' said Attwater. 'That was why I had her married. A man never knows when he may be inclined to be a fool about women; so when we were left alone, I had the pair of them to the chapel and performed the ceremony. She made a lot of fuss. I do not take at all the romantic view of marriage,' he explained.

'And that strikes you as a safeguard?' asked Herrick with amazement.

'Certainly. I am a plain man and very literal. *Whom God*

hath joined together, are the words, I fancy. So one married them, and respects the marriage,' said Attwater.

'Ah!' said Herrick.

'You see, I may look to make an excellent marriage when I go home,' began Attwater, confidentially. 'I am rich. This safe alone' – laying his hand upon it – 'will be a moderate fortune, when I have the time to place the pearls upon the market. Here are ten years' accumulation from a lagoon, where I have had as many as ten divers going all day long; and I went further than people usually do in these waters, for I rotted a lot of shell, and did splendidly. Would you like to see them?'

This confirmation of the captain's guess hit Herrick hard, and he contained himself with difficulty. 'No, thank you, I think not,' said he. 'I do not care for pearls. I am very indifferent to all these . . .'

'Gewgaws?' suggested Attwater. 'And yet I believe you ought to cast an eye on my collection, which is really unique, and which – oh! it is the case with all of us and everything about us! – hangs by a hair. Today it groweth up and flourisheth; tomorrow it is cut down and cast into the oven. Today it is here and together in this safe; tomorrow – tonight! – it may be scattered. Thou fool, this night thy soul shall be required of thee.'

'I do not understand you,' said Herrick.

'Not?' said Attwater.

'You seem to speak in riddles,' said Herrick, unsteadily. 'I do not understand what manner of man you are, nor what you are driving at.'

Attwater stood with his hands upon his hips, and his head bent forward. 'I am a fatalist,' he replied, 'and just now (if you insist on it) an experimentalist. Talking of which, by the bye, who painted out the schooner's name?' he said, with mocking softness, 'because, do you know? one thinks it should be done again. It can still be partly read; and whatever is worth doing, is surely worth doing well. You think with me? That is so nice! Well, shall we step on the verandah? I have a dry sherry that I would like your opinion of.'

Herrick followed him forth to where, under the light of the hanging lamps, the table shone with napery and crystal; followed him as the criminal goes with the hangman, or the sheep with the butcher; took the sherry mechanically, drank it, and spoke mechanical words of praise. The object of his terror had become suddenly inverted; till then he had seen Attwater trussed and gagged, a helpless victim, and had longed to run in and save him; he saw him now tower up mysterious and menacing, the angel of the Lord's wrath, armed with knowledge and threatening judgment. He set down his glass again, and was surprised to see it empty.

'You go always armed?' he said, and the next moment could have plucked his tongue out.

'Always,' said Attwater. 'I have been through a mutiny here; that was one of my incidents of missionary life.'

And just then the sound of voices reached them, and looking forth from the verandah they saw Huish and the captain drawing near.

NINE

The Dinner Party

They sat down to an island dinner, remarkable for its variety and excellence; turtle soup and steak, fish, fowls, a sucking pig, a cocoanut salad, and sprouting cocoanut roasted for dessert. Not a tin had been opened; and save for the oil and vinegar in the salad, and some green spears of onion which Attwater cultivated and plucked with his own hand, not even the condiments were European. Sherry, hock, and claret succeeded each other, and the *Farallone* champagne brought up the rear with the dessert.

It was plain that, like so many of the extremely religious in the days before teetotalism, Attwater had a dash of the epicure. For such characters it is softening to eat well; doubly so to have designed and had prepared an excellent meal for others; and the manners of their host were agreeably mollified in consequence. A cat of huge growth sat on his shoulders purring, and occasionally, with a deft paw, capturing a morsel in the air. To a cat he might be likened himself, as he lolled at the head of his table, dealing out attentions and innuendoes, and using the velvet and the claw indifferently. And both Huish and the captain fell progressively under the charm of his hospitable freedom.

Over the third guest, the incidents of the dinner may be said to have passed for long unheeded. Herrick accepted all that was offered him, ate and drank without tasting, and heard without comprehension. His mind was singly occupied in contemplating the horror of the circumstances in which he sat. What Attwater knew, what the captain designed, from which side treachery was to be first expected, these were the ground of his thoughts. There were times when he longed to throw down the table and flee into the night. And even that was debarred him; to do anything, to say anything, to move at all, were only to precipitate the barbarous tragedy; and he sat spellbound, eating with white lips. Two of his companions observed him narrowly, Attwater with raking, sidelong glances that did not interrupt his talk, the captain with a heavy and anxious consideration.

'Well, I must say this sherry is a really prime article,' said Huish. "Ow much does it stand you in, if it's a fair question?'

'A hundred and twelve shillings in London, and the freight to Valparaiso, and on again,' said Attwater. 'It strikes one as really not a bad fluid.'

'A 'undred and twelve!' murmured the clerk, relishing the wine and the figures in a common ecstasy: 'O my!'

'So glad you like it,' said Attwater. 'Help yourself, Mr Whish, and keep the bottle by you.'

'My friend's name is Huish and not Whish, sir,' said the captain with a flush.

'I beg your pardon, I am sure. Huish and not Whish, certainly,' said Attwater. 'I was about to say that I have still eight dozen,' he added, fixing the captain with his eye.

'Eight dozen what?' said Davis.

'Sherry,' was the reply. 'Eight dozen excellent sherry. Why, it seems almost worth it in itself; to a man fond of wine.'

The ambiguous words struck home to guilty consciences, and Huish and the captain sat up in their places and regarded him with a scare.

'Worth what?' said Davis.

'A hundred and twelve shillings,' replied Attwater.

The captain breathed hard for a moment. He reached out far and wide to find any coherency in these remarks; then, with a great effort, changed the subject.

'I allow we are about the first white men upon this island, sir,' said he.

Attwater followed him at once, and with entire gravity, to the new ground. 'Myself and Dr Symonds excepted, I should say the only ones,' he returned. 'And yet who can tell? In the course of the ages someone may have lived here, and we sometimes think that someone must. The cocoa palms grow all round the island, which is scarce like nature's planting. We found besides, when we landed, an unmistakable cairn upon the beach; use unknown; but probably erected in the hope of gratifying some mumbo jumbo whose very name is forgotten, by some thick-witted gentry whose very bones are lost. Then the island (witness the *Directory*) has been twice reported; and since my tenancy, we have had two wrecks, both derelict. The rest is conjecture.'

'Dr Symonds is your partner, I guess?' said Davis.

'A dear fellow, Symonds! How he would regret it, if he knew you had been here!' said Attwater.

''E's on the *Trinity 'All*, ain't he?' asked Huish.

'And if you could tell me where the *Trinity 'All* was, you would confer a favour, Mr Whish!' was the reply.

'I suppose she has a native crew?' said Davis.

'Since the secret has been kept ten years, one would suppose she had,' replied Attwater.

'Well, now, see 'ere!' said Huish. 'You have everything about you in no end style, and no mistake, but I tell you it wouldn't do for me. Too much of "the old rustic bridge by the mill"; too retired, by 'alf. Give me the sound of Bow Bells!'

'You must not think it was always so,' replied Attwater. 'This was once a busy shore, although now, hark! you can hear the solitude. I find it stimulating. And talking of the sound of bells kindly follow a little experiment of mine in silence.' There was a silver bell at his right hand to call the servants; he made them a sign to stand still, struck the bell with force, and leaned eagerly forward. The note rose clear and strong; it rang out clear and far into the night and over the deserted island; it died into the distance until there only lingered in the porches of the ear a vibration that was sound no longer. 'Empty houses, empty sea, solitary beaches!' said Attwater. 'And yet God hears the bell! And yet we sit in this verandah on a lighted stage with all heaven for spectators! And you call that solitude?'

There followed a bar of silence, during which the captain sat mesmerised.

Then Attwater laughed softly. 'These are the diversions of a lonely man,' he resumed, 'and possibly not in good taste. One tells oneself these little fairy tales for company. If there *should* happen to be anything in folk-lore, Mr Hay? But here comes the claret. One does not offer you Lafitte, captain, because I believe it is all sold to the railroad dining cars in your great country; but this Brâne-Mouton is of a good year, and Mr Whish will give me news of it.'

'That's a queer idea of yours!' cried the captain, bursting with a sigh from the spell that had bound him. 'So you mean to tell me now, that you sit here evenings and ring up . . . well, ring on the angels . . . by yourself?'

'As a matter of historic fact, and since you put it directly, one does not,' said Attwater. 'Why ring a bell, when there flows out from oneself and everything about one a far more momentous silence? the least beat of my heart and the least thought in my mind echoing into eternity for ever and for ever and for ever.'

'O look 'ere,' said Huish, 'turn down the lights at once, and the Band of 'Ope will oblige! This ain't a spiritual séance.'

'No folk-lore about Mr Whish – I beg your pardon, captain: Huish not Whish, of course,' said Attwater.

As the boy was filling Huish's glass, the bottle escaped from his hand and was shattered, and the wine spilt on the verandah floor. Instant grimness as of death appeared on the face of Attwater; he smote the bell imperiously, and the two brown natives fell into the attitude of attention and stood mute and trembling. There was just a moment of silence and hard looks; then followed a few savage words in the native; and, upon a gesture of dismissal, the service proceeded as before.

None of the party had as yet observed upon the excellent bearing of the two men. They were dark, undersized, and well set up; stepped softly, waited deftly, brought on the wines and dishes at a look, and their eyes attended studiously on their master.

'Where do you get your labour from anyway?' asked Davis.

'Ah, where not?' answered Attwater.

'Not much of a soft job, I suppose?' said the captain.

'If you will tell me where getting labour is!' said Attwater with a shrug. 'And of course, in our case, as we could name no destination, we had to go far and wide and do the best we could. We have gone as far west as the Kingsmills and as far south as Rapa-iti. Pity Symonds isn't here! He is full of yarns. That was his part, to collect them. Then began mine, which was the educational.'

'You mean to run them?' said Davis.

'Ay! to run them,' said Attwater.

'Wait a bit,' said Davis, 'I'm out of my depth. How was this? Do you mean to say you did it single-handed?'

'One did it single-handed,' said Attwater, 'because there was nobody to help one.'

'By God, but you must he a holy terror!' cried the captain, in a glow of admiration.

'One does one's best,' said Attwater.

'Well, now!' said Davis, 'I have seen a lot of driving in my time and been counted a good driver myself; I fought my way, third mate, round the Cape Horn with a push of packet rats that would have turned the devil out of hell and shut the door on him; and I tell you, this racket of Mr Attwater's takes the cake. In a ship, why, there ain't nothing to it! You've got the law with you, that's what does it. But put me down on this blame' beach alone, with nothing but a whip and a mouthful of bad words, and ask me to . . . no, *sir*! it's not good enough! I haven't got the sand for that!' cried Davis. 'It's the law behind,' he added; 'it's the law does it, every time!'

'The beak ain't as black as he's sometimes pynted,' observed Huish, humorously.

'Well, one got the law after a fashion,' said Attwater. 'One had to be a number of things. It was sometimes rather a bore.'

'I should smile!' said Davis. 'Rather lively, I should think!'

'I dare say we mean the same thing,' said Attwater. 'However, one way or another, one got it knocked into their heads that they *must* work, and they *did* . . . until the Lord took them!'

''Ope you made 'em jump,' said Huish.

'When it was necessary, Mr Whish, I made them jump,' said Attwater.

'You bet you did,' cried the captain. He was a good deal flushed, but not so much with wine as admiration; and his eyes drank in the huge proportions of the other with delight. 'You bet you did, and you bet that I can see you doing it! By God, you're a man, and you can say I said so.'

'Too good of you, I'm sure,' said Attwater.

'Did you – did you ever have crime here?' asked Herrick, breaking his silence with a pungent voice.

'Yes,' said Attwater, 'we did.'

'And how did you handle that, sir?' cried the eager captain.

'Well, you see, it was a queer case,' replied Attwater. 'It was a case that would have puzzled Solomon. Shall I tell it you? yes?'

The captain rapturously accepted.

'Well,' drawled Attwater, 'here is what it was. I dare say you know two types of natives, which may be called the obsequious and the sullen? Well, one had them, the types themselves, detected in the fact; and one had them together. Obsequiousness ran out of the first like wine out of a bottle, sullenness congested in the second. Obsequiousness was all smiles; he ran to catch your eye, he loved to gabble; and he had about a dozen words of beach English, and an eighth-of-an-inch veneer of Christianity. Sullens was industrious; a big down-looking bee. When he was spoken to, he answered with a black look and a shrug of one shoulder, but the thing would be done. I don't give him to you for a model of manners; there was nothing showy about Sullens; but he was strong and steady, and ungraciously obedient. Now Sullens got into trouble; no matter how; the regulations of the place were broken, and he was punished accordingly – without effect. So, the next day, and the next, and the day after, till I began to be weary of the business, and Sullens (I am afraid) particularly so. There came a day when he was in fault again, for the – oh, perhaps the thirtieth time; and he rolled a dull eye upon me, with a spark in it, and appeared to speak. Now the regulations of the place are formal upon one point: we allow no explanations; none are received, none allowed to be offered. So one stopped him instantly; but made a note of the circumstance. The next day, he was gone from the settlement. There could be nothing more annoying; if the labour took to running away, the fishery was wrecked. There are sixty miles of this island, you see, all in length like the Queen's Highway; the idea of pursuit in such a place was a piece of single-minded childishness, which one did not entertain. Two days later, I made a discovery; it came in upon me with a flash that Sullens had been unjustly punished from beginning to end, and the real culprit throughout had been Obsequiousness. The native who talks, like the woman who hesitates, is lost. You set him talking and lying; and he talks, and lies, and watches your face to see if he has pleased you; till at last, out comes the truth! It came out of Obsequiousness in the regular course. I said nothing to him; I dismissed him; and late as it was, for it was already night, set off to look for Sullens. I had not far to go: about two hundred yards up the island, the moon showed him to me. He was hanging in a cocoa palm – I'm not botanist enough to tell you how – but it's the way, in nine cases out of ten, these natives commit suicide. His tongue was out, poor devil, and the birds had got at him; I spare you details, he was an ugly sight! I gave the business six good hours of thinking in this verandah. My justice had been made a fool of; I don't suppose that I was ever angrier. Next day, I had the conch sounded and all hands out before sunrise. One took one's gun, and led the way, with Obsequiousness. He was very talkative; the beggar supposed that all was right now he had confessed; in the old schoolboy phrase, he was plainly 'sucking up' to me; full of protestations of goodwill and good behaviour; to which one answered one really can't remember what. Presently the tree came in sight, and the hanged man. They all burst out lamenting for their comrade in the island way, and Obsequiousness was the loudest of the mourners. He was quite genuine; a noxious creature, without any consciousness of guilt. Well, presently – to make a long story short – one told him to go up the tree. He stared a bit, looked at one with a trouble in his eye, and had rather a sickly smile; but went. He was obedient to the last; he had all the pretty virtues, but the truth was not in him. So soon as he was up, he looked down, and there was the rifle covering him; and at that he gave a whimper like a dog. You could hear a pin drop; no more keening now. There they all crouched upon the ground, with bulging eyes; there was he in the tree top, the colour of the lead; and between was the dead man, dancing a bit in the air. He was obedient to the last, recited his crime, recommended his soul to God. And then . . .'

Attwater paused, and Herrick, who had been listening attentively, made a convulsive movement which upset his glass.

'And then?' said the breathless captain.

'Shot,' said Attwater. 'They came to ground together.'

Herrick sprang to his feet with a shriek and an insensate gesture.

'It was a murder,' he screamed. 'A cold-hearted, bloody-minded murder! You monstrous being! Murderer and hypocrite – murderer and hypocrite – murderer and hypocrite— ' he repeated, and his tongue stumbled among the words.

The captain was by him in a moment. 'Herrick!' he cried, 'behave yourself! Here, don't be a blame' fool!'

Herrick struggled in his embrace like a frantic child, and suddenly bowing his face in his hands, choked into a sob, the first of many, which now convulsed his body silently, and now jerked from him indescribable and meaningless sounds.

'Your friend appears over-excited,' remarked Attwater, sitting unmoved but all alert at table.

'It must be the wine,' replied the captain. 'He ain't no drinking man, you see. I – I think I'll take him away. A walk'll sober him up, I guess.'

He led him without resistance out of the verandah and into the night, in which they soon melted; but still for some time, as they drew away, his comfortable voice was to be heard soothing and remonstrating, and Herrick answering, at intervals, with the mechanical noises of hysteria.

''E's like a bloomin' poultry yard!' observed Huish, helping himself to wine (of which he spilled a good deal) with gentlemanly ease. 'A man should learn to beyave at table,' he added.

'Rather bad form, is it not?' said Attwater. 'Well, well, we are left *tête-à-tête*. A glass of wine with you, Mr Whish!'

TEN

The Open Door

The captain and Herrick meanwhile turned their back upon the lights in Attwater's verandah, and took a direction towards the pier and the beach of the lagoon.

The isle, at this hour, with its smooth floor of sand, the pillared roof overhead, and the prevalent illumination of the lamps, wore an air of unreality like a deserted theatre or a public garden at midnight. A man looked about him for the statues and tables. Not the least air of wind was stirring among the palms, and the silence was emphasised by the continuous clamour of the surf from the seashore, as it might be of traffic in the next street.

Still talking, still soothing him, the captain hurried his patient on, brought him at last to the lagoon side, and leading him down the beach, laved his head and face with the tepid water. The paroxysm gradually subsided, the sobs became less convulsive and then ceased; by an odd but not quite unnatural conjunction, the captain's soothing current of talk died away at the same time and by proportional steps, and the pair remained sunk in silence. The lagoon broke at their feet in petty wavelets, and with a sound as delicate as a whisper; stars of all degrees looked down on their own images in that vast mirror; and the more angry colour of the *Farallone's* riding lamp burned in the middle distance. For long they continued to gaze on the scene before them, and hearken anxiously to the rustle and tinkle of that miniature surf, or the more distant and loud reverberations from the outer coast. For long speech was denied them; and when the words came at last, they came to both simultaneously.

'Say, Herrick . . .' the captain was beginning.

But Herrick, turning swiftly towards his companion, bent him down with the eager cry: 'Let's up anchor, captain, and to sea!'

'Where to, my son?' said the captain. 'Up anchor's easy saying. But where to?'

'To sea,' responded Herrick. 'The sea's big enough! To sea – away from this dreadful island and that, oh! that sinister man!'

'Oh, we'll see about that,' said Davis. 'You brace up, and we'll see about that. You're all run down, that's what's wrong with you; you're all nerves, like Jemimar; you've got to brace up good and be yourself again, and then we'll talk.'

'To sea,' reiterated Herrick, 'to sea tonight – now – this moment!'

'It can't be, my son,' replied the captain firmly. 'No ship of mine puts to sea without provisions, you can take that for settled.'

'You don't seem to understand,' said Herrick. 'The whole thing is over, I tell you. There is nothing to do here, when he knows all. That man there with the cat knows all; can't you take it in?'

'All what?' asked the captain, visibly discomposed. 'Why, he received us like a perfect gentleman and treated us real handsome, until you began with your foolery – and I must say I seen men shot for less, and nobody sorry! What more do you expect anyway?'

Herrick rocked to and fro upon the sand, shaking his head.

'Guying us,' he said, 'he was guying us – only guying us; it's all we're good for.'

'There was one queer thing, to be sure,' admitted the captain, with a misgiving of the voice; 'that about the sherry. Damned if I caught on to that. Say, Herrick, you didn't give me away?'

'Oh! give you away!' repeated Herrick with weary, querulous scorn. 'What was there to give away? We're transparent; we've got rascal branded on us: detected rascal – detected rascal! Why, before he came on board, there was the name painted out, and he saw the whole thing. He made sure we would kill him there and then, and stood guying you and Huish on the chance. He calls that being frightened! Next he had me ashore; a fine time I had! *The two wolves*, he calls you and Huish. – *What is the puppy doing with the two wolves?* he asked. He showed me his

pearls; he said they might be dispersed before morning, and
all hung by a hair – and smiled as he said it, such a smile! O,
it's no use, I tell you! He knows all, he sees through all; we
only make him laugh with our pretences – he looks at us
and laughs like God!'

There was a silence. Davis stood with contorted brows,
gazing into the night.

'The pearls?' he said suddenly. 'He showed them to you?
he has them?'

'No, he didn't show them; I forgot: only the safe they
were in,' said Herrick. 'But you'll never get them!'

'I've two words to say to that,' said the captain.

'Do you think he would have been so easy at table, unless
he was prepared?' cried Herrick. 'The servants were both
armed. He was armed himself; he always is; he told me.
You will never deceive his vigilance. Davis, I know it! It's
all up; all up. There's nothing for it, there's nothing to be
done: all gone: life, honour, love. Oh, my God, my God,
why was I born?'

Another pause followed upon this outburst.

The captain put his hands to his brow.

'Another thing!' he broke out. 'Why did he tell you all
this? Seems like madness to me!'

Herrick shook his head with gloomy iteration. 'You
wouldn't understand if I were to tell you,' said he.

'I guess I can understand any blame' thing that you can
tell me,' said the captain.

'Well, then, he's a fatalist,' said Herrick.

'What's that, a fatalist?' said Davis.

'Oh, it's a fellow that believes a lot of things,' said Herrick,
'believes that his bullets go true; believes that all falls out as
God chooses, do as you like to prevent it; and all that.'

'Why, I guess I believe right so myself,' said Davis.

'You do?' said Herrick.

'You bet I do!' says Davis.

Herrick shrugged his shoulders. 'Well, you must be a
fool,' said he, and he leaned his head upon his knees.

The captain stood biting his hands.

'There's one thing sure,' he said at last. 'I must get Huish
out of that. *He's* not fit to hold his end up with a man like
you describe.'

And he turned to go away. The words had been quite

simple; not so the tone; and the other was quick to catch it.

'Davis!' he cried, 'no! Don't do it. Spare *me*, and don't do it – spare yourself, and leave it alone – for God's sake, for your children's sake!'

His voice rose to a passionate shrillness; another moment, and he might be overheard by their not distant victim. But Davis turned on him with a savage oath and gesture; and the miserable young man rolled over on his face on the sand, and lay speechless and helpless.

The captain meanwhile set out rapidly for Attwater's house. As he went, he considered with himself eagerly, his thoughts racing. The man had understood, he had mocked them from the beginning; he would teach him to make a mockery of John Davis! Herrick thought him a god; give him a second to aim in, and the god was overthrown. He chuckled as he felt the butt of his revolver. It should be done now, as he went in. From behind? It was difficult to get there. From across the table? No, the captain preferred to shoot standing, so as you could be sure to get your hand upon your gun. The best would be to summon Huish, and when Attwater stood up and turned – ah, then would be the moment. Wrapped in his ardent prefiguration of events, the captain posted towards the house with his head down.

'Hands up! Halt!' cried the voice of Attwater.

And the captain, before he knew what he was doing, had obeyed. The surprise was complete and irremediable. Coming on the top crest of his murderous intentions, he had walked straight into an ambuscade, and now stood, with his hands impotently lifted, staring at the verandah.

The party was now broken up. Attwater leaned on a post, and kept Davis covered with a Winchester. One of the servants was hard by with a second at the port arms, leaning a little forward, round-eyed with eager expectancy. In the open space at the head of the stair, Huish was partly supported by the other native; his face wreathed in meaningless smiles, his mind seemingly sunk in the contemplation of an unlighted cigar.

'Well,' said Attwater, 'you seem to me to be a very twopenny pirate!'

The captain uttered a sound in his throat for which we have no name; rage choked him.

'I am going to give you Mr Whish – or the wine-sop that remains of him,' continued Attwater. 'He talks a great deal when he drinks, Captain Davis of the *Sea Ranger*. But I have quite done with him – and return the article with thanks. Now,' he cried sharply. 'Another false movement like that, and your family will have to deplore the loss of an invaluable parent; keep strictly still, Davis.'

Attwater said a word in the native, his eye still undeviatingly fixed on the captain; and the servant thrust Huish smartly forward from the brink of the stair. With an extraordinary simultaneous dispersion of his members, that gentleman bounded forth into space, struck the earth, ricocheted, and brought up with his arms about a palm. His mind was quite a stranger to these events; the expression of anguish that deformed his countenance at the moment of the leap was probably mechanical; and he suffered these convulsions in silence; clung to the tree like an infant; and seemed, by his dips, to suppose himself engaged in the pastime of bobbing for apples. A more finely sympathetic mind or a more observant eye might have remarked, a little in front of him on the sand, and still quite beyond reach, the unlighted cigar.

'There is your Whitechapel carrion!' said Attwater. 'And now you might very well ask me why I do not put a period to you at once, as you deserve. I will tell you why, Davis. It is because I have nothing to do with the *Sea Ranger* and the people you drowned, or the *Farallone* and the champagne that you stole. That is your account with God; He keeps it, and He will settle it when the clock strikes. In my own case, I have nothing to go on but suspicion, and I do not kill on suspicion, not even vermin like you. But understand! if ever I see any of you again, it is another matter, and you shall eat a bullet. And now take yourself off. March! and as you value what you call your life, keep your hands up as you go!'

The captain remained as he was, his hands up, his mouth open: mesmerised with fury.

'March!' said Attwater. 'One – two – three!'

And Davis turned and passed slowly away. But even as he went, he was meditating a prompt, offensive return. In the twinkling of an eye, he had leaped behind a tree; and was crouching there, pistol in hand, peering from either side of his place of ambush with bared teeth; a serpent already poised to strike. And already he was too late. Attwater and his servants had disappeared; and only the lamps shone on the deserted table and the bright sand about the house, and threw into the night in all directions the strong and tall shadows of the palms.

Davis ground his teeth. Where were they gone, the cowards? to what hole had they retreated beyond reach? It was in vain he should try anything, he, single and with a second-hand revolver, against three persons, armed with Winchesters, and who did not show an ear out of any of the apertures of that lighted and silent house? Some of them might have already ducked below it from the rear, and be drawing a bead upon him at that moment from the low-browed crypt, the receptacle of empty bottles and broken crockery. No, there was nothing to be done but to bring away (if it were still possible) his shattered and demoralised forces.

'Huish,' he said, 'come along.'

''S lose my ciga',' said Huish, reaching vaguely forward.

The captain let out a rasping oath. 'Come right along here,' said he.

''S all righ'. Sleep here 'th Atty-Attwa. Go boar' t'morr',' replied the festive one.

'If you don't come, and come now, by the living God, I'll shoot you!' cried the captain.

It is not to be supposed that the sense of these words in any way penetrated to the mind of Huish; rather that, in a fresh attempt upon the cigar, he overbalanced himself and came flying erratically forward: a course which brought him within reach of Davis.

'Now you walk straight,' said the captain, clutching him, 'or I'll know why not!'

''S lose my ciga',' replied Huish.

The captain's contained fury blazed up for a moment. He twisted Huish round, grasped him by the neck of the coat, ran him in front of him to the pier end, and flung him savagely forward on his face.

'Look for your cigar then, you swine!' said he, and blew his boat call till the pea in it ceased to rattle.

An immediate activity responded on board the *Farallone*;

far away voices, and soon the sound of oars, floated along the surface of the lagoon; and at the same time, from nearer hand, Herrick aroused himself and strolled languidly up. He bent over the insignificant figure of Huish, where it grovelled, apparently insensible, at the base of the figure-head.

'Dead?' he asked.

'No, he's not dead,' said Davis.

'And Attwater?' asked Herrick.

'Now you just shut your head!' replied Davis. 'You can do that, I fancy, and by God, I'll show you how! I'll stand no more of your drivel.'

They waited accordingly in silence till the boat bumped on the furthest piers; then raised Huish, head and heels, carried him down the gangway, and flung him summarily in the bottom. On the way out he was heard murmuring of the loss of his cigar; and after he had been handed up the side like baggage, and cast down in the alleyway to slumber, his last audible expression was: 'Splen'l fl' Attwa'!' This the expert construed into 'Splendid fellow, Attwater'; with so much innocence had this great spirit issued from the adventures of the evening.

The captain went and walked in the waist with brief, irate turns; Herrick leaned his arms on the taffrail; the crew had all turned in. The ship had a gentle, cradling motion; at times a block piped like a bird. On shore, through the colonnade of palm stems, Attwater's house was to be seen shining steadily with many lamps. And there was nothing else visible, whether in the heaven above or in the lagoon below, but the stars and their reflections. It might have been minutes or it might have been hours, that Herrick leaned there, looking in the glorified water and drinking peace. 'A bath of stars,' he was thinking; when a hand was laid at last on his shoulder.

'Herrick,' said the captain, 'I've been walking off my trouble.'

A sharp jar passed through the young man, but he neither answered nor so much as turned his head.

'I guess I spoke a little rough to you on shore,' pursued the captain; 'the fact is, I was real mad; but now it's over, and you and me have to turn to and think.'

'I will *not* think,' said Herrick.

'Here, old man!' said Davis, kindly; 'this won't fight, you know! You've got to brace up and help me get things straight. You're not going back on a friend? That's not like you, Herrick!'

'O yes, it is,' said Herrick.

'Come, come!' said the captain, and paused as if quite at a loss. 'Look here,' he cried, 'you have a glass of champagne. *I* won't touch it, so that'll show you if I'm in earnest. But it's just the pick-me-up for you; it'll put an edge on you at once.'

'O, you leave me alone!' said Herrick, and turned away.

The captain caught him by the sleeve; and he shook him off and turned on him, for the moment, like a demoniac.

'Go to hell in your own way!' he cried.

And he turned away again, this time unchecked, and stepped forward to where the boat rocked alongside and ground occasionally against the schooner. He looked about him. A corner of the house was interposed between the captain and himself; all was well; no eye must see him in that last act. He slid silently into the boat; thence, silently, into the starry water. Instinctively he swam a little; it would be time enough to stop by and by.

The shock of the immersion brightened his mind immediately. The events of the ignoble day passed before him in a frieze of pictures, and he thanked 'whatever Gods there be' for that open door of suicide. In such a little while he would be done with it, the random business at an end, the prodigal son come home. A very bright planet shone before him and drew a trenchant wake along the water. He took that for his line and followed it. That was the last earthly thing that he should look upon; that radiant speck, which he had soon magnified into a City of Laputa, along whose terraces there walked men and women of awful and benignant features, who viewed him with distant commiseration. These imaginary spectators consoled him; he told himself their talk, one to another; it was of himself and his sad destiny.

From such flights of fancy, he was aroused by the growing coldness of the water. Why should he delay? Here, where he was now, let him drop the curtain, let him seek the ineffable refuge, let him lie down with all races and generations of

men in the house of sleep. It was easy to say, easy to do.
To stop swimming: there was no mystery in that, if he
could do it. Could he? And he could not. He knew it
instantly. He was aware instantly of an opposition in his
members, unanimous and invincible, clinging to life with
a single and fixed resolve, finger by finger, sinew by sinew;
something that was at once he and not he – at once within
and without him; the shutting of some miniature valve in his
brain, which a single manly thought should suffice to open
– and the grasp of an external fate ineluctable as gravity.
To any man there may come at times a consciousness that
there blows, through all the articulations of his body, the
wind of a spirit not wholly his; that his mind rebels; that
another girds him and carries him whither he would not.
It came now to Herrick, with the authority of a revelation.
There was no escape possible. The open door was closed
in his recreant face. He must go back into the world and
amongst men without illusion. He must stagger on to the
end with the pack of his responsibility and his disgrace,
until a cold, a blow, a merciful chance ball, or the more
merciful hangman, should dismiss him from his infamy.
There were men who could commit suicide; there were
men who could not; and he was one who could not.

For perhaps a minute, there raged in his mind the coil
of this discovery; then cheerless certitude followed; and,
with an incredible simplicity of submission to ascertained
fact, he turned round and struck out for shore. There
was a courage in this which he could not appreciate;
the ignobility of his cowardice wholly occupying him. A
strong current set against him like a wind in his face; he
contended with it heavily, wearily, without enthusiasm,
but with substantial advantage; marking his progress the
while, without pleasure, by the outline of the trees. Once
he had a moment of hope. He heard to the southward of
him, towards the centre of the lagoon, the wallowing of
some great fish, doubtless a shark, and paused for a little,
treading water. Might not this be the hangman? he thought.
But the wallowing died away; mere silence succeeded; and
Herrick pushed on again for the shore, raging as he went
at his own nature. Ay, he would wait for the shark; but if
he had heard him coming! . . . His smile was tragic. He
could have spat upon himself.

About three in the morning, chance, and the set of the current, and the bias of his own right-handed body, so decided it between them that he came to shore upon the beach in front of Attwater's. There he sat down, and looked forth into a world without any of the lights of hope. The poor diving dress of self-conceit was sadly tattered! With the fairy tale of suicide, of a refuge always open to him, he had hitherto beguiled and supported himself in the trials of life; and behold! that also was only a fairy tale, that also was folk-lore. With the consequences of his acts he saw himself implacably confronted for the duration of life: stretched upon a cross, and nailed there with the iron bolts of his own cowardice. He had no tears; he told himself no stories. His disgust with himself was so complete that even the process of apologetic mythology had ceased. He was like a man cast down from a pillar, and every bone broken. He lay there, and admitted the facts, and did not attempt to rise.

Dawn began to break over the far side of the atoll, the sky brightened, the clouds became dyed with gorgeous colours, the shadows of the night lifted. And, suddenly, Herrick was aware that the lagoon and the trees wore again their daylight livery; and he saw, on board the *Farallone*, Davis extinguishing the lantern, and smoke rising from the galley.

Davis, without doubt, remarked and recognised the figure on the beach; or perhaps hesitated to recognise it; for after he had gazed a long while from under his hand, he went into the house and fetched a glass. It was very powerful; Herrick had often used it. With an instinct of shame, he hid his face in his hands.

'And what brings you here, Mr Herrick-Hay, or Mr Hay-Herrick?' asked the voice of Attwater. 'Your back view from my present position is remarkably fine, and I would continue to present it. We can get on very nicely as we are, and if you were to turn round, do you know? I think it would be awkward.'

Herrick slowly rose to his feet; his heart throbbed hard, a hideous excitement shook him, but he was master of himself. Slowly he turned, and faced Attwater and the muzzle of a pointed rifle. 'Why could I not do that last night?' he thought.

'Well, why don't you fire?' he said aloud, with a voice that trembled.

Attwater slowly put his gun under his arm, then his hands in his pockets.

'What brings you here?' he repeated.

'I don't know,' said Herrick; and then, with a cry: 'Can you do anything with me?'

'Are you armed?' said Attwater. 'I ask for the form's sake.'

'Armed? No!' said Herrick. 'O yes, I am, too!' And he flung upon the beach a dripping pistol.

'You are wet,' said Attwater.

'Yes, I am wet,' said Herrick. 'Can you do anything with me?'

Attwater read his face attentively.

'It would depend a good deal upon what you are,' said he.

'What I am? A coward!' said Herrick.

'There is very little to be done with that,' said Attwater. 'And yet the description hardly strikes one as exhaustive.'

'Oh, what does it matter?' cried Herrick. 'Here I am. I am broken crockery; I am a burst drum; the whole of my life is gone to water; I have nothing left that I believe in, except my living horror of myself. Why do I come to you? I don't know; you are cold, cruel, hateful; and I hate you, or I think I hate you. But you are an honest man, an honest gentleman. I put myself, helpless, in your hands. What must I do? If I can't do anything, be merciful and put a bullet through me; it's only a puppy with a broken leg!'

'If I were you, I would pick up that pistol, come up to the house, and put on some dry clothes,' said Attwater.

'If you really mean it?' said Herrick. 'You know they – we – they . . . But you know all.'

'I know quite enough,' said Attwater. 'Come up to the house.'

And the captain, from the deck of the *Farallone*, saw the two men pass together under the shadow of the grove.

ELEVEN

David and Goliath

Huish had bundled himself up from the glare of the day – his face to the house, his knees retracted. The frail bones in the thin tropical raiment seemed scarce more considerable than a fowl's; and Davis, sitting on the rail with his arm about a stay, contemplated him with gloom, wondering what manner of counsel that insignificant figure should contain. For since Herrick had thrown him off and deserted to the enemy, Huish, alone of mankind, remained to him to be a helper and oracle.

He considered their position with a sinking heart. The ship was a stolen ship; the stores, either from initial carelessness or ill administration during the voyage, were insufficient to carry them to any port except back to Papeete; and there retribution waited in the shape of a gendarme, a judge with a queer-shaped hat, and the horror of distant Noumea. Upon that side, there was no glimmer of hope. Here, at the island, the dragon was roused; Attwater with his men and his Winchesters watched and patrolled the house; let him who dare approach it. What else was then left but to sit there, inactive, pacing the decks – until the *Trinity Hall* arrived and they were cast into irons, or until the food came to an end, and the pangs of famine succeeded? For the *Trinity Hall* Davis was prepared; he would barricade the house, and die there defending it, like a rat in a crevice. But for the other? The cruise of the *Farallone*, into which he had plunged only a fortnight before, with such golden expectations, could this be the nightmare end of it? The ship rotting at anchor, the crew stumbling and dying in the scuppers? It seemed as if any extreme of hazard were to be preferred to so grisly a certainty; as if it would be better to up-anchor after all, put to sea at a venture, and, perhaps, perish at the hands of cannibals on one of the more obscure Paumotus. His eye roved swiftly over sea and sky in quest of any promise of wind, but the fountains of the Trade were empty. Where it had run yesterday and for weeks before, a roaring blue river charioting clouds, silence now reigned; and the whole height of the atmosphere stood balanced. On the endless ribbon of island that stretched out to either hand of him its array of golden and green and silvery palms, not the most volatile frond was to be seen stirring; they drooped to their stable images in the lagoon like things carved of metal, and already their long line began to reverberate heat. There was no escape possible that day, none probable on the morrow. And still the stores were running out!

Then came over Davis, from deep down in the roots of his being, or at least from far back among his memories of childhood and innocence, a wave of superstition. This run of ill luck was something beyond natural; the chances of the game were in themselves more various; it seemed as if the devil must serve the pieces. The devil? He heard again the clear note of Attwater's bell ringing abroad into the night, and dying away. How if God . . .?

Briskly, he averted his mind. Attwater: that was the point. Attwater had food and a treasure of pearls; escape made possible in the present, riches in the future. They must come to grips with Attwater; the man must die. A smoky heat went over his face, as he recalled the impotent figure he had made last night and the contemptuous speeches he must bear in silence. Rage, shame, and the love of life, all pointed the one way; and only invention halted: how to reach him? had he strength enough? was there any help in that misbegotten packet of bones against the house?

His eyes dwelled upon him with a strange avidity, as though he would read into his soul; and presently the sleeper moved, stirred uneasily, turned suddenly round, and threw him a blinking look. Davis maintained the same dark stare, and Huish looked away again and sat up.

'Lord, I've an 'eadache on me!' said he. 'I believe I was a bit swipey last night. W'ere's that cry-byby 'Errick?'

'Gone,' said the captain.

'Ashore?' cried Huish. 'Oh, I say! I'd 'a gone too.'

'Would you?' said the captain.

'Yes, I would,' replied Huish. 'I like Attwater. 'E's all right; we got on like one o'clock when you were gone. And ain't his sherry in it, rather? It's like Spiers and

Ponds' Amontillado! I wish I 'ad a drain of it now.' He sighed.

'Well, you'll never get no more of it – that's one thing,' said Davis, gravely.

''Ere! wot's wrong with you, Dyvis? Coppers 'ot? Well, look at *me*! *I* ain't grumpy,' said Huish; 'I'm as plyful as a canarybird, I am.'

'Yes,' said Davis, 'you're playful; I own that; and you were playful last night, I believe, and a damned fine performance you made of it.'

''Allo!' said Huish. ''Ow's this? Wot performance?'

'Well, I'll tell you,' said the captain, getting slowly off the rail.

And he did: at full length, with every wounding epithet and absurd detail repeated and emphasised; he had his own vanity and Huish's upon the grill, and roasted them; and as he spoke, he inflicted and endured agonies of humiliation. It was a plain man's masterpiece of the sardonic.

'What do you think of it?' said he, when he had done, and looked down at Huish, flushed and serious, and yet jeering.

'I'll tell you wot it is,' was the reply, 'you and me cut a pretty dicky figure.'

'That's so,' said Davis, 'a pretty measly figure, by God! And, by God, I want to see that man at my knees.'

'Ah!' said Huish. ''Ow to get him there?'

'That's it!' cried Davis. 'How to get hold of him! They're four to two; though there's only one man among them to count, and that's Attwater. Get a bead on Attwater, and the others would cut and run and sing out like frightened poultry – and old man Herrick would come round with his hat for a share of the pearls. No, *Sir*! it's how to get hold of Attwater! And we daren't even go ashore; he would shoot us in the boat like dogs.'

'Are you particular about having him dead or alive?' asked Huish.

'I want to see him dead,' said the captain.

'Ah, well!' said Huish, 'then I believe I'll do a bit of breakfast.'

And he turned into the house.

The captain doggedly followed him.

'What's this?' he asked. 'What's your idea, anyway?'

'Oh, you let me alone, will you?' said Huish, opening a bottle of champagne. 'You'll 'ear my idea soon enough. Wyte till I pour some cham on my 'ot coppers.' He drank a glass off, and affected to listen. ''Ark!' said he, ''ear it fizz. Like 'am fryin', I declyre. 'Ave a glass, do, and look sociable.'

'No!' said the captain, with emphasis; 'no, I will not! there's business.'

'You p'ys your money and you tykes your choice, my little man,' returned Huish. 'Seems rather a shyme to me to spoil your breakfast for wot's really ancient 'istory.'

He finished three parts of a bottle of champagne, and nibbled a corner of biscuit, with extreme deliberation; the captain sitting opposite and champing the bit like an impatient horse. Then Huish leaned his arms on the table and looked Davis in the face.

'W'en you're ready!' said he.

'Well, now, what's your idea?' said Davis, with a sigh.

'Fair play!' said Huish. 'What's yours?'

'The trouble is that I've got none,' replied Davis; and wandered for some time in aimless discussion of the difficulties in their path, and useless explanations of his own fiasco.

'About done?' said Huish.

'I'll dry up right here,' replied Davis.

'Well, then,' said Huish, 'you give me your 'and across the table, and say, "Gawd strike me dead if I don't back you up."'

His voice was hardly raised, yet it thrilled the hearer. His face seemed the epitome of cunning, and the captain recoiled from it as from a blow.

'What for?' said he.

'Luck,' said Huish. 'Substantial guarantee demanded.' And he continued to hold out his hand.

'I don't see the good of any such tomfoolery,' said the other.

'I do, though,' returned Huish. 'Gimme your 'and and say the words; then you'll 'ear my view of it. Don't, and you won't.'

The captain went through the required form, breathing short, and gazing on the clerk with anguish. What to fear, he knew not; yet he feared slavishly what was to fall from the pale lips.

'Now, if you'll excuse me 'alf a second,' said Huish, 'I'll go and fetch the byby.'

'The baby?' said Davis. 'What's that?'

'Fragile. With care. This side up,' replied the clerk with a wink, as he disappeared.

He returned, smiling to himself, and carrying in his hand a silk handkerchief. The long stupid wrinkles ran up Davis's brow, as he saw it. What should it contain? He could think of nothing more recondite than a revolver.

Huish resumed his seat.

'Now,' said he, 'are you man enough to take charge of 'Errick and the niggers? Because I'll take care of Hattwater.'

'How?' cried Davis. 'You can't!'

'Tut, tut!' said the clerk. 'You gimme time. Wot's the first point? The first point is that we can't get ashore, and I'll make you a present of that for a 'ard one. But 'ow about a flag of truce? Would that do the trick, d'ye think? or would Attwater simply blyze aw'y at us in the bloomin' boat like dawgs?'

'No,' said Davis, 'I don't believe he would.'

'No more do I,' said Huish; 'I don't believe he would either; and I'm sure I 'ope he won't! So then you can call us ashore. Next point is to get near the managin' direction. And for that I'm going to 'ave you write a letter, in w'ich you s'y you're ashamed to meet his eye, and that the bearer, Mr J. L. 'Uish, is empowered to represent you. Armed with w'ich seemin'ly simple expedient, Mr J. L. 'Uish will proceed to business.'

He paused, like one who had finished, but still held Davis with his eye.

'How?' said Davis. 'Why?'

'Well, you see, you're big,' returned Huish; ''e knows you 'ave a gun in your pocket, and anybody can see with 'alf an eye that you ain't the man to 'esitate about usin' it. So it's no go with you, and never was; you're out of the runnin', Dyvis. But he won't be afryde of me, I'm such a little un! I'm unarmed – no kid about that – and I'll hold my 'ands up right enough.' He paused. 'If I can manage to sneak up nearer to him as we talk,' he resumed, 'you

look out and back me up smart. If I don't, we go aw'y
again, and nothink to 'urt. See?'

The captain's face was contorted by the frenzied effort
to comprehend.

'No, I don't see,' he cried, 'I can't see. What do you
mean?'

'I mean to do for the Beast!' cried Huish, in a burst of
venomous triumph. 'I'll bring the 'ulkin' bully to grass.
He's 'ad his larks out of me; I'm goin' to 'ave my lark out
of 'im, and a good lark too!'

'What is it?' said the captain, almost in a whisper.

'Sure you want to know?' asked Huish.

Davis rose and took a turn in the house.

'Yes, I want to know,' he said at last with an effort.

'We'n your back's at the wall, you do the best you can,
don't you?' began the clerk. 'I s'y that, because I 'appen to
know there's a prejudice against it; it's considered vulgar,
awf'ly vulgar.' He unrolled the handkerchief and showed
a four-ounce jar. 'This 'ere's vitriol, this is,' said he.

The captain stared upon him with a whitening face.

'This is the stuff!' he pursued, holding it up. 'This'll burn
to the bone; you'll see it smoke upon 'im like 'ell fire! One
drop upon 'is bloomin' heyesight, and I'll trouble you for
Attwater!'

'No, no, by God!' exclaimed the captain.

'Now, see 'ere, ducky,' said Huish, 'this is my bean feast,
I believe? I'm goin' up to that man single-'anded, I am. 'E's
about seven foot high, and I'm five foot one. 'E's a rifle in
his 'and, 'e's on the look-out, 'e wasn't born yesterday. This
is Dyvid and Goliar, I tell you! If I'd ast you to walk up and
face the music I could understand. But I don't. I on'y ast
you to stand by and spifflicate the niggers. It'll all come in
quite natural; you'll see, else! Fust thing, you know, you'll
see him running round and 'owling like a good un . . .'

'Don't!' said Davis. 'Don't talk of it!'

'Well, you *are* a juggins!' exclaimed Huish. 'What did
you want? You wanted to kill him, and tried to last night.
You wanted to kill the 'ole lot of them and tried to, and
'ere I show you 'ow; and because there's some medicine
in a bottle you kick up this fuss!'

'I suppose that's so,' said Davis. 'It don't seem someways
reasonable, only there it is.'

'It's the happlication of science, I suppose?' sneered Huish.

'I don't know what it is,' cried Davis, pacing the floor; 'it's there! I draw the line at it. I can't put a finger to no such piggishness. It's too damned hateful!'

'And I suppose it's all your fancy pynted it,' said Huish, 'w'en you take a pistol and a bit o' lead, and copse a man's brains all over him? No accountin' for tystes.'

'I'm not denying it,' said Davis, 'it's something here, inside of me. It's foolishness; I dare say it's dam foolishness. I don't argue, I just draw the line. Isn't there no other way?'

'Look for yourself,' said Huish. 'I ain't wedded to this, if you think I am; I ain't ambitious; I don't make a point of playin' the lead; I offer to, that's all, and if you can't show me better, by Gawd, I'm goin' to!'

'Then the risk!' cried Davis.

'If you ast me straight, I should say it was a case of seven to one and no takers,' said Huish. 'But that's my look-out, ducky, and I'm gyme, that's wot I am: gyme all through.'

The captain looked at him. Huish sat there, preening his sinister vanity, glorying in his precedency in evil; and the villainous courage and readiness of the creature shone out of him like a candle from a lantern. Dismay and a kind of respect seized hold on Davis in his own despite. Until that moment, he had seen the clerk always hanging back, always listless, uninterested, and openly grumbling at a word of anything to do; and now, by the touch of an enchanter's wand, he beheld him sitting girt and resolved, and his face radiant. He had raised the devil, he thought; and asked who was to control him? and his spirits quailed.

'Look as long as you like,' Huish was going on. 'You don't see any green in my eye! I ain't afryde of Attwater, I ain't afryde of you, and I ain't afryde of words. You want to kill people, that's wot *you* want; but you want to do it in kid gloves, and it can't be done that w'y. Murder ain't genteel, it ain't easy, it ain't safe, and it tykes a man to do it. 'Ere's the man.'

'Huish!' began the captain with energy; and then stopped, and remained staring at him with corrugated brows.

'Well, hout with it!' said Huish. "Ave you anythink else
to put up? Is there any other chanst to try?'

The captain held his peace.

'There you are then!' said Huish with a shrug.

Davis fell again to his pacing.

'Oh, you may do sentry-go till you're blue in the mug,
you won't find anythink else,' said Huish.

There was a little silence; the captain, like a man launched
on a swing, flying dizzily among extremes of conjecture and
refusal.

'But see,' he said, suddenly pausing. 'Can you? Can the
thing be done? It – it can't be easy.'

'If I get within twenty foot of 'im it'll be done; so you look
out,' said Huish, and his tone of certainty was absolute.

'How can you know that?' broke from the captain in a
choked cry. 'You beast, I believe you've done it before!'

'Oh, that's private affyres,' returned Huish, 'I ain't a
talking man.'

A shock of repulsion struck and shook the captain;
a scream rose almost to his lips; had he uttered it,
he might have cast himself at the same moment on
the body of Huish, might have picked him up, and
flung him down, and wiped the cabin with him, in
a frenzy of cruelty that seemed half moral. But the
moment passed; and the abortive crisis left the man
weaker. The stakes were so high – the pearls on the
one hand – starvation and shame on the other. Ten
years of pearls! The imagination of Davis translated
them into a new, glorified existence for himself and his
family. The seat of this new life must be in London;
there were deadly reasons against Portland, Maine; and
the pictures that came to him were of English manners. He saw his boys marching in the procession of
a school, with gowns on, an usher marshalling them
and reading as he walked in a great book. He was
installed in a villa, semi-detached; the name, *Rosemore*,
on the gateposts. In a chair on the gravel walk, he
seemed to sit smoking a cigar, a blue ribbon in his
buttonhole, victor over himself and circumstances, and
the malignity of bankers. He saw the parlour with red
curtains and shells on the mantelpiece – and with the fine
inconsistency of visions, mixed a grog at the mahogany

table ere he turned in. With that the *Farallone* gave one of the aimless and nameless movements which (even in an anchored ship and even in the most profound calm) remind one of the mobility of fluids; and he was back again under the cover of the house, the fierce daylight besieging it all round and glaring in the chinks, and the clerk in a rather airy attitude, awaiting his decision.

He began to walk again. He aspired after the realisation of these dreams, like a horse nickering for water; the lust of them burned in his inside. And the only obstacle was Attwater, who had insulted him from the first. He gave Herrick a full share of the pearls, he insisted on it; Huish opposed him, and he trod the opposition down; and praised himself exceedingly. He was not going to use vitriol himself; was he Huish's keeper? It was a pity he had asked, but after all! . . . he saw the boys again in the school procession, with the gowns he had thought to be so 'tony' long since . . . And at the same time the incomparable shame of the last evening blazed up in his mind.

'Have it your own way!' he said hoarsely.

'Oh, I knew you would walk up,' said Huish. 'Now for the letter. There's paper, pens and ink. Sit down and I'll dictyte.'

The captain took a seat and the pen, looked a while helplessly at the paper, then at Huish. The swing had gone the other way; there was a blur upon his eyes. 'It's a dreadful business,' he said, with a strong twitch of his shoulders.

'It's rather a start, no doubt,' said Huish. 'Tyke a dip of ink. That's it. *William John Hattwater, Esq., Sir*': he dictated.

'How do you know his name is William John?' asked Davis.

'Saw it on a packing case,' said Huish. 'Got that?'

'No,' said Davis. 'But there's another thing. What are we to write?'

'O my golly!' cried the exasperated Huish. 'Wot kind of man do *you* call yourself? *I'm* goin' to tell you wot to write; that's *my* pitch; if you'll just be so bloomin' condescendin' as to write it down! *William John Attwater, Esq., Sir*':

he reiterated. And the captain at last beginning half mechanically to move his pen, the dictation proceeded:

It is with feelings of shyme and 'artfelt contrition that I approach you after the yumiliatin' events of last night. Our Mr 'Errick has left the ship, and will have doubtless communicated to you the nature of our 'opes. Needless to s'y, these are no longer possible: Fate 'as declyred against us, and we bow the 'ead. Well awyre as I am of the just suspicions with w'ich I am regarded, I do not venture to solicit the fyvour of an interview for myself, but in order to put an end to a situytion w'ich must be equally pyneful to all, I 'ave deputed my friend and partner, Mr J.L. Huish, to l'y before you my proposals, and w'ich by their moderytion, will, I trust, be found to merit your attention. Mr J.L. Huish is entirely unarmed, I swear to Gawd! and will 'old 'is 'ands over 'is 'ead from the moment he begins to approach you. I am your fytheful servant, John Davis.

Huish read the letter with the innocent joy of amateurs, chuckled gustfully to himself, and reopened it more than once after it was folded, to repeat the pleasure; Davis meanwhile sitting inert and heavily frowning.

Of a sudden he rose; he seemed all abroad. 'No!' he cried. 'No! it can't be! It's too much; it's damnation. God would never forgive it.'

'Well, and 'oo wants Him to?' returned Huish, shrill with fury. 'You were damned years ago for the *Sea Rynger*, and said so yourself. Well then, be damned for something else, and 'old your tongue.'

The captain looked at him mistily. 'No,' he pleaded, 'no, old man! don't do it.'

''Ere now,' said Huish, 'I'll give you my ultimytum. Go or st'y w'ere you are; I don't mind; I'm goin' to see that man and chuck this vitriol in his eyes. If you st'y I'll go alone; the niggers will likely knock me on the 'ead, and a fat lot you'll be the better! But there's one thing sure: I'll 'ear no more of your moonin', mullygrubbin' rot, and tyke it stryte.'

The captain took it with a blink and a gulp. Memory, with phantom voices, repeated in his ears something similar, something he had once said to Herrick – years ago it seemed.

'Now, gimme over your pistol,' said Huish. 'I 'ave to see all clear. Six shots, and mind you don't wyste them.'

The captain, like a man in a nightmare, laid down his revolver on the table, and Huish wiped the cartridges and oiled the works.

It was close on noon, there was no breath of wind, and the heat was scarce bearable, when the two men came on deck, had the boat manned, and passed down, one after another, into the stern-sheets. A white shirt at the end of an oar served as a flag of truce; and the men, by direction, and to give it the better chance to be observed, pulled with extreme slowness. The isle shook before them like a place incandescent; on the face of the lagoon blinding copper suns, no bigger than sixpences, danced and stabbed them in the eyeballs; there went up from sand and sea, and even from the boat, a glare of scathing brightness; and as they could only peer abroad from between closed lashes, the excess of light seemed to be changed into a sinister darkness, comparable to that of a thundercloud before it bursts.

The captain had come upon this errand for any one of a dozen reasons, the last of which was desire for its success. Superstition rules all men; semi-ignorant and gross natures, like that of Davis, it rules utterly. For murder he had been prepared; but this horror of the medicine in the bottle went beyond him, and he seemed to himself to be parting the last strands that united him to God. The boat carried him on to reprobation, to damnation; and he suffered himself to be carried passively consenting, silently bidding farewell to his better self and his hopes.

Huish sat by his side in towering spirits that were not wholly genuine. Perhaps as brave a man as ever lived, brave as a weasel, he must still reassure himself with the tones of his own voice; he must play his part to exaggeration, he must out-Herod Herod, insult all that was respectable, and brave all that was formidable, in a kind of desperate wager with himself.

'Golly, but it's 'ot!' said he. 'Cruel 'ot, I call it. Nice d'y to get your gruel in! I s'y, you know, it must feel awf'ly peculiar to get bowled over on a d'y like this. I'd rather 'ave it on a cowld and frosty morning, wouldn't you? (Singing) "'*Ere we go round the mulberry bush on a cowld and frosty*

mornin'." (Spoken) Give you my word, I 'aven't thought
o' that in ten year; used to sing it at a hinfant school in
'Ackney, 'Ackney Wick it was. (Singing) "*This is the way
the tyler does, the tyler does.*" (Spoken) Bloomin' 'umbug.
'Ow are you off now, for the notion of a future styte? Do
you cotton to the tea-fight views, or the old red 'ot boguey
business?'

'Oh, dry up!' said the captain.

'No, but I want to know,' said Huish. 'It's within the
sp'ere of practical politics for you and me, my boy; we
may both be bowled over, one up, t'other down, within
the next ten minutes. It would be rather a lark, now, if
you only skipped across, came up smilin' t'other side, and
a hangel met you with a B. and S. under his wing. 'Ullo,
you'd s'y: come, I tyke this kind.'

The captain groaned. While Huish was thus airing and
exercising his bravado, the man at his side was actually
engaged in prayer. Prayer, what for? God knows. But out
of his inconsistent, illogical, and agitated spirit, a stream
of supplication was poured forth, inarticulate as himself,
earnest as death and judgment.

'Thou Gawd seest me!' continued Huish. 'I remember I
had that written in my Bible. I remember the Bible too, all
about Abinadab and parties. Well, Gawd!' apostrophising
the meridian, 'you're goin' to see a rum start presently, I
promise you that!'

The captain bounded.

'I'll have no blasphemy!' he cried, 'no blasphemy in
my boat.'

'All right, cap,' said Huish. 'Anythink to oblige. Any
other topic you would like to sudgest, the rynegyge, the
lightnin' rod, Shykespeare, or the musical glasses? 'Ere's
conversation on a tap. Put a penny in the slot, and . . .
'ullo! 'ere they are!' he cried. 'Now or never is 'e goin' to
shoot?'

And the little man straightened himself into an alert and
dashing attitude, and looked steadily at the enemy.

But the captain rose half up in the boat with eyes
protruding.

'What's that?' he cried.

'Wot's wot?' said Huish.

'Those – blamed things,' said the captain.

And indeed it was something strange. Herrick and Attwater, both armed with Winchesters, had appeared out of the grove behind the figure-head; and to either hand of them, the sun glistened upon two metallic objects, locomotory like men, and occupying in the economy of these creatures the places of heads – only the heads were faceless. To Davis between wind and water, his mythology appeared to have come alive, and Tophet to be vomiting demons. But Huish was not mystified a moment.

'Divers' 'elmets, you ninny. Can't you see?' he said.

'So they are,' said Davis, with a gasp. 'And why? Oh, I see, it's for armour.'

'Wot did I tell you?' said Huish. 'Dyvid and Goliar all the w'y and back.'

The two natives (for they it was that were equipped in this unusual panoply of war) spread out to right and left, and at last lay down in the shade, on the extreme flank of the position. Even now that the mystery was explained, Davis was hatefully preoccupied, stared at the flame on their crests, and forgot, and then remembered with a smile, the explanation.

Attwater withdrew again into the grove, and Herrick, with his gun under his arm, came down the pier alone.

About half-way down he halted and hailed the boat.

'What do you want?' he cried.

'I'll tell that to Mr Attwater,' replied Huish, stepping briskly on the ladder. 'I don't tell it to you, because you played the trucklin' sneak. Here's a letter for him: tyke it, and give it, and be 'anged to you!'

'Davis, is this all right?' said Herrick.

Davis raised his chin, glanced swiftly at Herrick and away again, and held his peace. The glance was charged with some deep emotion, but whether of hatred or of fear, it was beyond Herrick to divine.

'Well,' he said, 'I'll give the letter.' He drew a score with his foot on the boards of the gangway. 'Till I bring the answer, don't move a step past this.'

And he returned to where Attwater leaned against a tree, and gave him the letter. Attwater glanced it through.

'What does that mean?' he asked, passing it to Herrick. 'Treachery?'

'Oh, I suppose so!' said Herrick.

'Well, tell him to come on,' said Attwater. 'One isn't a fatalist for nothing. Tell him to come on and to look out.'

Herrick returned to the figure-head. Half-way down the pier the clerk was waiting, with Davis by his side.

'You are to come along, Huish,' said Herrick. 'He bids you look out, no tricks.'

Huish walked briskly up the pier, and paused face to face with the young man.

'W'ere is 'e?' said he, and to Herrick's surprise, the low-bred, insignificant face before him flushed suddenly crimson and went white again.

'Right forward,' said Herrick, pointing. 'Now your hands above your head.'

The clerk turned away from him and towards the figure-head, as though he were about to address to it his devotions; he was seen to heave a deep breath; and raised his arms. In common with many men of his unhappy physical endowments, Huish's hands were disproportionately long and broad, and the palms in particular enormous; a four-ounce jar was nothing in that capacious fist. The next moment he was plodding steadily forward on his mission.

Herrick at first followed. Then a noise in his rear startled him, and he turned about to find Davis already advanced as far as the figure-head. He came, crouching and open-mouthed, as the mesmerised may follow the mesmeriser; all human considerations, and even the care of his own life, swallowed up in one abominable and burning curiosity.

'Halt!' cried Herrick, covering him with his rifle. 'Davis, what are you doing, man? *You* are not to come.'

Davis instinctively paused, and regarded him with a dreadful vacancy of eye.

'Put your back to that figure-head, do you hear me? and stand fast!' said Herrick.

The captain fetched a breath, stepped back against the figurehead, and instantly redirected his glances after Huish.

There was a hollow place of the sand in that part, and, as it were, a glade among the cocoa palms in which the direct noonday sun blazed intolerably. At the far end, in the shadow, the tall figure of Attwater was to be seen leaning on a tree; towards him, with his hands over his head, and his steps smothered in the sand, the clerk painfully waded. The surrounding glare threw out and exaggerated the man's smallness; it seemed no less perilous an enterprise, this that he was gone upon, than for a whelp to besiege a citadel.

'There, Mr Whish. That will do,' cried Attwater. 'From that distance, and keeping your hands up, like a good boy, you can very well put me in possession of the skipper's views.'

The interval betwixt them was perhaps forty feet; and Huish measured it with his eye, and breathed a curse. He was already distressed with labouring in the loose sand, and his arms ached bitterly from their unnatural position. In the palm of his right hand, the jar was ready; and his heart thrilled, and his voice choked, as he began to speak.

'Mr Hattwater,' said he, 'I don't know if ever you 'ad a mother . . .'

'I can set your mind at rest: I had,' returned Attwater; 'and henceforth, if I might venture to suggest it, her name need not recur in our communications. I should perhaps tell you that I am not amenable to the pathetic.'

'I am sorry, sir, if I 'ave seemed to tresparse on your private feelin's,' said the clerk, cringing and stealing a step. 'At least, sir, you will never pe'suade me that you are not a perfec' gentleman; I know a gentleman when I see him; and as such, I 'ave no 'esitation in throwin' myself on your merciful consideration. It *is* 'ard lines, no doubt; it's 'ard lines to have to hown yourself beat; it's 'ard lines to 'ave to come and beg to you for charity.'

'When, if things had only gone right, the whole place was as good as your own?' suggested Attwater. 'I can understand the feeling.'

'You are judging me, Mr Attwater,' said the clerk, 'and God knows how unjustly! *Thou Gawd seest me*, was the tex' I 'ad in my Bible, w'ich my father wrote it in with 'is own 'and upon the fly leaf.'

'I am sorry I have to beg your pardon once more,' said Attwater; 'but, do you know, you seem to me to be a trifle nearer, which is entirely outside of our bargain. And I would venture to suggest that you take one – two – three – steps back; and stay there.'

The devil, at this staggering disappointment, looked

out of Huish's face, and Attwater was swift to suspect. He frowned, he stared on the little man, and considered. Why should he be creeping nearer? The next moment, his gun was at his shoulder.

'Kindly oblige me by opening your hands. Open your hands wide – let me see the fingers spread, you dog – throw down that thing you're holding!' he roared, his rage and certitude increasing together.

And then, at almost the same moment, the indomitable Huish decided to throw, and Attwater pulled the trigger. There was scarce the difference of a second between the two resolves, but it was in favour of the man with the rifle; and the jar had not yet left the clerk's hand, before the ball shattered both. For the twinkling of an eye the wretch was in hell's agonies, bathed in liquid flames, a screaming bedlamite; and then a second and more merciful bullet stretched him dead.

The whole thing was come and gone in a breath. Before Herrick could turn about, before Davis could complete his cry of horror, the clerk lay in the sand, sprawling and convulsed.

Attwater ran to the body; he stooped and viewed it; he put his finger in the vitriol, and his face whitened and hardened with anger.

Davis had not yet moved; he stood astonished, with his back to the figure-head, his hands clutching it behind him, his body inclined forward from the waist.

Attwater turned deliberately and covered him with his rifle.

'Davis,' he cried, in a voice like a trumpet, 'I give you sixty seconds to make your peace with God!'

Davis looked, and his mind awoke. He did not dream of self-defence, he did not reach for his pistol. He drew himself up instead to face death, with a quivering nostril.

'I guess I'll not trouble the Old Man,' he said; 'considering the job I was on, I guess it's better business to just shut my face.'

Attwater fired; there came a spasmodic movement of the victim, and immediately above the middle of his forehead, a black hole marred the whiteness of the figure-head. A dreadful pause; then again the report, and the solid sound and jar of the bullet in the wood; and this time the captain

had felt the wind of it along his cheek. A third shot, and
he was bleeding from one ear; and along the levelled rifle
Attwater smiled like a Red Indian.

The cruel game of which he was the puppet was now
clear to Davis; three times he had drunk of death, and he
must look to drink of it seven times more before he was
despatched. He held up his hand.

'Steady!' he cried; 'I'll take your sixty seconds.'

'Good!' said Attwater.

The captain shut his eyes tight like a child: he held his
hands up at last with a tragic and ridiculous gesture.

'My God, for Christ's sake, look after my two kids,' he
said; and then, after a pause and a falter, 'for Christ's sake,
Amen.'

And he opened his eyes and looked down the rifle with
a quivering mouth.

'But don't keep fooling me long!' he pleaded.

'That's all your prayer?' asked Attwater, with a singular
ring in his voice.

'Guess so,' said Davis.

'So?' said Attwater, resting the butt of his rifle on the
ground, 'is that done? Is your peace made with Heaven?
Because it is with me. Go, and sin no more, sinful father.
And remember that whatever you do to others, God shall
visit it again a thousand-fold upon your innocents.'

The wretched Davis came staggering forward from his
place against the figure-head, fell upon his knees, and waved
his hands, and fainted.

When he came to himself again, his head was on
Attwater's arm, and close by stood one of the men in
divers' helmets, holding a bucket of water, from which his
late executioner now laved his face. The memory of that
dreadful passage returned upon him in a clap; again he
saw Huish lying dead, again he seemed to himself to totter
on the brink of an unplumbed eternity. With trembling
hands he seized hold of the man whom he had come to
slay; and his voice broke from him like that of a child
among the nightmares of fever: 'O! isn't there no mercy?
O! what must I do to be saved?'

'Ah!' thought Attwater, 'here's the true penitent.'

TWELVE

A Tail-Piece

On a very bright, hot, lusty, strongly blowing noon, a fortnight after the events recorded, and a month since the curtain rose upon this episode, a man might have been spied, praying on the sand by the lagoon beach. A point of palm trees isolated him from the settlement; and from the place where he knelt, the only work of man's hand that interrupted the expanse, was the schooner *Farallone*, her berth quite changed, and rocking at anchor some two miles to windward in the midst of the lagoon. The noise of the Trade ran very boisterous in all parts of the island; the nearer palm trees crashed and whistled in the gusts, those farther off contributed a humming bass like the roar of cities; and yet, to any man less absorbed, there must have risen at times over this turmoil of the winds, the sharper note of the human voice from the settlement. There all was activity. Attwater, stripped to his trousers and lending a strong hand of help, was directing and encouraging five Kanakas; from his lively voice, and their more lively efforts, it was to be gathered that some sudden and joyful emergency had set them in this bustle; and the Union Jack floated once more on its staff. But the suppliant on the beach, unconscious of their voices, prayed on with instancy and fervour, and the sound of his voice rose and fell again, and his countenance brightened and was deformed with changing moods of piety and terror.

Before his closed eyes, the skiff had been for some time tacking towards the distant and deserted *Farallone*; and presently the figure of Herrick might have been observed to board her, to pass for a while into the house, thence forward to the forecastle, and at last to plunge into the main hatch. In all these quarters, his visit was followed by a coil of smoke; and he had scarce entered his boat again and shoved off, before flames broke forth upon the schooner.

They burned gaily; kerosene had not been spared, and the bellows of the Trade incited the conflagration. About half way on the return voyage, when Herrick looked back, he beheld the *Farallone* wrapped to the topmasts in leaping arms of fire, and the voluminous smoke pursuing him along the face of the lagoon. In one hour's time, he computed, the waters would have closed over the stolen ship.

It so chanced that, as his boat flew before the wind with much vivacity, and his eyes were continually busy in the wake, measuring the progress of the flames, he found himself embayed to the northward of the point of palms, and here became aware at the same time of the figure of Davis immersed in his devotion. An exclamation, part of annoyance, part of amusement, broke from him: and he touched the helm and ran the prow upon the beach not twenty feet from the unconscious devotee. Taking the painter in his hand, he landed, and drew near, and stood over him. And still the voluble and incoherent stream of prayer continued unabated. It was not possible for him to overhear the suppliant's petitions, which he listened to some while in a very mingled mood of humour and pity: and it was only when his own name began to occur and to be conjoined with epithets, that he at last laid his hand on the captain's shoulder.

'Sorry to interrupt the exercise,' said he; 'but I want you to look at the *Farallone*.'

The captain scrambled to his feet, and stood gasping and staring. 'Mr Herrick, don't startle a man like that!' he said. 'I don't seem someways rightly myself since . . .' he broke off. 'What did you say anyway? O, the *Farallone*,' and he looked languidly out.

'Yes,' said Herrick. 'There she burns! and you may guess from that what the news is.'

'The *Trinity Hall*, I guess,' said the captain.

'The same,' said Herrick; 'sighted half an hour ago, and coming up hand over fist.'

'Well, it don't amount to a hill of beans,' said the captain with a sigh.

'O, come, that's rank ingratitude!' cried Herrick.

'Well,' replied the captain, meditatively, 'you mayn't just see the way that I view it in, but I'd 'most rather stay here upon this island. I found peace here, peace in believing.

Yes, I guess this island is about good enough for John Davis.'

'I never heard such nonsense!' cried Herrick. 'What! with all turning out in your favour the way it does, the *Farallone* wiped out, the crew disposed of, a sure thing for your wife and family, and you, yourself, Attwater's spoiled darling and pet penitent!'

'Now, Mr Herrick, don't say that,' said the captain gently; 'when you know he don't make no difference between us. But, O! why not be one of us? why not come to Jesus right away, and let's meet in yon beautiful land? That's just the one thing wanted; just say, Lord, I believe, help thou mine unbelief! And He'll fold you in His arms. You see, I know! I've been a sinner myself!'

THE WRECKER

by Robert Louis Stevenson
and
Lloyd Osbourne

Contents

In the Marquesas

It was about three o'clock of a winter's afternoon in Tai-o-hae, the French capital and port of entry of the Marquesas Islands. The trades blew strong and squally; the surf roared loud on the shingle beach; and the fifty-ton schooner of war, that carries the flag and influence of France about the islands of the cannibal group, rolled at her moorings under Prison Hill. The clouds hung low and black on the surrounding amphitheatre of mountains; rain had fallen earlier in the day, real tropic rain, a waterspout for violence; and the green and gloomy brow of the mountain was still seamed with many silver threads of torrent.

In these hot and healthy islands winter is but a name. The rain had not refreshed, nor could the wind invigorate the dwellers of Tai-o-hae: away at one end, indeed, the commandant was directing some changes in the residency garden beyond Prison Hill; and the gardeners, being all convicts, had no choice but to continue to obey. All other folks slumbered and took their rest: Vaekehu, the native Queen, in her trim house under the rustling palms; the Tahitian missionary, in his beflagged official residence; the merchants, in their deserted stores; and even the club-servant in the club, his head fallen forward on the bottle-counter, under the map of the world and the cards of navy officers. In the whole length of the single shoreside street, with its scattered board houses looking to the sea, its grateful shade of palms and green jungle of puraos, no moving figure could be seen. Only, at the end of the rickety pier, that once (in the prosperous days of the American rebellion) was used to groan under the cotton of John Hart, there might have been spied upon a pile of lumber the famous tattooed white man, the living curiosity of Tai-o-hae.

His eyes were open, staring down the bay. He saw

the mountains droop, as they approached the entrance, and break down in cliffs: the surf boil white round the two sentinel islets; and between, on the narrow bight of blue horizon, Ua-pu upraise the ghost of her pinnacled mountain-tops. But his mind would take no account of these familiar features; as he dodged in and out along the frontier line of sleep and waking, memory would serve him with broken fragments of the past: brown faces and white, of skipper and shipmate, king and chief, would arise before his mind and vanish; he would recall old voyages, old landfalls in the hour of dawn; he would hear again the drums beat for a man-eating festival; perhaps he would summon up the form of that island princess for the love of whom he had submitted his body to the cruel hands of the tattooer, and now sat on the lumber, at the pier-end of Tai-o-hae, so strange a figure of a European. Or perhaps, from yet further back, sounds and scents of England and his childhood might assail him; the merry clamour of cathedral bells, the broom upon the foreland, the song of the river on the weir.

It is bold water at the mouth of the bay; you can steer a ship about either sentinel, close enough to toss a biscuit on the rocks. Thus it chanced that, as the tattooed man sat dozing and dreaming, he was startled into wakefulness and animation by the appearance of a flying jib beyond the western islet. Two more headsails followed; and before the tattooed man had scrambled to his feet, a topsail schooner, of some hundred tons, had luffed about the sentinel, and was standing up the bay, close-hauled.

The sleeping city awakened by enchantment. Natives appeared upon all sides, hailing each other with the magic cry 'Ehippy' – ship; the Queen stepped forth on her verandah, shading her eyes under a hand that was a miracle of the fine art of tattooing; the commandant broke from his domestic convicts and ran into the residency for his glass; the harbour master, who was also the gaoler, came speeding down the Prison Hill; the seventeen brown Kanakas and the French boatswain's mate, that made up the complement of the war-schooner, crowded on the forward deck; and the various English, Americans, Germans, Poles, Corsicans, and Scots – the merchants and the clerks of Tai-o-hae – deserted their places of business, and gathered, according to invariable custom, on the road before the club.

So quickly did these dozen whites collect, so short are the distances in Tai-o-hae, that they were already exchanging guesses as to the nationality and business of the strange vessel, before she had gone about upon her second board towards the anchorage. A moment after, English colours were broken out at the main truck.

'I told you she was a Johnny Bull – knew it by her headsails,' said an evergreen old salt, still qualified (if he could anywhere have found an owner unacquainted with his story) to adorn another quarter-deck and lose another ship.

'She has American lines, anyway,' said the astute Scotch engineer of the gin-mill; 'it's my belief she's a yacht.'

'That's it,' said the old salt, 'a yacht! look at her davits, and the boat over the stern.'

'A yacht in your eye!' said a Glasgow voice. 'Look at her red ensign! A yacht! not much she isn't!'

'You can close the store, anyway, Tom,' observed a gentlemanly German. '*Bon jour, mon Prince!*' he added, as a dark, intelligent native cantered by on a neat chestnut. '*Vous allez boire un verre de bière?*'

But Prince Stanilas Moanatini, the only reasonably busy human creature on the island, was riding hotspur to view this morning's landslip on the mountain road; the sun already visibly declined; night was imminent; and if he would avoid the perils of darkness and precipice, and the fear of the dead, the haunters of the jungle, he must for once decline a hospitable invitation. Even had he been minded to alight, it presently appeared there would be difficulty as to the refreshment offered.

'Beer!' cried the Glasgow voice. 'No such a thing; I tell you there's only eight bottles in the club! Here's the first time I've seen British colours in this port! and the man that sails under them has got to drink that beer.'

The proposal struck the public mind as fair, though far from cheering; for some time back, indeed, the very name of beer had been a sound of sorrow in the club, and the evenings had passed in dolorous computation.

'Here is Havens,' said one, as if welcoming a fresh topic. 'What do you think of her, Havens?'

'I don't think,' replied Havens, a tall, bland, cool-looking, leisurely Englishman, attired in spotless duck, and deliberately dealing with a cigarette. 'I may say I know. She's consigned to me from Auckland by Donald and Edenborough. I am on my way aboard.'

'What ship is she?' asked the ancient mariner.

'Haven't an idea,' returned Havens. 'Some tramp they have chartered.'

With that, he placidly resumed his walk, and was soon seated in the stern-sheets of a whaleboat manned by uproarious Kanakas, himself daintily perched out of the way of the least maculation, giving his commands in an unobstrusive, dinner-table tone of voice, and sweeping neatly enough alongside the schooner.

A weather-beaten captain received him at the gangway.

'You are consigned to us, I think,' said he. 'I am Mr Havens.'

'That is right, sir,' replied the captain, shaking hands. 'You will find the owner, Mr Dodd, below. Mind the fresh paint on the house.'

Havens stepped along the alley-way, and descended the ladder into the main cabin.

'Mr Dodd, I believe,' said he, addressing a smallish, bearded gentleman, who sat writing at the table. 'Why,' he cried, 'it isn't Loudon Dodd?'

'Myself, my dear fellow,' replied Mr Dodd, springing to his feet with companionable alacrity. 'I had a half-hope it might be you, when I found your name on the papers. Well, there's no change in you; still the same placid, fresh-looking Britisher.'

'I can't return the compliment; for you seem to have become a Britisher yourself,' said Havens.

'I promise you, I am quite unchanged,' returned Dodd. 'The red tablecloth at the top of the stick is not my flag; it's my partner's. He is not dead, but sleepeth. There he is,' he added, pointing to a bust which formed one of the numerous unexpected ornaments of that unusual cabin.

Havens politely studied it. 'A fine bust,' said he; 'and a very nice-looking fellow.'

'Yes; he's a good fellow,' said Dodd. 'He runs me now. It's all his money.'

'He doesn't seem to be particularly short of it,' added the other, peering with growing wonder round the cabin.

'His money, my taste,' said Dodd. 'The black walnut

bookshelves are old English; the books all mine – mostly Renaissance French. You should see how the beach-combers wilt away when they go round them, looking for a change of seaside library novels. The mirrors are genuine Venice; that's a good piece in the corner. The daubs are mine – and his; the mudding mine.'

'Mudding? What is that?' asked Havens.

'These bronzes,' replied Dodd. 'I began life as a sculptor.'

'Yes; I remember something about that,' said the other. 'I think, too, you said you were interested in Californian real estate.'

'Surely, I never went so far as that,' said Dodd. 'Interested? I guess not. Involved, perhaps. I was born an artist; I never took an interest in anything but art. If I were to pile up this old schooner tomorrow,' he added, 'I declare I believe I would try the thing again!'

'Insured?' inquired Havens.

'Yes,' responded Dodd. 'There's some fool in 'Frisco who insures us, and comes down like a wolf on the fold on the profits; but we'll get even with him some day.'

'Well, I suppose it's all right about the cargo,' said Havens.

'Oh, I suppose so!' replied Dodd. 'Shall we go into the papers?'

'We'll have all tomorrow, you know,' said Havens; 'and they'll be rather expecting you at the club. *C'est l'heure de l'absinthe*. Of course, Loudon, you'll dine with me later on?'

Mr Dodd signified his acquiescence; drew on his white coat, not without a trifling difficulty, for he was a man of middle age, and well-to-do; arranged his beard and moustaches at one of the Venetian mirrors; and, taking a broad felt hat, led the way through the trade-room into the ship's waist.

The stern boat was waiting alongside – a boat of an elegant model, with cushions and polished hardwood fittings.

'You steer,' observed Loudon. 'You know the best place to land.'

'I never like to steer another man's boat,' replied Havens.

'Call it my partner's, and cry quits,' returned Loudon, getting nonchalantly down the side.

Havens followed and took the yoke lines without further protest.

'I am sure I don't know how you make this pay,' he said. 'To begin with, she is too big for the trade, to my taste; and then you carry so much style.'

'I don't know that she does pay,' returned Loudon. 'I never pretend to be a business man. My partner appears happy; and the money is all his, as I told you – I only bring the want of business habits.'

'You rather like the berth, I suppose?' suggested Havens.

'Yes,' said Loudon; 'it seems odd, but I rather do.'

While they were yet on board, the sun had dipped; the sunset gun (a rifle) cracked from the war-schooner, and the colours had been handed down. Dusk was deepening as they came ashore; and the *Cercle International* (as the club is officially and significantly named) began to shine, from under its low verandahs, with the light of many lamps. The good hours of the twenty-four drew on; the hateful, poisonous day-fly of Nukahiva was beginning to desist from its activity; the land-breeze came in refreshing draughts; and the club men gathered together for the hour of absinthe. To the commandant himself, to the man whom he was then contending with at billiards – a trader from the next island, honorary member of the club, and once carpenter's mate on board a Yankee war-ship – to the doctor of the port, to the Brigadier of Gendarmerie, to the opium farmer, and to all the white men whom the tide of commerce, or the chances of shipwreck and desertion, had stranded on the beach of Tai-o-hae, Mr Loudon Dodd was formally presented; by all (since he was a man of pleasing exterior, smooth ways, and an unexceptionable flow of talk, whether in French or English) he was excellently well received; and presently, with one of the last eight bottles of beer on a table at his elbow, found himself the rather silent centre-piece of a voluble group on the verandah.

Talk in the South Seas is all upon one pattern; it is a wide ocean, indeed, but a narrow world: you shall never talk long and not hear the name of Bully Hayes, a naval hero whose exploits and deserved extinction left Europe cold;

commerce will be touched on, copra, shell, perhaps cotton or fungus; but in a far-away, dilettante fashion, as by men not deeply interested; through all, the names of schooners and their captains will keep coming and going, thick as may-flies; and news of the last shipwreck will be placidly exchanged and debated. To a stranger, this conversation will at first seem scarcely brilliant; but he will soon catch the tone; and by the time he shall have moved a year or so in the island world, and come across a good number of the schooners, so that every captain's name calls up a figure in pyjamas or white duck, and becomes used to a certain laxity of moral tone which prevails (as in memory of Mr Hayes) on smuggling, ship-scuttling, barratry, piracy, the labour trade, and other kindred fields of human activity, he will find Polynesia no less amusing and no less instructive than Pall Mall or Paris.

Mr Loudon Dodd, though he was new to the group of the Marquesas, was already an old, salted trader; he knew the ships and the captains; he had assisted, in other islands, at the first steps of some career of which he now heard the culmination, or (*vice versâ*) he had brought with him from further south the end of some story which had begun in Tai-o-hae. Among other matter of interest, like other arrivals in the South Seas, he had a wreck to announce. The *John T. Richards*, it appeared, had met the fate of other island schooners.

'Dickinson piled her up on Palmerston Island,' Dodd announced.

'Who were the owners?' inquired one of the club men.

'Oh, the usual parties!' returned Loudon, 'Capsicum and Co.'

A smile and a glance of intelligence went round the group; and perhaps Loudon gave voice to the general sentiment by remarking—

'Talk of good business! I know nothing better than a schooner, a competent captain, and a sound reliable reef.'

'Good business! There's no such a thing!' said the Glasgow man. 'Nobody makes anything but the missionaries – dash it!'

'I don't know,' said another; 'there's a good deal in opium.'

'It's a good job to strike a tabooed pearl-island – say, about the fourth year,' remarked a third, 'skim the whole lagoon on the sly, and up stick and away before the French get wind of you.'

'A pig nokket of cold is good,' observed a German.

'There's something in wrecks, too,' said Havens. 'Look at that man in Honolulu, and the ship that went ashore on Waikiki Reef; it was blowing a kona, hard; and she began to break up as soon as she touched. Lloyd's agent had her sold inside an hour; and before dark, when she went to pieces in earnest, the man that bought her had feathered his nest. Three more hours of daylight, and he might have retired from business. As it was, he built a house on Beretania Street, and called it after the ship.'

'Yes, there's something in wrecks sometimes,' said the Glasgow voice; 'but not often.'

'As a general rule, there's deuced little in anything,' said Havens.

'Well, I believe that's a Christian fact,' cried the other. 'What I want is a secret, get hold of a rich man by the right place, and make him squeal.'

'I suppose you know it's not thought to be the ticket,' returned Havens.

'I don't care for that; it's good enough for me,' cried the man from Glasgow, stoutly. 'The only devil of it is, a fellow can never find a secret in a place like the South Seas: only in London and Paris.'

'McGibbon's been reading some dime-novel, I suppose,' said one club man.

'He's been reading "Aurora Floyd,"' remarked another.

'And what if I have?' cried McGibbon. 'It's all true. Look at the newspapers! It's just your confounded ignorance that sets you snickering. I tell you, it's as much a trade as underwriting, and a dashed sight more honest.'

The sudden acrimony of these remarks called Loudon (who was a man of peace) from his reserve. 'It's rather singular,' said he, 'but I seem to have practised about all these means of livelihood.'

'Tit you effer find a nokket?' inquired the inarticulate German, eagerly.

'No. I have been most kinds of fool in my time,' returned

Loudon, 'but not the gold-digging variety. Every man has a sane spot somewhere.'

'Well, then,' suggested someone, 'did you ever smuggle opium?'

'Yes, I did,' said Loudon.

'Was there money in that?'

'All the way,' responded Loudon.

'And perhaps you bought a wreck?' asked another.

'Yes, sir,' said Loudon.

'How did that pan out?' pursued the questioner.

'Well, mine was a peculiar kind of wreck,' replied Loudon. 'I don't know, on the whole, that I can recommend that branch of industry.'

'Did she break up?' asked someone.

'I guess it was rather I that broke down,' says Loudon. 'Head not big enough.'

'Ever try the blackmail?' inquired Havens.

'Simple as you see me sitting here!' responded Dodd.

'Good business?'

'Well, I'm not a lucky man, you see,' returned the stranger. 'It ought to have been good.'

'You had a secret?' asked the Glasgow man.

'As big as the State of Texas.'

'And the other man was rich?'

'He wasn't exactly Jay Gould, but I guess he could buy these islands if he wanted.'

'Why, what was wrong, then? Couldn't you get hands on him?'

'It took time, but I had him cornered at last; and then— '

'What then?'

'The speculation turned bottom up. I became the man's bosom friend.'

'The deuce you did!'

'He couldn't have been particular, you mean?' asked Dodd, pleasantly. 'Well, no; he's a man of rather large sympathies.'

'If you're done talking nonsense, Loudon,' said Havens, 'let's be getting to my place for dinner.'

Outside, the night was full of the roaring of the surf. Scattered lights glowed in the green thicket. Native women came by twos and threes out of the darkness, smiled and ogled the two whites, perhaps wooed them with a strain of laughter, and went by again, bequeathing to the air a heady perfume of palm-oil and frangipani blossom. From the club to Mr Haven's residence was but a step or two, and to any dweller in Europe they must have seemed steps in fairyland. If such an one could but have followed our two friends into the wide-verandahed house, sat down with them in the cool trellised room, where the wine shone on the lamp-lighted tablecloth; tasted of their exotic food – the raw fish, the bread-fruit, the cooked bananas, the roast pig served with the inimitable miti, and that king of delicacies palm-tree salad; seen and heard by fits and starts, now peering round the corner of the door, now railing within against invisible assistants, a certain comely young native lady in a sacque, who seemed too modest to be a member of the family, and too imperious to be less; and then if such an one were whisked again through space to Upper Tooting, or wherever else he honoured the domestic gods, 'I have had a dream,' I think he would say, as he sat up, rubbing his eyes, in the familiar chimney-corner chair, 'I have had a dream of a place, and I declare I believe it must be heaven,' But to Dodd and his entertainer, all this amenity of the tropic night, and all these dainties of the island table, were grown things of custom; and they fell to meat like men who were hungry, and drifted into idle talk like men who were a trifle bored.

The scene in the club was referred to.

'I never heard you talk so much nonsense, Loudon,' said the host.

'Well, it seemed to me there was sulphur in the air, so I talked for talking,' returned the other. 'But it was none of it nonsense.'

'Do you mean to say it was true?' cried Havens – 'that about the opium and the wreck, and the blackmailing, and the man who became your friend?'

'Every last word of it,' said Loudon.

'You seem to have been seeing life,' returned the other.

'Yes, it's a queer yarn,' said his friend; 'if you think you would like, I'll tell it you.'

Here follows the yarn of Loudon Dodd, not as he told it to his friend, but as he subsequently wrote it.

PART II
THE YARN

CHAPTER ONE

A Sound Commercial Education

The beginning of this yarn is my poor father's character. There never was a better man, nor a handsomer, nor (in my view) a more unhappy – unhappy in his business, in his pleasures, in his place of residence, and (I am sorry to say it) in his son. He had begun life as a land-surveyor, soon became interested in real estate, branched off into many other speculations, and had the name of one of the smartest men in the State of Muskegon. 'Dodd has a big head,' people used to say; but I was never so sure of his capacity. His luck, at least, was beyond doubt for long; his assiduity, always. He fought in that daily battle of money-grubbing, with a kind of sad-eyed loyalty like a martyr's; rose early, ate fast, came home dispirited and over-weary, even from success; grudged himself all pleasure, if his nature was capable of taking any, which I sometimes wondered; and laid out, upon some deal in wheat or corner in aluminium, the essence of which was little better than highway robbery, treasures of conscientiousness and self-denial.

Unluckily, I never cared a cent for anything but art, and never shall. My idea of man's chief end was to enrich the world with things of beauty, and have a fairly good time myself while doing so. I do not think I mentioned that second part, which is the only one I have managed to carry out; but my father must have suspected the suppression, for he branded the whole affair as self-indulgence.

'Well,' I remember crying once, 'and what is your life? You are only trying to get money, and to get it from other people at that.'

He sighed bitterly (which was very much his habit), and shook his poor head at me.

'Ah, Loudon, Loudon!' said he, 'you boys think yourselves very smart. But, struggle as you please, a man has to work in this world. He must be an honest man or a thief, Loudon.'

You can see for yourself how vain it was to argue with my father. The despair that seized upon me after such an interview was, besides, embittered by remorse; for I was at times petulant, but he invariably gentle; and I was fighting, after all, for my own liberty and pleasure, he singly for what he thought to be my good. And all the time he never despaired. 'There is good stuff in you, Loudon,' he would say; 'there is the right stuff in you. Blood will tell, and you will come right in time. I am not afraid my boy will ever disgrace me; I am only vexed he should sometimes talk nonsense.' And then he would pat my shoulder or my hand with a kind of motherly way he had, very affecting in a man so strong and beautiful.

As soon as I had graduated from the high school, he packed me off to the Muskegon Commercial Academy. You are a foreigner, and you will have a difficulty in accepting the reality of this seat of education. I assure you before I begin that I am wholly serious. The place really existed, possibly exists today: we were proud of it in the State, as something exceptionally nineteenth century and civilised; and my father, when he saw me to the cars, no doubt considered he was putting me in a straight line for the Presidency and the New Jerusalem.

'Loudon,' said he, 'I am now giving you a chance that Julius Cæsar could not have given to his son – a chance to see life as it is, before your own turn comes to start in earnest. Avoid rash speculation, try to behave like a gentleman; and if you will take my advice, confine yourself to a safe, conservative business in railroads. Breadstuffs are tempting, but very dangerous; I would not try breadstuffs at your time of life; but you may feel your way a little in other commodities. Take a pride to keep your books posted, and never throw good money after bad. There, my dear boy, kiss me good-bye; and never forget that you are an only chick, and that your dad watches your career with fond suspense.'

The commercial college was a fine, roomy establishment, pleasantly situate among woods. The air was healthy, the food excellent, the premium high. Electric wires connected it (to use the words of the prospectus) with 'the various world centres.' The reading-room was well supplied with 'commercial organs.' The talk was that of Wall Street; and the pupils (from fifty to a hundred lads) were principally engaged in rooking or trying to rook one another for nominal sums in what was called 'college paper.' We had class hours, indeed, in the morning, when we studied German, French, book-keeping, and the like goodly matters; but the bulk of our day and the gist of the education centred in the exchange, where we were taught to gamble in produce and securities. Since not one of the participants possessed a bushel of wheat or a dollar's worth of stock, legitimate business was of course impossible from the beginning. It was cold-drawn gambling, without colour or disguise. Just that which is the impediment and destruction of all genuine commercial enterprise, just that we were taught with every luxury of stage effect. Our simulacrum of a market was ruled by the real markets outside, so that we might experience the course and vicissitude of prices. We must keep books, and our ledgers were overhauled at the month's end by the principal or his assistants. To add a spice of verisimilitude, 'college paper' (like poker chips) had an actual marketable value. It was bought for each pupil by anxious parents and guardians at the rate of one cent for the dollar. The same pupil, when his education was complete, resold, at the same figure, so much as was left him to the college; and even in the midst of his curriculum, a successful operator would sometimes realise a proportion of his holding, and stand a supper on the sly in the neighbouring hamlet. In short, if there was ever a worse education, it must have been in that academy where Oliver met Charlie Bates.

When I was first guided into the exchange to have my desk pointed out by one of the assistant teachers, I was overwhelmed by the clamour and confusion. Certain blackboards at the other end of the building were covered with figures continually replaced. As each new set appeared, the pupils swayed to and fro, and roared out aloud with a formidable and to me quite meaningless vociferation; leaping at the same time upon the desks and benches, signalling with arms and heads, and scribbling briskly in note books. I thought I had never beheld a scene more disagreeable; and when I considered that the whole traffic was illusory, and all the money then upon the market would scarce have sufficed to buy a pair of skates, I was at first astonished, although not for long. Indeed, I had no sooner called to mind how grown-up men and women of considerable estate will lose their temper about halfpenny points, than (making an immediate allowance for my fellow-students) I transferred the whole of my astonishment to the assistant teacher, who – poor gentleman – had quite forgot to show me to my desk, and stood in the midst of this hurly-burly, absorbed and seemingly transported.

'Look, look,' he shouted in my ear; 'a falling market! The bears have had it all their own way since yesterday.'

'It can't matter,' I replied, making him hear with difficulty, for I was unused to speak in such a babel, 'since it is all fun.'

'True,' said he; 'and you must always bear in mind that the real profit is in the book-keeping. I trust, Dodd, to be able to congratulate you upon your books. You are to start in with ten thousand dollars of college paper, a very liberal figure, which should see you through the whole curriculum, if you keep to a safe, conservative business. . . . Why, what's that?' he broke off, once more attracted by the changing figures on the board. 'Seven, four, three! Dodd, you are in luck: this is the most spirited rally we have had this term. And to think that the same scene is now transpiring in New York, Chicago, St. Louis, and rival business centres! For two cents, I would try a flutter with the boys myself,' he cried, rubbing his hands; 'only it's against the regulations.'

'What would you do, sir?' I asked.

'Do?' he cried with glittering eyes. 'Buy for all I was worth!'

'Would that be a safe, conservative business?' I inquired, as innocent as a lamb.

He looked daggers at me. 'See that sandy-haired man in glasses?' he asked, as if to change the subject. 'That's Billson, our most prominent undergraduate. We build confidently on Billson's future. You could not do better, Dodd, than follow Billson.'

Presently after, in the midst of a still growing tumult, the figures coming and going more busily than ever on the board, and the hall resounding like Pandemonium with the howls of operators, the assistant teacher left me to my own resources at my desk. The next boy was posting up his ledger, figuring his morning's loss, as I discovered later on; and from this ungenial task he was readily diverted by the sight of a new face.

'Say, Freshman,' he said, 'what's your name? What? Son of Big Head Dodd? What's your figure? Ten thousand? O, you're away up! What a soft-headed clam you must be to touch your books!'

I asked him what else I could do, since the books were to be examined once a month.

'Why, you galoot, you get a clerk!' cries he. 'One of our dead beats – that's all they're here for. If you're a successful operator, you need never do a stroke of work in this old college.'

The noise had now become deafening; and my new friend, telling me that some one had certainly 'gone down,' that he must know the news, and that he would bring me a clerk when he returned, buttoned his coat and plunged into the tossing throng. It proved that he was right: some one had gone down; a prince had fallen in Israel; the corner in lard had proved fatal to the mighty; and the clerk who was brought back to keep my books, spare me all work, and get all my share of the education, at a thousand dollars a month, college paper (ten dollars, United States currency) was no other than the prominent Billson whom I could do not better than follow. The poor lad was very unhappy. It's the only good thing I have to say for Muskegon Commercial College, that we were all, even the small fry, deeply mortified to be posted as defaulters; and the collapse of a merchant prince like Billson, who had ridden pretty high in his days of prosperity, was, of course, particularly hard to bear. But the spirit of make-believe conquered even the bitterness of recent shame; and my clerk took his orders, and fell to his new duties, with decorum and civility.

Such were my first impressions in this absurd place of education; and, to be frank, they were far from disagreeable. As long as I was rich, my evenings and afternoons would be my own; the clerk must keep my books, the clerk could do the jostling and bawling in the exchange; and I could turn my mind to landscape-painting and Balzac's novels, which were then my two preoccupations. To remain rich, then, became my problem; or, in other words, to do a safe, conservative line of business. I am looking for that line still; and I believe the nearest thing to it in this imperfect world is the sort of speculation sometimes insidiously proposed to childhood, in the formula, 'Heads I win; tails you lose.' Mindful of my father's parting words, I turned my attention timidly to railroads; and for a month or so maintained a position of inglorious security, dealing for small amounts in the most inert stocks, and bearing (as best I could) the scorn of my hired clerk. One day I had ventured a little further by way of experiment; and, in the sure expectation they would continue to go down, sold several thousand dollars of Pan-Handle Preference (I think it was). I had no sooner made this venture than some fools in New York began to bull the market; Pan-Handles rose like a balloon; and in the inside of half an hour I saw my position compromised. Blood will tell, as my father said; and I stuck to it gallantly: all afternoon I continued selling that infernal stock, all afternoon it continued skying. I suppose I had come (a frail cockle-shell) athwart the hawse of Jay Gould; and, indeed, I think I remember that this vagary in the market proved subsequently to be the first move in a considerable deal. That evening, at least, the name of H. Loudon Dodd held the first rank in our collegiate gazette, and I and Billson (once more thrown upon the world) were competing for the same clerkship. The present object takes the present eye. My disaster, for the moment, was the more conspicuous; and it was I that got the situation. So, you see, even in Muskegon Commercial College, there were lessons to be learned.

For my own part, I cared very little whether I lost or won at a game so random, so complex, and so dull; but it was sorry news to write to my poor father, and I employed all the resources of my eloquence. I told him (what was the truth) that the successful boys had none of the education; so that if he wished me to learn, he should rejoice at my misfortune. I went on (not very consistently) to beg him to set me up again, when I would solemnly promise to do a safe business in reliable railroads. Lastly (becoming somewhat carried away), I assured him I was totally unfit for business, and implored him to take me away from this abominable place, and let me go to Paris to study art. He answered briefly, gently, and sadly, telling me the vacation was near at hand, when we would talk things over.

When the time came, he met me at the depôt, and I was shocked to see him looking older. He seemed to have no thought but to console me and restore (what he supposed I had lost) my courage. I must not be down-hearted; many of the best men had made a failure in the beginning. I told him I had no head for business, and his kind face darkened. 'You must not say that, Loudon,' he replied; 'I will never believe my son to be a coward.'

'But I don't like it,' I pleaded. 'It hasn't got any interest for me, and art has. I know I could do more in art,' and I reminded him that a successful painter gains large sums; that a picture of Meissonier's would sell for many thousand dollars.

'And do you think, Loudon,' he replied, 'that a man who can paint a thousand-dollar picture has not grit enough to keep his end up in the stock market? No, sir; this Mason (of whom you speak) or our own American Bierstadt – if you were to put them down in a wheat-pit tomorrow, they would show their mettle. Come, Loudon, my dear; heaven knows I have no thought but your own good, and I will offer you a bargain. I start you again next term with ten thousand dollars; show yourself a man, and double it, and then (if you still wish to go to Paris, which I know you won't) I'll let you go. But to let you run away as if you were whipped, is what I am too proud to do.'

My heart leaped at this proposal, and then sank again. It seemed easier to paint a Meissonier on the spot than to win ten thousand dollars on that mimic stock exchange. Nor could I help reflecting on the singularity of such a test for a man's capacity to be a painter. I ventured even to comment on this.

He sighed deeply. 'You forget, my dear,' said he, 'I'm a judge of the one, and not of the other. You might have the genius of Bierstadt himself, and I would be none the wiser.'

'And then,' I continued, 'it's scarcely fair. The other boys are helped by their people, who telegraph and give them pointers. There's Jim Costello, who never budges without a word from his father in New York. And then, don't you see, if anybody is to win, somebody must lose?'

'I'll keep you posted,' cried my father, with unusual animation; 'I did not know it was allowed. I'll wire you in the office cipher, and we'll make it a kind of partnership business, Loudon – Dodd and Son, eh?' and he patted my shoulder and repeated, 'Dodd and Son, Dodd and Son,' with the kindliest amusement.

If my father was to give me pointers, and the commercial college was to be a stepping-stone to Paris, I could look my future in the face. The old boy, too, was so pleased at the idea of our association in this foolery that he immediately plucked up spirit. Thus it befell that those who had met at the depôt like a pair of mutes, sat down to table with holiday faces.

And now I have to introduce a new character that never said a word nor wagged a finger, and yet shaped my whole subsequent career. You have crossed the States, so that in all likelihood you have seen the head of it, parcel-gilt and curiously fluted, rising among trees from a wide plain; for this new character was no other than the State capitol of Muskegon, then first projected. My father had embraced the idea with a mixture of patriotism and commercial greed, both perfectly genuine. He was on all the committees, he had subscribed a great deal of money, and he was making arrangements to have a finger in most of the contracts. Competitive plans had been sent in; at the time of my return from college my father was deep in their consideration; and as the idea entirely occupied his mind, the first evening did not pass away before he had called me into council. Here was a subject at last into which I could throw myself with pleasurable zeal. Architecture was new to me, indeed; but it was at least an art; and for all the arts I had a taste naturally classical, and that capacity to take delighted pains which some famous idiot has supposed to be synonymous with genius. I threw myself headlong into my father's work, acquainted myself with all the plans, their merits and defects, read besides in special books, made myself a master of the theory of strains, studied the current prices of materials, and (in one word) 'devilled' the whole business so thoroughly, that when the plans came up for consideration, Big Head Dodd was supposed to have earned fresh laurels. His arguments carried the day, his choice was approved by the committee, and I had the anonymous satisfaction to know that arguments and choice were wholly mine. In the re-casting of the plan which followed, my part was even larger; for I designed and cast with my own hand a hot-air grating for the offices, which had the luck or merit to be accepted. The energy and aptitude which I displayed throughout delighted and surprised my father, and I believe, although I say it, whose tongue should be tied, that they alone prevented Muskegon capitol from being the eyesore of my native State.

Altogether, I was in a cheery frame of mind when I returned to the commercial college; and my earlier operations were crowned with a full measure of success. My father wrote and wired to me continually. 'You are to exercise your own judgment, Loudon,' he would say. 'All that I do is to give you the figures; but whatever operation you take up must be upon your own responsibility, and whatever you earn will be entirely due to your own dash and forethought.' For all that, it was always clear what he intended me to do, and I was always careful to do it. Inside of a month I was at the head of seventeen or eighteen thousand dollars, college paper. And here I fell a victim to one of the vices of the system. The paper (I have already explained) had a real value of one per cent.; and cost, and could be sold for, currency. Unsuccessful speculators were thus always selling clothes, books, banjos, and sleeve-links, in order to pay their differences; the successful, on the other hand, were often tempted to realise, and enjoy some return upon their profits. Now I wanted thirty dollars' worth of artist-truck, for I was always sketching in the woods; my allowance was for the time exhausted; I had begun to regard the exchange (with my father's help) as a place where money was to be got for stooping; and in an evil hour I realised three thousand dollars of the college paper and bought my easel.

It was a Wednesday morning when the things arrived, and set me in the seventh heaven of satisfaction. My father (for I can scarcely say myself) was trying at this time a 'straddle' in wheat between Chicago and New York; the operation so called is, as you know, one of the most tempting and least safe upon the chess-board of finance. On the Thursday, luck began to turn against my father's calculations; and by the Friday evening I was posted on the boards as a defaulter for the second time. Here was a rude blow: my father would have taken it ill enough in any case; for however much a man may resent the incapacity of an only son, he will feel his own more sensibly. But it chanced that, in our bitter cup of failure, there was one ingredient that might truly be called poisonous. He had been keeping the run of my position; he missed the three thousand dollars, paper; and in his view, I had stolen thirty dollars, currency. It was an extreme view perhaps; but in some senses, it was just; and my father, although (to my judgment) quite reckless of honesty in the essence of his operations, was the soul of honour as to their details. I had one grieved letter from him, dignified and tender; and during the rest of that wretched term, working as a clerk, selling my clothes and sketches to make futile speculations, my dream of Paris quite vanished. I was cheered by no word of kindness and helped by no hint of counsel from my father.

All the time he was no doubt thinking of little else but his son, and what to do with him. I believe he had been really appalled by what he regarded as my laxity of principle, and began to think it might be well to preserve me from temptation; the architect of the capitol had, besides, spoken obligingly of my design; and while he was thus hanging between two minds, Fortune suddenly stepped in, and Muskegon State capitol reversed my destiny.

'Loudon,' said my father, as he met me at the depôt, with a smiling countenance, 'if you were to go to Paris, how long would it take you to become an experienced sculptor?'

'How do you mean, father?' I cried, – 'experienced?'

'A man that could be entrusted with the highest styles,' he answered; 'the nude, for instance; and the patriotic and emblematical styles.'

'It might take three years,' I replied.

'You think Paris necessary?' he asked. 'There are great advantages in our own country; and that man Prodgers appears to be a very clever sculptor, though I suppose he stands too high to go around giving lessons.'

'Paris is the only place,' I assured him.

'Well, I think myself it will sound better,' he admitted. 'A Young Man, a Native of this State, Son of a Leading Citizen, Studies Prosecuted under the Most Experienced Masters in Paris,' he added, relishingly.

'But, my dear dad, what is it all about?' I interrupted. 'I never even dreamed of being a sculptor.'

'Well, here it is,' said he. 'I took up the statuary contract on our new capitol; I took it up at first as a deal; and then it occurred to me it would be better to keep it in the family. It meets your idea; there's considerable money in the thing; and it's patriotic. So, if you say the word, you shall go to Paris, and come back in three years to decorate the capitol of your native State. It's a big chance for you, Loudon; and I'll tell you what – every dollar you earn, I'll put another alongside of it. But the sooner you go, and the harder you work, the better; for if the first half-dozen statues aren't in a line with public taste in Muskegon, there will be trouble.'

CHAPTER TWO

Roussillon Wine

My mother's family was Scotch, and it was judged fitting I should pay a visit, on my way Paris-ward, to my uncle Adam Loudon, a wealthy retired grocer of Edinburgh. He was very stiff and very ironical; he fed me well, lodged me sumptuously, and seemed to take it out of me all the time, cent. per cent., in secret entertainment which caused his spectacles to glitter and his mouth to twitch. The ground of this ill-suppressed mirth (as well as I could make out) was simply the fact that I was an American. 'Well,' he would say, drawing out the word to infinity, 'and I suppose now in your country things will be so and so.' And the whole group of my cousins would titter joyously. Repeated receptions of this sort must be at the root, I suppose, of what they call the Great American Jest; and I know I was myself goaded into saying that my friends went naked in the summer months, and that the Second Methodist Episcopal Church in Muskegon was decorated with scalps. I cannot say that these flights had any great success; they seemed to awaken little more surprise than the fact that my father was a Republican, or that I had been taught in school to spell *colour* without the *u*. If I had told them (what was, after all, the truth) that my father had paid a considerable annual sum to have me brought up in a gambling hell, the tittering and grinning of this dreadful family might perhaps have been excused.

I cannot deny but I was sometimes tempted to knock my Uncle Adam down; and indeed I believe it must have come to a rupture at last, if they had not given a dinner party at which I was the lion. On this occasion I learned (to my surprise and relief) that the incivility to which I had been subjected was a matter for the family circle, and might be regarded almost in the light of an endearment. To strangers I was presented with consideration; and the account given of 'my American brother-in-law, poor Janie's man, James K. Dodd, the well-known millionaire of Muskegon,' was calculated to enlarge the heart of a proud son.

An aged assistant of my grandfather's, a pleasant, humble creature with a taste for whiskey, was at first deputed to be my guide about the city. With this harmless but hardly aristocratic companion I went to Arthur's Seat and the Calton Hill, heard the band play in the Princes Street Gardens, inspected the regalia and the blood of Rizzio, and fell in love with the great castle on its cliff, the innumerable spires of churches, the stately buildings, the broad prospects, and those narrow and crowded lanes of the old town where my ancestors had lived and died in the days before Columbus.

But there was another curiosity that interested me more deeply – my grandfather, Alexander Loudon. In his time the old gentleman had been a working mason, and had risen from the ranks – more, I think, by shrewdness than by merit. In his appearance, speech, and manners he bore broad marks of his origin, which were gall and wormwood to my Uncle Adam. His nails, in spite of anxious supervision, were often in conspicuous mourning; his clothes hung about him in bags and wrinkles, like a ploughman's Sunday coat; his accent was rude, broad, and dragging. Take him at his best, and even when he could be induced to hold his tongue, his mere presence in a corner of the drawing-room, with his open-air wrinkles, his scanty hair, his battered hands, and the cheerful craftiness of his expression, advertised the whole gang of us for a self-made family. My aunt might mince and my cousins bridle, but there was no getting over the solid, physical fact of the stonemason in the chimney-corner.

That is one advantage of being an American. It never occurred to me to be ashamed of my grandfather, and the old gentleman was quick to mark the difference. He held my mother in tender memory, perhaps because he was in the habit of daily contrasting her with Uncle Adam, whom he detested to the point of frenzy; and he set down to inheritance from his favourite my own becoming treatment of himself. On our walks abroad, which soon became daily, he would sometimes (after duly warning me to keep the matter dark from 'Aadam') skulk into some old familiar pot-house, and there (if had the luck to encounter any of his veteran cronies) he would present me to the company with manifest pride, casting at the same time a covert slur on the rest of his descendants. 'This is my Jeannie's yin,' he would say. 'He's a fine fallow, him.' The purpose of our excursions was not to seek antiquities or to enjoy famous prospects, but to visit one after another a series of doleful suburbs, for which it was the old gentleman's chief claim to renown that he had been the sole contractor, and too often the architect besides. I have rarely seen a more shocking exhibition: the brick seemed to be blushing in the walls, and the slates on the roof to have turned pale with shame; but I was careful not to communicate these impressions to the aged artificer at my side; and when he would direct my attention to some fresh monstrosity – perhaps with the comment, 'There's an idee of mine's; it's cheap and tasty, and had a graand run; the idee was soon stole, and there's whole deestricts near Glesgie with the goathic adeetion and that plunth,' I would civilly make haste to admire and (what I found particularly delighted him) to inquire into the cost of each adornment. It will be conceived that Muskegon capitol was a frequent and a welcome ground of talk. I drew him all the plans from memory; and he, with the aid of a narrow volume full of figures and tables, which answered (I believe) to the name of Molesworth, and was his constant pocket companion, would draw up rough estimates and make imaginary offers on the various contracts. Our Muskegon builders he pronounced a pack of cormorants; and the congenial subject, together with my knowledge of architectural terms, the theory of strains, and the prices of materials in the States, formed a strong bond of union between what might have been otherwise an ill-assorted pair, and led my grandfather to pronounce me, with emphasis, 'a real intalligent kind of a cheild.' Thus a second time, as you will presently see, the capitol of my native State had influentially affected the current of my life.

I left Edinburgh, however, with not the least idea that I had done a stroke of excellent business for myself, and singly delighted to escape out of a somewhat dreary house and plunge instead into the rainbow city of Paris. Every man has his own romance; mine clustered exclusively about the practice of the arts, the life of Latin Quarter students, and the world of Paris as depicted by that grimy wizard, the author of the *Comédie Humaine*. I was not disappointed – I could not have been; for I did not see the facts, I brought them with me ready-made. Z. Marcas lived next door to me in my ungainly, ill-smelling hotel on the Rue Racine; I dined at my villainous restaurant with Lousteau and with Rastignac: if a curricle nearly ran me down at a street-crossing, Maxime de Trailles would be the driver. I dined, I say, at a poor restaurant and lived in a poor hotel; and this was not from need, but sentiment. My father gave me a profuse allowance, and I might have lived (had I chosen) in the Quartier de l'Étoile and driven to my studies daily. Had I done so, the glamour must have fled: I should still have been but Loudon Dodd; whereas now I was a Latin Quarter student, Murger's successor, living in flesh and blood the life of one of those romances I had loved to read, to re-read, and to dream over, among the woods of Muskegon.

At this time we were all a little Murger-mad in the Latin Quarter. The play of the *Vie de Bohème* (a dreary, snivelling piece) had been produced at the Odéon, had run an unconscionable time – for Paris – and revived the freshness of the legend. The same business, you may say, or there and thereabout, was being privately enacted in consequence in every garret of the neighbourhood, and a good third of the students were consciously impersonating Rodolphe or Schaunard, to their own incommunicable satisfaction. Some of us went far, and some farther. I always looked with awful envy (for instance) on a certain countryman of my own who had a studio in the Rue Monsieur le Prince, wore boots, and long hair in a net, and could be seen tramping off, in this guise, to the worst eating-house of the quarter, followed by a Corsican model, his mistress, in the conspicuous costume of her race and calling. It takes some greatness of soul to carry even folly to such heights as these; and for my own part, I had to content myself by pretending very arduously to be poor, by wearing a smoking-cap on the streets, and by pursuing, through a series of misadventures, that extinct mammal the grisette. The most grievous part was the eating and the drinking. I was born with a dainty tooth and a palate for wine; and only a genuine devotion to romance could have supported me under the cat-civets that I had to swallow, and the red ink of Bercy I must wash them down withal. Every now and again, after a hard day at the studio, where I was steadily and far from unsuccessfully industrious, a wave of distaste would overbear me; I would slink away from my haunts and companions, indemnify myself for weeks of self-denial with fine wines and dainty dishes; seated perhaps on a terrace, perhaps in an arbour in a garden, with a volume of one of my favourite authors propped open in front of me, and now consulted awhile, and now forgotten: so remain, relishing my situation, till night fell and the lights of the city kindled; and thence stroll homeward by the riverside, under the moon or stars, in a heaven of poetry and digestion.

One such indulgence led me in the course of my second year into an adventure which I must relate: indeed, it is the very point I have been aiming for, since that was what brought me in acquaintance with Jim Pinkerton. I sat down alone to dinner one October day when the rusty leaves were falling and scuttling on the boulevard, and the minds of impressionable men inclined in about an equal degree towards sadness and conviviality. The restaurant was no great place, but boasted a considerable cellar and a long printed list of vintages. This I was perusing with the double zest of a man who is fond of wine and a lover of beautiful names, when my eye fell (near the end of the card) on that not very famous or familiar brand, Roussillon. I remembered it was a wine I had never tasted, ordered a bottle, found it excellent, and when I had discussed the contents, called (according to my habit) for a final pint. It appears they did not keep Roussillon in half-bottles. 'All right,' said I, 'another bottle.' The tables at this eating-house are close together; and the next thing I can remember, I was in somewhat loud conversation with my nearest neighbours. From these I must have gradually extended my attentions; for I have a clear recollection of gazing about a room in which every chair was half turned round and every face turned smilingly to mine. I can even remember what I was saying at the moment; but after twenty years the embers of shame are still alive, and I prefer to give your imagination the cue by simply mentioning that my

muse was the patriotic. It had been my design to adjourn
for coffee in the company of some of these new friends;
but I was no sooner on the sidewalk than I found myself
unaccountably alone. The circumstance scarce surprised
me at the time, much less now; but I was somewhat
chagrined a little after to find I had walked into a kiosque.
I began to wonder if I were any the worse for my last bottle,
and decided to steady myself with coffee and brandy. In
the Café de la Source, where I went for this restorative,
the fountain was playing, and (what greatly surprised me)
the mill and the various mechanical figures on the rockery
appeared to have been freshly repaired and performed the
most enchanting antics. The café was extraordinarily hot
and bright, with every detail of a conspicuous clearness –
from the faces of the guests, to the type of the newspapers
on the tables – and the whole apartment swang to and fro
like a hammock, with an exhilarating motion. For some
while I was so extremely pleased with these particulars that
I thought I could never be weary of beholding them: then
dropped of a sudden into a causeless sadness; and then,
with the same swiftness and spontaneity, arrived at the
conclusion that I was drunk and had better get to bed.

It was but a step or two to my hotel, where I got my lighted
candle from the porter, and mounted the four flights to my
own room. Although I could not deny that I was drunk, I
was at the same time lucidly rational and practical. I had but
one preoccupation – to be up in time on the morrow for my
work; and when I observed the clock on my chimney-piece
to have stopped, I decided to go downstairs again and give
directions to the porter. Leaving the candle burning and
my door open, to be a guide to me on my return, I set forth
accordingly. The house was quite dark; but as there were
only the three doors on each landing, it was impossible to
wander, and I had nothing to do but descend the stairs
until I saw the glimmer of the porter's night-light. I counted
four flights: no porter. It was possible, of course, that I had
reckoned incorrectly; so I went down another and another,
and another, still counting as I went, until I had reached
the preposterous figure of nine flights. It was now quite
clear that I had somehow passed the porter's lodge without
remarking it; indeed, I was, at the lowest figure, five pairs
of stairs below the street, and plunged in the very bowels

of the earth. That my hotel should thus be founded upon catacombs was a discovery of considerable interest; and if I had not been in a frame of mine entirely businesslike, I might have continued to explore all night this subterranean empire. But I was bound I must be up betimes on the next morning, and for that end it was imperative that I should find the porter. I faced about accordingly, and counting with painful care, remounted towards the level of the street. Five, six, and seven flights I climbed, and still there was no porter. I began to be weary of the job, and reflecting that I was now close to my own room, decided I should go to bed. Eight, nine, ten, eleven, twelve, thirteen flights I mounted; and my open door seemed to be as wholly lost to me as the porter and his floating dip. I remembered that the house stood but six stories at its highest point, from which it appeared (on the most moderate computation) I was now three stories higher than the roof. My original sense of amusement was succeeded by a not unnatural irritation. 'My room has just *got* to be here,' said I, and I stepped towards the door with outspread arms. There was no door and no wall; in place of either there yawned before me a dark corridor, in which I continued to advance for some time without encountering the smallest opposition. And this in a house whose extreme area scantily contained three small rooms, a narrow landing; and the stair! The thing was manifestly nonsense; and you will scarcely be surprised to learn that I now began to lose my temper. At this juncture I perceived a filtering of light along the floor, stretched forth my hand, which encountered the knob of a door-handle, and without further ceremony entered a room. A young lady was within: she was going to bed, and her toilet was far advanced – or the other way about, if you prefer.

'I hope you will pardon this intrusion,' said I; 'but my room is No. 12, and something has gone wrong with this blamed house.'

She looked at me a moment; and then, 'If you will step outside for a moment, I will take you there,' says she.

Thus, with perfect composure on both sides, the matter was arranged. I waited awhile outside her door. Presently she rejoined me, in a dressing-gown, took my hand, led me up another flight, which made the fourth above the level of the roof, and shut me into my own room, where (being quite weary after these contraordinary explorations) I turned in, and slumbered like a child.

I tell you the thing calmly, as it appeared to me to pass; but the next day, when I awoke and put memory in the witness-box, I could not conceal from myself that the tale presented a good many improbable features. I had no mind for the studio, after all, and went instead to the Luxembourg gardens, there, among the sparrows and the statues and the falling leaves, to cool and clear my head. It is a garden I have always loved. You sit there in a public place of history and fiction. Barras and Fouché have looked from these windows. Lousteau and De Banville (one as real as the other) have rhymed upon these benches. The city tramples by without the railings to a lively measure; and within and about you, trees rustle, children and sparrows utter their small cries, and the statues look on for ever. Here, then, in a seat opposite the gallery entrance, I set to work on the events of the last night, to disengage (if it were possible) truth from fiction.

The house, by daylight, had proved to be six stories high, the same as ever. I could find, with all my architectural experience, no room in its altitude for those interminable stairways, no width between its walls for that long corridor, where I had tramped at night. And there was yet a greater difficulty. I had read somewhere an aphorism that everything may be false to itself save human nature. A house might elongate or enlarge itself – or seem to do so to a gentleman who had been dining. The ocean might dry up, the rocks melt in the sun, the stars fall from heaven like autumn apples; and there was nothing in these incidents to boggle the philosopher. But the case of the young lady stood upon a different foundation. Girls were not good enough, or not good that way, or else they were too good. I was ready to accept any of these views: all pointed to the same conclusion, which I was thus already on the point of reaching, when a fresh argument occurred, and instantly confirmed it. I could remember the exact words we had each said; and I had spoken, and she had replied, in English. Plainly, then, the whole affair was an illusion: catacombs, and stairs, and charitable lady, all were equally the stuff of dreams.

I had just come to this determination, when there blew a flaw of wind through the autumnal gardens; the dead leaves showered down, and a flight of sparrows, thick as a snowfall, wheeled above my head with sudden pipings. This agreeable bustle was the affair of a moment, but it startled me from the abstraction into which I had fallen like a summons. I sat briskly up, and as I did so my eyes rested on the figure of a lady in a brown jacket and carrying a paint-box. By her side walked a fellow some years older than myself, with an easel under his arm; and alike by their course and cargo I might judge they were bound for the gallery, where the lady was, doubtless, engaged upon some copying. You can imagine my surprise when I recognised in her the heroine of my adventure. To put the matter beyond question our eyes met, and she, seeing herself remembered, and recalling the trim in which I had last beheld her, looked swiftly on the ground with just a shadow of confusion.

I could not tell you today if she were plain or pretty; but she had behaved with so much good sense, and I had cut so poor a figure in her presence, that I became instantly fired with the desire to display myself in a more favourable light. The young man, besides, was possibly her brother; brothers are apt to be hasty, theirs being a part in which it is possible, at a comparatively early age, to assume the dignity of manhood; and it occurred to me it might be wise to forestall all possible complications by an apology.

On this reasoning I drew near to the gallery door, and had hardly got in position before the young man came out. Thus it was that I came face to face with my third destiny, for my career has been entirely shaped by these three elements – my father, the capitol of Muskegon, and my friend Jim Pinkerton. As for the young lady, with whom my mind was at the moment chiefly occupied, I was never to hear more of her from that day forward – an excellent example of the Blind Man's Buff that we call life.

CHAPTER THREE

To Introduce Mr Pinkerton

The stranger, I have said, was some years older than myself: a man of a good stature, a very lively face, cordial, agitated manners, and a grey eye as active as a fowl's.

'May I have a word with you?' said I.

'My dear sir,' he replied, 'I don't know what it can be about, but you may have a hundred if you like.'

'You have just left the side of a young lady,' I continued, 'towards whom I was led (very unintentionally) into the appearance of an offence. To speak to herself would be only to renew her embarrassment, and I seize the occasion of making my apology, and declaring my respect, to one of my own sex who is her friend, and perhaps,' I added, with a bow, 'her natural protector.'

'You are a countryman of mine; I know it!' he cried: 'I am sure of it by your delicacy to a lady. You do her no more than justice. I was introduced to her the other night at tea, in the apartment of some people, friends of mine; and meeting her again this morning, I could not do less than carry her easel for her. My dear sir, what is your name?'

I was disappointed to find he had so little bond with my young lady; and but that it was I who had sought the acquaintance, might have been tempted to retreat. At the same time something in the stranger's eye engaged me.

'My name,' said I, 'is Loudon Dodd; I am a student of sculpture here from Muskegon.'

'Of sculpture?' he cried, as though that would have been his last conjecture. 'Mine is James Pinkerton; I am delighted to have the pleasure of your acquaintance.'

'Pinkerton!' it was now my turn to exclaim. 'Are you Broken-Stool Pinkerton?'

He admitted his identity with a laugh of boyish delight;

35

and indeed any young man in the quarter might have been proud to own a sobriquet thus gallantly acquired.

In order to explain the name, I must here digress into a chapter of the history of manners in the nineteenth century, very well worth commemoration for its own sake. In some of the studios at that date, the hazing of new pupils was both barbarous and obscene. Two incidents, following one on the heels of the other, tended to produce an advance in civilisation by the means (as so commonly happens) of a passing appeal to savage standards. The first was the arrival of a little gentleman from Armenia. He had a fez upon his head and (what nobody counted on) a dagger in his pocket. The hazing was set about in the customary style, and, perhaps in virtue of the victim's head-gear, even more boisterously than usual. He bore it at first with an inviting patience; but upon one of the students proceeding to an unpardonable freedom, plucked out his knife and suddenly plunged it in the belly of the jester. This gentleman, I am pleased to say, passed months upon a bed of sickness before he was in a position to resume his studies. The second incident was that which had earned Pinkerton his reputation. In a crowded studio, while some very filthy brutalities were being practised on a trembling débutant, a tall pale fellow sprang from his stool and (without the smallest preface or explanation) sang out, 'All English and Americans to clear the shop!' Our race is brutal, but not filthy; and the summons was nobly responded to. Every Anglo-Saxon student seized his stool; in a moment the studio was full of bloody coxcombs, the French fleeing in disorder for the door, the victim liberated and amazed. In this feat of arms, both English-speaking nations covered themselves with glory; but I am proud to claim the author of the whole for an American, and a patriotic American at that, being the same gentleman who had subsequently to be held down in the bottom of a box during a performance of *L'Oncle Sam*, sobbing at intervals, 'My country, O my country!' while yet another (my new acquaintance, Pinkerton) was supposed to have made the most conspicuous figure in the actual battle. At one blow he had broken his own stool, and sent the largest of his opponents back foremost through what we used to call a 'conscientious nude.' It appears that, in the continuation of his flight, this fallen warrior issued on the boulevard still framed in the burst canvas.

It will be understood how much talk the incident aroused in the students' quarter, and that I was highly gratified to make the acquaintance of my famous countryman. It chanced I was to see more of the Quixotic side of his character before the morning was done; for, as we continued to stroll together, I found myself near the studio of a young Frenchman whose work I had promised to examine, and in the fashion of the quarter carried up Pinkerton along with me. Some of my comrades of this date were pretty obnoxious fellows. I could almost always admire and respect the grown-up practitioners of art in Paris; but many of those who were still in a state of pupilage were sorry specimens – so much so that I used often to wonder where the painters came from, and where the brutes of students went to. A similar mystery hangs over the intermediate stages of the medical profession, and must have perplexed the least observant. The ruffian, at least, whom I now carried Pinkerton to visit, was one of the most crapulous in the quarter. He turned out for our delectation a huge 'crust' (as we used to call it) of St Stephen, wallowing in red upon his belly in an exhausted receiver, and a crowd of Hebrews in blue, green, and yellow, pelting him – apparently with buns; and while we gazed upon this contrivance, regaled us with a piece of his own recent biography, of which his mind was still very full, and which he seemed to fancy represented him in an heroic posture. I was one of those cosmopolitan Americans who accept the world (whether at home or abroad) as they find it, and whose favourite part is that of the spectator; yet even I was listening with ill-suppressed disgust, when I was aware of a violent plucking at my sleeve.

'Is he saying he kicked her downstairs?' asked Pinkerton, white as St Stephen.

'Yes,' said I: 'his discarded mistress; and then he pelted her with stones. I suppose that's what gave him the idea for his picture. He has just been alleging the pathetic excuse that she was old enough to be his mother.'

Something like a sob broke from Pinkerton. 'Tell him,' he gasped – 'I can't speak this language, though I understand a little; I never had any proper education – tell him I'm going to punch his head.'

'For God's sake do nothing of the sort!' I cried; 'they don't understand that sort of thing here;' and I tried to bundle him out.

'Tell him first what we think of him,' he objected. 'Let me tell him what he looks in the eyes of a pure-minded American.'

'Leave that to me,' said I, thrusting Pinkerton clear through the door.

'*Qu'est-ce qu'il a?*'[1] inquired the student.

'*Monsieur se sent mal au coeur d'avoir trop regardé votre croute,*'[2] said I, and made my escape, scarce with dignity, at Pinkerton's heels.

'What did you say to him?' he asked.

'The only thing that he could feel,' was my reply.

After this scene, the freedom with which I had ejected my new acquaintance, and the precipitation with which I had followed him, the least I could do was to propose luncheon. I have forgot the name of the place to which I led him, nothing loath; it was on the far side of the Luxembourg at least, with a garden behind, where we were speedily set face to face at table, and began to dig into each other's history and character, like terriers after rabbits, according to the approved fashion of youth.

Pinkerton's parents were from the Old Country; there, too, I incidentally gathered, he had himself been born, though it was a circumstance he seemed prone to forget. Whether he had run away, or his father had turned him out, I never fathomed; but about the age of twelve he was thrown upon his own resources. A travelling tin-type photographer picked him up, like a haw out of a hedgerow, on a wayside in New Jersey; took a fancy to the urchin; carried him on with him in his wandering life; taught him all he knew himself – to take tin-types (as well as I can make out) and doubt the Scriptures; and died at last in Ohio at the corner of a road. 'He was a grand specimen,' cried Pinkerton; 'I wish you could have seen him, Mr Dodd. He had an appearance of magnanimity that used to remind me of the patriarchs.'

1. 'What's the matter with him?'
2. 'The gentleman is sick at his stomach from having looked too long at your daub.'

On the death of this random protector, the boy inherited the plant and continued the business. 'It was a life I could have chosen, Mr Dodd!' he cried. 'I have been in all the finest scenes of that magnificent continent that we were born to be the heirs of. I wish you could see my collection of tin-types; I wish I had them here. They were taken for my own pleasure and to be a memento; and they show Nature in her grandest as well as her gentlest moments.' As he tramped the Western States and Territories, taking tin-types, the boy was continually getting hold of books, good, bad, and indifferent, popular and abstruse, from the novels of Sylvanus Cobb to Euclid's Elements, both of which I found (to my almost equal wonder) he had managed to peruse: he was taking stock by the way, of the people, the products, and the country, with an eye unusually observant and a memory unusually retentive; and he was collecting for himself a body of magnanimous and semi-intellectual nonsense, which he supposed to be the natural thoughts and to contain the whole duty of the born American. To be pure-minded, to be patriotic, to get culture and money with both hands and with the same irrational fervour – these appeared to be the chief articles of his creed. In later days (not of course upon this first occasion) I would sometimes ask him why; and he had his answer pat. 'To build up the type!' he would cry. 'We're all committed to that; we're all under bond to fulfil the American Type! Loudon, the hope of the world is there. If we fail, like these old feudal monarchies, what is left?'

The trade of a tin-typer proved too narrow for the lad's ambition; it was insusceptible of expansion, he explained; it was not truly modern; and by a sudden conversion of front he became a railroad-scalper. The principles of this trade I never clearly understood; but its essence appears to be to cheat the railroads out of their due fare. 'I threw my whole soul into it; I grudged myself food and sleep while I was at it; the most practised hands admitted I had caught on to the idea in a month and revolutionised the practice inside of a year,' he said. 'And there's interest in it, too. It's amusing to pick out someone going by, make up your mind about his character and tastes, dash out of the office, and hit him flying with an offer of the very place he wants to go to. I don't think there was a scalper on the continent made fewer blunders. But I took it only as a stage. I was saving every dollar; I was looking ahead. I knew what I wanted – wealth, education, a refined home, and a conscientious cultured lady for a wife; for, Mr Dodd' – this with a formidable outcry – 'every man is bound to marry above him: if the woman's not the man's superior, I brand it as mere sensuality. There was my idea, at least. That was what I was saving for; and enough, too! But it isn't every man, I know that – it's far from every man – could do what I did: close up the livest agency in Saint Jo, where he was coining dollars by the pot, set out alone, without a friend or a word of French, and settle down here to spend his capital learning art.'

'Was it an old taste?' I asked him, 'or a sudden fancy?'

'Neither, Mr Dodd,' he admitted. 'Of course, I had learned in my tin-typing excursions to glory and exult in the works of God. But it wasn't that. I just said to myself, "What is most wanted in my age and country? More culture and more art," I said; and I chose the best place, saved my money, and came here to get them.'

The whole attitude of this young man warmed and shamed me. He had more fire in his little toe than I in my whole carcase; he was stuffed to bursting with the manly virtues; thrift and courage glowed in him; and even if his artistic vocation seemed (to one of my exclusive tenets) not quite clear, who could predict what might be accomplished by a creature so full-blooded and so inspired with animal and intellectual energy? So, when he proposed that I should come and see his work (one of the regular stages of a Latin Quarter friendship), I followed him with interest and hope.

He lodged parsimoniously at the top of a tall house near the Observatory, in a bare room, principally furnished with his own trunks and papered with his own despicable studies. No man has less taste for disagreeable duties than myself; perhaps there is only one subject on which I cannot flatter a man without a blush; but upon that, upon all that touches art, my sincerity is Roman. Once and twice I made the circuit of his walls in silence, spying in every corner for some spark of merit; he meanwhile following close at my heels, reading the verdict in my face with furtive glances, presenting some fresh study for my inspection with undisguised anxiety, and (after it had been silently weighed in the balances and found wanting) whisking it away with an open gesture of despair. By the time the second round was completed, we were both extremely depressed.

'Oh!' he groaned, breaking the long silence, 'it's quite unnecessary you should speak!'

'Do you want me to be frank with you? I think you are wasting time,' said I.

'You don't see any promise?' he inquired, beguiled by some return of hope, and turning upon me the embarrassing brightness of his eye. 'Not in this still-life here of the melon? One fellow thought it good.'

It was the least I could do to give the melon a more particular examination; which, when I had done, I could but shake my head. 'I am truly sorry, Pinkerton,' said I, 'but I can't advise you to persevere.'

He seemed to recover his fortitude at the moment, rebounding from disappointment like a man of india-rubber. 'Well,' said he stoutly, 'I don't know that I'm surprised. But I'll go on with the course; and throw my whole soul into it too. You mustn't think the time is lost. It's all culture; it will help me to extend my relations when I get back home; it may fit me for a position on one of the illustrateds; and then I can always turn dealer,' he said, uttering the monstrous proposition, which was enough to shake the Latin Quarter to the dust, with entire simplicity. 'It's all experience, besides,' he continued; 'and it seems to me there's a tendency to underrate experience, both as net profit and investment. Never mind. That's done with. But it took courage for you to say what you did, and I'll never forget it. Here's my hand, Mr Dodd. I'm not your equal in culture or talent.'

'You know nothing about that,' I interrupted. 'I have seen your work, but you haven't seen mine.'

'No more I have,' he cried; 'and let's go see it at once! But I know you are away up; I can feel it here.'

To say truth, I was almost ashamed to introduce him to my studio – my work, whether absolutely good or bad, being so vastly superior to his. But his spirits were now quite restored; and he amazed me, on the way, with his light-hearted talk and new projects. So that I began at last to understand how matters lay: that this was not an artist who had been deprived of the practice of his single art; but only a business man of very extended interests, informed (perhaps something of the most suddenly) that one investment out of twenty had gone wrong.

As a matter of fact, besides (although I never suspected it), he was already seeking consolation with another of the muses, and pleasing himself with the notion that he would repay me for my sincerity, cement our friendship, and (at one and the same blow) restore my estimation of his talents. Several times already, when I had been speaking of myself, he had pulled out a writing-pad and scribbled a brief note; and now, when we entered the studio, I saw it in his hand again, and the pencil go to his mouth, as he cast a comprehensive glance round the uncomfortable building.

'Are you going to make a sketch of it?' I could not help asking, as I unveiled the Genius of Muskegon.

'Ah, that's my secret,' said he. 'Never you mind. A mouse can help a lion.'

He walked round my statue, and had the design explained to him. I had represented Muskegon as a young, almost a stripling mother, with something of an Indian type; the babe upon her knees was winged, to indicate our soaring future; and her seat was a medley of sculptured fragments, Greek, Roman, and Gothic, to remind us of the older worlds from which we trace our generation.

'Now, does this satisfy you, Mr Dodd?' he inquired, as soon as I had explained to him the main features of the design.

'Well,' I said, 'the fellows seem to think it's not a bad *bonne femme* for a beginner. I don't think it's entirely bad, myself. Here is the best point; it builds up best from here. No, it seems to me it has a kind of merit,' I admitted; 'but I mean to do better.'

'Ah, that's the word!' cried Pinkerton. 'There's the word I love!' and he scribbled in his pad.

'What in creation ails you?' I inquired. 'It's the most commonplace expression in the English language.'

'Better and better!' chuckled Pinkerton. 'The unconsciousness of genius. Lord, but this is coming in beautiful!' and he scribbled again.

'If you're going to be fulsome,' said I, 'I'll close the place of entertainment;' and I threatened to replace the veil upon the Genius.

'No, no,' said he; 'don't be in a hurry. Give me a point or two. Show me what's particularly good.'

'I would rather you found that out for yourself,' said I.

'The trouble is,' said he, 'that I've never turned my attention to sculpture – beyond, of course, admiring it, as everybody must who has a soul. So do just be a good fellow, and explain to me what you like in it, and what you tried for, and where the merit comes in. It'll be all education for me.'

'Well, in sculpture, you see, the first thing you have to consider is the masses. It's, after all, a kind of architecture,' I began, and delivered a lecture on that branch of art, with illustrations from my own masterpiece there present – all of which, if you don't mind, or whether you mind or not, I mean to conscientiously omit. Pinkerton listened with a fiery interest, questioned me with a certain uncultivated shrewdness, and continued to scratch down notes, and tear fresh sheets from his pad. I found it inspiring to have my words thus taken down like a professor's lecture; and having had no previous experience of the press, I was unaware that they were all being taken down wrong. For the same reason (incredible as it must appear in an American) I never entertained the least suspicion that they were destined to be dished up with a sauce of penny-a-lining gossip; and myself, my person, and my works of art butchered to make a holiday for the readers of a Sunday paper. Night had fallen over the Genius of Muskegon before the issue of my theoretic eloquence was stayed, nor did I separate from my new friend without an appointment for the morrow.

I was, indeed, greatly taken with this first view of my countryman, and continued, on further acquaintance, to be interested, amused, and attracted by him in about equal proportions. I must not say he had a fault, not only because my mouth is sealed by gratitude, but because those he had sprang merely from his education, and you could see he had cultivated and improved them like virtues. For all that, I can never deny he was a troublous friend to me, and the trouble began early.

It may have been a fortnight later that I divined the secret of the writing-pad. My wretch (it leaked out) wrote letters for a paper in the West, and had filled a part of one of them with descriptions of myself. I pointed out to him that he had no right to do so without asking my permission.

'Why, this is just what I hoped!' he exclaimed. 'I thought you didn't seem to catch on; only it seemed too good to be true.'

'But, my good fellow, you were bound to warn me,' I objected.

'I know it's generally considered etiquette,' he admitted; 'but between friends, and when it was only with a view of serving you, I thought it wouldn't matter. I wanted it (if possible) to come on you as a surprise; I wanted you just to waken, like Lord Byron, and find the papers full of you. You must admit it was a natural thought. And no man likes to boast of a favour beforehand.'

'But heavens and earth! how do you know I think it a favour?' I cried.

He became immediately plunged in despair. 'You think it a liberty,' said he; 'I see that. I would rather have cut off my hand. I would stop it now, only it's too late; it's published by now. And I wrote it with so much pride and pleasure!'

I could think of nothing but how to console him. 'Oh, I daresay it's all right,' said I. 'I know you meant it kindly, and you would be sure to do it in good taste.'

'That you may swear to,' he cried. 'It's a pure, bright, A number 1 paper; the St Jo *Sunday Herald*. The idea of the series was quite my own, I interviewed the editor, put it to him straight; the freshness of the idea took him, and I walked out of that office with the contract in my pocket, and did my first Paris letter that evening in Saint Jo. The editor did no more than glance his eye down the headlines. "You're the man for us," said he.'

I was certainly far from reassured by this sketch of the class of literature in which I was to make my first appearance; but I said no more, and possessed my soul in patience, until the day came when I received a copy of a newspaper marked in the corner, 'Compliments of J.P.' I opened it with sensible shrinkings; and there, wedged between an account of a prize-fight and a skittish article upon chiropody – think of chiropody treated with a leer! – I came upon a column and a half in which myself and my poor statue were embalmed. Like the editor with the first of the series, I did but glance my eye down the head-lines, and was more than satisfied.

ANOTHER OF PINKERTON'S SPICY CHATS.
ART PRACTITIONERS IN PARTS.
MUSKEGON'S COLUMNED CAPITOL.
SON OF MILLIONAIRE DODD,
PATRIOT AND ARTIST.
'HE MEANS TO DO BETTER.'

In the body of the text, besides, my eye caught, as it passed, some deadly expressions: 'Figure somewhat fleshy,' 'bright, intellectual smile,' 'the unconsciousness of genius,' 'Now, Mr Dodd,' resumed the reporter, 'what would be your idea of a distinctively American quality in sculpture?' It was true the question had been asked; it was true, alas! that I had answered; and now here was my reply, or some strange hash of it, gibbetted in the cold publicity of type. I thanked God that my French fellow-students were ignorant of English; but when I thought of the British – of Myner (for instance) or the Stennises – I think I could have fallen on Pinkerton and beat him.

To divert my thoughts (if it were possible) from this calamity, I turned to a letter from my father which had arrived by the same post. The envelope contained a strip of newspaper cutting; and my eye caught again, 'Son of Millionaire Dodd – Figure somewhat fleshy,' and the rest of the degrading nonsense. What would my father think of it? I wondered, and opened his manuscript. 'My dearest boy,' it began, 'I send you a cutting which has pleased me, very much, from a St Joseph paper of high standing. At last you seem to be coming fairly to the front; and I cannot but reflect with delight and gratitude how very few youths of your age occupy nearly two columns of press-matter all to themselves. I only wish your dear mother had been here to read it over my shoulder; but we will hope she shares my grateful emotion in a better place. Of course I have sent a copy to your grandfather and uncle in Edinburgh; so you can keep the one I enclose. This Jim Pinkerton seems a valuable acquaintance; he has certainly great talent; and it is a good general rule to keep in with pressmen.'

I hope it will be set down to the right side of my account, but I had no sooner read these words, so touchingly silly, than my anger against Pinkerton was swallowed up in gratitude. Of all the circumstances of my career – my birth, perhaps, excepted – not one had given my poor father so profound a pleasure as this article in the *Sunday Herald*. What a fool, then, was I to be lamenting! when I had at last, and for once, and at the cost of only a few blushes, paid back a fraction of my debt of gratitude. So that, when I next met Pinkerton, I took things very lightly; my father was pleased, and thought the letter very clever, I told him; for my own part, I had no taste for publicity: thought the public had no concern with the artist, only with his art; and though I owned he had handled it with great consideration, I should take it as a favour if he never did it again.

'There it is,' he said, despondingly. 'I've hurt you. You can't deceive me, Loudon. It's the want of tact, and it's incurable.' He sat down, and leaned his head upon his hand. 'I had no advantages when I was young, you see,' he added.

'Not in the least, my dear fellow,' said I. 'Only the next time you wish to do me a service, just speak about my work; leave my wretched person out, and my still more wretched conversation: and above all,' I added, with an irrepressible shudder, 'don't tell them how I said it! There's that phrase, now. "With a proud, glad smile." Who cares whether I smiled or not?'

'Oh, there now, Loudon, you're entirely wrong,' he broke in. 'That's what the public likes; that's the merit of the thing, the literary value. It's to call up the scene before them; it's to enable the humblest citizen to enjoy that afternoon the same as I did. Think what it would have been to me when I was tramping around with my tin-types to find a column and a half of real, cultured conversation – an artist, in his studio abroad, talking of his art – and to know how he looked as he did it, and what the room was like, and what he had for breakfast; and to tell myself, eating tinned beans beside a creek, that if all went well, the same sort of thing would, sooner or later, happen to myself: why, Loudon, it would have been like a peephole into heaven!'

'Well, if it gives so much pleasure,' I admitted, 'the sufferers shouldn't complain. Only give the other fellows a turn.'

The end of the matter was to bring myself and the journalist in a more close relation. If I know anything at all of human nature – and the *if* is no mere figure of speech, but stands for honest doubt – no series of benefits conferred, or even dangers shared, would have so rapidly confirmed our friendship as this quarrel avoided, this fundamental difference of taste and training accepted and condoned.

CHAPTER FOUR

In which I Experience Extremes of Fortune

Whether it came from my training and repeated bankruptcy at the Commercial College, or by direct inheritance from old Loudon, the Edinburgh mason, there can be no doubt about the fact that I was thrifty. Looking myself impartially over, I believe that is my only manly virtue. During my first two years in Paris I not only made it a point to keep well inside of my allowance, but accumulated considerable savings in the bank. You will say, with my masquerade of living as a penniless student, it must have been easy to do so: I should have had no difficulty, however, in doing the reverse. Indeed, it is wonderful I did not; and early in the third year, or soon after I had known Pinkerton, a singular incident proved it to have been equally wise. Quarter-day came, and brought no allowance. A letter of remonstrance was despatched, and, for the first time in my experience, remained unanswered. A cablegram was more effectual; for it brought me at least a promise of attention. 'Will write at once,' my father telegraphed; but I waited long for his letter. I was puzzled, angry, and alarmed; but, thanks to my previous thrift, I cannot say that I was ever practically embarrassed. The embarrassment, the distress, the agony, were all for my unhappy father at home in Muskegon, struggling for life and fortune against untoward chances, returning at night, from a day of ill-starred shifts and ventures, to read and perhaps to weep over that last harsh letter from his only child, to which he lacked the courage to reply.

Nearly three months after time, and when my economies were beginning to run low, I received at last a letter with the customary bills of exchange.

'My dearest boy,' it ran, 'I believe, in the press of anxious business, your letters and even your allowance have been somewhile neglected. You must try to forgive your poor old dad, for he has had a trying time; and now when it is over, the doctor wants me to take my shotgun and go to the Adirondacks for a change. You must not fancy I am sick, only overdriven and under the weather. Many of our foremost operators have gone down: John T. M'Brady skipped to Canada with a trunkful of boodle; Billy Sandwith, Charlie Downs, Joe Kaiser, and many others of our leading men in this city bit the dust. But Big Head Dodd has again weathered the blizzard, and I think I have fixed things so that we may be richer than ever before autumn.

'Now I will tell you, my dear, what I propose. You say you are well advanced with your first statue; start in manfully and finish it, and if your teacher – I can never remember how to spell his name – will send me a certificate that it is up to market standard, you shall have ten thousand dollars to do what you like with, either at home or in Paris. I suggest, since you say the facilities for work are so much greater in that city, you would do well to buy or build a little home; and the first thing you know, your dad will be dropping in for a luncheon. Indeed, I would come now – for I am beginning to grow old, and I long to see my dear boy – but there are still some operations that want watching and nursing. Tell your friend, Mr Pinkerton, that I read his letters every week; and though I have looked in vain lately for my Loudon's name, still I learn something of the life he is leading in that strange Old World depicted by an able pen.'

Here was a letter that no young man could possibly digest in solitude. It marked one of those junctures when the confidant is necessary; and the confidant selected was none other than Jim Pinkerton. My father's message may have had an influence in this decision; but I scarce suppose so, for the intimacy was already for advanced. I had a genuine and lively taste for my compatriot; I laughed at, I scolded, and I loved him. He, upon his side, paid me a kind of doglike service of admiration, gazing at me from afar off, as at one who had liberally enjoyed those 'advantages' which he envied for himself. He followed at heel; his laugh was ready chorus; our friends gave him the nickname of 'The Henchman.' It was in this insidious form that servitude approached me.

Pinkerton and I read and re-read the famous news: he,

I can swear, with an enjoyment as unalloyed and far more vocal than my own. The statue was nearly done: a few days' work sufficed to prepare it for exhibition; the master was approached; he gave his consent; and one cloudless morning of May beheld us gathered in my studio for the hour of trial. The master wore his many-hued rosette; he came attended by two of my French fellow-pupils – friends of mine, and both considerable sculptors in Paris at this hour. 'Corporal John' (as we used to call him), breaking for once those habits of study and reserve which have since carried him so high in the opinion of the world, had left his easel of a morning to countenance a fellow-countryman in some suspense. My dear old Romney was there by particular request; for who that knew him would think a pleasure quite complete unless he shared it, or not support a mortification more easily if he were present to console? The party was completed by John Myner, the Englishman; by the brothers Stennis – Stennis-*ainé* and Stennis-*frère*, as they used to figure on their accounts at Barbizon – a pair of hare-brained Scots; and by the inevitable Jim, as white as a sheet and bedewed with the sweat of anxiety.

I suppose I was little better myself when I unveiled the Genius of Muskegon. The master walked about it seriously; then he smiled.

'It is already not so bad,' said he, in that funny English of which he was so proud; 'no, already not so bad.'

We all drew a deep breath of relief; and Corporal John (as the most considerable junior present) explained to him it was intended for a public building, a kind of prefecture.

'*Hé! quoi?*' cried he, relapsing into French. '*Qu'est-ce que vous me chantez là?* Oh, in América,' he added, on further information being hastily furnished. 'That is anozer sing. Oh, véry good – véry good.'

The idea of the required certificate had to be introduced to his mind in the light of a pleasantry – the fancy of a nabob little more advanced than the red Indians of 'Fénnimore Cooperr'; and it took all our talents combined to conceive a form of words that would be acceptable on both sides. One was found, however: Corporal John engrossed it in his undecipherable hand, the master lent it the sanction of his name and flourish, I slipped it into an envelope along with one of the two letters I had ready prepared in my pocket, and as the rest of us moved off along the boulevard to breakfast, Pinkerton was detached in a cab and duly committed it to the post.

The breakfast was ordered at Lavenue's, where no one need be ashamed to entertain even the master; the table was laid in the garden; I had chosen the bill of fare myself; on the wine question we held a council of war, with the most fortunate results; and the talk, as soon as the master laid aside his painful English, became fast and furious. There were a few interruptions, indeed, in the way of toasts. The master's health had to be drunk, and he responded in a little well-turned speech, full of neat allusions to my future and to the United States; my health followed; and then my father's must not only be proposed and drunk, but a full report must be despatched to him at once by cablegram – an extravagance which was almost the means of the master's dissolution. Choosing Corporal John to be his confidant (on the ground, I presume, that he was already too good an artist to be any longer an American except in name) he summed up his amazement in one oft-repeated formula – '*C'est barbare!*' Apart from these genial formalities, we talked, talked of art, and talked of it as only artists can. Here in the South Seas we talk schooners most of the time; in the Quarter we talked art with the like unflagging interest, and perhaps as much result.

Before very long the master went away; Corporal John (who was already a sort of young master) followed on his heels; and the rank and file were naturally relieved by their departure. We were now among equals; the bottle passed, the conversation sped. I think I can still hear the Stennis brothers pour forth their copious tirades; Dijon, my portly French fellow-student, drop witticisms, well-conditioned like himself; and another (who was weak in foreign languages) dash hotly into the current of talk with some '*Je trove que pore oon sontimong de delicacy, Corot . . .*' or some '*Pour moi Corot est le plou . . .*' and then, his little raft of French foundering at once, scramble silently to shore again. He at least could understand; but to Pinkerton, I think the noise, the wine, the sun, the shadows of the leaves, and the esoteric glory of being seated at a foreign festival, made up the whole available means of entertainment.

We sat down about half-past eleven; I suppose it was two

when, some point arising and some particular picture being instanced, an adjournment to the Louvre was proposed. I paid the score, and in a moment we were trooping down the Rue de Renne. It was smoking hot; Paris glittered with that superficial brilliancy which is so agreeable to the man in high spirits, and in moods of dejection so depressing; the wine sang in my ears, it danced and brightened in my eyes. The pictures that we saw that afternoon, as we sped briskly and loquaciously through the immortal galleries, appear to me, upon a retrospect, the loveliest of all; the comments we exchanged to have touched the highest mark of criticism, grave or gay.

It was only when we issued again from the museum that a difference of race broke up the party. Dijon proposed an adjournment to a café, there to finish the afternoon on beer; the elder Stennis revolted at the thought, moved for the country – a forest, if possible – and a long walk. At once the English speakers rallied to the name of any exercise; even to me, who have been often twitted with my sedentary habits, the thought of country air and stillness proved invincibly attractive. It appeared, upon investigation, we had just time to hail a cab and catch one of the fast trains for Fontainebleau. Beyond the clothes we stood in all were destitute of what is called, with dainty vagueness, personal effects; and it was earnestly mooted, on the other side, whether we had not time to call upon the way and pack a satchel? But the Stennis boys exclaimed upon our effeminacy. They had come from London, it appeared, a week before with nothing but great-coats and tooth-brushes. No baggage – there was the secret of existence. It was expensive, to be sure, for every time you had to comb your hair a barber must be paid, and every time you changed your linen one shirt must be bought and another thrown away; but anything was better, argued these young gentlemen, than to be the slaves of haversacks. 'A fellow has to get rid gradually of all material attachments: that was manhood,' said they; 'and as long as you were bound down to anything – house, umbrella, or portmanteau – you were still tethered by the umbilical cord.' Something engaging in this theory carried the most of us away. The two Frenchmen, indeed, retired scoffing to their bock, and Romney, being too poor to join the excursion on his own resources and too proud to borrow, melted unobtrusively away. Meanwhile the remainder of the company crowded the benches of a cab; the horse was urged, as horses have to be, by an appeal to the pocket of the driver; the train caught by the inside of a minute; and in less than an hour and a half we were breathing deep of the sweet air of the forest, and stretching our legs up the hill from Fontainebleau octroi, bound for Barbizon. That the leading members of our party covered the distance in fifty-one minutes and a half is, I believe, one of the historic landmarks of the colony; but you will scarce be surprised to learn that I was somewhat in the rear. Myner, a comparatively philosophic Briton, kept me company in my deliberate advance; the glory of the sun's going down, the fall of the long shadows, the inimitable scent, and the inspiration of the woods, attuned me more and more to walk in a silence which progressively infected my companion; and I remember that, when at last he spoke, I was startled from a deep abstraction.

'Your father seems to be a pretty good kind of a father,' said he. 'Why don't he come to see you?' I was ready with some dozen of reasons, and had more in stock; but Myner, with that shrewdness which made him feared and admired, suddenly fixed me with his eye-glass and asked, 'Ever press him?'

The blood came in my face. No, I had never pressed him; I had never even encouraged him to come. I was proud of him, proud of his handsome looks, of his kind gentle ways, of that bright face he could show when others were happy; proud, too – meanly proud, if you like – of his great wealth and startling liberalities. And yet he would have been in the way of my Paris life, of much of which he would have disapproved. I had feared to expose to criticism his innocent remarks on art; I had told myself, I had even partly believed, he did not want to come; I had been, and still am, convinced that he was sure to be unhappy out of Muskegon; in short, I had a thousand reasons, good and bad, not all of which could alter one iota of the fact that I knew he only waited for my invitation.

'Thank you, Myner,' said I; 'you're a much better fellow than ever I supposed. I'll write tonight.'

'Oh, you're a pretty decent sort yourself,' returned

Myner, with more than his usual flippancy of manner, but, as I was gratefully aware, not a trace of his occasional irony of meaning.

Well, these were brave days, on which I could dwell for ever. Brave, too, were those that followed, when Pinkerton and I walked Paris and the suburbs, viewing and pricing houses for my new establishment, or covered ourselves with dust and returned laden with Chinese gods and brass warming-pans from the dealers in antiquities. I found Pinkerton well up in the situation of these establishments as well as in the current prices, and with quite a smattering of critical judgment. It turned out he was investing capital in pictures and curiosities for the States, and the superficial thoroughness of the creature appeared in the fact that although he would never be a connoisseur, he was already something of an expert. The things themselves left him as near as may be cold, but he had a joy of his own in understanding how to buy and sell them.

In such engagements the time passed until I might very well expect an answer from my father. Two mails followed each other, and brought nothing. By the third I received a long and almost incoherent letter of remorse, encouragement, consolation, and despair. From this pitiful document, which (with a movement of piety) I burned as soon as I had read it, I gathered that the bubble of my father's wealth was burst, that he was now both penniless and sick; and that I, so far from expecting ten thousand dollars to throw away in juvenile extravagance, must look no longer for the quarterly remittances on which I lived. My case was hard enough; but I had sense enough to perceive, and decency enough to do, my duty. I sold my curiosities – or, rather, I sent Pinkerton to sell them; and he had previously bought, and now disposed of them, so wisely that the loss was trifling. This, with what remained of my last allowance, left me at the head of no less than five thousand francs. Five hundred I reserved for my own immediate necessities: the rest I mailed inside of the week to my father at Muskegon, where they came in time to pay his funeral expenses.

The news of his death was scarcely a surprise and scarce a grief to me. I could not conceive my father a poor man. He had led too long a life of thoughtless and generous profusion to endure the change; and though I grieved for myself, I was able to rejoice that my father had been taken from the battle. I grieved, I say, for myself; and it is probable there were at the same date many thousands of persons grieving with less cause. I had lost my father; I had lost the allowance; my whole fortune (including what had been returned from Muskegon) scarce amounted to a thousand francs; and, to crown my sorrows, the statuary contract had changed hands. The new contractor had a son of his own, or else a nephew; and it was signified to me, with business-like plainness, that I must find another market for my pigs. In the meanwhile I had given up my room, and slept on a truckle-bed in the corner of the studio, where, as I read myself to sleep at night, and when I awoke in the morning, that now useless bulk, the Genius of Muskegon, was ever present to my eyes. Poor stone lady! born to be enthroned under the gilded, echoing dome of the new capitol, whither was she now to drift? for what base purposes be ultimately broken up, like an unseaworthy ship? and what should befall her ill-starred artificer, standing with his thousand francs on the threshold of a life so hard as that of the unbefriended sculptor?

It was a subject often and earnestly debated by myself and Pinkerton. In his opinion I should instantly discard my profession. 'Just drop it, here and now,' he would say. 'Come back home with me, and let's throw our whole soul into business. I have the capital; you bring the culture. *Dodd and Pinkerton* – I never saw a better name for an advertisement; and you can't think, Loudon, how much depends upon a name.' On my side I would admit that a sculptor should possess one of three things – capital, influence, or an energy only to be qualified as hellish. The first two I had now lost; to the third I never had the smallest claim; and yet I wanted the cowardice (or, perhaps, it was the courage) to turn my back on my career without a fight. I told him, besides, that however poor my chances were in sculpture, I was convinced they were yet worse in business, for which I equally lacked taste and aptitude. But upon this head he was my father over again; assured me that I spoke in ignorance; that any intelligent and cultured person was bound to succeed; that I must, besides, have inherited some of my father's fitness; and, at any rate, that I had been regularly trained for that career in the commercial college.

'Pinkerton,' I said, 'can't you understand that, as long as I was there, I never took the smallest interest in any stricken thing? The whole affair was poison to me.'

'It's not possible,' he would cry; 'it can't be; you couldn't live in the midst of it and not feel the charm; with all your poetry of soul, you couldn't help! Loudon,' he would go on, 'you drive me crazy. You expect a man to be all broken up about the sunset, and not to care a dime for a place where fortunes are fought for and made and lost all day; or for a career that consists in studying up life till you have it at your finger-ends, spying out every cranny where you can get your hand in and a dollar out, and standing there in the midst – one foot on bankruptcy, the other on a borrowed dollar, and the whole thing spinning round you like a mill – raking in the stamps, in spite of fate and fortune.'

To this romance of dickering I would reply with the romance (which is also the virtue) of art: reminding him of those examples of constancy through many tribulations, with which the *rôle* of Apollo is illustrated – from the case of Millet, to those of many of our friends and comrades, who had chosen this agreeable mountain path through life, and were now bravely clambering among rocks and brambles, penniless and hopeful.

'You will never understand it, Pinkerton,' I would say. 'You look to the result, you want to see some profit of your endeavours: that is why you could never learn to paint, if you lived to be Methusalem. The result is always a fizzle: the eyes of the artist are turned in; he lives for a frame of mind. Look at Romney now. There is the nature of the artist. He hasn't a cent; and if you offered him tomorrow the command of an army, or the presidentship of the United States, he wouldn't take it, and you know he wouldn't.'

'I suppose not,' Pinkerton would cry, scouring his hair with both his hands; 'and I can't see why; I can't see what in fits he would be after, not to; I don't seem to rise to these views. Of course it's the fault of not having had advantages in early life; but, Loudon, I'm so miserably low that it seems to me silly. The fact is,' he might add with a smile, 'I don't seem to have the least use for a frame of mind without square meals; and you can't get it out of my head that it's a man's duty to die rich, if he can.'

'What for?' I asked him once.

'Oh, I don't know,' he replied. 'Why in snakes should anybody want to be a sculptor, if you come to that? I would love to sculp myself. But what I can't see is why you should want to do nothing else. It seems to argue a poverty of nature.'

Whether or not he ever came to understand me – and I have been so tossed about since then that I am not very sure I understand myself – he soon perceived that I was perfectly in earnest; and after about ten days of argument, suddenly dropped the subject, and announced that he was wasting capital, and must go home at once. No doubt he should have gone long before, and had already lingered over his intended time for the sake of our companionship and my misfortune; but man is so unjustly minded that the very fact, which ought to have disarmed, only embittered my vexation. I resented his departure in the light of a desertion; I would not say, but doubtless I betrayed it; and something hang-dog in the man's face and bearing led me to believe he was himself remorseful. It is certain at least that, during the time of his preparations, we drew sensibly apart – a circumstance that I recall with shame. On the last day he had me to dinner at a restaurant which he knew I had formerly frequented, and had only forsworn of late from considerations of economy. He seemed ill at ease; I was myself both sorry and sulky; and the meal passed with little conversation.

'Now, Loudon,' said he, with a visible effort, after the coffee was come and our pipes lighted, 'you can never understand the gratitude and loyalty I bear you. You don't know what a boon it is to be taken up by a man that stands on the pinnacle of civilisation; you can't think how it's refined and purified me, how it's appealed to my spiritual nature; and I want to tell you that I would die at your door like a dog.'

I don't know what answer I tried to make, but he cut me short.

'Let me say it out!' he cried. 'I revere you for your whole-souled devotion to art; I can't rise to it, but there's a strain of poetry in my nature, Loudon, that

responds to it. I want you to carry it out, and I mean
to help you.'

'Pinkerton, what nonsense is this?' I interrupted.

'Now don't get mad, Loudon; this is a plain piece of
business,' said he; 'it's done every day; it's even typical.
How are all those fellows over here in Paris, Henderson,
Sumner, Long? – it's all the same story: a young man
just plum full of artistic genius on the one side, a man
of business on the other who doesn't know what to do
with his dollars— '

'But, you fool, you're as poor as a rat,' I cried.

'You wait till I get my irons in the fire!' returned
Pinkerton. 'I'm bound to be rich; and I tell you I mean
to have some of the fun as I go along. Here's your first
allowance; take it at the hand of a friend; I'm one that
holds friendship sacred, as you do yourself. It's only a
hundred francs; you'll get the same every month, and as
soon as my business begins to expand we'll increase it to
something fitting. And so far from it's being a favour,
just let me handle your statuary for the American market,
and I'll call it one of the smartest strokes of business in
my life.'

It took me a long time, and it had cost us both much
grateful and painful emotion, before I had finally managed
to refuse his offer and compounded for a bottle of particular
wine. He dropped the subject at last suddenly with a 'Never
mind; that's all done with'; nor did he again refer to the
subject, though we passed together the rest of the afternoon,
and I accompanied him, on his departure, to the doors of the
waiting-room at St Lazare. I felt myself strangely alone; a
voice told me that I had rejected both the counsels of wisdom
and the helping hand of friendship; and as I passed through
the great bright city on my homeward way, I measured it
for the first time with the eye of an adversary.

CHAPTER FIVE

In which I am down on my Luck in Paris

In no part of the world is starvation an agreeable business; but I believe it is admitted there is no worse place to starve in than this city of Paris. The appearances of life are there so especially gay, it is so much a magnified beer-garden, the houses are so ornate, the theatres so numerous, the very pace of the vehicles is so brisk, that a man in any deep concern of mind or pain of body is constantly driven in upon himself. In his own eyes, he seems the one serious creature moving in a world of horrible unreality; voluble people issuing from a café, the *queue* at theatre doors, Sunday cabfuls of second-rate pleasure-seekers, the bedizened ladies of the pavement, the show in the jewellers' windows – all the familiar sights contributing to flout his own unhappiness, want, and isolation. At the same time, if he be at all after my pattern, he is perhaps supported by a childish satisfaction. 'This is life at last,' he may tell himself; 'this is the real thing. The bladders on which I was set swimming are now empty; my own weight depends upon the ocean; by my own exertions I must perish or succeed; and I am now enduring in the vivid fact, what I so much delighted to read of in the case of Lonsteau or Lucien, Rodolphe or Schaunard.'

Of the steps of my misery, I cannot tell at length. In ordinary times what were politically called 'loans' (although they were never meant to be repaid) were matters of constant course among the students, and many a man has partly lived on them for years. But my misfortune befell me at an awkward juncture. Many of my friends were gone; others were themselves in a precarious situation. Romney (for instance) was reduced to tramping Paris in a pair of country sabots, his only suit of clothes so imperfect (in spite of cunningly-adjusted pins) that the authorities at the Luxembourg suggested his withdrawal from the gallery. Dijon, too, was on a leeshore, designing clocks and gas-brackets for a dealer; and the most he could do was to offer me a corner of his studio where I might work. My own studio (it will be gathered) I had by that time lost; and in the course of my expulsion the Genius of Muskegon was finally separated from her author. To continue to possess a full-sized statue, a man must have a studio, a gallery, or at least the freedom of a back garden. He cannot carry it about with him, like a satchel, in the bottom of a cab, nor can he cohabit in a garret ten by fifteen with so momentous a companion. It was my first idea to leave her behind at my departure. There, in her birthplace, she might lend an inspiration, methought, to my successor. But the proprietor, with whom I had unhappily quarrelled, seized the occasion to be disagreeable, and called upon me to remove my property. For a man in such straits as I now found myself, the hire of a lorry was a consideration; and yet even that I could have faced, if I had had anywhere to drive to after it was hired. Hysterical laughter seized upon me as I beheld (in imagination) myself, the waggoner, and the Genius of Muskegon, standing in the public view of Paris, without the shadow of a destination; perhaps driving at last to the nearest rubbish heap, and dumping there, among the ordures of a city, the beloved child of my invention. From these extremities I was relieved by a seasonable offer, and I parted from the Genius of Muskegon for thirty francs. Where she now stands, under what name she is admired or criticised, history does not inform us; but I like to think she may adorn the shrubbery of some suburban tea-garden, where holiday shop-girls hang their hats upon the mother, and their swains (by way of an approach of gallantry) identify the winged infant with the god of love.

In a certain cabman's eating-house on the outer boulevard I got credit for my midday meal. Supper I was supposed not to require, sitting down nightly to the delicate table of some rich acquaintances. This arrangement was extremely ill-considered. My fable, credible enough at first, and so long as my clothes were in good order, must have seemed worse than doubtful after my coat became frayed about the edges, and my boots began to squelch and pipe along the restaurant floors. The allowance of one meal a day, besides, though suitable enough to the state of my finances, agreed poorly with my stomach. The restaurant was a place I had often visited experimentally, to taste the life of students then more unfortunate than myself; and I had never in those days entered it without disgust, or left it without nausea. It was strange to find myself sitting down with avidity, rising up with satisfaction, and counting the hours that divided me from my return to such a table. But hunger is a great magician; and so soon as I had spent my ready cash, and could no longer fill up on bowls of chocolate or hunks of bread, I must depend entirely on that cabman's eating-house, and upon certain rare, long-expected, long-remembered windfalls. Dijon (for instance) might get paid for some of his pot-boiling work, or else an old friend would pass through Paris; and then I would be entertained to a meal after my own soul, and contract a Latin Quarter loan, which would keep me in tobacco and my morning coffee for a fortnight. It might be thought the latter would appear the more important. It might be supposed that a life, led so near the confines of actual famine, should have dulled the nicety of my palate. On the contrary, the poorer a man's diet, the more sharply is he set on dainties. The last of my ready cash, about thirty francs, was deliberately squandered on a single dinner; and a great part of my time when I was alone was passed upon the details of imaginary feasts.

One gleam of hope visited me – an order for a bust from a rich Southerner. He was free-handed, jolly of speech, merry of countenance; kept me in good humour through the sittings, and, when they were over, carried me off with him to dinner and the sights of Paris. I ate well, I laid on flesh; by all accounts, I made a favourable likeness of the being, and I confess I thought my future was assured. But when the bust was done, and I had despatched it across the Atlantic, I could never so much as learn of its arrival. The blow felled me; I should have lain down and tried no stroke to right myself, had not the honour of my country been involved. For Dijon improved the opportunity in the European style, informing me (for the first time) of the manners of America: how it was a den of banditti without the smallest rudiment of law or order, and debts could be there only collected with a shotgun. 'The whole world knows it,' he would say; 'you are alone, *mon petit* Loudon – you are alone, to be in ignorance of these facts. The judges of the

Supreme Court fought but the other day with stilettos on the
bench at Cincinnati. You should read the little book of one
of my friends, "Le Touriste dans le Far-West"; you will see
it all there in good French.' At last, incensed by days of such
discussion, I undertook to prove to him the contrary, and
put the affair in the hands of my late father's lawyer. From
him I had the gratification of hearing, after a due interval,
that my debtor was dead of the yellow fever in Key West,
and had left his affairs in some confusion. I suppress his
name; for though he treated me with cruel nonchalance,
it is probable he meant to deal fairly in the end.

Soon after this a shade of change in my reception at
the cabman's eating-house marked the beginning of a new
phase in my distress. The first day I told myself it was but
fancy; the next, I made quite sure it was a fact; the third,
in mere panic I stayed away, and went for forty-eight hours
fasting. This was an act of great unreason; for the debtor
who stays away is but the more remarked, and the boarder
who misses a meal is sure to be accused of infidelity. On
the fourth day, therefore, I returned, inwardly quaking.
The proprietor looked askance upon my entrance; the
waitresses (who were his daughters) neglected my wants,
and sniffed at the affected joviality of my salutations; last
and most plain, when I called for a *suisse* (such as was
being served to all the other diners), I was bluntly told
there were no more. It was obvious I was near the end
of my tether; one plank divided me from want, and now
I felt it tremble. I passed a sleepless night, and the first
thing in the morning took my way to Myner's studio. It
was a step I had long meditated and long refrained from;
for I was scarce intimate with the Englishman; and though
I knew him to possess plenty of money, neither his manner
nor his reputation were the least encouraging to beggars.

I found him at work on a picture, which I was able
conscientiously to praise, dressed in his usual tweeds –
plain, but pretty fresh, and standing out in disagreeable
contrast to my own withered and degraded outfit. As we
talked, he continued to shift his eyes watchfully between
his handiwork and the fat model, who sat at the far end
of the studio in a state of nature, with one arm gallantly
arched above her head. My errand would have been difficult
enough under the best of circumstances: placed between

Myner, immersed in his art, and the white, fat, naked female in a ridiculous attitude, I found it quite impossible. Again and again I attempted to approach the point, again and again fell back on commendations of the picture; and it was not until the model had enjoyed an interval of repose, during which she took the conversation in her own hands and regaled us (in a soft weak voice) with details as to her husband's prosperity, her sister's lamented decline from the paths of virtue, and the consequent wrath of her father, a peasant of stern principles, in the vicinity of Chalons on the Marne – it was not, I say, until after this was over, and I had once more cleared my throat for the attack, and once more dropped aside into some commonplace about the picture, that Myner himself brought me suddenly and vigorously to the point.

'You didn't come here to talk this rot,' said he.

'No,' I replied sullenly; 'I came to borrow money.'

He painted awhile in silence.

'I don't think we were ever very intimate?' he asked.

'Thank you,' said I. 'I can take my answer,' and I made as if to go, rage boiling in my heart.

'Of course you can go if you like,' said Myner, 'but I advise you to stay and have it out.'

'What more is there to say?' I cried. 'You don't want to keep me here for a needless humiliation?'

'Look here, Dodd; you must try and command your temper,' said he. 'This interview is of your own seeking, and not mine; if you suppose it's not disagreeable to me, you're wrong; and if you think I will give you money without knowing thoroughly about your prospects, you take me for a fool. Besides,' he added, 'if you come to look at it, you've got over the worst of it by now: you have done the asking, and you have every reason to know I mean to refuse. I hold out no false hopes, but it may be worth your while to let me judge.'

Thus – I was going to say – encouraged, I stumbled through my story; told him I had credit at the cabman's eating-house, but began to think it was drawing to a close; how Dijon lent me a corner of his studio, where I tried to model ornaments, figures for clocks, Time with the scythe, Leda and the swan, musketeers for candlesticks, and other kickshaws, which had never (up to that day) been honoured with the least approval.

'And your room?' asked Myner.

'Oh, my room is all right, I think,' said I. 'She is a very good old lady, and has never even mentioned her bill.'

'Because she is a very good old lady, I don't see why she should be fined,' observed Myner.

'What do you mean by that?' I cried.

'I mean this,' said he. 'The French give a great deal of credit amongst themselves; they find it pays on the whole, or the system would hardly be continued; but I can't see where *we* come in; I can't see that it's honest of us Anglo-Saxons to profit by their easy ways, and then skip over the Channel or (as you Yankees do) across the Atlantic.'

'But I'm not proposing to skip,' I objected.

'Exactly,' he replied. 'And shouldn't you? There's the problem. You seem to me to have a lack of sympathy for the proprietors of cabmen's eating-houses. By your own account you're not getting on; the longer you stay, it'll only be the more out of the pocket of the dear old lady at your lodgings. Now I'll tell you what I'll do: if you consent to go, I'll pay your passage to New York, and your railway fare and expenses to Muskegon (if I have the name right), where your father lived, where he must have left friends, and where, no doubt, you'll find an opening. I don't seek any gratitude, for of course you'll think me a beast; but I do ask you to pay it back when you are able. At any rate, that's all I can do. It might be different if I thought you a genius, Dodd; but I don't, and I advise you not to.'

'I think that was uncalled for, at least,' said I.

'I daresay it was,' he returned, with the same steadiness. 'It seemed to me pertinent; and, besides, when you ask me for money upon no security, you treat me with the liberty of a friend, and it's to be presumed that I can do the like. But the point is, do you accept?'

'No, thank you,' said I; 'I have another string to my bow.'

'All right,' says Myner; 'be sure it's honest.'

'Honest? honest?' I cried. 'What do you mean by calling my honesty in question?'

'I won't, if you don't like it,' he replied. 'You seem to

think honesty as easy as Blind Man's Buff: I don't. It's some difference of definition.'

I went straight from this irritating interview, during which Myner had never discontinued painting, to the studio of my old master. Only one card remained for me to play, and I was now resolved to play it: I must drop the gentleman and the frock-coat, and approach art in the workman's tunic.

'*Tiens*, this little Dodd!' cried the master; and then, as his eye fell on my dilapidated clothing, I thought I could perceive his countenance to darken.

I made my plea in English; for I knew, if he were vain of anything, it was of his achievement of the island tongue. 'Master,' said I, 'will you take me in your studio again – but this time as a workman?'

'I sought your fazér was immensely reech?' said he.

I explained to him that I was now an orphan and penniless.

He shook his head. 'I have better workmen waiting at my door,' said he, 'far better workmen.'

'You used to think something of my work, sir,' I pleaded.

'Somesing, somesing – yés!' he cried; 'énough for a son of a reech man – not énough for an orphan. Besides, I sought you might learn to be an artist; I did not sink you might learn to be a workman.'

On a certain bench on the outer boulevard, not far from the tomb of Napoleon – a bench shaded at that date by a shabby tree, and commanding a view of muddy roadway and blank wall – I sat down to wrestle with my misery. The weather was cheerless and dark; in three days I had eaten but once; I had no tobacco; my shoes were soaked, my trousers horrid with mire; my humour and all the circumstances of the time and place lugubriously attuned. Here were two men who had both spoken fairly of my work while I was rich and wanted nothing; now that I was poor and lacked all: 'No genius,' said the one; 'not enough for an orphan,' the other; and the first offered me my passage like a pauper immigrant, and the second refused me a day's wage as a hewer of stone – plain dealing for an empty belly. They had not been insincere in the past; they were not insincere today: change of circumstance had introduced a new criterion, that was all.

But if I acquitted my two Job's comforters of insincerity, I was yet far from admitting them infallible. Artists had been contemned before, and had lived to turn the laugh on their contemners. How old was Corot before he struck the vein of his own precious metal? When had a young man been more derided (or more justly so) than the god of my admiration, Balzac? Or, if I required a bolder inspiration, what had I to do but turn my head to where the gold dome of the Invalides glittered against inky squalls, and recall the tale of him sleeping there: from the day when a young artillery-sub could be giggled at and nicknamed Puss-in-Boots by frisky misses, on to the days of so many crowns and so many victories, and so many hundred mouths of cannon, and so many thousand war-hoofs trampling the roadways of astonished Europe eighty miles in front of the grand army? To go back, to give up, to proclaim myself a failure, an ambitious failure – first a rocket, then a stick! I, Loudon Dodd, who had refused all other livelihoods with scorn, and been advertised in the Saint Joseph *Sunday Herald* as a patriot and an artist, to be returned upon my native Muskegon like damaged goods, and go the circuit of my father's acquaintance, cap in hand, and begging to sweep offices! No, by Napoleon! I would die at my chosen trade; and the two who had that day flouted me should live to envy my success, or to weep tears of unavailing penitence behind my pauper coffin.

Meantime, if my courage was still undiminished, I was none the nearer to a meal. At no great distance my cabman's eating-house stood, at the tail of a muddy cab-rank, on the shores of a wide thoroughfare of mud, offering (to fancy) a face of ambiguous invitation. I might be received, I might once more fill my belly there; on the other hand, it was perhaps this day the bolt was destined to fall, and I might be expelled instead, with vulgar hubbub. It was policy to make the attempt, and I knew it was policy; but I had already, in the course of that one morning, endured too many affronts, and I felt I could rather starve than face another. I had courage and to spare for the future, none left for that day; courage for the main campaign, but not a spark of it for that preliminary skirmish of the cabman's restaurant. I continued accordingly to sit upon my bench, not far from the ashes of Napoleon, now drowsy, now light-headed, now in complete mental obstruction, or only conscious of an animal pleasure in quiescence; and now thinking, planning, and remembering with unexampled clearness, telling myself tales of sudden wealth, and gustfully ordering and greedily consuming imaginary meals, in the course of which I must have dropped asleep.

It was towards dark that I was suddenly recalled to famine by a cold souse of rain, and sprang shivering to my feet. For a moment I stood bewildered; the whole train of my reasoning and dreaming passed afresh through my mind; I was again tempted, drawn as if with cords, by the image of the cabman's eating-house, and again recoiled from the possibility of insult. '*Qui dort dîne*,' thought I to myself; and took my homeward way with wavering footsteps, through rainy streets in which the lamps and the shop-windows now began to gleam, still marshalling imaginary dinners as I went.

'Ah, Monsieur Dodd,' said the porter, 'there has been a registered letter for you. The facteur will bring it again tomorrow.'

A registered letter for me, who had been so long without one? Of what it could possibly contain I had no vestige of a guess, nor did I delay myself guessing; far less form any conscious plan of dishonesty: the lies flowed from me like a natural secretion.

'Oh,' said I, 'my remittance at last! What a bother I should have missed it! Can you lend me a hundred francs until tomorrow?'

I had never attempted to borrow from the porter till that moment; the registered letter was, besides, my warranty; and he gave me what he had – three napoleons and some francs in silver. I pocketed the money carelessly, lingered awhile chaffing, strolled leisurely to the door; and then (fast as my trembling legs could carry me) round the corner to the Café Cluny. French waiters are deft and speedy; they were not deft enough for me: and I had scarce decency to let the man set the wine upon the table or put the butter alongside the bread, before my glass and my mouth were filled. Exquisite bread of the Café Cluny, exquisite first glass of old Pomard tingling to my wet feet, indescribable first olive culled from the *hors d'œuvre* – I suppose, when I come to lie dying, and the lamp begins to grow dim, I shall still recall your savour. Over the rest of that meal, and the rest of the evening, clouds lie thick; clouds perhaps of Burgundy: perhaps, more properly, of famine and repletion.

I remember clearly, at least, the shame, the despair, of the next morning, when I reviewed what I had done, and how I had swindled the poor honest porter; and, as if that were not enough, fairly burnt my ships, and brought bankruptcy home to that last refuge, my garret. The porter would expect his money; I could not pay him; here was scandal in the house; and I knew right well the cause of scandal would have to pack. 'What do you mean by calling my honesty in question?' I had cried the day before, turning upon Myner. Ah, that day before! the day before Waterloo, the day before the Flood; the day before I had sold the roof over my head, my future, and my self-respect, for a dinner at the Café Cluny!

In the midst of these lamentations the famous registered letter came to my door, with healing under its seals. It bore the postmark of San Francisco, where Pinkerton was already struggling to the neck in multifarious affairs; it renewed the offer of an allowance, which his improved estate permitted him to announce at the figure of two hundred francs a month; and in case I was in some immediate pinch, it enclosed an introductory draft for forty dollars. There are a thousand excellent reasons why a man, in this self-helpful epoch, should decline to be dependent on another; but the most numerous and cogent considerations all bow to a necessity as stern as mine; and the banks were scarce open ere the draft was cashed.

It was early in December that I thus sold myself into slavery, and for six months I dragged a slowly lengthening chain of gratitude and uneasiness. At the cost of some debt I managed to excel myself and eclipse the Genius of Muskegon, in a small but highly patriotic 'Standard Bearer' for the Salon; whither it was duly admitted, where it stood the proper length of days entirely unremarked, and whence it came back to me as patriotic as before. I threw my whole soul (as Pinkerton would have phrased it) into clocks and candlesticks; the devil a candlestick-maker would have anything to say to my designs. Even when Dijon, with his infinite good humour and infinite scorn for all such journey-work, consented to peddle them in indiscriminately with his own, the dealers still detected and rejected mine. Home they returned to me, true as the Standard Bearer, who now, at the head of quite a regiment of lesser idols, began to grow an eyesore in the scanty studio of my friend. Dijon and I have sat by the hour, and gazed upon that company of images. The severe, the frisky, the classical, the Louis Quinze, were there – from Joan of Arc in her soldierly cuirass to Leda with the swan; nay – and God forgive me for a man that knew better! – the humorous was represented also. We sat and gazed, I say; we criticised, we turned them hither and thither; even upon the closest inspection they looked quite like statuettes; and yet nobody would have a gift of them!

Vanity dies hard; in some obstinate cases it outlives the man: but about the sixth month, when I already owed near two hundred dollars to Pinkerton, and half as much again in debts scattered about Paris, I awoke one morning with a horrid sentiment of oppression, and found I was alone: my vanity had breathed her last during the night. I dared not plunge deeper in the bog; I saw no hope in my poor statuary; I owned myself beaten at last; and sitting down in my nightshirt beside the window, whence I had a glimpse of the tree-tops at the corner of the boulevard, and where the music of its early traffic fell agreeably upon my ear, I penned my farewell to Paris, to art, to my whole past life, and my whole former self. 'I give in,' I wrote. 'When the next allowance arrives, I shall go straight out West, where you can do what you like with me.'

It is to be understood that Pinkerton had been, in a sense, pressing me to come from the beginning; depicting his isolation among new acquaintances, 'who have none of them your culture,' he wrote; expressing his friendship in terms so warm that it sometimes embarrassed me to think how poorly I could echo them; dwelling upon his need for assistance; and the next moment turning about to commend my resolution and press me to remain in Paris. 'Only remember, Loudon,' he would write, 'if you ever *do* tire of it, there's plenty of work here for you – honest, hard, well-paid work, developing the resources of this practically virgin State. And, of course, I needn't say what a pleasure it would be to me if we were going at it *shoulder to shoulder*.' I marvel, looking back, that I could so long have resisted these appeals, and continue to sink my friend's money in a manner that I knew him to dislike. At least, when I did awake to any sense of my position, I awoke to it entirely, and determined not only to follow his counsel for the future, but, even as regards the past, to rectify his losses. For in this juncture of affairs I called to mind that I was not without a possible resource, and resolved, at whatever cost of mortification, to beard the Loudon family in their historic city.

In the excellent Scots phrase, I made a moonlight flitting, a thing never dignified, but in my case unusually easy. As I had scarce a pair of boots worth portage I deserted the whole of my effects without a pang. Dijon fell heir to Joan of Arc, the Standard Bearer, and the Musketeers. He was present when I bought and frugally stocked my new portmanteau, and it was at the door of the trunk-shop that I took my leave of him, for my last few hours in Paris must be spent alone. It was alone, and at a far higher figure than my finances warranted, that I discussed my dinner; alone that I took my ticket at Saint Lazare; all alone, though in a carriage full of people, that I watched the moon shine on the Seine flood with its tufted isles, on Rouen with her spires, and on the shipping in the harbour of Dieppe. When the first light of the morning called me from troubled slumbers on the deck, I beheld the dawn at first with pleasure; I watched with pleasure the green shores of England rising out of rosy haze; I too the salt air with delight into my nostrils; and then all came back to me – that I was no longer an artist, no longer myself; that I was leaving all I cared for, and returning to all that I detested, the slave of debt and gratitude, a public and a branded failure.

From this picture of my own disgrace and wretchedness it is not wonderful if my mind turned with relief to the thought of Pinkerton waiting for me, as I knew, with unwearied affection, and regarding me with a respect that I had never deserved, and might therefore fairly hope that I should never forfeit. The inequality of our relation struck me rudely. I must have been stupid, indeed, if I could have considered the history of that friendship without shame – I who had given so little, who had accepted and profited by so much. I had the whole day before me in London, and I determined, at least in words, to set the balance somewhat straighter. Seated in the corner of a public place, and calling for sheet after sheet of paper, I poured forth the expression of my gratitude, my penitence for the past, my resolutions for the future. Till now, I told him, my course had been mere selfishness. I had been selfish to my father and to my friend, taking their help and denying them (which was all they asked) the poor gratification of my company and countenance.

Wonderful are the consolations of literature! As soon as that letter was written and posted the consciousness of virtue glowed in my veins like some rare vintage.

CHAPTER SIX

In which I Go West

I reached my uncle's door next morning in time to sit down with the family to breakfast. More than three years had intervened – almost without mutation in that stationary household – since I had sat there first, a young American freshman, bewildered among unfamiliar dainties (finnan haddock, kippered salmon, baps, and mutton ham), and had wearied my mind in vain to guess what should be under the tea-cosy. If there were any change at all, it seemed that I had risen in the family esteem. My father's death once fittingly referred to, with a ceremonial lengthening of Scotch upper lips and wagging of the female head, the party launched at once (God help me!) into the more cheerful topic of my own successes. They had been so pleased to hear such good accounts of me; I was quite a great man now; where was that beautiful statue of the Genuis of Something or other? 'You haven't it here? Not here? Really?' asks the sprightliest of my cousins, shaking curls at me; as though it were likely I had brought it in the cab, or kept it concealed about my person like a birthday surprise. In the bosom of this family, unaccustomed to the tropical nonsense of the West, it became plain the *Sunday Herald* and poor blethering Pinkerton had been accepted for their face. It is not possible to invent a circumstance that could have more depressed me; and I am conscious that I behaved all through that breakfast like a whipped schoolboy.

At length, the meal and family prayers being both happily over, I requested the favour of an interview with Uncle Adam on 'the state of my affairs.' At sound of this ominous expression, the good man's face conspicuously lengthened; and when my grandfather, having had the proposition repeated to him (for he was hard of hearing), announced his intention of being present at the interview,

I could not but think that Uncle Adam's sorrow kindled into momentary irritation. Nothing, however, but the usual grim cordiality appeared upon the surface; and we all three passed ceremoniously to the adjoining library, a gloomy theatre for a depressing piece of business. My grandfather charged a clay pipe, and sat tremulously smoking in a corner of the fireless chimney; behind him, although the morning was both chill and dark, the window was partly open and the blind partly down: I cannot depict what an air he had of being out of place, like a man shipwrecked there. Uncle Adam had his station at the business table in the midst. Valuable rows of books looked down upon the place of torture; and I could hear sparrows chirping in the garden, and my sprightly cousin already banging the piano and pouring forth an acid stream of song from the drawing-room overhead.

It was in these circumstances that, with all brevity of speech and a certain boyish sullenness of manner, looking the while upon the floor; I informed my relatives of my financial situation: the amount I owed Pinkerton; the hopelessness of any maintenance from sculpture; the career offered me in the States; and how, before becoming more beholden to a stranger, I had judged it right to lay the case before my family.

'I am only sorry you did not come to me at first,' said Uncle Adam. 'I take the liberty to say it would have been more decent.'

'I think so too, Uncle Adam,' I replied; 'but you must bear in mind I was ignorant in what light you might regard my application.'

'I hope I would never turn my back on my own flesh and blood,' he returned with emphasis; but, to my anxious ear, with more of temper than affection. 'I could never forget you were my sister's son. I regard this as a manifest duty. I have no choice but to accept the entire responsibility of the position you have made.'

I did not know what else to do but murmur 'Thank you.'

'Yes,' he pursued, 'and there is something providential in the circumstance that you come at the right time. In my old firm there is a vacancy; they call themselves Italian Warehousemen now,' he continued, regarding me with a twinkle of humour; 'so you may think yourself in luck: we were only grocers in my day. I shall place you there tomorrow.'

'Stop a moment, Uncle Adam,' I broke in. 'This is not at all what I am asking. I ask you to pay Pinkerton, who is a poor man. I ask you to clear my feet of debt, not to arrange my life or any part of it.'

'If I wished to be harsh, I might remind you that beggars cannot be choosers,' said my uncle; 'and as to managing your life, you have tried your own way already, and you see what you have made of it. You must now accept the guidance of those older and (whatever you may think of it) wiser than yourself. All these schemes of your friend (of whom I know nothing, by-the-bye) and talk of openings in the West, I simply disregard. I have no idea whatever of your going troking across a continent on a wild-goose chase. In this situation, which I am fortunately able to place at your disposal, and which many a well-conducted young man would be glad to jump at, you will receive, to begin with, eighteen shillings a week.'

'Eighteen shillings a week!' I cried. 'Why, my poor friend gave me more than that for nothing!'

'And I think it is this very friend you are now trying to repay?' observed my uncle, with an air of one advancing a strong argument.

'Aadam,' said my grandfather.

'I'm vexed you should be present at this business,' quoth Uncle Adam, swinging rather obsequiously towards the stonemason; 'but I must remind you it is of your own seeking.'

'Aadam!' repeated the old man.

'Well, sir, I am listening,' says my uncle.

My grandfather took a puff or two in silence; and then, 'Ye're makin' an awfu' poor appearance, Aadam,' said he.

My uncle visibly reared at the affront. 'I'm sorry you should think so,' said he, 'and still more sorry you should say so before present company.'

'A believe that; A ken that, Aadam,' returned old Loudon, dryly; 'and the curiis thing is, I'm no very carin'. See here, ma man,' he continued, addressing himself to me. 'A'll your grandfaither, amn't I not?

Never you mind what Aadam says. A'll see justice din ye. A'm rich.'

'Father,' said Uncle Adam, 'I would like one word with you in private.'

I rose to go.

'Set down upon your hinderlands,' cried my grandfather, almost savagely. 'If Aadam has anything to say, let him say it. It's me that has the money here; and by Gravy! I'm goin' to be obeyed.'

Upon this scurvy encouragement, it appeared that my uncle had no remark to offer: twice challenged to 'speak out and be done with it,' he twice sullenly declined; and I may mention that about this period of the engagement I began to be sorry for him.

'See here, then, Jeannie's yin!' resumed my grandfather. 'A'm goin' to give ye a set-off. Your mither was always my fav'rite, for A never could agree with Aadam. A like ye fine yoursel'; there's nae noansense aboot ye; ye've a fine nayteral idee of builder's work; ye've been to France, where, they tell me, they're grand at the stuccy. A splendid thing for ceilin's, the stuccy! and it's a vailyable disguise, too; A don't believe there's a builder in Scotland has used more stuccy than me. But, as A was sayin', if ye'll follie that trade, with the capital that A'm goin' to give ye, ye may live yet to be as rich as mysel'. Ye see, ye would have always had a share of it when A was gone; it appears ye're needin' it now; well, ye'll get the less, as is only just and proper.'

Uncle Adam cleared his throat. 'This is very handsome, father,' said he; 'and I am sure Loudon feels it so. Very handsome, and, as you say, very just; but will you allow me to say that it had better, perhaps, be put in black and white?'

The enmity always smouldering between the two men, at this ill-judged interruption almost burst in flame. The stonemason turned upon his offspring, his long upper lip pulled down for all the world like a monkey's. He stared awhile in virulent silence; and then, 'Get Gregg!' said he.

The effect of these words was very visible. 'He will be gone to his office,' stammered my uncle.

'Get Gregg!' repeated my grandfather.

'I tell you, he will be gone to his office,' reiterated Adam.

'And I tell ye, he's takin' his smoke,' retorted the old man.

'Very well, then,' cried my uncle, getting to his feet with some alacrity, as upon a sudden change of thought, 'I will get him myself.'

'Ye will not!' cried my grandfather. 'Ye will sit there upon your hinderland.'

'Then how the devil am I to get him?' my uncle broke forth, with not unnatural petulance.

My grandfather (having no possible answer) grinned at his son with the malice of a schoolboy; then he rang the bell.

'Take the garden key,' said Uncle Adam to the servant; 'go over to the garden, and if Mr Gregg the lawyer is there (he generally sits under the red hawthorn), give him old Mr Loudon's compliments, and will he step in here for a moment?'

'Mr Gregg the lawyer!' At once I understood (what had been puzzling me) the significance of my grandfather and the alarm of my poor uncle: the stonemason's will, it was supposed, hung trembling in the balance.

'Look here, grandfather,' I said, 'I didn't want any of this. All I wanted was a loan of, say, two hundred pounds. I can take care of myself; I have prospects and opportunities, good friends in the States— '

The old man waved me down. 'It's me that speaks here,' he said curtly; and we waited the coming of the lawyer in a triple silence. He appeared at last, the maid ushering him in – a spectacled, dry but not ungenial looking man.

'Here, Gregg,' cried my grandfather, 'just a question. What has Aadam got to do with my will?'

'I'm afraid I don't quite understand,' said the lawyer, staring.

'What has he got to do with it?' repeated the old man, smiting with his fist upon the arm of his chair. 'Is my money mine's, or is it Aadam's? Can Aadam interfere?'

'Oh, I see,' said Mr Gregg. 'Certainly not. On the marriage of both of your children a certain sum was paid down and accepted in full of legitim. You have surely not forgotten the circumstance, Mr Loudon?'

'So that, if I like,' concluded my grandfather, hammering out his words, 'I can leave every doit I die possessed of to the Great Magunn?' – meaning probably the Great Mogul.

'No doubt of it,' replied Gregg, with a shadow of a smile.

'Ye hear that, Aadam?' asked my grandfather.

'I may be allowed to say I had no need to hear it,' said my uncle.

'Very well,' says my grandfather. 'You and Jeannie's yin can go for a bit walk. Me and Gregg has business.'

When once I was in the hall alone with Uncle Adam, I turned to him, sick at heart. 'Uncle Adam,' I said, 'you can understand, better than I can say, how very painful all this is to me.'

'Yes, I am sorry you have seen your grandfather in so unamiable a light,' replied this extraordinary man. 'You shouldn't allow it to affect your mind, though. He has sterling qualities, quite an extraordinary character; and I have no fear but he means to behave handsomely to you.'

His composure was beyond my imitation: the house could not contain me, nor could I even promise to return to it: in concession to which weakness, it was agreed that I should call in about an hour at the office of the lawyer, whom (as he left the library) Uncle Adam should waylay and inform of the arrangement. I suppose there was never a more topsy-turvy situation; you would have thought it was I who had suffered some rebuff, and that iron-sided Adam was a generous conqueror who scorned to take advantage.

It was plain enough that I was to be endowed: to what extent and upon what conditions I was now left for an hour to meditate in the wide and solitary thoroughfares of the new town, taking counsel with street-corner statues of George IV, and William Pitt, improving my mind with the pictures in the window of a music-shop, and renewing my acquaintance with Edinburgh east wind. By the end of the hour I made my way to Mr Gregg's office, where I was placed, with a few appropriate words, in possession of a cheque for two thousand pounds and a small parcel of architectural works.

'Mr Loudon bids me add,' continued the lawyer, consulting a little sheet of notes, 'that although these volumes are very valuable to the practical builder, you must be careful not to lose originality. He tells you also not to be "hadden doun" – his own expression – by the theory of strains, and that Portland cement, properly sanded, will go a long way.'

I smiled, and remarked that I supposed it would.

'I once lived in one of my excellent client's houses,' observed the lawyer; 'and I was tempted, in that case, to think it had gone far enough.'

'Under these circumstances, sir,' said I, 'you will be rather relieved to hear that I have no intention of becoming a builder.'

At this he fairly laughed; and, the ice being broken, I was able to consult him as to my conduct. He insisted I must return to the house – at least, for luncheon, and one of my walks with Mr Loudon. 'For the evening, I will furnish you with an excuse, if you please,' said he, 'by asking you to a bachelor dinner with myself. But the luncheon and the walk are unavoidable. He is an old man, and, I believe, really fond of you; he would naturally feel aggrieved if there were any appearance of avoiding him; and as for Mr Adam, do you know, I think your delicacy out of place . . . And now, Mr Dodd, what are you to do with this money?'

Ay, there was the question. With two thousand pounds – fifty thousand francs – I might return to Paris and the arts, and be a prince and millionaire in that thrifty Latin Quarter. I think I had the grace with one corner of my mind, to be glad that I had sent the Loudon letter: I know very well that with the rest and worst of me, I repented bitterly of that precipitate act. On one point, however, my whole multiplex estate of man was unanimous: the letter being gone, there was no help but I must follow. The money was accordingly divided in two unequal shares: for the first, Mr Gregg got me a bill in the name of Dijon to meet my liabilities in Paris; for the second, as I had already cash in hand for the expenses of my journey, he supplied me with drafts on San Francisco.

The rest of my business in Edinburgh, not to dwell on a very agreeable dinner with the lawyer or the horrors of the family luncheon, took the form of an excursion with the stonemason, who led me this time to no suburb or work of his old hands, but with an impulse both natural and pretty, to that more enduring home which he had chosen for his clay. It was in a cemetery, by some strange chance immured within the bulwarks of a prison; standing, besides, on the margin of a cliff, crowded with elderly stone memorials, and green with turf and ivy. The east wind (which I thought too harsh for the old man) continually shook the boughs, and the thin sun of a Scottish summer drew their dancing shadows.

'I wanted ye to see the place,' said he. 'Yon's the stane. *Euphemia Ross*: that was my goodwife, your grandmither – hoots! I'm wrong; that was my first yin; I had no bairns by her; – yours is the second, *Mary Murray, Born* 1819, *Died* 1850: that's her – a fine, plain, decent sort of a creature, tak' her athegether. *Alexander London, Born Seventeen Ninety-Twa, Died* – and then a hole in the ballant: that's me. Alexander's my name. They ca'd me Ecky when I was a boy. Eh, Ecky! ye're an awfu' auld man!'

I had a second and sadder experience of graveyards at my next alighting-place, the city of Muskegon, now rendered conspicuous by the dome of the new capitol encaged in scaffolding. It was late in the afternoon when I arrived, and raining; and as I walked in great streets, of the very name of which I was quite ignorant – double, treble, and quadruple lines of horse-cars jingling by – hundred-fold wires of telegraph and telephone matting heaven above my head – huge, staring houses, garish and gloomy, flanking me from either hand – the thought of the Rue Racine, ay, and of the cabman's eating-house brought tears to my eyes. The whole monotonous Babel had grown – or, I should rather say, swelled – with such a leap since my departure that I must continually inquire my way; and the very cemetery was brand-new. Death, however, had been active; the graves were already numerous, and I must pick my way in the rain among the tawdry sepulchres of millionaires, and past the plain black crosses of Hungarian labourers, till chance or instinct led me to the place that was my father's. The stone had been erected (I knew already) 'by admiring friends'; I could now judge their taste in monuments. Their taste in literature, methought, I could imagine, and I refrained from drawing near enough to read the terms of the inscription. But the name was in larger letters and stared at me – *James*

K. Dodd. 'What a singular thing is a name!' I thought; 'how it clings to a man, and continually misrepresents, and then survives him!' And it flashed across my mind, with a mixture of regret and bitter mirth, that I had never known, and now probably never should know, what the *K* had represented. King, Kilter, Kay, Kaiser, I went, running over names at random, and then stumbled, with ludicrous misspelling, on Kornelius, and had nearly laughed aloud. I have never been more childish; I suppose (although the deeper voices of my nature seemed all dumb) because I have never been more moved. And at this last incongruous antic of my nerves I was seized with a panic of remorse, and fled the cemetery.

Scarce less funereal was the rest of my experience in Muskegon, where, nevertheless, I lingered, visiting my father's circle, for some days. It was in piety to him I lingered; and I might have spared myself the pain. His memory was already quite gone out. For his sake, indeed, I was made welcome; and for mine the conversation rolled awhile with laborious effort on the virtues of the deceased. His former comrades dwelt, in my company, upon his business talents or his generosity for public purposes: when my back was turned, they remembered him no more. My father had loved me; I had left him alone, to live and die among the indifferent; now I returned to find him dead and buried and forgotten. Unavailing penitence translated itself in my thoughts to fresh resolve. There was another poor soul who loved me – Pinkerton. I must not be guilty twice of the same error.

A week perhaps had been thus wasted, nor had I prepared my friend for the delay. Accordingly, when I had changed trains at Council Bluffs, I was aware of a man appearing at the end of the car with a telegram in his hand and inquiring whether there were anyone aboard 'of the name of *London* Dodd?' I thought the name near enough, claimed the despatch, and found it was from Pinkerton: 'What day do you arrive? Awfully important.' I sent him an answer, giving day and hour, and at Ogden found a fresh despatch awaiting me: 'That will do. Unspeakable relief. Meet you at Sacramento.' In Paris days I had a private name for Pinkerton: 'The Irrepressible' was what I had called him in hours of bitterness, and the name rose once more on my lips. What mischief was he up to now? What new bowl was my benignant monster brewing for his Frankenstein? In what new imbroglio should I alight on the Pacific coast? My trust in the man was entire, and my distrust perfect. I knew he would never mean amiss; but I was convinced he would almost never (in my sense) do aright.

I suppose these vague anticipations added a shade of gloom to that already gloomy place of travel: Nebraska, Wyoming, Utah, Nevada, scowled in my face at least, and seemed to point me back again to that other native land of mine, the Latin Quarter. But when the Sierras had been climbed, and the train, after so long beating and panting, stretched itself upon the downward track – when I beheld that vast extent of prosperous country rolling seaward from the woods and the blue mountains, that illimitable spread of rippling corn, the trees growing and blowing in the merry weather, the country boys thronging aboard the train with figs and peaches, and the conductors, and the very darky stewards, visibly exulting in the change – up went my soul like a balloon; Care fell from his perch upon my shoulders; and when I spied my Pinkerton among the crowd at Sacramento, I thought of nothing but to shout and wave for him, and grasp him by the hand, like what he was – my dearest friend.

'Oh, Loudon!' he cried; 'man, how I've pined for you! And you haven't come an hour too soon. You're known here and waited for; I've been booming you already: you're billed for a lecture tomorrow night: "Student Life in Paris, Grave and Gay": twelve hundred places booked at the last stock! Tut, man, you're looking thin! Here, try a drop of this.' And he produced a case bottle, staringly labelled PINKERTON'S THIRTEEN STAR GOLDEN STATE BRANDY, WARRANTED ENTIRE.

'God bless me!' said I, gasping and winking after my first plunge into this fiery fluid; 'and what does "Warranted Entire" mean?'

'Why, Loudon, you ought to know that!' cried Pinkerton. 'It's real, copper-bottomed English; you see it on all the old-time wayside hostelries over there.'

'But if I'm not mistaken, it means something Warranted Entirely different,' said I, 'and applies to the public-house, and not the beverages sold.'

'It's very possible,' said Jim, quite unabashed. 'It's effective, anyway; and I can tell you, sir, it has boomed that spirit:
it goes now by the gross of cases. By the way, I hope you
won't mind; I've got your portrait all over San Francisco for
the lecture, enlarged from that carte de visite: "H. Loudon
Dodd, the Americo-Parisienne Sculptor." Here's a proof of
the small handbills; the posters are the same, only in red
and blue, and the letters fourteen by one.'

I looked at the handbill, and my head turned. What
was the use of words? why seek to explain to Pinkerton
the knotted horrors of 'Americo-Parisienne'? He took an
early occasion to point it out as 'rather a good phrase; gives
the two sides at a glance: I wanted the lecture written up
to that.' Even after we had reached San Francisco, and at
the actual physical shock of my own effigy placarded on
the streets I had broken forth in petulant words, he never
comprehended in the least the ground of my aversion.

'If I had only known you disliked red lettering!' was as
high as he could rise. 'You are perfectly right: a clear-cut
black is preferable, and shows a great deal further. The only
thing that pains me is the portrait: I own I thought that a
success. I'm dreadfully and truly sorry, my dear fellow: I
see now it's not what you had a right to expect; but I did
it, Loudon, for the best; and the press is all delighted.'

At the moment, sweeping through green tule swamps, I
fell direct on the essential. 'But, Pinkerton,' I cried, 'this
lecture is the maddest of your madnesses. How can I prepare
a lecture in thirty hours?'

'All done, Loudon!' he exclaimed in triumph. 'All ready.
Trust me to pull a piece of business through. You'll find it
all type-written in my desk at home. I put the best talent
of San Francisco on the job: Harry Miller, the brightest
pressman in the city.'

And so he rattled on, beyond reach of my modest
protestations, blurting out his complicated interests, crying
up his new acquaintances, and ever and again hungering
to introduce me to some 'whole-souled, grand fellow, as
sharp as a needle,' from whom, and the very thought of
whom, my spirit shrank instinctively.

Well, I was in for it – in for Pinkerton, in for the portrait,
in for the type-written lecture. One promise I extorted –
that I was never again to be committed in ignorance.

Even for that, when I saw how its extortion puzzled and depressed the Irrepressible, my soul repented me, and in all else I suffered myself to be led uncomplaining at his chariot-wheels. The Irrepressible, did I say? The Irresistible were nigher truth.

But the time to have seen me was when I sat down to Harry Miller's lecture. He was a facetious dog, this Harry Miller. He had a gallant way of skirting the indecent, which in my case produced physical nausea, and he could be sentimental and even melodramatic about grisettes and starving genius. I found he had enjoyed the benefit of my correspondence with Pinkerton; adventures of my own were here and there horridly misrepresented, sentiments of my own echoed and exaggerated till I blushed to recognise them. I will do Harry Miller justice: he must have had a kind of talent, almost of genius; all attempts to lower his tone proving fruitless, and the Harry-Millerism ineradicable. Nay, the monster had a certain key of style, or want of style, so that certain milder passages, which I sought to introduce, discorded horribly and impoverished, if that were possible, the general effect.

By an early hour of the numbered evening I might have been observed at the sign of 'The Poodle Dog' dining with my agent – so Pinkerton delighted to describe himself. Thence, like an ox to the slaughter, he led me to the hall, where I stood presently alone, confronting assembled San Francisco, with no better allies than a table, a glass of water, and a mass of manuscript and typework, representing Harry Miller and myself. I read the lecture; for I had lacked both time and will to get the trash by heart – read it hurriedly, humbly, and with visible shame. Now and then I would catch in the auditorium an eye of some intelligence, now and then in the manuscript would stumble on a richer vein of Harry Miller, and my heart would fail me, and I gabbled. The audience yawned, it stirred uneasily, it muttered, grumbled, and broke forth at last in articulate cries of 'Speak up!' and 'Nobody can hear!' I took to skipping, and, being extremely ill-acquainted with the country, almost invariably cut in again in the unintelligible midst of some new topic. What struck me as extremely ominous, these misfortunes were allowed to pass without a laugh. Indeed, I was beginning to fear the worst, and even personal indignity, when all at once the humour of the thing broke upon me strongly. I could have laughed aloud, and, being again summoned to speak up, I faced my patrons for the first time with a smile. 'Very well,' I said, 'I will try, though I don't suppose anybody wants to hear, and I can't see why anybody should.' Audience and lecturer laughed together till the tears ran down, vociferous and repeated applause hailed my impromptu sally. Another hit which I made but a little after, as I turned three pages of the copy – 'You see, I am leaving out as much as I possibly can' – increased the esteem with which my patrons had begun to regard me; and when I left the stage at last, my departing form was cheered with laughter, stamping, shouting, and the waving of hats.

Pinkerton was in the waiting-room, feverishly jotting in his pocket-book. As he saw me enter, he sprang up, and I declare the tears were trickling on his cheeks.

'My dear boy,' he cried, 'I can never forgive myself, and you can never forgive me. Never mind, I did it for the best. And how nobly you clung on! I dreaded we should have had to return the money at the doors.'

'It would have been more honest if we had,' said I.

The pressmen followed me, Harry Miller in the front ranks; and I was amazed to find them, on the whole, a pleasant set of lads, probably more sinned against than sinning, and even Harry Miller apparently a gentleman. I had in oysters and champagne – for the receipts were excellent – and, being in a high state of nervous tension, kept the table in a roar. Indeed, I was never in my life so well inspired as when I described my vigil over Harry Miller's literature or the series of my emotions as I faced the audience. The lads vowed I was the soul of good company and the prince of lecturers; and – so wonderful an institution is the popular press – if you had seen the notices next day in all the papers you must have supposed my evening's entertainment an unqualified success.

I was in excellent spirits when I returned home that night, but the miserable Pinkerton sorrowed for us both.

'Oh, Loudon,' he said, 'I shall never forgive myself. When I saw you didn't catch on to the idea of the lecture, I should have given it myself!'

CHAPTER SEVEN

Irons in the Fire

OPES STREPITUMQUE

The food of the body differs not so greatly for the fool or the sage, the elephant or the cock-sparrow; and similar chemical elements, variously disguised, support all mortals. A brief study of Pinkerton in his new setting convinced me of a kindred truth about that other and mental digestion by which we extract what is called 'fun for our money' out of life. In the same spirit as a schoolboy deep in Mayne Reid handles a dummy gun and crawls among imaginary forests, Pinkerton sped through Kearney Street upon his daily business, representing to himself a highly-coloured part in life's performance, and happy for hours if he should have chanced to brush against a millionaire. Reality was his romance; he gloried to be thus engaged; he wallowed in his business. Suppose a man to dig up a galleon on the Coromandel coast, his rakish schooner keeping the while an offing under easy sail, and he, by the blaze of a great fire of wreckwood, to measure ingots by the bucketful on the uproarious beach; such an one might realise a greater material spoil; he should have no more profit of romance than Pinkerton when he cast up his weekly balance-sheet in a bald office. Every dollar gained was like something brought ashore from a mysterious deep; every venture made was like a diver's plunge; and as he thrust his bold hand into the plexus of the money-market he was delightedly aware of how he shook the pillars of existence, turned out men, as at a battle-cry, to labour in far countries, and set the gold twitching in the drawers of millionaires.

I could never fathom the full extent of his speculations; but there were five separate businesses which he avowed and carried like a banner. The *Thirteen Star Golden State Brandy, Warranted Entire* (a very flagrant distillation) filled a great part of his thoughts, and was kept before the public in an eloquent but misleading treatise, 'Why Drink French Brandy? A Word to the Wise.' He kept an office for advertisers, counselling, designing, acting as middleman with printers and bill-stickers, for the inexperienced or the uninspired: the dull haberdasher came to him for ideas, the smart theatrical agent for his local knowledge, and one and all departed with a copy of his pamphlet, 'How, When and Where; or, The Advertiser's Vade-Mecum.' He had a tug chartered every Saturday afternoon and night, carried people outside the Heads, and provided them with lines and bait for six hours' fishing, at the rate of five dollars a person. I am told that some of them (doubtless adroit anglers) made a profit on the transaction. Occasionally he bought wrecks and condemned vessels; these latter (I cannot tell you how) found their way to sea again under aliases, and continued to stem the waves triumphantly enough under the colours of Bolivia or Nicaragua. Lastly, there was a certain agricultural engine, glorying in a great deal of vermilion and blue paint, and filling (it appeared) a 'long-felt want,' in which his interest was something like a tenth.

This for the face or front of his concerns. 'On the outside,' as he phrased it, he was variously and mysteriously engaged. No dollar slept in his possession; rather, he kept all simultaneously flying, like a conjurer with oranges. My own earnings, when I began to have a share, he would but show me for a moment, and disperse again, like those illusive money gifts which are flashed in the eyes of childhood, only to be entombed in the missionary-box. And he would come down radiant from a weekly balance-sheet, clap me on the shoulder, declare himself a winner by Gargantuan figures, and prove destitute of a quarter for a drink.

'What on earth have you done with it?' I would ask.

'Into the mill again; all re-invested!' he would cry, with infinite delight. 'Investment' was ever his word. He could not bear what he called gambling. 'Never touch stocks, Loudon,' he would say; 'nothing but legitimate business.' And yet, Heaven knows, many an indurated gambler might have drawn back appalled at the first hint of some of Pinkerton's investments! One which I succeeded in tracking home, and instance for a specimen, was a seventh share in the charter of a certain ill-starred

schooner bound for Mexico – to smuggle weapons on the
one trip, and cigars upon the other. The latter end of this
enterprise, involving (as it did) shipwreck, confiscation,
and a lawsuit with the underwriters, was too painful to
be dwelt upon at length. 'It's proved a disappointment,'
was as far as my friend would go with me in words; but
I knew, from observation, that the fabric of his fortunes
tottered. For the rest, it was only by accident I got wind
of the transaction; for Pinkerton, after a time, was shy of
introducing me to his arcana: the reason you are to hear
presently.

The office which was (or should have been) the point of
rest for so many evolving dollars stood in the heart of the city
– a high and spacious room, with many plate-glass windows.
A glazed cabinet of polished redwood offered to the eye
a regiment of some two hundred bottles, conspicuously
labelled. These were all charged with Pinkerton's Thirteen
Star, although from across the room it would have required
an expert to distinguish them from the same number of
bottles of Courvoisier. I used to twit my friend with this
resemblance, and propose a new edition of the pamphlet,
with the title thus improved, 'Why Drink French Brandy,
When We give You the same Labels?' The doors of the
cabinet revolved all day upon their hinges; and if there
entered anyone who was a stranger to the merits of the
brand, he departed laden with a bottle. When I used to
protest at this extravagance, 'My dear Loudon,' Pinkerton
would cry, 'you don't seem to catch on to business principles! The prime cost of the spirit is literally nothing. I
couldn't find a cheaper advertisement if I tried.' Against
the side post of the cabinet there leaned a gaudy umbrella,
preserved there as a relic. It appears that when Pinkerton
was about to place Thirteen Star upon the market, the
rainy season was at hand. He lay dark, almost in penury,
awaiting the first shower, at which, as upon a signal, the
main thoroughfares became dotted with his agents, vendors
of advertisements; and the whole world of San Francisco,
from the business man fleeing for the ferry-boat, to the
lady waiting at the corner for her car, sheltered itself under
umbrellas with this strange device: *Are you wet? Try Thirteen
Star.* 'It was a mammoth boom,' said Pinkerton, with a sigh
of delighted recollection. 'There wasn't another umbrella

to be seen. I stood at this window, Loudon, feasting my eyes; and I declare, I felt like Vanderbilt.' And it was to this neat application of the local climate that he owed, not only much of the sale of Thirteen Star, but the whole business of his advertising agency.

The large desk (to resume our survey of the office) stood about the middle, knee-deep in stacks of hand-bills and posters of 'Why Drink French Brandy?' and 'The Advertiser's Vade-Mecum.' It was flanked upon the one hand by two female type-writers, who rested not between the hours of nine and four, and upon the other by a model of the agricultural machine. The walls, where they were not broken by telephone-boxes and a couple of photographs – one representing the wreck of the *James L. Moody* on a bold and broken coast, the other the Saturday tug alive with amateur fishers – almost disappeared under oil-paintings gaudily framed. Many of these were relics of the Latin Quarter, and I must do Pinkerton the justice to say that none of them were bad, and some had remarkable merit. They went off slowly, but for handsome figures; and their places were progressively supplied with the work of local artists. These last it was one of my first duties to review and criticise. Some of them were villainous, yet all were saleable. I said so; and the next moment saw myself, the figure of a miserable renegade, bearing arms in the wrong camp. I was to look at pictures thenceforward, not with the eye of the artist, but the dealer; and I saw the stream widen that divided me from all I loved.

'Now, Loudon,' Pinkerton had said, the morning after the lecture, – 'now, Loudon, we can go at it shoulder to shoulder. This is what I have longed for: I wanted two heads and four arms; and now I have 'em. You'll find it's just the same as art – all observation and imagination; only more movement. Just wait till you begin to feel the charm!'

I might have waited long. Perhaps I lack a sense; for our whole existence seemed to me one dreary bustle, and the place we bustled in fitly to be called the Place of Yawning. I slept in a little den behind the office; Pinkerton, in the office itself, stretched on a patent sofa which sometimes collapsed, his slumbers still further menaced by an imminent clock with an alarm. Roused by this diabolical contrivance, we rose early, went forth early to breakfast, and returned by nine to what Pinkerton called work, and I distraction. Masses of letters must be opened, read, and answered; some by me at a subsidiary desk which had been introduced on the morning of my arrival; others by my bright-eyed friend, pacing the room like a caged lion as he dictated to the tinkling type-writers. Masses of wet proof had to be overhauled and scrawled upon with a blue pencil – 'rustic'; 'six-inch caps'; 'bold spacing here'; or sometimes terms more fervid – as, for instance, this (which I remember Pinkerton to have spirted on the margin of an advertisement of Soothing Syrup), 'Throw this all down. Have you never printed an advertisement? I'll be round in half-an-hour.' The ledger and sale-book, besides, we had always with us. Such was the backbone of our occupation, and tolerable enough; but the far greater proportion of our time was consumed by visitors – whole-souled, grand fellows no doubt, and as sharp as a needle, but to me unfortunately not diverting. Some were apparently half-witted, and must be talked over by the hour before they could reach the humblest decision, which they only left the office to return again (ten minutes later) and rescind. Others came with a vast show of hurry and despatch, but I observed it to be principally show. The agricultural model, for instance, which was practicable, proved a kind of flypaper for these busybodies. I have seen them blankly turn the crank of it for five minutes at a time, simulating (to nobody's deception) business interest: 'Good thing this, Pinkerton? Sell much of it? Ha! Couldn't use it, I suppose, as a medium of advertisement for my article'? – which was perhaps toilet soap. Others (a still worse variety) carried us to neighbouring saloons to dice for cocktails and (after the cocktails were paid) for dollars on a corner of the counter. The attraction of dice for all these people was, indeed, extraordinary: at a certain club where I once dined in the character of 'my partner, Mr Dodd,' the dice-box came on the table with the wine, an artless substitute for after-dinner wit.

Of all our visitors, I believe I preferred Emperor Norton; the very mention of whose name reminds me I am doing scanty justice to the folks of San Francisco. In what other city would a harmless madman who supposed himself emperor of the two Americas have been so fostered and encouraged? Where else would even the people of the streets have respected the poor soul's illusion? Where else would bankers and merchants have received his visits, cashed his cheques, and submitted to his small assessments? Where else would he have been suffered to attend and address the exhibition days of schools and colleges? Where else, in God's green earth, have taken his pick of restaurants, ransacked the bill of fare, and departed scatheless? They tell me he was even an exacting patron, threatening to withdraw his custom when dissatisfied; and I can believe it, for his face wore an expression distinctly gastronomical. Pinkerton had received from this monarch a cabinet appointment; I have seen the brevet, wondering mainly at the good nature of the printer who had executed the forms, and I think my friend was at the head either of foreign affairs or education: it mattered, indeed, nothing, the prestation being in all offices identical. It was at a comparatively early date that I saw Jim in the exercise of his public functions. His Majesty entered the office – a portly, rather flabby man, with the face of a gentleman, rendered unspeakably pathetic and absurd by the great sabre at his side and the peacock's feather in his hat.

'I have called to remind you, Mr Pinkerton, that you are somewhat in arrear of taxes,' he said, with old-fashioned, stately courtesy.

'Well, your Majesty, what is the amount?' asked Jim; and when the figure was named (it was generally two or three dollars), paid upon the nail and offered a bonus in the shape of Thirteen Star.

'I am always delighted to patronise native industries,' said Norton the First. 'San Francisco is public-spirited in what concerns its emperor; and indeed, sir, of all my domains, it is my favourite city.'

'Come,' said I, when he was gone, 'I prefer that customer to the lot.'

'It's really rather a distinction,' Jim admitted. 'I think it must have been the umbrella racket that attracted him.'

We were distinguished under the rose by the notice of other and greater men. There were days when Jim wore an air of unusual capacity and resolve, spoke with more brevity, like one pressed for time, and took often on his tongue such phrases as 'Longhurst told me so this

morning,' or 'I had it straight from Longhurst himself.'
It was no wonder, I used to think, that Pinkerton was
called to council with such Titans; for the creature's
quickness and resource were beyond praise. In the early
days when he consulted me without reserve, pacing the
room, projecting, ciphering, extending hypothetical interests, trebling imaginary capital, his 'engine' (to renew an
excellent old word) labouring full steam ahead, I could
never decide whether my sense of respect or entertainment
were the stronger. But these good hours were destined to
curtailment.

'Yes, it's smart enough,' I once observed. 'But, Pinkerton,
do you think it's honest?'

'You don't think it's honest?' he wailed. 'O dear me,
that ever I should have heard such an expression on
your lips.'

At sight of his distress I plagiarised unblushingly from
Myner. 'You seem to think honesty as simple as Blind
Man's Buff,' said I. 'It's a more delicate affair than that:
delicate as any art.'

'Oh well, at that rate!' he exclaimed, with complete relief;
'that's casuistry.'

'I am perfectly certain of one thing; that what you propose
is dishonest,' I returned.

'Well, say no more about it; that's settled,' he replied.

Thus, almost at a word, my point was carried. But
the trouble was that such differences continued to recur,
until we began to regard each other with alarm. If there
were one thing Pinkerton valued himself upon, it was his
honesty; if there were one thing he clung to, it was my
good opinion; and when both were involved, as was the
case in these commercial cruces, the man was on the rack.
My own position, if you consider how much I owed him,
how hateful is the trade of fault-finder, and that yet I
lived and fattened on these questionable operations, was
perhaps equally distressing. If I had been more sterling or
more combative, things might have gone extremely far.
But, in truth, I was just base enough to profit by what
was not forced on my attention, rather than seek scenes;
Pinkerton quite cunning enough to avail himself of my
weakness; and it was a relief to both when he began to
involve his proceedings in a decent mystery.

Our last dispute, which had a most unlooked-for consequence, turned on the refitting of condemned ships. He had bought a miserable hulk, and came, rubbing his hands, to inform me she was already on the slip, under a new name, to be repaired. When first I had heard of this industry I suppose I scarcely comprehended; but much discussion had sharpened my faculties, and now my brow became heavy.

'I can be no party to that, Pinkerton,' said I.

He leaped like a man shot. 'What next?' he cried. 'What ails you anyway? You seem to me to dislike everything that's profitable.'

'This ship has been condemned by Lloyd's agent,' said I.

'But I tell you it's a deal. The ship's in splendid condition; there's next to nothing wrong with her but the garboard streak and the sternpost. I tell you, Lloyd's is a ring, like everybody else; only it's an English ring, and that's what deceives you. If it was American, you would be crying it down all day. It's Anglomania – common Anglomania,' he cried, with growing irritation.

'I will not make money by risking men's lives,' was my ultimatum.

'Great Cæsar! isn't all speculation a risk? Isn't the fairest kind of shipowning to risk men's lives? And mining – how's that for risk? And look at the elevator business – there's danger if you like! Didn't I take my risk when I bought her? She might have been too far gone; and where would I have been? Loudon,' he cried, 'I tell you the truth: you're too full of refinement for this world!'

'I condemn you out of your own lips,' I replied. '"The fairest kind of shipowning," says you. If you please, let us only do the fairest kind of business.'

The shot told; the Irrepressible was silenced; and I profited by the chance to pour in a broadside of another sort. He was all sunk in money-getting, I pointed out; he never dreamed of anything but dollars. Where were all his generous, progressive sentiments? Where was his culture? I asked. And where was the American Type?

'It's true, Loudon,' he cried, striding up and down the room, and wildly scouring at his hair. 'You're perfectly right. I'm becoming materialised. Oh, what a thing to have to say,

what a confession to make! Materialised! Me! Loudon, this
must go on no longer. You've been a loyal friend to me once
more; give me your hand – you've saved me again. I must do
something to rouse the spiritual side; something desperate;
study something, something dry and tough. What shall it
be? Theology? Algebra? What's algebra?'

'It's dry and tough enough,' said I; '$a^2 + 2ab + b^2$.'

'It's stimulating, though?' he inquired.

I told him I believed so, and that it was considered
fortifying to Types.

'Then that's the thing for me. I'll study algebra,' he
concluded.

The next day, by application to one of his typewriting
women, he got word of a young lady, one Miss Mamie
McBride, who was willing and able to conduct him in
these bloomless meadows; and, her circumstances being
lean, and terms consequently moderate, he and Mamie
were soon in agreement for two lessons in the week. He
took fire with unexampled rapidity; he seemed unable to
tear himself away from the symbolic art; an hour's lesson
occupied the whole evening; and the original two was soon
increased to four, and then to five. I bade him beware of
female blandishments. 'The first thing you know, you'll
be falling in love with the algebraist,' said I.

'Don't say it, even in jest,' he cried. 'She's a lady I
revere. I could no more lay a hand upon her than I could
upon a spirit. Loudon, I don't believe God ever made a
purer-minded woman.'

Which appeared to me too fervent to be reassuring.

Meanwhile I had been long expostulating with my friend
upon a different matter. 'I'm the fifth wheel,' I kept telling
him. 'For any use I am, I might as well be in Senegambia.
The letters you give me to attend to might be answered by
a sucking child. And I tell you what it is, Pinkerton; either
you've got to find me some employment, or I'll have to
start in and find it for myself.'

This I said with a corner of my eye in the usual
quarter, toward the arts, little dreaming what destiny was
to provide.

'I've got it, Loudon,' Pinkerton at last replied. 'Got the
idea on the Potrero cars. Found I hadn't a pencil, borrowed
one from the conductor, and figured on it roughly all

the way in town. I saw it was the thing at last; gives you a real show. All your talents and accomplishments come in. Here's a sketch advertisement. Just run your eye over it. "*Sun, Ozone and Music!* PINKERTON'S HEBDOMADARY PICNICS!" (That's a good, catching phrase, "hebdomadary," though it's hard to say. I made a note of it when I was looking in the dictionary how to spell *hectagonal*. "Well, you're a boss word," I said. "Before you're very much older, I'll have you in type as long as yourself." And here it is, you see.) "*Five dollars a head, and ladies free.* MONSTER OLIO OF ATTRACTIONS." (How does that strike you?) "*Free luncheon under the greenwood tree. Dance on the elastic sward. Home again in the Bright Evening Hours. Manager and Honorary Steward, H. Loudon Dodd, Esq., the well-known connoisseur.*'"

Singular how a man runs from Scylla to Charybdis! I was so intent on securing the disappearance of a single epithet that I accepted the rest of the advertisement and all that it involved without discussion. So it befell that the words 'well-known connoisseur' were deleted; but that H. Loudon Dodd became manager and honorary steward of Pinkerton's Hebdomadary Picnics, soon shortened, by popular consent, to The Dromedary.

By eight o'clock, any Sunday morning, I was to be observed by an admiring public on the wharf. The garb and attributes of sacrifice consisted of a black frockcoat, rosetted, its pockets bulging with sweetmeats and inferior cigars, trousers of light blue, a silk hat like a reflector, and a varnished wand. A goodly steamer guarded my one flank, panting and throbbing, flags fluttering fore and aft of her, illustrative of the Dromedary and patriotism. My other flank was covered by the ticket-office, strongly held by a trusty character of the Scots persuasion, rosetted like his superior, and smoking a cigar to mark the occasion festive. At half-past, having assured myself that all was well with the free luncheons, I lit a cigar myself, and awaited the strains of the 'Pioneer Band.' I had never to wait long – they were German and punctual – and by a few minutes after the half-hour I would hear them booming down street with a long military roll of drums, some score of gratuitous asses prancing at the head in bearskin hats and buckskin aprons, and conspicuous with resplendent axes. The band, of course, we paid for; but so strong is the San Franciscan passion for public masquerade, that the asses (as I say) were all gratuitous, pranced for the love of it, and cost us nothing but their luncheon.

The musicians formed up in the bows of my steamer, and struck into a skittish polka; the asses mounted guard upon the gangway and the ticket-office; and presently after, in family parties of father, mother, and children, in the form of duplicate lovers or in that of solitary youth, the public began to descend upon us by the carful at a time; four to six hundred perhaps, with a strong German flavour, and all merry as children. When these had been shepherded on board, and the inevitable belated two or three had gained the deck amidst the cheering of the public, the hawser was cast off, and we plunged into the bay.

And now behold the honorary steward in the hour of duty and glory; see me circulate amid the crowd, radiating affability and laughter, liberal with my sweetmeats and cigars. I say unblushing things to hobbledehoy girls, tell shy young persons this is the married people's boat, roguishly ask the abstracted if they are thinking of their sweethearts, offer paterfamilias a cigar, am struck with the beauty and grow curious about the age of mamma's youngest, who (I assure her gaily) will be a man before his mother; or perhaps it may occur to me, from the sensible expression of her face, that she is a person of good counsel, and I ask her earnestly if she knows any particularly pleasant place on the Saucelito or San Rafael coast – for the scene of our picnic is always supposed to be uncertain. The next moment I am back at my giddy badinage with the young ladies, wakening laughter as I go, and leaving my wake applausive comments of 'Isn't Mr Dodd a funny gentleman?' and 'Oh, I think he's just too nice!'

An hour having passed in this airy manner, I start upon my rounds afresh, with a bag full of coloured tickets, all with pins attached, and all with legible inscriptions: 'Old Germany,' 'California,' 'True Love,' 'Old Fogies,' 'La Belle France,' 'Green Erin,' 'The Land of Cakes,' 'Washington,' 'Blue Jay,' 'Robin Red-Breast' – twenty of each denomination; for when it comes to the luncheon we sit down by twenties. These are distributed with anxious tact – for, indeed, this is the most delicate part of my functions – but outwardly with reckless unconcern, amidst the gayest flutter and confusion; and are immediately after sported upon hats and bonnets, to the extreme diffusion of cordiality, total strangers hailing each other by 'the number of their mess' – so we humorously name it – and the deck ringing with cries of, 'Here, all Blue Jays to the rescue!' or, 'I say, am I alone in this blame' ship? Ain't there no more Californians?'

By this time we are drawing near to the appointed spot. I mount upon the bridge, the observed of all observers.

'Captain,' I say, in clear, emphatic tones, heard far and wide, 'the majority of the company appear to be in favour of the little cove beyond One-Tree Point.'

'All right, Mr Dodd,' responds the captain, heartily; 'all one to me. I am not exactly sure of the place you mean; but just you stay here and pilot me.'

I do, pointing with my wand. I do pilot him, to the inexpressible entertainment of the picnic, for I am (why should I deny it?) the popular man. We slow down off the mouth of a grassy valley, watered by a brook and set in pines and redwoods. The anchor is let go, the boats are lowered – two of them already packed with the materials of an impromptu bar – and the Pioneer Band, accompanied by the resplendent asses, fill the other, and move shoreward to the inviting strains of 'Buffalo Gals, won't you come out tonight?' It is a part of our programme that one of the asses shall, from sheer clumsiness, in the course of this embarkation, drop a dummy axe into the water, whereupon the mirth of the picnic can hardly be assuaged. Upon one occasion the dummy axe floated, and the laugh turned rather the wrong way.

In from ten to twenty minutes the boats are alongside again, the messes are marshalled separately on the deck, and the picnic goes ashore, to find the band and the impromptu bar awaiting them. Then come the hampers, which are piled up on the beach, and surrounded by a stern guard of stalwart asses, axe on shoulder. It is here I take my place, note-book in hand, under a banner bearing the legend, 'Come here for hampers.' Each hamper contains a complete outfit for a separate twenty – cold provender, plates, glasses, knives, forks, and spoons. An agonised printed appeal from the fevered pen of Pinkerton, pasted on the inside of the lid, beseeches that care be taken of the glass and silver. Beer, wine, and lemonade are flowing already from the bar, and the various clans of twenty file away into the woods, with bottles under their arms and the hampers strung upon a stick. Till one they feast there, in a very moderate seclusion, all being within earshot of the band. From one till four dancing takes place upon the grass; the bar does a roaring business; and the honorary steward, who has already exhausted himself to bring life into the dullest of the messes, must now indefatigably dance with the plainest of the women. At four a bugle-call is sounded, and by half-past behold us on board again – Pioneers, corrugated iron bar, empty bottles, and all; while the honorary steward, free at last, subsides into the captain's cabin over a brandy and soda and a book. Free at last, I say; yet there remains before him the frantic leave-takings at the pier, and a sober journey up to Pinkerton's office with two policemen and the day's takings in a bag.

What I have here sketched was the routine. But we appealed to the taste of San Francisco more distinctly in particular fêtes. 'Ye Olde Time Pycke-Nycke,' largely advertised in hand-bills beginning 'Oyez, Oyez!' and largely frequented by knights, monks, and cavaliers, was drowned out by unseasonable rain, and returned to the city one of the saddest spectacles I ever remember to have witnessed. In pleasing contrast, and certainly our chief success, was 'The Gathering of the Clans,' or Scottish picnic. So many milk-white knees were never before simultaneously exhibited in public, and, to judge by the prevalence of 'Royal Stewart' and the number of eagles' feathers, we were a high-born company. I threw forward the Scottish flank of my own ancestry, and passed muster as a clansman with applause. There was, indeed, but one small cloud on this red-letter day. I had laid in a large supply of the national beverage in the shape of the '"Rob Roy MacGregor O" Blend, Warranted Old and Vatted'; and this must certainly have been a generous spirit, for I had some anxious work between four and half-past, conveying on board the inanimate forms of chieftains.

To one of our ordinary festivities, where he was the life and soul of his own mess, Pinkerton himself came incognito, bringing the algebraist on his arm. Miss Mamie proved to be a well-enough-looking mouse, with a large limpid eye, very good manners, and a flow of the most correct expressions I have ever heard upon the human lip. As Pinkerton's incognito was strict, I had little opportunity to cultivate the lady's acquaintance, but I was informed afterwards that she considered me 'the wittiest gentleman she had ever met.' 'The Lord mend your taste in wit!' thought I; but I cannot conceal that such was the general impression. One of my pleasantries even went the round of San Francisco, and I have heard it (myself, all unknown) bandied in saloons. To be unknown began at last to be a rare experience; a bustle woke upon my passage, above all, in humble neighbourhoods. 'Who's that?' one would ask, and the other would cry, 'That! why, Dromedary Dodd!' or, with withering scorn, 'Not know Mr Dodd of the picnics? Well!' and, indeed, I think it marked a rather barren destiny; for our picnics, if a trifle vulgar, were as gay and innocent as the age of gold. I am sure no people divert themselves so easily and so well, and even with the cares of my stewardship I was often happy to be there.

Indeed, there were but two drawbacks in the least considerable. The first was my terror of the hobbledehoy girls, to whom (from the demands of my situation) I was obliged to lay myself so open. The other, if less momentous, was more mortifying. In early days – at my mother's knee, as a man may say – I had acquired the unenviable accomplishment (which I have never since been able to lose) of singing 'Just before the Battle.' I have what the French call a fillet of voice – my best notes scarce audible about a dinner-table, and the upper register rather to be regarded as a higher power of silence. Experts tell me, besides, that I sing flat; nor, if I were the best singer in the world, does 'Just before the Battle' occur to my mature taste as the song that I would choose to sing. In spite of all which considerations, at one picnic, memorably dull, and after I had exhausted every other art of pleasing, I gave, in desperation, my one song. From that hour my doom was gone forth. Either we had a chronic passenger (though I could never detect him), or the very wood and iron of the steamer must have retained the tradition. At every successive picnic word went round that Mr Dodd was a singer; that Mr Dodd sang 'Just before the Battle'; and, finally, that now was the time

when Mr Dodd sang 'Just before the Battle.' So that the
thing became a fixture, like the dropping of the dummy axe;
and you are to conceive me, Sunday after Sunday, piping
up my lamentable ditty, and covered, when it was done,
with gratuitous applause. It is a beautiful trait in human
nature that I was invariably offered an encore.

I was well paid, however, even to sing. Pinkerton and I,
after an average Sunday, had five hundred dollars to divide.
Nay, and the picnics were the means, although indirectly,
of bringing me a singular windfall. This was at the end of
the season, after the 'Grand Farewell Fancy Dress Gala.'
Many of the hampers had suffered severely; and it was
judged wiser to save storage, dispose of them, and lay in
a fresh stock when the campaign reopened. Among my
purchasers was a working man of the name of Speedy,
to whose house, after several unavailing letters, I must
proceed in person, wondering to find myself once again
on the wrong side, and playing the creditor to someone
else's debtor. Speedy was in the belligerent stage of fear.
He could not pay. It appeared he had already resold the
hampers, and he defied me to do my worst. I did not like
to lose my own money; I hated to lose Pinkerton's; and
the bearing of my creditor incensed me.

'Do you know, Mr Speedy, that I can send you to the
penitentiary?' said I, willing to read him a lesson.

The dire expression was overheard in the next room.
A large, fresh, motherly Irishwoman ran forth upon the
instant, and fell to besiege me with caresses and appeals.
'Sure now, and ye couldn't have the heart to ut, Mr Dodd
– you, that's so well known' to be a pleasant gentleman;
and it's a pleasant face ye have, and the picture of me own
brother that's dead and gone. It's a truth that he's been
drinking. Ye can smell it off of him, more blame to him.
But, indade, and there's nothing in the house beyont the
furnicher, and Thim Stock. It's the stock that ye'll be taking,
dear. A sore penny it has cost me, first and last, and, by all
tales, not worth an owld tobacco pipe.' Thus adjured, and
somewhat embarrassed by the stern attitude I had adopted,
I suffered myself to be invested with a considerable quantity
of what is called 'wild-cat stock,' in which this excellent
if illogical female had been squandering her hard-earned
gold. It could scarce be said to better my position, but

the step quieted the woman; and, on the other hand, I could not think I was taking much risk, for the shares in question (they were those of what I will call the Catamount Silver Mine) had fallen some time before to the bed-rock quotation, and now lay perfectly inert, or were only kicked (like other waste-paper) about the kennel of the exchange by bankrupt speculators.

A month or two after, I perceived by the stock-list that Catamount had taken a bound; before afternoon 'thim stock' were worth a quite considerable pot of money; and I learned, upon inquiry, that a bonanza had been found in a condemned lead, and the mine was now expected to do wonders. Remarkable to philosophers how bonanzas are found in condemned leads, and how the stock is always at freezing-point immediately before! By some stroke of chance the Speedys had held on to the right thing; they had escaped the syndicate; yet a little more, if I had not come to dun them, and Mrs Speedy would have been buying a silk dress. I could not bear, of course, to profit by the accident, and returned to offer restitution. The house was in a bustle; the neighbours (all stock-gamblers themselves) had crowded to condole; and Mrs Speedy sat with streaming tears, the centre of a sympathetic group. 'For fifteen year I've been at ut,' she was lamenting as I entered, 'and grudging the babes the very milk – more shame to me! – to pay their dhirty assessments. And now, my dears, I should be a lady, and driving in my coach, if all had their rights; and a sorrow on that man Dodd! As soon as I set eyes on him, I seen the divil was in the house.'

It was upon these words that I made my entrance, which was therefore dramatic enough, though nothing to what followed. For when it appeared that I was come to restore the lost fortune, and when Mrs Speedy (after copiously weeping on my bosom) had refused the restitution, and when Mr Speedy (summoned to that end from a camp of the Grand Army of the Republic) had added his refusal, and when I had insisted, and they had insisted, and the neighbours had applauded and supported each of us in turn; and when at last it was agreed we were to hold the stock together, and share the proceeds in three parts – one for me, one for Mr Speedy, and one for his spouse – I will leave you to conceive the enthusiasm that reigned in that

small bare apartment, with the sewing-machine in the one
corner, and the babes asleep in the other, and pictures of
Garfield and the Battle of Gettysburg on the yellow walls.
Port wine was had in by a sympathiser, and we drank it
mingled with tears.

'And I dhrink to your health, my dear,' sobbed
Mrs Speedy, especially affected by my gallantry in the
matter of the third share; 'and I'm sure we all dhrink to
his health – Mr Dodd of the picnics, no gentleman better
known than him; and it's my prayer, dear, the good God
may be long spared to see ye in health and happiness!'

In the end I was the chief gainer; for I sold my third
while it was worth five thousand dollars, but the Speedys
more adventurously held on until the syndicate reversed
the process, when they were happy to escape with perhaps
a quarter of that sum. It was just as well; for the bulk of the
money was (in Pinkerton's phrase) reinvested; and when
next I saw Mrs Speedy, she was still gorgeously dressed
from the proceeds of the late success, but was already
moist with tears over the new catastrophe. 'We're froze
out, me darlin'! All the money we had, dear, and the
sewing-machine, and Jim's uniform, was in the Golden
West; and the vipers has put on a new assessment.'

By the end of the year, therefore, this is how I stood. I
had made

By Catamount Silver Mine	$5,000
By the picnics	3,000
By the lecture	600
By profit and loss on capital in Pinkerton's business	1,350
	$9,950

to which must be added

What remained of my grandfather's donation	8,500
	$18,450

It appears, on the other hand, that

I had spent	4,000
Which thus left me to the good	$14,450

A result on which I am not ashamed to say I looked
with gratitude and pride. Some eight thousand (being late
conquest) was liquid and actually tractile in the bank; the

rest whirled beyond reach and even sight (save in the mirror of a balance-sheet) under the compelling spell of wizard Pinkerton. Dollars of mine were tacking off the shores of Mexico, in peril of the deep and the guarda-costas; they rang on saloon counters in the city of Tombstone, Arizona; they shone in faro-tents among the mountain diggings; the imagination flagged in following them, so wide were they diffused, so briskly they span to the turning of the wizard's crank. But here, there, or everywhere I could still tell myself it was all mine, and – what was more convincing – draw substantial dividends. My fortune, I called it; and it represented, when expressed in dollars or even British pounds, an honest pot of money; when extended into francs, a veritable fortune. Perhaps I have let the cat out of the bag; perhaps you see already where my hopes were pointing, and begin to blame my inconsistency. But I must first tell you my excuse, and the change that had befallen Pinkerton.

About a week after the picnic to which he escorted Mamie, Pinkerton avowed the state of his affections. From what I had observed on board the steamer – where, methought, Mamie waited on him with her limpid eyes – I encouraged the bashful lover to proceed; and the very next evening he was carrying me to call on his affianced.

'You must befriend her, Loudon, as you have always befriended me,' he said, pathetically.

'By saying disagreeable things? I doubt if that be the way to a young lady's favour,' I replied; 'and since this picnicking I begin to be a man of some experience.'

'Yes, you do nobly there; I can't describe how I admire you,' he cried. 'Not that she will ever need it; she has had every advantage. God knows what I have done to deserve her. O man, what a responsibility this is for a rough fellow and not always truthful!'

'Brace up, old man – brace up!' said I.

But when we reached Mamie's boarding-house, it was almost with tears that he presented me. 'Here is Loudon, Mamie,' were his words. 'I want you to love him; he has a grand nature.'

'You are certainly no stranger to me, Mr Dodd,' was her gracious expression. 'James is never weary of descanting on your goodness.'

'My dear lady,' said I, 'when you know our friend a little better, you will make a large allowance for his warm heart. My goodness has consisted in allowing him to feed and clothe and toil for me when he could ill afford it. If I am now alive, it is to him I owe it; no man had a kinder friend. You must take good care of him,' I added, laying my hand on his shoulder, 'and keep him in good order, for he needs it.'

Pinkerton was much affected by this speech, and so, I fear, was Mamie. I admit it was a tactless performance. 'When you know our friend a little better,' was not happily said; and even 'keep him in good order, for he needs it,' might be construed into matter of offence. But I lay it before you in all confidence of your acquittal: was the general tone of it 'patronising'? Even if such was the verdict of the lady, I cannot but suppose the blame was neither wholly hers nor wholly mine; I cannot but suppose that Pinkerton had already sickened the poor woman of my very name; so that if I had come with the songs of Apollo, she must still have been disgusted.

Here, however, were two finger-posts to Paris – Jim was going to be married, and so had the less need of my society; I had not pleased his bride, and so was, perhaps, better absent. Late one evening I broached the idea to my friend. It had been a great day for me; I had just banked my five thousand Catamountain dollars; and as Jim had refused to lay a finger on the stock, risk and profit were both wholly mine, and I was celebrating the event with stout and crackers. I began by telling him that if it caused him any pain or any anxiety about his affairs, he had but to say the word, and he should hear no more of my proposal. He was the truest and best friend I ever had or was ever like to have; and it would be a strange thing if I refused him any favour he was sure he wanted. At the same time I wished him to be sure; for my life was wasting in my hands. I was like one from home: all my true interests summoned me away. I must remind him, besides, that he was now about to marry and assume new interests, and that our extreme familiarity might be even painful to his wife. 'Oh no, Loudon; I feel you are wrong there,' he interjected warmly; 'she *does* appreciate your nature.' 'So much the better, then,' I continued; and went on to point out that our separation need not be for long; that, in the way affairs were going, he might join me in two years with a fortune – small, indeed, for the States, but in France almost conspicuous; that we might unite our resources, and have one house in Paris for the winter and a second near Fontainebleau for summer, where we could be as happy as the day was long, and bring up little Pinkertons as practical artistic workmen, far from the money-hunger of the West. 'Let me go, then,' I concluded; 'not as a deserter, but as the vanguard, to lead the march of the Pinkerton men.'

So I argued and pleaded, not without emotion; my friend sitting opposite, resting his chin upon his hand and (but for that single interjection) silent. 'I have been looking for this, Loudon,' said he, when I had done. 'It does pain me, and that's the fact – I'm so miserably selfish. And I believe it's a deathblow to the picnics; for it's idle to deny that you were the heart and soul of them with your wand and your gallant bearing, and wit and humour and chivalry, and throwing that kind of society atmosphere about the thing. But, for all that, you're right, and you ought to go. You may count on forty dollars a week; and if Depew City – one of nature's centres for this State – pan out the least as I expect, it may be double. But it's forty dollars anyway; and to think that two years ago you were almost reduced to beggary!'

'I *was* reduced to it,' said I.

'Well, the brutes gave you nothing, and I'm glad of it now!' cried Jim. 'It's the triumphant return I glory in! Think of the master, and that cold-blooded Myner too! Yes, just let the Depew City boom get on its legs, and you shall go; and two years later, day for day, I'll shake hands with you in Paris, with Mamie on my arm, God bless her!'

We talked in this vein far into the night. I was myself so exultant in my new-found liberty, and Pinkerton so proud of my triumph, so happy in my happiness, in so warm a glow about the gallant little woman of his choice, and the very room so filled with castles in the air and cottages at Fontainebleau, that it was little wonder if sleep fled our eyelids, and three had followed two upon the office clock before Pinkerton unfolded the mechanism of his patent sofa.

CHAPTER EIGHT

Faces on the City Front

It is very much the custom to view life as if it were exactly ruled in two, like sleep and waking – the provinces of play and business standing separate. The business side of my career in San Francisco has been now disposed of; I approach the chapter of diversion; and it will be found they had about an equal share in building up the story of the Wrecker – a gentleman whose appearance may be presently expected.

With all my occupations, some six afternoons and two or three odd evenings remained at my disposal every week: a circumstance the more agreeable as I was a stranger in a city singularly picturesque. From what I had once called myself, 'The Amateur Parisian,' I grew (or declined) into a waterside prowler, a lingerer on wharves, a frequenter of shy neighbourhoods, a scraper of acquaintance with eccentric characters. I visited Chinese and Mexican gambling-hells, German secret societies, sailors' boarding-houses, and 'dives' of every complexion of the disreputable and dangerous. I have seen greasy Mexican hands pinned to the table with a knife for cheating, seamen (when blood-money ran high) knocked down upon the public street and carried insensible on board short-handed ships, shots exchanged, and the smoke (and the company) dispersing from the doors of the saloon. I have heard cold-minded Polacks debate upon the readiest method of burning San Francisco to the ground, hot-headed working men and women bawl and swear in the tribune at the Sandlot, and Kearney himself open his subscription for a gallows, name the manufacturers who were to grace it with their dangling bodies; and read aloud to the delighted multitude a telegram of adhesion from a member of the State legislature: all which preparations of proletarian war were (in a moment) breathed upon and abolished by the mere name and fame of Mr Coleman. That lion of the Vigilantes had but to rouse himself and shake his ears, and the whole brawling mob was silenced. I could not but reflect what a strange manner of man this was, to be living unremarked there as a private merchant, and to be so feared by a whole city; and if I was disappointed, in my character of looker-on, to have the matter end ingloriously without the firing of a shot or the hanging of a single millionaire, philosophy tried to tell me that this sight was truly the more picturesque. In a thousand towns and different epochs I might have had occasion to behold the cowardice and carnage of street-fighting; where else, but only there and then, could I have enjoyed a view of Coleman (the intermittent despot) walking meditatively up hill in a quiet part of town, with a very rolling gait, and slapping gently his great thigh?

Minora canamus. This historic figure stalks silently through a corner of the San Francisco of my memory. The rest is bric-à-brac, the reminiscences of a vagrant sketcher. My delight was much in slums. 'Little Italy' was a haunt of mine. There I would look in at the windows of small eating-shops transported bodily from Genoa or Naples, with their macaroni, and chianti flasks, and portraits of Garibaldi, and coloured political caricatures; or (entering in) hold high debate with some ear-ringed fisher of the bay as to the designs of 'Mr Owstria' and 'Mr Rooshia.' I was often to be observed (had there been any to observe me) in that dis-peopled, hillside solitude of 'Little Mexico,' with its crazy wooden houses, endless crazy wooden stairs, and perilous mountain-goat paths in the sand. Chinatown by a thousand eccentricities drew and held me; I could never have enough of its ambiguous, interracial atmosphere, as of a vitalised museum; never wonder enough at its outlandish, necromantic-looking vegetables set forth to sell in commonplace American shop-windows, its temple doors open and the scent of the joss-stick streaming forth on the American air, its kites of Oriental fashion hanging fouled in Western telegraph-wires, its flights of paper prayers which the trade-wind hunts and dissipates along Western gutters. I was a frequent wanderer on North Beach, gazing at the straits, and the huge Cape Horners creeping out to sea, and imminent Tamalpais. Thence, on my homeward way, I might visit that strange and filthy shed, earth-paved and walled with the cages of wild animals and birds, where at a ramshackle counter, amid the yells of monkeys and a poignant atmosphere of menagerie, forty-rod whisky was administered by a proprietor as dirty as his beasts. Nor did I even neglect Nob Hill, which is itself a kind of slum, being the habitat of the mere millionaire. There they dwell upon the hill-top, high raised above man's clamour, and the trade-wind blows between their palaces about deserted streets.

But San Francisco is not herself only. She is not only the most interesting city in the Union, and the hugest smelting-pot of races and the precious metals. She keeps, besides, the doors of the Pacific, and is the port of entry to another world and an earlier epoch in man's history. Nowhere else shall you observe (in the ancient phrase) so many tall ships as here convene from round the Horn, from China, from Sydney, and the Indies. But, scarce remarked amid that crowd of deep-sea giants, another class of craft, the Island schooner, circulates – low in the water, with lofty spars and dainty lines, rigged and fashioned like a yacht, manned with brown-skinned, soft-spoken, sweet-eyed native sailors, and equipped with their great double-ender boats that tell a tale of boisterous sea-beaches. These steal out and in again, unnoted by the world or even the newspaper press, save for the line in the clearing column, 'Schooner So-and-so for Yap and South Sea Islands' – steal out with nondescript cargoes of tinned salmon, gin, bolts of gaudy cotton stuff, women's hats, and Waterbury watches, to return, after a year, piled as high as to the eaves of the house with copra, or wallowing deep with the shells of the tortoise or the pearl oyster. To me, in my character of the Amateur Parisian, this island traffic, and even the island world, were beyond the bounds of curiosity, and how much more of knowledge. I stood there on the extreme shore of the West and of today. Seventeen hundred years ago, and seven thousand miles to the east, a legionary stood, perhaps, upon the wall of Antoninus, and looked northward toward the mountains of the Picts. For all the interval of time and space I, when I looked from the cliff-house on the broad Pacific, was that man's heir and analogue: each of us standing on the verge of the Roman Empire (or, as we now call it, Western civilisation), each of us gazing onward into zones unromanised. But I was dull. I looked rather backward, keeping a kind eye on Paris; and it required a series of converging incidents to change my attitude of nonchalance for one of interest, and even longing, which I little dreamed that I should live to gratify.

The first of these incidents brought me in acquaintance with a certain San Francisco character, who had something of a name beyond the limits of the city, and was known to many lovers of good English. I had discovered a new slum, a place of precarious sandy cliffs, deep sandy cuttings, solitary ancient houses, and the butt-ends of streets. It was already environed. The ranks of the street-lamps threaded it unbroken. The city, upon all sides of it, was tightly packed, and growled with traffic. Today, I do not doubt the very landmarks are all swept away; but it offered then, within narrow limits, a delightful peace, and (in the morning, when I chiefly went there) a seclusion almost rural. On a steep sand-hill in this neighbourhood toppled, on the most insecure foundation, a certain row of houses, each with a bit of garden, and all (I have to presume) inhabited. Thither I used to mount by a crumbling footpath, and in front of the last of the houses would sit down to sketch.

The very first day I saw I was observed out of the ground-floor window by a youngish, good-looking fellow, prematurely bald, and with an expression both lively and engaging. The second, as we were still the only figures in the landscape, it was no more than natural that we should nod. The third he came out fairly from his entrenchments, praised my sketch, and with the impromptu cordiality of artists carried me into his apartment; where I sat presently in the midst of a museum of strange objects – paddles, and battle-clubs, and baskets, rough-hewn stone images, ornaments of threaded shell, cocoanut bowls, snowy cocoanut plumes – evidences and examples of another earth, another climate, another race, and another (if a ruder) culture. Nor did these objects lack a fitting commentary in the conversation of my new acquaintance. Doubtless you have read his book. You know already how he tramped and starved, and had so fine a profit of living in his days among the islands; and meeting him as I did, one artist with another, after months of offices and picnics, you can imagine with what charm he would speak, and with what pleasure I would hear. It was in such talks, which we were both eager to repeat, that I first heard the names – first fell under the spell – of the islands; and it was from one of the first of them that I returned (a happy man) with 'Omoo' under one arm, and my friend's own adventures under the other.

The second incident was more dramatic, and had, besides, a bearing on my future. I was standing one day near a boat-landing under Telegraph Hill. A large barque, perhaps of eighteen hundred tons, was coming more than usually close about the point to reach her moorings; and I was observing her with languid inattention, when I observed two men to stride across the bulwarks, drop into a shore boat, and, violently dispossessing the boatman of his oars, pull toward the landing where I stood. In a surprisingly short time they came tearing up the steps, and I could see that both were too well dressed to be foremast hands – the first even with research, and both, and specially the first, appeared under the empire of some strong emotion.

'Nearest police office!' cried the leader.

'This way,' said I, immediately falling in with their precipitate pace. 'What's wrong? What ship is that?'

'That's the *Gleaner*,' he replied. 'I am chief officer, this gentleman's third, and we've to get in our depositions before the crew. You see, they might corral us with the captain, and that's no kind of berth for me. I've sailed with some hard cases in my time, and seen pins flying like sand on a squally day – but never a match to our old man. It never let up from the Hook to the Farallones, and the last man was dropped not sixteen hours ago. Packet rats our men were, and as tough a crowd as ever sand-bagged a man's head in; but they looked sick enough when the captain started in with his fancy shooting.'

'Oh, he's done up,' observed the other. 'He won't go to sea no more.'

'You make me tired,' retorted his superior. 'If he gets ashore in one piece, and isn't lynched in the next ten minutes, he'll do yet. The owners have a longer memory than the public, they'll stand by him; they don't find as smart a captain every day in the year.'

'Oh, he's a son of a gun of a fine captain; there ain't no

doubt of that,' concurred the other, heartily. 'Why, I don't suppose there's been no wages paid aboard that *Gleaner* for three trips.'

'No wages?' I exclaimed, for I was still a novice in maritime affairs.

'Not to sailor-men before the mast,' agreed the mate. 'Men cleared out; wasn't the soft job they maybe took it for. She isn' the first ship that never paid wages.'

I could not but observe that our pace was progressively relaxing; and, indeed, I have often wondered since whether the hurry of the start were not intended for the gallery alone. Certain it is at least, that when we had reached the police office, and the mates had made their deposition, and told their horrid tale of five men murdered – some with savage passion, some with cold brutality – between Sandy Hook and San Francisco, the police were despatched in time to be too late. Before we arrived, the ruffian had slipped out upon the dock, had mingled with the crowd, and found a refuge in the house of an acquaintance; and the ship was only tenanted by his late victims. Well for him that he had been thus speedy; for when word began to go abroad among the shore-side characters, when the last victim was carried by to the hospital, when those who had escaped (as by miracle) from that floating shambles, began to circulate and show their wounds in the crowd, it was strange to witness the agitation that seized and shook that portion of the city. Men shed tears in public; bosses of lodging-houses, long inured to brutality – and, above all, brutality to sailors – shook their fists at heaven. If hands could have been laid on the captain of the *Gleaner*, his shrift would have been short. That night (so gossip reports) he was headed up in a barrel and smuggled across the bay. In two ships already he had braved the penitentiary and the gallows; and yet, by last accounts, he now commands another on the Western Ocean.

As I have said, I was never quite certain whether Mr Nares (the mate) did not intend that his superior should escape. It would have been like his preference of loyalty to law; it would have been like his prejudice, which was all in favour of the after-guard. But it must remain a matter of conjecture only. Well as I came to know him in the sequel, he was never communicative on that point

– nor, indeed, on any that concerned the voyage of the *Gleaner*. Doubtless he had some reason for his reticence. Even during our walk to the police office he debated several times with Johnson, the third officer, whether he ought not to give up himself, as well as to denounce the captain. He had decided in the negative, arguing that 'it would probably come to nothing; and even if there was a stink, he had plenty good friends in San Francisco.' And to nothing it came; though it must have very nearly come to something, for Mr Nares disappeared immediately from view, and was scarce less closely hidden than his captain.

Johnson, on the other hand, I often met. I could never learn this man's country; and though he himself claimed to be American, neither his English nor his education warranted the claim. In all likelihood he was of Scandinavian birth and blood, long pickled in the forecastles of English and American ships. It is possible that, like so many of his race in similar positions, he had already lost his native tongue. In mind, at least, he was quite denationalised; thought only in English – to call it so; and though by nature one of the mildest, kindest, and, most feebly playful of mankind, he had been so long accustomed to the cruelty of sea discipline that his stories (told perhaps with a giggle) would sometimes turn me chill. In appearance he was tall, light of weight, bold and high-bred of feature, dusky-haired, and with a face of a clean even brown – the ornament of outdoor men. Seated in a chair, you might have passed him off for a baronet or a military officer; but let him rise, and it was Fo'c's'le Jack that came rolling toward you, crab-like; let him but open his lips, and it was Fo'c's'le Jack that piped and drawled his ungrammatical gibberish. He had sailed (among other places) much among the islands; and after a Cape Horn passage with its snow-squalls and its frozen sheets, he announced his intention of 'taking a turn among them Kanakas.' I thought I should have lost him soon; but, according to the unwritten usage of mariners, he had first to dissipate his wages. 'Guess I'll have to paint this town red,' was his hyperbolical expression; for, sure, no man ever embarked upon a milder course of dissipation, most of his days being passed in the little parlour behind Black Tom's public-house, with a select corps of old particular acquaintances, all from the South Seas, and all patrons of a long yarn, a short pipe, and glasses round.

Black Tom's, to the front, presented the appearance of a fourth-rate saloon, devoted to Kanaka seamen, dirt, negro-head tobacco, bad cigars, worse gin, and guitars and banjos in a state of decline. The proprietor, a powerful coloured man, was at once a publican, a ward politician, leader of some brigade of 'lambs' or 'smashers,' at the wind of whose clubs the party bosses and the mayor were supposed to tremble, and (what hurt nothing) an active and reliable crimp. His front quarters, then, were noisy, disreputable, and not even safe. I have seen worse-frequented saloons where there were fewer scandals; for Tom was often drunk himself: and there is no doubt the Lambs must have been a useful body, or the place would have been closed. I remember one day, not long before an election, seeing a blind man, very well dressed, led up to the counter and remain a long while in consultation with the negro. The pair looked so ill-assorted, and the awe with which the drinkers fell back and left them in the midst of an impromptu privacy was so unusual in such a place, that I turned to my next neighbour with a question. He told me the blind man was a distinguished party boss, called by some the King of San Francisco, but perhaps better known by his picturesque Chinese nickname of the Blind White Devil. 'The Lambs must be wanted pretty bad, I guess,' my informant added. I have here a sketch of the Blind White Devil leaning on the counter; on the next page, and taken the same hour, a jotting of Black Tom threatening a whole crowd of customers with a long Smith and Wesson – to such heights and depths we rose and fell in the front parts of the saloon!

Meanwhile, away in the back quarters, sat the small informal South Sea club, talking of another world and surely of a different century. Old schooner captains they were, old South Sea traders, cooks, and mates; fine creatures, softened by residence among a softer race: full men besides, though not by reading, but by strange experience; and for days together I could hear their yarns with an unfading pleasure. All had, indeed, some touch of the poetic; for the beach-comber, when not a mere ruffian, is the poor relation of the artist. Even though Johnson's inarticulate speech, his 'Oh yes, there ain't no harm in them Kanakas,' or 'Oh yes, that's a son of a gun of a fine island, mountainious right down; I didn't never ought to have left that island,' there pierced a certain gusto of appreciation; and some of the rest were master-talkers. From their long tales, their traits of character and unpremeditated landscape, there began to piece itself together in my head some image of the islands and the island life; precipitous shores, spired mountain-tops, the deep shade of hanging forests, the unresting surf upon the reef, and the unending peace of the lagoon; sun, moon, and stars of an imperial brightness; man moving in these scenes scarce fallen, and woman lovelier than Eve; the primal curse abrogated, the bed made ready for the stranger, life set to perpetual music, and the guest welcomed, the boat urged, and the long night beguiled with poetry and choral song. A man must have been an unsuccessful artist; he must have starved on the streets of Paris; he must have been yoked to a commercial force like Pinkerton, before he can conceive the longings that at times assailed me. The draughty, rowdy city of San Francisco, the bustling office where my friend Jim paced like a caged lion daily between ten and four, even (at times) the retrospect of Paris, faded in comparison. Many a man less tempted would have thrown up all to realise his visions; but I was by nature unadventurous and uninitiative; to divert me from all former paths and send me cruising through the isles of paradise, some force external to myself must be exerted; Destiny herself must use the fitting wedge; and, little as I deemed it, that tool was already in her hand of brass.

I sat, one afternoon, in the corner of a great, glassy, silvered saloon, a free lunch at my one elbow, at the other a 'conscientious nude' from the brush of local talent; when, with the tramp of feet and a sudden buzz of voices, the swing-doors were flung broadly open and the place carried as by storm. The crowd which thus entered (mostly seafaring men, and all prodigiously excited) contained a sort of kernel or general centre of interest, which the rest merely surrounded and advertised, as children in the Old World surround and escort the Punch-and-Judy man; and word went round the bar like wildfire, that these were Captain Trent and the survivors of the British brig *Flying Scud*, picked up by a British war-ship on Midway Island, arrived that morning in San Francisco Bay, and now fresh from making the necessary declarations. Presently I had a good sight of them; four brown, seamanlike fellows, standing by the counter, glass in hand, the centre of a score of questioners. One was a Kanaka – the cook, I was informed; one carried a cage with a canary, which occasionally trilled into thin song; one had his left arm in a sling, and looked gentlemanlike and somewhat sickly, as though the injury had been severe and he was scarce recovered; and the captain himself – a red-faced, blue-eyed, thick-set man of five-and-forty – wore a bandage on his right hand. The incident struck me; I was struck particularly to see captain, cook, and foremast hands walking the street and visiting saloons in company; and, as when anything impressed me, I got my sketch-book out, and began to steal a sketch of the four castaways. The crowd, sympathising with my design, made a clear lane across the room; and I was thus enabled, all unobserved myself, to observe with a still growing closeness the face and the demeanour of Captain Trent.

Warmed by whiskey and encouraged by the eagerness of the bystanders, that gentleman was now rehearsing the history of his misfortune. It was but scraps that reached me: how he 'filled her on the starboard tack,' and how 'it came up sudden out of the nor'nor'west,' and 'there she was, high and dry.' Sometimes he would appeal to one of the men – 'That was how it was, Jack?' – and the man would reply, 'That was the way of it, Captain Trent.' Lastly, he started a fresh tide of popular sympathy by enunciating the sentiment, 'Damn all these Admirality Charts, and that's what I say!' From the nodding of heads and the murmurs of assent that followed, I could see that Captain Trent had established himself in the public mind as a gentleman and a thorough navigator: about which period, my sketch of the four men and the canary-bird being finished, and all (especially the canary-bird) excellent likenesses, I buckled up my book, and slipped from the saloon.

Little did I suppose that I was leaving Act I., Scene 1, of the drama of my life; and yet the scene – or, rather, the captain's face – lingered for some time in my memory. I was no prophet, as I say; but I was something else – I was an observer; and one thing I knew – I knew when a man was terrified. Captain Trent, of the British brig *Flying Scud* had been glib; he had been ready; he had been loud; but in his blue eyes I could detect the chill, and in the lines of his countenance spy the agitation, of perpetual terror. Was he trembling for his certificate? In my judgment it was some livelier kind of fear that thrilled in the man's marrow as he turned to drink. Was it the result of recent shock, and had he not yet recovered the disaster to his brig? I remembered how a friend of mine had been in a railway accident, and shook and started for a month; and although Captain Trent of the *Flying Scud* had none of the appearance of a nervous man, I told myself, with incomplete conviction, that his must be a similar case.

CHAPTER NINE

The Wreck of the 'Flying Scud'

The next morning I found Pinkerton, who had risen before me, seated at our usual table, and deep in the perusal of what I will call the *Daily Occidental*. This was a paper (I know not if it be so still) that stood out alone among its brethren in the West. The others, down to their smallest item, were defaced with capitals, head-lines, alliterations, swaggering misquotations, and the shoddy picturesque and unpathetic pathos of the Harry Millers: the *Occidental* alone appeared to be written by a dull, sane, Christian gentleman, singly desirous of communicating knowledge. It had not only this merit – which endeared it to me – but was admittedly the best informed on business matters, which attracted Pinkerton.

'Loudon,' said he, looking up from the journal, 'you sometimes think I have too many irons in the fire. My notion, on the other hand, is, when you see a dollar lying, pick it up! Well, here I've tumbled over a whole pile of 'em on a reef in the middle of the Pacific.'

'Why, Jim, you miserable fellow!' I exclaimed; 'haven't we Depew City, one of God's green centres for this State? haven't we— '

'Just listen to this,' interrupted Jim. 'It's miserable copy; these *Occidental* reporter fellows have no fire; but the facts are right enough, I guess.' And he began to read:-

WRECK OF THE BRITISH BRIG 'FLYING SCUD.'

H.B.M.S. *Tempest*, which arrived yesterday at this port, brings Captain Trent and four men of the British brig *Flying Scud*, cast away February 12th on Midway Island, and most providentially rescued the next day. The *Flying Scud* was of 200 tons burthen, owned in London, and has been out nearly two years tramping. Captain Trent left Hong Kong December

8th, bound for this port in rice and a small mixed cargo of silks, teas, and China notions, the whole valued at $10,000, fully covered by insurance. The log shows plenty of fine weather, with light airs, calms, and squalls. In lat. 28 N., long. 177 W., his water going rotten, and misled by Hoyt's 'North Pacific Directory,' which informed him there was a coaling station on the island, Captain Trent put in to Midway Island. He found it a literal sandbank, surrounded by a coral reef mostly submerged. Birds were very plenty, there was good fish in the lagoon, but no firewood; and the water, which could be obtained by digging, brackish. He found good holding-ground off the north end of the larger bank in fifteen fathoms water; bottom sandy, with coral patches. Here he was detained seven days by a calm, the crew suffering severely from the water, which was gone quite bad; and it was only on the evening of the 12th that a little wind sprang up, coming puffy out of N.N.E. Late as it was, Captain Trent immediately weighed anchor and attempted to get out. While the vessel was beating up to the passage, the wind took a sudden lull, and then veered squally into N. and even N.N.W., driving the brig ashore on the sand at about twenty minutes before six o'clock. John Wallen, a native of Finland, and Charles Holdorsen, a native of Sweden, were drowned alongside, in attempting to lower a boat, neither being able to swim, the squall very dark, and the noise of the breakers drowning everything. At the same time John Brown, another of the crew, had his arm broken by the falls. Captain Trent further informed the *Occidental* reporter that the brig struck heavily at first bows on, he supposes upon coral; that she then drove over the obstacle, and now lies in sand, much down by the head, and with a list to starboard. In the first collision she must have sustained some damage, as she was making water forward. The rice will probably be all destroyed: but the more valuable part of the cargo is fortunately in the afterhold. Captain Trent was preparing his long-boat for sea, when the providential arrival of the *Tempest*, pursuant to Admiralty orders to call at islands in her course for castaways, saved the gallant captain from all further danger. It is scarcely necessary to add that both the officers and men of the unfortunate vessel speak in high terms of the kindness they received on board the man-of-war. We print a list of the survivors: Jacob Trent, master, of Hull, England; Elias Goddedaal, mate, native of Christiansand, Sweden; Ah Wing, cook, native of Sana, China; John Brown, native of Glasgow, Scotland; John Hardy, native of London, England. The *Flying Scud* is ten years old, and this morning will be sold as she stands, by order of Lloyd's agent, at public auction for the benefit of the underwriters. The auction will take place in the Merchants' Exchange at ten o'clock.

Farther Particulars. – Later in the afternoon the *Occidental* reporter found Lieutenant Sebright, first officer of H.B.M.S. *Tempest*, at the Palace Hotel. The gallant officer was somewhat pressed for time, but confirmed the account given by Captain Trent in all particulars. He added that the *Flying Scud* is in an excellent berth, and, except in the highly improbable event of a heavy N.W. gale, might last until next winter.

'You will never know anything of literature,' said I, when Jim had finished. 'That is a good, honest, plain piece of work, and tells the story clearly. I see only one mistake: the cook is not a Chinaman; he is a Kanaka, and, I think, a Hawaiian.'

'Why, how do you know that?' asked Jim.

'I saw the whole gang yesterday in a saloon,' said I. 'I even heard the tale, or might have heard it, from Captain Trent himself, who struck me as thirsty and nervous.'

'Well, that's neither here nor there,' cried Pinkerton; 'the point is, how about these dollars lying on a reef?'

'Will it pay?' I asked.

'Pay like a sugar trust!' exclaimed Pinkerton. 'Don't you see what this British officer says about the safety? Don't you see the cargo's valued at ten thousand? Schooners are begging just now; I can get my pick of them at two hundred and fifty a month; and how does that foot up? It looks like three hundred per cent. to me.'

'You forget,' I objected, 'the captain himself declares the rice is damaged.'

'That's a point, I know,' admitted Jim. 'But the rice is the sluggish article, anyway; it's little more account than ballast; it's the tea and silks that I look to: all we have to find is the proportion, and one look at the manifest will settle that. I've rung up Lloyd's on purpose; the captain is to meet me there in an hour, and then I'll be as posted on that brig as if I built her. Besides, you've no idea what pickings there are about a wreck – copper, lead, rigging, anchors, chains, even the crockery, Loudon!'

'You seem to me to forget one trifle,' said I. 'Before you pick that wreck, you've got to buy her, and how much will she cost?'

'One hundred dollars,' replied Jim, with the promptitude of an automaton.

'How on earth do you guess that?' I cried.

'I don't guess; I know it,' answered the Commercial Force. 'My dear boy, I may be a galoot about literature, but you'll always be an outsider in business. How do you suppose I bought the *James L. Moody* for two hundred and fifty, her boats alone worth four times the money? Because my name stood first in the list. Well, it stands there again; I have the naming of the figure, and I name a small one because of the distance: but it wouldn't matter what I named; that would be the price.'

'It sounds mysterious enough,' said I. 'Is this public auction conducted in a subterranean vault? Could a plain citizen – myself, for instance – come and see?'

'Oh, everything's open and above board!' he cried, indignantly. 'Anybody can come, only nobody bids against us; and if he did, he would get frozen out. It's been tried before now, and once was enough. We hold the plant; we've got the connection; we can afford to go higher than any outsider; there's two million dollars in the ring; and we stick at nothing. Or suppose anybody did buy over our head – I tell you, Loudon, he would think this town gone crazy; he could no more get business through on the city front than I can dance; schooners, divers, men – all he wanted – the prices would fly right up and strike him.'

'But how did you get in?' I asked. 'You were once an outsider like your neighbours, I suppose?'

'I took hold of that thing, Loudon, and just studied it up,' he replied. 'It took my fancy; it was so romantic, and then I saw there was boodle in the thing; and I figured on the business till no man alive could give me points. Nobody knew I had an eye on wrecks till one fine morning I dropped in upon Douglas B. Longhurst in his den, gave him all the facts and figures, and put it to him straight: "Do you want me in this ring? or shall I start another?" He took half an hour, and when I came back, "Pink," says he, "I've put your name on." The first time I came to the top, it was that *Moody* racket; now it's the *Flying Scud*.'

Whereupon Pinkerton, looking at his watch, uttered an exclamation, made a hasty appointment with myself for the doors of the Merchants' Exchange, and fled to examine manifests and interview the skipper. I finished my cigarette with the deliberation of a man at the end of many picnics; reflecting to myself that of all forms of the dollar-hunt, this wrecking had by far the most address to my imagination. Even as I went down town, in the brisk bustle and chill of the familiar San Francisco thoroughfares, I was haunted by a vision of the wreck, baking so far away in the strong sun, under a cloud of sea-birds; and even then, and for no better reason, my heart inclined towards the adventure. If not myself, something that was mine, some one at least in my employment should voyage to that ocean-bounded pin-point and descend to that deserted cabin.

Pinkerton met me at the appointed moment, pinched of lip, and more than usually erect of bearing, like one conscious of great resolves.

'Well?' I asked.

'Well,' said he, 'it might be better, and it might be worse. This Captain Trent is a remarkably honest fellow – one out of a thousand. As soon as he knew I was in the market, he owned up about the rice in so many words. By his calculation, if there's thirty mats of it saved, it's an outside figure. However, the manifest was cheerier. There's about five thousand dollars of the whole value in silks and teas and nut-oils and that, all in the lazarette, and as safe as if it was in Kearney Street. The brig was new coppered a year ago. There's upwards of a hundred and fifty fathom away-up chain. It's not a bonanza, but there's boodle in it; and we'll try it on.'

It was by that time hard on ten o'clock, and we turned at once into the place of sale. The *Flying Scud*, although so important to ourselves, appeared to attract a very humble share of popular attention. The auctioneer was surrounded by perhaps a score of lookers-on – big fellows for the most part, of the true Western build, long in the leg, broad in the shoulder, and adorned (to a plain man's taste) with needless finery. A jaunty ostentatious comradeship prevailed. Bets were flying, and nicknames. 'The boys' (as they would have called themselves) were very boyish; and it was plain they were here in mirth, and not on business. Behind, and certainly in strong contrast to these gentlemen, I could detect the figure of my friend Captain Trent, come (as I could very well imagine that a captain would) to hear the last of his old vessel. Since yesterday he had rigged himself anew in ready-made black clothes, not very aptly fitted; the upper left-hand pocket showing a corner of silk handkerchief, the lower, on the other side, bulging with papers. Pinkerton had just given this man a high character. Certainly he seemed to have been very frank, and I looked at him again to trace (if possible) that virtue in his face. It was red and broad and flustered and (I thought) false. The whole man looked sick with some unknown anxiety; and as he stood there, unconscious of my observation, he tore at his nails, scowled on the floor, or glanced suddenly, sharply, and fearfully at passers-by. I was still gazing at the man in a kind of fascination, when the sale began.

Some preliminaries were rattled through, to the irreverent, uninterrupted gambolling of the boys; and then, amid a trifle more attention, the auctioneer sounded for some two or three minutes the pipe of the charmer. 'Fine brig – new copper – valuable fittings – three fine boats – remarkably choice cargo – what the auctioneer would call a perfectly safe investment; nay, gentlemen, he would go further, he would put a figure on it: he had no hesitation (had that bold auctioneer) in putting it in figures; and in his view, what with this and that, and one thing and another, the purchaser might expect to clear a sum equal to the entire estimated value of the cargo; or, gentlemen, in other words, a sum of ten thousand dollars.' At this modest computation the roof immediately above the speaker's head (I suppose, through the intervention of a spectator of ventriloquial tastes) uttered a clear 'Cock-a-doodle-doo!' – whereat all laughed, the auctioneer himself obligingly joining.

'Now, gentlemen, what shall we say?' resumed that gentleman, plainly ogling Pinkerton, – 'what shall we say for this remarkable opportunity?'

'One hundred dollars,' said Pinkerton.

'One hundred dollars from Mr Pinkerton,' went the auctioneer, 'one hundred dollars. No other gentleman inclined to make any advance? One hundred dollars, only one hundred dollars— '

The auctioneer was droning on to some such tune as this, and I, on my part, was watching with something between sympathy and amazement the undisguised emotion of Captain Trent, when we were all startled by the interjection of a bid.

'And fifty,' said a sharp voice.

Pinkerton, the auctioneer, and the boys, who were all equally in the open secret of the ring, were now all equally and simultaneously taken aback.

'I beg your pardon,' said the auctioneer; 'anybody bid?'

'And fifty,' reiterated the voice, which I was now able to trace to its origin, on the lips of a small unseemly rag of human-kind. The speaker's skin was gray and blotched; he spoke in a kind of broken song, with much variety of key; his gestures seemed (as in the disease called Saint Vitus's dance) to be imperfectly under control; he was badly dressed; he carried himself with an air of shrinking assumption, as though he were proud to be where he was and to do what he was doing, and yet half expected to be called in question and kicked out. I think I never saw a man more of a piece; and the type was new to me: I had never before set eyes upon his parallel, and I thought instinctively of Balzac and the lower regions of the *Comédie Humaine*.

Pinkerton stared a moment on the intruder with no friendly eye, tore a leaf from his note-book, and scribbled a line in pencil, turned, beckoned a messenger boy, and whispered 'To Longhurst.' Next moment the boy had sped upon his errand, and Pinkerton was again facing the auctioneer.

'Two hundred dollars,' said Jim.

'And fifty,' said the enemy.

'This looks lively,' whispered I to Pinkerton.

'Yes; the little beast means cold-drawn biz,' returned

my friend. 'Well, he'll have to have a lesson. Wait till I see Longhurst. Three hundred,' he added aloud.

'And fifty,' came the echo.

It was about this moment when my eye fell again on Captain Trent. A deeper shade had mounted to his crimson face; the new coat was unbuttoned and all flying open, the new silk handkerchief in busy requisition; and the man's eye, of a clear sailor blue, shone glassy with excitement. He was anxious still, but now (if I could read face) there was hope in his anxiety.

'Jim,' I whispered, 'look at Trent. Bet you what you please he was expecting this.'

'Yes,' was the reply, 'there's some blame' thing going on here;' and he renewed his bid.

The figure had run up into the neighbourhood of a thousand when I was aware of a sensation in the faces opposite, and, looking over my shoulder, saw a very large, bland, handsome man come strolling forth and make a little signal to the auctioneer.

'One word, Mr Borden,' said he; and then to Jim, 'Well, Pink, where are we up to now?'

Pinkerton gave him the figure. 'I ran up to that on my own responsibility, Mr Longhurst,' he added, with a flush. 'I thought it the square thing.'

'And so it was,' said Mr Longhurst, patting him kindly on the shoulder, like a gratified uncle. 'Well, you can drop out now; we take hold ourselves. You can run it up to five thousand; and if he likes to go beyond that, he's welcome to the bargain.'

'By-the-bye, who is he?' asked Pinkerton. 'He looks away down.'

'I've sent Billy to find out;' and at the very moment Mr Longhurst received from the hands of one of the expensive young gentlemen a folded paper. It was passed round from one to another till it came to me, and I read: 'Harry D. Bellairs, Attorney-at-Law; defended Clara Varden: twice nearly disbarred.'

'Well, that gets me!' observed Mr Longhurst. 'Who can have put up a shyster[1] like that? Nobody with money, that's

---

1. A low lawyer.

a sure thing. Suppose you tried a big bluff? I think I would, Pink. Well, ta-ta! Your partner, Mr Dodd? Happy to have the pleasure of your acquaintance, sir;' and the great man withdrew.

'Well, what do you think of Douglas B.?' whispered Pinkerton, looking reverently after him as he departed. 'Six foot of perfect gentleman and culture to his boots.'

During this interview the auction had stood transparently arrested – the auctioneer, the spectators, and even Bellairs, all well aware that Mr Longhurst was the principal, and Jim but a speaking-trumpet. But now that the Olympian Jupiter was gone, Mr Borden thought proper to affect severity.

'Come, come, Mr Pinkerton; any advance?' he snapped.

And Pinkerton, resolved on the big bluff, replied, 'Two thousand dollars.'

Bellairs preserved his composure. 'And fifty,' said he. But there was a stir among the onlookers, and – what was of more importance – Captain Trent had turned pale and visibly gulped.

'Pitch it in again, Jim,' said I. 'Trent is weakening.'

'Three thousand,' said Jim.

'And fifty,' said Bellairs.

And then the bidding returned to its original movement by hundreds and fifties; but I had been able in the meanwhile to draw two conclusions. In the first place, Bellairs had made his last advance with a smile of gratified vanity, and I could see the creature was glorying in the *kudos* of an unusual position and secure of ultimate success. In the second, Trent had once more changed colour at the thousand leap, and his relief when he heard the answering fifty was manifest and unaffected. Here, then, was a problem: both were presumably in the same interest, yet the one was not in the confidence of the other. Nor was this all. A few bids later it chanced that my eye encountered that of Captain Trent, and his, which glittered with excitement, was instantly, and I thought guiltily, withdrawn. He wished, then, to conceal his interest? As Jim had said, there was some blamed thing going on. And for certain here were these two men, so strangely united, so strangely divided, both sharp-set to keep the wreck from us, and that at an exorbitant figure.

Was the wreck worth more than we supposed? A sudden heat was kindled in my brain; the bids were nearing

Longhurst's limit of five thousand; another minute and all would be too late. Tearing a leaf from my sketch-book, and inspired (I suppose) by vanity in my own powers of inference and observation, I took the one mad decision of my life. 'If you care to go ahead,' I wrote, 'I'm in for all I'm worth.'

Jim read and looked round at me like one bewildered; then his eyes lightened, and turning again to the auctioneer he bid, 'Five thousand one hundred dollars.'

'And fifty,' said monotonous Bellairs.

Presently Pinkerton scribbled, 'What can it be?' and I answered, still on paper: 'I can't imagine, but there's something. Watch Bellairs; he'll go up to the ten thousand, see if he don't.'

And he did, and we followed. Long before this word had gone abroad that there was battle royal. We were surrounded by a crowd that looked on wondering, and when Pinkerton had offered ten thousand dollars (the outside value of the cargo, even were it safe in San Francisco Bay) and Bellairs, smirking from ear to ear to be the centre of so much attention, had jerked out his answering 'And fifty,' wonder deepened to excitement.

'Ten thousand one hundred,' said Jim; and even as he spoke he made a sudden gesture with his hand, his face changed, and I could see that he had guessed, or thought that he had guessed, the mystery. As he scrawled another memorandum in his note-book, his hand shook like a telegraph operator's.

'Chinese ship,' ran the legend; and then in big, tremulous half-text, and with a flourish that overran the margin, 'Opium!'

'To be sure,' thought I, 'this must be the secret.' I knew that scarce a ship came in from any Chinese port but she carried somewhere, behind a bulkhead or in some cunning hollow of the beams, a nest of the valuable poison. Doubtless there was some such treasure on the *Flying Scud*. How much was it worth? We knew not; we were gambling in the dark. But Trent knew, and Bellairs; and we could only watch and judge.

By this time neither Pinkerton nor I were of sound mind. Pinkerton was beside himself, his eyes like lamps; I shook in every member. To any stranger entering, say, in the course of the fifteenth thousand, we should probably have cut a ·poorer figure than Bellairs himself. But we did not pause; and the crowd watched us – now in silence, now with a buzz of whispers.

Seventeen thousand had been reached, when Douglas B. Longhurst, forcing his way into the opposite row of faces, conspicuously and repeatedly shook his head at Jim. Jim's answer was a note of two words: 'My racket!' which, when the great man had perused he shook his finger warningly and departed – I thought, with a sorrowful countenance.

Although Mr Longhurst knew nothing of Bellairs, the shady lawyer knew all about the Wrecker Boss. He had seen him enter the ring with manifest expectation; he saw him depart, and the bids continue, with manifest surprise and disappointment. 'Hullo,' he plainly thought, 'this is not the ring I'm fighting, then?' And he determined to put on a spurt.

'Eighteen thousand,' said he.

'And fifty,' said Jim, taking a leaf out of his adversary's book.

'Twenty thousand,' from Bellairs.

'And fifty,' from Jim, with a little nervous titter.

And with one consent they returned to the old pace – only now it was Bellairs who took the hundreds, and Jim who did the fifty business. But by this time our idea had gone abroad. I could hear the word 'opium' pass from mouth to mouth, and by the looks directed at us I could see we were supposed to have some private information. And here an incident occurred highly typical of San Francisco. Close at my back there had stood for some time a stout middle-aged gentleman, with pleasant eyes, hair pleasantly grizzled, and a ruddy pleasing face. All of a sudden he appeared as a third competitor, skied the *Flying Scud* with four fat bids of a thousand dollars each, and then as suddenly fled the field, remaining thenceforth (as before) a silent, interested spectator.

Ever since Mr Longhurst's useless intervention Bellairs had seemed uneasy, and at this new attack he began (in his turn) to scribble a note between the bids. I imagined, naturally enough, that it would go to Captain Trent; but when it was done, and the writer turned and looked behind him in the crowd, to my unspeakable amazement he did not seem to remark the captain's presence.

'Messenger boy, messenger boy!' I heard him say. 'Somebody call me a messenger boy.'

At last somebody did, but it was not the captain.

'*He's sending for instructions,*' I wrote to Pinkerton.

'*For money,*' he wrote back. '*Shall I strike out? I think this is the time.*'

I nodded.

'Thirty thousand,' said Pinkerton, making a leap of close upon three thousand dollars.

I could see doubt in Bellairs's eye; then, sudden resolution. 'Thirty-five thousand,' said he.

'Forty thousand,' said Pinkerton.

There was a long pause, during which Bellairs's countenance was as a book; and then, not much too soon for the impending hammer, 'Forty thousand and five dollars,' said he.

Pinkerton and I exchanged eloquent glances. We were of one mind. Bellairs had tried a bluff; now he perceived his mistake, and was bidding against time; he was trying to spin out the sale until the messenger boy returned.

'Forty-five thousand dollars,' said Pinkerton: his voice was like a ghost's and tottered with emotion.

'Forty-five thousand and five dollars,' said Bellairs.

'Fifty thousand,' said Pinkerton.

'I beg your pardon, Mr Pinkerton. Did I hear you make an advance, sir?' asked the auctioneer.

'I – I have a difficulty in speaking,' gasped Jim. 'It's fifty thousand, Mr Borden.'

Bellairs was on his feet in a moment. 'Auctioneer,' he said, 'I have to beg the favour of three moments at the telephone. In this matter I am acting on behalf of a certain party to whom I have just written— '

'I have nothing to do with any of this,' said the auctioneer, brutally. 'I am here to sell this wreck. Do you make any advance on fifty thousand?'

'I have the honour to explain to you, sir,' returned Bellairs, with a miserable assumption of dignity, 'fifty thousand was the figure named by my principal; but if you will give me the small favour of two moments at the telephone— '

'Oh, nonsense!' said the auctioneer. 'If you make no advance, I'll knock it down to Mr Pinkerton.'

'I warn you,' cried the attorney, with sudden shrillness. 'Have a care what you're about. You are here to sell for the underwriters, let me tell you – not to act for Mr Douglas Longhurst. This sale has been already disgracefully interrupted to allow that person to hold a consultation with his minions; it has been much commented on.'

'There was no complaint at the time,' said the auctioneer, manifestly discountenanced. 'You should have complained at the time.'

'I am not here to conduct this sale,' replied Bellairs; 'I am not paid for that.'

'Well, I am, you see,' retorted the auctioneer, his impudence quite restored; and he resumed his sing-song. 'Any advance on fifty thousand dollars? No advance on fifty thousand? No advance, gentlemen? Going at fifty thousand, the wreck of the brig *Flying Scud* – going – going – gone!'

'My God, Jim, can we pay the money?' I cried, as the stroke of the hammer seemed to recall me from a dream.

'It's got to be raised,' said he, white as a sheet. 'It'll be a hell of a strain, Loudon. The credit's good for it, I think; but I shall have to get around. Write me a cheque for your stuff. Meet you at the Occidental in an hour.'

I wrote my cheque at a desk, and I declare I could never have recognised my signature. Jim was gone in a moment; Trent had vanished even earlier; only Bellairs remained, exchanging insults with the auctioneer; and, behold! as I pushed my way out of the exchange, who should run full tilt into my arms but the messenger boy!

It was by so near a margin that we became the owners of the *Flying Scud*.

CHAPTER TEN

In which the Crew Vanish

At the door of the exchange I found myself alongside of the short middle-aged gentleman who had made an appearance, so vigorous and so brief, in the great battle.

'Congratulate you, Mr Dodd,' he said. 'You and your friend stuck to your guns nobly.'

'No thanks to you, sir,' I replied, 'running us up a thousand at a time, and tempting all the speculators in San Francisco to come and have a try.'

'Oh, that was temporary insanity,' said he; 'and I thank the higher powers I am still a free man. Walking this way, Mr Dodd? I'll walk along with you. It's pleasant for an old fogey like myself to see the young bloods in the ring; I've done some pretty wild gambles in my time in this very city, when it was a smaller place and I was a younger man. Yes, I know you, Mr Dodd. By sight, I may say I know you extremely well, you and your followers, the fellows in the kilts, eh? Pardon me. But I have the misfortune to own a little box on the Saucelito shore. I'll be glad to see you there any Sunday – without the fellows in kilts, you know; and I can give you a bottle of wine, and show you the best collection of Arctic voyages in the States. Morgan is my name – Judge Morgan – a Welshman and a forty-niner.'

'Oh, if you're a pioneer,' cried I, 'come to me, and I'll provide you with an axe.'

'You'll want your axes for yourself, I fancy,' he returned, with one of his quick looks. 'Unless you have private knowledge, there will be a good deal of rather violent wrecking to do before you find that – opium, do you call it?'

'Well, it's either opium, or we are stark staring mad,' I replied. 'But I assure you we have no private information. We went in (as I suppose you did yourself) on observation.'

'An observer, sir?' inquired the judge.

'I may say it is my trade – or, rather, was,' said I.

'Well now, and what did you think of Bellairs?' he asked.

'Very little indeed,' said I.

'I may tell you,' continued the judge, 'that to me the employment of a fellow like that appears inexplicable. I knew him: he knows me, too; he has often heard from me in court; and I assure you the man is utterly blown upon; it is not safe to trust him with a dollar, and here we find him dealing up to fifty thousand. I can't think who can have so trusted him, but I am very sure it was a stranger in San Francisco.'

'Someone for the owners, I suppose,' said I.

'Surely not!' exclaimed the judge. 'Owners in London can have nothing to say to opium smuggled between Hong Kong and San Francisco. I should rather fancy they would be the last to hear of it – until the ship was seized. No; I was thinking of the captain. But where would he get the money – above all, after having laid out so much to buy the stuff in China? – unless, indeed, he were acting for some one in 'Frisco; and in that case – here we go round again in the vicious circle – Bellairs would not have been employed.'

'I think I can assure you it was not the captain,' said I, 'for he and Bellairs are not acquainted.'

'Wasn't that the captain with the red face and coloured handkerchief? He seemed to me to follow Bellairs's game with the most thrilling interest,' objected Mr Morgan.

'Perfectly true,' said I. 'Trent is deeply interested; he very likely knew Bellairs, and he certainly knew what he was there for; but I can put my hand in the fire that Bellairs didn't know Trent.'

'Another singularity,' observed the judge. 'Well, we have had a capital forenoon. But you take an old lawyer's advice, and get to Midway Island as fast as you can. There's a pot of money on the table, and Bellairs and Co. are not the men to stick at trifles.'

With this parting counsel Judge Morgan shook hands and made off along Montgomery Street, while I entered the Occidental Hotel, on the steps of which we had finished our conversation. I was well known to the clerks, and as soon as it was understood that I was there to wait for Pinkerton and lunch, I was invited to a seat inside the counter. Here, then, in a retired corner, I was beginning to come a little to myself after these so violent experiences, when who should come hurrying in, and (after a moment with a clerk) fly to one of the telephone-boxes but Mr Henry D. Bellairs in person! Call it what you will, but the impulse was irresistible, and I rose and took a place immediately at the man's back. It may be some excuse that I had often practised this very innocent form of eavesdropping upon strangers and for fun. Indeed, I scarce know anything that gives a lower view of man's intelligence than to overhear (as you thus do) one side of a communication.

'Central,' said the attorney, '2241 and 584 B' (or some such numbers) – 'Who's that? – All right – Mr Bellairs – Occidental; the wires are fouled in the other place – Yes, about three minutes – Yes – Yes – Your figure, I am sorry to say – No – I had no authority – Neither more nor less – I have every reason to suppose so – Oh, Pinkerton, Montana Block – Yes – Yes – Very good, sir – As you will, sir – Disconnect 584 B.'

Bellairs turned to leave; at sight of me behind him, up flew his hands, and he winced and cringed, as though in fear of bodily attack. 'Oh, it's you!' he cried; and then, somewhat recovered, 'Mr Pinkerton's partner, I believe? I am pleased to see you, sir – to congratulate you on your late success;' and with that he was gone, obsequiously bowing as he passed.

And now a madcap humour came upon me. It was plain Bellairs had been communicating with his principal; I knew the number, if not the name. Should I ring up at once? It was more than likely he would return in person to the telephone. Why should not I dash (vocally) into the presence of this mysterious person, and have some fun for my money? I pressed the bell.

'Central,' said I, 'connect again 2241 and 584 B.'

A phantom central repeated the numbers; there was a pause, and then 'Two two four one,' came in a tiny voice into my ear – a voice with the English sing-song – the voice plainly of a gentleman. 'Is that you again, Mr Bellairs?' it trilled. 'I tell you it's no use. Is that you, Mr Bellairs? Who is that?'

'I only want to put a single question,' said I, civilly. 'Why do you want to buy the *Flying Scud*?'

No answer came. The telephone vibrated and hummed in miniature with all the numerous talk of a great city; but the voice of 2241 was silent. Once and twice I put my question; but the tiny sing-song English voice I heard no more. The man, then, had fled – fled from an impertinent question. It scarce seemed natural to me – unless on the principle that the wicked fleeth when no man pursueth. I took the telephone list and turned the number up: '2241, Mrs Keane, res. 942, Mission Street.' And that, short of driving to the house and renewing my impertinence in person, was all that I could do.

Yet, as I resumed my seat in the corner of the office, I was conscious of a new element of the uncertain, the underhand, perhaps even the dangerous, in our adventure; and there was now a new picture in my mental gallery, to hang beside that of the wreck under its canopy of sea-birds and of Captain Trent mopping his red brow – the picture of a man with a telephone dice-box to his ear, and at the small voice of a single question struck suddenly as white as ashes.

From these considerations I was awakened by the striking of the clock. An hour and nearly twenty minutes had elapsed since Pinkerton departed for the money: he was twenty minutes behind time; and to me, who knew so well his gluttonous despatch of business, and had so frequently admired his iron punctuality, the fact spoke volumes. The twenty minutes slowly stretched into an hour; the hour had nearly extended to a second; and I still sat in my corner of the office, or paced the marble pavement of the hall, a prey to the most wretched anxiety and penitence. The hour for lunch was nearly over before I remembered that I had not eaten. Heaven knows I had no appetite; but there might still be much to do – it was needful I should keep myself in proper trim, if it were only to digest the now too probable bad news; and leaving word at the office for Pinkerton, I sat down to table and called for soup, oysters, and a pint of champagne.

I was not long set before my friend returned. He looked pale and rather old, refused to hear of food, and called for tea.

'I suppose all's up?' said I, with an incredible sinking.

'No,' he replied; 'I've pulled it through, Loudon – just pulled it through. I couldn't have raised another cent in all 'Frisco. People don't like it; Longhurst even went back on me; said he wasn't a three-card-monte man.'

'Well, what's the odds?' said I. 'That's all we wanted, isn't it?'

'Loudon, I tell you I've had to pay blood for that money,' cried my friend, with almost savage energy and gloom. 'It's all on ninety days, too; I couldn't get another day – not another day. If we go ahead with this affair, Loudon, you'll have to go yourself and make the fur fly. I'll stay, of course – I've got to stay and face the trouble in this city; though, I tell you, I just long to go. I would show these fat brutes of sailors what work was; I would be all through that wreck and out at the other end, before they had boosted themselves upon the deck! But you'll do your level best, Loudon; I depend on you for that. You must be all fire and grit and dash from the word "go." That schooner, and the boodle on board of her, are bound to be here before three months, or it's B U S T – bust.'

'I'll swear I'll do my best, Jim; I'll work double tides,' said I. 'It is my fault that you are in this thing, and I'll get you out again, or kill myself. But what is that you say? "If we go ahead?" Have we any choice, then?'

'I'm coming to that,' said Jim. 'It isn't that I doubt the investment. Don't blame yourself for that; you showed a fine sound business instinct: I always knew it was in you, but then it ripped right out. I guess that little beast of an attorney knew what he was doing; and he wanted nothing better than to go beyond. No, there's profit in the deal; it's not that; it's these ninety-day bills, and the strain I've given the credit – for I've been up and down borrowing, and begging and bribing to borrow. I don't believe there's another man but me in 'Frisco,' he cried, with a sudden fervour of self-admiration, 'who could have raised that last ten thousand! Then there's another thing. I had hoped you might have peddled that opium through the islands, which is safer and more profitable. But with this three-month limit, you must make tracks for Honolulu straight, and communicate by steamer. I'll try to put up something for you there; I'll have a man spoken to who's posted on that line of biz. Keep a bright look-out for him as soon's you make the islands; for it's on the cards he might pick you up at sea in a whaleboat or a steam-launch, and bring the dollars right on board.'

It shows how much I had suffered morally during my sojourn in San Francisco that even now, when our fortunes trembled in the balance, I should have consented to become a smuggler – and (of all things) a smuggler of opium. Yet I did, and that in silence; without a protest, not without a twinge.

'And suppose,' said I, 'suppose the opium is so securely hidden that I can't get hands on it?'

'Then you will stay there till that brig is kindling-wood, and stay and split that kindling-wood with your penknife,' cried Pinkerton. 'The stuff is there; we know that; and it must be found. But all this is only the one string to our bow – though I tell you I've gone into it head-first, as if it was our bottom dollar. Why, the first thing I did before I'd raised a cent, and with this other notion in my head already – the first thing I did was to secure the schooner. The *Norah Creina* she is, sixty-four tons – quite big enough for our purpose since the rice is spoiled, and the fastest thing of her tonnage out of San Francisco. For a bonus of two hundred, and a monthly charter of three, I have her for my own time; wages and provisions, say four hundred more: a drop in the bucket. They began firing the cargo out of her (she was part loaded) near two hours ago; and about the same time John Smith got the order for the stores. That's what I call business.'

'No doubt of that,' said I; 'but the other notion.'

'Well, here it is,' said Jim. 'You agree with me that Bellairs was ready to go higher?'

I saw where he was coming. 'Yes – and why shouldn't he?' said I. 'Is that the line?'

'That's the line, Loudon Dodd,' assented Jim. 'If Bellairs and his principal have any desire to go me better, I'm their man.'

A sudden thought, a sudden fear, shot into my mind. What if I had been right? What if my childish pleasantry had frightened the principal away, and thus destroyed our chance? Shame closed my mouth; I began instinctively a long course of reticence; and it was without a word of my meeting with Bellairs, or my discovery of the address in Mission Street, that I continued the discussion.

'Doubtless fifty thousand was originally mentioned as a round sum,' said I, 'or, at least, so Bellairs supposed. But at the same time it may be an outside sum; and to cover the expenses we have already incurred for the money and the schooner – I am far from blaming you; I see how needful it was to be ready for either event – but to cover them we shall want a rather large advance.'

'Bellairs will go to sixty thousand; it's my belief, if he were properly handled, he would take the hundred,' replied Pinkerton. 'Look back on the way the sale ran at the end.'

'That is my own impression as regards Bellairs,' I admitted; 'the point I am trying to make is that Bellairs himself may be mistaken; that what he supposed to be a round sum was really an outside figure.'

'Well, Loudon, if that is so,' said Jim, with extraordinary gravity of face and voice, 'if that is so, let him take the *Flying Scud* at fifty thousand, and joy go with her! I prefer the loss.'

'Is that so, Jim? Are we dipped as bad as that?' I cried.

'We've put our hand farther out than we can pull it in again, Loudon,' he replied. 'Why, man, that fifty thousand dollars, before we get clear again, will cost us nearer seventy. Yes, it figures up overhead to more than ten per cent a month; and I could do no better, and there isn't the man breathing could have done as well. It was a miracle, Loudon. I couldn't but admire myself. Oh, if we had just the four months! And you know, Loudon, it may still be done. With your energy and charm, if the worst comes to the worst, you can run that schooner as you ran one of your picnics; and we may have luck. And O man! if we do pull it through, what a dashing operation it will be! What an advertisement! what a thing to talk of and remember all our lives! However,' he broke off suddenly, 'we must try the safe thing first. Here's for the shyster!'

There was another struggle in my mind, whether I should even now admit my knowledge of the Mission Street address. But I had let the favourable moment slip. I had now, which made it the more awkward, not merely the original discovery, but my late suppression to confess. I could not help reasoning, besides, that the more natural course was to approach the principal by the road of his agent's office; and there weighed upon my spirits a conviction that we were already too late, and that the man was gone two hours ago. Once more, then, I held my peace; and after an exchange of words at the telephone to assure ourselves he was at home, we set out for the attorney's office.

The endless streets of any American city pass, from one end to another, through strange degrees and vicissitudes of splendour and distress, running under the same name between monumental warehouses, the dens and taverns of thieves, and the sward and shrubbery of villas. In San Francisco the sharp inequalities of the ground, and the sea bordering on so many sides, greatly exaggerate these contrasts. The street for which we were now bound took its rise among blowing sands, somewhere in view of the Lone Mountain Cemetery; ran for a term across that rather windy Olympus of Nob Hill, or perhaps just skirted its frontier; passed almost immediately after through a stage of little houses, rather impudently painted, and offering to the eye of the observer this diagnostic peculiarity, that the huge brass plates upon the small and highly-coloured doors bore only the first names of ladies – Norah or Lily or Florence; traversed China Town, where it was doubtless undermined with opium cellars, and its blocks pierced, after the similitude of rabbit-warrens, with a hundred doors and passages and galleries; enjoyed a glimpse of high publicity at the corner of Kearney; and proceeded, among dives and warehouses, towards the City Front and the region of the water-rats. In this last stage of its career, where it was both grimy and solitary, and alternately quiet and roaring to the wheels of drays, we found a certain house of some pretension to neatness, and furnished with a rustic outside stair. On the pillar of the stair a black plate bore in gilded lettering this device: 'Harry D. Bellairs, Attorney-at-law. Consultations, 9 to 6.' On ascending the stairs a door was found to stand open on the balcony, with this further inscription, 'Mr Bellairs In.'

'I wonder what we do next,' said I.

'Guess we sail right in,' returned Jim, and suited the action to the word.

The room in which we found ourselves was clean, but extremely bare. A rather old-fashioned secretaire stood by the wall, with a chair drawn to the desk; in one corner was a shelf with half-a-dozen law books; and I can remember literally not another stick of furniture. One inference imposed itself: Mr Bellairs was in the habit of sitting down himself and suffering his clients to stand. At the far end, and veiled by a curtain of red baize, a second door communicated with the interior of the house. Hence, after some coughing and stamping, we elicited the shyster, who came timorously forth, for all the world like a man in fear of bodily assault, and then, recognising his guests, suffered from what I can only call a nervous paroxysm of courtesy.

'Mr Pinkerton and partner!' said he. 'I will go and fetch you seats.'

'Not the least,' said Jim. 'No time. Much rather stand. This is business, Mr Bellairs. This morning, as you know, I bought the wreck *Flying Scud*.'

The lawyer nodded.

'And bought her,' pursued my friend, 'at a figure out of all proportion to the cargo and the circumstances, as they appeared.'

'And now you think better of it, and would like to be off with your bargain? I have been figuring upon this,' returned the lawyer. 'My client, I will not hide from you, was displeased with me for putting her so high. I think we were both too heated, Mr Pinkerton: rivalry – the spirit of competition. But I will be quite frank – I know when I am dealing with gentlemen – and I am almost certain, if you leave the matter in my hands, my client would relieve you of the bargain, so as you would lose' – he consulted our faces with gimlet-eyed calculation – 'nothing,' he added shrilly.

And here Pinkerton amazed me.

'That's a little too thin,' said he. 'I have the wreck. I know there's boodle in her, and I mean to keep her. What I want is some points which may save me needless expense, and which I'm prepared to pay for, money down. The thing for you to consider is just this, Am I to deal with you or direct with your principal? If you are prepared to give me the facts right off, why, name your figure. Only one thing,' added

Jim, holding a finger up, 'when I say "money down" I mean bills payable when the ship returns, and if the information proves reliable. I don't buy pigs in pokes.'

I had seen the lawyer's face light up for a moment, and then, at the sound of Jim's proviso, miserably fade. 'I guess you know more about this wreck than I do, Mr Pinkerton,' said he. 'I only know that I was told to buy the thing, and tried, and couldn't.'

'What I like about you, Mr Bellairs, is that you waste no time,' said Jim. 'Now then, your client's name and address.'

'On consideration,' replied the lawyer, with indescribable furtivity, 'I cannot see that I am entitled to communicate my client's name. I will sound him for you with pleasure, if you care to instruct me, but I cannot see that I can give you his address.'

'Very well,' said Jim, and put his hat on. 'Rather a strong step, isn't it?' (Between every sentence was a clear pause.) 'Not think better of it? Well, come, call it a dollar?'

'Mr Pinkerton, sir!' exclaimed the offended attorney; and, indeed, I myself was almost afraid that Jim had mistaken his man and gone too far.

'No present use for a dollar?' says Jim. 'Well, look here, Mr Bellairs – we're both busy men, and I'll go to my outside figure with you right away— '

'Stop this, Pinkerton,' I broke in. 'I know the address: 924, Mission Street.'

I do not know whether Pinkerton or Bellairs was the more taken aback.

'Why in snakes didn't you say so, Loudon?' cried my friend.

'You didn't ask for it before,' said I, colouring to my temples under his troubled eyes.

It was Bellairs who broke silence, kindly supplying me with all that I had yet to learn. 'Since you know Mr Dickson's address,' said he, plainly burning to be rid of us, 'I suppose I need detain you no longer.'

I do not know how Pinkerton felt, but I had death in my soul as we came down the outside stair from the den of this blotched spider. My whole being was strung, waiting for Jim's first question, and prepared to blurt out – I believe, almost with tears – a full avowal. But my friend asked nothing.

'We must hack it,' said he, tearing off in the direction of the nearest stand. 'No time to be lost. You saw how I changed ground. No use in paying the shyster's commission.'

Again I expected a reference to my suppression; again I was disappointed. It was plain Jim feared the subject, and I felt I almost hated him for that fear. At last, when we were already in the hack and driving towards Mission Street, I could bear my suspense so longer.

'You do not ask me about that address,' said I.

'No,' said he, quickly and timidly, 'what was it? I would like to know.'

The note of timidity offended me like a buffet; my temper rose as hot as mustard. 'I must request you do not ask me,' said I; 'it is a matter I cannot explain.'

The moment the foolish words were said, that moment I would have given worlds to recall them; how much more when Pinkerton, patting my hand, replied, 'All right, dear boy, not another word; that's all done; I'm convinced it's perfectly right!' To return upon the subject was beyond my courage; but I vowed inwardly that I should do my utmost in the future for this mad speculation, and that I would cut myself in pieces before Jim should lose one dollar.

We had no sooner arrived at the address than I had other things to think of.

'Mr Dickson? He's gone,' said the landlady.

Where had he gone?

'I'm sure I can't tell you,' she answered. 'He was quite a stranger to me.'

'Did he express his baggage, ma'am?' asked Pinkerton.

'Hadn't any,' was the reply. 'He came last night, and left again today with a satchel.'

'When did he leave?' I inquired.

'It was about noon,' replied the landlady. 'Someone rang up the telephone, and asked for him; and I reckon he got some news, for he left right away, although his rooms were taken by the week. He seemed considerable put out: I reckon it was a death.'

My heart sank; perhaps my idiotic jest had indeed driven him away; and again I asked myself, 'Why?'

and whirled for a moment in a vortex of untenable hypotheses.

'What was he like, ma'am?' Pinkerton was asking, when I returned to consciousness of my surroundings.

'A clean-shaved man,' said the woman, and could be led or driven into no more significant description.

'Pull up at the nearest drug-store,' said Pinkerton to the driver; and when there, the telephone was put in operation, and the message sped to the Pacific Mail Steamship Company's office – this was in the days before Spreckels had arisen – 'when does the next China steamer touch at Honolulu?'

'The *City of Pekin*; she cast off the dock today, at half-past one,' came the reply.

'It's a clear case of bolt,' said Jim. 'He's skipped, or my name's not Pinkerton. He's gone to head us off at Midway Island.'

Somehow I was not so sure; there were elements in the case, not known to Pinkerton – the fears of the captain, for example – that inclined me otherwise; and the idea that I had terrified Mr Dickson into flight, though resting on so slender a foundation, clung obstinately in my mind.

'Shouldn't we see the list of passengers?' I asked.

'Dickson is such a blamed common name,' returned Jim; 'and then, as like as not, he would change it.'

At this I had another intuition. A negative of a street scene, taken unconsciously when I was absorbed in other thought, rose in my memory with not a feature blurred: a view, from Bellairs's door as we were coming down, of muddy roadway, passing drays, matted telegraph wires, a China-boy with a basket on his head, and (almost opposite) a corner grocery with the name of Dickson in great gilt letters.

'Yes,' said I, 'you are right; he would change it. And anyway, I don't believe it was his name at all; I believe he took it from a corner grocery beside Bellairs's.'

'As like as not,' said Jim, still standing on the side-walk with contracted brows.

'Well, what shall we do next?' I asked.

'The natural thing would be to rush the schooner,' he replied. 'But I don't know. I telephoned the captain to go at it head down and heels in air; he answered like a little man; and I guess he's getting around. I believe, Loudon, we'll give Trent a chance. Trent was in it; he was in it up to the neck; even if he couldn't buy, he could give us the straight tip.'

'I think so, too,' said I. 'Where shall we find him?'

'British consulate of course,' said Jim. 'And that's another reason for taking him first. We can hustle that schooner up all evening; but when the consulate's shut, it's shut.'

At the consulate we learned that Captain Trent had alighted (such is, I believe, the classic phrase) at the What Cheer House. To that large and unaristocratic hostelry we drove, and addressed ourselves to a large clerk, who was chewing a toothpick and looking straight before him.

'Captain Jacob Trent?'

'Gone,' said the clerk.

'Where has he gone?' asked Pinkerton.

'Can't say,' said the clerk.

'When did he go?' I asked.

'Don't know,' said the clerk, and with the simplicity of a monarch offered us the spectacle of his broad back.

What might have happened next I dread to picture, for Pinkerton's excitement had been growing steadily, and now burned dangerously high; but we were spared extremities by the intervention of a second clerk.

'Why, Mr Dodd!' he exclaimed, running forward to the counter. 'Glad to see you, sir! Can I do anything in your way?'

How virtuous actions blossom! Here was a young man to whose pleased ears I had rehearsed 'Just before the Battle, Mother,' at some weekly picnic; and now, in that tense moment of my life, he came (from the machine) to be my helper.

'Captain Trent of the wreck? Oh yes, Mr Dodd; he left about twelve; he and another of the men. The Kanaka went earlier, by the *City of Pekin*; I know that; I remember expressing his chest. Captain Trent? I'll inquire, Mr Dodd. Yes, they were all here. Here are the names on the register; perhaps you would care to look at them while I go and see about the baggage?'

I drew the book toward me, and stood looking at the four names, all written in the same hand – rather a big, and rather a bad one: Trent, Brown, Hardy, and (instead of Ah Sing) Jos. Amalu.

'Pinkerton,' said I, suddenly, 'have you that *Occidental* in your pocket?'

'Never left me,' said Pinkerton, producing the paper.

I turned to the account of the wreck.

'Here,' said I, 'here's the name. "Elias Goddedaal, mate." Why do we never come across Elias Goddedaal?'

'That's so,' said Jim. 'Was he with the rest in that saloon when you saw them?'

'I don't believe it,' said I. 'They were only four, and there was none that behaved like a mate.'

At this moment the clerk returned with his report.

'The captain,' it appeared, 'came with some kind of an express wagon, and he and the man took off three chests and a big satchel. Our porter helped to put them on, but they drove the cart themselves. The porter thinks they went down town. It was about one.'

'Still in time for the *City of Pekin*,' observed Jim.

'How many of them were here?' I inquired.

'Three, sir, and the Kanaka,' replied the clerk. 'I can't somehow find out about the third, but he's gone too.'

'Mr Goddedaal, the mate, wasn't here then?' I asked.

'No, Mr Dodd, none but what you see,' says the clerk.

'Nor you never heard where he was?'

'No. Any particular reason for finding these men, Mr Dodd?' inquired the clerk.

'This gentleman and I have bought the wreck,' I explained; 'we wished to get some information, and it is very annoying to find the men all gone.'

A certain group had gradually formed about us, for the wreck was still a matter of interest; and at this, one of the bystanders, a rough seafaring man spoke suddenly.

'I guess the mate won't be gone,' said he. 'He's main sick; never left the sick-bay aboard the *Tempest*; so they tell *me*.'

Jim took me by the sleeve. 'Back to the consulate,' said he.

But even at the consulate nothing was known of Mr Goddedaal. The doctor of the *Tempest* had certified him very sick; he had sent his papers in, but never appeared in person before the authorities.

'Have you a telephone laid on to the *Tempest*?' asked Pinkerton.

'Laid on yesterday,' said the clerk.

'Do you mind asking, or letting me ask? We are very anxious to get hold of Mr Goddedaal.'

'All right,' said the clerk, and turned to the telephone. 'I'm sorry,' he said presently, 'Mr Goddedaal has left the ship, and no one knows where he is.'

'Do you pay the men's passage home?' I inquired, a sudden thought striking me.

'If they want it,' said the clerk; 'sometimes they don't. But we paid the Kanaka's passage to Honolulu this morning; and by what Captain Trent was saying, I understand the rest are going home together.'

'Then you haven't paid them?' said I.

'Not yet,' said the clerk.

'And you would be a good deal surprised if I were to tell you they were gone already?' I asked.

'Oh, I should think you were mistaken,' said he.

'Such is the fact, however,' said I.

'I am sure you must be mistaken,' he repeated.

'May I use your telephone one moment?' asked Pinkerton; and as soon as permission had been granted, I heard him ring up the printing-office where our advertisements were usually handled. More I did not hear, for, suddenly recalling the big bad hand in the register of the What Cheer House, I asked the consulate clerk if he had a specimen of Captain Trent's writing. Whereupon I learned that the captain could not write, having cut his hand open a little before the loss of the brig; that the latter part of the log even had been written up by Mr Goddedaal; and that Trent had always signed with his left hand. By the time I had gleaned this information Pinkerton was ready.

'That's all that we can do. Now for the schooner,' said he; 'and by tomorrow evening I lay hands on Goddedaal, or my name's not Pinkerton.'

'How have you managed?' I inquired.

'You'll see before you get to bed,' said Pinkerton, 'And now, after all this backwarding and forwarding, and that hotel clerk, and that bug Bellairs, it'll be a change and a kind of consolation to see the schooner. I guess things are humming there.'

But on the wharf, when we reached it, there was no sign of bustle, and, but for the galley smoke, no mark of life on the *Norah Creina*. Pinkerton's face grew pale and his mouth straightened as he leaped on board.

'Where's the captain of this—?' and he left the phrase unfinished, finding no epithet sufficiently energetic for his thoughts.

It did not appear whom or what he was addressing; but a head, presumably the cook's, appeared in answer at the galley door.

'In the cabin, at dinner,' said the cook deliberately, chewing as he spoke.

'Is that cargo out?'

'No, sir.'

'None of it?'

'Oh, there's some of it out. We'll get at the rest of it livelier tomorrow, I guess.'

'I guess there'll be something broken first,' said Pinkerton, and strode to the cabin.

Here we found a man, fat, dark, and quiet, seated gravely at what seemed a liberal meal. He looked up upon our entrance; and seeing Pinkerton continue to stand facing him in silence, hat on head, arms folded, and lips compressed, an expression of mingled wonder and annoyance began to dawn upon his placid face.

'Well!' said Jim; 'and so this is what you call rushing around?'

'Who are you?' cries the captain.

'Me! I'm Pinkerton!' retorted Jim, as though the name had been a talisman.

'You're not very civil, whoever you are,' was the reply. But still a certain effect had been produced, for he scrambled to his feet, and added hastily, 'A man must have a bit of dinner, you know, Mr Pinkerton.'

'Where's your mate?' snapped Jim.

'He's up town,' returned the other.

'Up town!' sneered Pinkerton. 'Now I'll tell you what you are – you're a Fraud; and if I wasn't afraid of dirtying my boot, I would kick you and your dinner into that dock.'

'I'll tell you something, too,' retorted the captain, duskily flushing. 'I wouldn't sail this ship for the man you are, if

you went upon your knees. I've dealt with gentlemen up
to now.'

'I can tell you the names of a number of gentlemen
you'll never deal with any more, and that's the whole of
Longhurst's gang,' said Jim. 'I'll put your pipe out in that
quarter, my friend. Here, rout out your traps as quick as
look at it, and take your vermin along with you. I'll have a
captain in, this very night, that's a sailor, and some sailors
to work for him.'

'I'll go when I please, and that's tomorrow morning,'
cried the captain after us, as we departed for the shore.

'There's something gone wrong with the world today;
it must have come bottom up!' wailed Pinkerton. 'Bellairs,
and then the hotel clerk, and now this Fraud! And what am
I to do for a captain, Loudon, with Longhurst gone home
an hour ago and the boys all scattered?'

'I know,' said I; 'jump in!' And then to the driver: 'Do
you know Black Tom's?'

Thither then we rattled, passed through the bar, and
found (as I had hoped) Johnson in the enjoyment of club
life. The table had been thrust upon one side; a South Sea
merchant was discoursing music from a mouth-organ in
one corner; and in the middle of the floor Johnson and
a fellow-seaman, their arms clasped about each other's
bodies, somewhat heavily danced. The room was both
cold and close; a jet of gas, which continually menaced
the heads of the performers, shed a coarse illumination;
the mouth-organ sounded shrill and dismal; and the faces
of all concerned were church-like in their gravity. It were,
of course, indelicate to interrupt these solemn frolics; so
we edged ourselves to chairs, for all the world like belated
comers in a concert-room, and patiently waited for the
end. At length the organist, having exhausted his supply
of breath, ceased abruptly in the middle of a bar. With
the cessation of the strain the dancers likewise came to
a full stop, swayed a moment, still embracing, and then
separated, and looked about the circle for applause.

'Very well danced!' said one; but it appears the compliment was not strong enough for the performers, who
(forgetful of the proverb) took up the tale in person.

'Well,' said Johnson, 'I mayn't be no sailor, but I can
dance!'

And his late partner, with an almost pathetic conviction, added, 'My foot is as light as a feather.'

Seeing how the wind set, you may be sure I added a few words of praise before I carried Johnson alone into the passage: to whom, thus mollified, I told so much as I judged needful of our situation, and begged him, if he would not take the job himself, to find me a smart man.

'Me!' he cried; 'I couldn't no more do it than I could try to go to hell!'

'I thought you were a mate?' said I.

'So I am a mate,' giggled Johnson, 'and you don't catch me shipping noways else. But I'll tell you what; I believe I can get you Arty Nares. You seen Arty; first-rate navigator, and a son of a gun for style.' And he proceeded to explain to me that Mr Nares, who had the promise of a fine barque in six months, after things had quieted down, was in the meantime living very private, and would be pleased to have a change of air.

I called out Pinkerton and told him. 'Nares!' he cried, as soon as I had come to the name, 'I would jump at the chance of a man that had had Nares's trousers on! Why, Loudon, he's the smartest deep-water mate out of San Francisco, and draws his dividends regular in service and out.' This hearty indorsation clinched the proposal; Johnson agreed to produce Nares before six the following morning; and Black Tom, being called into the consultation, promised us four smart hands for the same hour, and even (what appeared to all of us excessive) promised them sober.

The streets were fully lighted when we left Black Tom's: street after street sparkling with gas or electricity, line after line of distant luminaries climbing the steep sides of hills towards the overvaulting darkness; and on the other hand, where the waters of the bay invisibly trembled, a hundred riding lanterns marked the position of a hundred ships. The sea-fog flew high in heaven; and at the level of man's life and business it was clear and chill. By silent consent we paid the hack off, and proceeded arm-in-arm towards the 'Poodle Dog' for dinner.

At one of the first hoardings I was aware of a bill-sticker at work: it was a late hour for this employment, and I checked

Pinkerton until the sheet should be unfolded. This is what I read:-

TWO HUNDRED DOLLARS REWARD.

OFFICERS AND MEN OF THE
WRECKED BRIG 'FLYING SCUD'
APPLYING,
PERSONALLY OR BY LETTER,
AT THE OFFICE OF JAMES PINKERTON, MONTANA BLOOK,
BEFORE NOON TOMORROW, TUESDAY, 12TH,
WILL RECEIVE
TWO HUNDRED DOLLARS REWARD.

'This is your idea, Pinkerton!' I cried.

'Yes. They've lost no time; I'll say that for them – not like the Fraud,' said he. 'But mind you, Loudon, that's not half of it. The cream of the idea's here: we know our man's sick; well, a copy of that has been mailed to every hospital, every doctor, and every drug-store in San Francisco.'

Of course, from the nature of our business, Pinkerton could do a thing of the kind at a figure extremely reduced; for all that, I was appalled at the extravagance, and said so.

'What matter a few dollars now?' he replied sadly; 'it's in three months that the pull comes, Loudon.'

We walked on again in silence, not without a shiver. Even at the 'Poodle Dog' we took our food with small appetite and less speech; and it was not until he was warmed with a third glass of champagne that Pinkerton cleared his throat and looked upon me with a deprecating eye.

'Loudon,' said he,' there was a subject you didn't wish to be referred to. I only want to do so indirectly. It wasn't' – he faltered – 'it wasn't because you were dissatisfied with me?' he concluded, with a quaver.

'Pinkerton!' cried I.

'No, no, not a word just now,' he hastened to proceed; 'let me speak first. I appreciate, though I can't imitate, the delicacy of your nature; and I can well understand you would rather die than speak of it, and yet might feel disappointed. I did think I could have done better myself. But when I found how tight money was in this city, and a man like Douglas B. Longhurst – a forty-niner, the man that stood at bay in a corn patch for five hours against the San Diablo squatters – weakening on the operation, I tell you, Loudon, I began to despair; and – I may have made mistakes, no doubt there are thousands who could have done better – but I give you a loyal hand on it, I did my best.'

'My poor Jim,' said I, 'as if I ever doubted you! as if I didn't know you had done wonders! All day I've been admiring your energy and resource. And as for that affair— '

'No, Loudon, no more – not a word more! I don't want to hear,' cried Jim.

'Well, to tell you the truth, I don't want to tell you,' said I; 'for it's a thing I'm ashamed of.'

'Ashamed, Loudon? Oh, don't say that; don't use such an expression, even in jest!' protested Pinkerton.

'Do you never do anything you're ashamed of?' I inquired.

'No,' says he, rolling his eyes; 'why? I'm sometimes sorry afterwards, when it pans out different from what I figured. But I can't see what I would want to be ashamed for.'

I sat awhile considering with admiration the simplicity of my friend's character. Then I sighed. 'Do you know, Jim, what I'm sorriest for?' said I. 'At this rate I can't be best man at your marriage.'

'My marriage!' he repeated, echoing the sigh. 'No marriage for me now. I'm going right down tonight to break it to her. I think that's what's shaken me all day. I feel as if I had had no right (after I was engaged) to operate so widely.'

'Well, you know, Jim, it was my doing, and you must lay the blame on me,' said I.

'Not a cent of it!' he cried. 'I was as eager as yourself, only not so bright at the beginning. No; I've myself to thank for it; but it's a wrench.'

While Jim departed on his dolorous mission, I returned alone to the office, lit the gas, and sat down to reflect on the events of that momentous day: on the strange features of the tale that had been so far unfolded, the disappearances, the terrors, the great sums of money; and on the dangerous and ungrateful task that awaited me in the immediate future.

It is difficult, in the retrospect of such affairs, to avoid attributing to ourselves in the past a measure of the

knowledge we possess today. But I may say, and yet
be well within the mark, that I was consumed that night
with a fever of suspicion and curiosity; exhausted my fancy
in solutions, which I still dismissed as incommensurable
with the facts; and in the mystery by which I saw myself
surrounded, found a precious stimulus for my courage and
a convenient soothing draught for conscience. Even had all
been plain sailing, I do not hint that I should have drawn
back. Smuggling is one of the meanest of crimes, for by
that we rob a whole country *pro rata*, and are therefore
certain to impoverish the poor: to smuggle opium is an
offence particularly dark, since it stands related – not so
much to murder, as to massacre. Upon all these points I
was quite clear; my sympathy was all in arms against my
interest; and had not Jim been involved, I could have dwelt
almost with satisfaction on the idea of my failure. But Jim,
his whole fortune, and his marriage depended upon my
success; and I preferred the interests of my friend before
those of all the islanders in the South Seas. This is a poor,
private morality, if you like; but it is mine, and the best
I have; and I am not half so much ashamed of having
embarked at all on this adventure, as I am proud that
(while I was in it, and for the sake of my friend) I was
up early and down late, set my own hand to everything,
took dangers as they came, and for once in my life played
the man throughout. At the same time I could have desired
another field of energy; and I was the more grateful for
the redeeming element of mystery. Without that, though
I might have gone ahead and done as well, it would scarce
have been with ardour; and what inspired me that night with
an impatient greed of the sea, the island, and the wreck, was
the hope that I might stumble there upon the answer to a
hundred questions, and learn why Captain Trent fanned
his red face in the exchange, and why Mr Dickson fled
from the telephone in the Mission Street lodging-house.

CHAPTER ELEVEN

In which Jim and I Take Different Ways

I was unhappy when I closed my eyes; and it was to unhappiness that I opened them again next morning, to a confused sense of some calamity still inarticulate, and to the consciousness of jaded limbs and of a swimming head. I must have lain for some time inert and stupidly miserable before I became aware of a reiterated knocking at the door; with which discovery all my wits flowed back in their accustomed channels, and I remembered the sale and the wreck, and Goddedaal and Nares, and Johnson and Black Tom, and the troubles of yesterday and the manifold engagements of the day that was to come. The thought thrilled me like a trumpet in the hour of battle. In a moment I had leaped from bed, crossed the office where Pinkerton lay in a deep trance of sleep on the convertible sofa, and stood in the doorway, in my night gear, to receive our visitors.

Johnson was first, by way of usher, smiling. From a little behind, with his Sunday hat tilted forward over his brow and a cigar glowing between his lips, Captain Nares acknowledged our previous acquaintance with a succinct nod. Behind him again, in the top of the stairway, a knot of sailors, the new crew of the *Norah Creina*, stood polishing the wall with back and elbow. These I left without to their reflections. But our two officers I carried at once into the office, where (taking Jim by the shoulder) I shook him slowly into consciousness. He sat up, all abroad for the moment, and stared on the new captain.

'Jim,' said I, 'this is Captain Nares. Captain, Mr Pinkerton.'

Nares repeated his curt nod, still without speech; and I thought he held us both under a watchful scrutiny.

'Oh!' says Jim, 'this is Captain Nares, is it? Good-morning, Captain Nares. Happy to have the pleasure

of your acquaintance, sir. I know you well by reputation.'

Perhaps, under the circumstances of the moment, this
was scarce a welcome speech. At least, Nares received it
with a grunt.

'Well, Captain,' Jim continued, 'you know about the
size of the business? You're to take the *Norah Creina* to
Midway Island, break up a wreck, call at Honolulu, and
back to this port? I suppose that's understood?'

'Well,' returned Nares, with the same unamiable reserve,
'for a reason, which I guess you know, the cruise may suit
me; but there's a point or two to settle. We shall have to
talk, Mr Pinkerton. But whether I go or not, somebody
will. There's no sense in losing time; and you might give
Mr Johnson a note, let him take the hands right down,
and set to to overhaul the rigging. The beasts look sober,'
he added, with an air of great disgust, 'and need putting
to work to keep them so.'

This being agreed upon, Nares watched his subordinate
depart, and drew a visible breath.

'And now we're alone and can talk,' said he. 'What's this
thing about? It's been advertised like Barnum's museum;
that poster of yours has set the Front talking. That's an
objection in itself, for I'm laying a little dark just now;
and, anyway, before I take the ship, I require to know
what I'm going after.'

Thereupon Pinkerton gave him the whole tale, beginning
with a business-like precision, and working himself up, as he
went on, to the boiling-point of narrative enthusiasm. Nares
sat and smoked, hat still on head, and acknowledged each
fresh feature of the story with a frowning nod. But his pale
blue eyes betrayed him, and lighted visibly.

'Now you see for yourself,' Pinkerton concluded; 'there's
every last chance that Trent has skipped to Honolulu, and
it won't take much of that fifty thousand dollars to charter
a smart schooner down to Midway. Here's where I want
a man!' cried Jim, with contagious energy. 'That wreck's
mine; I've paid for it, money down; and if it's got to be
fought for, I want to see it fought for lively. If you're not
back in ninety days, I tell you plainly I'll make one of the
biggest busts ever seen upon this coast. It's life or death
for Mr Dodd and me. As like as not it'll come to grapples

on the island; and when I heard your name last night –
and a blame' sight more this morning when I saw the eye
you've got in your head – I said, "Nares is good enough
for me!"'

'I guess,' observed Nares, studying the ash of his cigar,
'the sooner I get that schooner outside the Farallones the
better you'll be pleased.'

'You're the man I dreamed of!' cried Jim, bouncing on
the bed. 'There's not five per cent of fraud in all your
carcase.'

'Just hold on,' said Nares. 'There's another point. I heard
some talk about a supercargo.'

'That's Mr Dodd here, my partner,' said Jim.

'I don't see it,' returned the captain, drily. 'One captain's
enough for any ship that ever I was aboard.'

'Now don't you start disappointing me,' said Pinkerton,
'for you're talking without thought. I'm not going to give
you the run of the books of this firm, am I? I guess not.
Well, this is not only a cruise, it's a business operation, and
that's in the hands of my partner. You sail that ship, you
see to breaking up that wreck and keeping the men upon
the jump, and you'll find your hands about full. Only, no
mistake about one thing; it has to be done to Mr Dodd's
satisfaction, for it's Mr Dodd that's paying.'

'I'm accustomed to give satisfaction,' said Mr Nares,
with a dark flush.

'And so you will here!' cried Pinkerton. 'I understand you.
You're prickly to handle, but you're straight all through.'

'The position's got to be understood, though,' returned
Nares, perhaps a trifle mollified. 'My position, I mean. I'm
not going to ship sailing-master; it's enough out of my way
already, to set a foot on this mosquito schooner.'

'Well, I'll tell you,' retorted Jim, with an indescribable
twinkle: 'you just meet me on the ballast, and we'll make
it a barquentine.'

Nares laughed a little; tactless Pinkerton had once more
gained a victory in tact. 'Then there's another point,'
resumed the captain, tacitly relinquishing the last. 'How
about the owners?'

'Oh, you leave that to me; I'm one of Longhurst's crowd,
you know,' said Jim, with sudden bristling vanity. 'Any man
that's good enough for me, is good enough for them.'

'Who are they?' asked Nares.

'M'Intyre and Spittal,' said Jim.

'Oh well, give me a card of yours,' said the captain; 'you needn't bother to write; I keep M'Intyre and Spittal in my vest-pocket.'

Boast for boast; it was always thus with Nares and Pinkerton – the two vainest men of my acquaintance. And having thus reinstated himself in his own opinion, the captain rose, and, with a couple of his stiff nods, departed.

'Jim,' I cried, as the door closed behind him, 'I don't like that man.'

'You've just got to, Loudon,' returned Jim. 'He's a typical American seaman – brave as a lion, full of resource, and stands high with his owners. He's a man with a record.'

'For brutality at sea,' said I.

'Say what you like,' exclaimed Pinkerton, 'it was a good hour we got him in: I'd trust Mamie's life to him tomorrow.'

'Well, and talking of Mamie?' says I.

Jim paused with his trousers half on. 'She's the gallantest little soul God ever made!' he cried. 'Loudon, I'd meant to knock you up last night, and I hope you won't take it unfriendly that I didn't. I went in and looked at you asleep; and I saw you were all broken up, and let you be. The news would keep, anyway; and even you, Loudon, couldn't feel it the same way as I did.'

'What news?' I asked.

'It's this way,' says Jim. 'I told her how we stood, and that I backed down from marrying. "Are you tired of me?" says she: God bless her! Well, I explained the whole thing over again, the chance of smash, your absence unavoidable, the point I made of having you for the best man, and that. "If you're not tired of me, I think I see one way to manage," says she. "Let's get married tomorrow, and Mr Loudon can be best man before he goes to sea." That's how she said it, crisp and bright, like one of Dickens's characters. It was no good for me to talk about the smash. "You'll want me all the more," she said. Loudon, I only pray I can make it up to her; I prayed for it last night beside your bed, while you lay sleeping – for you, and Mamie and myself; and – I don't know if you quite believe in prayer, I'm a bit Ingersollian myself – but a kind of sweetness came over me, and I couldn't help but think it was an answer. Never was a man so lucky! You and me and Mamie; it's a triple cord, Loudon. If either of you were to die! And she likes you so much, and thinks you so accomplished and distingué-looking, and was just as set as I was to have you for best man. "Mr Loudon," she calls you; seems to me so friendly! And she sat up till three in the morning fixing up a costume for the marriage; it did me good to see her, Loudon, and to see that needle going, going, and to say "All this hurry, Jim, is just to marry you!" I couldn't believe it; it was so like some blame' fairy story. To think of those old tin-type times about turned my head; I was so unrefined then, and so illiterate, and so lonesome; and here I am in clover, and I'm blamed if I can see what I've done to deserve it.'

So he poured forth with innocent volubility the fulness of his heart; and I, from these irregular communications, must pick out, here a little and there a little, the particulars of his new plan. They were to be married, sure enough, that day; the wedding breakfast was to be at Frank's; the evening to be passed in a visit of God-speed aboard the *Norah Creina*; and then we were to part, Jim and I – he to his married life, I on my sea-enterprise. If ever I cherished an ill-feeling for Miss Mamie, I forgave her now; so brave and kind, so pretty and venturesome, was her decision. The weather frowned overhead with a leaden sky, and San Francisco had never (in all my experience) looked so bleak and gaunt, and shoddy and crazy, like a city prematurely old; but through all my wanderings and errands to and fro, by the dockside or in the jostling street, among rude sounds and ugly sights, there ran in my mind, like a tiny strain of music, the thought of my friend's happiness.

For that was indeed a day of many and incongruous occupations. Breakfast was scarce swallowed before Jim must run to the City Hall and Frank's about the cares of marriage, and I hurry to John Smith's upon the account of stores, and thence, on a visit of certification, to the *Norah Creina*. Methought she looked smaller than ever, sundry great ships overspiring her from close without. She was already a nightmare of disorder; and the wharf alongside was piled with a world of casks and cases and tins, and tools and coils of rope, and miniature barrels of giant powder, such as it seemed no human ingenuity could stuff on board of her. Johnson was in the waist, in a red shirt and dungaree trousers, his eye kindled with activity. With him I exchanged a word or two; thence stepped aft along the narrow alleyway between the house and the rail, and down the companion to the main cabin, where the captain sat with the commissioner at wine.

I gazed with disaffection at the little box which for many a day I was to call home. On the starboard was a stateroom for the captain; on the port a pair of frowsy berths, one over the other, and abutting astern upon the side of an unsavoury cupboard. The walls were yellow and damp, the floor black and greasy; there was a prodigious litter of straw, old newspapers and broken packing-cases; and by way of ornament, only a glass rack, a thermometer presented 'with compliments' of some advertising whiskey-dealer, and a swinging lamp. It was hard to foresee that, before a week was up, I should regard that cabin as cheerful, lightsome, airy, and even spacious.

I was presented to the commissioner, and to a young friend of his whom he had brought with him for the purpose (apparently) of smoking cigars; and after we had pledged one another in a glass of California port, a trifle sweet and sticky for a morning beverage, the functionary spread his papers on the table, and the hands were summoned. Down they trooped, accordingly, into the cabin; and stood eyeing the ceiling or the floor, the picture of sheepish embarrassment, and with a common air of wanting to expectorate and not quite daring. In admirable contrast stood the Chinese cook, easy, dignified, set apart by spotless raiment, the hidalgo of the seas.

I daresay you never had occasion to assist at the farce which followed. Our shipping laws in the United States (thanks to the inimitable Dana) are conceived in a spirit of paternal stringency, and proceed throughout on the hypothesis that poor Jack is an imbecile, and the other parties to the contract, rogues and ruffians. A long and wordy paper of precautions, a fo'c's'le bill of rights, must be read separately to each man. I had now the benefit of hearing it five times in brisk succession; and you would suppose I was acquainted with its contents. But the commissioner (worthy man) spends his days in doing little else; and when we bear in mind the parallel case of the irreverent curate, we need not be surprised that he took the passage *tempo prestissimo*, in one roulade of gabble – that I, with the trained attention of an educated man, could gather but a fraction of its import – and the sailors nothing. No profanity in giving orders, no sheath-knives, Midway Island and any other port the master may direct, not to exceed six calendar months, and to this port to be paid off: so it seemed to run, with surprising verbiage; so ended. And with the end the commissioner, in each case, fetched a deep breath, resumed his natural voice, and proceeded to business. 'Now, my man,' he would say, 'you ship A. B. at so many dollars, American gold coin. Sign your name here, if you have one, and can write.' Whereupon, and the name (with infinite hard breathing) being signed, the commissioner would proceed to fill in the man's appearance, height, etc., on the official form. In this task of literary portraiture he seemed to rely wholly upon temperament; for I could not perceive him to cast one glance on any of his models. He was assisted, however, by a running commentary from the captain: 'Hair blue and eyes red, nose five foot seven, and stature broken' – jests as old, presumably, as the American marine; and, like the similar pleasantries of the billiard board, perennially relished. The highest note of humour was reached in the case of the Chinese cook, who was shipped under the name of 'One Lung,' to the sound of his own protests and the self-approving chuckles of the functionary.

'Now, captain,' said the latter, when the men were gone, and he had bundled up his papers, 'the law requires you to carry a slop-chest and a chest of medicines.'

'I guess I know that,' said Nares.

'I guess you do,' returned the commissioner, and helped himself to port.

But when he was gone, I appealed to Nares on the same subject, for I was well aware we carried none of these provisions.

'Well,' drawled Nares, 'there's sixty pounds of niggerhead on the quay, isn't there? and twenty pounds of salts; and I never travel without some pain-killer in my gripsack.'

As a matter of fact, we were richer. The captain had

the usual sailor's provision of quack medicines, with which, in the usual sailor fashion, he would daily drug himself, displaying an extreme inconstancy, and flitting from Kennedy's Red Discovery to Kennedy's White, and from Hood's Sarsaparilla to Mother Seigel's Syrup. And there were, besides, some mildewed and half-empty bottles, the labels obliterated, over which Nares would sometimes sniff and speculate. 'Seems to smell like diarrhœa stuff,' he would remark. 'I wish't I knew, and I would try it.' But the slop-chest was indeed represented by the plugs of niggerhead, and nothing else. Thus paternal laws are made, thus they are evaded; and the schooner put to sea, like plenty of her neighbours, liable to a fine of six hundred dollars.

This characteristic scene, which has delayed me overlong, was but a moment in that day of exercise and agitation. To fit out a schooner for sea and improvise a marriage between dawn and dusk, involves heroic effort. All day Jim and I ran and tramped, and laughed and came near crying, and fell in sudden anxious consultations, and were sped (with a prepared sarcasm on our lips) to some fallacious milliner, and made dashes to the schooner and John Smith's, and at every second corner were reminded (by our own huge posters) of our desperate estate. Between whiles I had found the time to hover at some half a dozen jewellers' windows; and my present, thus intemperately chosen, was graciously accepted. I believe, indeed, that was the last (though not the least) of my concerns, before the old minister, shabby and benign, was routed from his house and led to the office like a performing poodle; and there, in the growing dusk, under the cold glitter of Thirteen Star, two hundred strong, and beside the garish glories of the agricultural engine, Mamie and Jim were made one. The scene was incongruous, but the business pretty, whimsical, and affecting: the typewriters with such kindly faces and fine posies, Mamie so demure, and Jim – how shall I describe that poor, transfigured Jim? He began by taking the minister aside to the far end of the office. I knew not what he said, but I have reason to believe he was protesting his unfitness, for he wept as he said it; and the old minister, himself genuinely moved, was heard to console and encourage him, and at one time to use this expression: 'I assure you, Mr Pinkerton, there are not many who can say so much' – from which I gathered that my friend had tempered his self-accusations with at least one legitimate boast. From this ghostly counselling, Jim turned to me; and though he never got beyond the explosive utterance of my name and one fierce handgrip, communicated some of his own emotion, like a charge of electricity, to his best man. We stood up to the ceremony at last, in a general and kindly discomposure. Jim was all abroad; and the divine himself betrayed his sympathy in voice and demeanour, and concluded with a fatherly allocution, in which he congratulated Mamie (calling her 'my dear') upon the fortune of an excellent husband, and protested he had rarely married a more interesting couple. At this stage, like a glory descending, there was handed in, *ex machinâ*, the card of Douglas B. Longhurst, with congratulations and four dozen Perrier-Jouet. A bottle was opened, and the minister pledged the bride, and the bridesmaids simpered and tasted, and I made a speech with airy bacchanalianism, glass in hand. But poor Jim must leave the wine untasted. 'Don't touch it,' I had found the opportunity to whisper; 'in your state it will make you as drunk as a fiddler.' And Jim had wrung my hand with a 'God bless you, Loudon! – saved me again!'

Hard following upon this, the supper passed off at Frank's with somewhat tremulous gaiety; and thence, with one half of the Perrier-Jouet – I would accept no more – we voyaged in a hack to the *Norah Creina*.

'What a dear little ship!' cried Mamie, as our miniature craft was pointed out to her; and then, on second thought, she turned to the best man. 'And how brave you must be, Mr Dodd,' she cried, 'to go in the tiny thing so far upon the ocean!' And I perceived I had risen in the lady's estimation.

The 'dear little ship' presented a horrid picture of confusion, and its occupants of weariness and ill-humour. From the cabin the cook was storing tins into the lazarette, and the four hands, sweaty and sullen, were passing them from one to another from the waist. Johnson was three parts asleep over the table; and in his bunk, in his own cabin, the captain sourly chewed and puffed at a cigar.

'See here,' he said, rising; 'you'll be sorry you came. We can't stop work if we're to get away tomorrow. A ship getting ready for sea is no place for people, anyway. You'll only interrupt my men.'

I was on the point of answering something tart; but Jim, who was acquainted with the breed, as he was with most things that had a bearing on affairs, made haste to pour in oil.

'Captain,' he said, 'I know we're a nuisance here, and that you've had a rough time. But all we want is that you should drink one glass of wine with us, Perrier-Jouet, from Longhurst, on the occasion of my marriage, and Loudon's – Mr Dodd's – departure.'

'Well, it's your look-out,' said Nares. 'I don't mind half an hour. Spell, oh!' he added to the men; 'go and kick your heels for half an hour, and then you can turn to again a trifle livelier. Johnson, see if you can't wipe off a chair for the lady.'

His tone was no more gracious than his language; but when Mamie had turned upon him the soft fire of her eyes, and informed him that he was the first sea-captain she had ever met, 'except captains of steamers, of course' – she so qualified the statement – and had expressed a lively sense of his courage, and perhaps implied (for I suppose the arts of ladies are the same as those of men) a modest consciousness of his good looks, our bear began insensibly to soften; and it was already part as an apology, though still with unaffected heat of temper, that he volunteered some sketch of his annoyances.

'A pretty mess we've had,' said he. 'Half the stores were wrong; I'll wring John Smith's neck for him some of these days. Then two newspaper beasts came down, and tried to raise copy out of me, till I threatened them with the first thing handy; and then some kind of missionary bug, wanting to work his passage to Raiatea or somewhere. I told him I would take him off the wharf with the butt end of my boot, and he went away cursing. This vessel's been depreciated by the look of him.'

While the captain spoke, with his strange, humorous, arrogant abruptness, I observed Jim to be sizing him up, like a thing at once quaint and familiar, and with a scrutiny that was both curious and knowing.

'One word, dear boy,' he said, turning suddenly to me. And when he had drawn me on deck – 'That man,' says he, 'will carry sail till your hair grows white; but never you let on – never breathe a word. I know his line: he'll die before he'll take advice; and if you get his back up, he'll run you right under. I don't often jam in my advice, Loudon; and when I do, it means I'm thoroughly posted.'

The little party in the cabin, so disastrously begun, finished, under the mellowing influence of wine and woman, in excellent feeling and with some hilarity. Mamie, in a plush Gainsborough hat and a gown of wine-coloured silk, sat, an apparent queen, among her rude surroundings and companions. The dusky litter of the cabin set off her radiant trimness: tarry Johnson was a foil to her fair beauty; she glowed in that poor place, fair as a star; until even I, who was not usually of her admirers, caught a spark of admiration; and even the captain, who was in no courtly humour, proposed that the scene should be commemorated by my pencil. It was the last act of the evening. Hurriedly as I went about my task, the half-hour had lengthened out to more than three before it was completed: Mamie in full value, the rest of the party figuring in outline only, and the artist himself introduced in a back view, which was pronounced a likeness. But it was to Mamie that I devoted the best of my attention; and it was with her I made my chief success.

'Oh!' she cried, 'am I really like that? No wonder Jim . . .' She paused. 'Why, it's just as lovely as he's good!' she cried: an epigram which was appreciated, and repeated as we made our salutations, and called out after the retreating couple as they passed away under the lamplight on the wharf.

Thus it was that our farewells were smuggled through under an ambuscade of laughter, and the parting over ere I knew it was begun. The figures vanished, the steps died away along the silent city front; on board, the men had returned to their labours, the captain to his solitary cigar; and after that long and complex day of business and emotion, I was at last alone and free. It was, perhaps, chiefly fatigue that made my heart so heavy. I leaned, at least, upon the house, and stared at the foggy heaven, or over the rail at the wavering reflection of the lamps, like a man that was quite done with hope and would have welcomed the asylum of the grave. And all at once, as I thus stood, the *City of Pekin* flashed into my mind, racing her thirteen knots for Honolulu, with the hated Trent – perhaps with the mysterious Goddedaal – on board; and with the thought, the blood leaped and careered through all my body. It seemed no chase at all; it seemed we had no chance, as we lay there bound to iron pillars, and fooling away the precious moments over tins of beans. 'Let them get there first!' I thought. 'Let them! We can't be long behind.' And from that moment I date myself a man of a rounded experience: nothing had lacked but this – that I should entertain and welcome the grim thought of bloodshed.

It was long before the toil remitted in the cabin, and it was worth my while to get to bed; long after that, before sleep favoured me; and scarce a moment later (or so it seemed) when I was recalled to consciousness by bawling men and the jar of straining hawsers.

The schooner was cast off before I got on deck. In the misty obscurity of the first dawn I saw the tug heading us with glowing fires and blowing smoke, and heard her beat the roughened waters of the bay. Beside us, on her flock of hills, the lighted city towered up and stood swollen in the raw fog. It was strange to see her burn on thus wastefully, with half-quenched luminaries, when the dawn was already grown strong enough to show me, and to suffer me to recognise, a solitary figure standing by the piles.

Or was it really the eye, and not rather the heart, that identified that shadow in the dusk, among the shoreside lamps? I know not. It was Jim, at least; Jim, come for a last look; and we had but time to wave a valedictory gesture and exchange a wordless cry. This was our second parting, and our capacities were now reversed. It was mine to play the Argonaut, to speed affairs, to plan and to accomplish – if need were, at the price of life; it was his to sit at home, to study the calendar, and to wait. I knew, besides, another thing that gave me joy. I knew that my friend had succeeded in my education; that the romance of business, if our fantastic purchase merited the name, had at last stirred my dilettante nature; and as we swept under cloudy Tamalpais and through the roaring narrows of the bay, the Yankee blood sang in my veins with suspense and exultation.

Outside the heads, as if to meet my desire, we found it blowing fresh from the north-east. No time had been lost. The sun was not yet up before the tug cast off the hawser, gave us a salute of three whistles, and turned homeward toward the coast, which now began to gleam along its margin with the earliest rays of day. There was no other ship in view when the *Norah Creina*, lying over under all plain sail, began her long and lonely voyage to the wreck.

CHAPTER TWELVE

The 'Norah Creina'

I love to recall the glad monotony of a Pacific voyage, when the trades are not stinted, and the ship, day after day, goes free. The mountain scenery of trade-wind clouds, watched (and in my case painted) under every vicissitude of light – blotting stars, withering in the moon's glory, barring the scarlet eve, lying across the dawn collapsed into the unfeatured morning bank, or at noon raising their snowy summits between the blue roof of heaven and the blue floor of sea; the small, busy, and deliberate world of the schooner, with its unfamiliar scenes, the spearing of dolphin from the bowsprit end, the holy war on sharks, the cook making bread on the main hatch; reefing down before a violent squall, with the men hanging out on the foot-ropes; the squall itself, the catch at the heart, the opened sluices of the sky; and the relief, the renewed loveliness of life, when all is over, the sun forth again, and our out-fought enemy only a blot upon the leeward sea. I love to recall, and would that I could reproduce that life, the unforgetable, the unrememberable. The memory, which shows so wise a backwardness in registering pain, is besides an imperfect recorder of extended pleasures; and a long-continued well-being escapes (as it were, by its mass) our petty methods of commemoration. On a part of our life's map there lies a roseate, undecipherable haze, and that is all.

Of one thing, if I am at all to trust my own annals, I was delightedly conscious. Day after day, in the sun-gilded cabin, the whiskey-dealer's thermometer stood at 84°. Day after day the air had the same indescribable liveliness and sweetness, soft and nimble, and cool as the cheek of health. Day after day the sun flamed; night after night the moon beaconed, or the stars paraded their lustrous regiment. I was aware of a spiritual change, or, perhaps, rather a molecular reconstitution. My bones were sweeter to me. I had come home to my own climate, and looked back with pity on those damp and wintry zones, miscalled the temperate.

'Two years of this, and comfortable quarters to live in, kind of shake the grit out of a man,' the captain remarked; 'can't make out to be happy anywhere else. A townie of mine was lost down this way, in a coalship that took fire at sea. He struck the beach somewhere in the Navigators; and he wrote to me that when he left the place it would be feet first. He's well off, too, and his father owns some coasting craft Down East; but Billy prefers the beach, and hot rolls off the bread-fruit trees.'

A voice told me I was on the same track as Billy. But when was this? Our outward track in the *Norah Creina* lay well to the northward; and perhaps it is but the impression of a few pet days which I have unconsciously spread longer, or perhaps the feeling, grew upon me later, in the run to Honolulu. One thing I am sure: it was before I had ever seen an island worthy of the name that I must date my loyalty to the South Seas. The blank sea itself grew desirable under such skies; and wherever the trade-wind blows I know no better country than a schooner's deck.

But for the tugging anxiety as to the journey's end, the journey itself must thus have counted for the best of holidays. My physical well-being was over-proof; effects of sea and sky kept me for ever busy with my pencil; and I had no lack of intellectual exercise of a different order in the study of my inconsistent friend, the captain. I call him friend, here on the threshold; but that is to look well ahead. At first I was too much horrified by what I considered his barbarities, too much puzzled by his shifting humours, and too frequently annoyed by his small vanities, to regard him otherwise than as the cross of my existence. It was only by degrees, in his rare hours of pleasantness, when he forgot (and made me forget) the weaknesses to which he was so prone, that he won me to a kind of unconsenting fondness. Lastly, the faults were all embraced in a more generous view: I saw them in their place, like discords in a musical progression; and accepted them and found them picturesque, as we accept and admire, in the habitable face of nature, the smoky head of the volcano or the pernicious thicket of the swamp.

He was come of good people Down East, and had the beginnings of a thorough education. His temper had been ungovernable from the first; and it is likely the defect was inherited, and the blame of the rupture not entirely his. He ran away at least to sea; suffered horrible maltreatment, which seemed to have rather hardened than enlightened him; ran away again to shore in a South American port; proved his capacity and made money, although still a child; fell among thieves and was robbed; worked back a passage to the States, and knocked one morning at the door of an old lady whose orchard he had often robbed. The introduction appears insufficient; but Nares knew what he was doing. The sight of her old neighbourly depredator shivering at the door in tatters, the very oddity of his appeal, touched a soft spot in the spinster's heart. 'I always had a fancy for the old lady,' Nares said, 'even when she used to stampede me out of the orchard, and shake her thimble and her old curls at me out of the window as I was going by; I always thought she was a kind of pleasant old girl. Well, when she came to the door that morning, I told her so, and that I was stone-broke; and she took me right in, and fetched out the pie.' She clothed him, taught him, and had him to sea again in better shape, welcomed him to her hearth on his return from every cruise, and when she died bequeathed him her possessions. 'She was a good old girl,' he would say; 'I tell you, Mr Dodd, it was a queer thing to see me and the old lady taking a *pasear* in the garden, and the old man scowling at us over the pickets. She lived right next door to the old man, and I guess that's just what took me there. I wanted him to know that I was badly beat, you see, and would rather go to the devil than to him. What made the dig harder, he had quarrelled with the old lady about me and the orchard: I guess that made him rage. Yes, I was a beast when I was young; but I was always pretty good to the old lady.' Since then he had prospered, not uneventfully, in his profession; the old lady's money had fallen in during the voyage of the *Gleaner*, and he was now, as soon as the smoke of that engagement cleared away, secure of his ship. I suppose he was about thirty: a powerful, active man, with a blue eye, a thick head of hair, about the colour of oakum and growing low over the brow; clean-shaved and lean about the jaw; a good singer;

a good performer on that sea-instrument, the accordion; a quick observer, a close reasoner; when he pleased, of a really elegant address; and when he chose, the greatest brute upon the seas.

His usage the men, his hazing, his bullying, his perpetual fault-finding for no cause, his perpetual and brutal sarcasm, might have raised a munity in a slave galley. Suppose the steerman's eye to have wandered; 'You –, –, little, mutton-faced Dutchman,' Nares would bawl, 'you want a booting to keep you on your course! I know a little city-front slush when I see one. Just you glue your eye to that compass, or I'll show you round the vessel at the butt-end of my boot.' Or suppose a hand to linger aft, whither he had perhaps been summoned not a minute before. 'Mr Daniells, will you oblige me by stepping clear of that main-sheet?' the captain might begin, with truculent courtesy. 'Thank you. And perhaps you'll be so kind as to tell me what the hell you're doing on my quarter-deck? I want no dirt of your sort here. Is there nothing for you to do? Where's the mate? Don't you set *me* to find work for you, or I'll find you some that will keep you on your back a fortnight.' Such allocutions, conceived with a perfect knowledge of his audience, so that every insult carried home, were delivered with a mien so menacing, and an eye so fiercely cruel, that his unhappy subordinates shrank and quailed. Too often violence followed; too often I have heard and seen and boiled at the cowardly aggression; and the victim, his hands bound by law, has risen again from deck and crawled forward stupefied – I know not what passion of revenge in his wronged heart.

It seems strange I should have grown to like this tyrant. It may even seem strange that I should have stood by and suffered his excesses to proceed. But I was not quite such a chicken as to interfere in public, for I would rather have a man or two mishandled than one half of us butchered in a mutiny and the rest suffer on the gallows. And in private I was unceasing in my protests.

'Captain,' I once said to him, appealing to his patriotism, which was of a hardy quality, 'this is no way to treat American seamen. You don't call it American to treat men like dogs?'

'Americans?' he said, grimly. 'Do you call these

Dutchmen and Scattermouches[1] Americans? I've been fourteen years to sea, all but one trip under American colours, and I've never laid eye on an American foremast hand. There used to be such things in the old days, when thirty-five dollars were the wages out of Boston; and then you could see ships handled and run the way they want to be. But that's all past and gone, and nowadays the only thing that flies in an American ship is a belaying-pin. You don't know, you haven't a guess. How would you like to go on deck for your middle watch, fourteen months on end, with all your duty to do, and everyone's life depending on you, and expect to get a knife ripped into you as you come out of your state-room, or be sand-bagged as you pass the boat, or get tripped into the hold if the hatches are off in fine weather? That kind of shakes the starch out of the brotherly love and New Jerusalem business. You go through the mill, and you'll have a bigger grudge against every old shellback that dirties his plate in the three oceans than the Bank of California could settle up. No; it has an ugly look to it, but the only way to run a ship is to make yourself a terror.'

'Come, captain,' said I, 'there are degrees in everything. You know American ships have a bad name, you know perfectly well if it wasn't for the high wage and the good food, there's not a man would ship in one if he could help; and even as it is, some prefer a British ship, beastly food and all.'

'Oh, the lime-juicers?' said he. 'There's plenty booting in lime-juicers, I guess; though I don't deny but what some of them are soft.' And with that he smiled, like a man recalling something. 'Look here, that brings a yarn in my head,' he resumed, 'and for the sake of the joke I'll give myself away. It was in 1874 I shipped mate in the British ship *Maria*, from 'Frisco for Melbourne. She was the queerest craft in some ways that ever I was aboard of. The food was a caution; there was nothing fit to put your lips to but the lime-juice, which was from the end bin no doubt; it used to make me sick to see the men's dinners, and sorry to see my own. The old man was good enough,

---

1. In sea-lingo (Pacific) *Dutchman* includes all
   Teutons and folk from the basin of the Baltic;
   Scattermouch, all Latins and Levantines.

I guess. Green was his name – a mild, fatherly old galoot. But the hands were the lowest gang I ever handled, and whenever I tried to knock a little spirit into them the old man took their part. It was Gilbert and Sullivan on the high seas; but you bet I wouldn't let any man dictate to me. "You give me your orders, Captain Green," I said, "and you'll find I'll carry them out; that's all you've got to say. You'll find I do my duty," I said; "how I do it is my look-out, and there's no man born that's going to give me lessons." Well, there was plenty dirt on board that *Maria* first and last. Of course the old man put my back up, and of course he put up the crew's, and I had to regular fight my way through every watch. The men got to hate me, so's I would hear them grit their teeth when I came up. At last one day I saw a big hulking beast of a Dutchman booting the ship's boy. I made one shoot of it off the house and laid that Dutchman out. Up he came, and I laid him out again. "Now," I said, "if there's a kick left in you, just mention it, and I'll stamp your ribs in like a packing-case." He thought better of it and never let on; lay there as mild as a deacon at a funeral, and they took him below to reflect on his native Dutchland. One night we got caught in rather a dirty thing about 25 south. I guess we were all asleep, for the first thing I knew there was the fore-royal gone. I ran forward, bawling blue hell; and just as I came by the foremast something struck me right through the forearm and stuck there. I put my other hand up, and, by George, it was the grain; the beasts had speared me like a porpoise. "Cap'n!" I cried.— "What's wrong?" says he.— "They've grained me," says I.— "Grained you?" says he. "Well, I've been looking for that."— "And by God," I cried, "I want to have some of these beasts murdered for it!"— "Now, Mr Nares," says he, "you better go below. If I had been one of the men, you'd have got more than this. And I want no more of your language on deck. You've cost me my fore-royal already," says he; "and if you carry on, you'll have the three sticks out of her." That was old man Green's idea of supporting officers. But you wait a bit; the cream's coming. We made Melbourne right enough, and the old man said: "Mr Nares, you and me don't draw together. You're a first-rate seaman, no mistake of that; but you're the most disagreeable man I ever sailed with, and your language and your conduct to the crew I cannot stomach. I guess we'll separate." I didn't care about the berth, you may be sure; but I felt kind of mean, and if he made one kind of stink I thought I could make another. So I said I would go ashore and see how things stood; went, found I was all right, and came aboard again on the top rail.— "Are you getting your traps together, Mr Nares?" says the old man.— "No," says I, "I don't know as we'll separate much before 'Frisco – at least," I said, "it's a point for your consideration. I'm very willing to say good-bye to the *Maria*, but I don't know whether you'll care to start me out with three months' wages." He got his money-box right away. "My son," says he, "I think it cheap at the money." He had me there.'

It was a singular tale for a man to tell of himself; above all, in the midst of our discussion; but it was quite in character for Nares. I never made a good hit in our disputes, I never justly resented any act or speech of his, but what I found it long after carefully posted in his day-book and reckoned (here was the man's oddity) to my credit. It was the same with his father, whom he had hated; he would give a sketch of the old fellow, frank and credible, and yet so honestly touched that it was charming. I have never met a man so strangely constituted: to possess a reason of the most equal justice, to have his nerves at the same time quivering with petty spite, and to act upon the nerves and not the reason.

A kindred wonder in my eyes was the nature of his courage. There was never a braver man: he went out to welcome danger; an emergency (came it never so sudden) strung him like a tonic. And yet, upon the other hand, I have known none so nervous, so oppressed with possibilities, looking upon the world at large, and the life of a sailor in particular, with so constant and haggard a consideration of the ugly chances. All his courage was in blood, not merely cold, but icy with reasoned apprehension. He would lay our little craft rail under, and 'hang on' in a squall, until I gave myself up for lost, and the men were rushing to their stations of their own accord. 'There,' he would say, 'I guess there's not a man on board would have hung on as long as I did that time: they'll have to give up thinking me no schooner sailor. I guess I can shave just as near capsizing

as any other captain of this vessel, drunk or sober.' And
then he would fall to repining and wishing himself well out
of the enterprise, and dilate on the peril of the seas, the
particular dangers of the schooner rig, which he abhorred,
the various ways in which we might go to the bottom, and
the prodigious fleet of ships that have sailed out in the course
of history, dwindled from the eyes of watchers, and returned
no more. 'Well,' he would wind up, 'I guess it don't much
matter. I can't see what anyone wants to live for, anyway.
If I could get into someone else's apple-tree, and be about
twelve years old, and just stick the way I was, eating stolen
apples, I won't say. But there's no sense to this grown-up
business – sailorising, politics, the piety mill, and all the
rest of it. Good clean drowning is good enough for me.'
It is hard to imagine any more depressing talk for a poor
landsman on a dirty night; it is hard to imagine anything
less sailor-like (as sailors are supposed to be, and generally
are) than this persistent harping on the minor.

But I was to see more of the man's gloomy constancy
ere the cruise was at an end.

On the morning of the seventeenth day I came on deck,
to find the schooner under double reefs, and flying rather
wild before a heavy run of sea. Snoring trades and humming
sails had been our portion hitherto. We were already nearing
the island. My restrained excitement had begun again to
overmaster me; and for some time my only book had been
the patent log that trailed over the taffrail, and my chief
interest the daily observation and our caterpillar progress
across the chart. My first glance, which was at the compass,
and my second, which was at the log, were all that I could
wish. We lay our course; we had been doing over eight
since nine the night before, and I drew a heavy breath of
satisfaction. And then I know not what odd and wintry
appearance of the sea and sky knocked suddenly at my heart.
I observed the schooner to look more than usually small,
the men silent and studious of the weather. Nares, in one
of his rusty humours, afforded me no shadow of a morning
salutation. He, too, seemed to observe the behaviour of the
ship with an intent and anxious scrutiny. What I liked still
less, Johnson himself was at the wheel, which he span busily,
often with a visible effort; and as the seas ranged up behind
us, black and imminent, he kept casting behind him eyes

of animal swiftness, and drawing in his neck between his shoulders, like a man dodging a blow. From these signs, I gathered that all was not exactly for the best; and I would have given a good handful of dollars for a plain answer to the questions which I dared not put. Had I dared with the present danger signal in the captain's face, I should only have been reminded of my position as supercargo – an office never touched upon in kindness – and advised, in a very indigestible manner, to go below. There was nothing for it, therefore, but to entertain my vague apprehensions as best I should be able, until it pleased the captain to enlighten me of his own accord. This he did sooner than I had expected – as soon, indeed, as the Chinaman had summoned us to breakfast, and we sat face to face across the narrow board.

'See here, Mr Dodd,' he began, looking at me rather queerly, 'here is a business point arisen. This sea's been running up for the last two days, and now it's too high for comfort. The glass is falling, the wind is breezing up, and I won't say but what there's dirt in it. If I lay her to, we may have to ride out a gale of wind, and drift God knows where – on these French Frigate Shoals, for instance. If I keep her as she goes, we'll make that island tomorrow afternoon, and have the lee of it to lie under, if we can't make out to run in. The point you have to figure on, is whether you'll take the big chances of that Captain Trent making the place before you, or take the risk of something happening. I'm to run this ship to your satisfaction,' he added, with an ugly sneer. 'Well, here's a point for the supercargo.'

'Captain,' I returned, with my heart in my mouth, 'risk is better than certain failure.'

'Life is all risk, Mr Dodd,' he remarked. 'But there's one thing: it's now or never; in half an hour Archdeacon Gabriel couldn't lay her to, if he came downstairs on purpose.'

'All right,' said I; 'let's run.'

'Run goes,' said he; and with that he fell to breakfast, and passed half an hour in stowing away pie, and devoutly wishing himself back in San Francisco.

When we came on deck again, he took the wheel from Johnson – it appears they could trust none among the hands – and I stood close beside him, feeling safe in this proximity, and tasting a fearful joy from our surroundings and the consciousness of my decision. The breeze had already risen, and as it tore over our heads, it uttered at times a long hooting note that sent my heart into my boots. The sea pursued us without remission, leaping to the assault of the low rail. The quarter-deck was all awash, and we must close the companion doors.

'And all this, if you please, for Mr Pinkerton's dollars!' the captain suddenly exclaimed. 'There's many a fine fellow gone under, Mr Dodd, because of drivers like your friend. What do they care for a ship or two? Insured, I guess. What do they care for sailors' lives alongside of a few thousand dollars? What they want is speed between ports, and a damned fool of a captain that'll drive a ship under as I'm doing this one. You can put in the morning, asking why I do it.'

I sheered off to another part of the vessel as fast as civility permitted. This was not at all the talk that I desired, nor was the train of reflection which it started anyway welcome. Here I was, running some hazard of my life, and perilling the lives of seven others; exactly for what end, I was now at liberty to ask myself. For a very large amount of a very deadly poison, was the obvious answer; and I thought if all tales were true, and I were soon to be subjected to cross-examination at the bar of Eternal Justice, it was one which would not increase my popularity with the court. 'Well, never mind, Jim,' thought I; 'I'm doing it for you.'

Before eleven a third reef was taken in the mainsail, and Johnson filled the cabin with a storm-sail of No. 1 duck, and sat cross-legged on the streaming floor, vigorously putting it to rights with a couple of the hands. By dinner I had fled the deck, and sat in the bench corner, giddy, dumb, and stupefied with terror. The frightened leaps of the poor *Norah Creina*, spanking like a stag for bare existence, bruised me between the table and the berths. Overhead, the wild huntsman of the storm passed continuously in one blare of mingled noises; screaming wind, straining timber, lashing rope's-end, pounding block and bursting sea contributed; and I could have thought there was at times another, a more piercing, a more human note, that dominated all, like the wailing of an angel; I could have thought

I knew the angel's name, and that his wings were black. It seemed incredible that any creature of man's art could long endure the barbarous mishandling of the seas, kicked as the schooner was from mountainside to mountainside, beaten and blown upon and wrenched in every joint and sinew, like a child upon the rack. There was not a plank of her that did not cry aloud for mercy; and as she continued to hold together, I became conscious of a growing sympathy with her endeavours, a growing admiration for her gallant staunchness, that amused and at times obliterated my terrors for myself. God bless every man that swung a mallet on that tiny and strong hull! It was not for wages only that he laboured, but to save men's lives.

All the rest of the day, and all the following night, I sat in the corner or lay wakeful in my bunk; and it was only with the return of morning that a new phase of my alarms drove me once more on deck. A gloomier interval I never passed. Johnson and Nares steadily relieved each other at the wheel and came below. The first glance of each was at the glass, which he repeatedly knuckled and frowned upon; for it was sagging lower all the time. Then, if Johnson were the visitor, he would pick a snack out of the cupboard, and stand, braced against the table, eating it, and perhaps obliging me with a word or two of his heehaw conversation: how it was 'a son of a gun of a cold night on deck, Mr Dodd' (with a grin); how 'it wasn't no night for panjammers, he could tell me': having transacted all which, he would throw himself down in his bunk and sleep his two hours with compunction. But the captain neither ate nor slept. 'You there, Mr Dodd?' he would say, after the obligatory visit to the glass. 'Well, my son, we're one hundred and four miles' (or whatever it was) 'off the island, and scudding for all we're worth. We'll make it tomorrow about four, or not, as the case may be. That's the news. And now, Mr Dodd, I've stretched a point for you; you can see I'm dead tired; so just you stretch away back to your bunk again.' And with this attempt at geniality, his teeth would settle hard down on his cigar, and he would pass his spell below staring and blinking at the cabin lamp through a cloud of tobacco smoke. He has told me since that he was happy, which I should never have divined. 'You see,' he said, 'the wind we had was never anything out of the way; but the sea was really nasty, the schooner wanted a lot of humouring, and it was clear from the glass that we were close to some dirt. We might be running out of it, or we might be running right crack into it. Well, there's always something sublime about a big deal like that; and it kind of raises a man in his own liking. We're a queer kind of beasts, Mr Dodd.'

The morning broke with sinister brightness; the air alarmingly transparent, the sky pure, the rim of the horizon clear and strong against the heavens. The wind and the wild seas, now vastly swollen, indefatigably hunted us. I stood on deck, choking with fear; I seemed to lose all power upon my limbs; my knees were as paper when she plunged into the murderous valleys; my heart collapsed when some black mountain fell in avalanche beside her counter, and the water, that was more than spray, swept round my ankles like a torrent. I was conscious of but one strong desire – to bear myself decently in my terrors, and, whatever should happen to my life, preserve my character: as the captain said, we are a queer kind of beasts. Breakfast-time came, and I made shift to swallow some hot tea. Then I must stagger below to take the time, reading the chronometer with dizzy eyes, and marvelling the while what value there could be in observations taken in a ship launched (as ours then was) like a missile among flying seas. The forenoon dragged on in a grinding monotony of peril; every spoke of the wheel a rash but an obliged experiment – rash as a forlorn hope, needful as the leap that lands a fireman from a burning staircase. Noon was made; the captain dined on his day's work, and I on watching him; and our place was entered on the chart with a meticulous precision which seemed to me half pitiful and half absurd, since the next eye to behold that sheet of paper might be the eye of an exploring fish. One o'clock came, then two; the captain gloomed and chafed, as he held to the coaming of the house, and if ever I saw dormant murder in man's eye, it was in his. God help the hand that should have disobeyed him.

Of a sudden, he turned towards the mate, who was doing his trick at the wheel.

'Two points on the port bow,' I heard him say; and he took the wheel himself.

Johnson nodded, wiped his eyes with the back of his wet

hand, watched a chance as the vessel lunged up hill, and got to the main rigging, where he swarmed aloft. Up and up I watched him go, hanging on at every ugly plunge, gaining with every lull of the schooner's movement, until, clambering into the cross-trees and clinging with one arm around the masts, I could see him take one comprehensive sweep of the south-westernly horizon. The next moment he had slid down the backstay and stood on deck, with a grin, a nod, and a gesture of the finger that said 'yes'; the next again, and he was back sweating and squirming at the wheel, his tired face streaming and smiling, and his hair and the rags and corners of his clothes lashing round him in the wind.

Nares went below, fetched up his binocular, and fell into a silent perusal of the sea-line; I also, with my unaided eyesight. Little by little, in that white waste of water, I began to make out a quarter where the whiteness appeared more condensed: the sky above was whitish likewise, and misty like a squall; and little by little there thrilled upon my ears a note deeper and more terrible than the yelling of the gale – the long, thundering roll of breakers. Nares wiped his night-glass on his sleeve and passed it to me, motioning, as he did so, with his hand. An endless wilderness of ranging billows came and went and danced in the circle of the glass; now and then a pale corner of sky, or the strong line of the horizon rugged with the heads of waves; and then of a sudden – come and gone ere I could fix it, with a swallow's swiftness – one glimpse of what we had come so far and paid so dear to see: the masts and rigging of a brig pencilled on heaven, with an ensign streaming at the main, and the ragged ribbons of a topsail thrashing from the yard. Again and again, with toilful searching, I recalled that apparition. There was no sign of any land; the wreck stood between sea and sky, a thing the most isolated I had ever viewed; but as we drew nearer, I perceived her to be defended by a line of breakers which drew off on either hand and marked, indeed, the nearest segment of the reef. Heavy spray hung over them like a smoke, some hundred feet into the air; and the sound of their consecutive explosions rolled like a cannonade.

In half an hour we were close in; for perhaps as long again we skirted that formidable barrier toward its farther

side; and presently the sea began insensibly to moderate
and the ship to go more sweetly. We had gained the lee
of the island, as (for form's sake) I may call that ring of
foam and haze and thunder; and shaking out a reef, wore
ship and headed for the passage.

CHAPTER THIRTEEN

The Island and the Wreck

All hands were filled with joy. It was betrayed in their alacrity and easy faces: Johnson smiling broadly at the wheel, Nares studying the sketch chart of the island with an eye at peace, and the hands clustered forward, eagerly talking and pointing: so manifest was our escape, so wonderful the attraction of a single foot of earth after so many suns had set and risen on an empty sea! To add to the relief, besides, by one of those malicious coincidences which suggest for Fate the image of an underbred and grinning schoolboy, we had no sooner worn ship than the wind began to abate.

For myself, however, I did but exchange anxieties. I was no sooner out of one fear than I fell upon another; no sooner secure that I should myself make the intended haven, than I began to be convinced that Trent was there before me. I climbed into the rigging, stood on the board, and eagerly scanned that ring of coral reef and bursting breaker, and the blue lagoon which they enclosed. The two islets within began to show plainly – Middle Brooks and Lower Brooks Island, the Directory named them: two low, bush-covered, rolling strips of sand, each with glittering beaches, each perhaps a mile or a mile and a half in length running east and west, and divided by a narrow channel. Over these, innumerable as maggots, there hovered, chattered, screamed, and clanged, millions of twinkling sea-birds; white and black; the black by far the largest. With singular scintillations, this vortex of winged life swayed to and fro in the strong sunshine, whirled continually through itself, and would now and again burst asunder and scatter as wide as the lagoon: so that I was irresistibly reminded of what I had read of nebular convulsions. A thin cloud overspread the area of the reef and the adjacent sea – the dust, as I could not but fancy, of earlier explosions. And, a little apart, there was yet another focus of centrifugal and centripetal flight, where, hard by the deafening line of breakers, her sails (all but the tattered topsail) snugly furled down, and the red rag that marks Old England on the seas beating, union down, at the main – the *Flying Scud*, the fruit of so many toilers, a recollection in so many lives of men, whose tall spars had been mirrored in the remotest corners of the sea – lay stationary at last and for ever, in the first stage of naval dissolution. Towards her the taut *Norah Creina*, vulture-wise, wriggled to windward: come from so far to pick her bones. And, look as I pleased, there was no other presence of man or of man's handiwork; no Honolulu schooner lay there crowded with armed rivals, no smoke rose from the fire at which I fancied Trent cooking a meal of sea-birds. It seemed, after all, we were in time, and I drew a mighty breath.

I had not arrived at this reviving certainty before the breakers were already close aboard, the leadsman at his station, and the captain posted in the fore cross-trees to con us through the coral lumps of the lagoon. All circumstances were in our favour, the light behind, the sun low, the wind still fresh and steady, and the tide about the turn. A moment later we shot at racing speed between two pier heads of broken water; the lead began to be cast, the captain to bawl down his anxious directions, the schooner to tack and dodge among the scattered dangers of the lagoon; and at one bell in the first dog watch, we had come to our anchor off the northeast end of Middle Brooks Island, in five fathoms water. The sails were gasketed and covered, the boats emptied of the miscellaneous stores and odds and ends of sea-furniture, that accumulate in the course of a voyage, the kedge sent ashore, and the decks tidied down: a good three-quarters of an hour's work, during which I raged about the deck like a man with a strong toothache. The transition from the wild sea to the comparative immobility of the lagoon had wrought strange distress among my nerves: I could not hold still whether in hand or foot; the slowness of the men, tired as dogs after our rough experience outside, irritated me like something personal; and the irrational screaming of the sea-birds saddened me like a dirge. It was a relief when, with Nares, and a couple of hands, I might drop into the boat and move off at last for the *Flying Scud*.

'She looks kind of pitiful, don't she?' observed the captain, nodding towards the wreck, from which we were separated by some half a mile. 'Looks as if she didn't like her berth, and Captain Trent had used her badly. Give her ginger, boys,' he added to the hands, 'and you can all have shore liberty tonight to see the birds and paint the town red.'

We all laughed at the pleasantry, and the boat skimmed the faster over the rippling face of the lagoon. The *Flying Scud* would have seemed small enough beside the wharves of San Francisco, but she was some thrice the size of the *Norah Creina*, which had been so long our continent; and as we craned up at her wall-sides, she impressed us with a mountain magnitude. She lay head to the reef, where the huge blue wall of the rollers was for ever ranging up and crumbling down; and to gain her starboard side, we must pass below the stern. The rudder was hard aport, and we could read the legend –

FLYING SCUD,
HULL

On the other side, about the break of the poop, some half a fathom of rope ladder trailed over the rail, and by this we made our entrance.

She was a roomy ship inside, with a raised poop standing some three feet higher than the deck, and a small forward house, for the men's bunks and the galley, just abaft the foremast. There was one boat on the house, and another and larger one, in beds on deck, on either hand of it. She had been painted white, with tropical economy, outside and in; and we found, later on, that the stanchions of the rail, hoops of the scuttle butt, etc., were picked out with green. At that time, however, when we first stepped aboard, all was hidden under the droppings of innumerable sea-birds.

The birds themselves gyrated and screamed meanwhile among the rigging; and when we looked into the galley, their outrush drove us back. Savage-looking fowl they were, savagely beaked, and some of the black ones great as eagles. Half-buried in the slush, we were aware of a litter of kegs in the waist; and these, on being somewhat cleaned, proved to be water beakers and quarter-casks of mess beef with some colonial brand, doubtless collected there before the *Tempest* hove in sight, and while Trent and his men had no better expectation than to strike for Honolulu in the boats. Nothing else was notable on deck, save where the loose topsail had played some havoc with the rigging, and there hung, and swayed and sang in the declining wind, a raffle of intorted cordage.

With a shyness that was almost awe, Nares and I descended the companion. The stair turned upon itself and landed us just forward of a thwart-ship bulkhead that cut the poop in two. The fore part formed a kind of miscellaneous storeroom, with a double bunked division for the cook (as Nares supposed) and second mate. The after part contained, in the midst, the main cabin, running in a kind of bow into the curvature of the stern; on the port side, a pantry opening forward and a stateroom for the mate; and on the starboard, the captain's berth and water-closet. Into these we did but glance, the main cabin holding us. It was dark, for the sea-birds had obscured the skylight with their droppings; it smelt rank and fusty; and it was beset with a loud swarm of flies that beat continually in our faces. Supposing them close attendants upon man and his broken meat, I marvelled how they had found their way to Midway Reef; it was sure at least some vessel must have brought them, and that long ago, for they had multiplied exceedingly. Part of the floor was strewn with a confusion of clothes, books, nautical instruments, odds and ends of finery, and such trash as might be expected from the turning out of several seamen's chests, upon a sudden emergency and after a long cruise. It was strange in that dim cabin, quivering with the near thunder of the breakers and pierced with the screaming of the fowls, to turn over so many things that other men had coveted, and prized, and worn on their warm bodies – frayed old underclothing, pyjamas of strange design, duck suits in every stage of rustiness, oil skins, pilot coats, bottles of scent, embroidered shirts, jackets of Ponjee silk – clothes for the night watch at sea or the day ashore in the hotel verandah: and mingled among these, books, cigars, fancy pipes, quantities of tobacco, many keys, a rusty pistol, and a sprinkling of cheap curiosities – Benares brass, Chinese jars and pictures, and bottles of odd shells in cotton, each designed, no doubt, for somebody at home – perhaps in Hull, of which Trent had been a native and his ship a citizen.

Thence we turned our attention to the table, which stood spread, as if for a meal, with stout ship's crockery and the remains of food – a pot of marmalade, dregs of coffee in the mugs, unrecognisable remains of food, bread, some toast, and a tin of condensed milk. The table-cloth, originally of a red colour, was stained a dark brown at the captain's end, apparently with coffee; at the other end, it had been folded back, and a pen and ink-pot stood on the bare table. Stools were here and there about the table, irregularly placed, as though the meal had been finished and the men smoking and chatting; and one of the stools lay on the floor, broken.

'See! they were writing up the log,' said Nares, pointing to the ink-bottle. 'Caught napping, as usual. I wonder if there ever was a captain yet that lost a ship with his log-book up to date? He generally has about a month to fill up on a clean break, like Charles Dickens and his serial novels. What a regular, lime-juicer spread!' he added contemptuously. 'Marmalade – and toast for the old man! Nasty, slovenly pigs!'

There was something in this criticism of the absent that jarred upon my feelings. I had no love indeed for Captain Trent or any of his vanished gang; but the desertion and decay of this once habitable cabin struck me hard. The death of man's handiwork is melancholy like the death of man himself; and I was impressed with an involuntary and irrational sense of tragedy in my surroundings.

'This sickens me,' I said; 'let's go on deck and breathe.'

The captain nodded. 'It *is* kind of lonely, isn't it?' he said; 'but I can't go up till I get the code signals. I want to run up "Got Left" or something, just to brighten up this island home. Captain Trent hasn't been here yet, but he'll drop in before long; and it'll cheer him up to see a signal on the brig.'

'Isn't there some official expression we could use?' I asked, vastly taken by the fancy. '"Sold for the benefit of the underwriters: for further particulars apply to J. Pinkerton, Montana Block, S.F."'

'Well,' returned Nares, 'I won't say but what an old navy

quartermaster might telegraph all that, if you gave him a day to do it in and a pound of tobacco for himself. But it's above my register. I must try something short and sweet: KB, urgent signal, "Heave all aback;" or LM, urgent, "The berth you're now in is not safe;" or what do you say to PQH? – "Tell my owners the ship answers remarkably well."'

'It's premature,' I replied; 'but it seems calculated to give pain to Trent. PQH for me.'

The flags were found in Trent's cabin, neatly stored behind a lettered grating; Nares chose what he required, and (I following) returned on deck, where the sun had already dipped, and the dusk was coming.

'Here! don't touch that, you fool!' shouted the captain to one of the hands, who was drinking from the scuttle butt. 'That water's rotten!'

'Beg pardon, sir,' replied the man. 'Tastes quite sweet.'

'Let me see,' returned Nares, and he took the dipper and held it to his lips. 'Yes, it's all right,' he said. 'Must have rotted and come sweet again. Queer, isn't it, Mr Dodd? Though I've known the same on a Cape Horner.'

There was something in his intonation that made me look him in the face; he stood a little on tiptoe to look right and left about the ship, like a man filled with curiosity, and his whole expression and bearing testified to some suppressed excitement.

'You don't believe what you're saying!' I broke out.

'Oh, I don't know but what I do!' he replied, laying a hand upon me soothingly. 'The thing's very possible. Only, I'm bothered about something else.'

And with that he called a hand, gave him the code flags, and stepped himself to the main signal halliards, which vibrated under the weight of the ensign overhead. A minute later, the American colours, which we had brought in the boat, replaced the English red, and PQH was fluttering at the fore.

'Now, then,' said Nares, who had watched the breaking out of his signal with the old-maidish particularity of an American sailor, 'out with those handspikes, and let's see what water there is in the lagoon.'

The bars were shoved home; the barbarous cacophony of the clanking pump rose in the waist; and streams of ill-smelling water gushed on deck and made valleys in the slab guano. Nares leaned on the rail, watching the steady stream of bilge as though he found some interest in it.

'What is it that bothers you?' I asked.

'Well, I'll tell you one thing shortly,' he replied. 'But here's another. Do you see those boats there, one on the house and two on the beds? Well, where is the boat Trent lowered when he lost the hands?'

'Got it aboard again, I suppose,' said I.

'Well, if you'll tell me why!' returned the captain.

'Then it must have been another,' I suggested.

'She might have carried another on the main hatch, I won't deny,' admitted Nares, 'but I can't see what she wanted with it, unless it was for the old man to go out and play the accordion in, on moonlight nights.'

'It can't much matter, anyway,' I reflected.

'Oh, I don't suppose it does,' said he, glancing over his shoulder at the spouting of the scuppers.

'And how long are we to keep up this racket?' I asked. 'We're simply pumping up the lagoon. Captain Trent himself said she had settled down and was full forward.'

'Did he?' said Nares, with a significant dryness. And almost as he spoke the pumps sucked, and sucked again, and the men threw down their bars. 'There, what do you make of that?' he asked. 'Now, I'll tell, Mr Dodd,' he went on, lowering his voice, but not shifting from his easy attitude against the rail, 'this ship is as sound as the *Norah Creina*. I had a guess of it before we came aboard, and now I know.'

'It's not possible!' I cried. 'What do you make of Trent?'

'I don't make anything of Trent; I don't know whether he's a liar or only an old wife; I simply tell you what's the fact,' said Nares. 'And I'll tell you something more,' he added: 'I've taken the ground myself in deep-water vessels; I know what I'm saying; and I say that, when she first struck and before she bedded down, seven or eight hours' work would have got this hooker off, and there's no man that ever went two years to sea but must have known it.'

I could only utter an exclamation.

Nares raised his finger warningly. 'Don't let *them* get hold of it,' said he. 'Think what you like, but say nothing.'

I glanced round; the dusk was melting into early night;

the twinkle of a lantern marked the schooner's position in the distance; and our men, free from further labour, stood grouped together in the waist, their faces illuminated by their glowing pipes.

'Why didn't Trent get her off?' inquired the captain. 'Why did he want to buy her back in 'Frisco for these fabulous sums, when he might have sailed her into the bay himself?'

'Perhaps he never knew her value until then,' I suggested.

'I wish we knew her value now,' exclaimed Nares. 'However, I don't want to depress you; I'm sorry for you, Mr Dodd; I know how bothering it must be to you, and the best I can say's this: I haven't taken much time getting down, and now I'm here I mean to work this thing in proper style. I just want to put your mind at rest; you shall have no trouble with me.'

There was something trusty and friendly in his voice; and I found myself gripping hands with him, in that hard, short shake that means so much with English-speaking people.

'We'll do, old fellow,' said he. 'We've shaken down into pretty good friends, you and me; and you won't find me working the business any the less hard for that. And now let's scoot for supper.'

After supper, with the idle curiosity of the seafarer, we pulled ashore in a fine moonlight, and landed on Middle Brooks Island. A flat beach surrounded it upon all sides; and the midst was occupied by a thicket of bushes, the highest of them scarcely five feet high, in which the sea-fowl lived. Through this we tried at first to strike; but it were easier to cross Trafalgar Square upon a day of demonstration than to invade these haunts of sleeping sea-birds. The nests sank, and the eggs burst under footing; wings beat in our faces, beaks menaced our eyes, our minds were confounded with the screeching, and the coil spread over the island and mounted high into the air.

'I guess we'll saunter round the beach,' said Nares, when we had made good our retreat.

The hands were all busy after sea-birds' eggs, so there were none to follow us. Our way lay on the crisp sand by the margin of the water: on one side, the thicket from which we had been dislodged; on the other, the face of the

lagoon, barred with a broad path of moonlight, and beyond
that the line, alternately dark and shining, alternately hove
high and fallen prone, of the external breakers. The beach
was strewn with bits of wreck and drift: some redwood and
spruce logs, no less than two lower masts of junks, and the
stern-post of a European ship – all of which we looked on
with a shade of serious concern, speaking of the dangers
of the sea and the hard case of castaways. In this sober
vein we made the greater part of the circuit of the island;
had a near view of its neighbour from the southern end;
walked the whole length of the westerly side in the shadow
of the thicket; and came forth again into the moonlight at
the opposite extremity.

On our right, at the distance of about half a mile, the
schooner lay faintly heaving at her anchors. About half a
mile down the beach, at a spot still hidden from us by the
thicket, an upboiling of the birds showed where the men
were still (with sailor-like insatiability) collecting eggs. And
right before us, in a small indentation of the sand, we were
aware of a boat lying high and dry, and right side up.

Nares crouched back into the shadow of the bushes.

'What the devil's this?' he whispered.

'Trent,' I suggested, with a beating heart.

'We were damned fools to come ashore unarmed,' said
he. 'But I've got to know where I stand.' In the shadow,
his face looked conspicuously white, and his voice betrayed
a strong excitement. He took his boat's whistle from his
pocket. 'In case I might want to play a tune,' said he,
grimly, and thrusting it between his teeth, advanced into the
moonlit open, which we crossed with rapid steps, looking
guiltily about us as we went. Not a leaf stirred; and the
boat, when we came up to it, offered convincing proof
of long desertion. She was an eighteen-foot whaleboat of
the ordinary type, equipped with oars and thole-pins. Two
or three quarter-casks lay on the bilge amidships, one of
which must have been broached, and now stank horribly;
and these, upon examination, proved to bear the same New
Zealand brand as the beef on board the wreck.

'Well, here's the boat,' said I; 'here's one of your
difficulties cleared away.'

'H'm,' said he. There was a little water in the bilge, and
here he stooped and tasted it.

'Fresh,' he said. 'Only rain water.'

'You don't object to that?' I asked.

'No,' said he.

'Well, then, what ails you?' I cried.

'In plain United States, Mr Dodd,' he returned, 'a whale-boat, five ash sweeps, and a barrel of stinking pork.'

'Or, in other words, the whole thing?' I commented.

'Well, it's this way,' he condescended to explain. 'I've no use for a fourth boat at all; but a boat of this model tops the business. I don't say the type's not common in these waters; it's as common as dirt; the traders carry them for surf-boats. But the *Flying Scud*? a deep-water tramp, who was lime-juicing around between big ports, Calcutta and Rangoon and 'Frisco and the Canton River? No, I don't see it.'

We were leaning over the gunwale of the boat as we spoke. The captain stood nearest the bow, and he was idly playing with the trailing painter, when a thought arrested him. He hauled the line in hand over hand, and stared, and remained staring, at the end.

'Anything wrong with it?' I asked.

'Do you know, Mr Dodd,' said he, in a queer voice, this painter's been cut? A sailor always seizes a rope's end, but this is sliced short off with the cold steel. This won't do at all for the men,' he added. 'Just stand by till I fix it up more natural.'

'Any guess what it all means?' I asked.

'Well, it means one thing,' said he. 'It means Trent was a liar. I guess the story of the *Flying Scud* was a sight more picturesque than he gave out.'

Half an hour later the whaleboat was lying astern of the *Norah Creina*; and Nares and I sought our bunks, silent and half bewildered by our late discoveries.

CHAPTER FOURTEEN

The Cabin of the 'Flying Scud'

The sun of the morrow had not cleared the morning bank: the lake of the lagoon, the islets, and the wall of breakers now beginning to subside, still lay clearly pictured in the flushed obscurity of early day, when we stepped again upon the deck of the *Flying Scud*: Nares, myself, the mate, two of the hands, and one dozen bright, virgin axes, in war against that massive structure. I think we all drew pleasurable breath; so profound in man is the instinct of destruction, so engaging is the interest of the chase. For we were now about to taste, in a supreme degree, the double joys of demolishing a toy and playing 'Hide the handkerchief' – sports from which we had all perhaps desisted since the days of infancy. And the toy we were to burst in pieces was a deep-sea ship; and the hidden good for which we were to hunt was a prodigious fortune.

The decks were washed down, the main hatch removed, and a gun-tackle purchase rigged, before the boat arrived with breakfast. I had grown so suspicious of the wreck, that it was a positive relief to me to look down into the hold, and see it full, or nearly full of undeniable rice packed in the Chinese fashion in boluses of matting. Breakfast over, Johnson and the hands turned to upon the cargo; while Nares and I, having smashed open the skylight and rigged up a windsail on deck, began the work of rummaging the cabins.

I must not be expected to describe our first day's work, or (for that matter) any of the rest, in order and detail as it occurred. Such particularity might have been possible for several officers and a draft of men from a ship of war, accompanied by an experienced secretary with a knowledge of shorthand. For two plain human beings, unaccustomed to the use of the broad-axe and consumed with an impatient greed of the result, the whole business melts, in the retrospect, into a nightmare of exertion, heat, hurry, and bewilderment; sweat pouring from the face like rain, the scurry of rats, the choking exhalations of the bilge, and the throbs and splinterings of the toiling axes. I shall content myself with giving the cream of our discoveries in a logical rather than a temporal order; though the two indeed practically coincided and we had finished our exploration of the cabin, before we could be certain of the nature of the cargo.

Nares and I began operations by tossing up pell-mell through the companion, and piling in a squalid heap about the wheel, all clothes, personal effects, the crockery, the carpet, stale victuals, tins of meat, and in a word, all movables from the main cabin. Thence we transferred our attention to the captain's quarters on the starboard side. Using the blankets for a basket, we sent up the books, instruments, and clothes to swell our growing midden on the deck; and then Nares, going on hands and knees, began to forage underneath the bed. Box after box of Manilla cigars rewarded his search. I took occasion to smash some of these boxes open, and even to guillotine the bundles of cigars; but quite in vain – no secret *cache* of opium encouraged me to continue.

'I guess I've got hold of the dicky now!' exclaimed Nares, and turning round from my perquisitions, I found he had drawn forth a heavy iron box, secured to the bulkhead by chain and padlock. On this he was now gazing, not with the triumph that instantly inflamed my own bosom, but with a somewhat foolish appearance of surprise.

'By George, we have it now!' I cried, and would have shaken hands with my companion; but he did not see, or would not accept, the salutation.

'Let's see what's in it first,' he remarked dryly. And he adjusted the box upon its side, and with some blows of an axe burst the lock open. I threw myself beside him, as he replaced the box on its bottom and removed the lid. I cannot tell what I expected; a million's worth of diamonds might perhaps have pleased me; my cheeks burned, my heart throbbed to bursting; and lo! there was disclosed but a trayful of papers, neatly taped, and a cheque-book of the customary pattern. I made a snatch at the tray to see what was beneath, but the captain's hand fell on mine, heavy and hard.

'Now, boss!' he cried, not unkindly, 'is this to be run shipshape? or is it a Dutch grab-racket?'

And he proceeded to untie and run over the contents of the papers, with a serious face and what seemed an ostentation of delay. Me and my impatience it would appear he had forgotten; for when he was quite done, he sat awhile thinking, whistled a bar or two, refolded the papers, tied them up again; and then, and not before, deliberately raised the tray.

I saw a cigar-box, tied with a piece of fishing-line, and four fat canvas bags. Nares whipped out his knife, cut the line, and opened the box. It was about half full of sovereigns.

'And the bags?' I whispered.

The captain ripped them open one by one, and a flood of mixed silver coin burst forth and rattled in the rusty bottom of the box. Without a word, he set to work to count the gold.

'What is this?' I asked.

'It's the ship's money,' he returned, doggedly continuing his work.

'The ship's money?' I repeated. 'That's the money Trent tramped and traded with? And there's his cheque-book to draw upon his owners? And he has left it?'

'I guess he has,' said Nares austerely, jotting down a note of the gold; and I was abashed into silence till his task should be completed.

It came, I think, to three hundred and seventy-eight pounds sterling; some nineteen pounds of it in silver: all of which we turned again into the chest.

'And what do you think of that?' I asked.

'Mr Dodd,' he replied, 'you see something of the rumness of this job, but not the whole. The specie bothers you, but what gets me is the papers. Are you aware that the master of a ship has charge of all the cash in hand, pays the men advances, receives freight and passage money, and runs up bills in every port? All this he does as the owner's confidential agent, and his integrity is proved by his receipted bills. I tell you, the captain of a ship is more likely to forget his pants than these bills which guarantee his character. I've known men drown to save them – bad men, too; but this is the shipmaster's honour. And here this Captain Trent – not hurried, not threatened with anything but a free passage in a British man-of-war – has left them all behind. I don't want to express myself too strongly, because the facts appear against me, but the thing is impossible.'

Dinner came to us not long after, and we ate it on deck, in a grim silence, each privately racking his brain for some solution of the mysteries. I was indeed, so swallowed up in these considerations that the wreck, the lagoon, the islets, and the strident sea-fowl, the strong sun then beating on my head, and even the gloomy countenance of the captain at my elbow, all vanished from the field of consciousness. My mind was a blackboard, on which I scrawled and blotted out hypotheses, comparing each with the pictorial records in my memory – ciphering with pictures. In the course of this tense mental exercise I recalled and studied the faces of one memorial masterpiece, the scene of the saloon; and here I found myself, on a sudden, looking in the eyes of the Kanaka.

'There's one thing I can put beyond doubt, at all events,' I cried, relinquishing my dinner and getting briskly afoot. 'There was that Kanaka I saw in the bar with Captain Trent, the fellow the newspapers and ship's articles made out to be a Chinaman. I mean to rout his quarters out and settle that.'

'All right,' said Nares. 'I'll lazy off a bit longer, Mr Dodd; I feel pretty rocky and mean.'

We had thoroughly cleared out the three after-compartments of the ship; all the stuff from the main cabin and the mate's and captain's quarters lay piled about the wheel; but in the forward stateroom with the two bunks, where Nares had said the mate and cook most likely berthed, we had as yet done nothing. Thither I went. It was very bare; a few photographs were tacked on the bulkhead, one of them indecent; a single chest stood open, and like all we had yet found, it had been partly rifled. An armful of two-shilling novels proved to me beyond a doubt it was a European's; no Chinaman would have possessed any, and the most literate Kanaka conceivable in a ship's galley was not likely to have gone beyond one. It was plain, then, that the cook had not berthed aft, and I must look elsewhere.

The men had stamped down the nests and driven the birds from the galley, so that I could now enter without contest. One door had been already blocked with rice; the place was in part darkness, full of a foul stale smell, and a cloud of nasty flies; it had been left, besides, in some disorder, or else the birds, during their time of tenancy, had knocked the things about; and the floor, like the deck before we washed it, was spread with pasty filth. Against the wall, in the far corner, I found a handsome chest of camphor wood bound with brass, such as Chinamen and sailors love, and indeed all of mankind that plies in the Pacific. From its outside view I could thus make no deduction; and, strange to say, the interior was concealed. All the other chests, as I have said already, we had found gaping open and their contents scattered abroad; the same remark we found to apply afterwards in the quarters of the seamen; only this camphor-wood chest, a singular exception, was both closed and locked.

I took an axe to it, readily forced the paltry Chinese fastening, and, like a Custom House officer, plunged my hands among the contents. For some while I groped among linen and cotton. Then my teeth were set on edge with silk, of which I drew forth several strips covered with mysterious characters. And these settled the business, for I recognised them as a kind of bed-hanging, popular with the commoner class of the Chinese. Nor were farther evidences wanting, such as night-clothes of an extraordinary design, a three-stringed Chinese fiddle,' a silk handkerchief full of roots and herbs, and a neat apparatus for smoking opium, with a liberal provision of the drug. Plainly, then, the cook had been a Chinaman; and, if so, who was Jos. Amalu? Or had Jos. stolen the chest before he proceeded to ship under a false name and domicile? It was possible, as anything was possible in such a welter; but, regarded as a solution, it only led and left me deeper in the bog. For why should this chest have been deserted and neglected, when the others were rummaged or removed? and where had Jos. come by that second chest, with which (according to the clerk at the What Cheer) he had started for Honolulu?

'And how have *you* fared?' inquired the captain, whom I found luxuriously reclining in our mound of litter. And the accent on the pronoun, the heightened colour of the speaker's face, and the contained excitement in his tones, advertised me at once that I had not been alone to make discoveries.

'I have found a Chinaman's chest in the galley,' said I, 'and John (if there was any John) was not so much as at the pains to take his opium.'

Nares seemed to take it mighty quietly. 'That so?' said he. 'Now, cast your eyes on that and own you're beaten!' And with a formidable clap of his open hand, he flattened out before me, on the deck, a pair of newspapers.

I gazed upon them dully, being in no mood for fresh discoveries.

'Look at them, Mr Dodd,' cried the captain sharply. 'Can't you look at them?' And he ran a dirty thumb along the title. '"*Sydney Morning Herald*, November 26th," can't you make that out?' he cried, with rising energy. 'And don't you know, sir, that not thirteen days after this paper appeared in New South Wales, this ship we're standing in heaved her blessed anchors out of China? How did the *Sydney Morning Herald* get to Hong Kong in thirteen days? Trent made no land, he spoke no ship, till he got here. Then he either got it here or in Hong Kong. I give you your choice, my son!' he cried, and fell back among the clothes like a man weary of life.

'Where did you find them?' I asked. 'In that black bag?'

'Guess so,' he said. 'You needn't fool with it. There's nothing else but a lead-pencil and a kind of worked-out knife.'

I looked in the bag, however, and was well rewarded.

'Every man to his trade, captain,' said I. 'You're a sailor, and you've given me plenty of points; but I am an artist, and allow me to inform you this is quite as strange as all the rest. The knife is a palette knife; the pencil a Winsor and Newton, and a B B B at that. A palette knife and a B B B on a tramp brig! It's against the laws of nature.'

'It would sicken a dog, wouldn't it?' said Nares.

'Yes.' I continued, 'it's been used by an artist, too: see how it's sharpened – not for writing – no man could write with that. An artist, and straight from Sydney? How can he come in?'

'Oh, that's natural enough,' sneered Nares. 'They cabled him to come up and illustrate this dime novel.'

We fell awhile silent.

'Captain,' I said at last, 'there is something deuced underhand about this brig. You tell me you've been to sea a good part of your life. You must have seen shady things done on ships, and heard of more. Well, what is this? is it insurance? is it piracy? what is it *about*? what can it be *for*?'

'Mr Dodd,' returned Nares, 'you're right about me having been to sea the bigger part of my life. And you're right again when you think I know a good many ways in which a dishonest captain mayn't be on the square, nor do exactly the right thing by his owners, and altogether be just a little too smart by ninety-nine and three-quarters. There's a good many ways, but not so many as you'd think; and not one that has any mortal thing to do with Trent. Trent and his whole racket has got to do with nothing – that's the bed-rock fact; there's no sense to it, and no use in it, and no story to it – it's a beastly dream. And don't you run away with that notion that landsmen take about ships. A society actress don't go around more publicly than what a ship does, nor is more interviewed, nor more humbugged, nor more run after by all sorts of little fussinesses in brass buttons. And more than an actress, a ship has a deal to lose; she's capital, and the actress only character – if she's that. The ports of the world are thick with people ready to kick a captain into the penitentiary, if he's not as bright as a dollar and as honest as the morning star; and what with Lloyd keeping watch and watch in every corner of the three oceans, and the insurance leeches, and the consuls, and the Customs bugs, and the medicos, you can only get the idea by thinking of a landsman watched by a hundred and fifty detectives, or a stranger in a village down east.'

'Well, but at sea?' I said.

'You make me tired,' retorted the captain. 'What's the use – at sea? Everything's got to come to bearings at some port, hasn't it? You can't stop at sea for ever, can you? – No; the *Flying Scud* is rubbish; if it meant anything, it would have to mean something so almighty intricate that James G. Blaine hasn't got the brains to engineer it; and I vote for more axeing, pioneering, and opening up the

resources of this phenomenal brig, and less general fuss,'
he added, arising. 'The dime-museum symptoms will drop
in of themselves, I guess, to keep us cheery.'

But it appeared we were at the end of discoveries for
the day; and we left the brig about sundown, without
being further puzzled or further enlightened. The best
of the cabin spoils – books, instruments, papers, silks,
and curiosities – we carried along with us in a blanket,
however, to divert the evening hours; and when supper
was over, and the table cleared, and Johnson set down to
a dreary game of cribbage between his right hand and his
left, the captain and I turned out our blanket on the floor,
and sat side by side to examine and appraise the spoils.

The books were the first to engage our notice. These
were rather numerous (as Nares contemptuously put it)
'for a lime-juicer.' Scorn of the British mercantile marine
glows in the breast of every Yankee merchant captain; as
the scorn is not reciprocated, I can only suppose it justified
in fact; and certainly the Old Country mariner appears of
a less studious disposition. The more credit to the officers
of the *Flying Scud*, who had quite a library, both literary
and professional. There were Findlay's five directories of
the world – all broken-backed, as is usual with Findlay,
and all marked and scribbled over with corrections and
additions – several books of navigation, a signal code, and
an Admiralty book of a sort of orange hue, called 'Islands
of the Eastern Pacific Ocean,' Vol. III., which appeared
from its imprint to be the latest authority, and showed
marks of frequent consultation in the passages about the
French Frigate Shoals, the Harman, Cure, Pearl, and
Hermes Reefs, Lisiansky Island, Ocean Island, and the
place where we then lay – Brooks or Midway. A volume
of Macaulay's 'Essays,' and a shilling Shakespeare led
the van of the *belles lettres*; the rest were novels. Several
Miss Braddon's – of course, 'Aurora Floyd,' which has
penetrated to every island of the Pacific, a good many
cheap detective books, 'Rob Roy,' Auerbach's 'Auf der
Höhe,' in the German, and a prize temperance story,
pillaged (to judge by the stamp) from an Anglo-Indian
circulating library.

'The Admiralty man gives a fine picture of our island,'
remarked Nares, who had turned up Midway Island. 'He

draws the dreariness rather mild, but you can make out he knows the place.'

'Captain,' I cried, 'you've struck another point in this mad business. See here,' I went on eagerly, drawing from my pocket a crumpled fragment of the *Daily Occidental* which I had inherited from Jim: 'Misled by Hoyt's Pacific Directory'? Where's Hoyt?'

'Let's look into that,' said Nares. 'I got that book on purpose for this cruise.' Therewith he fetched it from the shelf in his berth, turned to Midway Island, and read the account aloud. It stated with precision that the Pacific Mail Company were about to form a depôt there, in preference to Honolulu, and that they had already a station on the island.

'I wonder who gives these directory men their information,' Nares reflected. 'Nobody can blame Trent after that. I never got in company with squarer lying; it reminds a man of a presidential campaign.'

'All very well,' said I; 'that's your Hoyt, and a fine, tall copy. But what I want to know is, where is Trent's Hoyt?'

'Took it with him,' chuckled Nares; 'he had left everything else, bills and money and all the rest: he was bound to take something, or it would have aroused attention on the *Tempest*. "Happy thought," says he, "let's take Hoyt."'

'And has it not occurred to you,' I went on, 'that all the Hoyts in creation couldn't have misled Trent, since he had in his hand that red Admiralty book, an official publication, later in date, and particularly full on Midway Island?'

'That's a fact!' cried Nares; 'and I bet the first Hoyt he ever saw was out of the mercantile library of San Francisco. Looks as if he had brought her here on purpose, don't it? But then that's inconsistent with the steam-crusher of the sale. That's the trouble with this brig racket; anyone can make half-a-dozen theories for sixty or seventy per cent. of it; but when they're made, there's always a fathom or two of slack hanging out of the other end.'

I believe our attention fell next on the papers, of which we had altogether a considerable bulk. I had hoped to find among these matter for a full-length character of Captain Trent; but here I was doomed, on the whole, to disappointment. We could make out he was an orderly man, for all his bills were docketed and preserved. That he was convivial, and inclined to be frugal even in conviviality, several documents proclaimed. Such letters as we found were, with one exception, arid notes from tradesmen. The exception, signed Hannah Trent, was a somewhat fervid appeal for a loan. 'You know what misfortunes I have had to bear,' wrote Hannah, 'and how much I am disappointed in George. The landlady appeared a true friend when I first came here, and I thought her a perfect lady. But she has come out since then in her *true colours*; and if you will not be softened by this last appeal, I can't think what is to become of your affectionate— ' and then the signature. This document was without place or date, and a voice told me that it had gone likewise without answer. On the whole, there were few letters anywhere in the ship; but we found one before we were finished, in a seaman's chest, of which I must transcribe some sentences. It was dated from some place on the Clyde. 'My dearist son,' it ran, 'this is to tell you your dearist father passed away, Jan twelft, in the peace of the Lord. He had your photo and dear David's lade upon his bed, made me sit by him. Let's be a' thegither, he said, and gave you all his blessing. Oh my dear laddie, why were nae you and Davie here? He would have had a happier passage. He spok of both of ye all night most beautiful, and how ye used to stravaig on the Saturday afternoons and of *auld Kelvinside*. Sooth the tune to me, he said, though it was the Sabbath, and I had to sooth him 'Kelvin Grove,' and he looked at his fiddle, the dear man. I cannae bear the sight of it, he'll never play it mair. Oh my lamb, come home to me, I'm all by my lane now.' The rest was in a religious vein and quite conventional. I have never seen any one more put out than Nares, when I handed him this letter. He had read but a few words, before he cast it down; it was perhaps a minute ere he picked it up again, and the performance was repeated the third time before he reached the end.

'It's touching, isn't it?' said I.

For all answer, Nares exploded in a brutal oath; and it was some half an hour later that he vouchsafed an explanation. 'I'll tell you what broke me up about that letter,' said he. 'My old man played the fiddle, played it all out of tune: one of the things he played was "Martyrdom," I remember

– it was all martyrdom to me. He was a pig of a father, and I was a pig of a son; but it sort of came over me I would like to hear that fiddle squeak again. Natural,' he added; 'I guess we're all beasts.'

'All sons are, I guess,' said I. 'I have the same trouble on my conscience: we can shake hands on that.' Which (oddly enough, perhaps) we did.

Amongst the papers we found a considerable sprinkling of photographs; for the most part either of very debonair-looking young ladies or old women of the lodging-house persuasion. But one among them was the means of our crowning discovery.

'They're not pretty, are they, Mr Dodd?' said Nares, as he passed it over.

'Who?' I asked, mechanically taking the card (it was a quarter-plate) in hand, and smothering a yawn; for the hour was late, the day had been labourious, and I was wearying for bed.

'Trent and Company,' said he. 'That's a historic picture of the gang.'

I held it to the light, my curiosity at a low ebb: I had seen Captain Trent once, and had no delight in viewing him again. It was a photograph of the deck of the brig, taken from forward: all in apple-pie order; the hands gathered in the waist, the officers on the poop. At the foot of the card was written, 'Brig *Flying Scud*, Rangoon,' and a date; and above or below each individual figure the name had been carefully noted.

As I continued to gaze, a shock went through me; the dimness of sleep and fatigue lifted from my eyes, as fog lifts in the channel; and I beheld with startled clearness, the photographic presentment of a crowd of strangers. '1. Trent, Master' at the top of the card directed me to a smallish, weazened man, with bushy eyebrows and full white beard, dressed in a frock coat and white trousers; a flower stuck in his button-hole, his bearded chin set forward, his mouth clenched with habitual determination. There was not much of the sailor in his looks, but plenty of the martinet: a dry, precise man, who might pass for a preacher in some rigid sect; and whatever he was, not the Captain Trent of San Francisco. The men, too, were all new to me: the cook, an unmistakable Chinaman, in his characteristic dress, standing apart on the poop steps. But perhaps I turned on the whole with the greatest curiosity to the figure labelled 'E. Goddedaal, 1st off.' He whom I had never seen, he might be the identical; he might be the clue and spring of all this mystery; and I scanned his features with the eye of a detective. He was of great stature, seemingly blonde as a Viking, his hair clustering round his head in frowsy curls, and two enormous whiskers, like the tusks of some strange animal, jutting from his cheeks. With these virile appendages and the defiant attitude in which he stood, the expression of his face only imperfectly harmonised. It was wild, heroic, and womanish-looking; and I felt I was prepared to hear he was a sentimentalist, and to see him weep.

For some while I digested my discovery in private, reflecting how best, and how with most of drama, I might share it with the captain. Then my sketch-book came in my head, and I fished it out from where it lay, with other miscellaneous possessions, at the foot of my bunk and turned to my sketch of Captain Trent and the survivors of the British brig *Flying Scud* in the San Francisco bar-room.

'Nares,' said I, 'I've told you how I first saw Captain Trent in that saloon in 'Frisco? how he came with his men, one of them a Kanaka with a canary-bird in a cage? and how I saw him afterwards at the auction, frightened to death, and as much surprised at how the figures skipped up as anybody there. Well,' said I, 'there's the man I saw' – and I laid the sketch before him – 'there's Trent of 'Frisco and there are his three hands. Find one of them in the photograph, and I'll be obliged.'

Nares compared the two in silence. 'Well,' he said at last, 'I call this rather a relief: seems to clear the horizon. We might have guessed at something of the kind from the double ration of chests that figured.'

'Does it explain anything?' I asked.

'It would explain everything,' Nares replied, 'but for the steam-crusher. It'll all tally as neat as a patent puzzle, if you leave out the way these people bid the wreck up. And there we come to a stone wall. But whatever it is, Mr Dodd, it's on the crook.'

'And looks like piracy,' I added.

'Looks like blind hookey!' cried the captain. 'No, don't you deceive yourself; neither your head nor mine is big enough to put a name on this business.'

CHAPTER FIFTEEN

The Cargo of the 'Flying Scud'

In my early days I was a man, the most wedded to his idols of my generation. I was a dweller under roofs; the gull of that which we call civilisation; a superstitious votary of the plastic arts; a cit, and a prop of restaurants. I had a comrade in those days, somewhat of an outsider, though he moved in the company of artists, and a man famous in our small world for gallantry, knee breeches, and dry and pregnant sayings. He, looking on the long meals and waxing bellies of the French, whom I confess I somewhat imitated, branded me as 'a cultivator of restaurant fat.' And I believe he had his finger on the dangerous spot; I believe, if things had gone smooth with me, I should be now swollen like a prize-ox in body, and fallen in mind to a thing perhaps as low as many types of *bourgeois* – the implicit or exclusive artist. That was a home word of Pinkerton's, deserving to be writ in letters of gold on the portico of every school of art: 'What I can't see is why you should want to do nothing else.' The dull man is made, not by the nature, but by the degree of his immersion in a single business. And all the more if that be sedentary, uneventful, and ingloriously safe. More than one half of him will then remain unexercised and undeveloped; the rest will be distended and deformed by over-nutrition, over-cerebration, and the heat of rooms. And I have often marvelled at the impudence of gentlemen who describe and pass judgment on the life of man, in almost perfect ignorance of all its necessary elements and natural careers. Those who dwell in clubs and studios may paint excellent pictures or write enchanting novels. There is one thing that they should not do: they should pass no judgment on man's destiny, for it is a thing with which they are unacquainted. Their own life is an excrescence of the moment, doomed, in the vicissitude of history, to pass and disappear. The eternal life of man, spent under sun and rain and in rude physical effort, lies upon one side, scarce changed since the beginning.

I would I could have carried along with me to Midway Island all the writers and the prating artists of my time. Day after day of hope deferred, of heat, of unremitting toil; night after night of aching limbs, bruised hands, and a mind obscured with the grateful vacancy of physical fatigue. The scene, the nature of my employment, the rugged speech and faces of my fellow-toilers, the glare of the day on deck, the stinking twilight in the bilge, the shrill myriads of the ocean-fowl; above all, the sense of our immitigable isolation from the world and from the current epoch – keeping another time, some eras old; the new day heralded by no daily paper, only by the rising sun; and the State, the churches, the peopled empires, war, and the rumours of war, and the voices of the arts, all gone silent as in the days ere they were yet invented. Such were the conditions of my new experience in life, of which (if I had been able) I would have had all my confrères and contemporaries to partake, forgetting, for that while, the orthodoxies of the moment, and devoted to a single and material purpose under the eye of heaven.

Of the nature of our task I must continue to give some summary idea. The forecastle was lumbered with ship's chandlery, the hold nigh full of rice, the lazarette crowded with the teas and silks. These must all be dug out; and that made but a fraction of our task. The hold was ceiled throughout; a part, where perhaps some delicate cargo was once stored, had been lined, in addition, with inch boards; and between every beam there was a movable panel into the bilge. Any of these, the bulkheads of the cabins, the very timbers of the hull itself, might be the place of hiding. It was therefore necessary to demolish, as we proceeded, a great part of the ship's inner skin and fittings, and to auscultate what remained, like a doctor sounding for a lung disease. Upon the return, from any beam or bulkhead, of a flat or doubtful sound, we must up axe and hew into the timber: a violent and – from the amount of dry rot in the wreck – a mortifying exercise. Every night saw a deeper inroad into the bones of the *Flying Scud* – more beams tapped and hewn in splinters, more planking peeled away and tossed aside – and every night saw us as far as ever from the end and object of our arduous devastation. In this perpetual disappointment, my courage did not fail me, but my spirits dwindled; and Nares himself grew silent and morose. At night, when supper was done, we passed an hour in the cabin, mostly without speech: I, sometimes dozing over a book; Nares, sullenly but busily drilling sea-shells with the instrument called a Yankee fiddle. A stranger might have supposed we were estranged; as a matter of fact, in this silent comradeship of labour, our intimacy grew.

I had been struck, at the first beginning of our enterprise upon the wreck, to find the men so ready at the captain's lightest word. I dare not say they liked, but I can never deny that they admired him thoroughly. A mild word from his mouth was more valued than flattery and half a dollar from myself; if he relaxed at all from his habitual attitude of censure, smiling alacrity surrounded him; and I was led to think his theory of captainship, even if pushed to excess, reposed upon some ground of reason. But even terror and admiration of the captain failed us before the end. The men wearied of the hopeless, unremunerative quest and the long strain of labour. They began to shirk and grumble. Retribution fell on them at once, and retribution multiplied the grumblings. With every day it took harder driving to keep them to the daily drudge; and we, in our narrow boundaries, were kept conscious every moment of the ill-will of our assistants.

In spite of the best care, the object of our search was perfectly well known to all on board; and there had leaked out, besides, some knowledge of those inconsistencies that had so greatly amazed the captain and myself. I could overhear the men debate the character of Captain Trent, and set forth competing theories of where the opium was stowed; and, as they seemed to have been eavesdropping on ourselves, I thought little shame to prick up my ears when I had the return chance of spying upon them, in this way. I could diagnose their temper and judge how far they were informed upon the mystery of the *Flying Scud*. It was after having thus overheard some almost mutinous speeches that a fortunate idea crossed my mind. At night, I matured it in my bed, and the first thing the next morning, broached it to the captain.

'Suppose I spirit up the hands a bit,' I asked, 'by the offer of a reward?'

'If you think you're getting your month's wages out of them the way it is, I don't,' was his reply. 'However, they are all the men you've got, and you're the supercargo.'

This, from a person of the captain's character, might be regarded as complete adhesion; and the crew were accordingly called aft. Never had the captain worn a front more menacing. It was supposed by all that some misdeed had been discovered, and some surprising punishment was to be announced.

'See here, you!' he threw at them over his shoulder as he walked the deck. 'Mr Dodd, here, is going to offer a reward to the first man who strikes the opium in that wreck. There's two ways of making a donkey go – both good, I guess; the one's kicks and the other's carrots. Mr Dodd's going to try the carrots. Well, my sons' – and here he faced the men for the first time with his hands behind him – 'if that opium's not found in five days, you can come to me for the kicks.'

He nodded to the present narrator, who took up the tale. 'Here is what I propose, men,' said I: 'I put up one hundred and fifty dollars. If any man can lay hands on the stuff right away, and off his own club, he shall have the hundred and fifty down. If any one can put us on the scent of where to look, he shall have a hundred and twenty-five, and the balance shall be for the lucky one who actually picks it up. We'll call it the Pinkerton´ Stakes, captain,' I added, with a smile.

'Call it the Grand Combination Sweep, then,' cries he. 'For I go you better. Look here, men, I make up this jack-pot to two hundred and fifty dollars, American gold coin.'

'Thank you, Captain Nares,' said I; 'that was hand-somely done.'

'It was kindly meant,' he returned.

The offer was not made in vain; the hands had scarce yet realised the magnitude of the reward, they had scarce begun to buzz aloud in the extremity of hope and wonder, ere the Chinese cook stepped forward with gracious gestures and explanatory smiles.

'Captain,' he began, 'I serv-um two year Melican navy; serv-um six year mail-boat steward. Savvy plenty.'

'Oho!' cried Nares, 'you savvy plenty, do you? (Beggar's seen this trick in the mail-boat, I guess.) Well, why you no savvy a little sooner, sonny?'

'I think bimeby make-um reward,' replied the cook, with smiling dignity.

'Well, you can't say fairer than that,' the captain admitted; 'and now the reward's offered you'll talk? Speak up then. Suppose you speak true you get reward. See?'

'I think long time,' replied the Chinaman. 'See plenty litty mat lice; too muchy plenty litty mat lice; sixty ton litty mat lice. I think all-e-time perhaps plenty opium plenty litty mat lice.'

'Well, Mr Dodd, how does that strike you?' asked the captain. 'He may be right, he may be wrong. He's likely to be right, for if he isn't where can the stuff be? On the other hand, if he's wrong we destroy a hundred and fifty tons of good rice for nothing. It's a point to be considered.'

'I don't hesitate,' said I. 'Let's get to the bottom of the thing. The rice is nothing; the rice will neither make nor break us.'

'That's how I expected you to see it,' returned Nares.

And we called the boat away and set forth on our new quest.

The hold was now almost entirely emptied; the mats (of which there went forty to the short ton) had been stacked on deck, and now crowded the ship's waist and forecastle. It was our task to disembowel and explore six thousand individual mats, and incidentally to destroy a hundred and fifty tons of valuable food. Nor were the circumstances of the day's business less strange than its essential nature. Each man of us, armed with a great knife, attacked the pile from his own quarter, slashed into the nearest mat, burrowed in it with his hands, and shed forth the rice upon the deck where it heaped up, overflowed, and was trodden down, poured at last into the scuppers, and occasionally spouted from the vents. About the wreck, thus transformed into an overflowing granary, the sea-fowl swarmed in myriads and with surprising insolence. The sight of so much food confounded them; they deafened us with their shrill tongues, swooped in our midst, dashed in our faces, and snatched the grain from between our fingers. The men – their hands bleeding from these assaults – turned savagely on the offensive, drove their knives into the birds, drew them out crimsoned, and turned again to dig among the rice, unmindful of the gawking creatures that struggled and died among their feet. We made a singular picture – the hovering and diving birds; the bodies of the dead discolouring the rice with blood; the scuppers vomiting breadstuff; the men, frenzied by the gold hunt, toiling, slaying, and shouting aloud; over all the lofty intricacy of rigging and the radiant heaven of the Pacific. Every man there toiled in the immediate hope of fifty dollars, and I of fifty thousand. Small wonder if we waded callously in blood and food.

It was perhaps about ten in the forenoon when the scene was interrupted. Nares, who had just ripped open a fresh mat, drew forth and slung at his feet, among the rice, a papered tin box.

'How's that?' he shouted.

A cry broke from all hands. The next moment, forgetting their own disappointment in that contagious sentiment of success, they gave three cheers that scared the sea-birds; and the next they had crowded round the captain, and were jostling together and groping with emulous hands in the new-opened mat. Box after box rewarded them, six in all; wrapped, as I have said, in a paper envelope, and the paper printed on in Chinese characters.

Nares turned to me and shook my hand. 'I began to think we should never see this day,' said he. 'I congratulate you, Mr Dodd, on having pulled it through.'

The captain's tones affected me profoundly; and when Johnson and the men pressed round me in turn with congratulations, the tears came in my eyes.

'These are five-tael boxes, more than two pounds,' said Nares, weighing one in his hand. 'Say two hundred and fifty dollars to the mat. Lay into it, boys! We'll make Mr Dodd a millionaire before dark.'

It was strange to see with what a fury we fell to. The men had now nothing to expect; the mere idea of great sums inspired them with disinterested ardour. Mats were slashed and disembowelled, the rice flowed to our knees in the ship's waist, the sweat ran in our eyes and blinded us, our arms ached to agony; and yet our fire abated not. Dinner came; we were too weary to eat, too hoarse for conversation; and yet dinner was scarce done, before we were afoot again and delving in the rice. Before nightfall not a mat was unexplored, and we were face to face with the astonishing result.

For of all the inexplicable things in the story of the *Flying Scud*, here was the most inexplicable. Out of the six thousand mats, only twenty were found to have been sugared; in each we found the same amount, about twelve pounds of drug; making a grand total of two hundred and forty pounds. By the last San Francisco quotation, opium was selling for a fraction over twenty dollars a pound; but it had been known not long before to bring as much as forty in Honolulu, where it was contrabrand.

Taking, then, this high Honolulu figure, the value of the opium on board the *Flying Scud* fell considerably short of ten thousand dollars, while at the San Francisco rate, it lacked a trifle of five thousand. And fifty thousand was the price that Jim and I had paid for it. And Bellairs had been eager to go higher! There is no language to express the stupor with which I contemplated this result.

It may be argued we were not yet sure; there might be yet another *cache*; and you may be certain in that hour of my distress the argument was not forgotten. There was never a ship more ardently perquested; no stone was left unturned, and no expedient untried; day after day of growing despair, we punched and dug in the brig's vitals, exciting the men with promises and presents; evening after evening Nares and I sat face to face in the narrow cabin, racking our minds for some neglected possibility of search. I could stake my salvation on the certainty of the result: in all that ship there was nothing left of value but the timber and the copper nails. So that our case was lamentably plain; we had paid fifty thousand dollars, borne the charges of the schooner, and paid fancy interest on money; and if things went well with us, we might realise fifteen per cent. of the first outlay. We were not merely bankrupt, we were comic bankrupts – a fair butt for jeering in the streets. I hope I bore the blow with a good countenance; indeed, my mind had long been quite made up, and since the day we found the opium I had known the result. But the thought of Jim and Mamie ached in me like a physical pain, and I shrank from speech and companionship.

I was in this frame of mind when the captain proposed that we should land upon the island. I saw he had something to say, and only feared it might be consolation, for I could just bear my grief, not bungling sympathy; and yet I had no choice but to accede to his proposal.

We walked awhile along the beach in silence. The sun overhead reverberated rays of heat; the staring sand, the glaring lagoon, tortured our eyes; and the birds and the boom of the far-away breakers made a savage symphony.

'I don't require to tell you the game's up?' Nares asked.

'No,' said I.

'I was thinking of getting to sea tomorrow,' he pursued.

'The best thing you can do,' said I.

'Shall we say Honolulu?' he inquired.

'Oh, yes; let's stick to the programme,' I cried. 'Honolulu be it!'

There was another silence, and then Nares cleared his throat.

'We've been pretty good friends, you and me, Mr Dodd,' he resumed. 'We've been going through the kind of thing that tries a man. We've had the hardest kind of work, we've been badly backed, and now we're badly beaten. And we've fetched through without a word of disagreement. I don't say this to praise myself: it's my trade; it's what I'm paid for, and trained for, and brought up to. But it was another thing for you; it was all new to you; and it did me good to see you stand right up to it and swing right into it – day in, day out. And then see how you've taken this disappointment, when everybody knows you must have been taughtened up to shying-point! I wish you'd let me tell you, Mr Dodd, that you've stood out mighty manly and handsomely in all this business, and made every one like you and admire you. And I wish you'd let me tell you, besides, that I've taken this wreck business as much to heart as you have; something kind of rises in my throat when I think we're beaten; and if I thought waiting would do it, I would stick on this reef until we starved.'

I tried in vain to thank him for these generous words, but he was beforehand with me in a moment.

'I didn't bring you ashore to sound my praises,' he

interrupted. 'We understand one another now, that's all; and I guess you can trust me. What I wished to speak about is more important, and it's got to be faced. What are we to do about the *Flying Scud* and the dime novel?'

'I really have thought nothing about that,' I replied; 'but I expect I mean to get at the bottom of it, and if the bogus Captain Trent is to be found on the earth's surface, I guess I mean to find him.'

'All you've got to do is talk,' said Nares; 'you can make the biggest kind of boom; it isn't often the reporters have a chance at such a yarn as this; and I can tell you how it will go. It will go by telegraph, Mr Dodd; it'll be telegraphed by the column, and head-lined, and frothed up, and denied by authority, and it'll hit bogus Captain Trent in a Mexican bar-room, and knock over bogus Goddedaal in a slum somewhere up the Baltic, and bowl down Hardy and Brown in sailors' music halls round Greenock. Oh, there's no doubt you can have a regular domestic Judgment Day. The only point is whether you deliberately want to.'

'Well,' said I, 'I deliberately don't want one thing: I deliberately don't want to make a public exhibition of myself and Pinkerton: so moral – smuggling opium; such damned fools – paying fifty thousand for a "dead horse"!'

'No doubt it might damage you in a business sense,' the captain agreed; 'and I'm pleased you take that view, for I've turned kind of soft upon the job. There's been some crookedness about, no doubt of it; but, law bless you! if we dropped upon the troupe, all the premier artists would slip right out with the boodle in their grip-sacks, and you'd only collar a lot of old mutton-headed shell-backs that didn't know the back of the business from the front. I don't take much stock in mercantile Jack, you know that, but, poor devil, he's got to go where he's told; and if you make trouble, ten to one it'll make you sick to see the innocents who have to stand the racket. It would be different if we understood the operation; but we don't, you see: there's a lot of queer corners in life, and my vote is to let the blame' thing lie.'

'You speak as if we had that in our power,' I objected.

'And so we have,' said he.

'What about the men?' I asked. 'They know too much by half, and you can't keep them from talking.'

'Can't I?' returned Nares. 'I bet a boarding-master can!

They can be all half-seas over when they get ashore, blind drunk by dark, and cruising out of the Golden Gate in different deep-sea ships by the next morning. Can't keep them from talking, can't I? Well, I can make 'em talk separate, leastways. If a whole crew came talking, parties would listen; but if it's only one lone old shell-back, it's the usual yarn. And at least, they needn't talk before six months, or – if we have luck, and there's a whaler handy – three years. And by that time, Mr Dodd, it's ancient history.'

'That's what they call Shanghaiing, isn't it?' I asked. 'I thought it belonged to the dime novel.'

'Oh, dime novels are right enough,' returned the captain. 'Nothing wrong with the dime novel, only that things happen thicker than they do in life, and the practical seamanship is off-colour.'

'So we can keep the business to ourselves,' I mused.

'There's one other person that might blab,' said the captain. 'Though I don't believe she has anything left to tell.'

'And who is *she*?' I asked.

'The old girl there,' he answered, pointing to the wreck; 'I know there's nothing in her; but somehow I'm afraid of someone else – it's the last thing you'd expect, so it's just the first that'll happen – someone dropping into this God-forgotten island where nobody drops in, waltzing into that wreck that we've grown old with searching, stooping straight down, and picking right up the very thing that tells the story. What's that to me? you may ask, and why am I gone Soft Tommy on this Museum of Crooks? They've smashed up you and Mr Pinkerton; they've turned my hair grey with conundrums; they've been up to larks, no doubt; and that's all I know of them – you say. Well, and that's just where it is. I don't know enough; I don't know what's uppermost; it's just such a lot of miscellaneous eventualities as I don't care to go stirring up; and I ask you to let me deal with the old girl after a patent of my own.'

'Certainly – what you please,' said I, scarce with attention, for a new thought now occupied my brain. 'Captain,' I broke out, 'you are wrong; we cannot hush this up. There is one thing you have forgotten.'

'What is that?' he asked.

'A bogus Captain Trent, a bogus Goddedaal, a whole bogus crew, have all started home,' said I. 'If we are right, not one of them will reach his journey's end. And do you mean to say that such a circumstance as that can pass without remark?'

'Sailors,' said the captain, 'only sailors! If they were all bound for one place in a body, I don't say so; but they're all going separate – to Hull, to Sweden, to the Clyde, to the Thames. Well, at each place, what is it? Nothing new. Only one sailor man missing: got drunk or got drowned, or got left – the proper sailor's end.'

Something bitter in the thought and in the speaker's tones struck me hard. 'Here is one that has got left!' I cried, getting sharply to my feet, for we had been some time seated. 'I wish it were the other. I don't – don't relish going home to Jim with this!'

'See here,' said Nares, with ready tact, 'I must be getting aboard. Johnson's in the brig annexing chandlery and canvas, and there's some things in the *Norah* that want fixing against we go to sea. Would you like to be left here in the chicken-ranch? I'll send for you to supper.'

I embraced the proposal with delight. Solitude, in my frame of mind, was not too dearly purchased at the risk of sunstroke or sand-blindness; and soon I was alone on the ill-omened islet. I should find it hard to tell of what I thought – of Jim, of Mamie, of our lost fortune, of my lost hopes, of the doom before me: to turn to at some mechanical occupation in some subaltern rank, and to toil there, unremarked and unamused, until the hour of the last deliverance. I was, at least, so sunk in sadness that I scarce remarked where I was going; and chance (or some finer sense that lives in us, and only guides us when the mind is in abeyance) conducted my steps into a quarter of the island where the birds were few. By some devious route, which I was unable to retrace for my return, I was thus able to mount, without interruption, to the highest point of land. And here I was recalled to consciousness by a last discovery.

The spot on which I stood was level, and commanded a wide view of the lagoon, the bounding reef, the round horizon. Nearer hand I saw the sister islet, the wreck, the *Norah Creina*, and the *Norah's* boat already moving shoreward. For the sun was now low, flaming on the sea's verge; and the galley chimney smoked on board the schooner.

It thus befell that though my discovery was both affecting and suggestive, I had no leisure to examine further. What I saw was the blackened embers of fire of wreck. By all the signs, it must have blazed to a good height and burned for days; from the scantling of a spar that lay upon the margin only half consumed, it must have been the work of more than one; and I received at once the image of a forlorn troop of castaways, houseless in that lost corner of the earth, and feeding there their fire of signal. The next moment a hail reached me from the boat; and bursting through the bushes and the rising sea-fowl, I said farewell (I trust for ever) to that desert isle.

CHAPTER SIXTEEN

In which I Turn Smuggler, and the Captain Casuist

The last night at Midway I had little sleep; the next morning, after the sun was risen, and the clatter of departure had begun to reign on deck, I lay a long while dozing; and when at last I stepped from the companion, the schooner was already leaping through the pass into the open sea. Close on her board, the huge scroll of a breaker unfurled itself along the reef with a prodigious clamour; and behind I saw the wreck vomiting into the morning air a coil of smoke. The wreaths already blew out far to leeward, flames already glittered in the cabin skylight, and the sea-fowl were scattered in surprise as wide as the lagoon. As we drew further off, the conflagration of the *Flying Scud* flamed higher; and long after we had dropped all signs of Midway Island, the smoke still hung in the horizon like that of a distant steamer. With the fading out of that last vestige, the *Norah Creina* passed again into the empty world of cloud and water by which she had approached; and the next features that appeared, eleven days later, to break the line of sky, were the arid mountains of Oahu.

It has often since been a comfortable thought to me that we had thus destroyed the tell-tale remnants of the *Flying Scud*; and often a strange one that my last sight and reminiscence of that fatal ship should be a pillar of smoke on the horizon. To so many others besides myself the same appearance had played a part in the various stages of that business; luring some to what they little imagined, filling some with unimaginable terrors. But ours was the last smoke raised in the story; and with its dying away the secret of the *Flying Scud* became a private property.

It was by the first light of dawn that we saw, close on board, the metropolitan island of Hawaii. We held along the coast, as near as we could venture, with a fresh breeze and under an unclouded heaven; beholding, as we went, the arid mountain sides and scrubby cocoa-palms of that somewhat melancholy archipelago. About four of the afternoon we turned Waimanolo Point, the westerly headland of the great bight of Honolulu; showed ourselves for twenty minutes in full view, and then fell again to leeward, and put in the rest of daylight, plying under shortened sail under the lee of Waimanolo.

A little after dark we beat once more about the point, and crept cautiously toward the mouth of the Pearl Lochs, where Jim and I had arranged I was to meet the smugglers. The night was happily obscure, the water smooth. We showed, according to instructions, no light on deck; only a red lantern dropped from either cathead to within a couple of feet of the water. A lookout was stationed on the bowsprit end, another in the crosstrees; and the whole ship's company crowded forward, scouting for enemies or friends. It was now the crucial moment of our enterprise; we were now risking liberty and credit, and that for a sum so small to a man in my bankrupt situation, that I could have laughed aloud in bitterness. But the piece had been arranged, and we must play it to the finish.

For some while we saw nothing but the dark mountain outline of the island, the torches of native fishermen glittering here and there along the foreshore, and right in the midst, that cluster of brave lights with which the town of Honolulu advertises itself to the seaward. Presently a ruddy star appeared inshore of us, and seemed to draw near unsteadily. This was the anticipated signal; and we made haste to show the countersign, lowering a white light from the quarter, extinguishing the two others, and laying the schooner incontinently to. The star approached slowly; the sounds of oars and of men's speech came to us across the water; and then a voice hailed us—

'Is that Mr Dodd?'

'Yes,' I returned. 'Is Jim Pinkerton there?'

'No, sir,' replied the voice. 'But there's one of his crowd here, name of Speedy.'

'I'm here, Mr Dodd,' added Speedy himself. 'I have letters for you.'

'All right,' I replied. 'Come aboard, gentlemen, and let me see my mail.'

A whaleboat accordingly ranged alongside, and three men boarded us: my old San Francisco friend the stock-gambler Speedy, a little wizened person of the name of Sharpe, and a big, flourishing, dissipated-looking man called Fowler. The two last (I learned afterward) were frequent partners; Sharpe supplied the capital, and Fowler, who was quite a character in the islands, and occupied a considerable station, brought activity, daring, and a private influence, highly necessary in the case. Both seemed to approach the business with a keen sense of romance; and I believe this was the chief attraction, at least with Fowler – for whom I early conceived a sentiment of liking. But in that first moment I had something else to think of than to judge my new acquaintances; and before Speedy had fished out the letters, the full extent of our misfortune was revealed.

'We've rather bad news for you, Mr Dodd,' said Fowler. 'Your firm's gone up.'

'Already?' I exclaimed.

'Well, it was thought rather a wonder Pinkerton held on as long as he did,' was the reply. 'The wreck deal was too big for your credit; you were doing a big business, no doubt, but you were doing it on precious little capital, and when the strain came, you were bound to go. Pinkerton's through all right: seven cents dividend, some remarks made, but nothing to hurt: the press let you down easy – I guess Jim had relations there. The only trouble is, that all this *Flying Scud* affair got in the papers with the rest; everybody's wide awake in Honolulu, and the sooner we get the stuff in and the dollars out, the better for all concerned.'

'Gentlemen,' said I, 'you must excuse me. My friend, the captain here, will drink a glass of champagne with you to give you patience; but as for myself, I am unfit even for ordinary conversation till I have read these letters.'

They demurred a little, and indeed the danger of delay seemed obvious; but the sight of my distress, which I was unable entirely to control, appealed strongly to their good-nature, and I was suffered at last to get by myself on deck, where, by the light of a lantern smuggled under shelter of the low rail, I read the following wretched correspondence: –

'MY DEAR LOUDON,' ran the first, 'this will be handed you by your friend Speedy of the *Catamount*. His sterling character and loyal devotion to yourself pointed him out as the best man for our purposes in Honolulu – the parties on the spot being difficult to manipulate. A man called Billy Fowler (you must have heard of Billy) is the boss; he is in politics some, and squares the officers. I have hard times before me in the city, but I feel as bright as a dollar and as strong as John L. Sullivan. What with Mamie here, and my partner speeding over the seas, and the bonanza in the wreck, I feel like I could juggle with the Pyramids of Egypt, same as conjurers do with aluminium balls. My earnest prayers follow you, Loudon, that you may feel the way I do – just inspired! My feet don't touch the ground; I kind of swim. Mamie is like Moses and Aaron that held up the other individual's arms. She carries me along like a horse and buggy. I am beating the record.

'Your true partner,
'J. PINKERTON.'

Number two was in a different style: –

'MY DEAREST LOUDON, – How am I to prepare you for this dire intelligence? Oh, dear me, it will strike you to the earth. The fiat has gone forth; our firm went bust at a quarter before twelve. It was a bill of Bradley's (for two hundred dollars) that brought these vast operations to a close, and evolved liabilities of upwards of two hundred and fifty thousand. Oh, the shame and pity of it, and you but three weeks gone! Loudon, don't blame your partner; if human hands and brains could have sufficed I would have held the thing together. But it just slowly crumbled; Bradley was the last kick, but the blamed business just *melted*. I give the liabilities – it's supposed they're all in – for the cowards were waiting, and the claims were filed like taking tickets to hear Patti. I don't quite have the hang of the assets yet, our interests were so extended; but I am at it day and night, and I guess will make a creditable dividend. If the wreck pans out only half the way it ought we'll turn the laugh still. I am as full of grit and work as ever, and just tower above our troubles. Mamie is a host in herself. Somehow I feel like it was only me that had gone bust, and you and she soared clear of it. Hurry up. That's all you have to do.

'Yours ever,
'J. PINKERTON.'

The third was yet more altered: –

'MY POOR LOUDON,' it began, 'I labour far into the night getting our affairs in order; you could not believe their vastness and complexity. Douglas B. Longhurst said humorously that the receiver's work would be cut out for him. I cannot deny that some of them have a speculative look. God forbid a sensitive, refined spirit like yours should ever come face to face with a Commissioner in Bankruptcy; these men get all the sweetness knocked right out of them. But I could bear up better if it weren't for press comments. Often and often, Loudon, I recall to mind your most legitimate critiques of the press system. They published an interview with me, not the least like what I said, and with *jeering* comments; it would make your blood boil, it was literally *inhumane*; I wouldn't have written it about a yellow dog that was in trouble like what I am. Mamie just winced, the first time she has turned a hair right through the whole catastrophe. How wonderfully true was what you said long ago in Paris about touching on people's personal appearance! The fellow said— ' And then these words had been scored through, and my distressed friend turned to another subject. 'I cannot bear to dwell upon our assets. They simply don't show up. Even *Thirteen Star*, as sound a line as can be produced upon this coast, goes begging. The wreck has thrown a blight on all we ever touched. And where's the use? God never made a wreck big enough to fill our deficit. I am haunted by the thought that you may blame me; I know how I despised your remonstrances. Oh, Loudon, don't be hard on your miserable partner. The funny-dog business is what kills. I fear your stern rectitude of mind like the eye of God. I cannot think but what some of my books seem mixed up; otherwise, I don't seem to see my way as plain as I could wish to. Or else my brain is gone soft. Loudon, if there should be any unpleasantness you can trust me to do the right thing and keep you clear. I've been telling them already how you had no business grip and never saw the books. Oh, I trust I have done right in this! I knew it was a liberty; I know you may justly complain, but it was some things that were said. And mind you, all legitimate business! Not even your shrinking sensitiveness could find fault with the first look of one of them if they had panned out right. And you know the

Flying Scud was the biggest gamble of the crowd, and that was your own idea. Mamie says she never could bear to look you in the face if that idea had been mine, she is *so* conscientious!

'Your broken-hearted
'JIM'.

The last began without formality: –

'This is the end of me commercially. I give up; my nerve has gone. I suppose I ought to be glad, for we're through the court. I don't know as ever I knew how, and I'm sure I don't remember. If it pans out – the wreck I mean – we'll go to Europe and live on the interest of our money. No more work for me. I shake when people speak to me. I have gone on, hoping and hoping, and working and working, and the lead has pinched right out. I want to lie on my back in a garden and read Shakespeare and E.P. Roe. Don't suppose it's cowardice, Loudon. I'm a sick man. Rest is what I must have. I've worked hard all my life; I never spared myself, every dollar I ever made I've coined my brains for it. I've never done a mean thing; I've lived respectable, and given to the poor. Who has a better right to a holiday than I have? And I mean to have a year of it straight out, and if I don't I shall lie right down here in my tracks, and die of worry and brain trouble. Don't mistake, that's so. If there are any pickings at all *trust Speedy*; don't let the creditors get wind of what there is. I helped you when you were down, help me now. Don't deceive yourself; you've got to help me right now or never. I am clerking, and *not fit to cipher*. Mamie's typewriting at the Phœnix Guano Exchange, down town. The light is right out of my life. I know you'll not like to do what I propose. Think only of this, that it's life or death for

'JIM PINKERTON.'

'P.S. – Our figure was seven per cent. Oh, what a fall was there! Well, well, it's past mending; I don't want to whine. But, Loudon, I do want to live. No more ambition; all I ask is life. I have so much to make it sweet to me. I am clerking, and *useless at that*. I know I would have fired such a clerk inside of forty minutes in *my* time. But my time's over. I can only cling on to you. Don't fail

'JIM PINKERTON.'

There was yet one more postscript, yet one more outburst of self-pity and pathetic adjuration; and a doctor's opinion, unpromising enough, was besides enclosed. I pass them both in silence. I think shame to have shown at so great length the half-baked virtues of my friend dissolving in the crucible of sickness and distress; and the effect upon my spirits can be judged already. I got to my feet when I had done, drew a deep breath, and stared hard at Honolulu. One moment the world seemed at an end, the next I was conscious of a rush of independent energy. On Jim I could rely no longer; I must now take hold myself. I must decide and act on my own better thoughts.

The word was easy to say; the thing, at the first blush, was undiscoverable. I was overwhelmed with miserable, womanish pity for my broken friend; his outcries grieved my spirit; I saw him then and now – then, so invincible; now, brought so low – and knew neither how to refuse, nor how to consent to his proposal. The remembrance of my father, who had fallen in the same field unstained, the image of his monument incongruously raising a fear of the law, a chill air that seemed to blow upon my fancy from the doors of prisons, and the imaginary clank of fetters, recalled me to a different resolve. And then again, the wails of my sick partner intervened. So I stood hesitating, and yet with a strong sense of capacity behind, sure, if I could but choose my path, that I should walk in it with resolution.

Then I remembered that I had a friend on board, and stepped to the companion.

'Gentlemen,' said I, 'only a few moments more: but these, I regret to say, I must make more tedious still by removing your companion. It is indispensable that I should have a word or two with Captain Nares.'

Both the smugglers were afoot at once, protesting. The business, they declared, must be despatched at once; they had run risk enough, with a conscience, and they must either finish now, or go.

'The choice is yours, gentlemen,' said I, 'and I believe, the eagerness. I am not yet sure that I have anything in your way; even if I have, there are a hundred things to be considered; and I assure you it is not at all my habit to do business with a pistol to my head.'

'That is all very proper, Mr Dodd; there is no wish to

coerce you, believe me,' said Fowler; 'only, please consider our position. It is really dangerous; we were not the only people to see your schooner off Waimanolo.'

'Mr Fowler,' I replied, 'I was not born yesterday. Will you allow me to express an opinion, in which I may be quite wrong, but to which I am entirely wedded? If the Custom House officers had been coming, they would have been here now. In other words, somebody is working the oracle, and (for a good guess) his name is Fowler.'

Both men laughed loud and long; and being supplied with another bottle of Longhurst's champagne, suffered the captain and myself to leave them without further word.

I gave Nares the correspondence, and he skimmed it through.

'Now, captain,' said I, 'I want a fresh mind on this. What does it mean?'

'It's large enough text,' replied the captain. 'It means you're to stake your pile on Speedy, hand him over all you can, and hold your tongue. I almost wish you hadn't shown it me,' he added wearily. 'What with the specie from the wreck and the opium money, it comes to a biggish deal.'

'That's supposing that I do it?' said I.

'Exactly,' said he, 'supposing you do it.'

'And there are pros and cons to that,' I observed.

'There's San Quentin, to start in with,' said the captain; 'and suppose you clear the penitentiary, there's the nasty taste in the mouth. The figure's big enough to make bad trouble, but it's not big enough to be picturesque; and I should guess a man always feels kind of small who has sold himself under six ciphers. That would be my way, at least; there's an excitement about a million that might carry me on; but the other way, I should feel kind of lonely when I woke in bed. 'Then there's Speedy. Do you know him well?'

'No, I do not,' said I.

'Well, of course he can vamoose with the entire speculation, if he chooses,' pursued the captain, 'and if he don't I can't see but what you've to support and bed and board with him to the end of time. I guess it would weary me. Then there's Mr Pinkerton, of course. He's been a good friend to you, hasn't he? Stood by you, and all that? and pulled you through for all he was worth?'

'That he has,' I cried; 'I could never begin telling you my debt to him!'

'Well, and that's a consideration,' said the captain. 'As a matter of principle, I wouldn't look at this business at the money. "Not good enough," would be my word. But even principle goes under when it comes to friends – the right sort, I mean. This Pinkerton is frightened, and he seems sick; the medico don't seem to care a cent about his state of health; and you've got to figure how you would like it if he came to die. Remember, the risk of this little swindle is all yours; it's no sort of risk to Mr Pinkerton. Well, you've got to put it that way plainly, and see how you like the sound of it: my friend Pinkerton is in danger of the New Jerusalem, I am in danger of San Quentin; which risk do I propose to run?'

'That's an ugly way to put it,' I objected, 'and perhaps hardly fair. There's right and wrong to be considered.'

'Don't know the parties,' replied Nares; 'and I'm coming to them, anyway. For it strikes me, when it came to smuggling opium, you walked right up?'

'So I did,' I said. 'Sick I am to have to say it.'

'All the same,' continued Nares, 'you went into the opium-smuggling with your head down; and a good deal of fussing I've listened to, that you hadn't more of it to smuggle. Now, maybe your partner's not quite fixed the same as you are; maybe he sees precious little difference between the one thing and the other.'

'You could not say truer: he sees none, I do believe,' cried I; 'and though I see one, I could never tell you how.'

'We never can,' said the oracular Nares; 'taste is all a matter of opinion. But the point is, how will your friend take it? You refuse a favour, and you take the high horse at the same time; you disappoint him, and you rap him over the knuckles. It won't do, Mr Dodd; no friendship can stand that. You must be as good as your friend, or as bad as your friend, or start on a fresh deal without him.'

'I don't see it!' said I. 'You don't know Jim.'

'Well, you *will* see,' said Nares. 'And now, here's another point. This bit of money looks mighty big to Mr Pinkerton; it may spell life or health to him; but among all your creditors, I don't see that it amounts to a hill of beans – I don't believe it'll pay their car-fares all round. And don't you think you'll ever get thanked. You were known to pay a long price for the chance of rummaging that wreck; you do the rummaging, you come home, and you hand over ten thousand – or twenty, if you like – a part of which you'll have to own up you made by smuggling; and, mind! you'll never get Billy Fowler to stick his name to a receipt. Now just glance at the transaction from the outside, and see what a clear case it makes. Your ten thousand is a sop; and people will only wonder you were so damned impudent as to offer such a small one! Whichever way you take it, Mr Dodd, the bottom's out of your character; so there's one thing less to be considered.'

'I daresay you'll scarce believe me,' said I, 'but I feel that a positive relief.'

'You must be made some way different from me, then,' returned Nares. 'And, talking about me, I might just mention how I stand. You'll have no trouble from me – you've trouble enough of your own; and I'm friend enough, when a friend's in need, to shut my eyes and go right where he tells me. All the same, I'm rather queerly fixed. My owners'll have to rank with the rest on their charter-party. Here am I, their representative! and I have to look over the ship's side while the bankrupt walks his assets ashore in Mr Speedy's hat-box. It's a thing I wouldn't do for James G. Blaine; but I'll do it for you, Mr Dodd, and only sorry I can't do more.'

'Thank you, captain; my mind is made up,' said I. 'I'll go straight, *ruat cælum*! I never understood that old tag before tonight.'

'I hope it isn't my business that decides you?' asked the captain.

'I'll never deny it was an element,' said I. 'I hope, I hope I'm not cowardly; I hope I could steal for Jim myself; but when it comes to dragging in you and Speedy, and this one and the other, why, Jim has got to die, and there's an end. I'll try and work for him when I get to 'Frisco, I suppose; and I suppose I'll fail, and look on at his death, and kick myself: it can't be helped – I'll fight it on this line.'

'I don't say as you're wrong,' replied Nares, 'and I'll be hanged if I know if you're right. It suits me anyway. And look here – hadn't you better just show our friends over the side?' he added; 'no good of being at the risk and worry of smuggling for the benefit of creditors.'

'I don't think of the creditors,' said I. 'But I've kept this pair so long I haven't got the brass to fire them now.'

Indeed, I believe that was my only reason for entering upon a transaction which was now outside my interest, but which (as it chanced) repaid me fifty-fold in entertainment. Fowler and Sharpe were both preternaturally sharp; they did me the honour in the beginning to attribute to myself their proper vices, and before we were done had grown to regard me with an esteem akin to worship. This proud position I attained by no more recondite arts than telling the mere truth and unaffectedly displaying my indifference to the result. I have doubtless stated the essentials of all good diplomacy, which may be rather regarded, therefore, as a grace of state, than the effect of management. For to tell the truth is not in itself diplomatic, and to have no care for the result a thing involuntary. When I mentioned, for instance, that I had but two hundred and forty pounds of drug, my smugglers exchanged meaning glances, as who should say, 'Here is a foeman worthy of our steel!' But when I carelessly proposed thirty-five dollars a pound, as an amendment to their offered twenty, and wound up with the remark: 'The whole thing is a matter of moonshine to me, gentlemen. Take it or want it, and fill your glasses' – I had the indescribable gratification to see Sharpe nudge Fowler warningly, and Fowler choke down the jovial acceptance that stood ready on his lips, and lamely substitute a 'No – no more wine, please, Mr Dodd!' Nor was this all: for when the affair was settled at thirty dollars a pound – a shrewd stroke of business for my creditors – and our friends had got on board their whaleboat and shoved off, it appeared they were imperfectly acquainted with the conveyance of sound upon still water, and I had the joy to overhear the following testimonial.

'Deep man, that Dodd,' said Sharpe.

And the bass-toned Fowler echoed, 'Damned if I understand his game.'

Thus we were left once more alone upon the *Norah Creina*; and the news of the night, and the lamentations of Pinkerton, and the thought of my own harsh decision, returned and besieged me in the dark. According to all the rubbish I had read, I should have been sustained by the warm consciousness of virtue. Alas, I had but the one feeling: that I had sacrificed my sick friend to the fear of prison-cells and stupid starers. And no moralist has yet advanced so far as to number cowardice amongst the things that are their own reward.

CHAPTER SEVENTEEN

Light from the Man of War

In the early sunlight of the next day, we tossed close off the buoy and saw the city sparkle in its groves about the foot of the Punch Bowl, and the masts clustering thick in the small harbour. A good breeze, which had risen with the sea, carried us triumphantly through the intricacies of the passage; and we had soon brought up not far from the landing-stairs. I remember to have remarked an ugly-horned reptile of a modern warship in the usual moorings across the port, but my mind was so profoundly plunged in melancholy that I paid no heed.

Indeed, I had little time at my disposal. Messieurs Sharpe and Fowler had left the night before in the persuasion that I was a liar of the first magnitude; the genial belief brought them aboard again with the earliest opportunity, proffering help to one who had proved how little he required it, and hospitality to so respectable a character. I had business to mind, I had some need both of assistance and diversion; I liked Fowler – I don't know why; and in short, I let them do with me as they desired. No creditor intervening, I spent the first half of the day inquiring into the conditions of the tea and silk market under the auspices of Sharpe; lunched with him in a private apartment at the Hawaiian Hotel – for Sharpe was a teetotaler in public; and about four in the afternoon was delivered into the hands of Fowler. This gentleman owned a bungalow on the Waikiki beach; and there in company with certain young bloods of Honolulu, I was entertained to a sea-bathe, indiscriminate cocktails, a dinner, a *hula-hula*, and (to round off the night), poker and assorted liquors. To lose money in the small hours to pale, intoxicated youth has always appeared to me a pleasure overrated. In my then frame of mind, I confess I found it even delightful; put up my money (or rather my creditors'), and put down Fowler's champagne with equal avidity and success; and awoke the next morning to a mild headache and the rather agreeable lees of the last night's excitement. The young bloods, many of whom were still far from sober, had taken the kitchen into their own hands, *vice* the Chinaman deposed; and since each was engaged upon a dish of his own, and none had the least scruple in demolishing his neighbour's handiwork, I became early convinced that many eggs would be broken and few omelets made. The discovery of a jug of milk and a crust of bread enabled me to stay my appetite; and since it was Sunday when no business could be done, and the festivities were to be renewed that night in the abode of Fowler, it occurred to me to slip silently away and enjoy some air and solitude.

I turned seaward under the dead crater known as Diamond Head. My way was for some time under the shade of certain thickets of green, thorny trees, dotted with houses. Here I enjoyed some pictures of the native life: wide-eyed, naked children, mingled with pigs; a youth asleep under a tree; an old gentleman spelling through glasses his Hawaiian Bible; the somewhat embarrassing spectacle of a lady at her bath in a spring; and the glimpse of gaudy coloured gowns in the deep shade of the houses. Thence I found a road along the beach itself, wading in sand, opposed and buffeted by the whole weight of the Trade: on one hand, the glittering and sounding surf, and the bay lively with many sails; on the other, precipitous, arid gullies and sheer cliffs, mounting towards the crater and the blue sky. For all the companionship of skimming vessels, the place struck me with a sense of solitude. There came in my head what I had been told the day before at dinner, of a cavern above in the bowels of the volcano, a place only to be visited with the light of torches, a treasure-house of the bones of priests and warriors, and clamorous with the voice of an unseen river pouring seaward through the crannies of the mountain. At the thought, it was revealed to me suddenly how the bungalows, and the Fowlers, and the bright, busy town and crowding ships, were all children of yesterday; and for centuries before, the obscure life of the natives, with its glories and ambitions, its joys and crimes and agonies, had rolled unseen, like the mountain river, in that sea-girt place. Not Chaldea appeared more ancient, nor the Pyramids of

Egypt more abstruse; and I heard time measured by 'the drums and tramplings' of immemorial conquests, and saw myself the creature of an hour. Over the bankruptcy of Pinkerton and Dodd, of Montana Block, S. F., and the conscientious troubles of the junior partner, the spirit of eternity was seen to smile.

To this mood of philosophic sadness, my excesses of the night before no doubt contributed, for more things than virtue are at times their own reward, but I was greatly healed at least of my distresses. And while I was yet enjoying my abstracted humour, a turn of the beach brought me in view of the signal-station, with its watch-house and flag-staff, perched on the immediate margin of a cliff. The house was new and clean and bald, and stood naked to the Trades. The wind beat about it in loud squalls; the seaward windows rattled without mercy; the breach of the surf below contributed its increment of noise; and the fall of my foot in the narrow verandah passed unheard by those within.

They were two on whom I thus entered unexpectedly: the look-out man, with grizzled beard, keen seaman's eyes, and that brand on his countenance that comes of solitary living; and a visitor, an oratorical fellow, in the smart tropical array of the British man-o'-war's man, perched on a table, and smoking a cigar. I was made pleasantly welcome, and was soon listening with amusement to the sea-lawyer.

'No, if I hadn't have been born an Englishman,' was one of his sentiments, 'damn me! I'd rather a' been born a Frenchy! I'd like to see another nation fit to black their boots.' Presently after, he developed his views on home politics with similar trenchancy. 'I'd rather be a brute beast than what I'd be a Liberal,' he said; 'carrying banners and that! a pig's got more sense. Why, look at our chief engineer – they do say he carried a banner with his own 'ands: "Hooroar for Gladstone!" I suppose, or "Down with the Aristocracy!" What 'arm does the aristocracy do? Show me a country any good without one! Not the States; why, it's the 'ome of corruption! I knew a man – he was a good man, 'ome born – who was signal quartermaster in the *Wyandotte*. He told me he could never have got there, if he hadn't have "run with the boys" – told it me as I'm telling you. Now we're all British subjects here— ' he was going on.

'I am afraid I am an American,' I said apologetically.

He seemed the least bit taken aback, but recovered himself; and with the ready tact of his betters, paid me the usual British compliment on the riposte. 'You don't say so!' he exclaimed; 'well, I give you my word of honour, I'd never have guessed it. Nobody could tell it on you,' said he, as though it were some form of liquor.

I thanked him, as I always do, at this particular stage, with his compatriots; not so much, perhaps, for the compliment to myself and my poor country, as for the revelation (which is ever fresh to me) of Britannic self-sufficiency and taste. And he was so far softened by my gratitude as to add a word of praise on the American method of lacing sails. 'You're ahead of us in lacing sails,' he said; 'you can say that with a clear conscience.'

'Thank you,' I replied; 'I shall certainly do so.'

At this rate we got along swimmingly; and when I rose to retrace my steps to the Fowlery, he at once started to his feet and offered me the welcome solace of his company for the return. I believe I discovered much alacrity at the idea, for the creature (who seemed to be unique, or to represent a type like that of the dodo) entertained me hugely. But when he had produced his hat, I found I was in the way of more than entertainment, for on the ribbon I could read the legend, 'H.M.S. Tempest.'

'I say,' I began, when our adieus were paid, and we were scrambling down the path from the look-out, 'it was your ship that picked up the men on board the *Flying Scud*, wasn't it?'

'You may say so,' said he. 'And a blessed good job for the Flying-Scuds. It's a God-forsaken spot, that Midway Island.'

'I've just come from there,' said I; 'it was I who bought the wreck.'

'Beg your pardon, sir,' cried the sailor: 'gen'lem'n in the white schooner?'

'The same,' said I.

My friend saluted, as though we were now for the first time formally introduced.

'Of course,' I continued, 'I am rather taken up with the whole story; and I wish you would tell me what you can of how the men were saved.'

'It was like this,' said he. 'We had orders to call at Midway after castaways, and had our distance pretty nigh run down the day before. We steamed half-speed all night, looking to make it about noon, for old Tootles – beg your pardon, sir, the captain – was precious scared of the place at night. Well, there's nasty, filthy currents round that Midway; *you* know, as has been there; and one on 'em must have set us down. Leastways, about six bells, when we had ought to been miles away, some one sees a sail, and lo and be'old, there was the spars of a full-rigged brig! We raised her pretty fast, and the island after her; and made out she was hard aground, canted on her bilge, and had her ens'n flying, union down. It was breaking 'igh on the reef, and we laid well out, and sent a couple of boats. I didn't go in neither; only stood and looked on: but it seems they was all badly scared and muddled, and didn't know which end was uppermost. One on 'em kep' snivelling and wringing of his 'ands; he come on board all of a sop like a monthly nurse. That Trent, he come first, with his 'and in a bloody rag. I was near 'em as I am to you; and I could make out he was all to bits – 'eard his breath rattle in his blooming lungs as he come down the ladder. Yes, they was a scared lot, small blame to 'em *I* say! The next after Trent, come him as was mate.'

'Goddedaal!' I exclaimed.

'And a good name for him, too,' chuckled the man-o'-war's man, who probably confounded the word with a familiar oath. 'A good name, too; only it weren't his. He was a gen'lem'n born, sir, as had gone maskewerading. One of our officers knowed him at 'ome, reckonises him, steps up, 'olds out his 'and right off, and says he, "Ullo, Norrie, old chappie!' he says. The other was coming up, as bold as look at it; didn't seem put out – that's where blood tells, sir! Well, no sooner does he 'ear his born name given him, than he turns as white as the Day of Judgment, stares at Mr Sebright like he was looking at a ghost, and then (I give you my word of honour) turned to, and doubled up in a dead faint. "Take him down to my berth," says Mr Sebright. "'Tis poor old Norrie Carthew," he says.'

'And what – what sort of a gentleman was this Mr Carthew?' I gasped.

'The ward-room steward told me he was come of the

best blood in England,' was my friend's reply: 'Eton and 'Arrow bred; and might have been a bar'net!'

'No, but to look at?' I corrected him.

'The same as you or me,' was the uncompromising answer: 'not much to look at. *I* didn't know he was a gen'lem'n; but then, I never see him cleaned up.'

'How was that?' I cried. 'Oh, yes, I remember: he was sick all the way to 'Frisco, was he not?'

'Sick, or sorry, or something,' returned my informant. 'My belief, he didn't hanker after showing up. He kep' close; the ward-room steward, what took his meals in, told me he ate nex' to nothing; and he was fetched ashore at 'Frisco on the quiet. Here was how it was. It seems his brother had took and died, him as had the estate. This one had gone in for his beer, by what I could make out; the old folks at 'ome had turned rusty; no one knew where he had gone to. Here he was, slaving in a merchant brig, shipwrecked on Midway, and packing up his duds for a long voyage in a open boat. He comes on board our ship, and by God, here he is a landed proprietor, and may be in Parliament tomorrow! It's no less than natural he should keep dark: so would you and me, in the same box.'

'I daresay,' said I. 'But you saw more of the others?'

'To be sure,' says he: 'no 'arm in them from what I see. There was one 'Ardy there: colonial born he was, and had been through a power of money. There was no nonsense about 'Ardy; he had been up, and he had come down, and took it so. His 'eart was in the right place; and he was well-informed, and knew French; and Latin, I believe, like a native! I liked that 'Ardy: he was a good-looking boy, too.'

'Did they say much about the wreck?' I asked.

'There wasn't much to say, I reckon,' replied the man-o'-war's man. 'It was all in the papers. 'Ardy used to yarn most about the coins he had gone through; he had lived with bookmakers, and jockeys, and pugs, and actors, and all that – a precious low lot,' added this judicious person. 'But it's about here my 'orse is moored, and by your leave I'll be getting ahead.'

'One moment,' said I. 'Is Mr Sebright on board?'

'No, sir, he's ashore today,' said the sailor. 'I took up a bag for him to the 'otel.'

With that we parted. Presently after my friend overtook and passed me on a hired steed which seemed to scorn its cavalier; and I was left in the dust of his passage, a prey to whirling thoughts. For I now stood, or seemed to stand, on the immediate threshold of these mysteries. I knew the name of the man Dickson – his name was Carthew; I knew where the money came from that opposed us at the sale – it was part of Carthew's inheritance; and in my gallery of illustrations to the history of the wreck, one more picture hung, perhaps the most dramatic of the series. It showed me the deck of a warship in that distant part of the great ocean, the officers and seamen looking curiously on: and a man of birth and education, who had been sailing under an alias on a trading brig, and was now rescued from desperate peril, felled like an ox by the bare sound of his own name. I could not fail to be reminded of my own experience at the Occidental telephone. The hero of three styles, Dickson, Goddedaal, or Carthew, must be the owner of a lively – or a loaded – conscience, and the reflection recalled to me the photograph found on board the *Flying Scud*; just such a man, I reasoned, would be capable of just such starts and crises, and I inclined to think that Goddedaal (or Carthew) was the mainspring of the mystery.

One thing was plain; as long as the *Tempest* was in reach, I must make the acquaintance of both Sebright and the doctor. To this end, I excused myself with Mr Fowler, returned to Honolulu, and passed the remainder of the day hanging vainly round the cool verandahs of the hotel. It was near nine o'clock at night before I was rewarded.

'That is the gentleman you were asking for,' said the clerk.

I beheld a man in tweeds, of an incomparable languor of demeanour, and carrying a cane with genteel effort. From the name, I had looked to find a sort of Viking and young ruler of the battle and the tempest; and I was the more disappointed, and not a little alarmed, to come face to face with this impracticable type.

'I believe I have the pleasure of addressing Lieutenant Sebright,' said I, stepping forward.

'Aw, yes,' replied the hero; 'but, aw! I dawn't knaw you, do I?' (He spoke for all the world like Lord Foppington in the old play – a proof of the perennial nature of man's affectations. But his limping dialect I scorn to continue to reproduce.)

'It was with the intention of making myself known that I have taken this step,' said I, entirely unabashed (for impudence begets in me its like – perhaps my only martial attribute). 'We have a common subject of interest, to me very lively; and I believe I may be in a position to be of some service to a friend of yours – to give him, at least, some very welcome information.'

The last clause was a sop to my conscience; I could not pretend, even to myself, either the power or the will to serve Mr Carthew; but I felt sure he would like to hear the *Flying Scud* was burned.

'I don't know – I – I don't understand you,' stammered my victim. 'I don't have any friends in Honolulu, don't you know?'

'The friend to whom I refer is English,' I replied. 'It is Mr Carthew, whom you picked up at Midway. My firm has bought the wreck; I am just returned from breaking her up; and – to make my business quite clear to you – I have a communication it is necessary I should make; and have to trouble you for Mr Carthew's address.'

It will be seen how rapidly I had dropped all hope of interesting the frigid British bear. He, on his side, was plainly on thorns at my insistence; I judged he was suffering torments of alarm lest I should prove an undesirable acquaintance; diagnosed him for a shy, dull, vain, unamiable animal, without adequate defence – a sort of dishoused snail; and concluded, rightly enough, that he would consent to anything to bring our interview to a conclusion. A moment later, he had fled, leaving with me a sheet of paper, thus inscribed: –

Norris Carthew,
Stallbridge-le-Carthew,
Dorset.

I might have cried victory, the field of battle and some of the enemy's baggage remaining in my occupation. As a matter of fact, my moral sufferings during the engagement had rivalled those of Mr Sebright. I was left incapable of fresh hostilities; I owned that the navy of old England was (for me) invincible as of yore; and giving up all thought of the doctor, inclined to salute her veteran flag, in the future, from a prudent distance. Such was my inclination when I retired to rest; and my first experience the next morning strengthened it to certainty. For I had the pleasure of encountering my fair antagonist on his way on board; and he honoured me with a recognition so disgustingly dry, that my impatience overflowed, and (recalling the tactics of Nelson) I neglected to perceive or to return it.

Judge of my astonishment, some half-hour later, to receive a note of invitation from the *Tempest*.

'Dear Sir,' it began, 'we are all naturally very much interested in the wreck of the *Flying Scud*, and as soon as I mentioned that I had the pleasure of making your acquaintance, a very general wish was expressed that you would come and dine on board. It will give us all the greatest pleasure to see you tonight, or in case you should be otherwise engaged, to luncheon either tomorrow or today. A note of the hours followed, and the document wound up with the name of 'J. Lascelles Sebright,' under an undeniable statement that he was sincerely mine.

'No, Mr Lascelles Sebright,' I reflected, 'you are not, but I begin to suspect that (like the lady in the song) you are another's. You have mentioned your adventure, my friend; you have been blown up; you have got your orders; this note has been dictated; and I am asked on board (in spite of your melancholy protests) not to meet the men, and not to talk about the *Flying Scud*, but to undergo the scrutiny of someone interested in Carthew – the doctor, for a wager. And for a second wager, all this springs from your facility in giving the address.' I lost no time in answering the billet, electing for the earliest occasion; and at the appointed hour, a somewhat blackguard-looking boat's crew from the *Norah Creina* conveyed me under the guns of the *Tempest*.

The ward-room appeared pleased to see me; Sebright's brother officers, in contrast to himself, took a boyish interest in my cruise; and much was talked of the *Flying Scud*; of how she had been lost, of how I had found her, and of the weather, the anchorage, and the currents about Midway Island. Carthew was referred to more than once without embarrassment; the parallel case of a late Earl of Aberdeen, who died mate on board a Yankee schooner, was adduced. If they told me little of the man, it was because they had not much to tell, and only felt an interest in his recognition and pity for his prolonged ill-health. I could never think the subject was avoided; and it was clear that the officers, far from practising concealment, had nothing to conceal.

So far, then, all seemed natural, and yet the doctor troubled me. This was a tall, rugged, plain man, on the wrong side of fifty, already grey, and with a restless mouth and bushy eyebrows: he spoke seldom, but then with gaiety; and his great, quaking, silent laughter was infectious. I could make out that he was at once the quiz of the ward-room and perfectly respected; and I made sure that he observed me covertly. It is certain I returned the compliment. If Carthew had feigned sickness – and all seemed to point in that direction – here was the man who knew all – or certainly knew much. His strong, sterling face progressively and silently persuaded of his full knowledge. That was not the mouth, these were not the eyes of one who would act in ignorance, or could be led at random. Nor again was it the face of a man squeamish in the case of malefactors; there was even a touch of Brutus there, and something of the hanging judge. In short, he seemed the last character for the part assigned him in my theories; and wonder and curiosity contended in my mind.

Luncheon was over, and an adjournment to the smoking-room proposed, when (upon a sudden impulse) I burned my ships, and pleading indisposition, requested to consult the doctor.

'There is nothing the matter with my body, Dr Urquart,' said I, as soon as we were alone.

He hummed, his mouth worked, he regarded me steadily with his grey eyes, but resolutely held his peace.

'I want to talk to you about the *Flying Scud* and Mr Carthew,' I resumed. 'Come, you must have expected this. I am sure you know all; you are shrewd, and must have a guess that I know much. How are we to stand to one another? and how am I to stand to Mr Carthew?'

'I do not fully understand you,' he replied, after a pause; and then, after another: 'it is the spirit I refer to, Mr Dodd.'

'The spirit of my inquiries?' I asked.

He nodded.

'I think we are at cross-purposes,' said I. 'The spirit is

precisely what I came in quest of. I bought the *Flying Scud* at a ruinous figure, run up by Mr Carthew through an agent; and I am, in consequence, a bankrupt. But if I have found no fortune in the wreck, I have found unmistakable evidences of foul play. Conceive my position: I am ruined through this man, whom I never saw; I might very well desire revenge or compensation; and I think you will admit I have the means to extort either.'

He made no sign in answer to this challenge.

'Can you not understand, then,' I resumed, 'the spirit in which I come to one who is surely in the secret, and ask him, honestly and plainly, How do I stand to Mr Carthew?'

'I must ask you to be more explicit,' said he.

'You do not help me much,' I retorted. 'But see if you can understand: my conscience is not very fine-spun; still, I have one. Now, there are degrees of foul play, to some of which I have no particular objection. I am sure with Mr Carthew, I am not at all the person to forego an advantage, and I have much curiosity. But on the other hand, I have no taste for persecution; and I ask you to believe that I am not the man to make bad worse, or heap trouble on the unfortunate.'

'Yes; I think I understand,' said he. 'Suppose I pass you my word that, whatever may have occurred, there were excuses – great excuses – I may say, very great?'

'It would have weight with me, doctor,' I replied.

'I may go further,' he pursued. 'Suppose I had been there or you had been there. After a certain event had taken place, it's a grave question what we might have done – it's even a question what we could have done – ourselves. Or take me. I will be plain with you, and own that I am in possession of the facts. You have a shrewd guess how I have acted in that knowledge. May I ask you to judge from the character of my action, something of the nature of that knowledge, which I have no call, nor yet no title, to share with you?'

I cannot convey a sense of the rugged conviction and judicial emphasis of Dr Urquart's speech. To those who did not hear him, it may appear as if he fed me on enigmas; to myself, who heard, I seemed to have received a lesson and a compliment.

'I thank you,' I said; 'I feel you have said as much as possible, and more than I had any right to ask. I take that as a mark of confidence, which I will try to deserve. I hope, sir, you will let me regard you as a friend.'

He evaded my proffered friendship with a blunt proposal to rejoin the mess; and yet a moment later contrived to alleviate the snub. For, as we entered the smoking-room, he laid his hand on my shoulder with a kind familiarity—

'I have just prescribed for Mr Dodd,' says he, 'a glass of our Madeira.'

I have never again met Dr Urquart; but he wrote himself so clear upon my memory that I think I see him still. And indeed I had cause to remember the man for the sake of his communication. It was hard enough to make a theory fit the circumstances of the *Flying Scud*; but one in which the chief actor should stand the least excused, and might retain the esteem or at least the pity of a man like Dr Urquart, failed me utterly. Here at least was the end of my discoveries. I learned no more, till I learned all; and my reader has the evidence complete. Is he more astute than I was? or, like me, does he give it up?

CHAPTER EIGHTEEN

Cross-Questions and Crooked Answers

I have said hard words of San Francisco; they must scarce be literally understood (one cannot suppose the Israelites did justice to the land of Pharaoh); and the city took a fine revenge of me on my return. She had never worn a more becoming guise; the sun shone, the air was lively, the people had flowers in their buttonholes and smiles upon their faces; and as I made my way towards Jim's place of employment, with some very black anxieties at heart, I seemed to myself a blot on the surrounding gaiety.

My destination was in a by-street in a mean, rickety building. 'The Franklin H. Dodge Steam Printing Company' appeared upon its front, and in characters of greater freshness, so as to suggest recent conversion, the watch-cry, 'White Labour Only.' In the office in a dusty pen Jim sat alone before a table. A wretched change had overtaken him in clothes, body, and bearing; he looked sick and shabby. He who had once rejoiced in his day's employment, like a horse among pastures, now sat staring on a column of accounts, idly chewing a pen, at times heavily sighing, the picture of inefficiency and inattention. He was sunk deep in a painful reverie; he neither saw nor heard me, and I stood and watched him unobserved. I had a sudden vain relenting. Repentance bludgeoned me. As I had predicted to Nares, I stood and kicked myself. Here was I come home again, my honour saved; there was my friend in want of rest, nursing, and a generous diet; and I asked myself, with Falstaff, 'What is in that word honour? what is that honour?' and, like Falstaff, I told myself that it was air.

'Jim!' said I.

'Loudon!' he gasped, and jumped from his chair and stood shaking.

The next moment I was over the barrier, and we were hand in hand.

'My poor old man!' I cried.

'Thank God, you're home at last!' he gulped, and kept patting my shoulder with his hand.

'I've no good news for you, Jim,' said I.

'You've come – that's the good news that I want,' he replied. 'Oh, how I have longed for you Loudon!'

'I couldn't do what you wrote me,' I said, lowering my voice. 'The creditors have it all. I couldn't do it.'

'S-s-h!' returned Jim. 'I was crazy when I wrote. I could never have looked Mamie in the face if we had done it. Oh, Loudon, what a gift that woman is? You think you know something of life; you just don't know anything. It's the *goodness* of the woman, it's a revelation!'

'That's all right,' said I. 'That's how I hoped to hear you, Jim.'

'And so the *Flying Scud* was a fraud,' he resumed. 'I didn't quite understand your letter, but I made out that.'

'Fraud is a mild term for it,' said I. 'The creditors will never believe what fools we were. And that reminds me,' I continued, rejoicing in the transition, 'how about the bankruptcy?'

'You were lucky to be out of that,' answered Jim, shaking his head; 'you were lucky not to see the papers. The *Occidental* called me a fifth-rate kerbstone broker with water on the brain; another said I was a tree-frog that had got into the same meadow with Longhurst, and had blown myself out till I went pop. It was rough on a man in his honeymoon; so was what they said about my looks, and what I had on, and the way I perspired. But I braced myself up with the *Flying Scud*. How did it exactly figure out anyway? I don't seem to catch on to that story, Loudon.'

'The devil you don't!' thinks I to myself; and then aloud, 'You see we had neither one of us good luck. I didn't do much more than cover current expenses, and you got floored immediately. How did we come to go so soon?'

'Well, we'll have to have a talk over all this,' said Jim with a sudden start. 'I should be getting to my books, and I guess you had better go up right away to Mamie. She's at Speedy's. She expects you with impatience. She regards you in the light of a favourite brother, Loudon.'

Any scheme was welcome which allowed me to postpone the hour of explanation, and avoid (were it only for a breathing space) the topic of the *Flying Scud*. I hastened accordingly to Bush Street. Mrs. Speedy, already rejoicing in the return of a spouse, hailed me with acclamation. 'And it's beautiful you're looking, Mr Dodd, my dear,' she was kind enough to say. 'And a miracle they naygur waheenies let ye lave the oilands. I have my suspicions of Shpeedy,' she added roguishly. 'Did ye see him after the naygresses now?'

I gave Speedy an unblemished character.

'The one of ye will niver bethray the other,' said the playful dame, and ushered me into a bare room, where Mamie sat working a type-writer.

I was touched by the cordiality of her greeting. With the prettiest gesture in the world she gave me both her hands, wheeled forth a chair, and produced from a cupboard a tin of my favourite tobacco, and a book of my exclusive cigarette papers.

'There!' she cried, 'you see, Mr Loudon, we were all prepared for you; the things were bought the very day you sailed.'

I imagined she had always intended me a pleasant welcome; but the certain fervour of sincerity, which I could not help remarking, flowed from an unexpected source. Captain Nares, with a kindness for which I can never be sufficiently grateful, had stolen a moment from his occupations, driven to call on Mamie, and drawn her a generous picture of my prowess at the wreck. She was careful not to breathe a word of this interview, till she had led me on to tell my adventures for myself.

'Ah! Captain Nares was better,' she cried, when I had done. 'From your account, I have only learned one new thing, that you are modest as well as brave.'

I cannot tell with what sort of disclamation I sought to reply.

'It is of no use,' said Mamie. 'I know a hero. And when I heard of you working all day like a common labourer, with your hands bleeding and your nails broken – and how you told the captain to "crack on" (I think he said) in the storm, when he was terrified himself – and the danger of that horrid mutiny' – (Nares had been obligingly dipping his brush in earthquake and eclipse) – 'and how it was all done, in part at least, for Jim and me – I felt we could never say how we admired and thanked you.'

'Mamie,' I cried, 'don't talk of thanks; it is not a word to be used between friends. Jim and I have been prosperous together; now we shall be poor together. We've done our best, and that's all that need be said. The next thing is for me to find a situation, and send you and Jim up country for a long holiday in the redwoods – for a holiday Jim has got to have.'

'Jim can't take your money, Mr Loudon,' said Mamie.

'Jim?' cried I. 'He's got to. Didn't I take his?'

Presently after, Jim himself arrived, and before he had yet done mopping his brow, he was at me with the accursed subject. 'Now, Loudon,' said he, 'here we are all together, the day's work done and the evening before us; just start in with the whole story.'

'One word on business first,' said I, speaking from the lips outward, and meanwhile (in the private apartments of my brain) trying for the thousandth time to find some plausible arrangement of my story. 'I want to have a notion how we stand about the bankruptcy.'

'Oh, that's ancient history,' cried Jim. 'We paid seven cents, and a wonder we did as well. The receiver— ' (methought a spasm seized him at the name of this official, and he broke off). 'But it's all past and done with anyway; and what I want to get at is the facts about the wreck. I don't seem to understand it; appears to me like as there was something underneath.'

'There was nothing *in* it anyway,' I said, with a forced laugh.

'That's what I want to judge of,' returned Jim.

'How the mischief is it I can never keep you to that bankruptcy? It looks as if you avoided it,' said I – for a man in my situation, with unpardonable folly.

'Don't it look a little as if you were trying to avoid the wreck?' asked Jim.

It was my own doing; there was no retreat. 'My dear fellow, if you make a point of it, here goes!' said I, and launched with spurious gaiety into the current of my tale. I told it with point and spirit; described the island and the wreck, mimicked Anderson and the Chinese, maintained the suspense . . . My pen has stumbled on the fatal word. I maintained the suspense so well that it was never relieved; and when I stopped – I dare not say concluded, where there was no conclusion – I found Jim and Mamie regarding me with surprise.

'Well?' said Jim.

'Well, that's all,' said I.

'But how do you explain it?' he asked.

'I can't explain it,' said I.

Mamie wagged her head ominously.

'But, great Cæsar's ghost, the money was offered!' cried Jim. 'It won't do, Loudon; it's nonsense on the face of it! I don't say but what you and Nares did your best; I'm sure, of course, you did; but I do say you got fooled. I say the stuff is in that ship today, and I say I mean to get it.'

'There is nothing in the ship, I tell you, but old wood and iron!' said I.

'You'll see,' said Jim. 'Next time I go myself. I'll take Mamie for the trip: Longhurst won't refuse me the expense of a schooner. You wait till I get the searching of her.'

'But you can't search her!' cried I. 'She's burned.'

'Burned!' cried Mamie, starting a little from the attitude of quiescent capacity in which she had hitherto sat to hear me, her hands folded in her lap.

There was an appreciable pause.

'I beg your pardon, Loudon,' began Jim at last, 'but why in snakes did you burn her?'

'It was an idea of Nares's,' said I.

'This is certainly the strangest circumstance of all,' observed Mamie.

'I must say, Loudon, it does seem kind of unexpected,' added Jim. 'It seems kind of crazy even. What did you – what did Nares expect to gain by burning her?'

'I don't know; it didn't seem to matter; we had got all there was to get,' said I.

'That's the very point,' cried Jim. 'It was quite plain you hadn't.'

'What made you so sure?' asked Mamie.

'How can I tell you?' I cried. 'We had been all through her. We *were* sure; that's all that I can say.'

'I begin to think you were,' she returned, with a significant emphasis.

Jim hurriedly intervened. 'What I don't quite make

out, Loudon, is that you don't seem to appreciate the peculiarities of the thing,' said he. 'It doesn't seem to have struck you same as it does me.'

'Pshaw! why go on with this?' cried Mamie, suddenly rising. 'Mr Dodd is not telling us either what he thinks or what he knows.'

'Mamie!' cried Jim.

'You need not be concerned for his feelings, James; he is not concerned for yours,' returned the lady. 'He dare not deny it, besides. And this is not the first time he has practised reticence. Have you forgotten that he knew the address, and did not tell it you until that man had escaped?'

Jim turned to me pleadingly – we were all on our feet. 'Loudon,' he said, 'you see Mamie has some fancy, and I must say there's just a sort of a shadow of an excuse; for it *is* bewildering – even to me, Loudon, with my trained business intelligence. For God's sake clear it up.'

'This serves me right,' said I. 'I should not have tried to keep you in the dark; I should have told you at first that I was pledged to secrecy; I should have asked you to trust me in the beginning. It is all I can do now. There is more of the story, but it concerns none of us, and my tongue is tied. I have given my word of honour. You must trust me and try to forgive me.'

'I daresay I am very stupid, Mr Dodd,' began Mamie, with an alarming sweetness, 'but I thought you went upon this trip as my husband's representative and with my husband's money? You tell us now that you are pledged, but I should have thought you were pledged first of all to James. You say it does not concern us; we are poor people, and my husband is sick, and it concerns us a great deal to understand how we come to have lost our money, and why our representative comes back to us with nothing. You ask that we should trust you; you do not seem to understand – the question we are asking ourselves is whether we have not trusted you too much.'

'I do not ask you to trust me,' I replied. 'I ask Jim. He knows me.'

'You think you can do what you please with James; you trust to his affection, do you not? And me, I suppose, you do not consider,' said Mamie. 'But it was perhaps an unfortunate day for you when we were married, for I at least am not blind. The crew run away, the ship is sold for a great deal of money, you know that man's address and you conceal it; you do not find what you were sent to look for, and yet you burn the ship; and now, when we ask explanations, you are pledged to secrecy! But I am pledged to no such thing; I will not stand by in silence and see my sick and ruined husband betrayed by his condescending friend. I will give you the truth for once. Mr Dodd, you have been bought and sold.'

'Mamie,' cried Jim, 'no more of this! It's me you're striking; it's only me you hurt. You don't know, you cannot understand these things. Why, today, if it hadn't been for Loudon, I couldn't have looked you in the face. He saved my honesty.'

'I have heard plenty of this talk before,' she replied. 'You are a sweet-hearted fool, and I love you for it. But I am a clear-headed woman; my eyes are open, and I understand this man's hypocrisy. Did he not come here today and pretend he would take a situation – pretend he would share his hard-earned wages with us until you were well? Pretend! It makes me furious! His wages! a share of his wages! That would have been your pittance, that would have been your share of the *Flying Scud* – you who worked and toiled for him when he was a beggar in the streets of Paris. But we do not want your charity; thank God, I can work for my own husband! See what it is to have obliged a gentleman! He would let you pick him up when he was begging; he would stand and look on, and let you black his shoes, and sneer at you. For you were always sneering at my James; you always looked down upon him in your heart, you know it!' She turned back to Jim. 'And now when he is rich,' she began, and then swooped again on me. 'For you are rich, I dare you to deny it; I defy you to look me in the face and try to deny that you are rich – rich with our money – my husband's money— '

Heaven knows to what a height she might have risen, being, by this time, bodily whirled away in her own hurricane of words. Heart-sickness, a black depression, a treacherous sympathy with my assailant, pity unutterable for poor Jim, already filled, divided, and abashed my spirit.

Flight seemed the only remedy; and making a private sign to Jim, as if to ask permission, I slunk from the unequal field.

I was but a little way down the street, when I was arrested by the sound of some one running, and Jim's voice calling me by name. He had followed me with a letter which had been long awaiting my return.

I took it in a dream. 'This has been a devil of a business,' said I.

'Don't think hard of Mamie,' he pleaded. 'It's the way she's made; it's her high-toned loyalty. And of course I know it's all right. I know your sterling character; but you didn't, somehow, make out to give us the thing straight, Loudon. Anybody might have – I mean it – I mean— '

'Never mind what you mean, my poor Jim,' said I. 'She's a gallant little woman, and a loyal wife: and I thought her splendid. My story was as fishy as the devil. I'll never think the less of either her or you.'

'It'll blow over, it must blow over,' said he.

'It never can,' I returned sighing: 'and don't you try to make it! Don't name me, unless it's with an oath. And get home to her right away. Good-bye, my best of friends. Good-bye, and God bless you. We shall never meet again.'

'Oh Loudon, that we should live to say such words!' he cried.

I had no views on life, beyond an occasional impulse to commit suicide, or to get drunk, and drifted down the street, semi-conscious, walking apparently on air, in the light-headedness of grief. I had money in my pocket, whether mine or my creditors' I had no means of guessing; and, the Poodle Dog lying in my path, I went mechanically in and took a table. A waiter attended me, and I suppose I gave my orders; for presently I found myself, with a sudden return of consciousness, beginning dinner. On the white cloth at my elbow lay the letter, addressed in a clerk's hand, and bearing an English stamp and the Edinburgh postmark. A bowl of bouillon and a glass of wine awakened in one corner of my brain (where all the rest was in mourning, the blinds down as for a funeral) a faint stir of curiosity; and while I waited the next course, wondering the while what I had ordered, I opened and began to read the epoch-making document.

'DEAR SIR, – I am charged with the melancholy duty of announcing to you the death of your excellent grandfather, Mr Alexander Loudon, on the 17th ult. On Sunday the 13th, he went to church as usual in the forenoon, and stopped on his way home, at the corner of Princes Street, in one of our seasonable east winds, to talk with an old friend. The same evening acute bronchitis declared itself; from the first, Dr M'Combie anticipated a fatal result, and the old gentleman appeared to have no illusion as to his own state. He repeatedly assured me it was "by" with him now; "and high time, too," he once added with characteristic asperity. He was not in the least changed on the approach of death: only (what I am sure must be very grateful to your feelings) he seemed to think and speak even more kindly than usual of yourself, referring to you as "Jeannie's yin," with strong expressions of regard. "He was the only one I ever liket of the hale jing-bang," was one of his expressions; and you will be glad to know that he dwelt particularly on the dutiful respect you had always displayed in your relations. The small codicil, by which he bequeaths you his Molesworth, and other professional works, was added (you will observe) on the day before his death; so that you were in his thoughts until the end. I should say that, though rather a trying patient, he was most tenderly nursed by your uncle, and your cousin, Miss Euphemia. I enclose a copy of the testament, by which you will see that you share equally with Mr Adam, and that I hold at your disposal a sum nearly approaching seventeen thousand pounds. I beg to congratulate you on this considerable acquisition, and expect your orders, to which I shall hasten to give my best attention. Thinking that you might desire to return at once to this country, and not knowing how you may be placed, I enclose a credit for six hundred pounds. Please sign the accompanying slip, and let me have it at your earliest convenience.

'I am, dear sir, yours truly,
'W. RUTHERFORD GREGG.'

'God bless the old gentleman!' I thought; 'and for that matter God bless Uncle Adam! and my cousin Euphemia!

and Mr Gregg!' I had a vision of that grey old life now brought to an end – 'and high time too' – a vision of those Sabbath streets alternately vacant and filled with silent people; of the babel of the bells, the long-drawn psalmody, the shrewd sting of the east wind, the hollow, echoing, dreary house to which 'Ecky' had returned with the hand of death already on his shoulder; a vision, too, of the long, rough country lad, perhaps a serious courtier of the lasses in the hawthorn den, perhaps a rustic dancer on the green, who had first earned and answered to that harsh diminutive. And I asked myself if, on the whole, poor Ecky had succeeded in life; if the last state of that man were not on the whole worse than the first; and the house in Randolph Crescent a less admirable dwelling than the hamlet where he saw the day and grew to manhood. Here was a consolatory thought for one who was himself a failure.

Yes, I declare the word came in my mind; and all the while, in another partition of the brain, I was glowing and singing for my new-found opulence. The pile of gold – four thousand two hundred and fifty double eagles, seventeen thousand ugly sovereigns, twenty-one thousand two hundred and fifty Napoleons – danced, and rang and ran molten, and lit up life with their effulgence, in the eye of fancy. Here were all things made plain to me: Paradise – Paris, I mean – regained, Carthew protected, Jim restored, the creditors . . .

'The creditors!' I repeated, and sank back benumbed. It was all theirs to the last farthing: my grandfather had died too soon to save me.

I must have somewhere a rare vein of decision. In that revolutionary moment I found myself prepared for all extremes except the one: ready to do anything, or to go anywhere, so long as I might save my money. At the worst, there was flight, flight to some of those blest countries where the serpent extradition has not yet entered in.

> On no condition is extradition
> Allowed in Callao!

– the old lawless words haunted me; and I saw myself hugging my gold in the company of such men as had once made and sung them, in the rude and bloody wharfside drinking shops of Chili and Peru. The run of my ill-luck, the breach of my old friendship, this bubble fortune flaunted for a moment in my eyes and snatched again, had made me desperate and (in the expressive vulgarism) ugly. To drink vile spirits among vile companions by the flare of a pine-torch; to go burthened with my furtive treasure in a belt; to fight for it knife in hand, rolling on a clay floor; to flee perpetually in fresh ships and to be chased through the sea from isle to isle, seemed, in my then frame of mind, a welcome series of events.

That was for the worst; but it began to dawn slowly on my mind that there was yet a possible better. Once escaped, once safe in Callao, I might approach my creditors with a good grace; and properly handled by a cunning agent, it was just possible they might accept some easy composition. The hope recalled me to the bankruptcy. It was strange, I reflected: often as I had questioned Jim, he had never obliged me with an answer. In his haste for news about the wreck, my own no less legitimate curiosity had gone disappointed. Hateful as the thought was to me, I must return at once and find out where I stood.

I left my dinner still unfinished, paying for the whole, of course, and tossing the waiter a gold piece. I was reckless; I knew not what was mine and cared not: I must take what I could get and give as I was able; to rob and to squander seemed the complimentary parts of my new destiny. I walked up Bush Street, whistling, brazening myself to confront Mamie in the first place, and the world at large and a certain visionary judge upon a bench in the second. Just outside I stopped and lighted a cigar to give me greater countenance; and puffing this and wearing what (I am sure) was a wretched assumption of braggadocio, I reappeared on the scene of my disgrace.

My friend and his wife were finishing a poor meal – rags of old mutton, the remainder cakes from breakfast eaten cold, and a starveling pot of coffee.

'I beg your pardon, Mrs Pinkerton,' said I. 'Sorry to inflict my presence where it cannot be desired; but there is a piece of business necessary to be discussed.'

'Pray do not consider me,' said Mamie, rising, and she sailed into the adjoining bedroom.

Jim watched her go and shook his head; he looked miserably old and ill.

'What is it now?' he asked.

'Perhaps you remember you answered none of my questions,' said I.

'Your questions?' faltered Jim.

'Even so, Jim; my questions,' I repeated. 'I put questions as well as yourself; and however little I may have satisfied Mamie with my answers, I beg to remind you that you gave me none at all.'

'You mean about the bankruptcy?' asked Jim.

I nodded.

He writhed in his chair. 'The straight truth is I was ashamed,' he said. 'I was trying to dodge you. I've been playing fast and loose with you, Loudon; I've deceived you from the first, I blush to own it. And here you came home and put the very question I was fearing. Why did we bust so soon? Your keen business eye had not deceived you. That's the point, that's my shame; that's what killed me this afternoon when Mamie was treating you so, and my conscience was telling me all the time, "Thou art the man."'

'What was it, Jim?' I asked,

'What I had been at all the time, Loudon,' he wailed; 'and I don't know how I'm to look you in the face and say it, after my duplicity. It was stocks,' he added in a whisper.

'And you were afraid to tell me that!' I cried. 'You poor, old, cheerless dreamer! what would it matter what you did or didn't? Can't you see we're doomed? And anyway, that's not my point. It's how I stand that I want to know. There is a particular reason. Am I clear? Have I a certificate, or what have I to do to get one? And when will it be dated? You can't think what hangs by it!'

'That's the worst of all,' said Jim, like a man in a dream, 'I can't see how to tell him!'

'What do you mean?' I cried, a small pang of terror at my heart.

'I'm afraid I sacrificed you, Loudon,' he said, looking at me pitifully.

'Sacrificed me?' I repeated. 'How? What do you mean by sacrifice?'

'I know it'll shock your delicate self-respect,' he said; 'but what was I to do? Things looked so bad. The receiver—' (as usual, the name stuck in his throat, and he began afresh). 'There was a lot of talk, the reporters were after me already; there was the trouble, and all about the Mexican business; and I got scared right out, and I guess I lost my head. You weren't there, you see, and that was my temptation.'

I did not know how long he might thus beat about the bush with dreadful hintings, and I was already beside myself with terror. What had he done? I saw he had been tempted; I knew from his letters that he was in no condition to resist. How had he sacrificed the absent?

'Jim,' I said, 'you must speak right out. I've got all that I can carry.'

'Well,' he said – 'I know it was a liberty – I made it out you were no business man, only a stone-broke painter; that half the time you didn't know anything anyway, particularly money and accounts. I said you never could be got to understand whose was whose. I had to say that because of some entries in the books— '

'For God's sake,' I cried, 'put me out of this agony! What did you accuse me of?'

'Accuse you of?' repeated Jim. 'Of what I'm telling you. And there being no deed of partnership, I made out you were only a kind of clerk that I called a partner just to give you taffy; and so I got you ranked a creditor on the estate for your wages and the money you had lent. And— '

I believe I reeled. 'A creditor!' I roared; 'a creditor! I'm not in the bankruptcy at all?'

'No,' said Jim. 'I know it was a liberty— '

'Oh damn your liberty! read that,' I cried, dashing the letter before him on the table, 'and call in your wife, and be done with eating this truck' – as I spoke, I slung the cold mutton in the empty grate – 'and let's all go and have a champagne supper. I've dined – I'm sure I don't remember what I had; I'd dine again ten scores of times upon a night like this. Read it, you blaying ass! I'm not insane. Here, Mamie,' I continued, opening the bedroom door, 'come out and make it up with me, and go and kiss your husband; and I'll tell you what, after the supper, let's go to some place where there's a band, and I'll waltz with you till sunrise.'

'What does it all mean?' cried Jim.

'It means we have a champagne supper tonight, and

all go to Vapor Valley or to Monterey tomorrow,' said I. 'Mamie, go and get your things on; and you, Jim, sit down right where you are, take a sheet of paper, and tell Franklin Dodge to go to Texas. Mamie, you were right, my dear; I was rich all the time, and didn't know it.'

CHAPTER NINETEEN

Travels with a Shyster

The absorbing and disastrous adventure of the *Flying Scud* was now quite ended; we had dashed into these deep waters and we had escaped again to starve; we had been ruined and were saved, had quarrelled and made up; there remained nothing but to sing *Te Deum*, draw a line, and begin on a fresh page of my unwritten diary. I do not pretend that I recovered all I had lost with Mamie, it would have been more than I had merited; and I had certainly been more uncommunicative than became either the partner or the friend. But she accepted the position handsomely; and during the week that I now passed with them, both she and Jim had the grace to spare me questions. It was to Calistoga that we went; there was some rumour of a Napa land-boom at the moment, the possibility of stir attracted Jim, and he informed me he would find a certain joy in looking on, much as Napoleon on St Helena took a pleasure to read military works. The field of his ambition was quite closed; he was done with action, and looked forward to a ranch in a mountain dingle, a patch of corn, a pair of kine, a leisurely and contemplative age in the green shade of forests. 'Just let me get down on my back in a hayfield,' said he, 'and you'll find there's no more snap to me than that much putty.'

And for two days the perfervid being actually rested. The third, he was observed in consultation with the local editor, and owned he was in two minds about purchasing the press and paper. 'It's a kind of a hold for an idle man,' he said pleadingly; 'and if the section was to open up the way it ought to, there might be dollars in the thing.' On the fourth day he was gone till dinner-time alone; on the fifth we made a long picnic drive to the fresh field of enterprise; and the sixth was passed entirely in the preparation of prospectuses. The pioneer of McBride City was already upright and self-reliant as of yore; the fire rekindled in his eye, the ring restored to his voice; a charger sniffing battle and saying ha-ha among the spears. On the seventh morning we signed a deed of partnership, for Jim would not accept a dollar of my money otherwise; and having once more engaged myself – or that mortal part of me, my purse – among the wheels of his machinery, I returned alone to San Francisco and took quarters in the Palace Hotel.

The same night I had Nares to dinner. His sunburnt face, his queer and personal strain of talk, recalled days that were scarce over and that seemed already distant. Through the music of the band outside, and the chink and clatter of the dining-room, it seemed to me as if I heard the foaming of the surf and the voices of the sea-birds about Midway Island. The bruises on our hands were not yet healed; and there we sat, waited on by elaborate darkies, eating pompino and drinking iced champagne.

'Think of our dinners on the *Norah*, captain, and then oblige me by looking round the room for contrast.'

He took the scene in slowly. 'Yes, it is like a dream,' he said: 'like as if the darkies were really about as big as dimes; and a great big scuttle might open up there, and Johnson stick in a great big head and shoulders, and cry, "Eight bells!" – and the whole thing vanish.'

'Well, it's the other thing that has done that,' I replied. 'It's all bygone now, all dead and buried. Amen! say I.'

'I don't know that, Mr Dodd; and to tell you the fact, I don't believe it,' said Nares. 'There's more *Flying Scud* in the oven; and the baker's name, I take it, is Bellairs. He tackled me the day we came in: sort of a razee of poor old humanity – jury clothes – full new suit of pimples: knew him at once from your description. I let him pump me till I saw his game. He knows a good deal that we don't know, a good deal that we do, and suspects the balance. There's trouble brewing for somebody.'

I was surprised I had not thought of this before. Bellairs had been behind the scenes; he had known Dickson; he knew the flight of the crew; it was hardly possible but what he should suspect; it was certain if he suspected, that he would seek to trade on the suspicion. And sure enough, I was not yet dressed the next morning ere the lawyer was knocking at my door. I let him in, for I was curious; and he, after some ambiguous prolegomena, roundly proposed I should go shares with him.

'Shares in what?' I inquired.

'If you will allow me to clothe my idea in a somewhat vulgar form,' said he, 'I might ask you, did you go to Midway for your health?'

'I don't know that I did,' I replied.

'Similarly, Mr Dodd, you may be sure I would never have taken the present step without influential grounds,' pursued the lawyer. 'Intrusion is foreign to my character. But you and I, sir, are engaged on the same ends. If we can continue to work the thing in company, I place at your disposal my knowledge of the law and a considerable practice in delicate negotiations similar to this. Should you refuse to consent, you might find in me a formidable and' – he hesitated –' and to my own regret, perhaps a dangerous competitor.'

'Did you get this by heart?' I asked genially.

'I advise *you* to!' he said, with a sudden sparkle of temper and menace, instantly gone, instantly succeeded by fresh cringing. 'I assure you, sir, I arrive in the character of a friend, and I believe you underestimate my information. If I may instance an example, I am acquainted to the last dime with what you made (or rather lost), and I know you have since cashed a considerable draft on London.'

'What do you infer?' I asked.

'I know where that draft came from,' he cried, wincing back like one who has greatly dared, and instantly regrets the venture.

'So?' said I.

'You forget I was Mr Dickson's confidential agent,' he explained. 'You had his address, Mr Dodd. We were the only two that he communicated with in San Francisco. You see my deductions are quite obvious; you see how open and frank I deal with you, as I should wish to do with any gentleman with whom I was conjoined in business. You see how much I know; and it can scarcely escape your strong common-sense how much better it would be if I knew all. You cannot hope to get rid of me at this time of day; I have my place in the affair, I cannot be shaken off; I am, if you will excuse a rather technical pleasantry, an encumbrance on the estate. The actual harm I can do I leave you to valuate for yourself. But without going so far, Mr Dodd, and without in any way inconveniencing myself, I could make things very uncomfortable. For instance, Mr Pinkerton's liquidation. You and I know, sir – and you better than I – on what a large fund you draw. Is Mr Pinkerton in the thing at all? It was you only who knew the address, and you were concealing it. Suppose I should communicate with Mr Pinkerton— '

'Look here!' I interrupted, 'communicate with him (if you will permit me to clothe my idea in a vulgar shape) till you are blue in the face. There is only one person with whom I refuse to allow you to communicate farther, and that is myself. Good-morning.'

He could not conceal his rage, disappointment, and surprise; and in the passage (I have no doubt) was shaken by St Vitus.

I was disgusted by this interview; it struck me hard to be suspected on all hands, and to hear again from this trafficker what I had heard already from Jim's wife; and yet my strongest impression was different and might rather be described as an impersonal fear. There was something against nature in the man's craven impudence; it was as though a lamb had butted me; such daring at the hands of such a dastard implied unchangeable resolve, a great pressure of necessity, and powerful means. I thought of the unknown Carthew, and it sickened me to see this ferret on his trail.

Upon inquiry I found the lawyer was but just disbarred for some malpractice, and the discovery added excessively to my disquiet. Here was a rascal without money or the means of making it, thrust out of the doors of his own trade, publicly shamed, and doubtless in a deuce of a bad temper with the universe. Here, on the other hand, was a man with a secret – rich, terrified, practically in hiding – who had been willing to pay ten thousand pounds for the bones of the *Flying Scud*. I slipped insensibly into a mental alliance with the victim. The business weighed on me all day long; I was wondering how much the lawyer knew, how much he guessed, and when he would open his attack.

Some of these problems are unsolved to this day; others were soon made clear. Where he got Carthew's name is still a mystery; perhaps some sailor on the *Tempest*, perhaps my own sea-lawyer served him for a tool; but I was actually at his elbow when he learned the address. It fell so. One evening when I had an engagement, and was killing time until the hour, I chanced to walk in the court of the hotel while the band played. The place was bright as day with the electric light, and I recognised, at some distance among the loiterers, the person of Bellairs in talk with a gentleman whose face appeared familiar. It was certainly someone I had seen, and seen recently; but who or where I knew not. A porter standing hard by gave me the necessary hint. The stranger was an English navy man invalided home from Honolulu, where he had left his ship; indeed, it was only from the change of clothes and the effects of sickness that I had not immediately recognised my friend and correspondent, Lieutenant Sebright.

The conjunction of these planets seeming ominous, I drew near; but it seemed Bellairs had done his business; he vanished in the crowd, and I found my officer alone.

'Do you know whom you have been talking to, Mr Sebright?' I began.

'No,' said he; 'I don't know him from Adam. Anything wrong?'

'He is a disreputable lawyer, recently disbarred,' said I. 'I wish I had seen you in time. I trust you told him nothing about Carthew?'

He flushed to his ears. 'I'm awfully sorry,' he said. 'He seemed civil, and I wanted to get rid of him. It was only the address he asked.'

'And you gave it?' I cried.

'I'm really awfully sorry,' said Sebright. 'I'm afraid I did.'

'God forgive you!' was my only comment, and I turned my back upon the blunderer.

The fat was in the fire now: Bellairs had the address, and I was the more deceived or Carthew would have news of him. So strong was this impression, and so painful, that the next morning I had the curiosity to pay the lawyer's den a visit. An old woman was scrubbing the stair, and the board was down.

'Lawyer Bellairs?' said the old woman; 'gone East this morning. There's Lawyer Dean next block up.'

I did not trouble Lawyer Dean, but walked slowly back

to my hotel, ruminating as I went. The image of the old woman washing that desecrated stair had struck my fancy; it seemed that all the water supply of the city and all the soap in the State would scarce suffice to cleanse it, it had been so long a clearing-house of dingy secrets and a factory of sordid fraud. And now the corner was untenanted; some judge, like a careful housewife, had knocked down the web, and the bloated spider was scuttling elsewhere after new victims. I had of late (as I have said) insensibly taken sides with Carthew; now when his enemy was at his heels, my interest grew more warm; and I began to wonder if I could not help. The drama of the *Flying Scud* was entering on a new phase. It had been singular from the first: it promised an extraordinary conclusion; and I who had paid so much to learn the beginning, might pay a little more and see the end. I lingered in San Francisco, indemnifying myself after the hardships of the cruise, spending money, regretting it, continually promising departure for the morrow. Why not go indeed, and keep a watch upon Bellairs? If I missed him, there was no harm done, I was the nearer Paris. If I found and kept his trail, it was hard if I could not put some stick in his machinery, and at the worst I could promise myself interesting scenes and revelations.

In such a mixed humour, I made up what it pleases me to call my mind, and once more involved myself in the story of Carthew and the *Flying Scud*. The same night I wrote a letter of farewell to Jim, and one of anxious warning to Dr Urquart begging him to set Carthew on his guard; the morrow saw me in the ferry-boat; and ten days later, I was walking the hurricane deck on the *City of Denver*. By that time my mind was pretty much made down again, its natural condition: I told myself that I was bound for Paris or Fontainebleau to resume the study of the arts; and I thought no more of Carthew or Bellairs, or only to smile at my own fondness. The one I could not serve, even if I wanted; the other I had no means of finding, even if I could have at all influenced him after he was found.

And for all that, I was close on the heels of an absurd adventure. My neighbour at table that evening was a 'Frisco man whom I knew slightly. I found he had crossed the plains two days in front of me, and this was the first steamer that had left New York for Europe since his arrival. Two days before me, meant a day before Bellairs; and dinner was scarce done before I was closeted with the purser.

'Bellairs?' he repeated. 'Not in the saloon, I am sure. He may be in the second class. The lists are not made out, but – Hullo! "Harry D. Bellairs?" That the name? He's there right enough.'

And the next morning I saw him on the forward deck, sitting in a chair, a book in his hand, a shabby puma skin rug about his knees: the picture of respectable decay. Off and on, I kept him in my eye. He read a good deal, he stood and looked upon the sea, he talked occasionally with his neighbours, and once when a child fell he picked it up and soothed it. I damned him in my heart; the book, which I was sure he did not read – the sea, to which I was ready to take oath he was indifferent – the child, whom I was certain he would as lieve have tossed overboard – all seemed to me elements in a theatrical performance; and I made no doubt he was already nosing after the secrets of his fellow-passengers. I took no pains to conceal myself, my scorn for the creature being as strong as my disgust. But he never looked my way, and it was night before I learned he had observed me.

I was smoking by the engine-room door, for the air was a little sharp, when a voice rose close beside me in the darkness.

'I beg your pardon, Mr Dodd,' it said.

'That you, Bellairs?' I replied.

'A single word, sir. Your presence on this ship has no connection with our interview?' he asked. 'You have no idea, Mr Dodd, of returning upon your determination?'

'None,' said I; and then, seeing he still lingered, I was polite enough to add 'Good-evening;' at which he sighed and went away.

The next day he was there again with the chair and the puma skin; read his book and looked at the sea with the same constancy; and though there was no child to be picked up, I observed him to attend repeatedly on a sick woman. Nothing fosters suspicion like the act of watching; a man spied upon can hardly blow his nose but we accuse him of designs; and I took an early opportunity to go forward and see the woman for myself. She was poor, elderly, and painfully plain; I stood abashed at the sight, felt I owed Bellairs amends for the injustice of my thoughts, and seeing him standing by the rail in his usual attitude of contemplation, walked up and addressed him by name.

'You seem very fond of the sea,' said I.

'I may really call it a passion, Mr Dodd,' he replied. '"*And the tall cataract haunted me like a passion*,"' he quoted. 'I never weary of the sea, sir. This is my first ocean voyage. I find it a glorious experience.' And once more my disbarred lawyer dropped into poetry: '"*Roll on, thou deep and dark blue ocean, roll!*"'

Though I had learned the piece in my reading-book at school, I came into the world a little too late on the one hand – and I daresay a little too early on the other – to think much of Byron; and the sonorous verse, prodigiously well delivered, struck me with surprise.

'You are fond of poetry, too?' I asked.

'I am a great reader,' he replied. 'At one time I had begun to amass quite a small but well selected library; and when that was scattered, I still managed to preserve a few volumes – chiefly of pieces designed for recitation – which have been my travelling companions.'

'Is that one of them?' I asked, pointing to the volume in his hand.

'No, sir,' he replied, showing me a translation of the 'Sorrows of Werther,' 'that is a novel I picked up some time ago. It has afforded me great pleasure though immoral.'

'Oh, immoral!' cried I, indignant as usual at any implication of art and ethics.

'Surely you cannot deny that, sir – if you know the book,' he said. 'The passion is illicit, although certainly drawn with a good deal of pathos. It is not a work one could possibly put into the hands of a lady; which is to be regretted on all accounts, for I do not know how it may strike you; but it seems to me – as a depiction, if I make myself clear – to rise high above its compeers – even famous compeers. Even in Scott, Dickens, Thackeray, or Hawthorne, the sentiment of love appears to me to be frequently done less justice to.'

'You are expressing a very general opinion,' said I.

'Is that so, indeed, sir?' he exclaimed, with unmistakable excitement. 'Is the book well known? and who was *Go-eath*? I am interested in that, because upon the title-page the usual initials are omitted, and it runs simply "by *Go-eath*." Was he an author of distinction? Has he written other works?'

Such was our first interview, the first of many; and in all he showed the same attractive qualities and defects. His taste for literature was native and unaffected; his sentimentality, although extreme and a thought ridiculous, was plainly genuine. I wondered at my own innocent wonder. I knew that Homer nodded, that Cæsar had compiled a jest-book, that Turner lived by preference the life of Puggy Booth, that Shelley made paper boats, and Wordsworth wore green spectacles! and with all this mass of evidence before me, I had expected Bellairs to be entirely of one piece, subdued to what he worked in, a spy all through. As I abominated the man's trade, so I had expected to detest the man himself; and behold, I liked him. Poor devil! he was essentially a man on wires, all sensibility and tremor, brimful of a cheap poetry, not without parts, quite without courage. His boldness was despair; the gulf behind him thrust him on; he was one of those who might commit a murder rather than confess the theft of a postage-stamp. I was sure that his coming interview with Carthew rode his imagination like a nightmare; when the thought crossed his mind, I used to think I knew of it, and that the qualm appeared in his face visibly. Yet he would never flinch. Necessity stalking at his back, famine (his old pursuer) talking in his ear; and I used to wonder whether I most admired, or most despised, this quivering heroism for evil. The image that occurred to me after his visit was just; I had been butted by a lamb, and the phase of life that I was now studying might be called the Revolt of a Sheep.

It could be said of him that he had learned in sorrow what he taught in song – or wrong; and his life was that of one of his victims. He was born in the back parts of the State of New York; his father a farmer, who became subsequently bankrupt and went West. The lawyer and money-lender who had ruined this poor family seems to have conceived in the end a feeling of remorse; he turned the father out indeed, but he offered, in compensation, to charge himself with one of the sons: and Harry, the fifth child and already sickly, was chosen to be left behind. He made himself useful in the office: picked up the scattered rudiments of an education; read right and left; attended and debated at the Young Men's Christian Association; and in all his early years, was the model for a good story-book. His landlady's daughter was his bane. He showed me her photograph; she was a big, handsome, dashing, dressy, vulgar hussy, without character, without tenderness, without mind, and (as the result proved) without virtue. The sickly and timid boy was in the house; he was handy; when she was otherwise unoccupied, she used and played with him – Romeo and Cressida; till in that dreary life of a poor boy in a country town, she grew to be the light of his days and the subject of his dreams. He worked hard, like Jacob, for a wife; he surpassed his patron in sharp practice; he was made head clerk; and the same night, encouraged by a hundred freedoms, depressed by the sense of his youth and his infirmities, he offered marriage and was received with laughter. Not a year had passed, before his master, conscious of growing infirmities, took him for a partner. He proposed again; he was accepted; led two years of troubled married life; and awoke one morning to find his wife had run away with a dashing drummer, and had left him heavily in debt. The debt, and not the drummer, was supposed to be the cause of the hegira; she had concealed her liabilities, they were on the point of bursting forth, she was weary of Bellairs; and she took the drummer as she might have taken a cab. The blow disabled her husband, his partner was dead; he was now alone in the business, for which he was no longer fit; the debts hampered him; bankruptcy followed; and he fled from city to city, falling daily into lower practice. It is to be considered that he had been taught, and had learned as a delightful duty, a kind of business whose highest merit is to escape the commentaries of the bench: that of the usurious lawyer in a county town. With this training, he was now shot, a penniless stranger, into the deeper gulfs of cities; and the result is scarce a thing to be surprised at.

'Have you heard of your wife again?' I asked.

He displayed a pitiful agitation. 'I am afraid you will think ill of me,' he said.

'Have you taken her back?' I asked.

'No, sir. I trust I have too much self-respect,' he answered, 'and, at least, I was never tempted. She won't come, she dislikes, she seems to have conceived a positive distaste for me, and yet I was considered an indulgent husband.'

'You are still in relations, then?' I asked.

'I place myself in your hands, Mr Dodd,' he replied. 'The world is very hard; I have found it bitter hard myself – bitter hard to live. How much worse for a woman, and one who has placed herself (by her own misconduct, I am far from denying that) in so unfortunate a position!'

'In short, you support her?' I suggested.

'I cannot deny it. I practically do,' he admitted. 'It has been a millstone round my neck. But I think she is grateful. You can see for yourself.'

He handed me a letter in a sprawling, ignorant hand, but written with violet ink on fine, pink paper, with a monogram. It was very foolishly expressed, and I thought (except for a few obvious cajoleries) very heartless and greedy in meaning. The writer said she had been sick, which I disbelieved; declared the last remittance was all gone in doctor's bills, for which I took the liberty of substituting dress, drink, and monograms; and prayed for an increase, which I could only hope had been denied her.

'I think she is really grateful?' he asked, with some eagerness, as I returned it.

'I daresay,' said I. 'Has she any claim on you?'

'Oh, no, sir. I divorced her,' he replied. 'I have a very strong sense of self-respect in such matters, and I divorced her immediately.'

'What sort of life is she leading now?' I asked.

'I will not deceive you, Mr Dodd. I do not know, I make a point of not knowing; it appears more dignified. I have been very harshly criticised,' he added, sighing.

It will be seen that I had fallen into an ignominious intimacy with the man I had gone out to thwart. My pity for the creature, his admiration for myself, his pleasure in my society, which was clearly unassumed, were the bonds with which I was fettered; perhaps I should add, in honesty, my own ill-regulated interest in the phases of life and human character. The fact is (at least) that we spent hours together daily, and that I was nearly as much on the forward deck as in the saloon. Yet all the while I could never forget he was a shabby trickster, embarked that very moment in a dirty enterprise. I used to tell myself at first that our acquaintance was a stroke of art, and that I was somehow fortifying Carthew. I told myself, I say; but I was no such fool as to believe it, even then. In these circumstances I displayed the two chief qualities of my character on the largest scale – my helplessness and my instinctive love of procrastination – and fell upon a course of action so ridiculous that I blush when I recall it.

We reached Liverpool one forenoon, the rain falling thickly and insidiously on the filthy town. I had no plans, beyond a sensible unwillingness to let my rascal escape; and I ended by going to the same inn with him, dining with him, walking with him in the wet streets, and hearing with him in a penny gaff that venerable piece, *The Ticket-of-Leave Man*. It was one of his first visits to a theatre, against which places of entertainment he had a strong prejudice; and his innocent, pompous talk, innocent old quotations, and innocent reverence for the character of Hawkshaw delighted me beyond relief. In charity to myself, I dwell upon and perhaps exaggerate my pleasures. I have need of all conceivable excuses when I confess that I went to bed without one word upon the matter of Carthew, but not without having covenanted with my rascal for a visit to Chester the next day. At Chester we did the cathedral, walked on the walls, discussed Shakespeare and the musical glasses – and made a fresh engagement for the morrow. I do not know, and I am glad to have forgotten, how long these travels were continued. We visited at least, by singular zigzags, Stratford, Warwick, Coventry, Gloucester, Bristol, Bath, and Wells. At each stage we spoke dutifully of the scene and its associations; I sketched, the Shyster spouted poetry and copied epitaphs. Who could doubt we were the usual Americans, travelling with a design of self-improvement? Who was to guess that one was a blackmailer, trembling to approach the scene of action – the other a helpless, amateur detective, waiting on events?

It is unnecessary to remark that none occurred, or none the least suitable with my design of protecting Carthew. Two trifles, indeed, completed though they scarcely changed my conception of the Shyster. The first was observed in Gloucester, where we spent Sunday, and I proposed we should hear service in the cathedral. To my surprise, the creature had an _ism_ of his own, to which he was loyal; and he left me to go alone to the cathedral – or perhaps not to go at all – and stole off down a deserted alley to some Bethel or Ebenezer of the proper shade. When we met again at lunch, I rallied him, and he grew restive.

'You need employ no circumlocutions with me, Mr Dodd,' he said suddenly. 'You regard my behaviour from an unfavourable point of view: you regard me, I much fear, as hypocritical.'

I was somewhat confused by the attack. 'You know what I think of your trade,' I replied lamely and coarsely.

'Excuse me, if I seem to press the subject,' he continued, 'but if you think my life erroneous, would you have me neglect the means of grace? Because you consider me in the wrong on one point, would you have me place myself on the wrong in all? Surely, sir, the church is for the sinner.'

'Did you ask a blessing on your present enterprise?' I sneered.

He had a bad attack of St Vitus, his face was changed, and his eyes flashed. 'I will tell you what I did,' he cried. 'I prayed for an unfortunate man and a wretched woman whom he tries to support.'

I cannot pretend that I found any repartee.

The second incident was at Bristol, where I lost sight of my gentleman some hours. From this eclipse he returned to me with thick speech, wandering footsteps, and a back all whitened with plaster. I had half expected, yet I could have wept to see it. All disabilities were piled on that weak back – domestic misfortune, nervous disease, a displeasing exterior, empty pockets, and the slavery of vice.

I will never deny that our prolonged conjunction was the result of double cowardice. Each was afraid to leave the other, each was afraid to speak, or knew not what to say. Save for my ill-judged allusion at Gloucester, the subject uppermost in both our minds was buried. Carthew, Stallbridge-le-Carthew, Stallbridge-Minster – which we had long since (and severally) identified to be the nearest station – even the name of Dorsetshire was studiously avoided. And yet we were making progress all the time, tacking across broad England like an unweatherly vessel on a wind; approaching our destination, not openly, but by a sort of flying sap. And at length, I can scarce tell how, we were set down by a dilatory butt-end of local train on the untenanted platform of Stallbridge-Minster.

The town was ancient and compact – a domino of tiled houses and walled gardens, dwarfed by the disproportionate bigness of the church. From the midst of the thoroughfare which divided it in half, fields and trees were visible at either end; and through the sally-port of every street, there flowed in from the country a silent invasion of green grass. Bees and birds appeared to make the majority of the inhabitants; every garden had its row of hives, the eaves of every house were plastered with the nests of swallows, and the pinnacles of the church were flickered about all day long by a multitude of wings. The town was of Roman foundation; and as I looked out that afternoon from the low windows of the inn, I should scarce have been surprised to see a centurion coming up the street with a fatigue draft of legionaires. In short, Stallbridge-Minster was one of those towns which appear to be maintained by England for the instruction and delight of the American rambler; to which he seems guided by an instinct not less surprising than the setter's; and which he visits and quits with equal enthusiasm.

I was not at all in the humour of the tourist. I had wasted weeks of time and accomplished nothing; we were on the eve of the engagement, and I had neither plans nor allies. I had thrust myself into the trade of private providence, and amateur detective; I was spending money and I was reaping disgrace. All the time I kept telling myself that I must at least speak; that this ignominious silence should have been broken long ago, and must be broken now. I should have broken it when he first proposed to come to Stallbridge-Minster; I should have broken it in the train; I should break it there and then, on the inn doorstep, as the omnibus rolled off. I turned toward him at the thought; he seemed to wince, the words died on my lips, and I proposed instead that we should visit the Minster.

While we were engaged upon this duty, it came on to rain in a manner worthy of the tropics. The vault reverberated; every gargoyle instantly poured its full discharge; we waded back to the inn, ankle deep in impromptu brooks; and the rest of the afternoon sat weatherbound, hearkening to the sonorous deluge. For two hours I talked of indifferent matters, laboriously feeding the conversation; for two hours my mind was quite made up to do my duty instantly – and at each particular instant I postponed it till the next. To screw up my faltering courage, I called at dinner for some sparkling wine. It proved when it came to be detestable; I could not put it to my lips; and Bellairs, who had as much palate as a weevil, was left to finish it himself. Doubtless the wine flushed him; doubtless he may have observed my embarrassment of the afternoon; doubtless he was conscious that we were approaching a crisis, and that that evening, if I did not join with him, I must declare myself an open enemy. At least he fled. Dinner was done; this was the time when I had bound myself to break my silence; no more delays were to be allowed, no more excuses received. I went upstairs after some tobacco, which I felt to be a mere necessity in the circumstances: and when I returned, the man was gone. The waiter told me he had left the house.

The rain still plumped, like a vast shower-bath, over the deserted town. The night was dark and windless: the street lit glimmeringly from end to end, lamps, house windows, and the reflections in the rain-pools all contributing. From a public-house on the other side of the way, I heard a harp twang and a doleful voice upraised in the 'Larboard Watch,' 'The Anchor's Weighed,' and other naval ditties. Where had my shyster wandered? In all likelihood to that lyrical tavern; there was no choice of diversion; in comparison with Stallbridge-Minster on a rainy night, a sheepfold would seem gay.

Again I passed in review the points of my interview, on which I was always constantly resolved so long as my adversary was absent from the scene, and again they struck me as inadequate. From this dispiriting exercise I turned to the native amusements of the inn coffee-room, and studied for some time the mezzotints that frowned upon the wall. The railway guide, after showing me how soon I could leave Stallbridge and how quickly I could reach Paris, failed to hold my attention. An illustrated advertisement book of hotels brought me very low indeed; and when it came to the local paper, I could have wept. At this point, I found a passing solace in a copy of Whitaker's Almanack, and obtained in fifty minutes more information than I have yet been able to use.

Then a fresh apprehension assailed me. Suppose Bellairs had given me the slip? Suppose he was now rolling on the road to Stallbridge-le-Carthew? or perhaps there already and laying before a very white-faced auditor his threats and propositions? A hasty person might have instantly pursued. Whatever I am, I am not hasty, and I was aware of three grave objections. In the first place, I could not be certain that Bellairs was gone. In the second, I had no taste whatever for a long drive at that hour of the night and in so merciless a rain. In the third, I had no idea how I was to get admitted if I went, and no idea what I should say if I got admitted. 'In short,' I concluded, 'the whole situation is the merest farce. You have thrust yourself in where you had no business and have no power. You would be quite as useful in San Francisco; far happier in Paris; and being (by the wrath of God) at Stallbridge-Minster, the wisest thing is to go quietly to bed.' On the way to my room, I saw (in a flash) that which I ought to have done long ago, and which it was now too late to think of – written to Carthew, I mean, detailing the facts and describing Bellairs, letting him defend himself if he were able, and giving him time to flee if he were not. It was the last blow to my self-respect; and I flung myself into my bed with contumely.

I have no guess what hour it was when I was wakened by the entrance of Bellairs carrying a candle. He had been drunk, for he was bedaubed with mire from head to foot; but he was now sober and under the empire of some violent emotion which he controlled with difficulty. He trembled visibly; and more than once, during the interview which followed, tears suddenly and silently overflowed his cheeks.

'I have to ask your pardon, sir, for this untimely visit,' he said. 'I make no defence, I have no excuse, I have disgraced myself, I am properly punished; I appear before you to appeal to you in mercy for the most trifling aid or, God help me! I fear I may go mad.'

'What on earth is wrong?' I asked.

'I have been robbed,' he said. 'I have no defence to offer; it was of my own fault, I am properly punished.'

'But, gracious goodness me!' I cried, 'who is there to rob you in a place like this?'

'I can form no opinion,' he replied. 'I have no idea. I was

lying in a ditch inanimate. This is a degrading confession, sir; I can only say in self-defence that perhaps (in your good-nature) you have made yourself partly responsible for my shame. I am not used to these rich wines.'

'In what form was your money? Perhaps it may be traced,' I suggested.

'It was in English sovereigns. I changed it in New York; I got very good exchange,' he said, and then, with a momentary outbreak, 'God in heaven, how I toiled for it!' he cried.

'That doesn't sound encouraging,' said I. 'It may be worth while to apply to the police, but it doesn't sound a hopeful case.'

'And I have no hope in that direction,' said Bellairs. 'My hopes, Mr Dodd, are all fixed upon yourself. I could easily convince you that a small, a very small advance, would be in the nature of an excellent investment; but I prefer to rely on your humanity. Our acquaintance began on an unusual footing; but you have now known me for some time, we have been some time – I was going to say we had been almost intimate. Under the impulse of instinctive sympathy, I have bared my heart to you, Mr Dodd, as I have done to few; and I believe – I trust – I may say that I feel sure – you heard me with a kindly sentiment. This is what brings me to your side at this most inexcusable hour. But put yourself in my place – how could I sleep – how could I dream of sleeping, in this blackness of remorse and despair? There was a friend at hand – so I ventured to think of you; it was instinctive: I fled to your side, as the drowning man clutches at a straw. These expressions are not exaggerated, they scarcely serve to express the agitation of my mind. And think, sir, how easily you can restore me to hope and, I may say, to reason. A small loan, which shall be faithfully repaid. Five hundred dollars would be ample.' He watched me with burning eyes. 'Four hundred would do. I believe, Mr Dodd, that I could manage with economy on two.'

'And then you will repay me out of Carthew's pocket?' I said. 'I am much obliged. But I will tell you what I will do: I will see you on board a steamer, pay your fare through to San Francisco, and place fifty dollars in the purser's hands, to be given you in New York.'

He drank in my words; his face represented an ecstasy

of cunning thought. I could read there, plain as print, that he but thought to overreach me.

'And what am I to do in 'Frisco?' he asked. 'I am disbarred, I have no trade, I cannot dig, to beg— ' he paused in the citation. 'And you know that I am not alone,' he added, 'others depend upon me.'

'I will write to Pinkerton,' I returned. 'I feel sure he can help you to some employment, and in the meantime, and for three months after your arrival, he shall pay to yourself personally, on the first and the fifteenth, twenty-five dollars.'

'Mr Dodd, I scarce believe you can be serious in this offer,' he replied. 'Have you forgotten the circumstances of the case? Do you know these people are the magnates of the section? They were spoken of tonight in the saloon; their wealth must amount to many millions of dollars in real estate alone; their house is one of the sights of the locality, and you offer me a bribe of a few hundred!'

'I offer you no bribe, Mr Bellairs, I give you alms,' I returned. 'I will do nothing to forward you in your hateful business; yet I would not willingly have you starve.'

'Give me a hundred dollars then, and be done with it,' he cried.

'I will do what I have said, and neither more nor less,' said I.

'Take care,' he cried. 'You are playing a fool's game; you are making an enemy for nothing; you will gain nothing by this, I warn you of it!' And then with one of his changes, 'Seventy dollars – only seventy – in mercy, Mr Dodd, in common charity. Don't dash the bowl from my lips! You have a kindly heart. Think of my position, remember my unhappy wife.'

'You should have thought of her before,' said I. 'I have made my offer, and I wish to sleep.'

'Is that your last word, sir? Pray consider; pray weigh both sides: my misery, your own danger. I warn you – I beseech you; measure it well before you answer,' so he half pleaded, half threatened me, with clasped hands.

'My first word, and my last,' said I.

The change upon the man was shocking. In the storm of anger that now shook him, the lees of his intoxication rose again to the surface; his face was deformed, his words insane with fury; his pantomime, excessive in itself, was distorted by an access of St. Vitus.

'You will perhaps allow me to inform you of my cold opinion,' he began, apparently self-possessed, truly bursting with rage: 'when I am a glorified saint, I shall see you howling for a drop of water and exult to see you. That your last word! Take it in your face, you spy, you false friend, you fat hypocrite! I defy, I defy and despise and spit upon you! I'm on the trail, his trail or yours, I smell blood, I'll follow it on my hands and knees, I'll starve to follow it! I'll hunt you down, hunt you, hunt you down! If I were strong, I'd tear your vitals out, here in this room – tear them out – I'd tear them out! Damn, damn, damn! You think me weak? I can bite, bite to the blood, bite you, hurt you, disgrace you . . .'

He was thus incoherently raging when the scene was interrupted by the arrival of the landlord and inn servants in various degrees of deshabille, and to them I gave my temporary lunatic in charge.

'Take him to his room,' I said, 'he's only drunk.'

These were my words; but I knew better. After all my study of Mr Bellairs, one discovery had been reserved for the last moment – that of his latent and essential madness.

CHAPTER TWENTY

Stallbridge-le-Carthew

Long before I was awake, the shyster had disappeared, leaving his bill unpaid. I did not need to inquire where he was gone, I knew too well, I knew there was nothing left me but to follow; and about ten in the morning, set forth in a gig for Stallbridge-le-Carthew.

The road, for the first quarter of the way, deserts the valley of the river, and crosses the summit of a chalk-down, grazed over by flocks of sheep and haunted by innumerable larks. It was a pleasant but a vacant scene, arousing but not holding the attention; and my mind returned to the violent passage of the night before. My thought of the man I was pursuing had been greatly changed. I conceived of him, somewhere in front of me, upon his dangerous errand, not to be turned aside, not to be stopped, by either fear or reason. I had called him a ferret; I conceived him now as a mad dog. Methought he would run, not walk; methought, as he ran, that he would bark and froth at the lips; methought, if the great wall of China were to rise across his path, he would attack it with his nails.

Presently the road left the down, returned by a precipitous descent into the valley of the Stall, and ran thenceforward among enclosed fields and under the continuous shade of trees. I was told we had now entered on the Carthew property. By and by, a battlemented wall appeared on the left hand, and a little after I had my first glimpse of the mansion. It stood in a hollow of a bosky park, crowded to a degree that surprised and even displeased me, with huge timber and dense shrubberies of laurel and rhododendron. Even from this low station and the thronging neighbourhood of the trees, the pile rose conspicuous like a cathedral. Behind, as we continued to skirt the park wall, I began to make out a straggling town of offices which became conjoined to the rear with those of the home farm.

On the left was an ornamental water sailed in by many swans. On the right extended a flower garden, laid in the old manner, and at this season of the year, as brilliant as stained glass. The front of the house presented a façade of more than sixty windows, surmounted by a formal pediment and raised upon a terrace. A wide avenue, part in gravel, part in turf, and bordered by triple alleys, ran to the great double gateways. It was impossible to look without surprise on a place that had been prepared through so many generations, had cost so many tons of minted gold, and was maintained in order by so great a company of emulous servants. And yet of these there was no sign but the perfection of their work. The whole domain was drawn to the line and weeded like the front plot of some suburban amateur; and I looked in vain for any belated gardener, and listened in vain for any sounds of labour. Some lowing of cattle and much calling of birds alone disturbed the stillness, and even the little hamlet, which clustered at the gates, appeared to hold its breath in awe of its great neighbour, like a troop of children who should have strayed into a king's anteroom.

The Carthew Arms, the small, but very comfortable inn, was a mere appendage and outpost of the family whose name it bore. Engraved portraits of bygone Carthews adorned the walls; Fielding Carthew, Recorder of the city of London; Major-General John Carthew in uniform, commanding some military operations; the Right Honourable Bailley Carthew, Member of Parliament for Stallbridge, standing by a table and brandishing a document; Singleton Carthew, Esquire, represented in the foreground of a herd of cattle – doubtless at the desire of his tenantry who had made him a compliment of this work of art; and the Venerable Archdeacon Carthew, D.D., LL.D., A.M., laying his hand on the head of a little child in a manner highly frigid and ridiculous. So far as my memory serves me, there were no other pictures in this exclusive hostelry; and I was not surprised to learn that the landlord was an ex-butler, the landlady an ex-lady's-maid from the great house; and that the bar-parlour was a sort of perquisite of former servants.

To an American, the sense of the domination of this family over so considerable tract of earth was even oppressive; and as I considered their simple annals, gathered from

the legends of the engravings, surprise began to mingle
with my disgust. 'Mr Recorder' doubtless occupies an
honourable post; but I thought that, in the course of so
many generations, one Carthew might have clambered
higher. The soldier had stuck at Major-General; the
churchman bloomed unremarked in an archdeaconate;
and though the Right Honourable Bailley seemed to have
sneaked into the Privy Council, I have still to learn what
he did when he had got there. Such vast means, so long a
start, and such a modest standard of achievement, struck
in me a strong sense of the dulness of that race.

I found that to come to the hamlet and not visit the Hall
would be regarded as a slight. To feed the swans, to see
the peacocks and the Raphaels – for these commonplace
people actually possessed two Raphaels – to risk life and
limb among a famous breed of cattle called the Carthew
Chillinghams, and to do homage to the sire (still living)
of Donibristle, a renowned winner of the Oaks: these, it
seemed, were the inevitable stations of the pilgrimage. I
was not so foolish as to resist, for I might have need,
before I was done, of general goodwill; and two pieces of
news fell in which changed my resignation to alacrity. It
appeared in the first place, that Mr Norris was from home
'travelling;' in the second, that a visitor had been before
me, and already made the tour of the Carthew curiosities.
I thought I knew who this must be, I was anxious to learn
what he had done and seen; and fortune so far favoured
me that the under-gardener singled out to be my guide had
already performed the same function for my predecessor.

'Yes, sir,' he said, 'an American gentleman right enough.
At least, I don't think he was quite a gentleman, but a very
civil person.'

The person, it seems, had been civil enough to be
delighted with the Carthew Chillinghams, to perform the
whole pilgrimage with rising admiration, and to have almost
prostrated himself before the shrine of Donibristle's sire.

'He told me, sir,' continued the gratified under-gardener,
'that he had often read of the "stately 'omes of England,"
but ours was the first he had the chance to see. When he
came to the 'ead of the long alley, he fetched his breath.
"This is indeed a lordly domain!" he cries. And it was
natural he should be interested in the place, for it seems

Mr Carthew had been kind to him in the States. In fact, he seemed a grateful kind of person, and wonderful taken up with flowers.'

I heard this story with amazement. The phrases quoted told their own tale; they were plainly from the shyster's mint. A few hours back I had seen him a mere bedlamite and fit for a strait waistcoat; he was penniless in a strange country; it was highly probable he had gone without breakfast; the absence of Norris must have been a crushing blow; the man (by all reason) should have been despairing. And now I heard of him, clothed and in his right mind, deliberate, insinuating, admiring vistas, smelling flowers, and talking like a book. The strength of character implied amazed and daunted me.

'This is curious,' I said to the under-gardener; 'I have had the pleasure of some acquaintance with Mr Carthew myself; and I believe none of our western friends ever were in England. Who can this person be? He couldn't – no, that's impossible, he could never have had the impudence. His name was not Bellairs?'

'I didn't 'ear the name, sir. Do you know anything against him?' cried my guide.

'Well,' said I, 'he is certainly not the person Carthew would like to have here in his absence.'

'Good gracious me!' exclaimed the gardener. 'He was so pleasant spoken, too; I thought he was some form of a schoolmaster. Perhaps, sir, you wouldn't mind going right up to Mr Denman? I recommended him to Mr Denman, when he had done the grounds. Mr Denman is our butler, sir,' he added.

The proposal was welcome, particularly as affording me a graceful retreat from the neighbourhood of the Carthew Chillinghams; and, giving up our projected circuit, we took a short cut through the shrubbery and across the bowling-green to the back quarters of the Hall.

The bowling-green was surrounded by a great hedge of yew, and entered by an archway in the quick. As we were issuing from this passage, my conductor arrested me.

'The Honourable Lady Ann Carthew,' he said, in an august whisper. And looking over his shoulder I was aware of an old lady with a stick, hobbling somewhat briskly along the garden path. She must have been extremely handsome in her youth; and even the limp with which she walked could not deprive her of an unusual and almost menacing dignity of bearing. Melancholy was impressed besides on every feature, and her eyes, as she looked straight before her, seemed to contemplate misfortune.

'She seems sad,' said I, when she had hobbled past and we had resumed our walk.

'She enjoys rather poor spirits, sir,' responded the under-gardener. 'Mr Carthew – the old gentleman, I mean – died less than a year ago; Lord Tillibody, her ladyship's brother, two months after; and then there was the sad business about the young gentleman. Killed in the 'unting-field, sir; and her ladyship's favourite. The present Mr Norris has never been so equally.'

'So I have understood,' said I persistently, and (I think) gracefully pursuing my inquiries and fortifying my position as a family friend. 'Dear, dear, how sad! And has this change – poor Carthew's return, and all – has this not mended matters?'

'Well, no, sir, not a sign of it,' was the reply. 'Worse, we think, than ever.'

'Dear, dear!' said I again.

'When Mr Norris arrived, she *did* seem glad to see him,' he pursued, 'and we were all pleased, I'm sure; for no one knows the young gentleman but what likes him. Ah, sir, it didn't last long! That very night they had a talk, and fell out or something; her ladyship took on most painful: it was like old days, but worse. And the next morning Mr Norris was off again upon his travels. "Denman," he said to Mr Denman, "Denman, I'll never come back," he said, and shook him by the 'and. I wouldn't be saying all this to a stranger, sir,' added my informant, overcome with a sudden fear lest he had gone too far.

He had indeed told me much, and much that was unsuspected by himself. On that stormy night of his return, Carthew had told his story; the old lady had more upon her mind than mere bereavements; and among the mental pictures on which she looked, as she walked staring down the path, was one of Midway Island and the *Flying Scud*.

Mr Denman heard my inquiries with discomposure, but informed me the shyster was already gone.

'Gone?' cried I. 'Then what can he have come for? One thing I can tell you, it was not to see the house.'

'I don't see it could have been anything else,' replied the butler.

'You may depend upon it it was,' said I. 'And whatever it was, he has got it. By the way, where is Mr Carthew at present? I was sorry to find he was from home.'

'He is engaged in travelling, sir,' replied the butler drily.

'Ah, bravo!' cried I. 'I laid a trap for you there, Mr Denman. Now I need not ask you; I am sure you did not tell this prying stranger.'

'To be sure not, sir,' said the butler.

I went through the form of 'shaking him by the 'and' – like Mr Norris – not, however, with genuine enthusiasm. For I had failed ingloriously to get the address for myself; and I felt a sure conviction that Bellairs had done better, or he had still been here and still cultivating Mr Denman.

I had escaped the grounds and the cattle; I could not escape the house. A lady with silver hair, a slender silver voice, and a stream of insignificant information not to be diverted, led me through the picture gallery, the music-room, the great dining-room, the long drawing-room, the Indian room, the theatre, and every corner (as I thought) of that interminable mansion. There was but one place reserved, the garden-room, whither Lady Ann had now retired. I paused a moment on the outside of the door, and smiled to myself. The situation was indeed strange, and those thin boards divided the secret of the *Flying Scud*.

All the while, as I went to and fro, I was considering the visit and departure of Bellairs. That he had got the address, I was quite certain; that he had not got it by direct questioning, I was convinced; some ingenuity, some lucky accident had served him. A similar chance, an equal ingenuity, was required; or I was left helpless, the ferret must run down his prey, the great oaks fall, the Raphaels be scattered, the house let to some stockbroker suddenly made rich, and the name which now filled the mouths of five or six parishes dwindle to a memory. Strange that such great matter, so old a mansion, a family so ancient and so dull, should come to depend for perpetuity upon the intelligence, the discretion, and the cunning of a Latin-Quartier student! What Bellairs had done, I must do likewise. Chance or ingenuity, ingenuity or chance – so I continued to ring the changes as I walked away down the avenue, casting back occasional glances at the red brick façade and the twinkling windows of the house. How was I to command chance? where was I to find the ingenuity?

These reflections brought me to the door of the inn. And here, pursuant to my policy of keeping well with all men, I immediately smoothed my brow, and accepted (being the only guest in the house) an invitation to dine with the family in the bar parlour. I sat down accordingly with Mr Higgs, the ex-butler, Mrs Higgs, the ex-lady's-maid, and Miss Agnes Higgs, their frowsy-headed little girl, the least promising and (as the event showed) the most useful of the lot. The talk ran endlessly on the great house and the great family; the roast beef, the Yorkshire pudding, the jam-roll, and the cheddar cheese came and went, and still the stream flowed on; near four generations of Carthews were touched upon without eliciting one point of interest; and we had killed Mr Henry in 'the 'unting field,' with a vast elaboration of painful circumstance, and buried him in the midst of a whole sorrowing county, before I could so much as manage to bring upon the stage my intimate friend, Mr Norris. At the name, the ex-butler grew diplomatic, and the ex-lady's maid tender. He was the only person of the whole featureless series who seemed to have accomplished anything worth mention; and his achievements, poor dog, seemed to have been confined to going to the devil and leaving some regrets. He had been the image of the Right Honourable Bailley, one of the lights of that dim house, and a career of distinction had been predicted of him in consequence almost from the cradle. But before he was out of long clothes, the cloven foot began to show; he proved to be no Carthew, developed a taste for low pleasures and bad company, went birdsnesting with a stable-boy before he was eleven, and when he was near twenty, and might have been expected to display at least some rudiments of the family gravity, rambled the county over with a knapsack, making sketches and keeping company in wayside inns. He had no pride about him, I was told; he would sit down with any man; and it was somewhat woundingly implied that I was indebted to this peculiarity for my own acquaintance with the hero. Unhappily, Mr Norris was not only eccentric, he was fast. His debts were still remembered at the University; still more, it appeared, the highly humorous circumstances attending his expulsion. 'He was always fond of his jest,' commented Mrs Higgs.

'That he were!' observed her lord.

But it was after he went into the diplomatic service that the real trouble began.

'It seems, sir, that he went the pace extraordinary,' said the ex-butler, with a solemn gusto.

'His debts were somethink awful,' said the lady's-maid. 'And as nice a young gentleman all the time as you would wish to see!'

'When word came to Mr Carthew's ears, the turn up was 'orrible,' continued Mr Higgs. 'I remember it as if it was yesterday. The bell was rung after her la'ship was gone, which I answered it myself, supposing it were the coffee. There was Mr Carthew on his feet. "'Iggs," he says, pointing with his stick, for he had a turn of the gout, "order the dog-cart instantly for this son of mine which has disgraced hisself." Mr Norris say nothink: he sit there with his 'ead down, making belief to be looking at a walnut. You might have bowled me over with a straw,' said Mr Higgs.

'Had he done anything very bad?' I asked.

'Not he, Mr Dodsley!' cried the lady – it was so she had conceived my name. 'He never did anythink to all really wrong in his poor life. The 'ole affair was a disgrace. It was all rank favouritising.'

'Mrs 'Iggs! Mrs 'Iggs!' cried the butler warningly.

'Well, what do I care?' retorted the lady, shaking her ringlets. 'You know it was yourself, Mr 'Iggs, and so did every member of the staff.'

While I was getting these facts and opinions, I by no means neglected the child. She was not attractive; but fortunately she had reached the corrupt age of seven, when half-a-crown appears about as large as a saucer and is fully as rare as the dodo. For a shilling down, sixpence in her money-box, and an American gold dollar which I happened to find in my pocket, I bought the creature soul and body. She declared her intention to accompany me to the ends of the earth; and had to be chidden by her sire for drawing comparisons between myself and her Uncle William, highly damaging to the latter.

Dinner was scarce done, the cloth was not yet removed, when Miss Agnes must needs climb into my lap with her stamp album, a relic of the generosity of Uncle William. There are few things I despise more than old stamps, unless perhaps it be crests; for cattle (from the Carthew Chillinghams down to the old gate-keeper's milk cow in the lane) contempt is far from being my first sentiment. But it seemed I was doomed to pass that day in viewing curiosities, and smothering a yawn, I devoted myself once more to tread the well-known round. I fancy Uncle William must have begun the collection himself and tired of it, for the book (to my surprise) was quite respectably filled. There were the varying shades of the English penny, Russians with the coloured heart, old undecipherable Thurn-und-Taxis, obsolete triangular Cape of Good Hopes, Swan Rivers with the Swan, and Guianas with the sailing ship. Upon all these I looked with the eyes of a fish and the spirit of a sheep; I think indeed I was at times asleep; and it was probably in one of these moments that I capsized the album, and there fell from the end of it, upon the floor, a considerable number of what I believe to be called 'exchanges.'

Here, against all probability, my chance had come to me; for as I gallantly picked them up, I was struck with the disproportionate amount of five-sous French stamps. Someone, I reasoned, must write very regularly from France to the neighbourhood of Stallbridge-le-Carthew. Could it be Norris? On one stamp I made out an initial C; upon a second I got as far as C H; beyond which point, the postmark used was in every instance undecipherable. C H, when you consider that about a quarter of the towns in France begin with 'chateau,' was an insufficient clue; and I promptly annexed the plainest of the collection in order to consult the post-office.

The wretched infant took me in the fact.

'Naughty man, to 'teal my 'tamp!' she cried; and when I would have brazened it off with a denial, recovered and displayed the stolen article.

My position was now highly false; and I believe it was in mere pity that Mrs Higgs came to my rescue with a welcome proposition. If the gentleman was really interested in stamps, she said, probably supposing me a monomaniac on the point, he should see Mr Denman's album. Mr Denman had been collecting forty years, and his collection was said to be worth a mint of money. 'Agnes,' she went on, 'if you were a kind little girl, you would run over to the 'All, tell Mr Denman there's a connaisseer in the 'ouse, and ask him if one of the young gentlemen might bring the album down.'

'I should like to see his exchanges too,' I cried, rising to the occasion. 'I may have some of mine in my pocket-book and we might trade.'

Half an hour later, Mr Denman arrived himself with a most unconscionable volume under his arm.

'Ah, sir,' he cried, 'when I 'eard you was a collector, I dropped all. It's a saying of mine, Mr Dodsley, that collecting stamps makes all collectors kin. It's a bond, sir; it creates a bond.'

Upon the truth of this, I cannot say; but there is no doubt that the attempt to pass yourself off for a collector falsely creates a precarious situation.

'Ah, here's the second issue!' I would say, after consulting the legend at the side. 'The pink – no, I mean the mauve – yes, that's the beauty of this lot. Though of course, as you say,' I would hasten to add, 'this yellow on the thin paper is more rare.'

Indeed I must certainly have been detected, had I not plied Mr Denman in self-defence with his favourite liquor – a port so excellent that it could never have ripened in the cellar of the Carthew Arms, but must have been transported, under cloud of night, from the neighbouring vaults of the great house. At each threat of exposure, and in particular whenever I was directly challenged for an opinion, I made haste to fill the butler's glass, and by the time we had got to the exchanges, he was in a condition in which no stamp collector need be seriously feared. God forbid I should hint that he was drunk; he seemed incapable of the necessary liveliness; but the man's eyes were set, and so long as he was suffered to talk without interruption, he seemed careless of my heeding him.

In Mr Denman's exchanges, as in those of little Agnes, the same peculiarity was to be remarked, an undue preponderance of that despicably common stamp, the French twenty-five centimes. And here joining them in stealthy review, I found the C and the CH; then something of an A just following; and then a terminal Y. Here was also the whole name spelt out to me; it seemed familiar, too; and yet for some time I could not bridge the imperfection. Then I came upon another stamp, in which an L was legible before the Y, and in a moment the word leaped up complete. Chailly, that was the name: Chailly-en-Bière, the post town of Barbizon – ah, there was the very place for any man to hide himself – there was the very place for Mr Norris, who had rambled over England making sketches – the very place for Goddedaal, who had left a palette-knife on board the *Flying Scud*. Singular, indeed, that while I was drifting over England with the shyster, the man we were in quest of awaited me at my own ultimate destination.

Whether Mr Denman had shown his album to Bellairs, whether, indeed, Bellairs could have caught (as I did) this hint from an obliterated postmark, I shall never know, and it mattered not. We were equal now; my task at Stallbridge-le-Carthew was accomplished; my interest in postage-stamps died shamelessly away; the astonished Denman was bowed out; and ordering the horse to be put in, I plunged into the study of the time-table.

CHAPTER TWENTY-ONE

Face to Face

I fell from the skies on Barbizon about two o'clock of a September afternoon. It is the dead hour of the day; all the workers have gone painting, all the idlers strolling, in the forest or the plain; the winding causewayed street is solitary, and the inn deserted. I was the more pleased to find one of my old companions in the dining-room; his town clothes marked him for a man in the act of departure; and indeed his portmanteau lay beside him on the floor.

'Why, Stennis,' I cried, 'you're the last man I expected to find here.'

'You won't find me here long,' he replied. '*King Pandion he is dead; all his friends are lapped in lead.* For men of our antiquity, the poor old shop is played out.'

'*I have had playmates, I have had companions,*' I quoted in return. We were both moved, I think, to meet again in this scene of our old pleasure parties so unexpectedly, after so long an interval, and both already so much altered.

'That is the sentiment,' he replied. '*All, all are gone, the old familiar faces.* I have been here a week, and the only living creature who seemed to recollect me was the Pharaon. Bar the Sirons, of course, and the perennial Bodmer.'

'Is there no survivor?' I inquired.

'Of our geological epoch? not one,' he replied. 'This is the city of Petra in Edom.'

'And what sort of Bedouins encamp among the ruins?' I asked.

'Youth, Dodd, youth; blooming, conscious youth,' he returned. 'Such a gang, such reptiles! to think we were like that! I wonder Siron didn't sweep us from his premises.'

'Perhaps we weren't so bad,' I suggested.

'Don't let me depress you,' said he. 'We were both Anglo-Saxons, anyway, and the only redeeming feature today is another.'

The thought of my quest, a moment driven out by this rencounter, revived in my mind. 'Who is he?' I cried. 'Tell me about him.'

'What, the Redeeming Feature?' said he. 'Well, he's a very pleasing creature, rather dim, and dull, and genteel, but really pleasing. He is very British, though, the artless Briton! Perhaps you'll find him too much so for the transatlantic nerves. Come to think of it, on the other hand, you ought to get on famously, he is an admirer of your great republic in one of its (excuse me) shoddiest features; he takes in and sedulously reads a lot of American papers. I warned you he was artless.'

'What papers are they?' cried I.

'San Francisco papers,' said he. 'He gets a bale of them about twice a week, and studies them like the Bible. That's one of his weaknesses; another is to be incalculably rich. He has taken Masson's old studio – you remember? – at the corner of the road; he has furnished it regardless of expense, and lives there surrounded with *vins fins* and works of art. When the youth of today goes up to the Caverne des Brigands to make punch – they do all that we did, like some nauseous form of ape (I never appreciated before what a creature of tradition mankind is) – this Madden follows with a basket of champagne. I told them he was wrong, and the punch tasted better; but he thought the boys liked the style of the thing, and I suppose they do. He is a very good-natured soul, and a very melancholy, and rather a helpless. Oh, and he has a third weakness which I came near forgetting. He paints. He has never been taught, and he's past thirty, and he paints.'

'How?' I asked.

'Rather well, I think,' was the reply. 'That's the annoying part of it. See for yourself. That panel is his.'

I stepped toward the window. It was the old familiar room, with the tables set like a Greek P, and the sideboard, and the aphasiac piano, and the panels on the wall. There were Romeo and Juliet, Antwerp from the river, Enfield's ships among the ice, and the huge huntsman winding a huge horn; mingled with them a few new ones, the thin crop of a succeeding generation, not better and not worse. It was to one of these I was directed – a thing coarsely and wittily handled, mostly with the palette-knife, and the colour in some parts excellent, the canvas in others loaded with mere clay. But it was the scene and not the art or want of it that riveted my notice. The foreground was of sand and scrub and wreckwood; in the middle distance the many-hued and smooth expanse of a lagoon, enclosed by a wall of breakers; beyond a blue strip of ocean. The sky was cloudless, and I could hear the surf break. For the place was Midway Island; the point of view the very spot at which I had landed with the captain for the first time, and from which I had re-embarked the day before we sailed. I had already been gazing for some seconds before my attention was arrested by a blur on the sea-line, and, stooping to look, I recognised the smoke of a steamer.

'Yes,' said I, turning toward Stennis, 'it has merit. What is it?'

'A fancy piece,' he returned. 'That's what pleased me. So few of the fellows in our time had the imagination of a garden snail.'

'Madden, you say his name is?' I pursued.

'Madden,' he repeated.

'Has he travelled much?' I inquired.

'I haven't an idea. He is one of the least autobiographical of men. He sits, and smokes, and giggles, and sometimes he makes small jests; but his contributions to the art of pleasing are generally confined to looking like a gentleman and being one. No,' added Stennis, 'he'll never suit you, Dodd; you like more head on your liquor. You'll find him as dull as ditch water.'

'Has he big blonde side whiskers like tusks?' I asked, mindful of the photograph of Goddedaal.

'Certainly not; why should he?' was the reply.

'Does he write many letters?' I continued.

'God knows,' said Stennis. 'What is wrong with you? I never saw you taken this way before.'

'The fact is I think I know the man,' said I. 'I think I'm looking for him. I rather think he is my long-lost brother.'

'Not twins, anyway,' returned Stennis.

And about the same time, a carriage driving up to the inn, he took his departure.

I walked till dinner-time in the plain, keeping to the fields; for I instinctively shunned observation, and was racked by

many incongruous and impatient feelings. Here was a man
whose voice I had once heard, whose doings had filled so
many days of my life with interest and distress, whom I
had lain awake to dream of like a lover, and now his
hand was on the door; now we were to meet; now I was
to learn at last the mystery of the substituted crew. The
sun went down over the plain of the Angelus, and as the
hour approached my courage lessened. I let the laggard
peasants pass me on the homeward way. The lamps were
lit, the soup was served, the company were all at table, and
the room sounded already with multitudinous talk before
I entered. I took my place and found I was opposite to
Madden. Over six feet high and well set up, the hair
dark and streaked with silver, the eyes dark and kindly,
the mouth very good-natured, the teeth admirable; linen
and hands exquisite; English clothes, an English voice, an
English bearing – the man stood out conspicuous from the
company. Yet he had made himself at home, and seemed
to enjoy a certain quiet popularity among the noisy boys
of the table d'hôte. He had an odd silver giggle of a laugh
that sounded nervous even when he was really amused,
and accorded ill with his big stature and manly melancholy
face. This laugh fell in continually all through dinner like
the note of the triangle in a piece of modern French music;
and he had at times a kind of pleasantry, rather of manner
than of words, with which he started or maintained the
merriment. He took his share in these diversions, not so
much like a man in high spirits, but like one of an approved
good-nature, habitually self-forgetful, accustomed to please
and to follow others. I have remarked in old soldiers much
the same smiling sadness and sociable self-effacement.

I feared to look at him, lest my glances should betray my
deep excitement, and chance served me so well that the soup
was scarce removed before we were naturally introduced.
My first sip of Château Siron, a vintage from which I had
been long estranged, startled me into speech.

'Oh, this'll never do!' I cried, in English.

'Dreadful stuff, isn't it?' said Madden, in the same
language. 'Do let me ask you to share my bottle. They
call it Chambertin, which it isn't; but it's fairly palatable, and there's nothing in this house that a man can
drink at all.'

I accepted; anything would do that paved the way to better knowledge.

'Your name is Madden, I think,' said I. 'My old friend Stennis told me about you when I came.'

'Yes, I am sorry he went; I feel such a Grandfather William, alone among all these lads,' he replied.

'My name is Dodd,' I resumed.

'Yes,' said he, 'so Madame Siron told me.'

'Dodd, of San Francisco,' I continued. 'Late of Pinkerton and Dodd.'

'Montana Block, I think?' said he.

'The same,' said I.

Neither of us looked at the other; but I could see his hand deliberately making bread pills.

'That's a nice thing of yours,' I pursued, 'that panel. The foreground is a little clayey, perhaps, but the lagoon is excellent.'

'You ought to know,' said he.

'Yes,' returned I, 'I'm rather a good judge of – that panel.'

There was a considerable pause.

'You know a man by the name of Bellairs, don't you?' he resumed.

'Ah!' cried I, 'you have heard from Doctor Urquart?'

'This very morning,' he replied.

'Well, there is no hurry about Bellairs,' said I. 'It's rather a long story and rather a silly one. But I think we have a good deal to tell each other, and, perhaps we had better wait till we are more alone.'

'I think so,' said he. 'Not that any of these fellows know English, but we'll be more comfortable over at my place. Your health, Dodd.'

And we took wine together across the table.

Thus had this singular introduction passed unperceived in the midst of more than thirty persons, art students, ladies in dressing-gowns and covered with rice powder, six foot of Siron whisking dishes over our head, and his noisy sons clattering in and out with fresh relays.

'One question more,' said I. 'Did you recognise my voice?'

'Your voice?' he repeated. 'How should I? I had never heard it – we have never met.'

'And yet, we have been in conversation before now,' said I, 'and I asked you a question which you never answered, and which I have since had many thousand better reasons for putting to myself.'

He turned suddenly white. 'Good God!' he cried, 'are you the man in the telephone?'

I nodded.

'Well, well!' said he. 'It would take a good deal of magnanimity to forgive you that. What nights I have passed! That little whisper has whistled in my ear ever since, like the wind in a keyhole. Who could it be? What could it mean? I suppose I have had more real, solid misery out of that . . .' He paused, and looked troubled. 'Though I had more to bother me, or ought to have,' he added, and slowly emptied his glass.

'It seems we were born to drive each other crazy with conundrums,' said I. 'I have often thought my head would split.'

Carthew burst into his foolish laugh. 'And yet neither you nor I had the worst of the puzzle,' he cried. 'There were others deeper in.'

'And who were they?' I asked.

'The underwriters,' said he.

'Why, to be sure,' cried I. 'I never thought of that. What could they make of it?'

'Nothing,' replied Carthew. 'It couldn't be explained. They were a crowd of small dealers at Lloyd's who took it up in syndicate; one of them has a carriage now; and people say he is a deuce of a deep fellow, and has the makings of a great financier. Another furnished a small villa on the profits. But they're all hopelessly muddled; and when they meet each other, they don't know where to look, like the Augurs.'

Dinner was no sooner at an end, than he carried me across the road to Masson's old studio. It was strangely changed. On the walls were tapestry, a few good etchings, and some amazing pictures – a Rousseau, a Corot, a really superb old Crome, a Whistler, and a piece which my host claimed (and I believe) to be a Titian. The room was furnished with comfortable English smoking-room chairs, some American rockers, and an elaborate business table; spirits and soda-water (with the mark of Schweppe, no less) stood ready on a butler's tray, and in one corner, behind a half-drawn curtain, I spied a camp-bed and a capacious tub. Such a room in Barbizon astonished the beholder, like the glories of the cave of Monte Cristo.

'Now,' said he, 'we are quiet. Sit down, if you don't mind, and tell me your story all through.'

I did as he asked, beginning with the day when Jim showed me the passage in the *Daily Occidental*, and winding up with the stamp album and the Chailly postmark. It was a long business; and Carthew made it longer, for he was insatiable of details; and it had struck midnight on the old eight-day clock in the corner, before I had made an end.

'And now,' said he, 'turn about: I must tell you my side, much as I hate it. Mine is a beastly story. You'll wonder how I can sleep. I've told it once before, Mr Dodd.'

'To Lady Ann?' I asked.

'As you suppose,' he answered; 'and to say the truth, I had sworn never to tell it again. Only, you seem somehow entitled to the thing; you have paid dear enough, God knows: and God knows I hope you may like it, now you've got it!'

With that he began his yarn. A new day had dawned, the cocks crew in the village and the early woodmen were afoot, when he concluded.

CHAPTER TWENTY-TWO

The Remittance Man

Singleton Carthew, the father of Norris, was heavily built and feebly vitalised, sensitive as a musician, dull as a sheep, and conscientious as a dog. He took his position with seriousness, even with pomp; the long rooms, the silent servants, seemed in his blue eyes like the observances of some religion of which he was the mortal god. He had the stupid man's intolerance of stupidity in others; the vain man's exquisite alarm lest it should be detected in himself. And on both sides Norris irritated and offended him. He thought his son a fool, and he suspected that his son returned the compliment with interest. The history of their relation was simple; they met seldom, they quarrelled often. To his mother, a fiery, pungent, practical woman, already disappointed in her husband and her elder son, Norris was only a fresh disappointment.

Yet the lad's faults were no great matter; he was diffident, placable, passive, unambitious, unenterprising; life did not much attract him; he watched it like a curious and dull exhibition, not much amused, and not tempted in the least to take a part. He beheld his father ponderously grinding sand, his mother fiercely breaking butterflies, his brother labouring at the pleasures of the Hawbuck with the ardour of a soldier in a doubtful battle; and the vital sceptic looked on wondering. They were careful and troubled about many things; for him there seemed not even one thing needful. He was born disenchanted, the world's promises awoke no echo in his bosom, the world's activities and the world's distinctions seemed to him equally without a base in fact. He liked the open air; he liked comradeship, it mattered not with whom, his comrades were only a remedy for solitude. And he had a taste for painted art. An array of fine pictures looked upon his childhood and from these roods of jewelled canvas he received an indelible impression. The gallery at

Stallbridge betokened generations of picture lovers; Norris was perhaps the first of his race to hold the pencil. The taste was genuine, it grew and strengthened with his growth; and yet he suffered it to be suppressed with scarce a struggle. Time came for him to go to Oxford, and he resisted faintly. He was stupid, he said; it was no good to put him through the mill; he wished to be a painter. The words fell on his father like a thunderbolt, and Norris made haste to give way. 'It didn't really matter, don't you know?' said he. 'And it seemed an awful shame to vex the old boy.'

To Oxford he went obediently, hopelessly; and at Oxford became the hero of a certain circle. He was active and adroit; when he was in the humour, he excelled in many sports; and his singular melancholy detachment gave him a place apart. He set a fashion in his clique. Envious undergraduates sought to parody his unaffected lack of zeal and fear; it was a kind of new Byronism more composed and dignified. 'Nothing really mattered;' among other things, this formula embraced the dons; and though he always meant to be civil, the effect on the college authorities was one of startling rudeness. His indifference cut like insolence; and in some outbreak of his constitutional levity (the complement of his melancholy) he was 'sent down' in the middle of the second year.

The event was new in the annals of the Carthews, and Singleton was prepared to make the most of it. It had been long his practice to prophesy for his second son a career of ruin and disgrace. There is an advantage in this artless parental habit. Doubtless the father is interested in his son; but doubtless also the prophet grows to be interested in his prophecies. If the one goes wrong, the others come true. Old Carthew drew from this source esoteric consolations; he dwelt at length on his own foresight; he produced variations hitherto unheard from the old theme 'I told you so,' coupled his son's name with the gallows and the hulks, and spoke of his small handful of college debts as though he must raise money on a mortgage to discharge them.

'I don't think that is fair, sir,' said Norris; 'I lived at college exactly as you told me. I am sorry I was sent down, and you have a perfect right to blame me for that; but you have no right to pitch into me about these debts.'

The effect upon a stupid man not unjustly incensed need scarcely be described. For a while Singleton raved.

'I'll tell you what, father,' said Norris at last, 'I don't think this is going to do. I think you had better let me take to painting. It's the only thing I take a spark of interest in. I shall never be steady as long as I'm at anything else.'

'When you stand here, sir, to the neck in disgrace,' said the father, 'I should have hoped you would have had more good taste than to repeat this levity.'

The hint was taken; the levity was never more obtruded on the father's notice, and Norris was inexorably launched upon a backward voyage. He went abroad to study foreign languages, which he learned, at a very expensive rate; and a fresh crop of debts fell soon to be paid, with similar lamentations, which were in this case perfectly justified, and to which Norris paid no regard. He had been unfairly treated over the Oxford affair; and with a spice of malice very surprising in one so placable, and an obstinacy remarkable in one so weak, refused from that day forward to exercise the least captaincy on his expenses. He wasted what he would; he allowed his servants to despoil him at their pleasure; he sowed insolvency; and when the crop was ripe, notified his father with exasperating calm. His own capital was put in his hands, he was planted in the diplomatic service, and told he must depend upon himself.

He did so till he was twenty-five; by which time he had spent his money, laid in a handsome choice of debts, and acquired (like so many other melancholic and uninterested persons) a habit of gambling. An Austrian colonel – the same who afterwards hanged himself at Monte Carlo – gave him a lesson which lasted two-and-twenty hours, and left him wrecked and helpless. Old Singleton once more repurchased the honour of his name, this time at a fancy figure; and Norris was set afloat again on stern conditions. An allowance of three hundred pounds in the year was to be paid to him quarterly by a lawyer in Sydney, New South Wales. He was not to write. Should he fail on any quarter-day to be in Sydney he was to be held for dead, and the allowance tacitly withdrawn. Should he return to Europe an advertisement publicly disowning him was to appear in every paper of repute.

It was one of his most annoying features as a son that he

was always polite, always just, and in whatever whirlwind of domestic anger always calm. He expected trouble; when trouble came he was unmoved; he might have said with Singleton, '*I told you so:*' he was content with thinking, '*Just as I expected.*' On the fall of these last thunderbolts he bore himself like a person only distantly interested in the event, pocketed the money and the reproaches, obeyed orders punctually; took ship and came to Sydney. Some men are still lads at twenty-five; and so it was with Norris. Eighteen days after he landed his quarter's allowance was all gone, and with the light-hearted hopefulness of strangers in what is called a new country he began to besiege offices and apply for all manner of incongruous situations. Everywhere, and last of all from his lodgings, he was bowed out; and found himself reduced, in a very elegant suit of summer tweeds, to herd and camp with the degraded outcasts of the city.

In this strait he had recourse to the lawyer who paid him his allowance.

'Try to remember that my time is valuable, Mr Carthew,' said the lawyer. 'It is quite unnecessary you should enlarge on the peculiar position in which you stand. *Remittance men*, as we call them here, are not so rare in my experience; and in such cases I act upon a system. I make you a present of a sovereign, here it is. Every day you choose to call my clerk will advance you a shilling; on Saturday, since my office is closed on Sunday, he will advance you half-a-crown. My conditions are these. That you do not come to me, but to my clerk, that you do not come here the worse of liquor; and you go away the moment you are paid and have signed a receipt. I wish you a good-morning.'

'I have to thank you, I suppose,' said Carthew. 'My position is so wretched that I cannot even refuse this starvation allowance.'

'Starvation!' said the lawyer smiling. 'No man will starve here on a shilling a day. I had on my hands another young gentleman who remained continuously intoxicated for six years on the same allowance.' And he once more busied himself with his papers.

In the time that followed the image of the smiling lawyer haunted Carthew's memory. 'That three minutes' talk was all the education I ever had worth talking of,' says he. 'It was all life in a nutshell. Confound it,'

I thought, 'have I got to the point of envying that ancient fossil?'

Every morning for the next two or three weeks the stroke of ten found Norris, unkempt and haggard, at the lawyer's door. The long day and longer night he spent in the Domain, now on a bench, now on the grass under a Norfolk Island pine, the companion of perhaps the lowest class on earth, the Larrikins of Sydney. Morning after morning, the dawn behind the lighthouse recalled him from slumber; and he would stand and gaze upon the changing east, the fading lenses, the smokeless city, and the many-armed and many-masted harbour growing slowly clear under his eyes. His bed-fellows (so to call them) were less active; they lay sprawled upon the grass and benches, the dingy men, the frowsy women, prolonging their late repose; and Carthew wandered among the sleeping bodies alone, and cursed the incurable stupidity of his behaviour. Day brought a new society of nursery-maids and children, and fresh-dressed and (I am sorry to say) tight-laced maidens, and gay people in rich traps; upon the skirts of which Carthew and 'the other black-guards' – his own bitter phrase – skulked, and chewed grass, and looked on. Day passed, the light died, the green and leafy precinct sparkled with lamps or lay in shadow, and the round of the night began again – the loitering women, the lurking men, the sudden outburst of screams, the sound of flying feet. 'You mayn't believe it,' says Carthew, 'but I got to that pitch that I didn't care a hang. I have been wakened out of my sleep to hear a woman screaming, and I have only turned upon my other side. Yes, it's a queer place, where the dowagers and the kids walk all day, and at night you can hear people bawling for help as if it was the Forest of Bondy, with the lights of a great town all round, and parties spinning through in cabs from Government House and dinner with my lord!'

It was Norris's diversion, having none other, to scrape acquaintance, where, how, and with whom he could. Many a long dull talk he held upon the benches or the grass; many a strange waif he came to know; many strange things he heard, and saw some that were abominable. It was to one of these last that he owed his deliverance from the Domain. For some time the rain had been merciless; one night after another he had been obliged to squander four-pence on a bed and reduce his board to the remaining eightpence; and he sat one morning near the Macquarrie Street entrance, hungry, for he had gone without breakfast, and wet, as he had already been for several days, when the cries of an animal in distress attracted his attention. Some fifty yards away, in the extreme angle of the grass, a party of the chronically unemployed had got hold of a dog, whom they were torturing in a manner not to be described. The heart of Norris, which had grown indifferent to the cries of human anger or distress, woke at the appeal of the dumb creature. He ran amongst the Larrikins, scattered them, rescued the dog, and stood at bay. They were six in number, shambling gallows-birds; but for once the proverb was right, cruelty was coupled with cowardice, and the wretches cursed him and made off. It chanced this act of prowess had not passed unwitnessed. On a bench near by there was seated a shopkeeper's assistant out of employ, a diminutive, cheerful, red-headed creature by the name of Hemstead. He was the last man to have interfered himself, for his discretion more than equalled his valour: but he made haste to congratulate Carthew, and to warn him he might not always be so fortunate.

'They're a dyngerous lot of people about this park. My word! it doesn't do to ply with them!' he observed, in that *rycy Austrylian* English, which (as it has received the imprimatur of Mr Froude) we should all make haste to imitate.

'Why, I'm one of that lot myself,' returned Carthew.

Hemstead laughed and remarked that he knew a gentleman when he saw one.

'For all that, I am simply one of the unemployed,' said Carthew, seating himself beside his new acquaintance, as he had sat (since this experience began) beside so many dozen others.

'I'm out of a plyce myself,' said Hemstead.

'You beat me all the way and back,' says Carthew. 'My trouble is that I have never been in one.'

'I suppose you've no tryde?' asked Hemstead.

'I know how to spend money,' replied Carthew, 'and I really do know something of horses and something of the sea. But the unions head me off; if it weren't for them, I might have had a dozen berths.'

'My word,' cried the sympathetic listener. 'Ever try the mounted police?' he inquired.

'I did, and was bowled out,' was the reply; 'couldn't pass the doctors.'

'Well, what do you think of the ryleways, then?' asked Hemstead.

'What do *you* think of them, if you come to that?' asked Carthew.

'Oh, *I* don't think of them; I don't go in for manual labour,' said the little man proudly. 'But if a man don't mind that, he's pretty sure of a job there.'

'By George, you tell me where to go!' cried Carthew, rising.

The heavy rains continued, the country was already overrun with floods; the railway system daily required more hands, daily the superintendent advertised; but 'the unemployed' preferred the resources of charity and rapine, and a navvy, even an amateur navvy, commanded money in the market. The same night, after a tedious journey, and a change of trains to pass a landslip, Norris found himself in a muddy cutting behind South Clifton, attacking his first shift of manual labour.

For weeks the rain scarce relented. The whole front of the mountain slipped seaward from above, avalanches of clay, rock, and uprooted forest spewed over the cliffs and fell upon the beach or in the breakers. Houses were carried bodily away and smashed like nuts; others were menaced and deserted, the doof locked, the chimney cold, the dwellers fled elsewhere for safety. Night and day the fire blazed in the encampment; night and day hot coffee was served to the overdriven toilers in the shift; night and day the engineer of the section made his round with words of encouragement, hearty and rough and well suited to his men. Night and day, too, the telegraph clicked with disastrous news and anxious inquiry. Along the terraced line of rail, rare trains came creeping and signalling; and paused at the threatened corner, like living things conscious of peril. The commandant of the post would hastily review his labours, make (with a dry throat) the signal to advance; and the whole squad line the way and look on in a choking silence, or burst into a brief cheer as the train cleared the point of danger and shot on, perhaps through the thin sunshine between squalls, perhaps with blinking lamps into the gathering, rainy twilight.

One such scene Carthew will remember till he dies. It blew great guns from the seaward; a huge surf bombarded, five hundred feet below him, the steep mountain's foot; close in was a vessel in distress, firing shots from a fowling-piece, if any help might come. So he saw and heard her the moment before the train appeared and paused, throwing up a Babylonian tower of smoke into the rain and oppressing men's hearts with the scream of her whistle. The engineer was there himself; he paled as he made the signal: the engine came at a foot's pace; but the whole bulk of mountain shook and seemed to nod seaward, and the watching navvies instinctively clutched at shrubs and trees: vain precautions, vain as the shots from the poor sailors. Once again fear was disappointed; the train passed unscathed; and Norris, drawing a long breath, remembered the labouring ship, and glanced below. She was gone.

So the days and the nights passed: Homeric labour in Homeric circumstance. Carthew was sick with sleeplessness and coffee; his hands, softened by the wet, were cut to ribbons; yet he enjoyed a peace of mind and health of body hitherto unknown. Plenty of open air, plenty of physical exertion, a continual instancy of toil, here was what had been hitherto lacking in that misdirected life, and the true cure of vital scepticism. To get the train through, there was the recurrent problem; no time remained to ask if it were necessary. Carthew, the idler, the spendthrift, the drifting dilettante, was soon remarked, praised, and advanced. The engineer swore by him and pointed him out for an example. 'I've a new chum, up here,' Norris overheard him saying, 'a young swell. He's worth any two in the squad.' The words fell on the ears of the discarded son like music; and from that moment, he not only found an interest, he took a pride, in his plebeian tasks.

The press of work was still at its highest when quarter-day approached. Norris was now raised to a position of some trust; at his discretion, trains were stopped or forwarded at the dangerous cornice near North Clifton; and he found in this responsibility both terror and delight. The thought of the seventy-five pounds that would soon await him at the lawyer's, and of his own obligation to be present every quarter-day in Sydney, filled him for a little with divided councils. Then he made up his mind, walked in a slack moment to the inn at Clifton, ordered a sheet of paper and a bottle of beer, and wrote, explaining that he held a good appointment which he would lose if he came to Sydney, and asking the lawyer to accept this letter as an evidence of his presence in the colony and retain the money till next quarter-day. The answer came in course of post, and was not merely favourable but cordial. 'Although what you propose is contrary to the terms of my instructions,' it ran, 'I willingly accept the responsibility of granting your request. I should say I am agreeably disappointed in your behaviour. My experience has not led me to found much expectations on gentlemen in your position.'

The rains abated, and the temporary labour was discharged; not Norris, to whom the engineer clung as to found money; not Norris, who found himself a ganger on the line in the regular staff of navvies. His camp was pitched in a grey wilderness of rock and forest, far from any house; as he sat with his mates about the evening fire, the trains passing on the track were their next, and indeed, their only neighbours, except the wild things of the wood. Lovely weather, light and monotonous employment, long hours of somnolent camp-fire talk, long sleepless nights, when he reviewed his foolish and fruitless career as he rose and walked in the moonlight forest, an occasional paper of which he would read all, the advertisements with as much relish as the text; such was the tenor of an existence which soon began to weary and harass him. He lacked and regretted the fatigue, the furious hurry, the suspense, the fires, the midnight coffee, the rude and mud-bespattered poetry of the first toilful weeks. In the quietness of his new surroundings, a voice summoned him from this exorbital part of life, and about the middle of October he threw up his situation and bade farewell to the camp of tents and the shoulder of Bald Mountain.

Clad in his rough clothes, with a bundle on his shoulder and his accumulated wages in his pocket, he entered Sydney for the second time, and walked with pleasure and some bewilderment in the cheerful streets, like a man landed from a voyage. The sight of the people led him on. He forgot his necessary errands, he forgot to eat. He wandered in moving multitudes like a stick upon a river. Last he came to the Domain and strolled there, and remembered his shame and sufferings, and looked with poignant curiosity at his successors. Hemstead, not much shabbier and no less cheerful than before, he recognised and addressed like an old family friend.

'That was a good turn you did me,' said he. 'That railway was the making of me. I hope you've had luck yourself.'

'My word, no!' replied the little man. 'I just sit here and read the *Dead Bird*. It's the depression in trýde, you see. There's no positions goin' that a man like me would care to look at.' And he showed Norris his certificates and written characters, one from a grocer in Wooloomooloo, one from an iron-monger, and a third from a billiard saloon. 'Yes,' he said, 'I tried bein' a billiard marker. It's no account; these lyte hours are no use for a man's health. I won't be no man's slyve,' he added firmly.

On the principle that he who is too proud to be a slave is usually not too modest to become a pensioner, Carthew gave him half a sovereign, and departed, being suddenly struck with hunger, in the direction of the Paris House. When he came to that quarter of the city, the barristers were trotting in the streets in wig and gown, and he stood to observe them with his bundle on his shoulder, and his mind full of curious recollections of the past.

'By George!' cried a voice, 'it's Mr Carthew!'

And turning about, he found himself face to face with a handsome sunburnt youth, somewhat fatted, arrayed in the finest of fine raiment, and sporting about a sovereign's worth of flowers in his buttonhole. Norris had met him during his first days in Sydney at a farewell supper; had even escorted him on board a schooner full of cockroaches and black-boy sailors, in which he was bound for six months among the islands; and had kept him ever since in entertained remembrance. Tom Hadden (known to the bulk of Sydney folk as *Tommy*) was heir to a considerable property, which a prophetic father had placed in the hands of rigorous trustees. The income supported Mr Hadden in splendour for about three months out of twelve; the rest of the year he passed in retreat among the islands. He was now about a week returned from his eclipse, pervading Sydney in hansom cabs and airing the first bloom of six new suits of clothes; and yet the unaffected creature hailed Carthew in his working jeans and with the damning bundle on his shoulder, as he might have claimed acquaintance with a duke.

'Come and have a drink?' was his cheerful cry.

'I'm just going to have lunch at the Paris House,' returned Carthew. 'It's a long time since I have had a decent meal.'

'Splendid scheme!' said Hadden. 'I've only had breakfast half an hour ago; but we'll have a private room, and I'll manage to pick something. It'll brace me up. I was on an awful tear last night, and I've met no end of fellows this morning.' To meet a fellow, and to stand and share a drink, were with Tom synonymous terms.

They were soon at table in the corner room upstairs, and paying due attention to the best fare in Sydney. The odd similarity of their positions drew them together, and they began soon to exchange confidences. Carthew related his privations in the Domain, and his toils as a navvy; Hadden gave his experience as an amateur copra merchant in the South Seas, and drew a humorous picture of life in a coral island. Of the two plans of retirement, Carthew gathered that his own had been vastly the more lucrative; but Hadden's trading outfit had consisted largely of bottled stout and brown sherry for his own consumption.

'I had champagne, too,' said Hadden, 'but I kept that in case of sickness, until I didn't seem to be going to be sick, and then I opened a pint every Sunday. Used to sleep all morning, then breakfast with my pint of fizz, and lie in a hammock and read Hallam's "Middle Ages." Have you read that? I always take something solid to the islands. There's no doubt I did the thing in rather a fine style; but if it was gone about a little cheaper, or there were two of us to bear the expense, it ought to pay hand over fist. I've got the influence, you see. I'm a chief now, and sit in the speak-house under my own strip of roof. I'd like to see them taboo *me*! They daren't try it; I've a strong party, I can tell you. Why, I've had upwards of thirty cowtops sitting in my front verandah eating tins of salmon.'

'Cowtops?' asked Carthew, 'what are they?'

'That's what Hallam would call feudal retainers,' explained Hadden, not without vainglory. 'They're My

Followers. They belong to My Family. I tell you, they come expensive, though; you can't fill up all these retainers on tinned salmon for nothing; but whenever I could get it, I would give 'em squid. Squid's good for natives, but I don't care for it, do you? – or shark either. It's like the working classes at home. With copra at the price it is, they ought to be willing to bear their share of the loss; and so I've told them again and again. I think it's a man's duty to open their minds, and I try to, but you can't get political economy into them; it doesn't seem to reach their intelligence.'

There was an expression still sticking in Carthew's memory, and he returned upon it with a smile. 'Talking of political economy,' said he, 'you said if there were two of us to bear the expense, the profits would increase. How do you make out that?'

'I'll show you! I'll figure it out for you!' cried Hadden, and with a pencil on the back of the bill of fare, proceeded to perform miracles. He was a man, or let us rather say a lad, of unusual projective power. Give him the faintest hint of any speculation, and the figures flowed from him by the page. A lively imagination, and a ready, though inaccurate memory supplied his data; he delivered himself with an inimitable heat that made him seem the picture of pugnacity; lavished contradiction; had a form of words, with or without significance, for every form of criticism; and the looker-on alternately smiled at his simplicity and fervour, or was amazed by his unexpected shrewdness. He was a kind of Pinkerton in play. I have called Jim's the romance of business; this was its Arabian tale.

'Have you any idea what this would cost?' he asked, pausing at an item.

'Not I,' said Carthew.

'Ten pounds ought to be ample,' concluded the projector.

'Oh, nonsense!' cried Carthew. 'Fifty at the very least.'

'You told me yourself this moment you knew nothing about it!' cried Tommy. 'How can I make a calculation, if you blow hot and cold? You don't seem able to be serious!'

But he consented to raise his estimate to twenty; and a little after, the calculation coming out with a deficit, cut it down again to five pounds ten, with the remark, 'I told you it was nonsense. This sort of thing has to be done strictly, or where's the use?'

Some of these processes struck Carthew as unsound; and he was at times altogether thrown out by the capricious startings of the prophet's mind. These plunges seemed to be gone into for exercise and by the way, like the curvets of a willing horse. Gradually the thing took shape; the glittering if baseless edifice arose; and the hare still ran on the mountains, but the soup was already served in silver plate. Carthew in a few days could command a hundred and fifty pounds; Hadden was ready with five hundred; why should they not recruit a fellow or two more, charter an old ship, and go cruising on their own account? Carthew was an experienced yachtsman; Hadden professed himself able to 'work an approximate sight.' Money was undoubtedly to be made, or why should so many vessels cruise about the islands? they, who worked their own ship, were sure of a still higher profit.

'And whatever else comes of it, you see,' cried Hadden, 'we get our keep for nothing. Come, buy some togs, that's the first thing you have to do of course; and then we'll take a hansom and go to the Currency Lass.'

'I'm going to stick to the togs I have,' said Norris.

'Are you?' cried Hadden. 'Well, I must say I admire you. You're a regular sage. It's what you call Pythagoreanism, isn't it? if I haven't forgotten my philosophy.'

'Well, I call it economy,' returned Carthew. 'If we are going to try this thing on, I shall want every sixpence.'

'You'll see if we're going to try it!' cried Tommy, rising radiant from table. 'Only, mark you, Carthew, it must be all in your name. I have capital, you see; but you're all right. You can play *vacuus viator*, if the thing goes wrong.'

'I thought we had just proved it was quite safe,' said Carthew.

'There's nothing safe in business, my boy,' replied the sage; 'not even bookmaking.'

The public-house and tea garden called the Currency Lass represented a moderate fortune gained by its proprietor, Captain Bostock, during a long, active, and occasionally historic career among the islands. Anywhere from Tonga to the Admiralty Isles, he knew the ropes and could lie in the native dialect. He had seen the end of sandal wood, the end of oil, and the beginning of copra; and he was himself a commercial pioneer, the first that ever carried human teeth into the Gilberts. He was tried for his life in Fiji in Sir Arthur Gordon's time; and if ever he prayed at all, the name of Sir. Arthur was certainly not forgotten. He was speared in seven places in New Ireland – the same time his mate was killed – the famous 'outrage on the brig *Jolly Roger*;' but the treacherous savages made little by their wickedness, and Bostock, in spite of their teeth, got seventy-five head of volunteer labour on board, of whom not more than a dozen died of injuries. He had a hand, besides, in the amiable pleasantry which cost the life of Patteson; and when the sham bishop landed, prayed, and gave his benediction to the natives, Bostock, arrayed in a female chemise out of the traderoom, had stood at his right hand and boomed amens. This, when he was sure he was among good fellows, was his favourite yarn. 'Two hundred head of labour for a hatful of amens,' he used to name the tale; and its sequel, the death of the real bishop, struck him as a circumstance of extraordinary humour.

Many of these details were communicated in the hansom, to the surprise of Carthew.

'Why do we want to visit this old ruffian?' he asked.

'You wait till you hear him,' replied Tommy. 'That man knows everything.'

On descending from the hansom at the Currency Lass, Hadden was struck with the appearance of the cabman, a gross, salt-looking man, red-faced, blue-eyed, short-handed and short-winded, perhaps nearing forty.

'Surely I know you?' said he. 'Have you driven me before?'

'Many's the time, Mr Hadden,' returned the driver. 'The last time you was back from the islands, it was me that drove you to the races, sir.'

'All right: jump down and have a drink then,' said Tom, and he turned and led the way into the garden.

Captain Bostock met the party: he was a slow, sour old man, with fishy eyes; greeted Tommy offhand, and (as was afterwards remembered) exchanged winks with the driver.

'A bottle of beer for the cabman there at that table,' said Tom. 'Whatever you please from shandygaff to champagne at this one here; and you sit down with us. Let me make you acquainted with my friend, Mr Carthew. I've come on business, Billy; I want to consult you as a friend; I'm going into the island trade upon my own account.'

Doubtless the captain was a mine of counsel, but opportunity was denied him. He could not venture on a statement, he was scarce allowed to finish a phrase, before Hadden swept him from the field with a volley of protest and correction. That projector, his face blazing with inspiration, first laid before him at inordinate length a question, and as soon as he attempted to reply, leaped at his throat, called his facts in question, derided his policy, and at times thundered on him from the heights of moral indignation.

'I beg your pardon,' he said once. 'I am a gentleman, Mr Carthew here is a gentleman, and we don't mean to do that class of business. Can't you see who you are talking to? Can't you talk sense? Can't you give us "a dead bird" for a good trade-room?'

'No, I don't suppose I can,' returned old Bostock; 'not when I can't hear my own voice for two seconds together. It was gin and guns I did it with.'

'Take your gin and guns to Putney,' cried Hadden. 'It was the thing in your times, that's right enough; but you're old now, and the game's up. I'll tell you what's wanted nowadays, Bill Bostock,' said he; and did, and took ten minutes to it.

Carthew could not refrain from smiling. He began to think less seriously of the scheme, Hadden appearing too irresponsible a guide; but on the other hand, he enjoyed himself amazingly. It was far from being the same with Captain Bostock.

'You know a sight, don't you?' remarked that gentleman bitterly, when Tommy paused.

'I know a sight more than you, if that's what you mean,' retorted Tom. 'It stands to reason I do. You're not a man of any education; you've been all your life at sea or in the islands; you don't suppose you can give points to a man like me.'

'Here's your health, Tommy,' returned Bostock. 'You'll make an A1 bake in the New Hebrides.'

'That's what I call talking,' cried Tom, not perhaps

grasping the spirit of this doubtful compliment. 'Now you give me your attention. We have the money and the enterprise, and I have the experience; what we want is a cheap, smart boat, a good captain, and an introduction to some house that will give us credit for the trade.'

'Well, I'll tell you,' said Captain Bostock. 'I have seen men like you baked and eaten, and complained of afterwards. Some was tough, and some hadn't no flaviour,' he added grimly.

'What do you mean by that,' cried Tom.

'I mean I don't care,' cried Bostock. 'It ain't any of my interests. I haven't underwrote your life. Only I'm blest if I'm not sorry for the cannibal as tries to eat your head. And what I recommend is a cheap, smart coffin and a good undertaker. See if you can find a house to give you credit for a coffin! Look at your friend there; *he's* got some sense; he's laughing at you so as he can't stand.'

The exact degree of ill-feeling in Mr Bostock's mind was difficult to gauge; perhaps there was not much, perhaps he regarded his remarks as a form of courtly badinage. But there is little doubt that Hadden resented them. He had even risen from his place, and the conference was on the point of breaking up when a new voice joined suddenly in the conversation.

The cabman sat with his back turned upon the party smoking a meerschaum pipe. Not a word of Tommy's eloquence had missed him, and he now faced suddenly about with these amazing words: –

'Excuse me, gentlemen; if you'll buy me the ship I want I'll get you the trade on credit.'

There was a pause.

'Well, what do *you* mean?' gasped Tommy.

'Better tell 'em who I am, Billy,' said the cabman.

'Think it safe, Joe?' inquired Mr Bostock.

'I'll take my risk of it,' returned the cabman.

'Gentlemen,' said Bostock, rising suddenly, 'let me make you acquainted with Captain Wicks of the *Grace Darling*.'

'Yes, gentlemen, that is what I am,' said the cabman. 'You know I've been in trouble, and I don't deny but what I struck the blow, and where was I to get evidence of my provocation? So I turned to and took a cab, and I've driven one for three year now and nobody the wiser.'

'I beg your pardon,' said Carthew, joining almost for the first time, 'I'm a new chum. What was the charge?'

'Murder,' said Captain Wicks, 'and I don't deny but what I struck the blow. And there's no sense in my trying to deny I was afraid to go to trial, or why would I be here? But it's a fact it was flat mutiny. Ask Billy here. He knows how it was.'

Carthew breathed long; he had a strange, half-pleasurable sense of wading deeper in the tide of life. 'Well,' said he, 'you were going on to say?'

'I was going on to say this,' said the captain sturdily. 'I've overheard what Mr Hadden has been saying, and I think he talks good sense. I like some of his ideas first chop. He's sound on traderooms; he's all there on the traderoom, and I see that he and I would pull together. Then you're both gentlemen, and I like that,' observed Captain Wicks. 'And then I'll tell you I'm tired of this cabbing cruise, and I want to get to work again. Now, here's my offer. I've a little money I can stake up – all of a hundred anyway. Then my old firm will give me trade, and jump at the chance; they never lost by me; they know what I'm worth as supercargo. And, last of all, you want a good captain to sail your ship for you. Well, here I am. I've sailed schooners for ten years. Ask Billy if I can handle a schooner.'

'No man better,' said Billy.

'And as for my character as a shipmate,' concluded Wicks, 'go and ask my old firm.'

'But, look here!' cried Hadden, 'how do you mean to manage? You can whisk round in a hansom and no questions asked; but if you try to come on a quarterdeck, my boy, you'll get nabbed.'

'I'll have to keep back till the last,' replied Wicks, 'and take another name.'

'But how about clearing? What other name?' asked Tommy, a little bewildered.

'I don't know yet,' returned the captain, with a grin. 'I'll see what the name is on my new certificate, and that'll be good enough for me. If I can't get one to buy, though I never heard of such a thing, there's old Kirkup, he's turned some sort of farmer down Bondi way; he'll hire me his.'

'You seemed to speak as if you had a ship in view,' said Carthew.

'So I have, too,' said Captain Wicks, 'and a beauty. Schooner yacht *Dream* – got lines you never saw the beat of, and a witch to go. She passed me once off Thursday Island, doing two knots to my one and laying a point and a half better, and the *Grace Darling* was a ship that I was proud of. I took and tore my hair. The *Dream's* been *my* dream ever since. That was in her old days, when she carried a blue ens'n. Grant Sanderson was the party as owned her; he was rich and mad, and got a fever at last somewhere about the Fly River and took and died. The captain brought the body back to Sydney and paid off. Well, it turned out Grant Sanderson had left any quantity of wills and any quantity of widows, and no fellow could make out which was the genuine article. All the widows brought lawsuits against all the rest, and every will had a firm of lawyers on the quarter-deck as long as your arm. They tell me it was one of the biggest turns-to that ever was seen, bar Tichborne; the Lord Chamberlain himself was floored, and so was the Lord Chancellor, and all that time the *Dream* lay rotting up by Glebe Point. Well, it's done now; they've picked out a widow and a will – tossed up for it, as like as not – and the *Dream's* for sale. She'll go cheap; she's had a long turn-to at rotting.'

'What size is she?'

'Well, big enough. We don't want her bigger. A hundred and ninety, going two hundred,' replied the captain. 'She's fully big for us three; it would be all the better if we had another hand, though it's a pity too, when you can pick up natives for half nothing. Then we must have a cook. I can fix raw sailor-men, but there's no going to sea with a new-chum cook. I can lay hands on the man we want for that: a Highway boy, an old shipmate of mine, of the name of Amalu. Cooks first rate, and it's always better to have a native; he ain't fly, you can turn him to as you please, and he don't know enough to stand out for his rights.'

From the moment that Captain Wicks joined in the conversation, Carthew recovered interest and confidence; the man (whatever he might have done) was plainly good-natured, and plainly capable; if he thought well of the enterprise, offered to contribute money, brought experience, and could thus solve at a word the problem of the trade, Carthew was content to go ahead. As for Hadden, his cup was full; he and Bostock forgave each other in champagne; toast followed toast; it was proposed and carried amid acclamation to change the name of the schooner (when she should be bought) to the *Currency Lass*; and the 'Currency Lass Island Trading Company' was practically founded before dusk.

Three days later, Carthew stood before the lawyer, still in his jean suit, received his hundred and fifty pounds, and proceeded rather timidly to ask for more indulgence.

'I have a chance to get on in the world,' he said. 'By tomorrow evening I expect to be part owner of a ship.'

'Dangerous property, Mr Carthew,' said the lawyer.

'Not if the partners work her themselves and stand to go down along with her,' was the reply.

'I conceive it possible you might make something of it in that way,' returned the other. 'But are you a seaman? I thought you had been in the diplomatic service.'

'I am an old yachtsman,' said Norris; and I must do the best I can. A fellow can't live in New South Wales upon diplomacy. But the point I wish to prepare you for is this. It will be impossible I should present myself here next quarter-day; we expect to make a six months' cruise of it among the islands.'

'Sorry, Mr Carthew: I can't hear of that,' replied the lawyer.

'I mean upon the same conditions as the last,' said Carthew.

'The conditions are exactly opposite,' said the lawyer. 'Last time I had reason to know you were in the colony, and even then I stretched a point. This time, by your own confession, you are contemplating a breach of the agreement; and I give you warning if you carry it out and I receive proof of it (for I will agree to regard this conversation as confidential), I shall have no choice but to do my duty. Be here on quarter-day, or your allowance ceases.'

'This is very hard and, I think, rather silly,' returned Carthew.

'It is not of my doing. I have my instructions,' said the lawyer.

'And you so read these instructions, that I am to be prohibited from making an honest livelihood?' asked Carthew.

'Let us be frank,' said the lawyer, 'I find nothing in these instructions about an honest livelihood. I have no reason to suppose my clients care anything about that. I have reason to suppose only one thing – that they mean you shall stay in this colony, and to guess another, Mr Carthew. And to guess another.'

'What do you mean by that?' asked Norris.

'I mean that I imagine, on very strong grounds, that your family desire to see no more of you,' said the lawyer. 'Oh, they may be very wrong; but that is the impression conveyed, that is what I suppose I am paid to bring about, and I have no choice but to try and earn my hire.'

'I would scorn to deceive you,' said Norris, with a strong flush, 'you have guessed rightly. My family refuse to see me; but I am not going to England, I am going to the islands. How does that affect the islands?'

'Ah, but I don't know that you are going to the islands,' said the lawyer, looking down, and spearing the blotting-paper with a pencil.

'I beg your pardon. I have the pleasure of informing you,' said Norris.

'I am afraid, Mr Carthew, that I cannot regard that communication as official,' was the slow reply.

'I am not accustomed to have my word doubted!' cried Norris.

'Hush! I allow no one to raise his voice in my office,' said the lawyer. 'And for that matter – you seem to be a young gentleman of sense – consider what I know of you. You are a discarded son; your family pays money to be shut of you. What have you done? I don't know. But do you not see how foolish I should be, if I exposed my business reputation on the safeguard of the honour of a gentleman of whom I know just so much and no more? This interview is very disagreeable. Why prolong it? Write home, get my instructions changed, and I will change my behaviour. Not otherwise.'

'I am very fond of three hundred a year,' said Norris, 'but I cannot pay the price required. I shall not have the pleasure of seeing you again.'

'You must please yourself,' said the lawyer. 'Fail to be here next quarter-day, and the thing stops. But I warn you, and I mean the warning in a friendly spirit. Three months later you will be here begging, and I shall have no choice but to show you in the street.'

'I wish you a good-evening,' said Norris.

'The same to you, Mr Carthew,' retorted the lawyer, and rang for his clerk.

So it befell that Norris during what remained to him of arduous days in Sydney, saw not again the face of his legal adviser; and he was already at sea, and land was out of sight, when Hadden brought him a Sydney paper, over which he had been dozing in the shadow of the galley, and showed him an advertisement.

'Mr Norris Carthew is earnestly entreated to call without delay at the office of Mr—, where important intelligence awaits him.'

'It must manage to wait for me six months,' said Norris lightly enough, but yet conscious of a pang of curiosity.

CHAPTER TWENTY-THREE

The Budget of the 'Currency Lass'

Before noon, on the 26th November, there cleared from the port of Sydney the schooner *Currency Lass*. The owner, Norris Carthew, was on board in the somewhat unusual position of mate; the master's name purported to be William Kirkup; the cook was a Hawaiian boy, Joseph Amalu; and there were two hands before the mast, Thomas Hadden and Richard Hemstead, the latter chosen partly because of his humble character, partly because he had an odd-jobman's handiness with tools. The *Currency Lass* was bound for the South Sea Islands, and first of all for Butaritari in the Gilberts, on a register; but it was understood about the harbour that her cruise was more than half a pleasure trip. A friend of the late Grant Sanderson (of Auchentroon and Kilclarty) might have recognised in that tall-masted ship, the transformed and rechristened *Dream*; and the Lloyd's surveyor, had the services of such a one been called in requisition, must have found abundant subject of remark.

For time, during her three years' inaction, had eaten deep into the *Dream* and her fittings; she had sold in consequence a shade above her value as old junk; and the three adventurers had scarce been able to afford even the most vital repairs. The rigging, indeed, had been partly renewed, and the rest set up; all Grant Sanderson's old canvas had been patched together into one decently serviceable suit of sails; Grant Sanderson's masts still stood, and might have wondered at themselves. 'I haven't the heart to tap them,' Captain Wicks used to observe, as he squinted up their height or patted their rotundity; and 'as rotten as our foremast' was an accepted metaphor in the ship's company. The sequel rather suggests it may have been sounder than was thought; but no one knew for certain, just as no one except the captain appreciated the dangers of the cruise. The captain, indeed, saw with clear eyes and spoke his mind aloud; and though a man of an astonishing hot-blooded courage, following life and taking its dangers in the spirit of a hound upon the slot, he had made a point of a big whaleboat. 'Take your choice,' he had said; 'either new masts and rigging or that boat. I simply ain't going to sea without the one or the other. Chicken coops are good enough, no doubt, and so is a dinghy; but they ain't for Joe.' And his partners had been forced to consent, and saw six-and-thirty pounds of their small capital vanish in the turn of a hand.

All four had toiled the best part of six weeks getting ready; and though Captain Wicks was of course not seen or heard of, a fifth was there to help them, a fellow in a bushy red beard, which he would sometimes lay aside when he was below, and who strikingly resembled Captain Wicks in voice and character. As for Captain Kirkup, he did not appear till the last moment, when he proved to be a burly mariner, bearded like Abou Ben Adhem. All the way down the harbour and through the Heads, his milk-white whiskers blew in the wind and were conspicuous from shore; but the *Currency Lass* had no sooner turned her back upon the lighthouse, than he went below for the inside of five seconds and reappeared clean shaven. So many doublings and devices were required to get to sea with an unseaworthy ship and a captain that was 'wanted.' Nor might even these have sufficed, but for the fact that Hadden was a public character, and the whole cruise regarded with an eye of indulgence as one of Tom's engaging eccentricities. The ship, besides, had been a yacht before: and it came the more natural to allow her still some of the dangerous liberties of her old employment.

A strange ship they had made of it, her lofty spars disfigured with patched canvas, her panelled cabin fitted for a traderoom with rude shelves. And the life they led in that anomalous schooner was no less curious than herself. Amalu alone berthed forward; the rest occupied staterooms, camped upon the satin divans, and sat down in Grant Sanderson's parquetry smoking-room to meals of junk and potatoes, bad of their kind and often scant in quantity. Hemstead grumbled; Tommy had occasional moments of revolt and increased the ordinary by a few haphazard tins or a bottle of his own brown sherry. But

Hemstead grumbled from habit, Tommy revolted only for the moment, and there was underneath a real and general acquiescence in these hardships. For besides onions and potatoes, the *Currency Lass* may be said to have gone to sea without stores. She carried two thousand pounds' worth of assorted trade, advanced on credit, their whole hope and fortune. It was upon this that they subsisted – mice in their own granary. They dined upon their future profits; and every scanty meal was so much in the savings bank.

Republican as were their manners, there was no practical, at least no dangerous, lack of discipline. Wicks was the only sailor on board, there was none to criticise; and besides, he was so easy-going, and so merry-minded, that none could bear to disappoint him. Carthew did his best, partly for the love of doing it, partly for love of the captain; Amalu was a willing drudge, and even Hemstead and Hadden turned to upon occasion with a will. Tommy's department was the trade and traderoom; he would work down in the hold or over the shelves of the cabin, till the Sydney dandy was unrecognisable come up at last, draw a bucket of sea-water, bathe, change, and lie down on deck over a big sheaf of Sydney *Heralds* and *Dead Birds*, or perhaps with a volume of Buckle's 'History of Civilisation,' the standard work selected for that cruise. In the latter case, a smile went round the ship, for Buckle almost invariably laid his student out, and when Tom awoke again he was almost always in the humour for brown sherry. The connection was so well established that 'a glass of Buckle' or 'a bottle of civilisation' became current pleasantries on board the *Currency Lass*.

Hemstead's province was that of the repairs, and he had his hands full. Nothing on board but was decayed in a proportion: the lamps leaked, so did the decks; door-knobs came off in the hand, mouldings parted company with the panels, the pump declined to suck, and the defective bathroom came near to swamp the ship. Wicks insisted that all the nails were long ago consumed, and that she was only glued together by the rust. 'You shouldn't make me laugh so much, Tommy,' he would say. 'I'm afraid I'll shake the sternpost out of her.' And, as Hemstead went to and fro with his tool basket on an endless round of tinkering, Wicks lost no opportunity of chaffing him upon his duties. 'If you'd turn to at sailoring or washing paint or something useful, now,' he would say, 'I could see the fun of it. But to be mending things that haven't no insides to them, appears to me the height of foolishness.' And doubtless these continual pleasantries helped to reassure the landsmen, who went to and fro unmoved, under circumstances that might have daunted Nelson.

The weather was from the outset splendid, and the wind fair and steady. The ship sailed like a witch. 'This *Currency Lass* is a powerful old girl, and has more complaints than I would care to put a name on,' the captain would say, as he pricked the chart; 'but she could show her blooming heels to anything of her size in the Western Pacific.' To wash decks, relieve the wheel, do the day's work after dinner on the smoking-room table, and take in kites at night – such was the easy routine of their life. In the evening – above all, if Tommy had produced some of his civilisation – yarns and music were the rule. Amalu had a sweet Hawaiian voice; and Hemstead, a great hand upon the banjo, accompanied his own quavering tenor with effect. There was a sense in which the little man could sing. It was great to hear him deliver 'My Boy Tammie' in Austrylian; and the words (some of the worst of the ruffian Macneil's) were hailed in his version with inextinguishable mirth.

> Where hye ye been a' dye?

he would ask, and answer himself: –

> I've been by burn and flowery brye,
> Meadow green and mountain grye,
> Courtin' o' this young thing,
>   Just come frye her mammie.

It was the accepted jest for all hands to greet the conclusion of this song with the simultaneous cry, 'My word!' thus winging the arrow of ridicule with a feather from the singer's wing. But he had his revenge with 'Home, Sweet Home,' and 'Where is my Wandering Boy Tonight?' – ditties into which he threw the most intolerable pathos. It appeared he had no home, nor had ever had one, nor yet any vestige of a family, except a truculent uncle, a baker in Newcastle, N.S.W. His domestic sentiment was therefore wholly in the air, and expressed an unrealised ideal. Or perhaps, of all his experiences, this of the *Currency Lass*, with its kindly, playful, and tolerant society, approached it the most nearly.

It is perhaps because I know the sequel, but I can never think upon this voyage without a profound sense of pity and mystery; of the ship (once the whim of a rich blackguard) faring with her battered fineries and upon her homely errand, across the plains of ocean, and past the gorgeous scenery of dawn and sunset; and the ship's company, so strangely assembled, so Britishly chuckle-headed, filling their days with chaff in place of conversation; no human book on board with them except Hadden's Buckle, and not a creature fit either to read or to understand it; and the one mark of any civilised interest being when Carthew filled in his spare hours with the pencil and the brush: the whole unconscious crew of them posting in the meanwhile towards so tragic a disaster.

Twenty-eight days out of Sydney, on Christmas Eve, they fetched up to the entrance of the lagoon, and plied all that night outside, keeping their position by the lights of fishers on the reef and the outlines of the palms against the cloudy sky. With the break of day, the schooner was hove to, and the signal for a pilot shown. But it was plain her lights must have been observed in the darkness by the native fishermen, and word carried to the settlement, for a boat was already underweigh. She came towards them across the lagoon under a great press of sail, lying dangerously down, so that at times, in the heavier puffs, they thought she would turn turtle; covered the distance in fine style, luffed up smartly alongside, and emitted a haggard looking white man in pyjamas.

'Good-mornin', cap'n,' said he, when he had made good his entrance. 'I was taking you for a Fiji man-of-war, what with your flush decks and them spars. Well, gen'lemen all, here's wishing you a merry Christmas and a happy New Year,' he added, and lurched against a stay.

'Why, you're never the pilot?' exclaimed Wicks, studying him with a profound disfavour. 'You've never taken a ship in – don't tell me!'

'Well, I should guess I have,' returned the pilot. 'I'm Captain Dobbs, I am; and when I take charge, the captain of that ship can go below and shave.'

'But, man alive! you're drunk, man!' cried the captain.

'Drunk!' repeated Dobbs. 'You can't have seen much life if you call me drunk. I'm only just beginning. Come night, I won't say; I guess I'll be properly full by then. But now I'm the soberest man in all Big Muggin.'

'It won't do,' retorted Wicks. 'Not for Joseph, sir. I can't have you piling up my schooner.'

'All right,' said Dobbs, 'lay and rot where you are, or take and go in and pile her up for yourself like the captain of the *Leslie*. That's business, I guess; grudged me twenty dollars' pilotage, and lost twenty thousand in trade and a brand new schooner; ripped the keel right off of her, and she went down in the inside of four minutes, and lies in twenty fathom, trade and all.'

'What's all this?' cried Wicks. 'Trade? What vessel was this *Leslie*, anyhow?'

'Consigned to Cohen and Co., from 'Frisco,' returned the pilot, 'and badly wanted. There's a barque inside filling up for Hamburg – you see her spars over there; and there's two more ships due, all the way from Germany, one in two months, they say, and one in three; Cohen and Co.'s agent (that's Mr Topelius) has taken and lain down with the jaundice on the strength of it. I guess most people would, in his shoes; no trade, no copra, and twenty hundred ton of shipping due. If you've any copra on board, cap'n, here's your chance. Topelius will buy, gold down and give three cents. It's all found money to him, the way it is, whatever he pays for it. And that's what come of going back on the pilot.'

'Excuse me one moment, Captain Dobbs. I wish to speak with my mate,' said the captain, whose face had begun to shine and his eyes to sparkle.

'Please yourself,' replied the pilot. 'You couldn't think of offering a man a nip, could you? just to brace him up. This kind of thing looks damned inhospitable, and gives a schooner a bad name.'

'I'll talk about that after the anchor's down,' returned Wicks, and he drew Carthew forward. 'I say,' he whispered, 'here's a fortune.'

'How much do you call that?' asked Carthew.

'I can't put a figure on it yet – I daren't!' said the captain. 'We might cruise twenty years and not find the match of it.

And suppose another ship came in tonight? Everything's possible! And the difficulty is this Dobbs. He's as drunk as a marine. How can we trust him? We ain't insured, worse luck!'

'Suppose you took him aloft and got him to point out the channel?' suggested Carthew. 'If he tallied at all with the chart, and didn't fall out of the rigging, perhaps we might risk it.'

'Well, all's risk here,' returned the captain. 'Take the wheel yourself, and stand by. Mind, if there's two orders, follow mine, not his. Set the cook for'ard with the heads'ls, and the two others at the main sheet, and see they don't sit on it.' With that he called the pilot; they swarmed aloft in the fore rigging, and presently after there was bawled down the welcome order to ease sheets and fill away.

At a quarter before nine o'clock on Christmas morning the anchor was let go.

The first cruise of the *Currency Lass* had thus ended in a stroke of fortune almost beyond hope. She had brought two thousand pounds' worth of trade, straight as a homing pigeon, to the place where it was most required. And Captain Wicks (or, rather, Captain Kirkup) showed himself the man to make the best of his advantage. For hard upon two days he walked a verandah with Topelius; for hard upon two days his partners watched from the neighbouring public-house the field of battle; and the lamps were not yet lighted on the evening of the second before the enemy surrendered. Wicks came across to the Sans Souci, as the saloon was called, his face nigh black, his eyes almost closed and all bloodshot, and yet bright as lighted matches.

'Come out here, boys,' he said; and when they were some way off among the palms, 'I hold twenty-four,' he added in a voice scarcely recognisable, and doubtless referring to the venerable game of cribbage.

'What do you mean?' asked Tommy.

'I've sold the trade,' answered Wicks; 'or, rather, I've sold only some of it, for I've kept back all the mess beef, and half the flour and biscuit, and, by God, we're still provisioned for four months! By God, it's as good as stolen!'

'My word!' cried Hemstead.

'But what have you sold it for?' gasped Carthew, the captain's almost insane excitement shaking his nerve.

'Let me tell it my own way,' cried Wicks, loosening his neck. 'Let me get at it gradual or I'll explode. I've not only sold it, boys, I've wrung out a charter on my own terms to 'Frisco and back, on my own terms. I made a point of it. I fooled him first by making believe I wanted copra, which, of course, I knew he wouldn't hear of – couldn't, in fact; and whenever he showed fight I trotted out the copra, and that man dived! I would take nothing but copra, you see; and so I've got the blooming lot in specie – all but two short bills on 'Frisco. And the sum? Well, this whole adventure, including two thousand pounds of credit, cost us two thousand seven hundred and some odd. That's all paid back; in thirty days' cruise we've paid for the schooner and the trade. Heard ever any man the match of that? And it's not all! For besides that,' said the captain, hammering his words, 'we've got thirteen blooming hundred pounds of profit to divide. I bled him in four thou.!' he cried, in a voice that broke like a schoolboy's.

For a moment the partners looked upon their chief with stupefaction, incredulous surprise their only feeling. Tommy was the first to grasp the consequences.

'Here,' he said in a hard business tone, 'come back to that saloon: I've got to get drunk.'

'You must please excuse me, boys,' said the captain earnestly. 'I daren't taste nothing. If I was to drink one glass of beer it's my belief I'd have the apoplexy. The last scrimmage and the blooming triumph pretty nigh hand done me.'

'Well, then, three cheers for the captain,' proposed Tommy.

But Wicks held up a shaking hand. 'Not that either, boys,' he pleaded. 'Think of the other buffer, and let him down easy. If I'm like this, just fancy what Topelius is. If he heard us singing out he'd have the staggers.'

As a matter of fact, Topelius accepted his defeat with a good grace; but the crew of the wrecked *Leslie*, who were in the same employment and loyal to their firm, took the thing more bitterly. Rough words and ugly looks were common. Once even they hooted Captain Wicks from the saloon verandah; the Currency Lasses drew out on the other side; for some minutes there had like to have been a battle in Butaritari; and though the occasion passed off without blows it left on either side an increase of ill-feeling.

No such small matter could affect the happiness of the successful traders. Five days more the ship lay in the lagoon, with little employment for anyone but Tommy and the captain, for Topelius's natives discharged cargo and brought ballast. The time passed like a pleasant dream; the adventurers sat up half the night debating and praising their good fortune, or strayed by day in the narrow isle gaping like Cockney tourists, and on the first of the new year the *Currency Lass* weighed anchor for the second time and set sail for 'Frisco, attended by the same fine weather and good luck. She crossed the doldrums with but small delay; on a wind and in ballast of broken coral she outdid expectations; and what added to the happiness of the ship's company, the small amount of work that fell on them to do was now lessened by the presence of another hand. This was the boatswain of the *Leslie*. He had been on bad terms with his own captain, had already spent his wages in the saloons of Butaritari, had wearied of the place, and while all his shipmates coldly refused to set foot on board the *Currency Lass* he had offered to work his passage to the coast. He was a north of Ireland man, between Scotch and Irish, rough, loud, humorous, and emotional, not without sterling qualities, and an expert and careful sailor. His frame of mind was different indeed from that of his new shipmates. Instead of making an unexpected fortune he had lost a berth, and he was besides disgusted with the rations, and really appalled at the condition of the schooner. A state-room door had stuck the first day at sea, and Mac (as they called him) laid his strength to it and plucked it from the hinges.

'Glory!' said he, 'this ship's rotten!'

'I believe you, my boy,' said Captain Wicks.

The next day the sailor was observed with his nose aloft.

'Don't you get looking at these sticks,' the captain said, 'or you'll have a fit and fall overboard.'

Mac turned towards the speaker with rather a wild eye. 'Why, I see what looks like a patch of dry rot up yonder, that I bet I could stick my fist into,' said he.

'Looks as if a fellow could stick his head into it, don't

it?' returned Wicks. 'But there's no good prying into things that can't be mended.'

'I think I was a Currency Ass to come on board of her!' reflected Mac.

'Well, I never said she was seaworthy,' replied the captain; 'I only said she could show her blooming heels to anything afloat. And besides, I don't know that it's dry rot; I kind of sometimes hope it isn't. Here; turn to and heave the log; that'll cheer you up.'

'Well, there's no denying it, you're a holy captain,' said Mac.

And from that day on, he made but the one reference to the ship's condition; and that was whenever Tommy drew upon his cellar. 'Here's to the junk trade!' he would say, as he held out his can of sherry.

'Why do you always say that?' asked Tommy.

'I had an uncle in the business,' replied Mac, and launched at once into a yarn, in which an incredible number of the characters were 'laid out as nice as you would want to see,' and the oaths made up about two-fifths of every conversation.

Only once he gave them a taste of his violence; he talked of it, indeed, often; 'I'm rather a violent man,' he would say, not without pride; but this was the only specimen. Of a sudden he turned on Hemstead in the ship's waist, knocked him against the foresail boom, then knocked him under it, and had set him up and knocked him down once more, before anyone had drawn a breath.

'Here! Belay that!' roared Wicks, leaping to his feet. 'I won't have none of this.'

Mac turned to the captain with ready civility. 'I only want to learn him manners,' said he. 'He took and called me Irishman.'

'Did he?' said Wicks. 'Oh, that's a different story! What made you do it, you tomfool? You ain't big enough to call any man that.'

'I didn't call him it,' spluttered Hemstead, through his blood and tears. 'I only mentioned-like he was.'

'Well, let's have no more of it,' said Wicks.

'But you *are* Irish, ain't you?' Carthew asked of his new shipmate shortly after.

'I may be,' replied Mac, 'but I'll allow no Sydney duck

to call me so. No,' he added, with a sudden heated countenance, 'nor any Britisher that walks! Why, look here,' he went on, 'you're a young swell, aren't you? Suppose I called you that! "I'll show you," you would say, and turn to and take it out of me straight.'

On the 28th of January, when in lat. 27° 20′ N., long. 177° W., the wind chopped suddenly into the west, not very strong, but puffy and with flaws of rain. The captain, eager for easting, made a fair wind of it and guyed the booms out wing and wing. It was Tommy's trick at the wheel, and as it was within half an hour of the relief (7.30 in the morning), the captain judged it not worth while to change him.

The puffs were heavy, but short; there was nothing to be called a squall, no danger to the ship, and scarce more than usual to the doubtful spars. All hands were on deck in their oilskins, expecting breakfast; the galley smoked, the ship smelt of coffee, all were in good humour to be speeding eastward a full nine; when the rotten foresail tore suddenly between two cloths and then split to either hand. It was for all the world as though some archangel with a huge sword had slashed it with the figure of a cross; all hands ran to secure the slatting canvas; and in the sudden uproar and alert, Tommy Hadden lost his head. Many of his days have been passed since then in explaining how the thing happened; of these explanations it will be sufficient to say that they were all different, and none satisfactory; and the gross fact remains that the main boom gybed, carried away the tackle, broke the mainmast some three feet above the deck and whipped it overboard. For near a minute the suspected foremast gallantly resisted; then followed its companion; and by the time the wreck was cleared, of the whole beautiful fabric that enabled them to skim the seas, two ragged stumps remained.

In these vast and solitary waters, to be dismasted is perhaps the worst calamity. Let the ship turn turtle and go down, and at least the pang is over. But men chained on a hulk may pass months scanning the empty sea line and counting the steps of death's invisible approach. There is no help but in the boats, and what a help is that! There heaved the *Currency Lass*, for instance, a wingless lump, and the nearest human coast (that of Kauai in the Sandwiches) lay about a thousand miles to south and east of her. Over the way there, to men contemplating that passage in an open boat, all kinds of misery, and the fear of death and of madness, brooded.

A serious company sat down to breakfast; but the captain helped his neighbours with a smile.

'Now, boys,' he said, after a pull at the hot coffee, 'we're done with this *Currency Lass*, and no mistake. One good job; we made her pay while she lasted, and she paid first rate; and if we were to try our hand again, we can try in style. Another good job; we have a fine, stiff, roomy boat, and you know who you have to thank for that. We've got six lives to save, and a pot of money; and the point is, where are we to take 'em?'

'It's all two thousand miles to the nearest of the Sandwiches, I fancy,' observed Mac.

'No, not so bad as that,' returned the captain. 'But it's bad enough; rather better'n a thousand.'

'I know a man who once did twelve hundred in a boat,' said Mac, 'and he had all he wanted. He fetched ashore in the Marquesas, and never set a foot on anything floating from that day to this. He said he would rather put a pistol to his head and knock his brains out.'

'Ay, ay!' said Wicks. 'Well I remember a boat's crew that made this very island of Kauai, and from just about where we lie, or a bit further. When they got up with the land, they were clean crazy. There was an iron-bound coast and an Old Bob Ridley of a surf on. The natives hailed 'em from fishing-boats, and sung out it couldn't be done at the money. Much they cared! there was the land, that was all they knew; and they turned to and drove the boat slap ashore in the thick of it, and was all drowned but one. No; boat trips are my eye,' concluded the captain gloomily.

The tone was surprising in a man of his indomitable temper. 'Come, captain,' said Carthew, 'you have something else up your sleeve; out with it.'

'It's a fact,' admitted Wicks. 'You see there's a raft of little bally reefs about here, kind of chicken-pox on the chart. Well, I looked 'em all up, and there's one – Midway or Brooks they call it, not forty mile from our assigned position – that I got news of. It turns out it's a coaling station of the Pacific Mail,' he said simply.

'Well, and I know it ain't no such a thing,' said Mac. 'I been quartermaster in that line myself.'

'All right,' returned Wicks. 'There's the book. Read what Hoyt says – read it aloud and let the others hear.'

Hoyt's falsehood (as readers know) was explicit; incredulity was impossible, and the news itself delightful beyond hope. Each saw in his mind's eye the boat draw in to a trim island with a wharf, coal-sheds, gardens, the Stars and Stripes and the white cottage of the keeper; saw themselves idle a few weeks in tolerable quarters, and then step on board the China mail, romantic waifs, and yet with pocketsful of money, calling for champagne and waited on by troops of stewards. Breakfast, that had begun so dully, ended amid sober jubilation, and all hands turned immediately to prepare the boat.

Now that all spars were gone, it was no easy job to get her launched. Some of the necessary cargo was first stowed on board: the specie, in particular, being packed in a strong chest and secured with lashings to the afterthwart in case of a capsize. Then a piece of the bulwark was razed to the level of the deck, and the boat swung thwart-ship, made fast with a slack line to either stump, and successfully run out. For a voyage of forty miles to hospitable quarters, not much food or water was required; but they took both in superfluity. Amalu and Mac, both ingrained sailor-men, had chests which were the headquarters of their lives; two more chests with hand-bags, oil-skins, and blankets supplied the others; Hadden, amid general applause, added the last case of the brown sherry; the captain brought the log, instruments, and chronometer; nor did Hemstead forget the banjo or a pinned handkerchief of Butaritari shells.

It was about three p.m. when they pushed off, and (the wind being still westerly) fell to the oars. 'Well, we've got the guts out of *you!*' was the captain's nodded farewell to the hulk of the *Currency Lass*, which presently shrank and faded in the sea. A little after a calm succeeded with much rain; and the first meal was eaten, and the watch below lay down to their uneasy slumber on the bilge under a roaring shower-bath. The twenty-ninth dawned overhead from out of ragged clouds; there is no moment when a boat at sea appears so trenchantly black and so conspicuously little; and the crew looked about them at the sky and water with a thrill of loneliness and fear. With sunrise the trade set in, lusty and true to the point; sail was made; the boat flew; and by about four of the afternoon, they were well up with the closed part of the reef, and the captain standing on the thwart, and holding by the mast, was studying the island through the binoculars.

'Well, and where's your station?' cried Mac.

'I don't someway pick it up,' replied the captain.

'No, nor never will!' retorted Mac, with a clang of despair and triumph in his tones.

The truth was soon plain to all. No buoys, no beacons, no lights, no coal, no station; the castaways pulled through a lagoon and landed on an isle, where was no mark of man but wreckwood, and no sound but of the sea. For the sea-fowl that harboured and lived there at the epoch of my visit were then scattered into the uttermost parts of the ocean, and had left no traces of their sojourn besides dropped feathers and addled eggs. It was to this they had been sent, for this they had stopped all night over the dripping oars, hourly moving further from relief. The boat, for as small as it was, was yet eloquent of the hands of men, a thing alone indeed upon the sea but yet in itself all human; and the isle, for which they had exchanged it, was ingloriously savage, a place of distress, solitude, and hunger unrelieved. There was a strong glare and shadow of the evening over all; in which they sat or lay, not speaking, careless even to eat, men swindled out of life and riches by a lying book. In the great good-nature of the whole party, no word of reproach had been addressed to Hadden, the author of these disasters. But the new blow was less magnanimously borne, and many angry glances rested on the captain.

Yet it was himself who roused them from their lethargy. Grudgingly they obeyed, drew the boat beyond tidemark, and followed him to the top of the miserable islet, whence a view was commanded of the whole wheel of the horizon, then part darkened under the coming night, part dyed with the hues of the sunset and populous with the sunset clouds. Here the camp was pitched and a tent run up with the oars, sails, and mast. And here Amalu, at no man's bidding, from the mere instinct of habitual service, built a fire and cooked a meal. Night was come, and the stars and the silver sickle of new moon beamed overhead, before the meal was ready.

The cold sea shone about them, and the fire glowed in their faces as they ate. Tommy had opened his case, and the brown sherry went the round; but it was long before they came to conversation.

'Well, is it to be Kauai, after all?' asked Mac suddenly.

'This is bad enough for me,' said Tommy. 'Let's stick it out where we are.'

'Well, I can tell ye one thing,' said Mac, 'if ye care to hear it. When I was in the China mail, we once made this island. It's in the course from Honolulu.'

'Deuce it is!' cried Carthew. 'That settles it, then. Let's stay. We must keep good fires going; and there's plenty wreck.'

'Lashings of wreck!' said the Irishman. 'There's nothing here but wreck and coffin boards.'

'But we'll have to make a proper blyze,' objected Hemstead. 'You can't see a fire like this, not any wye awye, I mean.'

'Can't you?' said Carthew. 'Look round.'

They did, and saw the hollow of the night, the bare, bright face of the sea, and the stars regarding them; and the voices died in their bosoms at the spectacle. In that huge isolation, it seemed they must be visible from China on the one hand and California on the other.

'My God, it's dreary!' whispered Hemstead.

'Dreary?' cried Mac, and fell suddenly silent.

'It's better than a boat, anyway,' said Hadden. 'I've had my bellyful of boat.'

'What kills me is that specie!' the captain broke out. 'Think of all that riches – four thousand in gold, bad silver, and short bills – all found money, too! – and no more use than that much dung!'

'I'll tell you one thing,' said Tommy. 'I don't like it being in the boat – don't care to have it so far away.'

'Why, who's to take it?' cried Mac, with a guffaw of evil laughter.

But this was not at all the feeling of the partners, who rose, clambered down the isle, brought back the inestimable treasure-chest slung upon two oars, and set it conspicuous in the shining of the fire.

'There's my beauty!' cried Wicks, viewing it with a cocked head; 'that's better than a bonfire. What! we have a chest here, and bills for close upon two thousand pounds; there's no show to that – it would go in your vest pocket – but the rest! upwards of forty pounds avoirdupois of coined gold, and close on two hundredweight of Chile silver! What! ain't that good enough to fetch a fleet? Do you mean to say that won't affect a ship's compass? Do you mean to tell me that the look-out won't turn to and *smell* it?' he cried.

Mac, who had no part nor lot in the bills, the forty pounds of gold, or the two hundred weight of silver, heard this with impatience, and fell into a bitter, choking laughter. 'You'll see!' he said harshly. 'You'll be glad to feed them bills into the fire before you're through with ut!' And he turned, passed by himself out of the ring of the firelight, and stood gazing seaward.

His speech and his departure extinguished instantly those sparks of better humour kindled by the dinner and the chest. The group fell again to an ill-favoured silence, and Hemstead began to touch the banjo, as was his habit of an evening. His repertory was small: the chords of 'Home, Sweet Home' fell under his fingers; and when he had played the symphony, he instinctively raised up his voice. 'Be it never so 'umble, there's no plyce like 'ome,' he sang. The last word was still upon his lips, when the instrument was snatched from him and dashed into the fire; and he turned with a cry to look into the furious countenance of Mac.

'I'll be damned if I stand this!' cried the captain leaping up belligerent.

'I told ye I was a voilent man,' said Mac, with a movement of deprecation very surprising in one of his character. 'Why don't he give me a chance, then? Haven't we enough to bear the way we are?' And to the wonder and dismay of all, the man choked upon a sob. 'It's ashamed of meself I am,' he said presently, his Irish accent twenty-fold increased. 'I ask all your pardons for me voilence; and especially the little man's, who is a harmless craytur, and here's me hand to'm, if he'll condescind to take me by't.'

So this scene of barbarity and sentimentalism passed off, leaving behind strange and incongruous impressions. True, everyone was perhaps glad when silence succeeded that all too appropriate music; true, Mac's apology and subsequent behaviour rather raised him in the opinion of his fellow-castaways. But the discordant note had been struck, and its harmonics tingled in the brain. In that savage, houseless isle, the passions of man had sounded, if only for the moment, and all men trembled at the possibilities of horror.

It was determined to stand watch and watch in case of passing vessels; and Tommy, on fire with an idea, volunteered to stand the first. The rest crawled under the tent, and were soon enjoying that comfortable gift of sleep, which comes everywhere and to all men, quenching anxieties and speeding time. And no sooner were all settled, no sooner had the drone of many snorers begun to mingle with and overcome the surf, than Tommy stole from his post with the case of sherry, and dropped it in a quiet cove in a fathom of water. But the stormy inconstancy of Mac's behaviour had no connection with a gill or two of wine; his passions, angry and otherwise, were on a different sail plan from his neighbours'; and there were possibilities of good and evil in that hybrid Celt beyond their prophecy.

About two in the morning, the starry sky – or so it seemed, for the drowsy watchman had not observed the approach of any cloud – brimmed over in a deluge; and for three days it rained without remission. The islet was a sponge, the castaways sops; the view all gone, even the reef concealed behind the curtain of the falling water. The fire was soon drowned out; after a couple of boxes of matches had been scratched in vain, it was decided to wait for better weather; and the party lived in wretchedness on raw tins and a ration of hard bread.

By the 2nd February, in the dark hours of the morning watch, the clouds were all blown by; the sun rose glorious; and once more the castaways sat by a quick fire, and drank hot coffee with the greed of brutes and sufferers. Thenceforward their affairs moved in a routine. A fire was constantly maintained; and this occupied one hand continuously, and the others for an hour or so in the day. Twice a day, all hands bathed in the lagoon, their chief, almost their only pleasure. Often they fished in the lagoon with good success. And the rest was passed in lolling, strolling, yarns, and disputation. The time of the China steamers was calculated to a nicety; which done, the thought was rejected and ignored. It was one that would not bear consideration. The boat voyage having been tacitly set aside, the desperate part chosen to wait there for the coming of help or of starvation, no man had courage left to look his bargain in the face, far less to discuss it with his neighbours. But the unuttered terror haunted them; in every hour of idleness, at every moment of silence, it returned, and breathed a chill about the circle, and carried men's eyes to the horizon. Then, in a panic of self-defence, they would rally to some other subject. And, in that lone spot, what else was to be found to speak of but the treasure?

That was indeed the chief singularity, the one thing conspicuous in their island life; the presence of that chest of bills and specie dominated the mind like a cathedral; and there were besides connected with it, certain irking problems well fitted to occupy the idle. Two thousand pounds were due to the Sydney firm; two thousand pounds were clear profit, and fell to be divided in varying proportions among six. It had been agreed how the partners were to range; every pound of capital subscribed, every pound that fell due in wages, was to count for one 'lay.' Of these, Tommy could claim five hundred and ten, Carthew one hundred and seventy, Wicks one hundred and forty, and Hemstead and Amalu ten apiece: eight hundred and forty 'lays' in all. What was the value of a lay? This was at first debated in the air and chiefly by the strength of Tommy's lungs. Then followed a series of incorrect calculations; from which they issued, arithmetically foiled, but agreed from weariness upon an approximate value of £2 7s. 7¹4d. The figures were admittedly incorrect; the sum of the shares came not to £2,000, but to £1,996 6s. – £3 14s. being thus left unclaimed. But it was the nearest they had yet found, and the highest as well, so that the partners were made the less critical by the contemplation of their splendid dividends. Wicks put in £100 and stood to draw captain's wages for two months; his taking was £333 3s. 6³4d. Carthew had put in £150: he was to take out £401 18s. 6¹2d. Tommy's £500 had grown to be £1,213 12s. 9³4d; and Amalu and Hemstead, ranking for wages only, had £22 16s. 0¹2d. each.

From talking and brooding on these figures it was but a step to opening the chest, and once the chest open the glamour of the cash was irresistible. Each felt that he must see his treasure separate with the eye of flesh, handle it in the hard coin, mark it for his own, and stand forth to himself the approved owner. And here an insurmountable difficulty barred the way. There were some seventeen shillings in English silver, the rest was Chile; and the Chile dollar, which had been taken at the rate of six to the pound sterling, was practically their smallest coin. It was decided, therefore, to divide the pounds only, and to throw the shillings, pence, and fractions in a common fund. This, with the three pound fourteen already in the heel, made a total of seven pounds one shilling.

'I'll tell you,' said Wicks. 'Let Carthew and Tommy and me take one pound apiece, and Hemstead and Amalu split the other four, and toss up for the odd bob.'

'Oh, rot!' said Carthew. 'Tommy and I are bursting already. We can take half a sov. each, and let the other three have forty shillings.'

'I'll tell you now, it's not worth splitting,' broke in Mac. 'I've cards in my chest. Why don't you play for the lump sum?'

In that idle place the proposal was accepted with delight. Mac, as the owner of the cards, was given a stake; the sum was played for in five games of cribbage; and when Amalu, the last survivor in the tournament, was beaten by Mac it was found the dinner-hour was past. After a hasty meal they fell again immediately to cards, this time (on Carthew's proposal) to Van John. It was then probably two p.m. of the 9th of February, and they played with varying chances for twelve hours, slept heavily, and rose late on the morrow to resume the game. All day of the 10th, with grudging intervals for food, and with one long absence on the part of Tommy, from which he returned dripping with the case of sherry, they continued to deal and stake. Night fell; they drew the closer to the fire. It was maybe two in the morning, and Tommy was selling his deal by auction, as usual with that timid player, when Carthew, who didn't intend to bid, had a moment of leisure and looked round him. He beheld the moonlight on the sea, the money piled and scattered in that incongruous place, the perturbed faces of the players. He felt in his own breast the familiar tumult; and it seemed as if there rose in his ears a sound of music, and the moon seemed still to shine upon a sea, but the sea was changed, and the Casino towered from among lamplit gardens, and the money clinked on the green board. 'Good God!' he thought, 'am I gambling again?' He looked the more curiously about the sandy table. He and Mac had played and won like gamblers; the mingled gold and silver lay by their places in the heap. Amalu and Hemstead had each more than held their own, but Tommy was cruel far to leeward, and the captain was reduced to perhaps fifty pounds.

'I say, let's knock off,' said Carthew.

'Give that man a glass of Buckle,' said someone, and a fresh bottle was opened, and the game went inexorably on.

Carthew was himself too heavy a winner to withdraw or to say more, and all the rest of the night he must look on at the progress of this folly, and make gallant attempts to lose with the not uncommon consequence of winning more. The first dawn of the 11th February found him well-nigh desperate. It chanced he was then dealer and still winning. He had just dealt a round of many tens; everyone had staked heavily. The captain had put up all that remained to him – twelve pounds in gold and a few dollars – and Carthew, looking privately at his cards before he showed them, found he held a natural.

'See here, you fellows,' he broke out, 'this is a sickening business, and I'm done with it for one.' So saying, he showed his cards, tore them across, and rose from the ground.

The company stared and murmured in mere amazement; but Mac stepped gallantly to his support.

'We've had enough of it, I do believe,' said he. 'But of course it was all fun, and here's my counters back. 'All counters in, boys!' and he began to pour his winnings into the chest, which stood fortunately near him.

Carthew stepped across and wrung him by the hand. 'I'll never forget this,' he said.

'And what are ye going to do with the Highway boy and the plumber?' inquired Mac, in a low tone of voice. 'They've both wan, ye see.'

'That's true!' said Carthew aloud. 'Amalu and Hemstead, count your winnings; Tommy and I pay that.'

It was carried without speech; the pair glad enough to receive their winnings, it mattered not from whence;

and Tommy, who had lost about five hundred pounds, delighted with the compromise.

'And how about Mac?' asked Hemstead. 'Is he to lose all?'

'I beg your pardon, plumber. I'm sure ye mean well,' returned the Irishman, 'but you'd better shut your face, for I'm not that kind of a man. If I t'ought I had wan that money fair, there's never a soul here could get it from me. But I t'ought it was in fun; that was my mistake, ye see; and there's no man big enough upon this island to give a present to my mother's son. So there's my opinion to ye, plumber, and you can put it in your pockut till required.'

'Well, I will say, Mac, you're a gentleman,' said Carthew, as he helped him to shovel back his winnings into the treasure chest.

'Divil a fear of it, sir! a drunken sailor-man,' said Mac.

The captain had sat somewhile with his face in his hands; now he rose mechanically, shaking and stumbling like a drunkard after a debauch. But as he rose, his face was altered, and his voice rang out over the isle, 'Sail, ho!'

All turned at the cry, and there, in the wild light of the morning, heading straight for Midway Reef, was the brig *Flying Scud* of Hull.

CHAPTER TWENTY-FOUR

A Hard Bargain

The ship which thus appeared before the castaways had long 'tramped' the ocean, wandering from one port to another as freights offered. She was two years out from London, by the Cape of Good Hope, India, and the Archipelago; and was now bound for San Francisco in the hope of working homeward round the Horn. Her captain was one Jacob Trent. He had retired some five years before to a suburban cottage, a patch of cabbages, a gig, and the conduct of what he called a Bank. The name appears to have been misleading. Borrowers were accustomed to choose works of art and utility in the front shop; loaves of sugar and bolts of broadcloth were deposited in pledge; and it was a part of the manager's duty to dash in his gig on Saturday evenings from one small retainer's to another, and to annex in each the bulk of the week's takings. His was thus an active life, and to a man of the type of a rat, filled with recondite joys. An unexpected loss, a lawsuit, and the unintelligent commentary of the judge upon the bench, combined to disgust him of the business. I was so extraordinarily fortunate as to find, in an old newspaper, a report of the proceedings in Lyall *v.* The Cardiff Mutual Accommodation Banking Co. 'I confess I fail entirely to understand the nature of the business,' the judge had remarked, while Trent was being examined in chief; a little after, on fuller information – 'They call it a bank,' he had opined, 'but it seems to me to be an unlicensed pawnshop;' and he wound up with this appalling allocution: 'Mr Trent, I must put you on your guard; you must be very careful, or we shall see you here again.' In the inside of a week the captain disposed of the bank, the cottage, and the gig and horse; and to sea again in the *Flying Scud*, where he did well and gave high satisfaction to his owners. But the glory clung to him; he was a plain sailor-man, he said, but he could never long allow you to forget that he had been a banker.

His mate, Elias Goddedaal, was a huge Viking of a man, six feet three and of proportionate mass, strong, sober, industrious, musical, and sentimental. He ran continually over into Swedish melodies, chiefly in the minor. He had paid nine dollars to hear Patti; to hear Nilsson, he had deserted a ship and two months' wages; and he was ready at any time to walk ten miles for a good concert or seven to a reasonable play. On board he had three treasures: a canary bird, a concertina, and a blinding copy of the works of Shakespeare. He had a gift, peculiarly Scandinavian, of making friends at sight: an elemental innocence commended him; he was without fear, without reproach, and without money or the hope of making it.

Holdorsen was second mate, and berthed aft, but messed usually with the hands.

Of one more of the crew, some image lives. This was a foremost hand out of the Clyde, of the name of Brown. A small, dark, thick-set creature, with dog's eyes, of a disposition incomparably mild and harmless, he knocked about seas and cities, the uncomplaining whiptop of one vice. 'The drink is my trouble, ye see,' he said to Carthew shyly; 'and it's the more shame to me because I'm come of very good people at Bowling down the wa'er.' The letter that so much affected Nares, in case the reader should remember it, was addressed to this man Brown.

Such was the ship that now carried joy into the bosoms of the castaways. After the fatigue and the bestial emotions of their night of play, the approach of salvation shook them from all self-control. Their hands trembled, their eyes shone, they laughed and shouted like children as they cleared their camp: and someone beginning to whistle 'Marching Through Georgia,' the remainder of the packing was conducted, amidst a thousand interruptions, to these martial strains. But the strong head of Wicks was only partly turned.

'Boys,' he said, 'easy all! We're going aboard of a ship of which we don't know nothing; we've got a chest of specie, and seeing the weight, we can't turn to and deny it. Now, suppose she was fishy; suppose it was some kind of a Bully

Hayes business! It's my opinion we'd better be on hand with the pistols.'

Every man of the party but Hemstead had some kind of a revolver; these were accordingly loaded and disposed about the persons of the castaways, and the packing was resumed and finished in the same rapturous spirit as it was begun. The sun was not yet ten degrees above the eastern sea, but the brig was already close in and hove to, before they had launched the boat and sped, shouting at the oars, towards the passage.

It was blowing fresh outside with a strong send of sea. The spray flew in the oarsmen's faces. They saw the Union Jack blow abroad from the *Flying Scud*, the men clustered at the rail, the cook in the galley door, the captain on the quarter-deck with a pith helmet and binoculars. And the whole familiar business, the comfort, company, and safety of a ship, heaving nearer at each stroke, maddened them with joy.

Wicks was the first to catch the line, and swarm on board, helping hands grabbing him as he came and hauling him across the rail.

'Captain, sir, I suppose?' he said, turning to the hard old man in the pith helmet.

'Captain Trent, sir,' returned the old gentleman.

'Well, I'm Captain Kirkup, and this is the crew of the Sydney schooner *Currency Lass*, dismasted at sea January 28th.'

'Ay, ay,' said Trent. 'Well, you're all right now. Lucky for you I saw your signal. I didn't know I was so near this beastly island, there must be a drift to the south'ard here; and when I came on deck this morning at eight bells, I thought it was a ship afire.'

It had been agreed that, while Wicks was to board the ship and do the civil, the rest were to remain in the whaleboat and see the treasure safe. A tackle was passed down to them; to this they made fast the invaluable chest, and gave the word to heave. But the unexpected weight brought the hand at the tackle to a stand; two others ran to tail on and help him, and the thing caught the eye of Trent.

''Vast heaving!' he cried sharply; and then to Wicks: 'What's that? I don't ever remember to have seen a chest weigh like that.'

'It's money,' said Wicks.

'It's what?' cried Trent.

'Specie,' said Wicks; 'saved from the wreck.'

Trent looked at him sharply. 'Here, let go that chest again, Mr Goddedaal,' he commanded, 'shove the boat off, and stream her with a line astern.'

'Ay, ay, sir!' from Goddedaal.

'What the devil's wrong?' asked Wicks.

'Nothing, I daresay,' returned Trent. 'But you'll allow it's a queer thing when a boat turns up in mid-ocean with half a ton of specie and everybody armed,' he added, pointing to Wicks's pocket. 'Your boat will lay comfortably astern, while you come below and make yourself satisfactory.'

'Oh, if that's all!' said Wicks. 'My log and papers are as right as the mail; nothing fishy about us.' And he hailed his friends in the boat, bidding them have patience, and turned to follow Captain Trent.

'This way, Captain Kirkup,' said the latter. 'And don't blame a man for too much caution; no offence intended; and these China rivers shake a fellow's nerve. All I want is just to see you're what you say you are; it's only my duty, sir, and what you would do yourself in the circumstances. I've not always been a ship-captain: I was a banker once, and I tell you that's the trade to learn caution in. You have to keep your weather-eye lifting Saturday nights.' And with a dry, business-like cordiality, he produced a bottle of gin.

The captains pledged each other; the papers were over-hauled; the tale of Topelius and the trade was told in appreciative ears and cemented their acquaintance. Trent's suspicions, thus finally disposed of, were succeeded by a fit of profound thought, during which he sat lethargic and stern, looking at and drumming on the table.

'Anything more?' asked Wicks.

'What sort of a place is it inside?' inquired Trent, sudden as though Wicks had touched a spring.

'It's a good enough lagoon – a few horses' heads, but nothing to mention,' answered Wicks.

'I've a good mind to go in,' said Trent. 'I was new rigged in China; it's given very bad, and I'm getting frightened for my sticks. We could set it up as good as new in a day. For I daresay your lot would turn to and give us a hand?'

'You see if we don't! said Wicks.

'So be it then,' concluded Trent. 'A stitch in time saves nine.'

They returned on deck; Wicks cried the news to the Currency Lasses; the foretopsail was filled again, and the brig ran into the lagoon lively, the whaleboat dancing in her wake, and came to single anchor off Middle Brooks Islands before eight. She was boarded by the castaways, breakfast was served, the baggage slung on board and piled in the waist, and all hands turned to upon the rigging. All day the work continued, the two crews rivalling each other in expense of strength. Dinner was served on deck, the officers messing aft under the slack of the spanker, the men fraternising forward. Trent appeared in excellent spirits, served out grog to all hands, opened a bottle of Cape wine for the after-table, and obliged his guests with many details of the life of a financier in Cardiff. He had been forty years at sea, had five times suffered shipwreck, was once nine months the prisoner of a pepper rajah, and had seen service under fire in Chinese rivers; but the only thing he cared to talk of, the only thing of which he was vain, or with which he thought it possible to interest a stranger, was his career as a money-lender in the slums of a seaport town.

The afternoon spell told cruelly on the Currency Lasses. Already exhausted as they were with sleeplessness and excitement, they did the last hours of this violent employment on bare nerves; and when Trent was at last satisfied with the condition of his rigging, expected eagerly the word to put to sea. But the captain seemed in no hurry. He went and walked by himself softly, like a man in thought. Presently he hailed Wicks.

'You're a kind of company, ain't you, Captain Kirkup?' he inquired.

'Yes, we're all on board on lays,' was the reply.

'Well, then, you won't mind if I ask the lot of you down to tea in the cabin?' asked Trent.

Wicks was amazed, but he naturally ventured no remark; and a little after, the six Currency Lasses sat down with Trent and Goddedaal to a spread of marmalade, butter, toast, sardines, tinned tongue, and steaming tea. The food was not very good, and I have no doubt Nares would have reviled it, but it was manna to the castaways. Goddedaal waited on them with a kindness far before courtesy, a kindness like that of some old, honest countrywoman in her farm. It was remembered afterwards that Trent took little share in these attentions, but sat much absorbed in thought, and seemed to remember and forget the presence of his guests alternately.

Presently he addressed the Chinaman.

'Clear out,' said he, and watched him till he had disappeared in the stair. 'Now, gentlemen,' he went on, 'I understand you're a joint-stock sort of crew, and that's why I've had you all down; for there's a point I want made clear. You see what sort of a ship this is – a good ship, though I say it, and you see what the rations are – good enough for sailormen.'

There was a hurried murmur of approval, but curiosity for what was coming next prevented an articulate reply.

'Well,' continued Trent, making bread pills and looking hard at the middle of the table, 'I'm glad of course to be able to give you a passage to 'Frisco; one sailor-man should help another, that's my motto. But when you want a thing in this world, you generally always have to pay for it.' He laughed a brief, joyless laugh. 'I have no idea of losing by my kindness.'

'We have no idea you should, captain,' said Wicks.

'We are ready to pay anything in reason,' added Carthew.

At the words, Goddedaal, who sat next to him, touched him with his elbow, and the two mates exchanged a significant look. The character of Captain Trent was given and taken in that silent second.

'In reason?' repeated the captain of the brig. 'I was waiting for that. Reason's between two people, and there's only one here. I'm the judge; I'm reason. If you want an advance you have to pay for it' – he hastily corrected himself – 'If you want a passage in my ship, you have to pay my price,' he substituted. 'That's business, I believe. I don't want you; you want me.'

'Well, sir,' said Carthew, 'and what *is* your price?'

The captain made bread pills. 'If I were like you,' he said, 'when you got hold of that merchant in the Gilberts, I might surprise you. You had your chance then; seems to me it's mine now. Turn about's fair play. What kind of mercy did you have on that Gilbert merchant?' he cried, with a sudden stridency. 'Not that I blame you. All's fair in love and business,' and he laughed again, a little frosty giggle.

'Well, sir?' said Carthew gravely.

'Well, this ship's mine, I think?' he asked sharply.

'Well, I'm of that way of thinking meself,' observed Mac.

'I say it's mine, sir!' reiterated Trent, like a man trying to be angry. 'And I tell you all, if I was a driver like what you are, I would take the lot. But there's two thousand pounds there that don't belong to you, and I'm an honest man. Give me the two thousand that's yours and I'll give you a passage to the coast, and land every man-jack of you in 'Frisco with fifteen pounds in his pocket, and the captain here with twenty-five.'

Goddedaal laid down his head on the table like a man ashamed.

'You're joking,' cried Wicks, purple in the face.

'Am I?' said Trent. 'Please yourselves. You're under no compulsion. This ship's mine, but there's that Brooks Island don't belong to me, and you can lay there till you die for what I care.'

'It's more than your blooming brig's worth!' cried Wicks.

'It's my price anyway,' returned Trent.

'And do you mean to say you would land us there to starve?' cried Tommy.

Captain Trent laughed the third time. 'Starve? I defy you to,' said he. 'I'll sell you all the provisions you want at a fair profit.'

'I beg your pardon, sir,' said Mac, 'but my case is by itself. I'm working me passage; I got no share in that two thousand pounds nor nothing in my pockut; and I'll be glad to know what you have to say to me?'

'I ain't a hard man,' said Trent; 'that shall make no difference. I'll take you with the rest, only of course you get no fifteen pound.'

The impudence was so extreme and startling, that all breathed deep, and Goddedaal raised up his face and looked his superior sternly in the eye.

But Mac was more articulate. 'And you're what ye call a British sayman, I suppose? the sorrow in your guts!' he cried.

'One more such word, and I clap you in irons!' said Trent, rising gleefully at the face of opposition.

'And where would I be the while you were doin' ut?' asked Mac. 'After you and your rigging, too! Ye ould puggy, ye haven't the civility of a bug, and I'll learn ye some.'

His voice did not even rise as he uttered the threat; no man present, Trent least of all, expected that which followed. The Irishman's hand rose suddenly from below the table, an open clasp-knife balanced on the palm; there was a movement swift as conjuring; Trent started half to his feet, turning a little as he rose so as to escape the table, and the movement was his bane. The missile struck him in the jugular; he fell forward, and his blood flowed among the dishes on the cloth.

The suddenness of the attack and the catastrophe, the instant change from peace to war and from life to death, held all men spellbound. Yet a moment they sat about the table staring open-mouthed upon the prostrate captain and the flowing blood. The next, Goddedaal had leaped to his feet, caught up the stool in which he had been sitting, and swung it high in air, a man transfigured, roaring (as he stood) so that men's ears were stunned with it. There was no thought of battle in the Currency Lasses; none drew his weapon; all huddled helplessly from before the face of the baresark Scandinavian. His first blow sent Mac to ground with a broken arm. His second dashed out the brains of Hemstead. He turned from one to another, menacing and trumpeting like a wounded elephant, exulting in his rage. But there was no counsel, no light of reason, in that ecstasy of battle; and he shied from the pursuit of victory to hail fresh blows upon the supine Hemstead, so that the stool was shattered and the cabin rang with their violence. The sight of that post-mortem cruelty recalled Carthew to the life of instinct, and his revolver was in hand and he had aimed and fired before he knew. The ear-bursting sound of the report was accompanied by a yell of pain; the colossus paused, swayed, tottered, and fell headlong on the body of his victim.

In the instant silence that succeeded, the sound of feet pounding on the deck and in the companion leaped into hearing; and a face, that of the sailor Holdorsen, appeared below the bulkheads in the cabin doorway.

Carthew shattered it with a second shot, for he was a marksman.

'Pistols!' he cried, and charged at the companion, Wicks at his heels, Tommy and Amalu following. They trod the body of Holdorsen underfoot, and flew upstairs and forth into the dusky blaze of a sunset red as blood. The numbers were still equal, but the Flying Scuds dreamed not of defence, and fled with one accord for the forecastle scuttle. Brown was first in flight; he disappeared below unscathed; the Chinaman followed head-foremost with a ball in his side; and the others shinned into the rigging.

A fierce composure settled upon Wicks and Carthew, their fighting second wind. They posted Tommy at the fore and Amalu at the main to guard the masts and shrouds, and going themselves into the waist, poured out a box of cartridges on deck and filled the chambers. The poor devils aloft bleated aloud for mercy. But the hour of any mercy was gone by; the cup was brewed and must be drunken to the dregs; since so many had fallen all must fall. The light was bad, the cheap revolvers fouled and carried wild, the screaming wretches were swift to flatten themselves against the masts and yards or find a momentary refuge in the hanging sails. The fell business took long, but it was done at last. Hardy the Londoner was shot on the fore-royal yard, and hung horribly suspended in the brails. Wallen, the other, had his jaw broken on the maintop-gallant crosstrees, and exposed himself, shrieking, till a second shot dropped him on the deck.

This had been bad enough, but worse remained behind. There was still Brown in the forepeak. Tommy, with a sudden clamour of weeping, begged for his life. 'One man can't hurt us,' he sobbed. 'We can't go on with this. I spoke to him at dinner. He's an awful decent little cad. It can't be done. Nobody can go into that place and murder him. It's too damned wicked.'

The sound of his supplications was perhaps audible to the unfortunate below.

'One left, and we all hang,' said Wicks. 'Brown must go the same road.' The big man was deadly white and trembled like an aspen; and he had no sooner finished speaking, than he went to the ship's side and vomited.

'We can never do it if we wait,' said Carthew. 'Now or never,' and he marched towards the scuttle.

'No, no, no!' wailed Tommy, clutching at his jacket.

But Carthew flung him off, and stepped down the ladder, his heart rising with disgust and shame. The Chinaman lay on the floor, still groaning; the place was pitch dark.

'Brown!' cried Carthew, 'Brown, where are you?'

His heart smote him for the treacherous apostrophe, but no answer came.

He groped in the bunks: they were all empty. Then he moved towards the forepeak, which was hampered with coils of rope and spare chandlery in general.

'Brown!' he said again.

'Here, sir,' answered a shaking voice; and the poor invisible caitiff called on him by name, and poured forth out of the darkness an endless, garrulous appeal for mercy. A sense of danger, of daring, had alone nerved Carthew to enter the forecastle; and here was the enemy crying and pleading like a frightened child. His obsequious 'Here, sir,' his horrid fluency of obtestation, made the murder tenfold more revolting. Twice Carthew raised the pistol, once he pressed the trigger (or thought he did) with all his might, but no explosion followed; and with that the lees of his courage ran quite out, and he turned and fled from before his victim.

Wicks sat on the fore hatch, raised the face of a man of seventy, and looked a wordless question. Carthew shook his head. With such composure as a man displays marching towards the gallows, Wicks arose, walked to the scuttle, and went down. Brown thought it was Carthew returning, and discovered himself, half-crawling from his shelter, with another incoherent burst of pleading. Wicks emptied his revolver at the voice, which broke into mouse-like whimperings and groans. Silence succeeded, and the murderer ran on deck like one possessed.

The other three were now all gathered on the fore hatch, and Wicks took his place beside them without question asked or answered. They sat close like children in the dark, and shook each other with their shaking. The dusk continued to fall; and there was no sound but the beating of the surf and the occasional hiccup of a sob from Tommy Hadden.

'God, if there was another ship!' cried Carthew of a sudden.

Wicks started and looked aloft with the trick of all seamen, and shuddered as he saw the hanging figure on the royal-yard.

'If I went aloft, I'd fall,' he said simply. 'I'm done up.'

It was Amalu who volunteered, climbed to the very truck, swept the fading horizon, and announced nothing within sight.

'No odds,' said Wicks. 'We can't sleep . . .'

'Sleep!' echoed Carthew; and it seemed as if the whole of Shakespeare's *Macbeth* thundered at the gallop through his mind.

'Well, then, we can't sit and chitter here,' said Wicks, 'till we've cleaned ship; and I can't turn to till I've had gin, and the gin's in the cabin, and who's to fetch it?'

'I will,' said Carthew, 'if anyone has matches.'

Amalu passed him a box, and he went aft and down the companion and into the cabin, stumbling upon bodies. Then he struck a match, and his looks fell upon two living eyes.

'Well?' asked Mac, for it was he who still survived in that shambles of a cabin.

'It's done; they're all dead,' answered Carthew.

'Christ!' said the Irishman, and fainted.

The gin was found in the dead captain's cabin; it was brought on deck, and all hands had a dram, and attacked their further task. The night was come, the moon would not be up for hours; a lamp was set on the main hatch to light Amalu as he washed down decks; and the galley lantern was taken to guide the others in their graveyard business. Holdorsen, Hemstead, Trent, and Goddedaal were first disposed of, the last still breathing as he went over the side; Wallen followed; and then Wicks, steadied by the gin, went aloft with a boathook and succeeded in dislodging Hardy. The Chinaman was their last task; he seemed to be light-headed, talked aloud in his unknown language as they brought him up, and it was only with the splash of his sinking body that the gibberish ceased. Brown, by common consent was left alone. Flesh and blood could go no farther.

All this time they had been drinking undiluted gin like

water; three bottles stood broached in different quarters; and none passed without a gulp. Tommy collapsed against the mainmast; Wicks fell on his face on the poop ladder and moved no more; Amalu had vanished unobserved. Carthew was the last afoot: he stood swaying at the break of the poop, and the lantern, which he still carried, swung with his movement. His head hummed; it swarmed with broken thoughts; memory of that day's abominations flared up and died down within him, like the light of a lamp in a strong draught. And then he had a drunkard's inspiration.

'There must be no more of this,' he thought, and stumbled once more below.

The absence of Holdorsen's body brought him to a stand. He stood and stared at the empty floor, and then remembered and smiled. From the captain's room he took the open case with one dozen and three bottles of gin, put the lantern inside, and walked precariously forth. Mac was once more conscious, his eyes haggard, his face drawn with pain and flushed with fever; and Carthew remembered he had never been seen to, had lain there helpless, and was so to lie all night, injured, perhaps dying. But it was now too late; reason had now fled from that silent ship. If Carthew could get on deck again, it was as much as he could hope; and casting on the unfortunate a glance of pity, the tragic drunkard shouldered his way up the companion, dropped the case overboard, and fell in the scuppers helpless.

CHAPTER TWENTY-FIVE

A Bad Bargain

With the first colour in the east, Carthew awoke and sat up. Awhile he gazed at the scroll of the morning bank and the spars and hanging canvas of the brig, like a man who wakes in a strange bed, with a child's simplicity of wonder. He wondered above all what ailed him, what he had lost, what disfavour had been done him, which he knew he should resent, yet had forgotten. And then, like a river bursting through a dam, the truth rolled on him its instantaneous volume: his memory teemed with speech and pictures that he should never again forget; and he sprang to his feet, stood a moment hand to brow, and began to walk violently to and fro by the companion. As he walked he wrung his hands. 'God – God – God,' he kept saying, with no thought of prayer, uttering a mere voice of agony.

The time may have been long or short, it was perhaps minutes, perhaps only seconds, ere he awoke to find himself observed, and saw the captain sitting up and watching him over the break of the poop, a strange blindness as of fever in his eyes, a haggard knot of corrugations on his brow. Cain saw himself in a mirror. For a flash they looked upon each other, and then glanced guiltily aside; and Carthew fled from the eye of his accomplice, and stood leaning on the taffrail.

An hour went by, while the day came brighter, and the sun rose and drank up the clouds: an hour of silence in the ship, an hour of agony beyond narration for the sufferers. Brown's gabbling prayers, the cries of the sailors in the rigging, strains of the dead Hemstead's minstrelsy, ran together in Carthew's mind with sickening iteration. He neither acquitted nor condemned himself: he did not think, he suffered. In the bright water into which he stared, the pictures changed and were repeated: the baresark rage of Goddedaal; the blood-red light of the sunset into which they had run forth; the face of the babbling Chinaman as they cast him over; the face of the captain, seen a moment since, as he awoke from drunkenness into remorse. And time passed, and the sun swam higher, and his torment was not abated.

Then were fulfilled many sayings, and the weakest of these condemned brought relief and healing to the others. Amalu the drudge awoke (like the rest) to sickness of body and distress of mind; but the habit of obedience ruled in that simple spirit, and, appalled to be so late, he went direct into the galley, kindled the fire, and began to get breakfast. At the rattle of dishes, the snapping of the fire, and the thin smoke that went up straight into the air, the spell was lifted. The condemned felt once more the good dry land of habit under foot; they touched again the familiar guide-ropes of sanity; they were restored to a sense of the blessed revolution and return of all things earthly. The captain drew a bucket of water and began to bathe. Tommy sat up, watched him awhile, and slowly followed his example; and Carthew, remembering his last thoughts of the night before, hastened to the cabin.

Mac was awake; perhaps had not slept. Over his head Goddedaal's canary twittered shrilly from its cage.

'How are you?' asked Carthew.

'Me arrum's broke,' returned Mac; 'but I can stand that. It's this place I can't abide. I was coming on deck anyway.'

'Stay where you are, though,' said Carthew. 'It's deadly hot above, and there's no wind. I'll wash out this— ' and he paused, seeking a word and not finding one for the grisly foulness of the cabin.

'Faith, I'll be obliged to ye, then,' replied the Irishman. He spoke mild and meek, like a sick child with its mother. There was now no violence in the violent man; and as Carthew fetched a bucket and swab and the steward's sponge, and began to cleanse the field of battle, he alternately watched him or shut his eyes and sighed like a man near fainting. 'I have to ask all your pardons,' he began again presently, 'and the more shame to me as I got ye into trouble and couldn't do nothing when it came. Ye saved me life, sir; ye're a clane shot.'

'For God's sake, don't talk of it!' cried Carthew. 'It

can't be talked of; you don't know what it was. It was nothing down here; they fought. On deck – Oh, – my God!' And Carthew, with the bloody sponge pressed to his face, struggled a moment with hysteria.

'Kape cool, Mr Cart'ew. It's done now,' said Mac; 'and ye may bless God ye're not in pain and helpless in the bargain.'

There was no more said by one or other, and the cabin was pretty well cleansed when a stroke on the ship's bell summoned Carthew to breakfast. Tommy had been busy in the meanwhile; he had hauled the whaleboat close aboard, and already lowered into it a small keg of beef that he found ready broached beside the galley door; it was plain he had but the one idea – to escape.

'We have a shipful of stores to draw upon,' he said. 'Well, what are we staying for? Let's get off at once for Hawaii. I've begun preparing already.'

'Mac has his arm broken,' observed Carthew; 'how would he stand the voyage?'

'A broken arm?' repeated the captain. 'That all? I'll set it after breakfast. I thought he was dead like the rest. That madman hit out like— ' and there, at the evocation of the battle, his voice ceased and the talk died with it.

After breakfast, the three white men went down into the cabin.

'I've come to set your arm,' said the captain.

'I beg your pardon, captain,' replied Mac; 'but the first thing ye got to do is to get this ship to sea We'll talk of me arrum after that.'

'Oh, there's no such blooming hurry,' returned Wicks.

'When the next ship sails in ye'll tell me stories!' retorted Mac.

'But there's nothing so unlikely in the world,' objected Carthew.

'Don't be deceivin' yourself,' said Mac. 'If ye want a ship, divil a one'll look near ye in six year; but if ye don't, ye may take my word for ut, we'll have a squadron layin' here.'

'That's what I say,' cried Tommy; 'that's what I call sense! Let's stock that whaleboat and be off.'

'And what will Captain Wicks be thinking of the whale-boat?' asked the Irishman.

'I don't think of it at all,' said Wicks. 'We've a

smart-looking brig under foot; that's all the whale-boat I want.'

'Excuse me!' cried Tommy. 'That's childish talk. You've got a brig to be sure, and what use is she? You daren't go anywhere in her. What port are you to sail for?'

'For the port of Davy Jones's Locker, my son,' replied the captain. 'This brig's going to be lost at sea. I'll tell you where, too, and that's about forty miles to windward of Kauai. We're going to stay by her till she's down; and once the masts are under, she's the *Flying Scud* no more, and we never heard of such a brig; and it's the crew of the schooner *Currency Lass* that comes ashore in the boat, and takes the first chance to Sydney.'

'Captain, dear, that's the first Christian word I've heard of ut!' cried Mac. 'And now, just let me arrum be, jewel, and get the brig outside.'

'I'm as anxious as yourself, Mac,' returned Wicks; 'but there's not wind enough to swear by. So let's see your arm, and no more talk.'

The arm was set and splinted; the body of Brown fetched from the forepeak, where it lay stiff and cold, and committed to the waters of the lagoon; and the washing of the cabin rudely finished. All these were done ere mid-day; and it was past three when the first cat's-paw ruffled the lagoon, and the wind came in a dry squall, which presently sobered to a steady breeze.

The interval was passed by all in feverish impatience, and by one of the party in secret and extreme concern of mind. Captain Wicks was a fore-and-aft sailor; he could take a schooner through a Scotch reel, felt her mouth and divined her temper like a rider with a horse; she, on her side, recognising her master and following his wishes like a dog. But by a not very unusual train of circumstance, the man's dexterity was partial and circumscribed. On a schooner's deck he was Rembrandt, or (at the least) Mr Whistler; on board a brig he was Pierre Grassou. Again and again in the course of the morning, he had reasoned out his policy and rehearsed his orders; and ever with the same depression and weariness. It was guess-work; it was chance; the ship might behave as he expected, and might not; suppose she failed him, he stood there helpless, beggared of all the proved resources of experience. Had not all hands been so weary, had he not feared to communicate his own misgivings, he could have towed her out. But these reasons sufficed, and the most he could do was to take all possible precautions. Accordingly he had Carthew aft, explained what was to be done with anxious patience, and visited along with him the various sheets and braces.

'I hope I'll remember,' said Carthew. 'It seems awfully muddled.'

'It's the rottenest kind of rig,' the captain admitted: 'all blooming pocket-handkerchiefs! And not one sailor-man on deck! Ah, if she'd only been a brigantine now! But it's lucky the passage is so plain; there's no manœuvring to mention. We get underweigh before the wind, and run right so till we begin to get fould of the island; then we haul our wind and lie as near south-east as may be till we're on that line; 'bout ship there and stand straight out on the port tack. Catch the idea?'

'Yes, I see the idea,' replied Carthew, rather dismally, and the two incompetents studied for a long time in silence the complicated gear above their heads.

But the time came when these rehearsals must be put in practice. The sails were lowered, and all hands heaved the anchor short. The whaleboat was then cut adrift, the upper topsails and the spanker set, the yards braced up, and the spanker sheet hauled out to starboard.

'Heave away on your anchor, Mr Carthew.'

'Anchor's gone, sir.'

'Set jibs.'

It was done, and the brig still hung enchanted. Wicks, his head full of a schooner's mainsail, turned his mind to the spanker. First he hauled in the sheet, and then he hauled it out, with no result.

'Brail the damned thing up!' he bawled at last, with a red face. 'There ain't no sense in it.'

It was the last stroke of bewilderment for the poor captain, that he had no sooner brailed up the spanker than the vessel came before the wind. The laws of nature seemed to him to be suspended; he was like a man in a world of pantomime tricks; the cause of any result, and the probable result of any action, equally concealed from him. He was the more careful not to shake the nerve of his amateur assistants. He stood there with a face like a torch; but he gave his orders with *aplomb*, and indeed, now the ship was under weigh, supposed his difficulties over.

The lower topsails and courses were then set, and the brig began to walk the water like a thing of life, her fore-foot discoursing music, the birds flying and crying over her spars. Bit by bit the passage began to open and the blue sea to show between the flanking breakers on the reef; bit by bit, on the starboard bow, the low land of the islet began to heave closer aboard. The yards were braced up, the spanker sheet hauled aft again; the brig was close hauled, lay down to her work like a thing in earnest, and had soon drawn near to the point of advantage, where she might stay and lie out of the lagoon in a single tack.

Wicks took the wheel himself, swelling with success. He kept the brig full to give her heels, and began to bark his orders: 'Ready about. Helm's a-lee. Tacks and sheets. Mainsail haul.' And then the fatal words: 'That'll do your mainsail; jump forrard and haul round your foreyards.'

To stay a square-rigged ship is an affair of knowledge and swift sight: and a man used to the succinct evolutions of a schooner will always tend to be too hasty with a brig. It was so now. The order came too soon; the topsails set flat aback; the ship was in irons. Even yet, had the helm been reversed, they might have saved her. But to think of a stern-board at all, far more to think of profiting by one, were foreign to the schooner-sailor's mind. Wicks made haste instead to wear ship, a manœuvre for which room was wanting, and the *Flying Scud* took ground on a bank of sand and coral about twenty minutes before five.

Wicks was no hand with a square-rigger, and he had shown it. But he was a sailor and a born captain of men for all homely purposes, where intellect is not required and an eye in a man's head and a heart under his jacket will suffice. Before the others had time to understand the misfortune, he was bawling fresh orders, and had the sails clewed up, and took soundings round the ship.

'She lies lovely,' he remarked, and ordered out a boat with the starboard anchor.

'Here! steady!' cried Tommy. 'You ain't going to turn us to, to warp her off?'

'I am though,' replied Wicks.

'I won't set a hand to such tomfoolery for one,' replied

Tommy. 'I'm dead beat.' He went and sat down doggedly on the main hatch. 'You got us on; get us off again,' he added.

Carthew and Wicks turned to each other.

'Perhaps you don't know how tired we are,' said Carthew.

'The tide's flowing!' cried the captain. 'You wouldn't have me miss a rising tide?'

'Oh, gammon! there's tides tomorrow!' retorted Tommy.

'And I'll tell you what,' added Carthew, 'the breeze is failing fast, and the sun will soon be down. We may get into all kinds of fresh mess in the dark and with nothing but light airs.'

'I don't deny it,' answered Wicks, and stood awhile as if in thought. 'But what I can't make out,' he began again, with agitation, 'what I can't make out is what you're made of! To stay in this place is beyond me. There's the bloody sun going down – and to stay here is beyond me!'

The others looked upon him with horrified surprise. This fall of their chief pillar – this irrational passion in the practical man, suddenly barred out of his true sphere – the sphere of action – shocked and daunted them. But it gave to another and unseen hearer the chance for which he had been waiting. Mac, on the striking of the brig, had crawled up the companion, and he now showed himself and spoke up.

'Captain Wicks,' said he, 'it's fne that brought this trouble on the lot of ye. I'm sorry for ut, I ask all your pardons, and if there's anyone can say "I forgive ye," it'll make my soul the lighter.'

Wicks stared upon the man in amaze; then his self-control returned to him. 'We're all in glass houses here,' he said; 'we ain't going to turn to and throw stones. I forgive you, sure enough; and much good may it do you!'

The others spoke to the same purpose.

'I thank ye for ut, and 'tis done like gentlemen,' said Mac. 'But there's another thing I have upon my mind. I hope we're all Prodestans here?'

It appeared they were; it seemed a small thing for the Protestant religion to rejoice in!

'Well, that's as it should be,' continued Mac. 'And why

shouldn't we say the Lord's Prayer? There can't be no hurt in ut.'

He had the same quiet, pleading, childlike way with him as in the morning; and the others accepted his proposal, and knelt down without a word.

'Knale if ye like!' said he. 'I'll stand.' And he covered his eyes.

So the prayer was said to the accompaniment of the surf and seabirds, and all rose refreshed and felt lightened of a load. Up to then, they had cherished their guilty memories in private, or only referred to them in the heat of a moment, and fallen immediately silent. Now they had faced their remorse in company, and the worst seemed over. Nor was it only that. But the petition 'Forgive us our trespasses,' falling in so apposite after they had themselves forgiven the immediate author of their miseries, sounded like an absolution.

Tea was taken on deck in the time of the sunset, and not long after the five castaways – castaways once more – lay down to sleep.

Day dawned windless and hot. Their slumbers had been too profound to be refreshing, and they woke listless, and sat up, and stared about them with dull eyes. Only Wicks, smelling a hard day's work ahead, was more alert. He went first to the well, sounded it once and then a second time, and stood awhile with a grim look, so that all could see he was dissatisfied. Then he shook himself, stripped to the buff, clambered on the rail, drew himself up and raised his arms to plunge. The dive was never taken. He stood, instead, transfixed, his eyes on the horizon.

'Hand up that glass,' he said.

In a trice they were all swarming aloft, the nude captain leading with the glass.

On the northern horizon was a finger of grey smoke, straight in the windless air like a point of admiration.

'What do you make it?' they asked of Wicks.

'She's truck down,' he replied; 'no telling yet. By the way the smoke builds, she must be heading right here.'

'What can she be?'

'She might be a China mail,' returned Wicks, 'and she might be a blooming man-of-war, come to look for castaways. Here! This ain't the time to stand staring. On deck, boys!'

He was the first on deck, as he had been the first aloft, handed down the ensign, bent it again to the signal halliards, and ran it up union down.

'Now hear me,' he said, jumping into his trousers, 'and everything I say you grip on to. If that's a man-of-war, she'll be in a tearing hurry; all these ships are what don't do nothing and have their expenses paid. That's our chance; for we'll go with them, and they won't take the time to look twice or to ask a question. I'm Captain Trent; Carthew, you're Goddedaal; Tommy, you're Hardy; Mac's Brown; Amalu – hold hard! we can't make a Chinaman of him! Ah, Wing must have deserted; Amalu stowed away; and I turned him to as cook, and was never at the bother to sign him. Catch the idea? Say your names.'

And that pale company recited their lesson earnestly.

'What were the names of the other two?' he asked. 'Him Carthew shot in the companion, and the one I caught in the jaw on the main top-gallant?'

'Holdorsen and Wallen,' said someone.

'Well, they're drowned,' continued Wicks; 'drowned alongside trying to lower a boat. We had a bit of a squall last night; that's how we got ashore.' He ran and squinted at the compass. 'Squall out of nor'-nor'-west-half-west; blew hard; every one in a mess, falls jammed, and Holdorsen and Wallen spilt overboard. See? Clear your blooming heads!' He was in his jacket now, and spoke with a feverish impatience and contention that rang like anger.

'But is it safe?' asked Tommy.

'Safe?' bellowed the captain. 'We're standing on the drop, you moon-calf! If that ship's bound for China (which she don't look to be), we're lost as soon as we arrive; if she's bound the other way, she comes from China, don't she? Well, if there's a man on board of her that ever clapped eyes on Trent or any blooming hand out of this brig, we'll all be in irons in two hours. Safe! no, it ain't safe; it's a beggarly last chance to shave the gallows, and that's what it is.'

At this convincing picture, fear took hold on all.

'Hadn't we a hundred times better stay by the brig?' cried Carthew. 'They would give us a hand to float her off.'

'You'll make me waste this holy day in chattering!' cried

Wicks. 'Look here, when I sounded the well this morning there was two foot of water there against eight inches last night. What's wrong? I don't know; might be nothing; might be the worst kind of smash. And then, there we are in for a thousand miles in an open boat, if that's your taste!'

'But it may be nothing, and anyway, their carpenters are bound to help us repair her,' argued Carthew.

'Moses Murphy!' cried the captain. 'How did she strike? Bows on, I believe. And she's down by the head now. If any carpenter comes tinkering here, where'll he go first? Down in the forepeak, I suppose! And then, how about all that blood among the chandlery? You would think you were a lot of members of Parliament discussing Plimsoll; and you're just a pack of murderers with the halter round your neck. Any other ass got any time to waste? No? Thank God for that! Now, all hands! I'm going below, and I leave you here on deck. You get the boat cover off that boat; then you turn to and open the specie chest. There are five of us; get five chests, and divide the specie equal among the five – put it at the bottom – and go at it like tigers. Get blankets, or canvas, or clothes, so it won't rattle. It'll make five pretty heavy chests, but we can't help that. You, Carthew – dash me! – You, Mr Goddedaal, come below. We've our share before us.'

And he cast another glance at the smoke, and hurried below with Carthew at his heels.

The logs were found in the main cabin behind the canary cage; two of them, one kept by Trent, one by Goddedaal. Wicks looked first at one, then at the other, and his lip stuck out.

'Can you forge hand of write?' he asked.

'No,' said Carthew.

'There's luck for you – no more can I!' cried the captain. 'Hullo! here's worse yet, here's this Goddedaal up to date; he must have filled it in before supper. See for yourself: "Smoke observed. – Captain Kirkup and five hands of the schooner *Currency Lass*." Ah! this is better,' he added, turning to the other log. 'The old man ain't written anything for a clear fortnight. We'll dispose of your log altogether, Mr Goddedaal, and stick to the old man's – to mine, I mean; only I ain't going to write it up, for reasons of my own. You are. You're going to sit down right here and fill it in the way I tell you.'

'How to explain the loss of mine?' asked Carthew.

'You never kept one,' replied the captain. 'Gross neglect of duty. You'll catch it.'

'And the change of writing?' resumed Carthew. 'You began; why do you stop and why do I come in? And you'll have to sign anyway.'

'Oh! I've met with an accident and can't write,' replied Wicks.

'An accident?' repeated Carthew. 'It don't sound natural. What kind of an accident?'

Wicks spread his hand face-up on the table, and drove a knife through his palm.

'That kind of an accident,' said he. 'There's a way to draw to windward of most difficulties, if you've a head on your shoulders.' He began to bind up his hand with a handkerchief, glancing the while over Goddedaal's log. 'Hullo!' he said, 'This'll never do for us – this is an impossible kind of a yarn. Here, to begin with, is this Captain Trent trying some fancy course, leastways he's a thousand miles to south'ard of the great circle. And here, it seems, he was close up with this island on the sixth, sails all these days and is close up with it again by daylight on the eleventh.'

'Goddedaal said they had the deuce's luck,' said Carthew.

'Well, it don't look like real life – that's all I can say,' returned Wicks.

'It's the way it was, though,' argued Carthew.

'So it is; and what the better are we for that, if it don't look so?' cried the captain, sounding unwonted depths of art criticism. 'Here! try and see if you can tie this bandage; I'm bleeding like a pig.'

As Carthew sought to adjust the handkerchief, his patient seemed sunk in a deep muse, his eye veiled, his mouth partly open. The job was yet scarce done, when he sprang to his feet.

'I have it,' he broke out, and ran on deck. 'Here, boys!' he cried, 'we didn't come here on the eleventh; we came in here on the evening of the sixth, and lay here ever since becalmed. As soon as you've done with these chests,' he added, 'you can turn to and roll out beef and water breakers; it'll look more shipshape – like as if we were getting ready for the boat voyage.'

And he was back again in a moment, cooking the new log. Goddedaal's was then carefully destroyed, and a hunt began for the ship's papers. Of all the agonies of that breathless morning, this was perhaps the most poignant. Here and there the two men searched, cursing, cannoning together, streaming with heat, freezing with terror. News was bawled down to them that the ship was indeed a man-of-war, that she was close up, that she was lowering a boat; and still they sought in vain. By what accident they missed the iron box with the money and accounts, is hard to fancy, but they did. And the vital documents were found at last in the pocket of Trent's shoregoing coat, where he had left them when last he came on board.

Wicks smiled for the first time that morning. 'None too soon,' said he. 'And now for it! Take these others for me; I'm afraid I'll get them mixed if I keep both.'

'What are they?' Carthew asked.

'They're the Kirkup and *Currency Lass* papers,' he replied. 'Pray God we need 'em again!'

'Boat's inside the lagoon, sir,' hailed down Mac, who sat by the skylight doing sentry while the others worked.

'Time we were on deck, then, Mr Goddedaal,' said Wicks.

As they turned to leave the cabin, the canary burst into piercing song.

'My God!' cried Carthew with a gulp, 'we can't leave that wretched bird to starve. It was poor Goddedaal's.'

'Bring the bally thing along!' cried the captain.

And they went on deck.

An ugly brute of a modern man-of-war lay just without the reef, now quite inert, now giving a flap or two with her propeller. Nearer hand, and just within, a big white boat came skimming to the stroke of many oars, her ensign blowing at the stern.

'One word more,' said Wicks, after he had taken in the scene. 'Mac, you've been in China ports? All right; then you can speak for yourself. The rest of you I kept on board all the time we were in Hong Kong, hoping you would desert; but you fooled me and stuck to the brig. That'll make your lying come easier.'

The boat was now close at hand; a boy in the stern sheets was the only officer, and a poor one plainly, for the men were talking as they pulled.

'Thank God, they've only sent a kind of a middy!' ejaculated Wicks. 'Here you, Hardy, stand for'ard! I'll have no deck hands on my quarter-deck,' he cried, and the reproof braced the whole crew like a cold douche.

The boat came alongside with perfect neatness, and the boy officer stepped on board, where he was respectfully greeted by Wicks.

'You the master of this ship?' he asked.

'Yes, sir,' said Wicks. 'Trent is my name, and this is the *Flying Scud* of Hull.'

'You seem to have got into a mess,' said the officer.

'If you'll step aft with me here, I'll tell you all there is of it,' said Wicks.

'Why, man, you're shaking!' cried the officer.

'So would you, perhaps, if you had been in the same berth,' returned Wicks; and he told the whole story of the rotten water, the long calm, the squall, the seamen drowned, glibly and hotly, talking, with his head in the lion's mouth, like one pleading in the dock. I heard the same tale from the same narrator in the saloon in San Francisco; and even then his bearing filled me with suspicion. But the officer was no observer.

'Well, the captain is in no end of a hurry,' said he; 'but I was instructed to give you all the assistance in my power, and signal back for another boat if more hands were necessary. What can I do for you?'

'Oh, we won't keep you no time,' replied Wicks cheerily. 'We're all ready, bless you – men's chests, chronometer, papers, and all.'

'Do you mean to leave her?' cried the officer. 'She seems to me to lie nicely; can't we get your ship off?'

'So we could, and no mistake; but how we're to keep her afloat's another question. Her bows is stove in,' replied Wicks.

The officer coloured to the eyes. He was incompetent and knew he was; thought he was already detected, and feared to expose himself again. There was nothing further from his mind than that the captain should deceive him; if the captain was pleased, why, so was he. 'All right,' he said. 'Tell your men to get their chests aboard.'

'Mr Goddedaal, turn the hands to to get the chests aboard,' said Wicks.

The four Currency Lasses had waited the while on tenter-hooks. This welcome news broke upon them like the sun at midnight; and Hadden burst into a storm of tears, sobbing aloud as he heaved upon the tackle. But the work went none the less briskly forward; chests, men, and bundles were got over the side with alacrity; the boat was shoved off; it moved out of the long shadow of the *Flying Scud*, and its bows were pointed at the passage.

So much, then, was accomplished. The sham wreck had passed muster; they were clear of her, they were safe away; and the water widened between them and her damning evidences. On the other hand, they were drawing nearer to the ship of war, which might very well prove to be their prison and a hangman's cart to bear them to the gallows of which they had not yet learned either whence she came or whither she was bound; and the doubt weighed upon their heart like mountains.

It was Wicks who did the talking. The sound was small in Carthew's ears, like the voices of men miles away, but the meaning of each word struck home to him like a bullet. 'What did you say your ship was?' inquired Wicks.

'*Tempest*, don't you know?' returned the officer.

'"Don't you know?" What could that mean? Perhaps nothing: perhaps that the ships had met already. Wicks took his courage in both hands. 'Where is she bound?' he asked.

'Oh, we're just looking in at all these miserable islands here,' said the officer. 'Then we bear up for San Francisco.'

'Oh, yes, you're from China ways, like us?' pursued Wicks.

'Hong Kong,' said the officer, and spat over the side.

Hong Kong. Then the game was up; as soon as they set foot on board, they would be seized: the wreck would be examined, the blood found, the lagoon perhaps dredged, and the bodies of the dead would reappear to testify. An impulse almost incontrollable bade Carthew rise from the thwart, shriek out aloud, and leap overboard; it seemed so vain a thing to dissemble longer, to dally with the inevitable, to spin out some hundred seconds more of agonised suspense, with shame and death thus visibly approaching. But the indomitable Wicks persevered. His face was like a skull, his voice scarce recognisable; the dullest of men and officers (it seemed) must have remarked that tell-tale countenance and broken utterance. And still he persevered, bent upon certitude.

'Nice place, Hong Kong?' he said.

'I'm sure I don't know,' said the officer. 'Only a day and a half there; called for orders and came straight on here. Never heard of such a beastly cruise.' And he went on describing and lamenting the untoward fortunes of the *Tempest*.

But Wicks and Carthew heeded him no longer. They lay back on the gunwale, breathing deep, sunk in a stupor of the body; the mind within still nimbly and agreeably at work, measuring the past danger, exulting in the present relief, numbering with ecstasy their ultimate chances of escape. For the voyage in the man-of-war they were now safe; yet a few more days of peril, activity and presence of mind in San Francisco, and the whole horrid tale was blotted out; and Wicks again became Kirkup, and Goddedaal became Carthew – men beyond all shot of possible suspicion, men who had never heard of the *Flying Scud*, who had never been in sight of Midway Reef.

So they came alongside, under many craning heads of seamen and projecting mouths of guns; so they climbed on board somnambulous, and looked blindly about them at the tall spars, the white decks, and the crowding ship's company, and heard men as from far away, and answered them at random.

And then a hand fell softly on Carthew's shoulder.

'Why, Norrie, old chappie, where have you dropped from? All the world's been looking for you. Don't you know you've come into your kingdom?'

He turned, beheld the face of his old schoolmate Sebright, and fell unconscious at his feet.

The doctor was attending him, awhile later, in Lieutenant Sebright's cabin, when he came to himself. He opened his eyes, looked hard in the strange face, and spoke with a kind of solemn vigour.

'Brown must go the same road,' he said, 'now or never.'

And then paused, and his reason coming to him with more clearness, spoke again: 'What was I saying? Where am I? Who are you?'

'I am the doctor of the *Tempest*,' was the reply. 'You are in Lieutenant Sebright's berth, and you may dismiss all concern from your mind. Your troubles are over, Mr Carthew.'

'Why do you call me that?' he asked. 'Ah, I remember – Sebright knew me! Oh!' and he groaned and shook. 'Send down Wicks to me; I must see Wicks at once!' he cried, and seized the doctor's wrist with unconscious violence.

'All right,' said the doctor. 'Let's make a bargain. You swallow down this draught, and I'll go and fetch Wicks.'

And he gave the wretched man an opiate that laid him out within ten minutes and in all likelihood preserved his reason.

It was the doctor's next business to attend to Mac; and he found occasion, while engaged upon his arm, to make the man repeat the names of the rescued crew. It was now the turn of the captain, and there is no doubt he was no longer the man that we have seen; sudden relief, the sense of perfect safety, a square meal and a good glass of grog, had all combined to relax his vigilance and depress his energy.

'When was this done?' asked the doctor, looking at the wound.

'More than a week ago,' replied Wicks, thinking singly of his log.

'Hey?' cried the doctor, and he raised his head and looked the captain in the eyes.

'I don't remember exactly,' faltered Wicks.

And at this remarkable falsehood, the suspicions of the doctor were at once quadrupled.

'By the way, which of you is called Wicks?' he asked easily.

'What's that?' snapped the captain, falling white as paper.

'Wicks,' repeated the doctor; 'which of you is he? That's surely a plain question.'

Wicks stared upon his questioner in silence.

'Which is Brown, then?' pursued the doctor.

'What are you talking of? what do you mean by this?'

cried Wicks, snatching his half-bandaged hand away, so that the blood sprinkled in the surgeon's face.

He did not trouble to remove it; looking straight at his victim, he pursued his questions. 'Why must Brown go the same way?' he asked.

Wicks fell trembling on a locker. 'Carthew told you,' he cried.

'No,' replied the doctor, 'he has not. But he and you between you have set me thinking, and I think there's something wrong.'

'Give me some grog,' said Wicks. 'I'd rather tell than have you find out. I'm damned if it's half as bad as what anyone would think.'

And with the help of a couple of strong grogs, the tragedy of the *Flying Scud* was told for the first time.

It was a fortunate series of accidents that brought the story to the doctor. He understood and pitied the position of these wretched men, and came wholeheartedly to their assistance. He and Wicks and Carthew (so soon as he was recovered) held a hundred councils and prepared a policy for San Francisco. It was he who certified 'Goddedaal' unfit to be moved, and smuggled Carthew ashore under cloud of night; it was he who kept Wicks's wound open that he might sign with his left hand; he who took all their Chile silver and (in the course of the first day) got it converted for them into portable gold. He used his influence in the wardroom to keep the tongues of the young officers in order, so that Carthew's identification was kept out of the papers. And he rendered another service yet more important. He had a friend in San Francisco, a millionaire; to this man he privately presented Carthew as a young gentleman come newly into a huge estate, but troubled with Jew debts which he was trying to settle on the quiet. The millionaire came readily to help; and it was with his money that the wrecker gang was to be fought. What was his name, out of a thousand guesses? It was Douglas Longhurst.

As long as the Currency Lasses could all disappear under fresh names, it did not greatly matter if the brig were bought, or any small discrepancies should be discovered in the wrecking. The identification of one of their number had changed all that. The smallest scandal must now direct attention to the movements of Norris. It would be asked how he who had sailed in a schooner from Sydney, had turned up so shortly after in a brig out of Hong Kong; and from one question to another all his original shipmates were pretty sure to be involved. Hence, arose naturally the idea of preventing danger, profiting by Carthew's new-found wealth, and buying the brig under an alias; and it was put in hand with equal energy and caution. Carthew took lodgings alone under a false name, picked up Bellairs at random, and commissioned him to buy the wreck.

'What figure, if you please?' the lawyer asked.

'I want it bought,' replied Carthew. 'I don't mind about the price.'

'Any price is no price,' said Bellairs. 'Put a name upon it.'

'Call it ten thousand pounds then, if you like!' said Carthew.

In the meanwhile, the captain had to walk the streets, appear in the consulate, be cross-examined by Lloyd's agent, be badgered about his lost accounts, sign papers with his left hand, and repeat his lies to every skipper in San Francisco; not knowing at what moment he might run into the arms of some old friend who should hail him by the name of Wicks, or some new enemy who should be in a position to deny him that of Trent. And the latter incident did actually befall him, but was transformed by his stout countenance into an element of strength. It was in the consulate (of all untoward places) that he suddenly heard a big voice inquiring for Captain Trent. He turned with the customary sinking at his heart.

'*You* ain't Captain Trent!' said the stranger, falling back. 'Why, what's all this? They tell me you're passing off as Captain Trent – Captain Jacob Trent – a man I knew since I was that high.'

'Oh, you're thinking of my uncle as had the bank in Cardiff,' replied Wicks, with desperate *aplomb*.

'I declare I never knew he had a nevvy!' said the stranger.

'Well, you see he has!' says Wicks.

'And how is the old man?' asked the other.

'Fit as a fiddle,' answered Wicks, and was opportunely summoned by the clerk.

This alert was the only one until the morning of the

sale, when he was once more alarmed by his interview with Jim; and it was with some anxiety that he attended the sale, knowing only that Carthew was to be represented, but neither who was to represent him nor what were the instructions given. I suppose Captain Wicks is a good life. In spite of his personal appearance and his own known uneasiness, I suppose he is secure from apoplexy, or it must have struck him there and then, as he looked on at the stages of that insane sale and saw the old brig and her not very valuable cargo knocked down at last to a total stranger for ten thousand pounds.

It had been agreed that he was to avoid Carthew, and above all Carthew's lodging, so that no connection might be traced between the crew and the pseudonymous purchaser. But the hour for caution was gone by, and he caught a tram and made all speed to Mission Street.

Carthew met him in the door.

'Come away, come away from here,' said Carthew; and when they were clear of the house, 'All's up!' he added.

'Oh, you've heard of the sale, then?' said Wicks.

'The sale!' cried Carthew. 'I declare I had forgotten it.' And he told of the voice in the telephone, and the maddening question: 'Why did you want to buy the *Flying Scud*?'

This circumstance, coming on the back of the monstrous improbabilities of the sale, was enough to have shaken the reason of Immanuel Kant. The earth seemed banded together to defeat them; the stones and the boys on the street appeared to be in possession of their guilty secret. Flight was their one thought. The treasure of the *Currency Lass* they packed in waist-belts, expressed their chests to an imaginary address in British Columbia, and left San Francisco the same afternoon, booked for Los Angeles.

The next day they pursued their retreat by the Southern Pacific route, which Carthew followed on his way to England; but the other three branched off for Mexico.

TO WILL H. LOW

Dear Low, – The other day (at Manihiki of all places) I
had the pleasure to meet Dodd. We sat some two hours
in the neat, little, toy-like church, set with pews after the
manner of Europe, and inlaid with mother-of-pearl in
the style (I suppose) of the New Jerusalem. The natives,
who are decidedly the most attractive inhabitants of this
planet, crowded round us in the pew, and fawned upon
and patted us; and here it was I put my questions, and
Dodd answered me.

I first carried him back to the night in Barbizon when
Carthew told his story, and asked him what was done
about Bellairs. It seemed he had put the matter to his
friend at once, and that Carthew had taken to it with
an inimitable lightness. 'He's poor and I'm rich,' he had
said. 'I can afford to smile at him. I go somewhere else,
that's all – somewhere that's far away and dear to get to.
Persia would be found to answer, I fancy. No end of a place,
Persia. Why not come with me?' And they had left the next
afternoon for Constantinople, on their way to Teheran. Of
the shyster, it is only known (by a newspaper paragraph)
that he returned somehow to San Francisco and died in
the hospital.

'Now there's another point,' said I. 'There you are off
to Persia with a millionaire, and rich yourself. How come
you here in the South Seas, running a trader?'

He said, with a smile, that I had not yet heard of Jim's
last bankruptcy. 'I was about cleaned out once more,' he
said; 'and then it was that Carthew had this schooner built
and put me in as supercargo. It's his yacht and it's my
trader; and as nearly all the expenses go to the yacht, I do
pretty well. As for Jim, he's right again; one of the best
businesses, they say, in the West – fruit, cereals, and real

estate; and he has a Tartar of a partner now – Nares, no less. Nares will keep him straight, Nares has a big head. They have their country places next door at Saucelito, and I stayed with them time about, the last time I was on the coast. Jim had a paper of his own – I think he has a notion of being senator one of these days – and he wanted me to throw up the schooner and come and write his editorials. He holds strong views on the State Constitution, and so does Mamie.'

'And what became of the other three Currency Lasses after they left Carthew?' I inquired.

'Well, it seems they had a huge spree in the city of Mexico,' said Dodd; 'and then Hadden and the Irishman took a turn at the gold fields in Venezuela, and Wicks went on alone to Valparaiso. There's a Kirkup in the Chilean navy to this day, I saw the name in the papers about the Balmaceda war. Hadden soon wearied of the mines, and I met him the other day in Sydney. The last news he had from Venezuela, Mac had been knocked over in an attack on the gold train. So there's only the three of them left, for Amalu scarcely counts. He lives on his own land in Maui, at the side of Hale-a-ka-la, where he keeps Goddedaal's canary; and they say he sticks to his dollars, which is a wonder in a Kanaka. He had a considerable pile to start with, for not only Hemstead's share but Carthew's was divided equally among the other four – Mac being counted.'

'What did that make for him altogether?' I could not help asking, for I had been diverted by the number of calculations in his narrative.

'One hundred and twenty-eight pounds nineteen shillings and eleven pence halfpenny,' he replied with composure; 'that's leaving out what little he won at Van John. It's something for a Kanaka, you know.'

And about that time we were at last obliged to yield to the solicitations of our native admirers, and go to the pastor's house to drink green cocoanuts. The ship I was in was sailing the same night, for Dodd had been beforehand and got all the shell in the island; and though he pressed me to desert and return with him to Auckland (whither he was now bound to pick up Carthew) I was firm in my refusal.

The truth is, since I have been mixed up with Havens

and Dodd in the design to publish the latter's narrative,
I seem to feel no want for Carthew's society. Of course, I
am wholly modern in sentiment, and think nothing more
noble than to publish people's private affairs at so much
a line. They like it, and if they don't, they ought to. But
a still small voice keeps telling me they will not like it
always, and perhaps not always stand it. Memory besides
supplies me with the face of a pressman (in the sacred
phrase) who proved altogether too modern for one of his
neighbours, and

Qui nunc it per iter tenebricosum

as it were, marshalling us our way. I am in no haste to

— nos præcedens —

be that man's successor. Carthew has a record as 'a clane
shot,' and for some years Samoa will be good enough
for me.

We agreed to separate, accordingly; but he took me on
board in his own boat with the hard-wood fittings, and
entertained me on the way with an account of his late visit
to Butaritari, whither he had gone on an errand for Carthew,
to see how Topelius was getting along, and, if necessary, to
give him a helping hand. But Topelius was in great force,
and had patronised and – well – out-manœuvred him.

'Carthew will be pleased,' said Dodd; 'for there's no
doubt they oppressed the man abominably when they were
in the *Currency Lass*. It's diamond cut diamond now.'

This, I think, was the most of the news I got from my friend
Loudon; and I hope I was well inspired, and have put all
the questions to which you would be curious to hear an
answer.

But there is one more that I daresay you are burning to
put to myself; and that is, what your own name is doing
in this place, cropping up (as it were uncalled-for) on the
stern of our poor ship? If you were not born in Arcadia,
you linger in fancy on its margin; your thoughts are busied
with the flutes of antiquity, with daffodils, and the classic
poplar, and the footsteps of the nymphs, and the elegant
and moving aridity of ancient art. Why dedicate to you a
tale of a cast so modern: – full of details of our barbaric

manners and unstable morals; full of the need and the lust of money, so that there is scarce a page in which the dollars do not jingle; full of the unrest and movement of our century, so that the reader is hurried from place to place and sea to sea, and the book is less a romance than a panorama – in the end, as blood-bespattered as an epic?

Well, you are a man interested in all problems of art, even the most vulgar; and it may amuse you to hear the genesis and growth of 'The Wrecker.' On board the schooner *Equator*, almost within sight of the Johnstone Islands (if anybody knows where these are) and on a moonlit night when it was a joy to be alive, the authors were amused with several stories of the sale of wrecks. The subject tempted them; and they sat apart in the alleyway to discuss its possibilities. 'What a tangle it would make,' suggested one, 'if the wrong crew were aboard. But how to get the wrong crew there?' – 'I have it!' cried the other; 'the so-and-so affair!' For not so many months before, and not so many hundred miles from where we were then sailing, a proposition almost tantamount to that of Captain Trent had been made by a British skipper to some British castaways.

Before we turned in, the scaffolding of the tale had been put together. But the question of treatment was as usual more obscure. We had long been at once attracted and repelled by that very modern form of the police novel or mystery story, which consists in beginning your yarn anywhere but at the beginning, and finishing it anywhere but at the end; attracted by its peculiar interest when done, and the peculiar difficulties that attend its execution; repelled by that appearance of insincerity and shallowness of tone, which seems its inevitable drawback. For the mind of the reader, always bent to pick up clues, receives no impression of reality or life, rather of an airless, elaborate mechanism; and the book remains enthralling, but insignificant, like a game of chess, not a work of human art. It seemed the cause might lie partly in the abrupt attack; and that if the tale were gradually approached, some of the characters introduced (as it were) beforehand, and the book started in the tone of a novel of manners and experience briefly treated, this defect might be lessened and our mystery seem to inhere in life. The tone of the age, its movement, the mingling of races and classes in the dollar hunt, the fiery and not quite unromantic struggle for existence with its changing trades and scenery, and two types in particular, that of the American handyman of business and that of the Yankee merchant sailor – we agreed to dwell upon at some length, and make the woof to our not very precious warp. Hence Dodd's father, and Pinkerton, and Nares, and the Dromedary picnics, and the railway work in New South Wales – the last an unsolicited testimonial from the powers that be, for the tale was half written before I saw Carthew's squad toil in the rainy cutting at South Clifton, or heard from the engineer of his 'young swell.' After we had invented at some expense of time this method of approaching and fortifying our police novel, it occurred to us it had been invented previously by someone else, and was in fact – however painfully different the results may seem – the method of Charles Dickens in his later work.

I see you staring. Here, you will say, is a prodigious quantity of theory to our halfpenny worth of police novel; and withal not a shadow of an answer to your question.

Well, some of us like theory. After so long a piece of practice, these may be indulged for a few pages. And the answer is at hand. It was plainly desirable, from every point of view of convenience and contrast, that our hero and narrator should partly stand aside from those with whom he mingles, and be but a pressed-man in the dollar hunt. Thus it was that Loudon Dodd became a student of the plastic arts, and that our globe-trotting story came to visit Paris and look in at Barbizon. And thus it is, dear Low, that your name appears in the address of this epilogue.

For sure, if any person can here appreciate and read between the lines, it must be you – and one other, our friend. All the dominos will be transparent to your better knowledge; the statuary contract will be to you a piece of ancient history; and you will not have now heard for the first time of the dangers of Roussillon. Dead leaves from the Bas Breau, echoes from Lavenue's and the Rue Racine, memories of a common past, let these be your bookmarkers as you read. And if you care for naught else in the story, be a little pleased to breathe once more for a moment the airs of our youth.

Books listed in alphabetical order by author.

The House with the Green Shutters
George Douglas Brown
ISBN 0 86241 549 7 £4.99
Witchwood John Buchan
ISBN 0 86241 202 1 £4.99
The Life of Robert Burns Catherine Carswell
ISBN 0 86241 292 7 £5.99
The Complete Brigadier Gerard Arthur Conan Doyle
ISBN 0 86241 534 9 £4.99
A Scots Quair: (Sunset Song, Cloud Howe, Grey Granite)
Lewis Grassic Gibbon
ISBN 0 86241 532 2 £5.99
Sunset Song Lewis Grassic Gibbon
ISBN 0 86241 179 3 £3.99
Memoirs of a Highland Lady vols. I&II
Elizabeth Grant of Rothiemurchus
ISBN 0 86241 396 6 £7.99
Highland River Neil M. Gunn
ISBN 0 86241 358 3 £5.99
Sun Circle Neil M. Gunn
ISBN 0 86241 587 X £5.99
The Well at the World's End Neil M. Gunn
ISBN 0 86241 645 0 £5.99
The Private Memoirs and Confessions of a Justified Sinner
James Hogg
ISBN 0 86241 340 0 £3.99
Fergus Lamont Robin Jenkins
ISBN 0 86241 310 9 £4.95
Just Duffy Robin Jenkins
ISBN 0 86241 551 9 £4.99
The Changeling Robin Jenkins
ISBN 0 86241 228 5 £4.99
Journey to the Hebrides (A Journey to the Western Isles of
Scotland, The Journal of a Tour to the Hebrides) Samuel
Johnson & James Boswell
ISBN 0 86241 588 8 £5.99
Private Angelo Eric Linklater
ISBN 0 86241 376 1 £5.95
Scottish Ballads Edited by Emily Lyle
ISBN 0 86241 477 6 £4.99
Nua-Bhardachd Ghaidhlig/Modern Scottish Gaelic Poems
Edited by Donald MacAulay
ISBN 0 86241 494 6 £4.99

The Early Life of James McBey James McBey
ISBN 0 86241 445 8 £5.99
The Devil and the Giro:
  Two Centuries of Scottish Stories
  Edited by Carl MacDougall
ISBN 0 86241 359 1 £8.99
St Kilda: Island on the Edge of the World
  Charles Maclean
ISBN 0 86241 388 5 £5.99
An Autobiography Edwin Muir
ISBN 0 86241 423 7 £5.99
The Wilderness Journeys (The Story of My Boyhood and Youth,
  A Thousand Mile Walk to the Gulf, My First Summer in the
  Sierra, Travels in Alaska, Stickeen) John Muir
ISBN 0 86241 586 1 £7.99
A Twelvemonth and a Day Christopher Rush
ISBN 0 86241 439 3 £4.99
Grampian Quartet (The Quarry Wood, The Weatherhouse, A Pass
in the Grampians, The Living Mountain) Nan Shepherd
ISBN 0 86241 589 6 £8.99
Consider the Lilies Iain Crichton Smith
ISBN 0 86241 415 6 £4.99
Listen to the Voice: Selected Stories Iain Crichton Smith
ISBN 0 86241 434 2 £5.99
Shorter Scottish Fiction Robert Louis Stevenson
ISBN 0 86241 555 1 £4.99
The Scottish Novels: (Kidnapped, Catriona, The Master of
  Ballantrae, Weir of Hermiston) Robert Louis Stevenson
ISBN 0 86241 533 0 £5.99
Tales of the South Seas (Island Landfalls, The Ebb-Tide,
The Wrecker) Robert Louis Stevenson
ISBN 0 86241 643 4 £7.99
The People of the Sea David Thomson
ISBN 0 86241 550 0 £4.99
City of Dreadful Night James Thomson
ISBN 0 86241 449 0 £4.99
Three Scottish Poets: MacCaig, Morgan, Lochead
ISBN 0 86241 400 8 £4.99
Black Lamb and Grey Falcon Rebecca West
ISBN 0 86241 428 8 £9.99

Most Canongate Classics are available at good bookshops. If you
experience difficulty in obtaining the title you want, please
contact us at 14 High Street, Edinburgh, EH1 1TE.